Jinny the Carrier by Israel Zangwill

Israel Zangwill was born in London on 21st January 1864, to a family of Jewish immigrants from the Russian Empire.

Zangwill was initially educated in Plymouth and Bristol. At age 9 he was enrolled in the Jews' Free School in Spitalfields in east London. Zangwill excelled here. He began to teach part-time at the school and eventually full time. Whilst teaching he also studied with the University of London and by 1884 had earned his BA with triple honours in philosophy, history, and the sciences.

His writing earned him the sobriquet "the Dickens of the Ghetto" primarily based on his much lauded novel 'Children of the Ghetto: A Study of a Peculiar People' in 1892 and its glimpse of the poverty-stricken life in London's Jewish quarter.

As a writer he was keen to reflect on his political and social outlooks. His simulation of Yiddish sentence structure in English aroused great interest. His mystery work, 'The Big Bow Mystery' (1892) was the first locked room mystery novel.

Zangwill was also involved with narrowly focused Jewish issues as an assimilationist, an early Zionist, and later a territorialist. In the early 1890s he had joined the Lovers of Zion movement in England. In 1897 he joined Theodor Herzl (considered the father of modern political Zionism) in founding the World Zionist Organization.

Zangwill quit the established philosophy of Zionism when his plan for a homeland in Uganda was rejected and founded his own organisation; the Jewish Territorialist Organization. Its stated goal was to create a Jewish homeland in whatever territory in the world could be found for them.

Amongst the challenges in his life he found time to write poetry. He had translated a medieval Jewish poet in 1903 and his volume 'Blind Children' in 1908 shows his promise in this new endeavour.

'The Melting Pot' in 1909 made Zangwill's name as an admired playwright. When the play opened in Washington D.C., former President Theodore Roosevelt leaned over the edge of his box and shouted, "That's a great play, Mr. Zangwill, that's a great play."

Israel Zangwill died on 1st August 1926 in Midhurst, West Sussex.

Index of Contents

EPISTLE DEDICATORY

DEAR MISTRESS OF BASSETTS,

You and Audrey have so often proclaimed the need—in our world of sorrow and care—of a "bland" novel, defining it as one to be read when in bed with a sore throat, that as an adventurer in letters I have frequently felt tempted to write one for you. But the spirit bloweth where it listeth, and seemed perversely to have turned against novels altogether, perhaps because I had been labelled "novelist," as though one had set up a factory. (Two a year is, I believe, the correct output.) However, here is a novel at last—my first this century—and there is a further reason for presuming to associate you with it, because it is largely from the vantage-point of your Essex homestead that I have, during the past twenty years, absorbed the landscape, character, and dialect which finally insisted on finding expression, first in a little play, and now in this elaborate canvas. How often have I passed over High Field and seen the opulent valley—tilth and pasture and ancient country seats—stretching before me like a great poem, with its glint of winding water, and the exquisite blue of its distances, and Bassetts awaiting me below, snuggling under its mellow moss-stained tiles, a true English home of "plain living and high thinking," and latterly of the rural Muse! I can only hope that some breath of the inspiration which has emanated from Bassetts in these latter days, and which has set its picturesquely clad poetesses turning rhymes as enthusiastically as clods, and weaving rondels as happily as they bound the sheaves, has been wafted over these more prosaic pages—something of that "wood-magic" which your granddaughter—soul of the idyllic band—has got into her song of your surroundings.

The glint of blue where the estuary flows,
Or a shimmering mist o'er the vale's green and gold:
A little grey church which 'mid willow-trees shows;
A house on the hillside so good to behold
With its yellow plaster and red tiles old,
The clematis climbing in purple and green,
And down in the garden 'mid hollyhocks bold
Sit Kathleen, Ursula, Helen, and Jean.

And yet it must not be thought that either "Bassetts" or "Little Baddow" figures in the "Little Bradmarsh" of my story. The artist cannot be tied down: he creates a composite landscape to his needs. Moreover, in these last four or five years a zealous constabulary can testify out of what odds and ends the strange inquiring figure, who walked, cycled, or rode in carriers' carts to forgotten hamlets or sea-marshes, has composed his background. Nor have I followed photographic realism even in my dialect, deeming the Cockneyish forms, except when unconsciously amusing, too ugly to the eye in a long sustained narrative, though enjoyable enough in those humorous sketches which my friend Bensusan, the true conquistador of Essex, pours forth so amazingly from his inexhaustible cornucopia. I differ—in all diffidence—from his transcription on the sole point that the Essex rustic changes "i" into "oi" in words like "while," though why on the other hand "boil" should go back to "bile" can be explained only by the perversity which insists on taking aspirates off the right words and clapping them on the wrong, much as Cockney youths and girls exchange hats on Bank Holiday. I have limited my own employment of this local vowelling mainly to the first person singular as sufficiently indicative of the rest. In the old vexed question of the use of dialect, my feeling is that its value is simply as colour, and that the rich old words, obsolete or unknown elsewhere, contribute this more effectively and far more beautifully than vagaries of pronunciation, itself a very shifting factor of language even in the best circles. It is not even necessary for the artistic effect that the reader should understand the provincial words, though the context should be so contrived as to make them fairly intelligible. In short, art is never nature, though it should conceal the fact. Even the slowness and minuteness of my method—imposed as it is by the attempt to seize the essence of Essex—are immeasurable velocity and breadth compared with the scale of reality.

In bringing this rustic complex under the category of comedy I clash, I am aware, with literary fashion, which demands that country folk should appear like toiling insects caught in the landscape as in a giant web of Fate, though why the inhabitants of Belgravia or Clapham escape this tragic convention I cannot understand. But I do not think that you, dear Aunt by adoption, see the life around you like that. Even, however, had you and I seen more gloomily, the fashionable fatalistic framework would have been clearly inconsistent with the "blandness" of your novel. Such a novel must, I conceive, begin with "once upon a time" and end with "they all lived happy ever after," so that my task was simply to fill in the lacuna between these two points, and supply the early-Victorian mottoes, while even the material was marked out for me by Dr. Johnson's definition of a novel as "a story mainly about love." I am hopeful that when you come to read it (not, I trust, with a sore throat), you will admit that I have at least tried to make my dear "Jinny" really "live happy ever after," even though—in the fierce struggle for literary survival—she is far from likely to do so. But at any rate, if only for the moment, I should be glad if I had succeeded in expressing through her my grateful appreciation of the beautiful country in which my lot, like Jinny's, has been cast, with its many lovable customs and simple, kindly people.

Your affectionate Nephew,

THE AUTHOR
SUSSEX
New Year 1919

PREAMBLE

I'll tell you who Time ambles withal.
"As You Like It."

Once upon a time—but then it was more than once, it was, in fact, every Tuesday and Friday—Jinny the Carrier, of Blackwater Hall, Little Bradmarsh, went the round with her tilt-cart from that torpid Essex village on the Brad, through Long Bradmarsh (over the brick bridge) to worldly, bustling Chipstone, and thence home again through the series of droughty hamlets with public pumps that curved back—if one did not take the wrong turning at the Four Wantz Way—to her too aqueous birthplace: baiting her horse, Methusalem, at "The Black Sheep" in Chipstone like the other carters and wagoners, sporting a dog with a wicked eye and a smart collar, and even blowing a horn as if she had been the red-coated guard of the Chelmsford coach sweeping grandly to his goal down the High Street of Chipstone.

Do you question more precisely when this brazen female flourished? The answer may be given with the empty exactitude of science and scholarship. Her climacteric was to the globe at large the annus mirabilis of the Great Exhibition, when the lion and the lamb lay down together in Hyde Park in a crystal cage. But though the advent of the world-trumpeted Millennium could not wholly fail to percolate even to Little Bradmarsh, a more veracious chronology, a history truer to local tradition, would date the climax of Jinny's unmaidenly career as "before the Flood."

Not, of course—as the mention of Methusalem might mislead you into thinking—the Flood which is still commemorated in toyshops and Babylonian tablets, and anent which German scholars miraculously contrive to be dry; but the more momentous local Deluge when the Brad, perversely swollen, washed away cattle, mangold clamps, and the Holy Sabbath in one fell surge, leaving the odd wooden gable of Frog Farm looming above the waste of waters as nautically as Noah's Ark.

In those antediluvian days, and in that sequestered hundred, farm-horses were the ruling fauna and set the pace; the average of which Methusalem, with his "jub" or cross between a lazy trot and a funeral procession, did little to elevate. It was not till the pride of life brought a giddier motion that the Flood— but we anticipate both moral and story. Let us go rather at the Arcadian amble of the days before the Deluge, when the bicycle—even of the early giant order—had not yet arisen to terrorize the countryside with its rotiferous mobility, still less the motor-mammoth swirling through the leafy lanes in a dust-fog and smelling like a super-skunk, or the air-monster out-soaring and out-Sataning the broomsticked witch. It is true that Bundock, Her Majesty's postman, had once brought word of a big-bellied creature, like a bloated Easter-egg, hovering over the old maypole as if meditating to impale itself thereon, like a bladder on a stick. But normally not even the mail or a post-chaise divided the road with Master Bundock; while, as for the snorting steam-horse that bore off the young Bradmarshians, once they had ventured as far as roaring railhead, it touched the postman's imagination no more than the thousand-ton sea-monsters with flapping membranes or cloud-spitting gullets that rapt them to the lands of barbarism and gold.

Blessèd Bundock, genial Mercury of those days before the Flood, if the rubbered wheel of the postdiluvian age might have better winged thy feet, yet thy susceptible eye—that rested all-embracingly on female gleaners—was never darkened by the sight of the soulless steel reaper, cropping close like a giant goose, and thou wast equally spared that mechanic flail-of-all-work that drones through the dog-days like a Brobdingnagian bumble-bee. For thine happier ear the cottages yet hummed with the last faint strains of the folk-song: unknown in thy sylvan perambulations that queer metallic parrot, hoarser even than the raucous reality, which now wakens and disenchants every sleepy hollow with echoes of the London music-hall.

Rural Essex was long the unchanging East, and there are still ploughmen who watch the airmen thunder by, then plunge into their prog again. The shepherds who pour their fleecy streams between its hedgerows are still as primitive as the herdsmen of Chaldea, and there are yokels who dangle sideways from their slow beasts as broodingly as the Bedouins of Palestine. Even to-day the spacious elm-bordered landscapes through which Jinny's cart rolled and her dog circumambiently darted, lie ignored of the picture postcard, and on the red spinal chimney-shaft of Frog Farm the doves settle with no air of perching for their photographs. Little Bradmarsh is still Little, still the most reclusive village of all that delectable champaign; the Brad still glides between its willows unruffled by picnic parties and soothed rather than disturbed by rusty, ancient barges. But when Gran'fer Quarles first brought little Jinny to these plashy bottoms, the region it watered—not always with discretion—was unknown even to the gipsy caravans and strolling showmen, and quite outside the circuit of the patterers and chaunters who stumped the country singing or declaiming lampoons on the early Victoria; not a day's hard tramp from Seven Dials where they bought their ribald broadsheets, yet as remote as Arabia Felix.

CHAPTER I

BUNDOCK ON HIS BEAT

I

It had rained that April more continuously than capriciously, but this morning April showed at last her fairer face. The sunshine held as yet no sense of heat, only the bracingness of a glad salt wave. Across the spacious blue of the Essex sky clouds floated and met and parted in a restful restlessness. The great valley swam in a blue sea of vapour. Men trod as on buoyant sunshine that bore them along. The buds were peeping out from every hedge and tree, the blackthorn was bursting into white, the whole world seemed like a child tiptoeing towards some delightful future. Primroses nestled in every hollow: the gorse lay golden on the commons. The little leaves of the trees seemed shy, scarcely grown familiar with the fluttering of the birds. All the misery, pain, and sadness had faded from creation like a bad dream: the stains and pollutions were washed out, leaving only the young clean beauty of the first day. It was a virgin planet, fresh from the hands of its Maker, trembling with morning dew—an earth that had never seen its own blossoming. And the pæan of all this peace and innocence throbbed exultingly in bird-music through all the great landscape. Over the orchard of Frog Farm there were only two larks, but you would have thought a whole orchestra.

A blot against this background seemed the blood-red shirt of Caleb Flynt in that same orchard; a wild undulating piece of primeval woodland where plum-trees and pear-trees indeed flourished, but not more so than oaks and chestnuts, briars and brambles, or fairy mists of bluebells. The task of regenerating it had been annually postponed, but now that Caleb was no longer the Frog Farm "looker," it formed, like his vegetable garden, his wheat patch, or his wife's piggery, a pleasant pottering-ground. He worked without coat or smock, chastening the ranker grass while the dew was still on it—or in his own idiom, "while the dag was on the herb." White-bearded and scythe-bearing, he suggested—although the beard was short and round and he wore a shapeless grey hat—a figure of Father Time, incarnadined from all his wars. But in sooth no creature breathed more at one with the earth's mood that morning than this ancient "Peculiar," whose parlour bore as its text of honour—in white letters on a lozenge of brown paper: "When He giveth quietness, who then can make trouble?"

Quietness was, indeed, all around him in this morning freshness: the swish of the scythe, the murmurous lapse of shorn grass, the drone of insects, the cooing of pigeons from the cote, the elusive cry of the new-come cuckoo, seemed forms of silence rather than of sound. And his inner peace matched his outer, for, as his arms automatically wielded the scythe, his soul was actually in heaven—or at least in the New Jerusalem which, according to his wife's novel Christadelphian creed, was to be let down from heaven for the virtuous remnant of earth—and at no distant date! Not that he definitely believed in her descending city, though he felt a certain proprietary interest in it. "Oi don't belong to Martha's Church," he reassured his brethren of the Peculiar faith, "but Oi belongs to she and she belongs to me."

In this mutual belonging he felt himself the brake and Martha the spirited mare who could never stand still. No doubt her argument that we were here to learn and to move forward was plausible enough— how could he traverse it, he who had himself changed from Churchman to Peculiar? But her rider: "We don't leave the doctrine, we carry it with us," struck him as somewhat shifty. And her move from "Sprinkling" to "Total Immersion"—even if the submergence did in a sense include the sprinkling—was surely enough progression for one lifetime. He did not like "this gospel of gooin' forrard": an obstinate instinct warned him to hold back, though with an uneasy recognition that her ceaseless explorations of her capacious Bible—to him a sealed book—must naturally yield discoveries denied to his less saintly and altogether illiterate self. Discoveries indeed had not been spared him. Ever since she had joined those new-fangled Christadelphians—"Christy Dolphins" as he called them—she had abounded in texts as crushing as they were unfamiliar; and even the glib Biblical patter he had picked up from the Peculiars was shown to imply at bottom the new teaching. Curtain lectures are none the less tedious when they are theological, and after a course of many months—each with its twenty-eight to thirty-one nights— Caleb Flynt was grown wearisomely learned in the bold doctrine launched by the great John Thomas that "the Kingdom of God on earth" actually meant on earth and must be brought about there and nowhere else, and that Immortality enjoyed except in one's terrestrial body—however spiritualized— was as absurd a notion as that it was lavished indiscriminately upon Tom, Giles, and Jerry.

The worst of it was he could never be sure Martha was not in the right—she had certainly modified his belief in "Sprinkling"—and he fluttered around her "New Jerusalem" like a moth around a lighthouse. Had anybody given a penny for his thoughts as he stooped now over his scythe, the fortunate investor would have come into possession of "the street of pure gold, as it were transparent glass," not to mention the sapphires and emeralds, the beryls and chrysolites and all the other shining swarms of precious stones catalogued in Revelation. If he had kept from her the rumour that had reached his own ears of such a treasure-city of glass actually arising in London at this very moment, it was not because he believed this was veritably her celestial city, but because it might possibly excite her credulity to the pitch of wishing to see it. And the thought of a journey was torture. Already Martha had dropped hints about the difficulties of "upbuilding" in the lack of local Christadelphians to institute a "Lightstand": the wild dream of some day breaking bread in an "Ecclesia" in London had been adumbrated: it was possible the restless female mind even contemplated London itself as a place to be seen before one died.

But surely the New Jerusalem, if it descended at all, would—he felt—descend here, at Little Bradmarsh. A heaven that meant girding up one's loins and wrenching out one's roots was a very problematic paradise, for all the splendour with which his inward eye was now, despite himself, dazzled.

II

From this jewelled Jerusalem Caleb was suddenly brought back to the breathing beauty of our imperfect earth, to pear-blossom and plum-blossom, to the sun-glinted shadows under his trees and the mellow tiles of his roof. The sound of his own name fell from on high—like the city of his daydream— accompanied by a great skirring of wings, and looking up dazedly, the pearly gates still shimmering, his eye followed the tarred side-wall of the farmhouse till, near the roof, it lit upon his wife's night-capped head protruded from the tiny diamond-paned casement that alone broke the sheer black surface of the wood.

A sense of the unusual quickened his pulses. It stole upon him, not mainly from Martha's face, which, despite its excited distension, wore—over wrinkles he never saw—the same russet complexion and was crowned by the same glory of unblanched brown hair that had gladdened his faithful eyes since the beginning of the century; but, more subtly and subconsciously, through the open lattice which framed this ever-enchanting vision. In the Flynt tradition, windows—restricted at best by the window tax still in force—were for light, not air. Had folks wanted air, they would have poked a hole in the wall; not built a section of it "of transparent glass." People so much under the sky as Caleb and Martha Flynt had no need to invite colds by artificial draughts. They were getting a change of air all day long. But their rooms—their small, low-ceiled rooms—were not thus vivified, even in their absence; the ground-floor windows were indeed immovable, and an immemorial mustiness made a sort of slum atmosphere in this spacious, sun-washed solitude. Hence Caleb's sense of a jar in his universe at the familiar, flat pattern of the wall dislocated into a third dimension by the out-flung casement: a prodigy which he was not surprised to find fluttering the dovecot, and which presaged, he felt, still vaster cataclysms. And to add to the auspices of change, he observed another piebald pigeon among his snowy flock.

"Yes, dear heart," he called up, disguising his uneasiness and shearing on.

Martha pointed a fateful finger towards the high-hedged, oozy path meandering beyond the orchard gate, and dividing the sown land from the pastures sloping to the Brad. "There's Bundock coming up the Green Lane!"

"Bundock?" gasped Caleb, the scythe stopping short. "You're a-dreamin'." That Brother Bundock, who had been prayed over for a decade by himself and every Peculiar in the vicinity, should at last have taken up his bed and walked, was too sudden a proof of their tenets, and the natural man blurted out his disbelief.

"But I see his red jacket," Martha protested, "his bag on his shoulder."

"Ow!" His tone was divided between relief and disappointment. "You mean Bundock's buoy-oy!" He drew out the word even longer than usual, and it rose even beyond the high pitch his Essex twang habitually gave to his culminating phrases. "Whatever can Posty be doin' in these pa-arts?" he went on, with a new wonder.

"And the chace that squashy," said Martha, who from her coign of vantage could see the elderly figure labouring in the remoter windings, "he's sinking into it at every step."

"Ay, the mud's only hazeled over. Whatever brings the silly youth when the roads be in that state?"

"It'll be the Census again!" groaned Martha.

Caleb's brow gloomed. He feared Martha was right, and anything official must have to do with that terrible paper-filling which had at last by the aid of Jinny been, they had hoped, finally accomplished some weeks before. Ever since the first English census had been taken in the first year of the century, Martha had been expecting a plague to fall upon the people as it had upon the Israelites when King

David numbered them. But although she had been disappointed, there was no doubt of the plague of the Census itself.

"Haps it's a letter for the shepherd," hazarded Caleb to comfort her.

"Who'd be writing Master Peartree a letter? He can't read."

"Noa!" he answered complacently, for his wife's learning seemed part of their mutual "belonging." The drawbacks of this vicarious erudition were, however, revealed by his next remark; for on Martha crying out that poor Bundock had sunk up to his knees, Caleb bade her be easy. "He won't be swallowed up like that minx Cora!"

But Martha's motherly heart was too agitated to recognize the Korah of her Biblical allusions—she vaguely assumed it was some scarlet woman englutted in the slimy saltings of Caleb's birthplace. "Run and lead him into the right path," she exhorted.

But Caleb's brain was not one for quick reactions. Inured for nigh seventy years to a world in which nothing happened too suddenly, even thunderbolts giving reasonable notice and bogs getting boggier by due degrees, he stood dazedly, his hands paralysed on the nibs of his arrested scythe. "Happen the logs Oi put have sunk down!" he soliloquized slowly.

"If I wasn't in my nightgown I'd go myself," said Martha impatiently. "'Tis a lesson from the Lord not to lay abed."

"The Lord allows for rheumaties, dear heart," said Caleb soothingly.

"He'll be up to his neck, if you don't stir your stumps."

"Not he, Martha. Unless he stands on his head." Caleb meant this as a literal contribution to the discussion. There was no wilful topsy-turveydom. He was as unconscious of his own humour as of other people's.

"But he'll spoil his breeches anyways," retorted Martha with equal gravity. "And the Lord just sending his wife a new baby."

"Bundock's breeches be the Queen's," said Caleb reassuringly. But laying down his scythe, he began to move mazedly adown the orchard, and before the postman's mud-cased leggings had floundered many more rods, the veteran was sitting astride his stile, dangling his top-boots over a rotten-planked brook, and waving in his hairy, mahogany hand his vast red handkerchief like a danger signal.

"Ahoy, Posty!"

Bundock responded with a cheerful blast on his bugle. "Ahoy, Uncle Flynt!"

"Turn back. Don't, ye'll strike a bog-hole."

"I never go back!" cried the dauntless Bundock. And even as he spoke, his stature shrank till his bag rested on the ooze.

"The missus was afeared you'd spoil the Queen's breeches," said Caleb sympathetically. "Catch hold of yon crab-apple branch."

"Better spoil her breeches than be unfaithful to her uniform," said the slimy hero, struggling up as directed. "I've got a letter for you."

Caleb's flag fell into the brook and startled a water-rat. "A letter for us!"

He splashed into the water, still dazedly, to rescue his handkerchief, avoiding the plank as a superfluous preliminary to the wetting; and, standing statuesque in mid-stream, more like Father Neptune now than Father Time, he continued incredulously: "Who'd be sendin' us a letter?"

"That's not my business," cried Bundock sternly. He came on heroically, disregarding a posterior consciousness of damp clay, and picking his way along the grassy, squashy strip that was starred treacherously with peaceful daisies and buttercups, over-hung by wild apple-trees, and hedged from the fields on either hand by a tall, prickly tangle and congestion—as of a vegetable slum—in which gorse, holly, speedwell, mustard, and lily of the valley (still in green sheaths), strove for breathing space. At the edge of a palpable mudhole he paused perforce. Caleb, who, when he recovered from his daze at the news of the letter, had advanced with dripping boots to meet him, was equally arrested at the opposite frontier, and the two men now faced each other across some fifteen feet of flowery ooze, two studies in red; Caleb, big-limbed and stolid, in his crimson shirt, and Bundock, dapper and peart, in his scarlet jacket.

The postman's face was lightly pockmarked, but found by females fascinating, especially under the quasi-military cap. Hairlessness was part of its open charm: his sun-tanned cheek kept him juvenile despite his half-century, and preserved from rust his consciousness of a worshipping womanhood. Caleb, on the contrary, was all hair, little bushes growing even out of his ears, and whiskers and beard and the silver-grey mop at his crown running into one another without frontiers—the "Nonconformist fringe" in a ragged edition.

"Sow sorry to give ye sow much ill-convenience," he called apologetically. "Oi count," he added, having had time for reflection, "one of our buoy-oys has written from furrin parts. And he wouldn't be knowing the weather here."

"'Tain't any of your boys," said Bundock crossly, "because it comes from London."

"That's a pity. The missus'll get 'sterical when she hears it's for us, and it's cruel hard to disappoint her. There ain't nobody else as we want letters from. Can't you send it back?"

"Not if I can deliver it," said Bundock stiffly.

"But ye can't—unless you chuck it over."

The slave of duty shook his head. "I daren't risk the Queen's mail like that."

"But it's my letter."

"Not yet, Uncle Flynt. When it reaches your hand it may be considered safely, legally, and constitutionally delivered. But, till then, 'tis the Queen's letter, and don't you forget it."

Caleb scratched his head.

"If 'twas the Queen's letter, she could read it," he urged obstinately.

"And so she can," rejoined Bundock. "She has the right to open any letter smelling of high treason, so to speak, and nobody can say her nay."

"But my letter ain't high treasony," said Caleb indignantly. "And if Wictoria wants to read it, why God bless her, says Oi."

Bundock sighed before the bovinity of the illiterate mind.

"The Queen has got better things to do than read every scribble her head's stuck on to."

"Happen Oi could ha' retched it with a rake," Caleb mused. "What a pity you ain't got spladges, like when Oi was a buoy-oy, and gatherin' pin-patches on the sands. And fine and fat they was too when ye got 'em on the pin!" His tongue clucked.

Bundock looked his contempt. "A pretty sight, Her Majesty's uniform lumbering along like a winkle-picker!"

"Bide a bit then," said Caleb, "and Oi'll thrash through the hedge and work through agen in your rear."

It was a chivalrous offer, for a deep ditch barred the way to the freshly ploughed land, and a tough and prickly chaos to the pasture land; but Bundock declined churlishly, if not unheroically, declaring there was a letter for Frog Cottage too. And when Caleb, recovering from this vindication of his wife's prophesyings, offered to transmit it to the shepherd, "What guarantee have I," asked Bundock, "that it reaches him safely, legally, and constitutionally? Nay, nay, uncle, a man must do his own jobs."

"Then work through the bushes yourself. Don't, ye'll be fit to grow crops on."

"Lord, how I hate going round—circumbendibus!" groaned Bundock. "I might as well be driving a post-cart."

"There's a mort of worser things than gooin' round," said Caleb. "And Oi do be marvelling a young chap like you should mind a bit of extra leg-work, bein' as how ye've got naught else to do but to put one leg afore the 'tother."

"Indeed?" snapped Bundock, this ignorant summary of his duties aggravating the moist clayey consciousness that resided at the seat of Her Majesty's trousers.

"Ef ye won't keep to the high roads, you ought to git a hoss what can clear everything," Caleb went on to advise.

"And break my neck?"

"Posty always had a hoss when I was a cad."

"Or lay in the road with a broken back and Her Majesty's mail at the mercy of every tramp?" pursued Bundock. "No, no, one cripple in a family is enough."

Caleb looked pained. "You dedn't ought to talk o' your feyther like that. And him pinchin' hisself and maybe injurin' his spinal collar to keep you at school till you was a large buoy-oy!"

III

Bundock's irritation at his Bœotian critic was suddenly diverted by the spectacle of a female figure bearing down upon him literally by leaps and bounds—it seemed as if the steeplechase method recommended by Caleb was already in action. The postman felt for his spectacles, discarded normally in the interests of manly fascination. "Lord!" he cried. "Has your missus joined the Jumpers?" Caleb turned his head, not unalarmed. With so skittish a theologian anything was possible. But his agitation subsided into a smile of admiration.

"She thinks of everything," he said.

The practical Martha was in fact advancing with an improvised leaping-pole that had already carried her neatly over the brook and would obviously bring Bundock over the boglet. But why—Caleb wondered—was she risking her "bettermost" skirt? His own mother, he remembered, had not hesitated to tuck up her petticoats when winkles had to be gathered. And why was Martha's hair massed in its black net cap with a Sunday stylishness?

"Morning, Mrs. Flynt," cried Bundock, becoming as genial as the weather. Females, even sexagenarian, so long as not utterly uncomely, turned him from an official into a man.

"Morning, Mr. Bundock!" Martha called back across the mudhole. "I hope your father's no worse!"

Bundock's brow clouded. Still harping on his father.

"He's not so active as you," he replied a bit testily.

"Thank the Lord!" said Caleb fervently. Then, colouring under Bundock's stare, "For the missus's legs," he explained.

And to cover his confusion he snatched the pole from her and hurled it towards Bundock, who had barely time to jump aside into a still squidgier patch. But in another instant the dauntless postman secured it, and with one brave bound—like Sir Walter Scott's stag—had cleared the slimiest section, and his staggering, sliding form was safely locked in Caleb's sanguineous shirt-sleeves. Safely but not contentedly, for at heart he was deeply piqued at this inglorious position of Her Majesty's envoy; the dignified newsbearer, the beguiler of loneliness, the gossip welcomed alike in the kitchens of the great and the parlours of the humble. Morbidly conscious of his unpresentable rear, he kept carefully behind the couple, while Caleb explained the situation to Martha, breaking and blunting the news at one hammer-blow.

"There's a letter for us! From Lunnon!"

Martha was wonderful. "What a piece! What a master!" he thought. One might live with a woman for half a century, yet never fathom her depths. Not a gasp, not a cry, not a sigh of vain yearning. Merely: "Then it'll be from Cousin Caroline. When she went back to London at Michaelmas she promised to let us know if she reached home safe, and if your brother George was better."

"Ay, ay!" he assented happily. "Oi'd disremembered Cousin Caroline."

It was a merciful oblivion, for his Cockney cousin had come from Limehouse in August and stayed two months, protesting that it was impossible to bide a day in a place where there wasn't a neighbour to speak to except a silly shepherd who was never at home; where water was scooped filthily from a green-scummy pond instead of flowing naturally from a tap; where on moonless nights you could break your leg at your own doorstep; where frogs croaked and cocks crowed and pigeons moaned and foxes barked at the unholiest hours; where disgusting vermin were nailed on the trees and where you broke out in itching blotches, which folks might ascribe to "harvesters," but which were susceptible of a more domestic explanation. Moreover, Cousin Caroline had brought a profuse and uninvited progeny, whose unexpected appearance in Jinny's cart, though vaguely comforting as recalling the days when the house resounded with child-life, was in truth at disturbing discord with the Quakerish calm into which Frog Farm had subsided after the flight of its teeming chicks. As Caleb came along now, convoying Bundock through the lush orchard grass, the echo of Cousin Caroline's querulous voice rasped his brain and made him wish she had pretermitted her promise to write. As for his ailing brother George, information about whom she was probably sending, it was obvious that he was no worse, else one would assuredly have heard of his funeral. Had not George carefully let him know when he got married? Caroline was a Churchwoman—he remembered suddenly—she had compromised Frog Farm by eking out Parson Fallow's miserable congregation. And now she had sent her letter just at a season to plague and muddy a worthy Dissenter.

"Sow sorry to give ye sow much ill-convenience, Mr. Bundock," he repeated, as they reached the farmhouse.

IV

Frog Farm, before which Bundock stood fumbling in his bag, was—as its name implies—situated in a batrachian region, croakily cheerless under a sullen sky, a region revealed under the plough as ancient sedge-land, black with rotted flags and rushes. But the scene was redeemed at its worst by the misty magnificence of great spaces, whose gentle undulations could not counteract a sublime flatness; not to mention the beauty of the Brad gliding like the snake in the grass it sometimes proved. The pasture land behind the farmhouse and sloping softly down to the river—across which, protected by a dyke and drained by little black mills working turbine wheels, lay the still lower Long Bradmarsh—was the salvage of a swamp roughly provided with a few, far-parted drains by some pioneer squatter, content—on the higher ground where a farmhouse was possible—to fell and slice his own timber and bake his own tiles. At the topmost rim, on a road artificially raised to take its wagons to the higher ground or "Ridge" of the village, rose this farmhouse with its buildings, all dyked off from the converted marsh by a three-foot wall of trunk-fragments and uncouth stones, bordered by bushes. The house turned its back on the Brad, and had not even hind eyes to see it—another effect of the window tax—and had the rear of the house not been relieved by the quaint red chimney bisecting it, the blankness would have been unbearable. But if little of good could have been said of its architecture behind its back, and if even in front it ended abruptly at one extremity like a sheer cliff or a halved haystack, with one gable crying for another to make both ends meet, it was as a whole picturesque enough with all that charm of rough wood, which still seems to keep its life-sap, and beside which your marble hall is a mere petrifaction. Weather-boarded and tarred, it faced you with a black beauty of its own, amid which its diamond-paned little lattices gleamed like an Ethiopian's eyes. In the foreground, haystacks, cornricks, and strawstacks gave grace and colour, fusing with the spacious landscape as naturally as the barns and byres and storehouses, the troughs and stables and cart-sheds and the mellow, immemorial dung.

But what surprised the stranger more than its lop-sidedness was the duplication of its front door, for there were two little doors, with twin sills and latches. It had, in fact, been partitioned to allow a couple of rooms to the shepherd-cowman, when that lone widower's cottage was needed for an extra horseman. Master Peartree's new home became known as Frog Cottage. The property was what was here called an "off-hand farm," the owner being "in parts," or engaged in other enterprises, and for more than a generation Caleb Flynt had lived there as "looker" to old Farmer Gale, the cute Cornish invader who had discovered the fatness of the oozy soil, and who had been glad to install a son of it as a reconciling link between Little Bradmarsh and "the furriner." Caleb belonged to that almost extinct species of managers who can dispense with reading and writing, and his semi-absentee employer found his honesty as meticulous as his memory. While the Flynt nestlings were growing up, the parent birds had found the nest a tight fit, but with the gradual flight of the brood to every quarter of the compass, the old pair had receded into its snugger recesses—living mainly by the kitchen fire under the hanging hams. Thus when last year Farmer Gale's son, succeeding to the property and foolishly desiring a more scientific and literate bailiff, delicately intimated that having bought all the adjoining land, he had been compelled to acquire therewith the rival looker, the old Flynts were glad enough to be allowed for a small rent the life-use of the farmhouse and the bits of waste land around it, subject to their providing living room for old Master Peartree, who was to pasture his flock of sheep and a few kine in the near meadows. Martha, indeed, always maintained that Caleb had made a bad bargain with the new master—did not the whole neighbourhood pronounce the young widower a skinflint?—but Caleb, who had magisterially negotiated with the new bailiff the swapping of his wood-ashes for straw for her pet pig, Maria, limited his discussions with her to theology. "When one talks law and high business," he maintained, "we must goo back to the days afore Eve was dug out of Adam."

V

Bundock, restored to his superiority by the deprecatory expectancy of the old couple, observed graciously that there was no need to apologize: anybody was liable to have a letter. Indeed, he added generously, with nine boys dotted about the world, Frog Farm might have been far more troublesome.

"Eleven, Mr. Bundock," corrected Martha with a quiver in her voice.

"I don't reckon the dead and buried, Mrs. Flynt. They don't write—not even to the dead-letter office." He cut short a chuckle, remembering this was no laughing matter.

"And the other nine might as well be dead for all the letters you bring me," Martha retorted bitterly.

"No news is good news, dear heart," Caleb put in, as though to shield the postman. He was not so sure now that this unfortunate letter had not disturbed her slowly won resignation. "We've always yeared of anything unpleasant—like when Daniel married the Kaffir lady."

"That was Christopher," said Martha.

"Ow, ay, Christopher. 'Tis a wonder he could take to a thick-lipped lady. Oi couldn't fancy a black-skinned woman, even if she was the Queen of Sheba. Oi shook hands with one once, though, and it felt soft. They rub theirselves with oil to keep theirselves lithe."

Martha replied only with a sigh. The Kaffir lady, for all her coloured and heathen horror, at least supplied a nucleus for visualization, whereas all her other stalwart sons, together with one married daughter, had vanished into the four corners of the Empire—building it up with an unconsciousness mightier than the sword—and only the children who had died young—two girls and a boy—remained securely hers, fixed against the flux of life and adventure. Occasionally indeed an indirect rumour of her live sons' doings came to her, but correspondence was not the habit of those days when even amid the wealthier classes a boy might go out to India and his safe arrival remain unknown for a semestrium or more. The foreign postage, too, was no inconsiderable check to the literary impulse or encouragement to the lazy. Indeed postage stamps were still confined to half a dozen countries. It was but a decade since they had come in at all and letters with envelopes or an extra sheet had ceased to be "double"; postcards were still unknown, and in many parts postmen came as infrequently as carriers, people often hastening to scrawl replies which the same men might convey to the mail-bags.

"Kaffirs ain't black," corrected Bundock. "They're coffee-coloured. That's what the name means."

Martha sighed again. So far had her brooding fantasy gone that she sometimes pictured baby grandchildren as innocently dusky as the hybrid young fantails which no solicitude could keep out of her dovecot, and which were a reminder that heaven knew no colour-boundaries.

"Don't be nervous," Bundock reassured her. "I'll find it."

"Oh, no hurry, no hurry!" said Caleb, beginning to perspire distressingly under the postman's exertions and to mop his hairy brow with his brook-sopped handkerchief. How these youngsters grew up! he was thinking. Brats one had seen spanked waxed into mighty officers of State. "Shall I brush your breeches, Posty?" he inquired tactlessly.

"What's the use till they're dry?" snapped Bundock.

"Come in and dry them before the kitchen fire," said Martha.

"This sun'll dry them," he said coldly.

"Not so slick as the fire," Caleb blundered on. "'Tain't like you was a serpent walking on your belly."

Bundock flushed angrily and right-wheeled to hide the seat of his trousers. "Why you should go and catch your letter when the roads are in that state—!" he muttered.

"You could ha' waited till they dried!" Caleb said deprecatingly.

"I did wait a post-day or so," said Bundock with undiminished resentment. "But there's such a thing, uncle, as duty to my Queen. Things might have got damper instead of drier, like the time the floods were out beyond Long Bradmarsh, and I might have had to swim out to you."

Caleb was impressed. "But can you swim?" he inquired.

"That's not the point," growled Bundock. "I don't say I'd ha' faced the elements for you, but if somebody with real traffic and entanglement were living here, e.g. the Duke of Wellington, I should have come through fire and water."

"The Dook at a farm!" Caleb smiled incredulously.

"In the Battle of Waterloo," said Bundock icily, "the whole fight was whether he or Boney should hold a farm."

"You don't say!" cried Caleb excitedly. "And who got it?"

"Well, it wasn't Froggy's Farm." And Bundock roared with glee and renewed self-respect. Caleb guffawed too, but merely for elation at the Frenchy's defeat.

The calm and piping voice of Martha broke in upon this robustious duet, pointing out that there was no Duke in residence and no need for natation, but that since Jinny called for orders every Friday he might have given her the letter.

"Give the Queen's mail to a girl!" Bundock looked apoplectic.

"Jinny never loses anything," said Martha, unimpressed.

"She'll lose her character if she ain't careful," he said viciously; "driving of a Sunday with Farmer Gale."

"That's onny to chapel," said Caleb.

"A man that rich'll never take her there!" sneered Bundock.

"Why, Jinny's only a child," said Martha, roused at last. "And the best girl breathing. Look how she slaves for her grandfather!"

"Jinny! Jinny!" Bundock muttered. "Nothing but Jinny all the day and all the way." How often indeed had she snatched the gossip from his mouth, staled his earth-shaking tidings, even as the Bellman anticipated his jokes! "Let me catch her carrying letters, that's all. I'll have the law on her, child or no child. I expect she blows that horn to make the old folks think she's got postal rights!" He did not mention that in his vendetta against the girl it was he who never hesitated to poach on the rival preserves, and that he was even now carrying a certain packet of tracts which he had found at "The Black Sheep" awaiting Jinny's day, and which he had bagged on the ground that he had a letter for the same address.

"Jinny would have saved your legs," said Martha dryly.

Caleb turned on her. "Ay, and his leggings too!" he burst forth with savage sarcasm. But at great moments deep calls to deep. "Women don't understand a man's duty. And Posty's every inch a man."

Bundock tried to look his full manhood: fortunately the discovery of the letter at this instant enabled him to gain an inch or two by throwing back his shoulders, so long bent under the royal yoke.

"Mrs. Flynt," he announced majestically.

"For me?" gasped Martha.

"For you," said Bundock implacably. "Mrs. Flynt, Frog Farm, Swash End, Little Bradmarsh, near Chipstone, Essex. Not that I hold it's proper to write to a man's wife while he's alive—but my feelings don't count." And he tendered her the letter.

"It does seem more becoming for Flynt to have his Cousin Caroline's letter," admitted Martha, shrinking back meekly.

Bundock relaxed in beams. "I'm wonderfully pleased with you, Mrs. Flynt," he said, handing Caleb the letter. "You're a shining example, for all you stand up for that chit. When I think of Deacon Mawhood's wife and how she defies him with that bonnet of hers—!"

"What sort of bonnet?" said Martha, pricking up her ears.

"You haven't heard?" Bundock's satisfaction increased. "It's like the Queen's—drat her! I mean, drat Mrs. Mawhood—made with that new plait—'Brilliant's' the name. They turn the border of one edge of the straw inwards and that makes it all splendiferous."

"Pomps and wanities," groaned Caleb. "And she a deacon's wife!"

Bundock sniggered. His sympathy with the husband was deeper and older than theology.

"I told you," Martha reminded Caleb, "what would come of electing a ratcatcher a deacon."

"A righteous ratcatcher," maintained Caleb sturdily, "be higher than a hungodly emperor."

"You haven't got any emperors," said the practical Martha.

"And how many kings have joined your Ecclesia?" put in Bundock.

"All the kings of righteousness!" answered Martha in trumpet-tones.

Bundock was quelled. "Well, I can't stop gammicking," he said, shouldering his bag.

"Won't you have a glass of pagles wine?" said Martha, relapsing to earth.

"No, thank you. I've got a letter for Frog Cottage too!"

"For Master Peartree!" cried Martha. "And all in one morning. Well, if that's not a miracle!"

"You and your miracles!" he said with a Tom Paine brutality. "Why I saved up yours till another came for Swash End. And so I've managed to kill—" His face suddenly changed. The brutal look turned beatific. But his sentence was frozen. The good couple regarded him dubiously.

"What's amiss?" cried Martha.

Bundock gasped for expression like a salmon on a slab. "To kill" burst from his lips again, but the rest was choked in a spasm of cachinnation.

"You'll kill yourself laughin'," said Caleb.

Bundock mastered himself with a mighty effort. "So as to kill—ha, ha, ha!—to kill—ha, ha, ha!—two frogs—ha, ha, ha!—with one stone!"

Martha corrected him coldly: "Two birds, you mean."

"Ay," corroborated Caleb, "the proverb be two birds."

"But here," Bundock explained between two convulsions, "it's two frogs."

Caleb shook his head. "Oi've lived here or by the saltings afore you was born, and brought up a mort o' childer here. Two birds, sonny, two birds."

Bundock's closing chuckles died into ineffable contempt.

"Good morning," he said firmly.

"You're sure you won't have a sip o' pagles wine?" repeated Martha.

He shook his head sternly. "If I had time for drinking I'd have time to tell you all the news." He turned on his heel, presenting the post-bag at them like a symbol of duty.

"Anything fresh?" murmured Martha.

Bundock veered round viciously. "D'you suppose all Bradmarsh is as sleepy as the Froggeries? Fresh? Why, there's things as fresh as the thatch on Farmer Gale's barn or the paint on Elijah Skindle's new dog-hospital or the black band on the chimney-sweep's Sunday hat."

"Is Mrs. Whitefoot dead?" inquired Martha anxiously.

"No, 'twas only his mother-in-law in London, and when he went up to the funeral he had his pocket picked. Quite spoilt his day, I reckon—ha, ha, ha!"

"Buryin' ain't a laughin' matter," rebuked Caleb stolidly.

"It depends who's buried," said Bundock. "I shouldn't cry over Mrs. Mawhood. Which reminds me that the Deacon sent out the Bellman to say he couldn't be responsible for her debts."

"Good!" cried Caleb. Martha paled, but was silent.

"Only the Bellman spoilt it as usual with his silly old jokes. Proclaimed that the Deacon had put his foot down on his wife's bonnet."

"He, he, he!" laughed the old couple.

Bundock turned a hopeless hump. "Good morning!"

"And thank you kindly for the letter," called Martha.

"Don't mention it," said Bundock. "And besides I killed—ho, ho, ho!—two frogs!"

They heard his explosions on the quiet air long after he and his royal hump had vanished along the Bradmarsh road.

VI

Caleb's eyes followed the heaving mail-bag.

"Bundock's buoy-oy fares to be jolly this mornin'."

"He does be lively sometimes," agreed Martha.

Suddenly Caleb became aware of the letter in his hand.

"Dash my buttons, Martha! We disremembered to ask him to read it."

It can no longer be concealed that despite her erudition Martha could not read writing nor write save by imitating print. The cursive alphabet was Phœnician to her.

"I didn't forget," she answered with her masterly calm. "Bundock's too leaky. You heard him tell all the gossip and scandal. And it ain't true about Jinny, for Master Peartree saw them riding in the other Sunday and Farmer Gale's little boy sat between them. Besides, Bundock's a man, and I don't want a man to read my letter from Caroline."

The point seemed arguable, but Caleb meekly suggested the little boy she had just mentioned—only a mile and a half away. He would be at school, Martha pointed out.

Caleb looked at the letter as a knifeless cook at an oyster.

"What's the clock-time?" he asked.

"Not quite certain. I set the clock by Jinny last Friday, but it stopped suddenly yesterday, when I was reading you St. Paul's Epistle to the Corinthians. Haven't you heard it not striking?"

Caleb shook his head.

"Afeared Oi'm gooin' deafish, dear heart. But we'll know the clock-time on Friday," he added philosophically. "And when Jinny comes she can read the letter likewise."

But Martha was blushing. "No, no, not Jinny! She's a young girl."

"Thank the Lord for her lively face!" agreed Caleb.

"Maybe she oughtn't to read a letter to a married woman," explained Martha shyly, "being a girl without mother or sisters, brought up by her grandfather."

"But Cousin Caroline wouldn't write naught improper."

"Of course not—but it mightn't be proper for an orphan girl to read. Maybe it's not even proper for you, and that's why she addressed it to me."

Caleb felt as bemused as before a Bundock witticism.

"Joulterhead!" said Martha, with a loving smile. "And you've had fourteen!"

The letter fell from his nerveless fingers. "Cousin Caroline confined again!" And the clacking of all those innumerable infants filled the air—like the barking of the black geese on the wintry mud-flats. But he recovered himself. "Why, she's a widow, not a pair."

"Widows can be re-paired," said Martha.

"Must have been a middlin' bold man to goo courtin' a family that size," Caleb reflected.

He picked up the letter and poised it in his hand.

"Don't feel as weighty as St. Paul's letters," he said.

"The text doesn't mean his letters were heavy," explained Martha. "'His letters, say they, are weighty and powerful'—that's what I was reading you when the clock stopped. Any fool can write a heavy letter—he's only got to write on a slate."

"That's a true word," said Caleb, admiring her.

"Whereas," pursued Martha, "the whole Bible has been got inside a nutshell."

"Lord!" said Caleb. "I suppose it was a cokernut!"

"Not at all. Only a walnut."

"Fancy! But was there walnuts in the Holy Land?"

"I didn't say 'twas done in Palestine."

"Then there wasn't walnuts there?" His face fell.

"I don't remember—oh, yes—Solomon asked his love to come into the garden of nuts."

"But it don't say walnuts?" he inquired wistfully.

"I can't say it does."

"Then maybe there won't be pickled walnuts in the New Jerusalem?"

"Not all the righteous have your carnal appetite," said Martha severely.

"You just said Solomon's sweetheart liked nuts," said Caleb stoutly. "And dedn't the Holy Land flow with milk and honey?" He had a vision of it, seamed and riddled like his native mud-flat, but with lacteal creeks and mellifluous pools.

"You put me out so," snapped Bundock, suddenly reappearing before the engrossed couple, "that I forgot to kill my two frogs after all!" And going to the Frog Cottage doorway, he knocked officially before opening it and committing the letter to the empty interior.

"You'll be witness that I delivered it constitutionally," he said, "for I can't be expected to come a third time."

"'Tis a windfall your coming a second," cried Caleb eagerly, "bein' as we can't read the letter."

Martha made facial contortions to remind him that Bundock was barred. "'Tain't you we want to read it," he hurriedly added, "but when a letter comes all of an onplunge, time a man's peacefully trimmin' the werges, he ain't prepared like. You haven't got a moment—did, Oi'd be glad o' your counsel on the matter."

"Well, since I've wasted so much of the Queen's time—!" said Bundock, flattered.

They adjourned to the parlour to give him a rest, and denuding himself of both cap and bag of office, he occupied oracularly the long-unused arm-chair, while Caleb, uncomfortably perched on a seat of slippery horsehair, started to unfold the situation.

"Take off your hat," broke in Martha. "Mr. Bundock will be thinking you've no manners."

"Oi'll be soon gooin' outside again," said Caleb obstinately, and re-started his story.

"Do let me explain," interrupted Martha at last.

"Do let me get a word in," cried Caleb.

"Well, take off your hat."

"Oi'll be gooin' outside soon, Oi tell ye."

"Then you can put it on again."

"Oi shall never make Bundock sensible, ef you keep interruptin' me."

"You see, Mr. Bundock, it's this way—" began Martha.

"Oi've told him all that," said Caleb. "Let me speak."

"Well, take off your hat," said Martha.

"Oi'll be gooin' outside agen, won't Oi?"

Bundock was examining the letter which had been laid on the table as for an operation.

"But it don't look like a woman's writing," he interrupted. "That would be spidery."

"'Tain't likely she could write herself in that condition," began Caleb, but Martha's face again hushed him down.

"There's neither seal nor sticking envelope," pursued the expert. "Nothing but a wafer. Comes from a poor man."

"Her new husband," said Caleb, and set Martha grimacing again.

"Oi'll be soon gooin' outside," he protested, misunderstanding.

"What you want," summed up Bundock judicially, "is a mixture of discretion with matrimony, seasoned with a sprinkle of learning."

"He talks like the Book!" said Caleb admiringly.

"But where is this mixture?" inquired Martha eagerly.

"She don't exist," said Bundock. "But Miss Gentry is the nearest lady that can read, and Fate is just sending me with a letter and a packet to her."

The couple looked doubtful.

"She ain't matrimony," said Caleb.

"No," admitted Bundock, "but I guess she's old enough to be, though I haven't seen her census paper—he, he! And besides she's a dressmaker!"

"What's that to do with it?" asked Caleb.

"I see your missus understands," said Bundock mysteriously.

"But she won't walk five miles to read my letter," urged the blushing Martha.

Caleb had one of the great inspirations of his life.

"And ain't it time you got a new gownd?"

Martha flushed up. "Oh, Caleb! Don't let us run to vanity!"

"Wanity, mother! It ain't tinkling ornaments nor cauls nor nose-jewels," protested Caleb, with a vague reminiscence of her Biblical readings. "And ye've had naught since the sucking-pig Oi bought ye for your sixtieth birthday."

But Martha shook her head, quoting firmly:

"Let me be dressed fine as I will, Birds, flowers, and worms exceed me still."

"Then why not a bonnet?" suggested Bundock. "That would be cheaper than a gown."

"Ay, a bonnet!" agreed Caleb, though he sounded it a "boarnt."

Martha flashed a resentful glance which, however, Bundock took for but another thrust at Caleb's obstinate hat.

"I don't want a new bonnet," she cried indignantly.

"It needn't be new," said Bundock helpfully. "Just have your old bonnet whitened. That's on her bill-paper:

'Bonnets Bleached As Good As New.'"

"That's a good notion," said Caleb. "You don't want it bran-span-new. Posty'll tell her to come over here to get your old boarnt and then we'll spring Cousin Caroline's letter on her for her to read!" He chuckled. Bundock chuckled too, swelling at the adoption of his advice.

"And now that I've stopped gammicking so long, I may as well sample that cowslip wine, Mrs. Flynt," he observed graciously.

But Martha had vanished.

VII

Miss Gentry had apartments in one of the most elegant cottages to be found in Little Bradmarsh. Protected by palings, it stood all alone on the high road, painted a vivid green, with three pollarded lime-trees in front like sentinel mops. At the base of the trim little garden the front door rose above two wooden steps with a little porch and ostentated a brass plate with the inscription:

MISS GENTRY
LATE OF COLCHESTER
PRACTICAL DRESSMAKER AND MILLINER.

In proof of which, from the cottage window, whose green shutters lay folded back, a visite or jacket of black silk, and a polka jacket, and a trio of straw bonnets, Tuscan or Leghorn, appealed to the passing eye: one of them a bonnet cap with a quilting of net and broad blue strings, another resplendent with purple ribbons and the new-treated straw plait that the Queen and Mrs. Mawhood favoured, and the third of drawn silk on little wires. The pictures of the period with a wonderful unanimity and monotony display a single style of bonnet, but artists in those days were men, and Miss Gentry could have told you better. "I've looked down from a pew in the gallery of my Colchester Church on Easter Sunday," she told Jinny once, "and tried in vain to find two fellow-bonnets."

But her professional door with its immaculate paint and shining brass was so forbiddingly respectable that clients mostly preferred to seek access through her landlady's back door, where the flutter of washing from the clothes-line on its green square poles in the little orchard was reassuring; not to mention her chickens.

"Practical" was the unfailing adjective in those parts. Miss Gentry was not undeserving of it, for her dresses were cheap without being vulgar, while her knack of whitening the straw enabled the poorest, in the succession of new bonnets, to keep pace with Victoria on the throne. A stranger might have thought another species of dressmaker existed, whose confections, though exquisite, would never fit, or who designed, but could not execute; whereas the only other person for miles round at all in the sartorial line was an equally "Practical Breeches-Maker," placarding from a flower-potted cottage window his "Strong, Stylish Pantaloons." But the thought of unpractical pantaloons—say, without buttons or belts—or of theoretical trousers, was simple compared with the image evoked by Mr. Henry Whitefoot's door-plate, proclaiming that victim of the London pick-pocket a "Practical Chimney-Sweep": as by contrast with some exquisite dream Ethiopian, only platonically black, darkly revolving flues and fireplaces, sweeping shadow-chimneys with fleckless brushes, and carrying off ideal bags of the soot that never was on sea or land.

But perhaps in Miss Gentry's case the word "Practical" was necessary to offset the business-damage of the tradition that had followed her from her native Colchester. For Miss Gentry had had a "revelation." It had occurred in her girlhood, but the halo of it still circled round her chignon. Seated in church, full of worldly thoughts—possibly studying the infinite variety of bonnets—she had seen the stained-glass angel move. What this flutter of wing and lifting of leg "revealed" had never been clear: unless—as a wag maintained—it portended the flight of Miss Gentry herself. That hegira of hers from Colchester to Bradmarsh had not, alas, increased her prophetic prestige: what right has a "furriner" to come with "revelations"? Even her fellow-Churchfolk—she was one of the few Bradmarshians that clung to the Establishment—looked askance on the miracle, feeling it indeed as reprehensibly Papish, and as lending colour to the suspicion that she was a "French" dressmaker: a suspicion strengthened at once by her elegant handiwork, and by her full-bosomed plenitude, swarthy complexion, and more than embryonic moustache. It was forgotten that if these did imply Gallic blood, it would have been, not the Papish, but that Huguenot strain whose inpour into the county had at one time carried the French liturgy into Essex churches. As a matter of fact Miss Gentry was so fanatical a Church woman that she supplemented all her bills and receipts by tracts in defence of the Establishment, purchased at her own expense from a mysterious reservoir in Colchester. Nevertheless, such is the contrariety of mankind, the large accession she represented to the parish church—where on wet Sundays only the Apostle's two or three were gathered together—was discounted by her felt queerness.

And it was, still more oddly, from the Peculiars that she received the bulk of her custom, and this despite her top-lofty airs towards them, and the tracts suggesting that souls, no less than bonnets, could be bleached as good as new. Possibly their more elastic spirituality vibrated more readily to the moving angel: perhaps the real bond of sympathy was that they knew her unpopular with the Church: like themselves a butt of legend, and lacking even their advantage of Bradmarsh birth.

But even the Churchwomen did not utterly deny patronage to this talented needlewoman, nor refuse her the deference due to weekday gloves, a parasol, and bills with printed headlines; they did not even discountenance her crusade against Dissent, though her copious allusions to Providence "moving in a mysterious way" were felt to be too broadly autobiographic. Moreover, in view of the caustic remarks upon cardinals, Puseyites, black-robed priests, and winking pictures, by which her tracts began to diversify the attack upon Dissent—for John Bull was getting alarmed at the new Roman invasion—it was a source of surprise that she failed to see the beam in her own eye. For if Virgins could not wink in Rimini, why should Angels wobble in Colchester? To add to her oddity, her brain was full of ancient maggots of astrology and medicine, crept in from "Culpeper's Herbal," her one bedside book.

That Bundock should be bringing a bonnet commission to this excellent and industrious, if freakish female, was the more laudable, inasmuch as he nourished a prejudice against her and her tracts. Not that he held with Catholic or evangelical Dissenters any more than with the Church proper. As a follower of Tom Paine, whose "Age of Reason" he read piously in bed every Sunday morning—the passage asserting that to make a true miracle Jonah should have swallowed the whale was a regular Lesson—he regarded himself as a great free spirit in an illiterate and priest-ridden world, one whose God was everywhere except in Church. Not that he could follow the Master's excursions into trigonometry or astronomy or knew anything of his idol's "Rights of Man," being indeed singularly free from the contemporary unrest of the industrial townsman, and combining, like greater men, a crusty conservatism for the old order with a radical rejection of its spinal creed. Possibly his devotion to the still youthful Queen was part of his softness for the sex, for the only part of "The Age of Reason" that left him unconvinced was its impugnment of the wisdom of Solomon, its contention that "seven hundred wives and three hundred concubines are worse than none." But it was not Tom Paine, nor even Bob Taylor's "The Devil's Chaplain," it was the long years of his father's paralysis that had first sapped his faith in the pharmacopœian aspects of prayer, though he considerately concealed his defection from his bed-ridden parent, and even the visiting elders withheld the racking information. The old Bundock was not, however, to be deceived, on this point at least.

"My son is moral, only moral," he would say, with a sigh.

To such a temperament Miss Gentry must needs be antipathetic, and to mark his distaste, Bundock was wont to leave the Colchester packets of tracts as well as the "practical" correspondence at the side door, shedding the light of his countenance only on the landlady. But on this occasion, having a message to deliver as well as a missive and a packet, he performed resoundingly on the green knocker, and Miss Gentry herself, attended by Squibs, her ebony cat, appeared in the narrow, little passage, frenziedly stitching at a feminine fabric. Behind her, through the open back door, was a gleam of blossoming orchard and dangling chemises.

"Good morning, Bundock," she said graciously; "lovely weather."

"It's all right overhead," he grumbled, "but underfoot, especially at Frog Farm—whew!"

"You had to go to Frog Farm?" she inquired sympathetically.

"Yes, but there was a letter for Frog Cottage too. So I—he, he!—I killed two frogs with one stone."

"Two birds, you mean," said Miss Gentry, embosoming her letter with a romantic air and laying her packet on a chair. She added in alarm: "Would you like a glass of water?"

"I don't need drink," said Bundock, mastering the apoplectic assault, "it's other folks that need brains."

"My, were the old Flynts unusually trying?" she asked sympathetically.

"They want you to clean the gammer's bonnet," he answered brusquely.

"That's not so foolish." Her needle was moving busily again. "Have you brought it?"

"No."

"That does seem foolish."

"I'm not a bonnet-bearer! They want you to fetch it."

"Me! Five miles to clean a bonnet! When I'm so busy! And in all that mud!"

"It ain't so muddy this side o' Swash End, and it's not two miles each way by the fields."

"Yes, with horrid cows!"

Bundock felt protective. "Cows ain't bulls."

"Well, I won't go. You tell Mrs. Flynt she must come to me."

"How can I tell her? I shan't likely be going that way for months, thank my stars." Miss Gentry quivered a little at the expression, wondering under what planet he was born.

"Well, I'll write to her," she said conclusively.

"What! And me take the letter!" In his indignation he almost blurted out that the same difficulty of reading it would arise.

"Then I'll tell Jinny to bring the bonnet!"

Bundock felt baffled. Instead of cunningly helping the Flynts to get their letter read, he had only secured that minx of a carrier a commission. He scowled at the dressmaker, seeing her moustache as big as a guardsman's and believing the worst of the legends about it: even that the real reason she left Colchester was that the bristly-bearded oysterman to whom she was engaged had refused to shave unless she did. "I'll be wishing you a good morning," he said icily, hitching up his bag.

"Good morning," said Miss Gentry. But she omitted to slam the door in his face as he expected, indeed she had gradually advanced into the porch, stitching unrelaxingly. And Bundock now became acutely aware that he could not turn his back on her without revealing the stain on Her Majesty's uniform, that even by lowering the mail-bag he had just hitched up, he could not cover up what certain rude ploughboys had already commented on. He understood it was green. In this dreadful situation he began backing slowly as from the presence of royalty, making desperate conversation to cover his retreat.

"I did give you your tracts, didn't I?" he babbled.

"If you mean the packet," said Miss Gentry in stern rebuke, "there it lies. I haven't opened it!"

"Do you mean that I have?" he asked indignantly, gaining another yard in this rear-guard action. "We don't have to open an oyster to know what's inside."

Miss Gentry's brow grew as swarthy as her moustache—at the reminder of her lost oysterman, Bundock supposed in dismay.

"Don't you always send out tracts after I bring you packets?" he explained hastily, still retreating with his face to the foe.

"Not when they're patterns," said Miss Gentry crushingly. "And how do you know it's not The Englishwomen's Magazine?"

She turned back into the passage, and he hoped she would slam the door on her triumph, but she took up the packet instead. "We shall soon see," and snipping the string with mysteriously produced scissors, she read out unctuously: "Ishmael and the Wilderness."

Bundock did not know which way to turn. Why in the name of propriety did she not go back to her workroom and close her door? Miss Gentry, without the clue to his lingering attitude, observed invitingly, tapping the packet: "If this won't make you see the beauties of the Establishment, nothing will."

He grinned uncomfortably. "Always willing to see the beauties of any establishment."

It was very strange. Give him a female, even with a moustache, even tepefied by tracts, and something from the deeps rose up to philander. Not that there wanted a lurid fascination in this exotic and literate lady: his very loathing was a tribute to a vivid personality.

Miss Gentry, however, was shocked. She put down the tracts. She knew herself "born under Venus," but romance and respectability were never disjoined in her day-dreams, and as the channel of a revelation she felt profaned. "Don't talk like that," she said sharply. "You're a married man."

"'Tis a married man knows how to appreciate beauty," he replied, receding farther nevertheless as in ironic commentary.

"For shame!" Her needle stabbed on. "And you setting up to be holy!"

"Me?" Surprise brought his strategic retreat to a standstill. "I never set up to be a stained-glass saint."

Again he had blundered. The black eyes flashed fire. "You who move mountains!" she cried angrily.

"Me move mountains?" Bundock was bewildered.

"A little grain of mustard-seed," he heard her saying more tremulously. "And if a sycamine-tree could move—! Surely you don't hold with the unbelievers!"

It was precisely whom Bundock did hold with, but the big black eyes seemed suddenly tearful and appealing, her needle seemed entering his breast, and she swam before him as a fine, voluptuous female. Through the passage he saw the apple-trees in bridal bloom and the white feminine washing, and the Master's remark on the apparent miracle of the extraction of electric flashes from the human body thrilled in his memory.

"Of course not," he heard himself saying soothingly, while his legs felt going forward, losing all the ground so laboriously won.

"Then you do believe the angel moved?" she asked eagerly.

"Don't I see her moving?" he replied.

Miss Gentry looked down from her doorstep more in sorrow than in anger. "You're a married man!" she reminded him again.

"And does marriage pick out a man's eyes—like a goat-sucker?" He felt too near her now to back out, and he put forth his hand for hers, not without nervousness at the needle. Could his father have seen him now, he might have thought his son not even "moral." But Miss Gentry dexterously met the amorous palm with a tract. "That'll open your eyes," she said.

To feel a flabby piece of paper instead of a warm hand is not conducive to theological persuasion: all Bundock's dissenting blood rushed to his head.

"There's two opinions about that," he snorted.

"There are two opinions," Miss Gentry assented placidly; "one wrong and the other mine."

"Oh, of course!" he sneered. "The Church is always infallible."

"We're eighteen and a half centuries old," said Miss Gentry freezingly.

"Did you put that in your census paper?" retorted the humorist.

Miss Gentry winced. She was weary of the jokes that had desolated Bradmarsh, yet she was conscious of having let her landlady's estimate of her age go by default.

"I had no paper to fill up," she reminded him frigidly. "But if there was a census of religions, you'd certainly be among the mushrooms."

"Better than being among the mummies." Bundock's father might have clapped his palsied hands, to hear this defender of the faith. But Miss Gentry mistook this fair retort in kind for another allusion to the personal census.

"I thought you could discuss like a gentleman!" It was a cunning shaft, and Squibs, seizing this moment to rub herself against the postman's leggings, he replied more mildly: "What's the use of going by age—except the Age of Reason?"

"Then be guided by Reason." Miss Gentry stitched implacably. "If the Almighty meant prayer to be medicine, why did He create castor-oil?"

Bundock was dumbfounded.

"Or Epsom salts?" she added triumphantly.

"They're for cattle which can't pray," he answered with an inspiration.

Miss Gentry's needle stabbed the air. But she recovered herself. "Then why do you eat rhubarb pie?"

"Because it's nice." He grinned.

"But rhubarb's a medicine!"

He countered cleverly. "We don't mind taking medicine—so long as we're well!" We! He was identifying himself with his despised Brethren: such is human nature under attack. But Miss Gentry was not at the end of her resources.

"Well, what do you do when you break your legs? Pray the bones straight?"

"But we don't break our legs. I never heard of a Peculiar breaking his leg."

"But why shouldn't a Peculiar break his leg?"

"That's not my affair. He don't. I've got Peculiars all over my beat, and never have I known one to break a leg. A broken heart, now—!"

"But if he did break a leg?" persisted Miss Gentry.

"If any one could break a leg, it would be me!" he said crossly.

"Well, then what would you do—if you broke your leg?"

Bundock was worn out. "What's the good of meeting troubles half-way?" he snapped, turning on his heel.

"Yours seem to have come more than half-way," scoffed Miss Gentry.

Bundock clapped his hand to the mud-patch, stung in his tenderest part. He wheeled round prestissimo, raging with repartee. But the door had closed—too late! Solitary, the sable Squibs dominated the doorstep—like a sardonic spirit.

Bundock was turning away angrily, though now fearlessly, when with a sudden thought he caught up the cat and plucked out one of her hairs. It was not revenge—it was merely that his youngest daughter had a sty, for which he believed the black hair an infallible remedy.

CHAPTER II

JINNY ON HER ROUNDS

Give me simple labouring folk,
Who love their work,
Whose virtue is a song
To cheer God along.
THOREAU.

I

Thus it was that the days passed without any literate and discreet female descending on Frog Farm or any rejuvenation appearing in Martha's bonnet; and the unread letter lay—guarded by two china dogs—on the parlour mantelpiece awaiting the carrier. For it had been decided, after nightly discussions that were a change for Caleb from the Christadelphian curtain-lectures, to fall back on Jinny after all. She was to read it to Martha in Caleb's careful absence, and was to be stopped if the improper seemed looming.

Alas, the best-laid schemes of mice and Marthas gang agley, and by the day that Jinny's horn resounded along the raised road that led to the farm, the world was changed for Caleb and Martha. There was, in fact—for the first time in Jinny's experience—neither of the twain to meet her as Methusalem ambled under the drooping witch-elms towards the twin doors.

It was a tilt-cart,—with two tall wheels, and although Jinny steered it and packed it and unpacked it, and scoured it and hitched Methusalem to it, its weather-beaten canvas blazoned in fading black letters the legend:

DANIEL QUARLES
CARRIER
LITTLE BRADMARSH.

You gather that she operated under the shadow of a great name, greatest as being masculine. Self-standing careers for women had not yet dawned on the world. If the first faint cloud of feminism had appeared that very year in New York, no bigger than a man's pants, the Bloomerites had but added to the gaiety of mankind, and in rural Essex, with the exception of dressmaking, wherein man appeared unnatural, women were the recognized practitioners only of witchcraft or fortune-telling or the concoction of philters; professions that were the peculiar province of crones scarcely to be considered sexed. Though women earned money by plaiting straw, they had husbands on the premises. Widows, of course, for whom there was no provision outside the Chipstone poorhouse, were allowed to maintain themselves more manfully than spinsters: but then they were "relicts" of the masculine, had served—so to speak—an apprenticeship under it. But the business of plying between Chipstone and Bradmarsh was a peculiarly male occupation, and even the venerable name of Daniel Quarles would not have sufficed to shield or install Jinny had she jumped into his place as abruptly as Nip was apt to jump into the cart.

No, Rome was not built in a day, nor could Jinny have become the carrier "all of an onplunge," as Caleb would have put it. That would have shocked the manners and morals of Bradmarsh, both Little and Long, and upset the decorum of Chipstone. A gradual preparation had been necessary, a transition by which Jinny changed into the carrier as imperceptibly as she had ripened into the girl. At first the small "furriner"—the carried and not the carrier—reposing in the cart because, after smallpox had snatched away both her parents in the same week, her grandfather, who had imported her, had nowhere else to put her; playing in the great canvas-covered playground that held as many heights, depths, and obstacles as a steeplechase course; petted by every client for her helplessness before her helpfulness gave her a second lease of favour; bearing a literally larger and larger hand in "Gran'fer's" transactions as he grew older and older; correcting with cautious tact his memories, his accounts, his muddled bookings and deliveries, in due course ousting the octogenarian even from his place on the driving-board and carrying him first by her side and then inside in his second childhood, just as he had carried her in her first—a stage in which his cackle with the customers carried on the continuity of the male tradition; leaving him at home on bad days—whether his own or Nature's—and then altogether in the winter, and then altogether in the spring, and then altogether in the autumn, and finally—when he reached his nineties—altogether in the summer; Jinny the Carrier was—it will be seen—a shock so subtly prepared and so long discounted as to have been practically imperceptible. She might crack Daniel's heavy whip, but nobody felt the flourish as other than vicarious, if not indeed a sort of play-acting evoking the pleasure a more sophisticated audience finds in Rosalind's swashbucklings. Not that she made any brazen pretences to equality in lifting boxes; she sat with due feminine humility while male muscles swelled and contracted under her presiding smile and the rippling music of her thanks.

Here was, in fact, the prosaic purpose of the little horn slung at her side—her one apparent embellishment of the tradition: it summoned her slavish superiors so that she might be spared alighting and re-climbing with goods. In face of the accuracy of her operations, this display of helplessness probably helped to remove the sting of an otherwise intolerable feminine sufficiency: it was perhaps the secret of her popularity. Even with the most Lilliputian packets nobody expected Jinny to descend and knock at their doors—one blast and old and young tumbled over one another to greet the coming or speed the parting parcel. It was indeed as if a good fairy should condescend to do your marketing, a fairy in a straw bonnet (piquantly tied under the chin in a bow with drooping ends), a fairy whose brilliant smile and teeth and flowing ringlets could convert even an order for jalap into poetry, nay, induce in the eternal masculine a craving for more. In fine, so topsy-turvily had this snail-paced transition worked, so slowly had Jinny's freedom broadened down from precedent to precedent, that when strangers expressed disapproval at these mannish courses, Little Bradmarsh was shocked, Long Bradmarsh surprised, and Chipstone scornful. Not that they were at all prepared to argue the question in the abstract. Their prejudice against carrying as a profession for women remained as rooted and unshaken as the critic's. Women? Who was speaking of women? Jinny was Jinny—a being unique and irreplaceable, "bless her bonny fice." It contributed to her unquestionability that the Quarleses had been carriers for a hundred years—and more.

Nor did Jinny, for her part, generalize on the other side or take any conscious interest in the emancipation of her sex. Her horn blew no challenge to the world. It did not even occur to her that she was doing anything out of the common—the tilt-cart had been her nursery, it was now her place of business. She had come into its foreground so unconsciously that it was not as a good fairy that she saw herself, nor even as an attractive asset of the Quarles concern, but as a busy toiler—driven from morning to night rather than driving—and handicapped not only by her household and garden work, her goats and poultry, but by a nonagenarian grandfather, shaky in health and immovable in opinion. Fortunately for her temper—and for the chastening of a tongue only too a-tingle with rustic wit—Jinny regarded the cantankerous patriarch as no more an object for back-talk than a suckling. It had become second nature to soothe and humour him; and she knew him as she knew the highways and byways in the dark or the snow: where to turn and where to go round, where to skirt a swamp and where to shave a ditch. By way of compensation there was his affection—as primitive as Nip's or Methusalem's—and evoking as primitive a response. For Jinny was none of your genteel heroines with ethereal emotions and complex aspirations.

It was not that Nature had not cast her for a poetic part—she was small and slender enough, and her light grey eyes behind dark lashes sufficiently subtilized her expression, and when she was hesitating between two words—not two opinions, for she always had one—her little mouth would purse itself enchantingly. There was gentility too about her toes. As her grandfather remarked with his archaic pronouns and plurals: "That has the smallest fitten I ever saw to a wench!" She certainly did not dress the part, for despite the witchery of the bonnet, her workaday skirt and stout shoes proclaimed the village girl, as her hands proclaimed the drudge who scoured and scrubbed and baked and dug and manured: indeed what with her own goats and her farmyard commissions, she was almost as familiar with the grosser aspects of animal life as that strangely romanticized modern figure, the hospital nurse. The delicate solicitude of Martha on her behalf was thus a pure morbidity, for in going to and fro like a weaver's shuttle, Jinny could scarcely remain ignorant that women were as liable to offspring as any other females, though it seemed a part of Nature's order that had no more to do with herself than the strange, hirsute growths on the masculine face—or for the matter of that on Miss Gentry's.

Mr. Fallow, the old pastor of Little Bradmarsh, who, though despised and rejected of Dissent, required—being human—comestibles, candles, and shoe-strings from Chipstone, as well as the disposal of his honey and his smaller tithes, was among Jinny's favourite clients, her original horror of Bradmarsh Church having been early modified by an accidental peep one weekday morning, which revealed its priest as its sole occupant. Yet, standing in his place in his white surplice, he was going through the service with such devout self-forgetfulness that the confused child wondered whether the Satan of worldliness had him so entirely gripped as she had been given to understand. She did not know that this very praying all to himself would have shocked Miss Gentry as savouring of the abhorred High Churchmanship. Indeed "little better than a Papist" the Chipstone curate had pronounced the harmless old widower.

He for his part had long admired the little carrier, and perceiving the fine shape of her calloused fingers, no less than the smallness of her sturdy shoes, and enjoying the tang of her tongue—for the cottage women, though nimbler than their lords, were not witty—he had indulged his antiquarian vein (and the abundant leisure due to the ravages of Dissent) by tracing for her a less plebeian and more Churchy pedigree. Foiled in the hope of connecting her with Francis Quarles of "Emblems" fame, he found in Norden's list of the Ancient Halls of Essex a Spring Elm Manor appertaining to one Jonathan Quarles. The flockless pastor had even journeyed in quest of this Hall and found illogical confirmation in the fact of its continued existence, in all the pride of mullioned windows and lily-strewn if muddy moat, though with its private chapel turned into a stable and its piscina bricked over. Henceforward he saw in the exuberant vitality and imperious obstinacy of Daniel Quarles only an impoverished reincarnation of hard-living but ecclesiastically correct squiredom, while in Jinny, with her generous visits to the ailing and bed-ridden on her route, he elected to behold a re-embodied Lady Bountiful, pride of a feudal parish. What was prosaically certain, however, was that Jinny had not even the education of Bundock's bunch of girls, the only school she had ever attended being the Peculiars' Sunday-school held at a house adjoining the chapel in an interval between the services. Thither, as to the services—her grandfather being a Wesleyan—she had been convoyed regularly by Caleb, packed into a cart with as many of the Flynt boys as had not yet flown off.

But the business itself forced reading and writing upon her, though when its sole responsibility devolved on her, and it was no longer necessary to confute the old man's memory by the written word or figure, she found herself agreeably able to dispense with the learned arts.

Welcomed at lonely farmyards where fierce dogs sometimes broke their chains for the joy of licking her hand or of flying at Nip's throat; not less welcome in village High Streets, where every other house would ply her fussily with orders that she took coolly and without a single note, her bosom knowledge of everybody's business and her dramatic interpretation of any abnormal commission infusing life into her work that saved her from slips of memory; adored by all the swains and yokels who hauled her goods and chattels up and down, but radiating only a frosty sunshine in return, for none had ever been able to pass the ice-barrier that separated her private self from her professional geniality; jumping down herself only to give Christian burial to hapless moles, rats, shrews, leverets, and blood-stained feathers, or to glean for lonely old women or the numerous and impoverished Pennymole family the unconscious largesse of more careless drivers—turnips, lumps of coal, wisps of hay; chaffering with beaming shopkeepers on behalf of her clients, and hail-fellow-well-met with her fellow-carriers, encountered at cross-roads or "The Black Sheep"; Jinny pursued her unmaidenly career in fine weather or foul, sometimes wayworn, wind-whipped, rain-drenched, and with aching forehead, but more often with a vital joy that was not least keen when Methusalem—cloud-exhaling and clogged by snow that sometimes raised the road as high as the hedges—had to plough his way along a track hewn out by labourers, with here and there a siding cut in the glittering mass for carts to pass each other by. Those were days not devoid of danger: road, hedge, ditch, and field obliterated in one snowy expanse. Once Jinny's cart had to be dug out like a crusted fossil of the Ice Age—and only the agonized howling of Nip had brought rescue.

III

It was the first time he had justified his air of managing the whole concern round which he barked and bounded and scurried as though Methusalem and Jinny were his minions. He had indeed commandeered them—jumping originally out of nowhere on to the tail-board—and however he strayed from the path of their duty in his numberless tangential excursions and expeditions, they knew he would never abandon them.

Like many other great characters Nip was a mongrel. His foundation was fox-terrier, and he had preserved the cleverness of the strain without its pluck. To strangers, indeed, he seemed a very David among dogs, attacking, as he sometimes did, canine Goliaths. But no dog is a hero to his mistress, and after he had adopted her, Jinny discovered that these resounding assaults on the bulkier were but bravado passages, based on his flair that the bigger dog was also the bigger coward. That was where his brains came in, as well as his baser breed. A sniff at a real fighter and Nip would evade combat, sauntering off with a nonchalant air. A splash of brown on his brainpan and about his ears, and a dab of black on his snout were—with his leathern collar—the sole touches of relief in his sleek whiteness. His head—beautifully poised and shaped—with its bright dark-brown eye, eloquently expressive and passing easily from love to greediness, from shyness to shame, invited many a pat from lovers of the soulful. Yet to hear him bolt a rabbit was to imagine a demon on the war-path: in a flash the cart would be left a furlong behind or athwart; his raucous staccato yells filled the meadows with echoes of blood-lust and revenge. But long experience had dulled Jinny's solicitude for Bunny: never once was there a sign of a kill. Sometimes, indeed, when Nip was hunting a rat, the creature would run across the path under his very nose, but that nose, pushing eagerly for far-off game, never seemed able to readjust itself to what was under it. All the which maladroitness was probably artfulness, Nip scenting shrewdly that a successful sports-dog would have been hounded out. He knew well the foolish, treacherous heart of his mistress, who actually misled the hunt those autumn mornings that brought the high-mettled hares across their path with ears taut and every muscle tragically astrain. Up would come the beagles, with a long processional flutter of waving white tails, nosing forlornly and barking dismally, while he—panting to put them right—was tied paw and paw. How they set him quivering, those horn-tootlings of the gorgeous Master, though they did not go to his bowels as much as those staccato chivies that suggested that the green-and-white gentleman was one of themselves rather than a biped, or as those more elaborately contorted cries and rousing thong-cracks of the Whipper-in. A fellow-feeling makes us wondrous kind. And when all these hunters—four-footed or two-footed—including the draggletail of fat, breathless farmers and wheezing females, were remorselessly sent the wrong way by his brutal mistress, the poor dog could not refrain from wailing.

Even when the hare did not cross her path, her horn, imitating the professional toot, would allure and misguide the distant dogs. Nip's own relatives, the foxhounds, more rarely came his way, but though his mistress's sympathies with the quarry were less marked—her chickens being precious—Nip was still held in. But amid all his disgust the cunning dog remembered that his days of foraging for himself—before he had picked up Jinny—had not been rosy and replete: caterers like Jinny, he realized, did not grow on every cart, not to mention the cushioned basket from which he could bark at everything on the road, or within which, with a huge grunt of satisfaction, he could curl into an odorous dream.

A contrast in all save colour was the stolid Methusalem, though he too was of hybrid stock. While his hairy fetlocks proclaimed a kinship with the draught-breed of the shire, he lacked that gross spirit, and while his flying mane and tail flaunted an affinity with the fiery Arab, he was equally deficient in that high mettle. By what romantic episode he had come into being, whether through the wild oats of an Arabian ancestor, or the indiscretion of a mere circus-horse, or whether his tossing hair and tail were the heritage from a Shetland pony—as his moderate stature suggested—is not recorded in any stud-book. But it was impossible to see him without the word "steed" coming into the mind, and equally impossible to sit behind him without thinking of a plough-horse. "When Oi first see that rollin' in the brook afore 'twas broke in," Gaffer Quarles would relate, "Oi was minded of the posters of Mazeppa at the Fair, and christened that accordin'." It was only when he discovered that this blonde beast was a whited sepulchre, that "Mazeppa" was exchanged for "Methusalem," as though that antediluvian worthy had always been a doddering millenarian, and not at one time in the prime of his hundreds. The name had at least the effect of banishing expectation; his mere amble was an agreeable surprise. As a matter of fact Methusalem had still his Mazeppa moments. They came on Tuesday and Friday evenings when he was loosed from the shafts; at which moments he would roll on his back, kick up his heels and gallop madly round the goat-pasture to the alarm of the tethered browsers. And even at his professional pace he always kept his mane flying. One accomplishment, however, Methusalem had which no "Mazeppa" steed could have bettered, nay, which made a circus pedigree plausible. He could lift the latch of gates with his nose and walk through. It was a trick which Jinny, with her habit of not alighting, had fostered in him: if the gate did not swing to, she could usually close it with the butt-end of her whip—through the cart-rear at the worst—a procedure which, with her further habit of using short cuts and even private tracks like that at Bellropes Park, saved not a little time, and was some compensation for Methusalem's general crawl.

If the local carrying business had grown indistinguishable from Jinny, it seemed no less bound up with her four-footed companions, whose ghostly figures, seen looming through the wintry dusk, sent a glow of warmth through the bleak countryside.

IV

But to-day Jinny's horn, Nip's yap, and Methusalem's pseudo-spirited pawing, were alike powerless to evoke the familiar forth-bustling of Caleb and Martha. Only cocks crowed and doves moaned, while from the river-slope came the lowing of cattle. Alarmed for the lonely and aged couple, Jinny jumped down and tapped at the door. Nobody replying, she lifted the latch and came from the joyous spring sunshine on a chill, silent piece of hall-way in which even the tall clock had stopped dead. She peeped perfunctorily into the musty parlour on her way to the kitchen—the lozenge-shaped motto: "When He giveth quietness, who then can make trouble?" seemed to have taken on a strange and solemn significance. But she knew that the kitchen was the likeliest lair, so not pausing to examine, the ominously unopened letter addressed to Mrs. Flynt which she espied on the mantelpiece, she pressed on to the rear. The kitchen, however, was still more desolate, not only of the couple, but of the habitual glow on the cavernous hearth. What wonder if Nip, who had followed her, set up an uncanny whining! She halloaed up the staircase, but that only aggravated the silence. She dashed next door to the shepherd's section—similar solitude! With a feeling of lead at her heart she rushed back into the ironic sunshine and towards the orchard—now unbearably beautiful in its blossoming—and as she was approaching a remote corner that harboured the pigsty in which Martha's pet sow carried on a lucrative maternity, she was half relieved to collide with Caleb who was moving houseward with haggard eyes and carpet slippers.

"Is anything the matter?" she gasped.

"Sow glad you've come. The missus keeps arxing for you. We've been up all night with her."

"With your wife?"

He looked astonished. "Noa, Maria!"

Jinny's full relief found vent in a peal of laughter.

"It's no laughin' matter—the missus wants ye to tell the wet to come at once."

"But what's the matter with her?" inquired Jinny, still unable to rise to his seriousness. "A snout-ache?"

"She's a goner," said Caleb solemnly. "We've reared up nine boys, but Maria's been more trouble than the lot. The missus would bring her up by hand, and Oi always prophesied she wouldn't live."

Amusedly aware that Maria's progeny had already exceeded sixty, Jinny offered to visit the patient.

"Do—that'll comfort the missus and ye'll know better what to tell Jorrow. Oi'll hold your hoss. You know the way—behind the red may-tree."

Jinny smiled again. The idea of Methusalem needing restraint amused her, but she did not dispel Caleb's romantic illusion.

The sick sty was visible through a half-door that gave at once air and view, and over which Nip at once bounded on to the startled Martha's back as she hung over the prostrate pig on its bed of dirty straw. Maria belonged to the Society of Large Black Pigs, and snuffed the world through a long, fine snout; but life had evidently lost its savour, for the poor sow was turning restlessly.

"Oh, Jinny!" moaned Martha. "She had thirteen last time, and I knew it was an unlucky number."

"Nonsense!" quoth Jinny gaily. "Twelve would have been less lucky—at the price I got you!"

"Yes, dearie, but I'm not thinking of prices. She was a birthday present for my loneliness."

"I know," said Jinny gently.

"No, you don't." She wrung her hands. The self-possession Caleb had admired when the letter broke on their lives was no longer hers. "You've got lots of Brethren and Sisters, but I've got nobody to break bread with, no fraternal gatherings to go to, and even Flynt won't be immersed, though he's in his sixty-nine and we must all fall asleep some day. So it was a comfort to have Maria following me about everywhere like Nip does you, and I do believe she's got more sense than the so-called Christians here, and would be the first to pray for the peace of Jerusalem with me if she could only speak. But now even Maria may be taken from me. You'll send Jorrow at once, won't you, dearie?"

"But what's the matter with her?"

"Can't you see? All night she kept rooting up the ground. Oh, I hope it isn't fever."

"Rubbish! Look at the skin of her ears. And she isn't coughing at all. What's she been overeating?"

"Nothing—only the grass Flynt has been cutting."

"Why don't you give her a dose of castor-oil?"

"She won't take it. She knows we've covered it up—I told you she's got as much brains as a Christian."

"Let me try and get it down."

"It is down. The piglets ate the mess up."

"Oh dear!" laughed Jinny. "That will need Jorrow. Anything else, Mrs. Flynt?"

"I can't think this morning. Ask Flynt."

Caleb, however, proved equally distraught.

"There was summat extra special, Oi know," he said, his red-shirted arm clinging heroically to Methusalem's bridle, "for here's the knot in my hankercher. But what it singafies Lord onny knows."

"It wasn't a new shirt?" she suggested slyly.

He shook his head. "Noa, noa; this keeps her colour as good as new. But the missus did make a talk about my Sunday neckercher."

"I'll get you a new one. Plain or speckled?"

"Oi leaves that to you, Jinny—you know more about stoylish things."

V

On her winding and much-halting way to Chipstone, Jinny took advantage of the absence of the noble family and the complaisance of her customer, the lodge-keeper, to smuggle her plebeian vehicle through Bellropes Park, which was not only a mile shorter, but dodged the turnpike with its aproned harpy of a tollman; she loved the great avenues of oaks, and the shining lake, the game of swans, and the sense of historic splendour; and Nip, as if with a sense of stolen sweets, sniffed never more happily, though when they got within view of the water, he had to be summoned back to his headquarters-basket by a stern military note, a combat between himself and the swans not commending itself to his mistress. Some of these irascible Graces floated now on the margin, meticulously picking their tail-feathers, contorting their necks. But vastly more exciting were those of the flock far out on that spacious sparkle of brown water. They seemed to be going spring-mad and threshing the scintillating water with their wings, oaring themselves thus along, each one infecting the other, till the water itself seemed to be leaping in a shimmering frenzy of froth. Even the ducks reared up or stood on their heads in a sort of intoxication. And this sense of the joy and beauty of the spring communicated itself to the girl, not in jubilance, but in some exquisite wistfulness: some craving of the blood for mysterious adventure. Something seemed calling at once out of the past and out of the future. And then her thoughts wandered back to Frog Farm and the Flynts and the far-scattered youths with whom she had formerly ridden to Sunday-school, and suddenly by a flash from her subconsciousness she recognized the writing of the unopened letter on Martha's mantelpiece: of the letter she had scarcely looked at. Surely, though the curves were bolder, it was the work of the very same male hand that had written on the fly-leaf of a Peculiar hymn-book the inspired quatrain—which she had admired from her childhood—beginning:

Steal not this book for fear of shame:

an admonition she thought peculiarly appropriate to the holy book it guarded. And with the memory of the fly-leaf surged up also the face—the long-forgotten, freckled face of the youngest and most headstrong of the Flynt boys: the Will, flouted as "Carrots," but in her opinion the handsomest of the batch, who had always loomed over her with such grown-up if genial grandeur, and had given her his bull-roarer and threaded birds' eggs for her before she had come to think their collection wicked. What a hullabaloo when the boy disappeared—he must have been hardly thirteen, she began computing—and she, the child of nine or so who could have comforted the distracted Martha, had dared say no word, because he had made her swear on that very hymn-book to keep his flight silent. Just as she was permeated by the solemnity of the book and the oath on it, he had thrown it away, she remembered, thrown it into the bushes from the wagon in which he was driving her home from chapel.

The details of that forgotten summer Sunday began to come back: most vividly of all, the boy struggling and sobbing when his buttons were cut off. He had been so proud of his new velvet jacket with its manifold rows of blue buttons, and lo! after Sunday-school his father had appeared with a somewhat crestfallen look and a pair of scissors, saying, "You don't want all this flummery," while Elder Mawhood—evidently the admonishing angel—had stood grimly by, intoning "Pride is abominable. Wanity must be rooted out."

The boy had choked back his sobs, and apparently found solace in the evening hymns, and was further soothed by being allowed at his own request to drive the party home. It was felt—especially by Martha—some compensation for the buttons was due to him. Thus when the wagon had reached Swash End and the bulk of the Flynt family got off according to custom—mud and weather permitting—and walked up to Frog Farm, leaving Jinny to be driven round the long detour to her home at Blackwater Hall, she was left alone with Will.

It was then that, having asked her if she could keep a secret and being assured she could, he informed her to her admiring horror that the moment he had safely delivered her on the road by the Common, he would turn his horse's head for Harwich, where (stabling the horse and wagon so that his parents might trace his intention) he would take ship as a cabin-boy or a stowaway for America, where he was sure to come across his brother Ben, and never would she see him again in Bradmarsh till he had made his fortune.

She could see him now, under a late sunset that was like his hair, with his flashing, freckled face, his blazing blue eyes, and his poor, defaced jacket, the thready stubs of the big buttons showing like scars. Their quaint dialogue came back vividly to her.

"Oh, Will, but can't you make your fortune here?"

"No, thank you—no more chapel for me!"

"I know it's hard—and you did look beautiful with the buttons—but isn't it more beautiful to please God?"

"Rubbish! What does God care about my buttons?"

"He's pleased, just as I like your giving me birds' eggs."

"But I didn't give my buttons—they were snatched from me—through that, beastly old Mawhood."

"But Elder Mawhood knows what God wants."

"Let him cut off his own nose and not go smelling into everybody's business. The other day he made poor old Sister Tarbox get riddy of her cat."

"That was kindness, because it had to be shut up alone all Sunday while she was at chapel."

"I believe it was only to make more rats for him to kill."

"That's not true, Will. You know Sister Tarbox is too poor to have her cottage cleared."

"Well, let him look after his rats and cats—not me."

"An elder must do his duty."

"I hate elders and deacons and hymn-books. Yah! I'm done with religion, thank God."

"Oh, Will, you mustn't speak like that!"

"Fancy stewing in chapel in weather like this!"

"Isn't this just the weather to thank God for?"

"No—it's all silliness."

"Oh, Will!"

"Yes, it is! You ask Brother Bundock—I don't mean old Mr. Bundock. I asked him once who wrote our hymn-book and he said, 'Twixt you and I, the village idiot!'"

"You are talking wickedly, Will"—there were tears in the voice now. "You mustn't run away, that's more wicked."

"Oh—I was an idiot myself to tell you. You are going to peach on me, I suppose."

"Peach?"

"Tell your grandfather about my running away."

"Not if you don't do it."

"But I shall do it! And you promised to keep the secret. To tell would be more wicked than me."

"I won't tell, but you mustn't go."

"I must. Swear not to betray me. Kiss my hymn-book."

It was with some soothed sense of restored sanctities that she had pressed her lips to the holy cover—she still remembered its smell and taste, salted with a tear of her own—but what a fresh and mightier shock, that throwing of the book into the bushes!

"Stop! Stop!" She heard the little girl's horror-struck cry over the years; remembered how, as he laughed and drove on furiously with her, the phrase "drive like the devil" had come to her mind, charged for the first time with meaning.

Wilful boy had had his way: he had escaped from England and even—despite his diabolism—by the aid of the ninepence she had insisted on bringing down from her money-box while he waited trustfully outside her grandfather's domain. But she had not responded in kind to the lordly kiss he had blown her as he drove off to America.

"Good-bye, little Jinny!"

"Good-bye, Will. Say your prayers!"

"Not me!"

"Then I shall pray for you!"

When the hue and cry was out, and bellmen were busy with his carroty head and velvet jacket with the buttons cut off, little Jinny had also gone a-hunting—but for the outraged hymn-book. It lay now still hidden in a drawer—the one secret of her life—unmentioned even when by the bulky clue of the horse and cart the fugitive had been traced, as he designed.

Yes, she must disinter this hymn-book of his from its hiding-place, compare the inscription—she knew by now the rhyme was not original—with her memory of Martha's letter. What was its postmark, she wondered. Well, she would find that out, indeed the whole contents, on her return to Frog Farm. Perhaps he was coming back—his fortune already made. And the revived sense of his wickedness was mixed with a sense of her own soon-forgotten resolve—or threat—to pray for him, and was blurred in some strange emotion, in which the glamorous freshness of child-feeling mingled with a leaping of the heart that was like the spring-joy of the swans.

VI

But Jorrow could not make the journey that day to that remote farm. There were more important animals more expensively endangered and more easily accessible. Old sows were so fussy, and to judge by the symptoms it was a mere case for castor-oil. But precisely because Jinny had herself recommended this drug-of-all-work she felt unconvinced: it seemed a mere glib formula for being "riddy" of her. There was another resource, Elijah Skindle, who, having settled in Chipstone only five years ago, practised only among parvenus like himself. It was not because he was a "furriner," nor even because he had started as a knacker and still had a nondescript status, that Jinny shrank from calling him in now: she had more than once deposited damaged dogs with him or deported them mended. But she objected to the appraising gaze he fixed upon her on these occasions, though to be sure her objection to these jaunts was not so strong as Nip's, who, seeing in every canine co-occupant of the cart a possible supplanter, bristled and whined and barked till the rival was safely discharged. But, on her way home, overcoming her repugnance—for Martha's sake, if not Maria's or duty's—she stopped her cart outside his pretentious black gauze blind and blew a rousing blast. A tall, black-eyed, grey-haired woman, issuing from the office door with a broom, who appeared to be Mr. Skindle's mother, informed her that 'Lijah was "full up": however, he could be found at the kennels if Jinny insisted on seeing him. She pointed vaguely to a field behind the house, visible through an unpaved alley yawning between the sober Skindle window and its flamboyant neighbour, the chemist's. But it was in vain that Jinny clucked to Methusalem to thread the alley. The beast refused absolutely.

Alighting with some dim understanding of his instinct, she walked to the field-gate over which a horse was gazing at her. Lifting the latch, she wandered among other happily scampering horses in search of the kennels, finding at first only a barn-like structure, a glance through whose doors at the flagstoned paving that sloped to a centre turned her sick. For a pyramid of horses' feet was the least repulsive indication, though even the homely skewers so agreeable to Squibs took on a sinister hue. The spectacle, however, served to make the kennels, when at last discovered, a lesser horror. But it was the first time she had seen dogs so far gone in distemper, and these rheumy-eyed skeletons, each chained in its niche, sullied the springtide and haunted her for days. She caught up Nip, who had come to heel, as though he too might pine suddenly into skin and bone. Nip himself, it must be confessed, regarded these shadows of his species with indifference, if not with satisfaction, as negligible competitors.

Elijah Skindle, discovered on his knees in the act of feeding a pathetic poodle, was as unstrung by the sight of Jinny as Jinny by the sight of the dogs. His black cutty pipe fell from his lips and he nearly stuck the dog's spoon into his own open mouth. But mastering himself, and without raising his cap or his pipe or changing his attitude, he gasped out: "Hullo! Nip ill?"

Jinny replied curtly—for there was a familiarity that repelled her in his calling Nip by his right name—, "No, a sow at Frog Farm—Little Bradmarsh, you know."

His heart leapt. Frog Farm meant an old inhabitant, local prejudice was then beginning to melt at last! But, "Rather out of my radius," he said with pretended indifference. "Besides," as he reached for his pipe, "my nag's gone lame."

"I could give you a lift," said Jinny, outwitted for once, since it never struck her that this was precisely what Elijah had fished for and why he had lamed his beast. The spoon trembled in his hand, but he replied grumblingly, "But then I should have to come at once."

"I'm afraid so," said Jinny.

Mr. Skindle rose and brushed his knees. "Anything to oblige a lady," he said.

"It isn't me, it's Maria," said Jinny icily.

VII

But Jinny was not altogether outmanœuvred, for while Mr. Skindle was getting his case of utensils, she filled up the rest of her seat—it was a stuffed seat covered with sacking—by means of a peculiarly precious parcel, needing a vigilant eye: no new device this, but her habitual protection against bores or adorers, and Skindle, she feared, was both. This swain-chaser or maid-protector was kept in a corner of the cart ready for emergencies, being an elongated package of stones, marked "Fragile." The stones had to be jagged and uncouth or Nip would have squatted on it and roused suspicion. This was the only parcel she lifted herself, and it figured in her own mind as "The Scarecrow."

And so, despite Mr. Skindle's offer to nurse it on his knees, she put him behind her—not as a Satan, for his seductiveness was small. He had, it is true, a good styside manner, and his slim figure, outlined by a trimly cut pepper-and-salt suit, effused a sense of vitality. But his straw-coloured moustache, which was not without its female votaries, was for Jinny more of a puzzle than a decoration, for she could not reconcile its flowingness with the desolating baldness that any shifting of his cap revealed. His cranium was, in fact, like the advertisement of a hair-restorer in the picture preceding the application thereof. As fixed a feature of his face as the grey cap which concealed his calvity was the black cutty pipe stuck in his stained teeth, nor had Jinny ever seen him without a large pearl horseshoe pin in his tie.

"Please don't smoke," she said, as he climbed in by the tail-board, "Gran'fer would smell it."

"And why shouldn't he?"

"He's a Wesleyan."

"Oh!" He laughed without comprehension, a shade scoffingly.

"And the smell might get into people's parcels," she added.

Bestowing himself under the tilt as well as he could on a box, grazed at his side by a ledge he considered too narrow to sit on, and threatened with decapitation through a plank holding the smaller parcels that ran athwart the cart just above his head, Mr. Skindle gazed up over this shelf at the glorious view of the back of Jinny's bonnet and feasted his eyes on her graceful dorsal curves and the more variegated motions of her driving arm, not to mention the succession of lovely rural backgrounds made for her figure by the arch of the awning. And his ill-humour melted, and though his pipe grew cold his heart began to glow. But Jinny took no more notice of him than if he had been himself a box. No wonder he began to feel closed and corded up, bursting though he knew himself to be with soul-riches. For a full mile, his extinct pipe in his teeth, he heard only the monotonous snap of Methusalem's hoofs as if everything along the road was snapping in a frost. The unjaded steed had actually started off at almost a trot, and as the Gaffer explained once, "a hoss what has long lopes knocks his fitten together." Then—as if to mark how completely her passenger was forgotten—one of her grandfather's songs began to steal from her lips. It was not "High Barbary" nor "Admiral Benbow," nor yet his favourite "Oi'm seventeen come Sunday," which the nonagenarian sang daily with growing conviction. It was—and Nip would have been the first to be surprised, had he understood it—the old English air:

The hunt is up, the hunt is up, and it is wellnigh day,
And Harry our King has gone huntynge, to bring the deer to bay.

Perhaps it was the influence of her horn; perhaps she was an artist who could enjoy in song what she could not suffer in life. Or perhaps she loved the lilt of the old song and never thought of the meaning, or only of the bravery of the spectacle and the gay coming of the dawn. For, all untrained as she was, she vibrated peculiarly to music, and one of the wonderful moments of her young life was when she first heard a hymn sung in parts at the Sunday-school; to her ear, accustomed only to the solo quavering of the Gaffer, was revealed harmony; a starry new universe and a blood-tickling enchantment in one.

Almost at the first outbreak of the hunting song Nip appeared at a run, and with two bounds he established himself in his mistress's lap—invidiously enough in Elijah's eyes. For that silvery little voice, rippling along the lonely road with the unconscious joyance of a blackbird's, completed the spell which the spring landscape—seen in that series of pictures framed by the arch of the tilt—was weaving on the doomed veterinary surgeon.

There were sheep, big and little, lying in the wide fields and great, newly ploughed spaces of red, freshly turned earth—for the first time Elijah felt the scarecrows as a degradation of all this primeval beauty. Apple-trees flowered in the cottage gardens and in the hedges was early May-blossom, and on the brinks primroses, anemones, and even a few precocious bluebells rioted in an intoxicating fertility of beauty. Larks rose palpitating with song, bumble-bees boomed, butterflies flittered, and ever and anon came the haunting cry of the cuckoo. And when Jinny's voice soared up too, Elijah Skindle's heart seemed melting down his spine.

VIII

"That's a lucky dog of yours," he said desperately, when the music ceased.

"That's what I thought at your place," she replied through the back of her head.

"Not had distemper yet?"

He saw her shoulders shudder. There was an awkward silence.

"You know I'd gladly look after him gratis," he blundered on, "and you too." Then, in a horrible consciousness of the pathological implication, he awaited the lash of her tongue.

But she must have been abstracted. For she only said politely: "Thanks very much. But I always go to Jorrow's."

Yes, he reflected bitterly, and always went there for other people unless Skindle's was expressly stipulated.

But they were now approaching the first village after Chipstone, and the outside world intruded on the idyll. A dozen times he vaulted up and down to prevent interloping young men—sometimes armed with nosegays—receiving parcels too proximately; and he had a proud and malicious pleasure in their disconcerted unspoken surmise as to his privileged situation. The small coin of conversation appertaining to these deliveries Jinny did not refuse him, and every cluck she gave to Methusalem, every ripple of laughter on her busy way, deepened the spell. The unexpected faces; the quaint cottage interiors; the cheerful-smiling women in high green aprons who received stay-laces or bobbins, sugar or tea-packets, in bare dough-powdered or soap-frothed arms; the panting figures that tolled after the cart with forgotten bundles; the dogs—the fiercer in their barrels and boxes, the milder waving free and friendly tails; the quaint commissions and monitions, the salutations and farewells—"I'll remember the twopence," "And tell my brother, won't you, about the christening," "I don't want any more of her puddings, they put the miller's eye out"—all this fascinating bustle and chatter, spiced with friendly laughter, seemed to belong to an enchanted earth of which gaiety was the ground-note, not animal groaning. The windings of her horn completed his sense of fairyland.

In the remoter woodland regions he was possessed alternately with a disapprobation of her recklessness in trusting herself thus alone with a male, far from help, and a surprise at his own passivity in so provoking and romantic a situation. Of course he was going to behave like the gentleman he was, but why was she so irritatingly sure of it? Did she think he wasn't flesh and blood? She might at least show some consciousness of his chivalry!

But his resentment at her professional nonchalance only served to confirm his long-standing suspicion that here at last was the girl for him: that he was choosing well if not wisely. Doubtless Chipstone and his mother would say he was marrying too much beneath him. But look at the farmers' daughters—what lumps beside her! He admitted, of course, that the Blanche of Foxearth Farm to whom his mother mainly aspired was an exception, but then this Purley minx was hopelessly out of reach, stuck up on her pedestal of beauty, conceit, and culture, and throwing over even her affianced wooers. As for his neighbour, the chemist's girl—what could his mother see in her except that annuity which would not even survive her, and she not looking particularly strong! No, with the present satisfactory amount of sheep-rot, glanders, and distemper he could afford to please himself. And if Jinny couldn't play the piano like the land-surveyor's widow, why one must content oneself with the horn, pending initiation into the higher life. Together they would work up the business. With Jinny's connexion—though of course she must give up carrying and become a lady—there would surely be a trail of sick beasts in her wake: Jorrow would soon be out-distanced. They would live away from his office; that could all be turned into dog-hospital.

Such were the kennels in the air built by the enamoured Elijah as he sat on boxes or hampers or panted under their weight in his officious deliveries: an officiousness which drove out of her head the keg of oil destined for Uckford Manor.

"Oh, dear!" she murmured suddenly, a mile later.

Forcing the explanation from her, he cried joyfully, "Let's go back."

Jinny shook her head. "No time," she said, and flicked at Methusalem.

"But I don't mind being late."

"I'm not thinking of you—but of the pig."

"Bother the pig."

"Is that the way you study your patients?"

"I've got better things to study." He could only say it to her back, but he threw enough intensity into it to come out on the other side of her.

"Indeed!" The back seemed impenetrable. "You going into another business?"

"Why ever should I when I'm getting on so famously—ten pound a week, if a penny." It was an opportunity made to his hand. "I know," he went on, as the back remained rigid, "that folks pretend it's not as high-class as real doctoring, but believe me it needs more brains."

"Does it?"

"Stands to reason. A human being can tell you what he feels and where the pain lays, but with a dumb beast you've got only your own sense and skill to go on: it's us vets that should really be at the top of the profession."

"But sick babies are dumb too," Jinny reminded him.

"Sick babies have talking mammas," he replied genteelly.

Jinny did not imitate them, and silence fell again, tempered by Methusalem's snappings. Really, it was very awkward, Elijah felt, thus proposing to a girl behind her back. But he struggled gallantly. "Take stomach staggers now—if those horses you saw waiting to be killed this evening had been treated in time—!"

"The horses in your field?" cried Jinny, shocked. "But they looked so lively."

"They're all like that," he explained. "Once out of harness they get a bit jaunty again, but they're worth more dead than alive."

"It's dreadful killing off a horse that has served one!" Jinny burst out. "Just for a few shillings!"

"A few shillings? Why there's horses over two-fifty pounds! Flesh, I mean," he explained, with a chuckle. "Not to mention the skin, hair and bones. Why, there's eighty pounds of intestines for sausage-skins!"

"Oh, do hold your tongue!" cried Jinny, feeling sick again.

"Yes, and what about his tongue!" retorted Elijah triumphantly. "It ain't only Frenchies that get that. And his tail waving for funerals! And his hoofs in your own shoe-buttons!"

Jinny felt indeed as though hoofs had descended on her feet, and she could almost have sacrificed Methusalem's high-waving tail to adorn her passenger's obsequies.

"My neighbour, the chemist—he buys the blood!" continued the ghoulish Elijah. "He makes it into—"

But just here at a cross-road Jinny's horn signalled to a smart young man in a velvet waistcoat, who was driving a trap, and brought him to a standstill. Would Barnaby deliver a keg of oil at Uckford Manor if he was passing that way?

That Manor was, it transpired, the one goal and purpose of Barnaby's journey.

Jinny—well aware young Purley was homeward bound for Foxearth Farm—gave him a radiant smile, and Elijah threw him the keg and a furious look, a reliable fellow-feeling informing him that the velvety liar was going at least two miles out of his way. Downright dishonest he felt it, seeing that neither the young man's time nor his trap was his own, but belonged to his father, the hurdle-maker. But what could you expect of Blanche's brother? Let Jinny beware of the family fickleness, let her lean on a less showy but manlier breast.

"I wonder you don't arrange your things village by village instead of letting 'em lay all over the vehicle," he observed as she drove on.

"I shan't forget where to drop you," came the answer over her cold shoulder.

Then silence fell more painfully than ever, and the monotonous tick-tack of Methusalem maddened his conscious ear. The monstrous possibility began to loom up that Jinny's affections were pre-engaged to some one of these numerous young men. His eye fell upon a coil of rope hung round a loose hoop of the tilt, and morbid thoughts of using it—whether on the young men or himself was not clear—floated vaguely in his usually serene soul. Presently he noted other coils on other ribs, and their plurality suggested it was for the young men, not himself, that rope was appropriate. What else were they there for, he wondered dully? Yes, let her fiancés go hang: engagements could always be broken off—nothing venture, nothing have!

To nerve himself for the great question he took advantage of the pause at Long Bradmarsh while Methusalem was drinking at the trough of "The King of Prussia." But this imitation of Methusalem on a stronger fluid was fatal, for in Jinny's persistent silence, the animal's tick-tacks now grew soothing: he settled himself more comfortably on the emptier floor of the cart, with his head on a soft bundle, and watched the nape of Jinny's neck till it faded into a great white sea of floating ice. He was struggling in it for hours, but at last the cold waves passed over his head, and Jinny, turning to throw out a parcel, saw that his cap had fallen off in his writhings, leaving his baldness almost indecently glaring.

So deep was he in his daymare that he was quite unaware of Jinny's colloquy with another male whom her horn had hailed as they passed over the bridge to Little Bradmarsh. Not that there was anything in Ephraim Bidlake to excite apprehension, for he was a stalwart Peculiar, safely married, and residing with his family and two twin-nieces of his wife's—Sophy and Sally—on board the billyboy whose great boomless black sail Jinny had espied darkening the water with its shadow. Bidlake's barge was a cross between a Norfolk wherry and a ferry-boat, and plied up and down the Brad, loading at the wharves with its half-lowered mast for crane, or carrying man and cattle across the bridgeless sections when it had nothing better to do. There was not much money coming in at the best, and it was often Jinny's privilege to eke out the barge's larder under pretence of presents for the motherless Sophy and Sally, so tragically fathered. For Ephraim Bidlake, a shaggy giant with doglike eyes, had brought the "little furriners" from Hampshire when their mother died after their father—Mrs. Bidlake's brother—had been transported to Botany Bay for burning a rick in some old agricultural riot against the introduction of machinery. The blot on their scutcheon had been concealed from the new neighbourhood, but had been gradually confided by Mrs. Bidlake to Jinny with protestations of her brother's innocence—had he not been made a constable in the very convict ship? By degrees, too, she had conveyed to the girl a vivid picture of the trial and deportation. For the devoted sister had walked the bulk of the way to Winchester, in the hope of proving his innocence by collecting testimonies to his character, and had joined the mob of weeping women who hung round the gaol gates night and day, or crowded the court, only to witness the sanctimonious cruelty of the bewigged judges, and the tragic exodus of the damned in the prison coach, guarded by a file of soldiers, to lie in the hulks at Southampton till they were shipped to savage Australia, there to be assigned to brutal stockowners. It was an experience which had cost Mrs. Bidlake dear; her next child had been stillborn, and to this day she had never reared but one more infant, and that a still delicate one. But for the comfort of the Peculiar faith it would have been a cheerless household. She was now again brought to bed: it was to inquire about her that Jinny had hailed the barge, and very sad she was to learn from Brother Bidlake—when he had punted within earshot—that the new baby had succumbed after a few hours, though the "missus," thank God, was recovering and the twins were "wunnerful good and helpful." She was not sorry, however, that the undoctored infant had departed with a precipitation which rendered an inquest unlikely, for inquests were the bane of the Brotherhood.

IX

It was twilight when Methusalem drew up again before the twin doors. This time Caleb did not fail.

"Sow glad you ain't brought the wet!"

"But I have—he's snoring inside," Jinny called down.

"Lord!" said Caleb, taking another look. "Oi did see his head, but by this owl-light Oi thought 'twas a cheese."

Jinny's laugh rippled out and Elijah Skindle started up and sneezed. He looked round dazedly for his cap.

"We've arrived?" he asked shamefacedly, clapping it on.

"Yes," said Jinny, "but the pig's all right. I fear you've had a wasted journey." She jumped down.

"Wasted?" He sat up ardently. "Don't say wasted."

"A good nap is a comfort," she agreed.

"I may have dozed off—your singing rocked me to sleep, I reckon. But all the while I've been trying to tell you—" His voice broke.

"I know," she said softly. "I heard you."

"Did I talk in my sleep?" he asked innocently.

"Through your nose."

He winced as at a blow on it. "That's—that's nature," he stammered: "I don't suppose even females are free from snoring."

"Maria isn't," observed Jinny, patting Methusalem.

Martha hurried out happily, with a piece of sugar for the same favoured beast.

"Maria's been walking with me!" she cried rapturously.

"And eating hearty," added Caleb. "If you ask me, she was drunk."

"Oh, Flynt!" cried Martha. "Aren't you ashamed to speak like that about your own pig; and before strangers?"

"But that rolled and kicked last night same as a sow Oi seen once that swallowed a thick wine. Happen Maria got swillin' at old Peartree's beer-barrel!"

"How could she do that?" Jinny protested.

"Turned on the tap like a Christian. Same as your Methusalem opens our gate."

Elijah picked up his pipe and his cap and scrambled down. "Appears to me I've been brought here under false pretences."

"We'll pay you all the same," said Caleb with dignity.

"But how am I to get back to Chipstone?" He had followed Maria in reckless abandonment, and now came the prose of life with its questions.

"If we're going to pay the gentleman," put in Martha, "he may as well have a look at Maria."

Mr. Skindle agreed it was as well to make a possible future patient's acquaintance, but repeated his inquiry.

"There's Shanks's mare," said Jinny blandly.

Caleb pointed towards the brook. "It's onny seven miles by Swash End through Plashy Walk."

"Plashy Hall has a dog," objected Elijah.

"Well, you're used to dogs," said Jinny.

"My instrument-case is too heavy. You'll have to give me a lift to your house."

"With pleasure," she said. "But Blackwater Hall is still farther from Chipstone."

"Anyhow I can get a trap from the village," he said firmly.

"No, you can't, and even if you walk to Long Bradmarsh it's a toss-up if you'll get anything at 'The King of Prussia.'"

"Well, take me as far as the bridge—I'll pay extra."

"I can't guarantee Methusalem will go back."

"That's all right," he said cheerfully. "Horses know I stand no nonsense. And now, Uncle, as soon as I've lit my pipe, I'll be ready for the pig. Got a match?"

To his disgust, Caleb produced a lucifer and a phial of sulphuric acid for dipping it in. The now well-established friction matches—that boon to the idle and extravagant—had not yet reached Frog Farm, where even flint and steel had been dispossessed but slowly. But the relit pipe was comforting.

"Wait a moment, Mr. Flynt," said Jinny, tendering a packet as he started convoying the vet. "Your neckerchief!"

"Neckerchief!" cried Martha. "And what about my new bonnet?"

"'Twas only to be cleaned," Caleb reminded her. "And by the same token, mother, don't forget we settled the wet was to read the letter."

Elijah raised his eyebrows.

"Ah, yes—I'll get it." And Martha hurried within.

"You see, Jinny," Caleb explained, "the missus got a letter from Cousin Caroline, and we thought the gentleman here could make one job of it with the pig."

"But why can't I read it?"

"You ain't married."

"No more is Mr. Skindle." Elijah flushed furiously.

"Noa—but ef it's too—too womanish, Oi'll arx him kindly to break it to me, sow Oi can break it to the missus when he's gone."

"Is this the letter?" asked Jinny, as Martha reappeared with it.

"That's her—came all of an onplunge," he repeated.

"But that's not from your Cousin Caroline!" said Jinny, with a thrill of excitement as she took it.

"Noa?" gasped Caleb, as if the world was tumbling about his ears. Then he smiled. "You're making game—you ain't opened her yet."

"But who else is it from?" cried Martha, catching her excitement.

"Can't you see? It's from Will."

"Will!" Martha gave a great cry, and clutched at the letter. "My baby Will!"

Caleb scratched his head. "Now which would be Will?"

"Will was the freckled, good-looking one," said Jinny.

"Oh, Jinny," said Martha. "They were all good-looking—took after Flynt. Dear heart, you can't ha' forgotten our tot after all that flurry. 'Tis only seven or eight years since he—"

"Ay, ay," cried Caleb. "Him what mowed the cat's whiskers."

"No, dear heart, that was Ben."

"To be sure. Ben's the barber in New York—or some such place."

"No, Caleb. That's Isaac."

"Isaac? Then Will 'ud be the one what married the coffee-coloured lady."

"I told you the other day that was Christopher."

"Ay, him in Australia."

"Africa surely," put in Elijah, puffing at his pipe with superior amusement.

"They furrin places be much of a muchness," said Caleb. "And my buoy-oys were as like as a baker's dozen."

"There were girls in the batch," corrected Martha. "But how you can forget that dreadful Sunday night, you who snipped the darling's buttons—!"

"If I don't see the pig soon," interrupted Elijah, losing patience, "the light'll be gone altogether."

"Oi'll git a lantern," said Caleb placidly. "Oi often used to set and wonder how they lads knowed theirselves, the one from the 'tother. Well, the Lord bless 'em all, says Oi, wherever they goo, and whichever they be."

"So you see," said Jinny, with a faint blush hardly visible by owl-light, "there's no need to waste Mr. Skindle's time over the letter."

"No more there ain't!" said Caleb dazedly. "Come along, sir!"

X

But Martha still clung strangely to the letter she had snatched back. "You mustn't strain your eyes, Jinny," she said. "I'll light the lamp. And you'll take a cup of tea first. You must be tired out."

"But I can see quite well," said Jinny. Indeed the sky, despite the risen moon, remained blue, and splashes of dying sunset burned magically through the yet empty branches of the quiet trees. There was a great sense of space and peace and beauty: a subtle waft from the stacks; the note of the thrush was full of evening restfulness. Jinny took the letter from the reluctant Martha.

"He must be back in England!" she cried. "Look at the stamp."

Martha staggered against the cart. "It's very good of God," she said simply.

Her emotion communicated itself to Jinny. Through misty eyes the girl watched a solitary heron winging on high through the great spaces, its legs sticking out like a tail.

"Ah, dearie," said Martha, recovering herself, "never forget, to say your prayers."

"I don't," said Jinny with equal simplicity. But she remembered with fresh remorse that she had forgotten those for the runaway.

"Ever since I was a little girl," said Martha, "I've wanted to please God. But of late, Jinny, I fear I've wanted Him to please me."

"Well, now He has," said Jinny. "You'll have Will as well as Maria," and plucking out a hairpin she inserted it to rip open the loose wafer-closed envelope.

"Stop!" cried Martha. "Suppose it's bad news."

"Nonsense, Mrs. Flynt! Look how firm the writing is."

"Firm—yes, he always was firm—even before he drove off with the cart. Don't you remember that night—no, 'twas before your grandfather fetched you to these parts—he wasn't seven, but that pig-headed he sulked in the wood all night—roosted up a tree like a bird, and never a move or a word when we came halloaing with torches!"

"Well, he's not hiding now, for the postmark's London and—"

"No, don't open it yet, Jinny—suppose he should be married like Christopher!"

Jinny laughed uneasily. "Two black daughters-in-law aren't very likely. Much more likely she'll be blonde."

"No, he can't be married," said Martha on reflection. "He never could abide girls. I don't mean you, dearie; you scarcely had your second teeth, had you?"

Jinny began to rip the envelope. "We shall soon see."

But Martha snatched away the letter again. "I'm sure you'll spoil your pretty eyes," she persisted. "Day-stars, Will called 'em once."

Jinny laughed still more uneasily. "Then I ought to be able to read by 'em. But I'll light my night-star." And she moved towards the cart-lamp.

"It isn't your lighting-up time yet, is it? You don't want to be wasteful."

"Well, come in and light me a candle a moment."

"You seem in a great hurry to read it!" said Martha fretfully.

"Me?" Jinny flushed furiously. "I thought you'd want to hear what he says."

"Don't I know what he says? That he is in England again and coming to see his old mother? Isn't that enough for one night?"

"It's a great deal, certainly. But suppose—he wants something."

"Ah, that's true!" Martha was visibly perplexed. She did not herself understand the suddenly awakened jealous instinct that resented Jinny's superior acquaintance with Will's handwriting, that was subconsciously urging her to hug this letter to her bosom and not share its sacred contents with a girl she at last—especially after Bundock's recent innuendo—realized as grown-up, and who seemed, moreover, to be claiming a co-proprietorship. And so it was difficult for her to frame an objection satisfactory to her conscious intelligence. But the letter was now in her possession, and that was a strong asset for her subconsciousness.

"'Tis a pity to tear open such a beautiful envelope," she said. "You have your cup o' tea. I'll steam it over the kettle."

"I'm afraid I haven't time for tea, especially having to take Mr. Skindle a bit back," said Jinny, almost as mystified as Martha herself. "I'm late already, and Gran'fer will be roaring for his supper. I must read it now or never."

"If it was anything unpleasant," wavered Martha, "Flynt would be very upset. And after sitting up all night with Maria—no, he must have a good sleep—better put it off till the morning."

"To-morrow, I won't be here. No, not till next Friday."

"But I've got to go to-morrow to Miss Gentry and she can read it."

"Oh!" said Jinny.

"Yes, Flynt wants to have my bonnet cleaned—vanity and waste, I call it."

"But won't that tire you—such a long walk? Why can't I take the bonnet to-night? I'll be passing her house."

"We haven't finished talking it over yet, Flynt and me," parried Martha. "I might be having a new bonnet, you see, dearie."

"Well, of course, it's just as you wish. But suppose it rains to-morrow."

"Rains?" repeated Martha, feeling—she knew not why—like an animal at bay. Then she drew a great breath of relief. Footsteps and voices were borne towards them. "Caleb!" she cried joyfully, "Will's in London—he's coming to see his old mother."

"Good buoy-oy!" cried Caleb jovially. It was only what he had expected the letter would say, but at heart he shrank from the change—he had finally equated himself to the dual solitude, and the home-coming prodigal loomed as menacing as Cousin Caroline.

"Good boy?" echoed Martha. "I should think he is—never cared for girls. And still unmarried."

"There's a chance for you, Jinny," chaffed Caleb.

"Oh, how can you talk such nonsense!" Jinny was furiously angry. "Basket, Nip," she called sharply, and climbed up to her seat almost as swiftly as he leapt into his.

"Are you coming, Mr. Skindle?" In her abstraction and to busy herself about something, she automatically removed the parcel of stones from the driving-seat.

"In a jiffy." Elijah did not bound as obediently as Nip—he could not lose the chance to pontificate before her. "Not at all so well as you think, Mrs. Flynt. We experts can see what even the breeder can't. Keep her upon corn and peas—give her just soft stuff." And he vaulted not ungracefully to Jinny's side.

"Thank you, sir," said Martha, impressed. "Have you paid him?" she inquired of Caleb in a formidable whisper.

"Dedn't Oi say Oi'd pay him for nawthen?" he answered still more audibly.

"Well, take off your hat for good-bye."

"But Oi ain't inside," said the obstinate, if confused, Caleb.

Jinny cracked her whip fiercely, and Methusalem joyously turned his nose for home.

"Good night, Jinny. Thank'ee for reading Cousin Caroline's letter," Caleb called after the receding vehicle.

XI

It was symptomatic of Jinny's new mood that she scarcely noticed that Mr. Skindle now shared her sacking. Her mind was wandering again over the ground covered by the Sunday-school wagon, and certain birds' eggs, losing their later cloud of guiltiness, lay suffused with childhood's holy light. Methusalem went unguided through quiet ways. The large, low moon, a pink clown's face, peered through leafless elms and gradually grew golden. To the right of the winding road rooks cawed persistently, and once a small flight flew towards the cart; to the left more melodious birds whistled slow, high notes, or thrilled and gurgled plaintively, or scurried off, startled, as the cart passed. One kept on crying "Quick, quick, quick," with a metallic sound as of shears snipping the grass, but Methusalem was not to be hurried. There was time to admire wherever a thatched cottage made a picturesque point or a pond mirrored the dying sunset; time to savour the subtle balm, where hayricks stood at the far margin of fields. Sometimes a little pig would run round terrified and finally squeeze itself under the fence, or a big gander would stand and hiss. Sometimes the road narrowed to a Gothic nave, but for the most part there was nothing but a far-diffused sense of keen air and great flat spaces, the dark blue circle of sky with rolling white clouds, the large green fields with their distant border of thin trees; a view unclosed and unbounded save by the horizon, though impalpably veiling itself as they journeyed.

Elijah Skindle's mood had changed no less than Jinny's. Though he now sat in the coveted proximity to her, and could propose to her profile instead of her nape—and her bonnet was of the narrow-flanked pattern, condemned by the more prudish of her sex, that left the profile visible—he was subtly conscious that he was really farther from her than before. Even when the delivery of the few remaining parcels necessitated a slight thawing on Jinny's part, the whole spirit seemed to have gone out of the adventure. It was grown tasteless as a thrice-warmed dish. The very horn had lost its thrill. Even if he found a vehicle at "The King of Prussia," he was thinking, it would be an expensive trip: they might charge him all Caleb's half-crown. He found himself morbidly counting the coils of cord—there were five in all, he made out. And when the rooks he called crows sailed towards him, they gave a still more sable hue to his thoughts. He counted them, too, remembering how his peasant mother—now installed as his woman-of-all-work—used to curtsy to a solitary magpie, and the rhyme she taught him about the crows: "One's unlucky, two lucky, three is health, four is wealth, five is sickness, and six is death." Odd that matrimony was not mentioned, unless it was included in "two." There were certainly five crows, he thought dismally—a sinister coincidence with the coils of cord. Then, cheering up, he interpreted the omened sickness as that of the local live-stock, a sickness greater than Jorrow could cope with, and he reflected that after all Jinny's was a hard and toilsome life and her frigidity was perhaps due to its never occurring to her that he was willing to raise her to his status. Perhaps she thought he was just itching to take liberties. Well, he could understand her coyness: other men might indeed exploit such a chance; but he, he assured himself again, was a gentleman.

"That's a slow couple," he said, boldly breaking the long silence.

"Seems to me they fly as fast as the other rooks," said Jinny.

"I mean the Flynts," he said.

"Oh!" said Jinny.

There was resentment in her tone. She had not liked his calling Caleb "Uncle," understanding well the urban contempt that lurked in declaring oneself a rustic's nephew, and feeling, too, that however slow in the uptake Caleb might be, his wealth of homely crafts, knacks, instincts, life-wisdom, and nature-knowledge gave him a richer and deeper quality than this pert townsman. But Elijah persisted in his urban appraisal.

"No go in them!"

"Dear old turtles!" sighed Jinny. "But so long as they go at the same pace—!"

"Ah!" he said eagerly. "You believe in like to like?"

"Well, fancy a turtle married to a hare!"

"But a pair of hares now—?" He seized his opportunity. "You and me, eh?"

"Speak for yourself, Mr.—Bunny!"

"I'm paying you a compliment, Jinny, classing you with me for smartness. There isn't a girl from Bradmarsh to Chipstone that can hold a candle to you. So that's why, seeing a man must marry somebody sometime, and looking around as becomes a man who's getting a bit—a bit—"

"Bald?" prompted Jinny blandly.

"And what does that matter?" he said, too intent now to be fobbed off by raillery. "The point is that with the practice and position I'm getting now, it would be a good lift for you."

"I thought I was giving you a lift," said Jinny icily.

"So you were—so you are—in that sense. But I didn't need even that. My nag wasn't really lame. I only made an excuse to talk this over. See?"

"A very lame excuse," flashed Jinny.

"There was never any way of talking to you—you always so busy with parcels and me with patients. I'm not one of your flirting kind with fancy waistcoats, I want to settle down, and I've taken a favour to you."

Even Jinny's ready tongue had no repartee to this massive complacency. She could only articulate: "Have you, now?"

"Yes, I have. And I'd like to see you driving of a Sunday in my smart trap. Come, what do you say?"

"Thank you," she said coldly. "I'd rather stay in my old cart."

"But it's such a shame—you so spruce and spry—tied to this ramshackle cart, when you might be adorning a higher sphere and sitting in my parlour instead of being at everybody's beck and call.'"

He had chosen precisely the worst form of appeal. Confronted with this picture of parlour-stodginess, her rôle of Jinny the Carrier—Jinny the pet and friend-in-need of the countryside—seemed infinitely dear and desirable. And what subtly added to her anger was some dim presentiment in herself of other forces coming into her life, forces threatening to emerge from their picture-past, and to trouble the placid current of her career. Like Caleb she shrank from change. To shuttle for ever 'twixt Bradmarsh and Chipstone; with her grandfather, Nip, Methusalem, all immortal and unchanging as herself—this was all she asked of heaven: this and not too much rain and wind.

"You want me to sit in your parlour?" she cried in white revolt.

He took off his cap and bowed gallantly: "In silks and satins." Then suddenly realizing his baldness, he clapped it on again.

"And give up my work!" There was an ominous light in Jinny's eyes. But love is blind! Even the bats now beginning to swoop in the dusk could see more clearly than Elijah.

"I promise you you shan't do a stroke!" said the fatuous young man. "As the wife of a veterinary surgeon, you'd be a lady."

"And what would become of Gran'fer?"

"He'd have warm corduroys and plenty of gruel in the Chipstone poorhouse."

"You heartless knacker! Get off my cart. Whoa! Methusalem, whoa!"

"How you fly at a man! I've already got my mother living with me, and she and your grandfather wouldn't get on, being of a different class. But I'd be willing to pay his rent and get a woman to look after him."

"Nobody shall look after him but me. And his business—who is to look after that?"

"Don't worry. Some other carrier'll crop up."

"There isn't going to be any other carrier here but Daniel Quarles, understand that."

"Well, if you think you'll find anybody to marry your grandfather—" he said sullenly.

"Who wants to marry? I shall never give up the road."

"If you're so fond of driving, there's always my trap."

"No good setting traps for me. I'll hang in a cage in no man's parlour. I must fly about in the woods like now—free!"

"Birds in the woods are sometimes hungry," her wooer reminded her. "Suppose your business falls off—or things go to famine prices like five or six years ago. The gallon loaf ain't always a shilling. Ten years ago I remember flour was two and ten the stone, and that only seconds, and tea was five shillings. With me you'd be sure of the fat of the land always—there's no difference with me 'twixt Sundays and weekdays."

"Oh, it's a stuffed bird you want for your parlour."

"Rubbish, I've got six stuffed birds in my parlour—in the loveliest glass cases!"

"But they don't sing!" And Jinny burst mockingly into a song that had hitherto been a mere tune to her:

"I'll be no submissive wife,
No, not I—"

He lost his temper. "Oh, you needn't make such a fuss over yourself. I dare say I can find plenty of wives—with my connexion."

"Among pigs?" she said sweetly. She jumped down and began to light the lamp. "This is your getting-out place."

"It's nothing of the sort—I go on to the bridge."

"Impossible. My horse is lame."

"I know all about that." And snatching up the reins she had dropped, "Gee-up!" he called suddenly.

But Methusalem knew better.

"You'll never get home that way," said Jinny, smiling.

"Then how the hell—?" he began furiously.

"Shanks's mare," she reminded him again. "That's not lame."

He gave her a long, nasty look as though meditating the law of the stronger. But he tried pleading first.

"By the time I walk home, my mother'll have locked up; thinking I'm sitting up with a patient."

"There's the poorhouse!"

He winced. "You've got to carry me," he said sullenly, "or I'll have the law on you."

"There's no law to make me carry aught save goods." And she sang on carelessly:

"Should a humdrum husband say,
That at home I ought to stay—"

The little voice, rippling through those demure lips, wellnigh stung him to close her mouth with the masterful gag of kisses, but a remnant of sanity warned him not to spoil a fine animal practice by a scandal. Besides Jinny had her whip, and what was still more formidable, her horn.

"I'll be even with you for this!" And jumping down, he strode off furiously.

"Hullo! Mr. Skindle! Hullo!"

"Keep away from me!" It was at once an appeal and a warning.

"Don't you want your case of instruments? Not that you'll be in time to kill those poor horses to-night."

With an unsmothered oath he turned back and clambered into the interior, upsetting Nip's basket in his fury; the result of which neglect to let sleeping dogs lie was that the unsagacious animal mounted growling guard over the instrument-case, as before a burglar.

"You'd best get it for me," he said sullenly. "And by the way, how much do I owe you?"

"Never mind," she said blandly, handing him his burden. "You promised to be even with me."

"The little vixen!" he thought, as he trudged towards a farm where he remembered doctoring a horse. "She ought to be put in the ducking-pond! What a lucky escape!"

CHAPTER III

JINNY AT HER HOMES

I remember the black wharves and the slips
And the sea-tides tossing free,
And Spanish sailors with bearded lips
And the beauty and mystery of the ships
And the magic of the sea.
LONGFELLOW, "My Lost Youth."

I

Blackwater Hall, the home of Daniel Quarles and his granddaughter, was none of your old manor-houses with mullioned windows and carven music-galleries, fallen in grandeur and rent. It had barely done yeoman's service, being just a low whitewashed and thatched cottage, whose upper windows under the overhanging eaves seemed deep-set eyes under jutting brows. Nor was it near the Blackwater, though from its comparatively high ground the broadening river first began to glimmer on the view when you came to the edge of Bradmarsh Common and looked across its brown expanse towards the bluish haze of the background.

It was in reality nearer the Brad, which as seen foreshortened from it seemed to lave the roof of Frog Farm and sentinel it with its willows. Blackwater Hall should in fact—Jinny would jest—have been called Common Cottage. For it was just a way of living on the Common, protected from the elements, yet sucked up into them: a sort of transparent, transpirable shell amid this universal flying, fluttering, hopping, creeping, crawling, soaring, swooping, scampering, twisting, droning, humming, buzzing, barking, chirping, croaking, cawing, and singing: a human nest niched on the edge of a chaos of twigs, roots, old amorphous trunks, tangled faded fern-branches, mossy patches, gorse, ferruginous-leaved oaks, shrubs, ant-heaps innumerable, rabbit-warrens, wild apple, wild plum, black heather, and endless stubs to catch the feet, or branches to whip the face, or thorns to prick the fingers. A garden path to the Hall lay between homely flowers, periwinkle and marigold and the like.

Behind the Hall lay the Quarles estate of an acre and a lug or two, with its poultry-run, its tethered goats, its vegetables, its clothes-lines, its thatched stables, its odd sheds and little barn, and its well. If Daniel Quarles was not nid-nodding over his big Bible or on the bench in the front porch, or pruning the vine over the kitchen door, or exercising his lopping and topping rights on the Common, it was here the nonagenarian was to be found pottering: planting, hoeing, watering, or weeding. He would usually groom Methusalem of a morning—it was his way of asserting his hold over the business—and on Tuesday and Friday evenings, when the wayworn Jinny drove up along the grassy path 'twixt cottage and Common, rutted only from her own wheels, he would generally rub down Methusalem after high tea. Otherwise the multiform labour of house and land, of cooking and bread-baking and goat-milking and scrubbing and washing, all fell upon the little Carrier. And even the work the Gaffer did was far outbalanced by the work he made.

And yet it was Daniel's personality, not Jinny's, that was impressed on the house, even as his name remained on the cart. Her own exiguous claim upon life combined with piety and affection to leave everything as she had found it when he brought her here; not only in the big attic where eight had once huddled and which he now occupied in solitary state, sadly conscious of the great, snoreless silences, but in both the ground-floor rooms over which it stretched. The one with the window was the living-room, and the other—on which the front door opened and where a Dutch clock with hanging weights greeted the visitor with a cheery tick that relieved its deadness—was piled pell-mell with old cypress chests and other-litter of the progeny he had outlived, as well as with a few boxes or parcels left by neighbouring clients or as yet undelivered to them. These two rooms communicating, the box-room served both as a business office and a passage to the living-room, from the rear of which you ascended by a door the wriggling staircase to the patriarch's big bedroom, or tumbled down two steps from another doorway to a combination of kitchen, larder, wood-cellar, and scullery, lit up and aired by one small swinging pane, a den which even Jinny could not keep free of cobwebs and smells. Here was the Gaffer's beer-barrel, and the thumb-hole tray, painted with tigers, on which she brought in his morning draught from it. Here also were the jug and basin of her toilette, for bedroom Jinny had none; the need of disturbing the ancient chests or the office—which would have been a sad blow to her grandfather—being avoided through the fortunate talent of the chest of drawers in the living-room for turning into a bed. Its drawers, in which the bedding was concealed, would come out and hook on to one another, while legs would swivel out from beneath them.

It was not gay—this room-of-all-work—despite its over-population of china shepherdesses with their swains and hounds and its rank growth of dried grass in vases—all doubled and distorted by the cracked, fustily gilt mirror on the mantelpiece—for the oaken beams of the ceiling, from which hung a gigantic rusty key, had been plastered over, and the walls—in a similar quest of gentility—dulled with a grey paper, sedulously rematched when it fell to pieces; far livelier was the staircase paper—all hearts and roses—if only you could have seen it in the dusky windings and under the menacing bulge of the plaster ceiling.

Apart from the shepherdesses and vases, among which Jinny was not sorry to see a growing mortality, as the Gaffer fumbled for his spectacles, the room was not over-furnished, a small carved wooden settle by the cavernous hearth, a small square, central table without flaps, two squat and cushioned arm-chairs, with one prim wooden chair, and a little lamp with a monstrous fat globe, constituting almost the minimum of necessaries; even their united libraries, the Gaffer's Family Bible and Jinny's "Peculiar Hymn-Book" and "Universal Spelling-Book," being constrained to repose, like the shepherdesses, on top of the chest of drawers—that shifty piece of furniture whose mysterious recesses secreted also the hymn-book recovered from the bushes. That article of bigotry and virtue, hurled from him by the angry boy, lay—long-forgotten—in the top drawer behind the rolled-up wire mattress that uncoiled by a spring.

Yet this shabby room with its drab paper and squat furniture—vivified most of the year only by that tireless tick of the Dutch clock from the office, or the purring of the kettle from the kitchen—made for Jinny the holy conception of home. The very cracks in the mirror had become second nature; a glass that looked one squarely in the face would have put her eye out, and if in an utterly impossible moment the Gaffer had considerately replaced the old one, the tresses she tamed into seemliness by it would have been a sorry sight. Here, without books or friends, mere living was a happiness, especially at night after Gran'fer, whose big Bible invariably turned from a table-book into a pillow, had woke up and remarked he was getting sleepy, and been steered up the corkscrew staircase to his bed. Then, in a silence broken by no human sound—save the snoring of the Gaffer from above—and in a security symbolized by the unlocked gates and doors, Jinny would sit in delicious relaxation with her sewing or knitting or bonnet-trimming, finding compensation for the long laborious day: listening in summer to the late singing birds or gazing in winter at the glowing logs with their delicate flicker of blue, while Nip in his virtuous basket snored in harmony with the Gaffer or uttered joyous yells in his dream-hunting.

In those hours Jinny demanded nothing of man or God, though when she had produced her bed like a conjurer out of its mahogany recesses, prayers came automatically to the sleepy little figure kneeling beside it, with the dark hair flowing over the white shoulders.

That was a pretty sight, but only the cracked mirror saw it.

II

Yet back, deep back in Jinny's baby consciousness, lay another home altogether, a home richer in comfort and love; giving not on a tumbling common, but on a strange, flat waterside—with stately dream-ships in swelling white, and black barges, and little boats with ochre or orange sails, and a pervading savour of salt and mud; the real Blackwater Hall she felt dimly, though its name escaped her.

In this overlaid life there was a filmy female figure that fed and bathed and rocked one, and kissed the place one had banged, and sometimes held one as passionately as if against some monster that was trying to tear one's face from that flower-soft cheek; it could scarcely be that burly figure, spasmodically appearing and disappearing, for that too was kind in its different way, and had a knee less cumbered by clothes across which one could ride astride, and pullable hair on its face and curling smoke issuing from its mouth more profusely than from the kettle's. Out of this general background, like mountains from a plain, stood out a few episodes of peculiar vividness, but of no apparent significance—in one she sat on a rough sea-wall playing with innumerable tiny white shells while a bird hovered over her crying, as if trying to induce her to follow it seaward, but before she could do so the female figure had appeared, frantically scolding and caressing, and had carried her, struggling and kicking, back to a cot. In another she was carried by the burly being to a little room with a strange little bulbous window and a queer smell, where she was kissed by an elderly figure with a cocked hat and a fixed eye that had a strange affinity to the window. Later she seemed to be living in the strange building that held this room: it had a canvas roof, a flag at one end and a mast with ropes at the other, yet puzzlingly was not a ship, for she saw herself running down the stairs to pat Methusalem in the road.

But these shadowy and usually submerged images all leapt into renewed vitality one delectable Wednesday when, clad in a new black dress, hurriedly stitched together by Miss Gentry, she divided the driving-board with her grandfather (looking odd in his white funeral smock beside her blackness), while Methusalem, equally refreshed and exhilarated by the novel roads, almost hurried them by square-towered hamlets and dear little bridges spanning crawling streams to the quaint cemetery where the old man's sister was to lie. How Nip would have loved the expedition she thought in after days! But he had not yet adopted her.

It was on this trip that she began to hear things that solidified the filmy figures—but it was only from the Gaffer's spasms of imprecation tailing off into anecdote that she was able in the course of years to piece together her parental history. Boldero, she learnt incidentally, was her real name, not Quarles: a correction that mattered less, since nobody had ever called her anything but Jinny. She gathered that the Gaffer had purposely neglected to perpetuate her father's name: he was cancelled and annulled.

Roger Boldero, she came gradually to understand, was one of those superior souls of uncertain status who, having got command of a little sailing vessel, were wafted joyously to and fro, exchanging the silks and spirits of France and the tobacco of Holland for the coins of England without any regard for the benighted principles handicapping human intercourse by taxation. Although her father finally came to own the cargoes he ran, he was at first the mere carrier for speculative capitalists; under cover, moreover, of an honest freight of non-dutiable articles. Carrying was thus in Jinny's blood, both by land and sea, and it is no marvel she made a success of it. But the conjuncture of the two bloods came by the queerest of accidents. The Tommy Devil—the fearsome name of Roger Boldero's boat was only the Essex name for the swift that flew gigantically in gay wood over its cutwater—being caught one night in a sudden gale at a season of high tides, found herself driven towards a lee shore of her native county. It was a perilous situation, and rather than be dashed on the beach broadside on, Skipper Boldero put his helm up and daringly essayed to land nose first on the mud. But the lugger, whose lightness was so admirable against the King's cutters, and which had been still further lightened of her ankers of brandy and stone bottles of Schiedam—these, through an interruption by the blockade men, "waiting to be called for" in certain "fleets" and ditches farther along the coast—could not keep her head against the veering welter. With desperate resourcefulness Boldero improvised a drogue by lashing spars and a spare sail to a rope and trailing it at the stern, and, thus steadied before the wind, the Tommy Devil escaped broaching to, and despite the following sea that tilted her figurehead into the depths, she was finally dumped high and wet on the beach, on the very verge of the sea-wall—both uninjured.

It was a fine piece of seamanship (though aided by the rare steepness of this bit of beach and the high water), and the storm beginning to abate and the water to recede, the sails were lowered and the skipper and crew turned thankfully in. They were not wanting in men—carrying of this kind needed large and able-minded crews—yet all hands being worn out by hours of battling with wind and wave— "dilvered," as old Daniel put it—a watch was deemed superfluous for a vessel no longer at sea, and the Tommy Devil reposed from stem to stern with all the soundness of conscious virtue watched over by Providence.

Now it happened that Lieutenant Dap, commander of His Majesty's Revenue Cutter, then prowling in the offing in quest of gin-tubs—he had been pressed as a youth, served under Nelson, and had exchanged to the Preventive Service when he married that rustic beauty Susannah Quarles, sister of Daniel—was returning with a lantern at the first peep of dawn to the "Leather Bottel," to knock up his boat's crew. His anxious day in Brandy Hole Creek—as everybody called the little place—had ended happily: Susannah's seventh baby had been safely and punctually launched—and the proud and prolific father was anxious to be back sweeping up the prizes that led to preferment. It being a high occasion, and to impress Mrs. Dap's neighbours, he had come ashore in a cocked hat, and he felt almost knocked into one when he beheld, towering over the sea-wall, the great masts of a vessel that loomed gigantic in that place and light. He rubbed his one eye—the other he had lost in his original struggle against the pressgang—but the mysterious jetsam remained, and a closer inspection showed it the kind of longish craft whose huge lugsails his clumsier man-o'-war could rarely overtake, despite his square sail yards. But boldly, as befitted a man with a Nelsonic eye, and without waiting even to summon his men, he hailed the stranded stranger. No reply. Nor did even a shower of such small stones as the muddy beach afforded have any effect on the uncanny bark. There was nothing left but to board her—which the hero achieved single-handed, clambering over the sagging bulwark and standing alone on the slanting deck.

Roger Boldero, aroused to find himself challenged by the cocked hat and stony eye of the Law, displayed, though blinking at the lantern, as great a sang-froid as in the presence of the elements. There was, in fact, far less danger. Of the forbidden articles only lace was left on board, and lace has been designed by the said watchful Providence to occupy small space and be easily invisible. A wink to his second in command, and two of the crew who were in excess of the legal number for that small tonnage, smuggled themselves overboard—here being one of the advantages of terra firma. The few odd kegs, flagons, and cigar-boxes were the ship's own stores Boldero maintained, and he would be very glad if the "Commodore" would join him in sampling them now. Softened by the title, the bold Dap nevertheless declined: the vessel was his prize, he declared.

"And what is to prevent us taking you as our prize?" asked Roger blandly, having by now discovered that Dap was alone.

"You can't move an inch," said Dap.

"But we shall float off as soon as the tide rises."

"Precisely. But it won't come as high again, not till the next spring tide. Meanwhiles I've a gig's crew ashore and a cutter within gunshot."

Boldero was taken aback. He realized that he was—in nautical parlance—"neaped." What a miserable misadventure! What a reward for his seamanship! But, masking his consternation, he rejoined with a smile, "Then you can't take your prize in tow either." He proceeded to point out laughingly that there was no question of capture on either side, that there was not a tittle of evidence against him, that he was an honest trader, as his manifest and cargo would show—and that even if His Majesty, through his admirable if over-zealous representative, insisted on taxing his own little modicum of alcohol and tobacco, it had not been technically landed. The nice point whether a cargo which lands inside its ship instead of outside can be said to have landed, side-tracked the question of the status of the ship herself, and entailed so great a consumption of the cheroots and liquor—despite the unearthly hour—that their fiscal value must have been considerably reduced. But the obdurate Dap still insisting they were dutiable, Roger Boldero invited him to seal them up till he sailed, as he had certainly no intention of landing them here. He pointed out, however, that though the tide, like Time, waited for no man, he would have to wait for the tide; and that during this disagreeable interval the hope of again offering the "Commodore" the cordial, if lop-sided, hospitality of his cabin must disappear if the fomenters of friendship were put in bond. Even this argument might have shattered itself against Dap's fuddled sense of duty had not the twice aforesaid Providence now sent on board a rival cocked hat with a feather salient. With the growing light the local exciseman—of the shoregoing branch of the service—had likewise discovered the strange quarry. But the gleam in the hunter's eye died when Lieutenant Dap introduced him to his friend Boldero, who was celebrating with him the birth of his seventh baby, and whose society for the next month would, he was sure, add to the amenities of life in Brandy Hole Creek.

And "my friend Boldero" did not fail to become it, for Lieutenant Dap's cruising was confined to the waters on whose border he had built his nest: and he was frequently hove to. And during those tedious four weeks, made still more tedious by rain, Boldero had himself rowed out more than once to the "Channel groper" whose black hull, copious white boats, formidable guns and flaming-flannelled red-capped crew were plainly visible from the beached lugger; and he moved genially among the blue-trousered tars and did full justice to the Lieutenant's gin-toddy and had his fingers often in the Lieutenant's snuff-box and lent a sympathetic ear to his methods and devices against those rascally smugglers with their manœuvre of rowing dead to windward.

Their spirit-casks were slung with ropes, the Lieutenant explained, so that their confederates on shore could load them easily on their horses, but only the other night the blockade-men had discomfited a formidable shore-gang of fifty who, despite their stout ashpoles, had been unable to carry off anything except their wounded. He would have caught the lugger, too, had she not kept doubling.

The commander of the amphibious Tommy Devil even shared in an exciting, if unsuccessful, chase after a suspicious landing-party, going out with a galley-crew in a rain-storm in a borrowed tarpaulin petticoat. And once the one-eyed hero—who felt himself none the less a Nelson because his eye had been lost in resisting entry into the navy—returned Roger Boldero's visit, and after broaching sundry of the happily unsealed kegs, the two skippers repaired arm in arm—the attitude was necessary—to see the seventh baby and present the fond mother with material for a lace cap.

Now while Daniel Quarles's sister had been lying as helpless as the lugger, his last unmarried daughter, Emma, a beauty still more engaging, was housekeeping for Aunt Susannah and minding the other four children (two were dead). She had come in Daniel Quarles's cart, and her father was to fetch her again as soon as Susannah was up (or down). He should already have come for her, but the rains had made such glue of the roads that a queerly spelt letter came instead, saying he would wait till they hardened. This delay, brief as it was, sufficed to bring the neaped mariner under the spell of the landlocked village maid, so sweet to look on, so serviceable about a house, and so motherly with a baby that the novel thought of matrimony was popped into a rover's head. She, for her part, was still more swiftly subjugated by the jolly Roger and the Tommy Devil, and the mutual confession was precipitated by the opposite menaces of tide and cart, each threatening to bear them apart. It was a race between these and the course of true love, which must flow rapid to flow at all. But it did not flow smooth, for when Daniel Quarles arrived to convey his daughter home and found a rival vehicle waiting uncouthly on the beach to bear her off, he roundly damned the "furriner" who aspired to be his son-in-law, and he included in his maledictions the Preventive Service and all its works, especially the new baby, not to mention the times and the tides. For though he had long ago found grace and become a Wesleyan, he had embraced the new doctrine with the old robustiousness. The natural man was no more to be mitigated than a hedgehog. Had he become a Quaker, he would have turned the other cheek in a violent collision with the striker's jaw. He enjoyed being angry, and that his wrath was "righteous" only added to its zest. And "righteous" it now was.

The trouble was not that Captain Boldero was a Churchman: the fellow was flippantly ready to embrace anything on earth that included Emma. It was not even that Daniel "suspicioned" him a smuggler. Smuggling—even if you had a brother-in-law in the Government—was quite as respectable as poaching, and in days when the rural labourer could not have lived had he not eked out his obolus by occasional rabbits (with the necessary vegetables), only an obtuse squirearchy could hold that sinful.

But even the squire had no opprobrium for the smuggler: gentry and peasantry were at one in backing up the manly patriot who thwarted a wicked Government, supplied Britons with the cup that cheers and their country with a fine naval reserve and early information of Froggy's movements. The shores of Essex as of all Britain were honeycombed—apart from their large natural resources and their ruins and haunted houses—with artificial hiding-places, cellars, vaults, and secret passages, and every man's hand was against the Ishmael of the Customs House. Farmers left their gates open at night to facilitate the cavalcades and coaches-and-six, and were but little surprised to find tea or tobacco coming up overnight on their fields like mushrooms. Even parsons were disposed to regard such treasures as drifted their way as heaven-sent flotsam, and Government circles themselves—in that era of purchasable votes and votable purchases—had not the ethical toploftiness which characterizes all Governments to-day. No, it was not Boldero the Smuggler, but Boldero the Smoker that found himself hurled into outer darkness the day poor shrinking Emma was borne off in her father's cart. "No puffing pirate shall cross my threshold," swore Daniel, but the accent was on the puffing, not the pirate. For tobacco had become tabu in the Wesleyan ranks: the godless practice of smoking was formally forbidden to the ministers. Swiss Protestantism indeed had once included its prohibition in the Ten Commandments. If Methodism did not thus re-edit the Decalogue, its horror of the abomination was no less keen, and a change of practice being always easier than a change of heart, Daniel Quarles had poured a deal of spiritual energy into the sacrifice of his pipe. The "rapscallion Boldero," he declared, not only sinned himself, but was the cause of sin in others, trafficking as he did in the unholy weed. If Emma insisted on a "smoker," wasn't there the miller at Long Bradmarsh, he inquired with grim facetiousness, meaning that the grotesque Griggs had a vote by living in a house with a chimney.

But Emma for all her gentle airs had proved "obstropolus." She had discovered that Susannah's husband smoked as prodigally as Roger—though it had been hidden from the old man on his rare visits—and that so far from bedevilling men, tobacco tended to angelicize them. Would indeed that her father haloed himself with these clouds! Besides, she shrewdly suspected that even a Wesleyan archangel, appearing suddenly as a suitor, would have fared similarly, and that the smoke was only a cover for a wish to keep his last girl. And so, though the lover was left lamenting, and the Tommy Devil duly floated off without the lass, it was not long that Emma was left stranded in Blackwater Hall. With a parent removed by Providence every Tuesday and Friday, even the flabbiest female may be stiffened, and the end was smuggled matrimony; though very soon the blessing of a minister brought Methodism into their madness. Roger Boldero not only became a Wesleyan like his wife and her father, but was one of the first Dissenters to be married in their own chapel by their own clergy under the new Act.

The odd union had turned out happy, but with one dismal drawback—the Bolderos could not rear children. They fared worse even than the Bidlakes, and with no such obvious reason. One hapless infant after another died, and when at last, in their late middle years, little Jinny was safely steered through three winters, it was they who were taken as if in lieu of their progeny.

The pair had finally settled down by the same waterside that had united them—the attractions of "Brandy Hole Creek" having been enhanced by the perpetual presence of their relative by marriage, Commander Dap, who with the subsidence of spirit duties and smuggling had found his mobile cutter replaced by the moored "Watch Vessel 23." Here with Susannah and his children and five satellites (and their wives and families) the veteran lived in domestic beatitude under the title of Chief Coast Guard Officer. High on the beach, and boarded by a commodious staircase, the houseboat seemed a standing reminder of the adventure of the Tommy Devil. Under its challenging eye, that adventurous bark had sailed out and home, till that last fatal voyage when the lugger foundered almost within sight of a little Sussex port, which for weeks after was mysteriously littered with washed-up tobacco-bales. Though Roger Boldero was rescued, it had been the beginning of the end of his prosperity, already undermined by the diminution of duties, and a few years later both he and Emma were dead simultaneously of smallpox. Again the carrier's cart must fare to the Creek to fetch the penniless little orphan, and there— soon after Will Flynt's flight—Daniel brought her back for the burial of his sister Susannah. It was what buried Will's memory too and replaced him in her prayers by a new being, conceived as her "Angel Mother."

The moment she saw and smelt the creek she knew she had carried it in her soul all along: the white hut with its flagged mast, the great Watch Vessel, the tumble of cottages, sheds, barrels, pecking fowls, grubbing black pigs, recumbent ladders, discoloured boats with their keels upwards, black rotting barges, and rigged smacks stranded on hard steep mud. The sea came in sluggishly through a broad green chine, half slime, half green water, spitted with gaunt encrusted poles to mark the channel. The water seemed even wider than she remembered, and yet not so wide, for it was split by an island or a promontory that gave a second sail-dotted expanse between her and the farther shore. She yearned now towards that ultimate hump of hazy woodland, and it was to remain for ever bathed in the quiet beauty which wrapped it around as Methusalem toiled up to the "Leather Bottel." They were to stay the night there, for Daniel would have none of the Commander's hospitality, he being still unforgiven. Besides, the child might be afraid of the corpse.

It was while sitting on that sea-wall with the octogenarian that evening, her great grown-up fingers toying once again with tiny white shells that strewed its top, and pewits again trying to lead her from their young, that she first heard in broken outlines how these waters had washed her into being. Something, too, she gleaned from her refound relative-in-law, the chief mourner, whose cocked hat, tattooed arm and genial senescence—not to mention his house-boat—were one of the pleasantest impressions or re-impressions of the funeral; and whose fascinating trick of rolling one eye while the other was fixed in a glassy stare almost made the child lose the sense of what he was saying. The death of his wife had reminded the veteran of the death of Nelson—nearly forty years before—and his tremulous tones grew still shakier as he recalled how the flags over the hut and the Watch Vessel and every other flag in England had flown at half-mast, though of course there were more joyous aspects of "Trafalgar" to be celebrated in bottles of Bony's own brandy. He frankly admitted he had himself been "three sheets in the wind"—an image of bed-linen fluttering on a clothes-line that long puzzled her. He took her abaft the Watch Vessel—it was a way of leaving Daniel Quarles alone with his dead sister—and recounted his astonishment at seeing her father's boat spued up like Jonah out of the whale.

"A handsome man," he told her to her pleasure. But he spoilt it all by adding, "though he would talk the hind leg off a dog."

"But wasn't that cruel?" the little girl faltered.

Dap laughed. "He never did it really, dearie, and if the leg had come off, he'd have helped the lame dog over a stile. And so many lingos—parleyvooing in French and swearing in Double Dutch. I don't wonder your angel mother fell in love with him."

"My angel mother!" echoed Jinny excitedly. "Was my mother an angel?"

The veteran was taken aback. For a child who must be past nine such primitiveness was startling. He had spoken loosely, hardly knowing whether he alluded to Emma's present heavenly abode or to her sweet-temperedness on earth. He did not know that little Jinny read nothing but literature in which angels were a common feature of the landscape, and that Miss Gentry had not measured her for her blacks without dwelling on her own stained-glass specimen.

"She was as pretty as one," said the Commander after an instant, "and now she is one." Thus it was that Jinny's mother, already felt as a hovering sweetness, took on definite wings, and even when Jinny's maturer experience amputated them from her earthly existence, they were what she still hovered over her child with.

"Susannah and she'll make a pair now," he added, feeling suddenly disloyal to the corpse at home.

"Susannah?" queried Jinny, for her grandfather had been calling his sister "Pegs"—"poor Pegs!"

"Your mother's aunt."

It was a new idea, an angel's aunt. She saw the twain flying, Susannah sailing with more sweeping pinions, her mother softly rustling.

The funeral was in style, and Jinny helped to set out the refreshments in the saloon. There was some dispute as to whether her grandfather could join the grand procession in his tilt-cart, but though he urged that squires were proud to be buried from farm-wagons, he consented to ride—like a fish out of water—inside a mourning-coach, and not even on the box.

The Commander and Jinny shared his dismal grandeur, she sitting bodkin though there was an empty seat opposite, which "the seventh baby" had been expected to occupy. But Toby had not arrived from his ship—he was a gunner—in time, and the earlier progeny were still more scattered.

The widower held his handkerchief in his fist, but owing to the heat of a discussion on the manner the Navy had gone to the dogs—or returned from them—since the Admiralty had set up a gunnery school on a Portsmouth ship, he used it only to mop his brow.

"Excellent, indeed!" He was mocking at the ship's name. "The ruination of the sarvice I tell you. It all comes from doing away with the pressgang—stands to reason they picked out the finest chaps—" here the Gaffer snorted—"Oh you may sniff, but for fighting you want guts and muscle. Look what England was in them days and what she is coming to now."

"To my lookin'-at-it-an'-thinkin'-o't-too"—the Gaffer made one breathless word of it—"'tis a blessin' to be riddy of all them gaolbirds, swearers, drinkers, smokers, and fornicators."

"Hush!" The Commander tried to wink his glass eye towards Jinny.

"She don't understand. Oi remember, the year my good-for-nawthen Gabriel smashed up a threshin'-machine (and the poor farmer dedn't git no compensation neither, though ef his furniture had been smashed 'twould have come on the Hundred) that wery same year Ebenezer Wagstaff—for 'twas the coronation year of King William, Oi remember, just afore my Emma desarted me—"

"That was a Sailor King," interrupted Dap, half to stave off fulminations against Jinny's dead mother. "Began as middy under Cap'n Digby in the unlucky Royal George—a ninety-eight gun ship she was—"

"Ye put me off the track, drat ye, aldoe it leads back to Ebenezer Wagstaff all the same, seein' as the Prince might ha' rubbed showlders with a thief as was sentenced for stealin' half-a-suvran from a barge on the Brad. He could ha' been hanged for it in them days, mind you—the case bein' as clear as day or rather as black as night. But they marcifully brought him in guilty to stealin' nine and 'levenpence and that saved his neck, being a navigable river, and the judge give him the option of gaol or jinin' the Navy."

"And a proper thing too. Set a thief to catch a Frenchy, and him used to taking prizes by water. Nowadays before the captain hoists his pennant he's got a crew dumped on him that's no choice of his—mealy-mouthed lubbers, full of book-larnin', who don't know a brigantine from a topsail schooner: it's the red ensign that gets all the good stuff, not the white. You mark me, it'll be the downfall of England."

"England'll never fall down while she's got God-fearin' congregations," maintained Daniel Quarles, and Jinny's devout little heart thrilled to hear it.

In the pleasant sunny graveyard there were apiaries and a dismantled tower almost smothered by blackberry-bushes, and the tombs and gravestones passed imperceptibly into a garden of monkey-trees and weeping willows. These wrought in her no stirring of memories, but as she had got off the coach, the standing church tower, square and ivy-wrapped, had composed beautifully with ricks of all sorts, with trees, old tiles, and thatch, into a picture that seemed as much hers as the waterside.

The parson—Susannah had remained a Churchwoman—was some minutes late, and Jinny was gratified to note how strong her grandfather was: how pillar-like he stood in his long black mourner's cloak under the weight of the coffin at the churchyard gate, while all the other bearers, his obvious juniors, shifted and sweated. Nor did he blubber either like the Commander, whose weakness, considering how often she had been adjured to be "spunky," and not—now that she was "grown up"—to cry, was as disconcerting as the double existence of his wife in the coffin and the empyrean. However, Dap grew "good" again when the thrilling if still more disconcerting episode of lowering his Susannah as far as possible from the skies and banking her safely against ascent, was over; and—Daniel Quarles having gone vaguely roving over the churchyard—the widower led her stealthily in his absence to a stone behind the ruined tower—in the "unconsecrated" or Dissenting area—and read to her the inscription, following it for her confirmation with his black-gloved forefinger:

HERE LIES ROGER BOLDERO
AFTER MANY STORMY VOYAGES
SAFELY NEAPED IN CHRIST.

He arrested himself suddenly and whisked her round the tower.

"But we didn't read it all," she protested.

"Oh, it only says: 'And also Emma Boldero, Wife of the Above.' But don't tell your grandfather."

The child wondered why she was to keep Emma's relationship to the Above a secret—she had already gathered from her grandfather that he knew it—and she was distressed as well as puzzled at the strange quarrel that broke out in the homeward coach.

"It ain't at all a proper word," said Daniel Quarles. "You might as well put 'carted to Christ' on mine."

"That'll be your affair," persisted the widower, "but this ain't. And how you came to see it gets over me."

The Gaffer flushed uneasily. "Oi've got two eyes, I suppose," he jerked.

The naval veteran glared glassily. "Them that pay the piper call the tune," he retorted defensively. "Besides," he added more gently, "Emma always said she'd have it somehow on her tombstone."

"Emma was a silly."

"Hush!" Dap again indicated the child with his glassy eye, now trickling without the other as in half-mourning.

"Oi won't hush it up. That's got to goo. The mason's got to cut another for me. Who arxed you to pay pipers?"

"Such a handsome stone to be torn up! It's a desecration, it's unlawful."

"Unlawful? Whose darter is she, mine or yourn?"

"Not yours. You cut her off."

"She cut me off. And ef poor Pegs and you had done your duty by my gal, he'd ha' never crossed your doorstep."

"He'd ha' met her on the sea-wall. I couldn't help his beholding her looks, any more than you could help having a handsome daughter—or for the matter of that, a handsome sister." His handkerchief came out again.

"Oi'm not denying their looks—a man with half an eye could see that. 'Tis just the handsome gals as seems to throw theirselves away," he added musingly.

"Maybe they are unhappy at home," suggested the widower, with equal philosophic aloofness.

"Or in the housen they stays at," assented the Gaffer. "But let bygones by bygones. It may be the Lord dumped him down for our good. All Oi say is, that word's got to goo. A Churchman may not see the blasphemy, but think o' what John Wesley would ha' said to it."

"He'd ha' said 'twas a wicked extravagance to waste such a fine stone."

"The mason'll take it back. Happen there'll be another Roger Boldero dead and neaped some day."

"Very likely," sneered the veteran. "And also an Emma, Wife of the Above."

"Hush!" The little maid nudged him, wondering he should forget his own monition.

"That has more sense than you!" cried the Gaffer in high glee. "Out of the mouths of babes and sucklings!" And drawing the astonished Jinny to his bristly beard, he kissed her lips with a hearty smack.

Despite these half-understood discords, Jinny was very sorry to leave the stony-eyed veteran and the motley waterside.

"Sometimes," she confided to the more sympathetic swivel eye, as her grandfather was harnessing Methusalem for their return, "I wish I had never come to earth at all."

Again Dap was startled by her simplicity—had not Daniel been telling him what a useful little body she was in the business?

"But then you'd never have had your grandfather—or me," he said, stroking her cheek.

"I should have had God—and my angel mother!"

IV

"Noa, arter she run away with her Boldero Oi'd never cross her doorstep, never," confessed the old carrier, picking up the story later, as she rode beside him on their day's work. He was getting so old now that he preferred to talk of twenty rather than of two years before, and the veneer of book-education which his unexpected inheritance of the business had necessitated had fallen away, and he was speaking more and more in the idioms of his illiterate youth, curiously tempered at times by the magnificent English of his Bible.

"But that was wicked!" said Jinny decisively. She felt it wrong indeed that a father should thus cut off his daughter, but to have done this when that daughter was an angel (even if only in the making), still more when that daughter was her own mother, seemed to her confused consciousness the climax of iniquity.

"Wicked! The contrairy! Oi'd taken my Bible oath never to set foot over her doorstep. So Oi dedn't have no chance, you see."

Jinny was silenced. She herself had succumbed to an oath, and that indeed on a less awful book.

"Arter she had lost two childer," he went on, "and the third got measles, she sent a man on hossback to beg me to take off the spell. Thought, d'ye see, dearie, that for her frowardness and disobedience Oi'd laid a curse on 'em all. Like one of our Methody preachers, the chap seemed, with all the texts to his tongue's tip, and pleaded that wunnerful he 'most made me believe Oi did have the evil eye. But though of course Oi hadn't no more to do wi' the deaths of your little brothers and sisters than a babe unborn—or you yourself, for the matter o' that, as was a babe unborn—Oi couldn't break my oath and goo and pretend to cure the wean, and so when the measles turned to pneumonia and it died, she got woundily distracted, and writ me two sheets sayin' as Oi was a child-murderer. That didn't worrit me no more than the child's death, seein' as the Lord does everything for the best, though Oi had to pay double on the letter. But one fine arternoon the preachin' chap comes again and says she'd been layin' paralysed-like for a month and wouldn't Oi come and forgive her afore she kicked the bucket!"

"Oh, Gran'fer!" Jinny protested.

"Oi'm givin' you his words," said the Gaffer defensively. "At least that was the meanin', though 'haps he put it different, me not havin' his gift o' the gab. But bein' never a man to nuss rancour, when folks own up, Oi said that even ef Oi could forgive my darter, never could Oi enter a house harbourin' that rascal Boldero—"

"Oh, Gran'fer!" she protested again.

"There's no call to bristle up—he wasn't your father yet. 'But Boldero ain't at home, he's off on a jarney,' says the chap. 'D'ye swear that?' says Oi. 'By God, Oi will,' says he. 'Then od rabbet, Oi'll goo,' says Oi."

"But," urged Jinny, "if you had taken your oath—"

"You wait till Oi've broke it! Oi knew 'twould be dead o' night by the time Oi got to Brandy Hole Crick and Oi made him swear too he wouldn't let on to a soul, partic'ler to that rascal Boldero or my sister Pegs and her cock-eyed son of a cocked hat; and off we scuttles in a twinklin', him on his hoss and me on mine—"

"Methusalem?"

"Noa, Jezebel. Methusalem and you wasn't born yet!"

"Were we both in heaven, then?"

"Hosses don't come from heaven."

"From where then?"

"From stables o' course. And you should see them two animals gallopin' like hell. 'Twas a race for the Crick. We went down this wery road like fleck and turned off by the smithy—"

"And who won?" asked Jinny breathlessly.

"He hadn't a chance, his hoss bein' that winded already, and him a heavyweight; Oi had the best part of an hour with your mother afore he crossed the doorstep."

"But how could you break your Bible oath?" persisted Jinny.

He chuckled. "Oi dedn't cross her doorstep. Oi'd sworn not to, and a Quarles never breaks even his plain word, bein' a forthright family. 'Twas gettin' on to bull's-noon and like pitch, but Oi could see her bedroom above by the light in it, and up Oi climbs on Jezebel's back and lifted myself up by the sill and got my knee acrost it and pushed open the casement. Lord, how she screamed! Up she flew from her dyin'-bed—no more paralysis or sich-like maggots and molligrubs Oi warrant you!" And his chuckle broadened into a hearty laugh.

Jinny was strangely relieved. "Then she didn't die!"

"How could she die, silly, when you wasn't there yet? Od rabbet, wasn't your feyther flabbergasted to see her up and bobbish and me holdin' her hand!"

"My father! But he was on a journey!"

"Yes, to me, the great ole sinner. You ain't guessed 'twas him with the gift o' the gab? But no more did Daniel Quarles, never conceivin' a sailor on hossback and him swelled in the stomach with prodigal livin' since the day he diddled Pegs's husband and tried to diddle me out o' my darter. But Oi'll do him the justice to say he never did blab to the Daps about my comin'—and no more dedn't your mother."

Jinny's hand sought her grandfather's, though through the whip-handle in his she could only secure a finger. "But why should you hide your goodness, Gran'fer?"

"'Twasn't no goodness, only nat'ral, Emma bein' punished and chastised enough from on high. Why, if Pegs and her false-eyed mannikin'd a-got wind as we'd made it up, Emma and me and Roger, they'd ha' come to think they was in the right arter all, lettin' Emma be kidnapped by a furriner. And that 'ud ha' been the last straw. As ill luck would have it Dap come knockin' there that wery dead o' night, he havin' just come home from a trip and heard from Pegs as her niece was dyin'. Oi shan't soon forget the start Oi got at that knockin', all on us settin' so hearty at supper, and Emma in her scarlet dressin'-gownd, smart as a carrot. Noigh quackled Oi was, with the brandy gooin' the wrong way. Your feyther he goes to the door with his face full o' lobster and sputters through the crack as they'd got a new doctor who was operatin' on her and wery 'opeful." He chuckled again. "And Oi count 'twas a better doctor than any in Brandy Hole Crick, for wery soon there was a new baby—though that died too, Oi'm thankful to say!"

"You aren't!" The little listener loosed his finger.

"Yes, Oi am, dearie." He cracked his whip. "Otherwise wouldn't Pegs ha' gone to her grave believin' it was my onforgiveness laid a spell on the tothers? That's what womenkind be. Same as when the Faith Healers got hold of her. Arter you was oiled and prayed over, they said 'twas want o' faith had killed all the tothers."

"Was I oiled and prayed over?"

"Well, you see when you come, poor Emma felt elders and oils was all there was left to try—there's a rare lot of you Peculiars down them parts and all the way to Southend, and they'd been gettin' round her like gulls round the plough—so the instant you started barkin'—"

"Barking?" gasped the little girl.

"You had the croup—so she turned Peculiar," he explained. "Like you," he added reproachfully. "And a wery dangerous thing to do, bein' as you might ha' died like the tothers. Did, she'd ha' been had up for child-murder—what she accused me of."

"And why weren't the doctors had up, that didn't save all my little brothers and sisters?" asked Jinny.

"That's just how your mother used to argufy," he said angrily, flicking at poor Methusalem. "Turnin' everything topsy-tivvy, Oi says. And what was the result? Two years arter you was prayed and oiled out o' croup, she was took herself with smallpox and wouldn't see a soul except elders and deacons and sich-like truck. Oi will say for your father though, that he was allus firm with her; naught she could say could turn him from his Wesleyan principles, and when he caught her smallpox he had the doctor in like blazes and took all the medicine he could lay hands on. But Emma would stick to her own way—though she died of it, poor thing."

"But didn't you tell me father died the same day as my angel mother?"

"Ain't that why Oi come for you in my cart, bein' as the creditors sold up everythin' except the infected beddin'?"

"I know, Gran'fer," she interrupted. "But then didn't father die of his way just as much as mother of hers?"

"That's a nat'ral death when you die with a doctor," he maintained.

"And were you there when they died?" said the child after a mournful pause.

His brow clouded obstinately. "How could Oi be, dearie, bein' as Oi'd taken my Bible oath?"

"You could ha' gone through the window?"

"With folks lookin' on and nusses about, as 'ud ha' thought me loony. Why, 'twas impossible for me even to goo to the funeral."

"Oh, Gran'fer!"

He looked fiercer, and poor Methusalem got another flick. "Wouldn't Pegs be there, she havin' her nat'ral feelin'? Could Oi let her think Oi'd come 'cos Oi was sorry Oi hadn't made it up with my darter afore she died? Nay, that 'ud a-been right-down deceit, bein' as there wasn't no ground for remorse. Happen he'd a-been at the churchyard too with his fish-eye—dedn't you see the stone he put up, drat his imperence, as ef Emma and Roger was aught of hisn—mebbe he'd a-preached to me as Oi ought to ha' forgiven my darter time she was still alive. 'Twas on the cards he'd say Oi'd broken your mother's heart, the blinkin'-fool, he not knowin' 'twas me as raised her from the dead and had her goffling lobster with your feyther in a scarlet dressin'-gownd time he was knockin' at her door to make inquirations—"

"Yes, I've heard about that," she interrupted.

"Who told you?" he said suspiciously. "There was only three of us inside the door and two's dead."

"You told me."

"Me! Oi never told a soul—Oi'll take my Bible oath."

"You told me just a minute ago."

"Ah!" He was appeased. "That may be. But Oi never told you afore—Oi'll take my oath."

"No, never before, Gran'fer."

There was a pause of peace.

Jinny was afraid to stir up the subject for weeks. But her little brain had been busy with the story, and finally taking advantage of a not unfriendly reference to Roger Boldero, she asked: "And was that the last time you saw father, when he was eating lobster with my angel mother in the dead of night?"

"Nay, nay, Oi seen lots of 'em both, afore Oi was shet out agen by molloncholy circumstances."

"Ah!" Jinny brightened up. "And did you always go in by the window?"

"'Twasn't in the house: 'twas on board the Tommy Devil. And that ain't got no doorstep." He laughed gleefully.

"Then did you go in by the porthole?" asked Jinny, smiling.

"Lord, missie, wherever did ye get that word? Ah, Oi mind me now—you was aboard the Watch Wessel the time we buried poor Pegs. No, dearie, Oi just shinned up the ladder, loight as a bird with that liddle ole oath off my showlders. But Pegs and her one-eyed fool of a pardner never suspicioned naught, for Oi never would set foot on the Tommy Devil except she was layin' up in coves and cricks where the Gov'ment turned its glass eye—he, he, he! Not that Oi had much stomach for his etarnal brandy—you can't take a satisfactory swig o' that and keep your sea-legs—but your feyther he kept a cask o' beer special for me, and Emma she 'ad allus cold roasts and kickshaws to be washed down with it. Oi reckon Oi was on board with your parents nigh once a month."

"Then what a pity they didn't invite you on board years before!"

"Ay, 'twas a pity. Only none of us 'ad never thought o' that way out."

"Or that way in," added Jinny excitedly. "Why, you might have gone to my mother the day after your oath!"

The Gaffer sighed. "Mebbe that 'ud only ha' ruined your folks quicker. For Oi ain't been on the lugger a dozen times afore she went down and your feyther was picked up by the revenue cutter, bein' the onny toime he was took at sea—he, he, he! Thussins there wasn't no place to meet in, and to goo over Emma's window-sill was too risky, for Pegs and her friends was allus spyin' around, and there wasn't a sharper eye in the Gov'ment than that dirty little Dap's—when he was off duty."

"But why didn't they come to see you at Blackwater Hall?"

"Nay, they couldn't do that. That was in my oath too. Never shall they cross my doorstep, neither—Oi'd sworn it on the Book!"

"But why didn't they come in through our window? There's hardly ever anybody on the common?"

"We never thought o' that, neither." He heaved a deeper sigh. "Ay, 'twas a pity," he repeated.

That night Jinny caught his eye resting more than once on the vases of dried grass before their casement.

"He was a bonkka man, your feyther," he observed at last. "Wery big-built, and it's a middlin' weeny window."

V

Though Jinny winced at her grandfather's attacks on the Peculiar Faith of her angel mother, she grew in time to understand the odd magnanimity he had evinced in letting her go to Sunday-school with the Flynt family and pick up the doctrine. That her one surviving child should be brought up of the sect that had saved it, was, it transpired, poor Emma's dying request, as conveyed by his sister Susannah Dap to the unforgiving father, whose oath never to cross his daughter's doorstep still held when he drew up Methusalem at it after the double funeral, and found the house empty even of Jinny.

"'Child-stealin', that's what it is,' Oi told Pegs when Oi boarded the Watch Wessel," he recounted once to his granddaughter in the cart. "'Ain't you got enough o' your own?' says Oi. "'Twas through your havin' one too many that Jinny's here at all,' Oi says. 'Then,' says she, sharp as a needle, 'the more reason she's mine. You cut off her mother,' says she, 'and now, Daniel, Jinny cuts you off.' 'Not so fast, sister,' says Oi. 'Whatever my conduct to Emma—and folks with stone eyes don't allus see through stone walls—the poor little brat haven't enough sense to cut me off, and Oi don't cut her off, for Oi ain't got to wisit sins to the fourth generation, not bein' the Almighty, thank the Lord. That's my lawful property, Pegs,' Oi says, 'and same as you don't hand her over, Oi'll summons you and carry off two o' yourn in my cart—and what's more Oi'll ill-treat 'em cruel and hide 'em twice a day with my whip.'"

"You didn't mean it," said Jinny.

"Dedn't Oi, though?"

"But they were your nephews and nieces!"

"The more right to wallop 'em. You should ha' seen Pegs climb down. She know'd well as Oi never broke my word, she bein' o' the same forthright family. Right up and down, Jo Perry, as the sayin' goos. Do to others as they'd like to do to you—that's good Christian gospel. Pegs she went as pale as a white butterfly and hiked you out on deck in your little yaller frock lookin' as pritty as a gay. Lord, Oi reckonized you on the nail, though Oi'd never clapped eyes on you afore."

"You'd never seen me before?" cried Jinny, amazed.

"How could Oi see you—you came arter the Tommy Devil was at the bottom, and your feyther never got the dubs from the insurance company, bein' a flaw in the articles as swallered up all the rest of his cash in the lawsuit. But you'd got his ways and your mother's looks"—Jinny flushed with pleasure—"and 'steddy cuttin' me off, you—ha, ha, ha!—made straight for my great ole beard and pulled out a great ole fistful."

"Ought I to have cut it off?" laughed Jinny happily.

"'D'ye see that, Pegs,' says Oi, 'blood's thicker than water. Will you come along o' your gran'fer, liddle maid?' says Oi."

"And what did I say?" asked Jinny breathlessly.

"You dedn't say naught—you bust into tears, bein' as you thought Oi was the auctioneerer and you'd been sold with everything else, poor liddle ole orphan, and then Pegs catches hold o' you and says you was clinging to her. But Oi soon stopped that lob-loll, for Oi holds you over the rail and shows you Methusalem all prancin' in his pride, and 'Won't you go with your gran'fer's hoss, liddle maid?' says Oi."

"And what did I say then?"

"You dedn't say naught, but in a twinklin' you jumps out o' Susannah's arms, scrambles down the accommodation ladder, and was rubbin' noses with Methusalem. And Oi count his was as damp as yourn, bein' as he'd come without a stop."

"Dear old Methusalem!" And nothing would content Jinny but she must jump down and rub noses with him now, and again both noses were damp. But as Methusalem had seized the opportunity to come to a standstill, and Jinny, lost in shadowy memories, continued the caress ten seconds too long, the old carrier declared with sudden querulousness that he hadn't got time for foolishness, and that since he had burdened himself with Jinny his business had gone "to rack and ruination."

"Peculiar, Pegs warned me, Oi'd have to bring you up," he added, as Jinny hastily clambered back to his side. "And Peculiar's the word for your gooin's on. Not that Methusalem's got more sense nor you. Oi count ef there was churches for cattle, he'd a-stoyled hisself Brother Methusalem and kicked over his drench."

It was the Gaffer's instinctive conviction that faith went with the father. In thus yielding to Emma's dying breath he may, apart from the pressure of death-bed wishes, have found vent for a lingering resentment against the seductive Boldero. Or was it that he had a lurking apprehension that the one child of Emma's which had at least survived prayer, might really be a testimony to the teaching, and as such entitled to share it? Jinny at any rate had absolute faith in the doctrine. It rested on the fifth chapter of James as clearly as the big Bible containing that chapter rested on the chest of drawers. Once indeed when the Gaffer was unbearably mocking, she had been goaded to read him the basal verses:

"Is any sick among you? let him call for the elders of the church; and let them pray over him, anointing him with oil in the name of the Lord:

"And the prayer of faith shall save the sick, and the Lord shall raise him up: and if he have committed sins, they shall be forgiven him."

But the Gaffer had not collapsed as she expected. It only meant a spiritual saving, in case he died, Daniel Quarles maintained, unruffled: otherwise why speak of his sins being forgiven? Moreover it didn't say you couldn't have a doctor, too.

Crestfallen, the child wept in a corner and did not recover her spirits till at Sunday-school Elder Mawhood had supplied her for the first part of the Gaffer's contention with Mark xvi. 18: "They shall lay hands on the sick and they shall recover"; while Martha, who was still at that date a Peculiar, comforted and equipped her against the second part with Asa, King of Judah, who (II Chronicles xvi) was diseased in his feet: "yet sought not to the Lord but to the physicians." The Lord's wishes in the matter were thus seen to be clearly indicated. "And the Lord's the same now as then, isn't He?" Martha wound up crushingly. "You ask your grandfather that."

The courage to launch this counter-attack never came to her, however, and henceforward she and her grandfather lived in that kindly toleration of each other's folly which comes from holding the proofs of it, yet letting sleeping dogmas lie. What after all was the old man's obduracy, Jinny told herself, but part of the perverseness and obstinacy of age? The fact that she now never needed either doctors or elders saved her from any personal problem. Such waverings as she had felt at fifteen were not towards Wesleyanism, but towards Martha's mushroom doctrine. The texts of this convert to the latest thing in creeds were certainly staggering, and her scorn for the still unconverted, sublime. "We don't take some bits o' the Word and leave others." That was an argument not easy to answer, and the bits now exhumed in support of Christadelphianism by the tireless discoverer of King Asa were ever accumulating. Fortunately Jinny was far too busy for religious discussions or doubts, and the "angel mother," softly hovering, made a restful background for the one true Faith.

VI

And a sensational episode in the history of the local Brethren came to strengthen the sect as well as to add to the number of Jinny's homes: came too, at the very crisis when the impossibility of carrying the Carrier with her through the coming winter threatened to leave her stranded alone at "The Black Sheep" during the midday rest at Chipstone. It would have been easy enough in summer to sit in her cart in the courtyard munching her bread and cheese, while Methusalem was lost in his nosebag, and clients were coming with commissions, but the parcel-shed had no stove, and to wait in the bar or taproom or even the parlour—all alike masculine haunts where one could hardly dump the "scarecrow" or swain-chaser beside one—was not a pleasant prospect.

Jinny's and the Brotherhood's good fortune began—such are the ways of Providence—with the death of the landlord.

Mother Gander—so everybody called Jeff Gander's buxom spouse—had fought like a lioness to save him. "Not a doctor for miles around," as the paralysed old Bundock put it triumphantly from his bed-of-all-news, "but she carted him over, and set 'em all consulting and quarrelling. There was two from London, one of 'em a bart, and all wasted. Charlie the potboy, as he was then, feelingly told my boy, the postman, that he could ha' set up a public-house with the fees. Not that I approve o' public-houses, but leastways they give you more waluable drinks than doctors does. And when poor Jeff was gone, and Mother Gander was carrying on like crazy, comes the Parson and tells her 'tis the Lord's will.

"'Then if it's the Lord's will,' says she, like lightning, for she was always quick in the uptake, 'why do you run down the Peculiars as just begs the Lord to alter His will, instead o' throwing their hard-earned gold to the doctors?' That was the way her eyes opened to the Truth, and she learnt how to save her soul as well as her money."

The Peculiars, they often lamented, were "not strong enough" in Chipstone: they looked yearningly "over the water"—to Rochford where the great Banyard himself was prophesying; or to Woodham where no less than five hundred Brethren and Sisters fevered themselves in a hall too small for the throngs that sought admission. But their own meetings, though, if we may trust Caleb, "noice things were brought out," were numerically disheartening. The capture of "The Black Sheep"—a hostelry to which all social roads radiated—was thus an event of considerable importance.

Nevertheless the dismay of the Congregationalists, of whose community Mother Gander was a fallen pillar, was not counter-poised in jubilation by the Brethren. For if a stronghold had been captured, the devil had not been dispossessed. Mother Gander doffed her gold chain, but Sister Gander gave no sign of emptying her liquor into the gutters, and to be proud of a convert against whose establishment you have to admonish one another is not simple. The Peculiars managed it, however, after some heart-searching. It was true old Bundock had been wont to make great play with Banyard's declaration—universally admired as a gem of humour—"If you want to get me to a public-house, you'll have to take a horse and hook me." But after all, Elder Mawhood pointed out, "The Black Sheep" was far more than a public-house: as the headquarters for the mail-coach it was part of the constitution of the country, and it was better for the farmers to eat their ordinary under a God-fearing roof—even if they would drink with it—than for the profits of their custom to go to a rival house which would contribute no farthing to the Brethren's treasury. It was Brother Flynt, however, who supplied the finest soothing-powder. "Oi used to condemn myself," he said, "but 'twasn't no good. You must drink when you're harvestin'. Don't, you'll be drippin' as you goo." If he did not drink now that his harvesting days were over, that did not prove other drinkers were wicked. You had to consider circumstances. And playing the Sancho Panza still more unexpectedly, he hinted that there was such a thing as over-zeal. "They used to call me a Banyard as a revilin' word, them as made fun of us, but to tell the truth Oi've never got out o' my warm bed in the middle o' the noight to pray as he exhorted—leastways, not in winter. We've got to be thankful for Sister Gander, and not expect her to goo all the way at the start. She don't want to lose her business as well as her husband."

But it appeared that Mother Gander did not want to go without a husband either. She suddenly, and before her year of mourning was up, married Charley Mott, the aforesaid potboy, not half her age, and this was a fresh upset for the Brethren, modified only by the conversion of Charley. The Congregationalists took the opportunity to give the couple "rough music," and the whole neighbourhood joined in with kettles and pokers. Brother Bundock from his omniscient bed at first proclaimed the scandal as a divine chastisement on his Brethren for having failed to "admonish" her to give up purveying "beer and 'bacca"—he himself would have dared it, he declared without fear of contradiction, had he only had his legs—but finally, when the storm blew over, he would relate with gusto how she had weathered it.

"What with hating us and hating her marriage and hating the new landlord with his jackanip's airs, they quit her, nearly all her customers, and them as was faithful looked askance at her between the drinks. So she offs with her silks and on with her apron and up with her sleeves, and back to the kitchen! She'd been poor Jeff's cook, you know, in the long, long ago, and 'twas her steak and kidney puddens and her gravies and sauces that he married, and now she was back at the old game. Whether 'twas partly to escape the sour looks that she burrowed in her kitchen or whether the whole thing was female artfulness I don't pretend to say, but in two months she'd cooked 'em all back again. Don't come in good time, you couldn't get a chair at the ordinary for all the tips at Chipstone, and my boy, the postman, he told me he hears everybody joking over the rhubarb tart and saying as the Lord's will is best. And she never come out o' that kitchen till she'd cooked it all down."

It was during the dark interval that Jinny and Sister Mott alias Mother Gander were first drawn together, the girl being summoned to the kitchen to receive instructions for such purchases from local tradesmen as the lady-hermit found indispensable yet dreaded to make in person. The fact that the little carrier was of the despised sect cemented the relationship. Jinny passed her midday respite in the warm kitchen, even sharing the cook's meal. And when at last Sister Mott resumed her blue silk bodice and faced her tradesmen and her customers, new and old, the run of the kitchen and the freedom of the joint remained gratuitous to the lucky Jinny. Here under the great bacon-hung oak beams of the ancient apartment, before a huge fire mirroring itself rosily in the copper pans and skillets, she could sit thawing her toes beside the clanking smokejack, while the wind howled through the arch of the sleety courtyard.

CHAPTER IV

WILL ON HIS WAY

Permit me of these unknown lands t'inquire,
Lands never till'd, where thou hast wandering been,
And all the marvels thou hast heard and seen:
Do tell me something of the miseries felt
In climes where travellers freeze, and where they melt.
CRABBE, "Tales of the Hall."

I

The coach from railhead to Chipstone was an hour and a half late, and not all the flourish of its horn as it thundered into the courtyard of "The Black Sheep" could disguise the fact. Not that it was the fault of the coach: it had waited for the mail train, and this, for those parts, parvenu monster had found an obstruction on the line, and was helpless to go round it, as the driver and the guard complacently pointed out. Their glory and their tips were shrunk like their circuit—unchanged along the short route, they could no longer prod the slumbering traveller with insinuatory farewells: they knew themselves, these Chipstone worthies, a last lingering out-of-the-way survival of the old order, doomed like the broad coaching road and the old hostelries to decay; already they had seen the horned guard decline in places to the omnibus cad, even as the ancient "shooter" of highwaymen had sunk to the key-bugler; yet they preserved the grand manner before the revolution that was deposing them—the Tom Pratt and Dick Burrage of a generation of travellers—and while dispensing their conversation like decorations and drinking your health as a concession, they retailed with gloomy satisfaction every railway collision and holocaust, as though coaches never overturned, and declared the English breed of horses would be ruined. And when certain lines set up third-class carriages they denounced the cruelty of packing the poor in roofless, seatless trucks, as though they themselves had never brought into port frost-bitten peers or dames sodden through their oilskin umbrellas.

But to-day "Powerful warrum" was the grumble of the passengers, even of those on the roof, the majority being—thus early in May—still smothered in box-coats; as for the unfortunates compressed inside, who had likewise not yet cast a clout, and had similarly mistrusted the sunshiny spell with which that pouring April had ended, they mopped their brows and cursed the fickle British climate. But though the sun had suddenly become hot enough to sour milk, it could not sour the temper of the bronzed young man—his face nigh as ruddy as his hair—who sat on the box-seat and conversed with Tom Pratt almost as an equal. Even the long delay on the line had left him unruffled, thanks largely to the blue-eyed girl in the train who before his clean-shaven cosmopolitan air had shown signs of tenderness, and whose address his purse now held—more precious than a fiver. Verily a pleasant change after the Eveless back-blocks of Canada.

And the idea of calling this "warrum"! He smiled to think of the hells he had known—Montreal with mosquitoes, New York in a damp heat. Why, this couldn't even melt a man's collar. And how refreshing was the trimness of the Essex countryside—the comfortable air of immemorial cultivation—after the giant untidiness of the New World. How soothing these long, green, white-sprinkled hedgerows with their ancient elms, this old, historic highway with thatch and tile, steeple and tower, after the corduroy roads of round logs or the muddy, dusty, sandy tracks. How adorable these creeper-covered cottages after log-cabins in backwoods; rotting floors on rotten sleepers and the mud paste fallen out of the walls. He forgot that it was precisely this that he had fled from nearly a decade ago—this dead, walled-in life, so petty and pietistic—and he congratulated himself afresh on the wisdom of that abrupt resolution to sell his clearing to a second-hand pioneer and to farm at home with the profits.

His clothes alone would have kept him in good humour. Not only were the heavier in what he had learned to call his trunk, but those on his back were the first he had ever had made to measure. And they were made too—like the neckcloth and shawl and fal-lals he was bringing to his parents "from America"—by the world-famous firm of "Moses & Son" (opposite Aldgate Church), whose imposingness was enhanced in his eyes by finding it—on the Saturday he first hied thither—haughtily aloof: a blank wilderness of shutters in a roaring world, with no gleam through their chinks from the seven hundred gas-burners. But he had finally stormed the "Private Hall," toiling—as invited by rhyme—up "the stairs of solid oak," and had gained the heights "where orders were bespoke," and there—in that rich-carpeted "showroom with the giant chandelier," in a setting of Corinthian columns, sculptured panels, and arabesque ceilings—dark enchanters with tape-measures like serpents over their shoulders had made obeisance to him and enfolded him with their coils. Even his billycock hat verified the bardic boast:

There's not another Hat-mart in the town
Which casts such lustre on the human crown.

Left to himself he would have liked a wideawake, but that arbiter elegantiarum, the small boy, he was warned, had not quite acquiesced in that. If it was not a coat of many buttons that he now sported, it was scrimp enough to show off the fine lines of his figure; for the movement towards ample waistcoats and wide trousers was not yet encouraged by his Aldgate mentors, and pockets on the hips had been conceded him with reluctance. In his large American trunk reposed a still grander suit of Sunday sable, though he had shied at a frock coat, and was glad to learn from these hierophants of the mode that morning jackets were no longer confined to the stable-yard or the barrack-room, but were permissible even in the country house—and there was no question but Frog Farm was that. He had already worn his blacks once, on his visit to the Great Exhibition, and they made, he found, a distinct difference to the policemen in top-hats whose guidance he sought in the labyrinths of the metropolis.

The delay in this visit to the Exhibition—the goal of his journey to London—had turned out an advantage, he felt, giving him time for these measured elegancies. If he had been unable to be in at the opening, as he had grandly designed in Canada when ignorant that this involved guineas and season-tickets, he had managed to squeeze for a glimpse of the Queen outside if not inside the Park, and the first five-shilling day—after all, only the fourth—was grandeur enough for a whilom ploughboy and cabin-boy. Although nine ten-pound notes made a warm waistcoat-lining, he was not under the illusion that he had returned with more than a competence.

One would have thought London itself a Greater Exhibition to a young man who had never seen it before: especially London at carnival with its colossal crowds swollen by visitors from all countries in all complexions and costumes: London with its numberless gay 'buses (plying mostly to Hyde Park), its swifter gliding cabriolets of the new pattern invented by Mr. Hansom, and the more stolid procession of four-wheeled clarences, not to mention the fashionable and civic carriages with the scarlet-and-gold pomp of flunkeys and outriders: London with its countless curious street-criers, costermongers, ballad-mongers, watercress sellers, muffin and hot-pie men, birdcage dealers, tract-peddling Lascars in white robes, and vendors of everything from corn-salves to speeches on the scaffold; blowsy, rowdy London that turned into a dream-city when those strange figures with rods glided through the twilight, flecking the long, grey streets with points of fire.

But though Will Flynt was not insensitive to these fascinating phenomena, and even rode about recklessly in the cabriolets at eightpence a mile, yet London had not the spell to hold him. Only the Great Exhibition had drawn him across the Atlantic. While awaiting impatiently for the five-shilling day, he duly did the Tower and the Zoo (sixpence extra for Mr. Gould's humming-birds in the twenty-five glass cases), paid twopence to go into St. Paul's, and a shilling to see the Great Globe in Leicester Square, patronized Phelps at Sadler's Wells, and the horses at Astley's, had a peep at Vauxhall, enjoyed "Rush, the Norwich Murderer," at Madame Tussaud's, and submitted the boots these operations begrimed to the red-coated shoeblacks of the Ragged Schools—London's new word in philanthropy. But though he liked the quarter in which his quaint galleried hotel, "The Flower Pot," was situated, with the Spitalfields Market and the tall old houses of the silk-weavers, whose vast casements with their little panes rose story on story, he was no sooner through with the visit to the Exhibition than without a day's delay—as promised in that letter to Martha—he took train and coach to Little Bradmarsh.

Beholding him thus on the County Flyer hurrying towards Frog Farm, after only a single visit to the stupendous spectacle, one may suspect that he did not know his own heart as well as he imagined. But he himself had no doubt of the magnet he obeyed, and he had found on his boat not a few rich Canadians—and the Dominion already boasted four thousand carriage-folk—who confessed to have yielded to the same irresistible attraction. There was indeed little else talked of on the voyage: even the wonders of the boat itself—a new Yankee iron and screw steamer of nearly two thousand tons and quite five hundred horse-power that brought them to Liverpool in eleven days from Halifax, and had spittoons and wedding-berths like the Yankee river-steamers, and to see which the Liverpudlians had flocked with their sixpences—paling before the world-marvel awaiting them in London.

And London itself was talking of it no less: for once London was staggered. And if London was thus shaken, how much more the provinces and the world at large? Did not indeed the flags of all nations wave over the great glass building, whose mere material would have been enough to set the globe agog, even if it had not contained contributions from every corner of civilization except Germany, which in that antediluvian age figured in the catalogue only as "The States of the Zollverein." What wonder if with all the excursions and alarums and millennial visions that attended its birth, the Press reeking with paragraphs, poems, discussions, wrangles, skits, prophecies, and forebodings, crowds equal to the population of provincial towns gathered at the Park to watch it rise, and to stare at the endlessly inrolling vans and the sappers and miners at work in their uniforms. One M.P.—military and moustachio'd—won the immortality of the comic prints by fulminating against the invasion of Freethinking foreigners who would pillage London and ruin the honour of British womanhood: more sober minds feared the Chartist mobs and the Red Republicans: even the Catholics, already flaunting their cardinals and ringing their unhallowed church bells, would profit by the Continental wave. The

House of Lords resounded with protests and petitions against the profanation of the Park, and apprehensions as to the fate of the building erected therein were equally rife: the great glass roof would be splintered by hailstones, the walls would be overturned by the wind, the galleries would collapse under the swarming multitudes, and Anarchism would seize its opportunity amid the dismantled treasures of the globe. But one unfailing factor was on the Exhibition's side: the scheme was attacked by the Times. And so Paxton's building rose steadily till the great day when through an avenue of three-quarters of a million spectators the Queen and "that Queen's indefatigable husband"—as a panegyrist of the period put it—drove to declare it open to the elect thirty thousand who had already found it so, while through glittering nave and transept, with their fountains, trees, flowers, and statues, the "Hallelujah Chorus" thundered from a thousand voices, two hundred orchestral instruments, and a dozen giant organs; and the millennial hope welled up in a grand climax of universal emotion. And hoary grandsires should hereafter tell—proclaimed the poet of the Great Catalogue—what in this famous century befell: grey Time should chronicle the victories gained, since Mercy o'er the world and Justice reigned:

What time the Crystal Hall sent forth her dove
And signed the League of Universal Love.

But although our Canadian pioneer had thus ample excuse for the unrest that forbade him to miss this Messianic spectacle, it was not—even he would have admitted—the Great Exhibition which had first unsettled his stolid labours. That oscillation had been communicated some two years earlier, and by a shock that had set the New World rattling even more noisily than the Old was shaken by the Great Exhibition. The discovery of gold in California was a seismic vibration that depopulated Eastern towns, shot sober lawyers into wagons, sent clergymen flying along mule-trails, swept timid tradesmen across the foodless and robber-haunted Rocky Mountains, whirled schoolmasters fifteen thousand miles round Cape Horn, and dumped them all waist-high in auriferous mud and shimmering water, to be fed by Indian squaws. It was under the lure of the Californian legend that Will had originally looked about for a purchaser of his cleared acres. But by the time the farm was off his hands, the glamour of easy gold had faded, and with a sum in his pockets sufficient for a little respite, life seemed suddenly larger than lucre, and he found himself possessed by a strange craving not to be away from the old country in that year of years—the year of the Great Exhibition.

II

Chipstone had seemed strangely shrivelled as the County Flyer tore through it; the High Street unexpectedly narrow and the great, gorgeous shops, against whose panes he had flattened his youthful nose, curiously small and drab, with diminutive sun-blinds; yet the quaint, blistered bulge of the old timbered houses was fascinatingly as he remembered it, and when the spirited quartet of tinkling steeds slackened under the archway crowned by the ironwork sign of "The Black Sheep," he saw through a warm dimness that the ancient inn still gave on the stable-yard with this same Tudor bulge, and that the courtyard itself was little less rambling than the picture he carried in his memory. There was the same mass-meeting of cocks crowing on the same golden dunghill, the same litter of barrels, boxes, baskets, and parcels of laundry-work, while the gardens of the whitewashed old cottages backing the black-tarred stables and cartsheds seemed caught up as incongruously as ever in the horsey medley. Why, there was the very shed which had sheltered the farm-wagon the Sunday he was to drive it to Harwich. And there—yes, actually there on the same doorstep, under the same hanging ironwork lamp, was Ostler Joe, the shambling, bottle-nosed hunchback, whose figure—in its reassurance of stability—struck him as positively beautiful, and whose head seemed aureoled by the mist. But where was that more expected face, where was the hair-swathed visage of Caleb Flynt? Brushing the mist from his eyes, he looked anxiously round the seething, sun-drenched courtyard. "Hullo, Joey," he said at last. "Wouldn't my dad wait?" It was a pleasant voice with something of a twang: but the twang was no longer local.

"Oi dunno your feyther from Adam," said Joe cheerfully, mopping his face with his shirt-sleeve.

"Yes, you do—old Mr. Flynt—Frog Farm."

Joe shook his head—it seemed no longer a saint's. "Oi never heerd nobody mention Frog Farm nowadays. It's a dead place." He shambled off on his many tasks with an aliveness that tightened the contraction Will felt at his heart. His father dead?

"But look here, Joe!" He pursued the factotum. "You remember me—little Will Flynt?"

"Can't say as Oi does—moind that box now."

"It's my box—and I wrote to dad to meet me with a trap. Guess he got tired of fooling around."

"There's warious traps." The hunchback waved a busy hand.

"No—he's not here. And how am I to get my trunk home?"

"Bradmarsh carrier goos at three—you're in luck."

He heaved a parcel now into a driverless tilt-cart, where a little white dog boisterously mounted guard. "That's 'er!" he said. "Take you too if you're smart."

"Daniel Quarles!" A fresh wave of reassurance radiated from that old household word on the familiar tilt. So the venerable carrier was still plying, how then could the comparatively juvenile Caleb be extinct? The May Day ribbons not removed from Daniel's horse, and making it a snow-white steed from fairyland, dispelled the last funereal images. Surely had Caleb Flynt really died, old Quarles would never have left so lively a topic untapped with Joey.

But here Will's meditations were agreeably cut short by another vision from auld lang syne—the laced mob-cap and blonde kiss-curls of Mother Gander, to whom Dick Burrage was gloating over the train's misadventure. There were pouches under the blue eyes, and no gold chain now heaved with her blue silk bosom: otherwise she was her old comely self. But fresh from his grand hotel in Spital Square, Will no longer regarded her as an awful and aristocratic personage, able to eat meat at every meal. An easy accost and inquiry about the old Flynts of Frog Farm brought him soothing information. Lord bless his soul, people living a healthy life like that never died—unless they took medicine. She couldn't say they had been to chapel lately—indeed she had gathered from the postman that the old wife had taken up with some New Jerusalem crankiness. "But you'll find the Bradmarsh carrier in the parcel-shed—that black one. You ask her!" And with a wave towards the arch she turned again to the beaming Dick Burrage.

Will thought the "her" referred to a chambermaid who was just passing, but he saw no need of such guidance—the parcel-shed was obvious enough. His mind was occupied with the odd fact that Mother

Gander had apparently become a sister in the spirit to his own father, while his mother had moved on to another eccentric doctrine. Ah well, changes were bound to come. Not everybody could be of the same immutable granite as himself.

He found the parcel-shed deserted save for a young girl who, busily heaping up parcels into the willing arms of Joey, did not even look up. Somewhat depressed by the chapel-memories the landlady had conjured up, he stood a moment, absently watching the operation, and wondering why the agreeably pretty creature should be dispatching so many parcels—wedding-cake came into his mind, though the oddly varying shape of the parcels was not consistent with the hypothesis. He would willingly have loitered—the chapel-cloud was dissipating—but the carrier was clearly not here, and, as the church clock opposite was booming three, he was afraid old Daniel might be starting off without him, so he hurried back to the pranked and pawing steed, only to find himself derided and defied by the little dog, which he now observed was also adorned with a May Day bow.

And then he remembered he was hungry. The block on the line had robbed him of his dinner, and he wondered whether to go off with that grim Gaffer Quarles would be so enjoyable as walking—after a square meal. No, why should he be thus whisked off? Why not a leisurely spread at "The Black Sheep" preceded by another glimpse of the girl in the shed, and then a long stroll home by the dear old field-paths, through Plashy Walk and Swash End, dry enough doubtless under this sun? Besides, his slow old parent might be on the way after all—there was no certainty the carrier with his compulsory windings and detours would not miss him. Yes, it would be kinder to his father to give him another hour or so. "The May Queen" he murmured to the air, brooding over Methusalem's belated ribbons. Yes, they would surely have made her that; though perhaps the old custom was no longer kept up. True, she hadn't the blue eyes or the plumpness of the girl in the train, and was not stately enough for a queen—though of course you couldn't really tell how Victoria looked outside her royal carriage. But then you couldn't imagine the blue-eyed minx in a royal carriage at all: you placed her smiling behind bars, manipulating beer-handles.

"It's all right," Joey startled him by announcing, toppling his tower of parcels into the cart. "Oi've made inquirations. The old Flynt chap be aloive and kickin'."

"Oh, thank you." Will's last shade of uneasiness vanished. He slipped a sixpence into Joey's palm. "Put my box in—I'm not going myself—say it's for Frog Farm." And he jostled back to the parcel-shed, through the bustle of boxes and jangling of bells, barging into other carriers from other circuits, stumbling over dogs that yelped, tangling himself in the whip of a postboy who was frantically buttoning his waistcoat, and nearly run over by the great coach just wheeling round. He was more disappointed than surprised when he at last reached the shed to find it empty, though far fuller than before of mere people. Still, there was always dinner.

III

But dinner was not always.

"No, I'm afraid it's all gone," said Mother Gander. She was blocking the way at the foot of the stairs, where a painted hand under pendent stag-horns directed you upwards to the "Parlour"—"The Black Sheep" would have none of your new-fangled "Coffee Rooms"—and Will Flynt, sniffing up the odours of beer, sand, tobacco, gin, snuff, and tallow like an ambrosial air, felt a further elation in the thought of its being now a beckoning not a monitory hand: to ascend to those unexplored heights, mysteriously grand to the boy, seemed symbolic of his rise in life.

"But haven't you got anything?" His face fell.

"Nothing fit to offer," said the landlady.

"But I'm hungry—and I've got to wait here."

"You're not staying for the night?" she queried.

"I may," he said, to encourage her to produce some food.

"Oh, but we haven't a room empty."

He reddened. Was it possible she recognized the hobnailed lad of yore, refused to serve him or to allow him up her aristocratic stairs?

"You haven't a room empty?" he repeated incredulously.

"There's a poky garret," she said, "and another man would have to go through it to his bedroom, and he goes to bed very late and gets up very early. But even our best rooms are stuffy and our corridors are that dingy people are always tumbling against the brooms the maids leave about; when they're not tumbling down the stairs. Look how steep they are! The whole house is badly built—it was never meant for an hotel—and the service is disgraceful."

Will, overwhelmed, stammered out deprecation of her abuse. The inn was most picturesque, he urged, and it was not the fault of the house if the coach was late; as for himself a crust of bread and cheese would suffice to stay his pangs.

"Well, go up and see what you can get," she rejoined sceptically, moving aside. Relieved to find the barrier raised, he ascended the dog-legged staircase; his boyish awe resurging. Alas! even the landlady's disparagement had not prepared him for this dishevelled scene—dirty plates and greasy knives and forks and tobacco-stoppers and sloppy pewter pots that had stamped bleary rims on the fly-haunted table-cloth, and a waiter in his shirt-sleeves dining, like a gentleman, off the ruins.

"Wegetables and pastry is hoff!" murmured this disturbed gentleman.

Will was retreating—bread and cheese at the bar amid the glinting bottles and shining beer-handles seemed more appetizing—but the waiter had sprung up, his mouth still masticating but his coat conjured on, and had him fixed instanter on a Windsor chair at a clean little sun-splashed table by a side window that was refreshingly open and gave on the cheery courtyard.

A cut of the devastated joint, strong mustard pickles, a hunch of good bread, a pint of porter and the freedom of the cheese to follow, soon dispelled the dismalness of the room; an effect to which the attendant magician contributed more literally by his great trick of vanishing crumbs and disappearing plates, including his own half-eaten meal. How good it was, this cold roast beef of old England, how equally redolent of the dear old country those hunting pictures on the low wainscoted walls, with all their gay bravado. There were four of them: The Meet, Breaking Cover, Full Cry, The Death; all populous with spirited pink gentlemen and violently animated dogs and horses, culminating in the leading dog tearing the fox, and the leading gentleman waving his tall hat in rapture. He quaffed voluptuously at his frothing pewter pot. To the Queen of the May—ay, why not drink to her?

"How's Mr. Gander?" he asked irrelevantly, with a sudden image of the bull-necked landlord and his massive gold scarfpin.

The waiter—on the point of disappearing—materialized himself again, and stared at the questioner.

"He ain't anyhow," he gasped at last. "At least that's a secret 'twixt him and his Maker."

"Dead?" It was Will's turn to gasp. Could so much gross vitality be extinct, or even rarefied?

"Dead and married over. She's Mrs. Mott now, though the old customers will keep on with the Mother Gander, just as I have to bite my tongue not to call her husband Charley." He lowered his voice. "He was the potboy once."

Will whistled. "What women are!" was in that knowing note. How pleasant it was thus to discuss—with beer and pickles!—life and death and the sex.

"Yes, sir—the potboy, and busting with pride if I let him hand up the plates at the Bowling Club dinner." A sigh accented the cruel change. "You've been away, sir, I presoom."

"Half round the world," said Will with airy inaccuracy. "But why didn't you go in for her?"

"Me! With my old woman! Besides I wasn't going to turn Peculiar—no, not for ten 'Black Sheep.' You've heard o' Peculiars, sir?"

"Ye-es." A cayenne pod in the pickles made him cough.

"Thick as blackberries about these parts—and as full of texts as the bush of prickles." The waiter's voice sank again. "She made poor Charley into one of 'em. He's got to go to chapel three times every Sunday and once on Wednesday."

"Poor chap!" There was sympathy as well as mockery in Will's tone. "But can you tell me"—he had a sudden remembrance—"why she runs down this place so? Is it her Peculiar conscience?"

"Ah! I've heard others arx that too. My opinion ain't worth a woman's tip, but I can't help fancying it's more defiance than conscience. Time was, you see, sir, folks kept away, and it sort o' soured her. I don't want your rotten custom, she as good as says to all and sundry. Take it to landladies who've arxed your permission to marry. And so they come all the more, sir, yes, and cringing to have rooms, and pays her whatever she asks. There was lots o' grumbling in the old days: now you never hear a complaint, except from herself. My stars, the money she's making! But I can't say I envy Charley—not even when he bullies me. Although in marriage if it's not one cross it's another, ain't it, sir? Or perhaps you're one o' the lucky ones."

"I'm not married at all."

"That's what I mean." And the waiter sighed again. "Got all you want, sir?"

"Everything, thank you—not wanting a wife."

His laugh, gurgling away into his pewter pot, evoked only a deeper sigh, on which the waiter seemed wafted without.

IV

Simultaneously—through the opening or closing door—something was wafted within. Our complacent young man at his place in the sun, with the glow of freedom at his heart and of porter at his throat, was startled by something leaping on his knees, which, automatically fended and thrust away, was felt as clinging claws scraping down his new trousers. Coughing and spluttering, and with the beery glow changing to a choke, he perceived that it was the carrier's little white dog, the very same that had warned him off its master's goods; unmistakable by its pink bow. So the doddering patriarch had not yet started, he thought lazily, though he must now be back in his cart or his canine sentry would not have gone off for a farewell prowl. He helped himself to another cut of beef, and his thoughts wandered from Mother Gander to a builder's widow he had known in a Montreal boarding-house, a widow to whom he could certainly have played the Charley had he cared to go so far. He seemed to hear her foolish whimpering the day he left for the backwoods, but he became aware that it was only the carrier's dog whining.

It was begging so prettily on its hind legs, looking so appealing in its pink bow, that he was soon feeding it rather than himself, and morsel after morsel fell to it, each gulped down with such celerity that from the creature's instantly renewed and unchangingly pathetic posture of supplication, an absent-minded man would have doubted if he had fed the brute at all. But finally the young man pushed away his cheese-plate, and dropping with plenary satisfaction upon a horsehair and mahogany arm-chair that stood by the empty grate, he lit his cherrywood pipe with a brimstone match and followed his springtide fancies in clouds of his own making. Thus the second pounce of the dog on to his knees found him acquiescent, even caressing, and with a beatific grunt the animal curled itself up as to an æon of repose.

Then a horn sounded, and with a convulsive start the creature was off his lap and scratching and yapping at the closed door. Will, too, had a moment of wild wishing he had engaged a seat in the cart— the thought of walking in this heat was no longer alluring—but it was equally unimaginable to get up now and rush like the animal. Besides, he hadn't paid his bill, he remembered not discontentedly. Meanwhile the distracted little dog had darted back to the window and leapt on the sill, but it was obviously cowering before the depth of the jump. He was feeling he really must get up and do its will, when to the satisfaction of the slothful man and the bliss of the active beast, the door opened, and like a streak of lightning the white figure had forked across the room and vanished. He turned his head lazily to the window to see if it would catch its cart, but was only in time to see the tail-board with his own box disappearing through the archway, pursued by Joe with a belated bundle. Then the new-comers claimed his languorous attention.

V

Strictly speaking, there was only one new-comer and he was hanging back at the sight of the London-tailored guest, being himself in moleskins and bent and fusty, though Mother Gander was clearly beckoning him forward. "The gentleman's just going," she said sweetly. Will knew not whether to be drowsily pleased at the status he had achieved in his own neighbourhood, or sluggishly wrathful at this renewed attempt to be rid of him.

"Plenty left," he observed encouragingly, puffing immovably.

"Oi reckon, sister, Oi'll feed in the taproom." The voice sent strange vibrations of resentment through Will's being, and particularly through his nostrils, where a mysterious smell of aniseed was called up, whether from memory or the actual moleskins he could not make out.

"You'll do no such thing," said Mother Gander sharply. "It's less trouble here. Remember what James says."

Who was James—was her husband not Charley?—Will was wondering dreamily.

"Chapter two, warse two—Oi take your p'int," answered this odd figure, whose wizened face with the straggling whiskers seemed loathsomely familiar. But though the beady eyes under the moleskin cap were turned for a moment full on his, remembrance stirred but feebly through his after-dinner lethargy, and it was not till the intruder had sinuously and softly skirted the great dining-table and begun solemnly turning the faces of the hunting pictures to the wall, like naughty schoolchildren, that he was dully conscious of the secret of his abhorrence. There—on the very first day of his return—was Joshua Mawhood, the button-snipping villain of his story!

Mother Gander stood by silent, as one properly censured. Neither did she protest when, slashing a giant gobbet off the beef, he carried it on the point of the carving-knife to Will's mustard-strewn meat-plate, and bearing the same with its dirty knife and fork to the remotest corner of the table, fell to with audible enjoyment.

"I'll send you your milk, Deacon," she said, turning to leave the room.

"Don't copy Jael too far," he answered, with a grimace.

"Copy who?" asked Mother Gander, mystified.

"Jael, the wife of Heber the Kenite—her as killed Sisera. Like me he asked for water, and, like you, she gave him milk. But she meant to nail him like a stoat."

"Me murder you!" said Mother Gander with a scandalized air. But she was clearly impressed by his erudition.

"'Tis onny my fun. But you look up Judges, chapter fower. They're beacons to us—they old Hebrews and Hebrewesses—beacons."

"Would you rather not have the milk?" Mother Gander was still a little puzzled.

"'Tain't for me to refuse a sister's kindness. And the best way to repay her is to take it with rum. Bein' as there's a wisitor, the leetlest drop o' rum in it, to show Oi don't howd with your rebukers in that regard. Send the bottle separate, to be plain to all beholders."

"And send me another pint of porter, please," added Will. He felt he must justify his stay even as the Deacon must justify his drink. The ecclesiastical preferment that had come to Elder Mawhood amused him—his boyish resentment faded suddenly, and the respectable rat-catcher—after all, the motor-impulse of his fortunes—now loomed through a cloud of kindly indulgence; even touched with the glamour of early memories, with the magic of those far-off winters whose approach had brought the expert to Frog Farm, as surely as it brought in from the hedges the creatures against whom he waged cunning battle in the war-zone of the barns and outbuildings. How thrilled the boy had been by the great traps and the pack of ferrets—nay, had not the strange old man seemed himself a larger ferret, with his tight-fitting moleskins, sidling motions, and curiously small shining eyes? What a joy his annual visit—with what fearful interest the bunch of children had listened to the annual contract, made for gross sums, or for particular buildings, sometimes calculated per tail of rats! The Elder had always made a point of the cost of the shoe-leather involved in the isolation of Frog Farm. Aniseed, Will suddenly remembered, had played a considerable part in beguiling the victims, and the scent of it, coming up again,—dream-whiff or reality—was now incongruously mingled with a flavour of youth and innocence, touching our rustic Ulysses almost to tears. He wheeled his arm-chair window-wards to hide his emotion, and puffed into the courtyard.

"Oi don't object to your smokin'," mumbled the Deacon.

"Thank you," said Will. "You don't remember me, I'm afraid, Mr. Mawhood." "Deacon" he could not bring his tongue to. "I'm Will Flynt, the looker's boy you were always so kind to. You let me set your traps and dose the bait."

The Deacon shot a beady look at him, but shook his head.

"Why, you let me smell your ferret once, don't you remember, when it came out of the hole by the Brad, and you said that though I hadn't heard a squeak or a scamper, your nose could tell there had been rats in the run."

"There was swarms of boys at Frog Farm, all bad 'uns. Oi never knew 'em by tail—but Oi dessay Oi do remember ye in the rough."

Will was strangely disappointed. "Don't you remember I lent you my slate to hide the trap from that cute old rascal?"

"Ay, warmints allus runs to cover," said the Deacon vaguely.

"And when caught he wouldn't eat the bait, surely you remember?"

"They never does. Rats has more sperrit than lions," said the Deacon with enthusiasm.

The abortive attempt to recall himself to the rat-catcher was ended by the return of the waiter, whose delicate balance of rum-bottle, milk-glass, and pewter pot on the tiniest of trays, was almost upset by the sight of the blank backs of the hunting pictures. He seemed as startled as though he was not in the conjuring line himself. Depositing the drinks, with his usual sleight of hand, at both ends of the room simultaneously, he made as if to reverse the pictures. But the Deacon emitted a sibilance so terrifying that he did the vanishing trick instead. The old man then produced from either pocket a pale-yellow, pink-eyed creature, and emptied the milk-glass into a saucer. "How thirsty they gets this weather," he observed, as they lapped greedily at the milk. "Pore things—their need is greater than mine."

VI

Will was sipping his porter piano, and the Deacon his rum strepitoso—the ferrets back in his pockets—when the door opened afresh, and a new figure protruded through it, likewise drawing back when the room which should have been empty at that hour was seen to be in occupation. This was, however, a very different figure from the Deacon's: a figure jovial and ponderous, sporting a floral dressing-gown and carpet slippers, and with all the air of having just left an adjacent bedroom.

"Come in—don't mind me," called Will cheerfully.

The smoker's invitation not being negatived by the muncher and bibber, the massive visitor padded forwards, revealing more clearly his heavy-jowled hairless rubicund face and the motley multitude of stains on his gay dressing-gown, and waving a roll of clammy-smelling posters. "Just come by the coach—and in the nick o' time," he observed genially. And espying in the reversed pictures a favourable background for his operations, he circumvented the table (not without surprise and disgust at the corner where the moleskinned man grunted, guzzled, and guttled), and hung up two of the bills on the nails without any observable astonishment at the state of the pictures or any apparent attention to anything but his own interests; stepping backwards to survey the effect with such absorption of mind that through the girdle of his dressing-gown his spine collided with the table.

"No, my boy!" he addressed Will. "They can't print like that in Chipstone."

From his arm-chair Will could easily read the more glaring headlines:

TO-NIGHT AT SEVEN—LIFE-SIZE
DUKE'S MARIONETTES
Hamlet And The Ghost
MARGARET CATCHPOLE
Pantomime-Ballet

THE MISTLETOE BOUGH
The Beggar of Bethnal Green
EDMUND, ORPHAN OF THE CASTLE
The High Road to Marriage

AS PERFORMED BEFORE ALL THE CROWNED HEADS
Of Europe, America, and Australia

N.B.—Miss Arabella Flippance at the Piano

"Sounds bully," he observed politely.

"Bully's the word, my young American friend," said the Showman. "What a pity the mail-coach was late—we might have had 'em stuck up for the ordinary and caught some shilling patrons. You're staying here for the night, I hope."

"No—I've got to go on."

"What a pity! I was about to offer you a front seat."

"Me? Why?"

"Must fill up somehow," said the Showman frankly. "People never go to a play unless they think they can't get in. And as we only open to-night, there's not been time to advertise our bumper houses. You see, sonny, we lay up here for the winter, and if we'd started before this heat-wave we'd have caught more colds than coppers."

"Is it open-air then?"

"No, but the next thing to it—a tent! By squinting out of that window you'll see the whole caboodle rising on the meadows like a giant mushroom. Why not stop here and pick up a young lady? I'll give you two seats."

"Don't want more than one seat when I've got a girl," laughed Will. Then the face of the girl in the parcel-shed came up, at once alluring and rebuking, and he repeated that seriously he must be off.

"Never mind—better luck next act," said the Showman, and tugged furiously at the bell-pull, and the waiter appeared with a glass of brandy and water, as though he added thought-reading to his conjuring accomplishments.

"Well, here's to our better—!" began the Showman. His eye, raised towards Will at the window, caught suddenly something in the courtyard, and setting down his untasted glass and snatching up his posters he disappeared almost as frantically as the dog.

"He's forgot he ain't dressed," chuckled the waiter.

"Seems to be a merry gent," said Will.

"Lives here all the while the show is on," said the waiter, not without pride. "Pays me a shilling every time I go in."

"I hope on the same principle Mother Gander will pay me," said Will, laughing, and ordered his bill: which he found as unreasonable as the food was excellent. He did not, however, mulct the waiter of the handsome tip, designed to show him not a woman but a man and a gentleman at that, and the waiter finally disappeared with congees instead of with conjurings.

"I know you will excuse me, old fellow," said the Showman, re-entering, "but business before pleasure. Fact is, I got up too late to catch the carriers, but now I've got the postman to leave my bills at all the public-houses on his next round. Good fellow, Bundock, though why he should boast so over killing two frogs with one stone, I don't understand. It seems an operation as cruel as it is simple." Here he swigged at his neglected glass. "He made a point, too, of my not employing the Bellman."

"You'd have done better with the Bellman here in Chipstone and over at Latchem," volunteered Will. "Where Bundock mostly goes, you'll never get 'em to come."

"That's what Bundock said. But don't you believe it, sonny." He held up a huge hairy forefinger, half gilded with a great ring. "They're only a canting lot o' sons of slow-coaches. They've never had the chance of knowing what they like. Temptation's the thing."

The diaconal sibilance that greeted this sinister sentiment fell unheeded on the Showman's ear, or rather he did not distinguish it from the worthy Mawhood's general medley of guttural and nasal noises.

"There's no greater temptation," added the Showman, "than Shakespeare and the Ballet."

Will shook his head. "They don't know one from t'other. Did—I mean, if they did"—he had slipped into the old idiom—"they'd be scandalized. Why, I went to see a piece of Shakespeare at Sadler's Wells myself last week, and I'm bound to say 'twas a bit thick—though splendidly acted, mind you."

"You needn't tell me that. Phelps!" He smacked his fleshy lips voluptuously. "Lord! What a job that man had to clear out the beer-sellers, babies, and filthy-mouthed roughs, and now it's the quietest show in London. What was the piece?"

"Can't remember the name—about a nigger."

"Othello?"

"That's it—sounded a rather Irish name for a nigger I thought."

"Irish? Ah, yes—ha, ha, ha! You had me there! By Jove, that's a new wheeze!" And he roared genially, while the innocent, and it is to be feared sadly illiterate, Will tried to look like a successful humorist. "Anyhow," he said, "you won't get 'em from Little Bradmarsh, no, nor Long Bradmarsh either. They think all actors are wicked."

"And so they be!" burst forth the Deacon at last. "Hobs and jills ought to be kept apart!" He stuck his knife towards the poster. "The High Road to Marriage, indeed! High road to Hell!"

"Hear, hear," agreed the Showman surprisingly, rattling his glass. "Well put, old cock. But these ain't actors; only puppets. You can't be wicked in wood."

"I'm afraid I must be off," said Will, rising.

"Then here's luck to you." He finished his glass. "And may you die before you're buried!"

"Thanks, I hope I shan't do either, Mr. Duke." He took his hat and stick.

"Not Duke, old man. Flippance, Anthony Flippance, universally docked to Tony Flip. Duke only goes with the Marionettes. I bought 'em lock, stock, and barrel—-the oldest circuit in East Anglia, and the name going well with the crowned heads."

"But there are no crowned heads in America," said Will, smiling.

"Pardon me, sonny," contradicted Mr. Flippance.

"But I've just come from there," said Will crushingly.

"And how about the Emperor of Brazil?"

"Oh!" said Will blankly. He seemed really to have heard of this personage. Then recovering, he said: "But have you played before him?"

"That's not my affair," said Mr. Flippance. "It ain't my responsibility what Duke's done or left undone—if Duke was his name, which I take leave to question. 'Twixt you and I, I doubt if it would pay to work Brazil. But, as I said, I bought it as a going concern, lock, stock—"

"And lies," snapped the Deacon.

Mr. Flippance turned his large red face benevolently towards the moleskins.

"Lies is a harsh word. Legends, old cock, legends."

"Oi bain't a bird," rasped the Deacon. "Stick to the truth."

"Lord love us, a Quaker!" Mr. Flippance winked at Will, who smiled—man of the world to man of the world. "As if anybody would take a thing that size and smell for a rooster!"

The Deacon reached for the rum-bottle in deadly silence. Will, with a fear—soon proved superfluous— that he meant it for a missile, hastened to remark that anyhow there were no crowned heads in Australia.

"Where were you educated, sonny?" retorted Mr. Flippance. And he began whistling the then favourite air: "The King of the Cannibal Islands." He broke off to point out that kings and queens were as thick in the man-eating islands round Australia as old cocks in Essex, though they didn't wear moleskins, or indeed anything but their own skins. Besides, he added as an afterthought, wasn't Queen Victoria monarch of Australia too?

Will, taken aback again, had to admit it. "But you haven't played before Victoria?" he murmured.

Mr. Flippance winked more widely as he explained that a study of the posters would show that the Marionettes themselves never claimed to have performed before crowned heads. It was the plays that had been performed. He turned suddenly upon the rum-soothed Deacon. "You're not denying, my Quaker friend, that Queen Victoria's seen Hamlet?"

"You leave me and the Queen out of it," growled the Deacon.

"Ha! Then you admit she's seen Hamlet?"

"Oi don't know nawthen about it. Why should she see Hamlet?"

"Because he was the Prince of Denmark," said Tony, winking again at his now bosom friend. "But you Methody Quaker dead-alive go-to-meeting sons of Sundayfied slugs crawl about thinking yourselves holier than Victoria, God bless her, even when it's wood, never having seen society or ever had a drink outside Chipstone."

The Deacon was roused at last. "Never had a drink outside Chipstone!" His breast heaved with a sinister movement—was it a wheeze of wrath or of laughter? "Oi'll goo bail my round is bigger nor yourn. There ain't scarce a barn in East Anglia what don't know me."

Tony's great jaw fell. "A barnstormer! You! Rats! What do you play?"

"It ain't play—it's work."

"Yes, I know—but what's your repertory?"

"My what?"

"Your pieces."

"Oi bain't onny a piece-worker."

"In what?"

"In what you said. It ain't always per tail."

"Retail, do you mean?" said the puzzled Tony.

Will, who had listened to the conversation with an ever-expanding grin, here burst into a guffaw. Tony turned on him.

"Is he kidding me?" he asked half angrily, half amicably.

The answer—like Will's departure from this enthralling parlour—was staved off by the advent of yet another head popped into the doorway. This time it was a heavily greased head with scrupulously parted hair, and was attached to a spruce young man with a spring posy in his buttonhole. But his bear's-grease out smelt his primroses.

"Hullo, Tony!" cried the aromatic apparition. "Up already!"

"I've got to work for my living," Mr. Flippance retorted. "The dormouse season is over. You coming in, Charley, to see the show to-night?"

"Me! I've got better things to do, old boy." The young landlord turned to the Deacon. "Can you let me have five or six live 'uns?"

The Deacon shook his head. "Oi don't want to disoblige brother. Oi do my duty according to Peter—'nat'ral brute beasts made to be taken and destroyed'—but they bain't meant by the Almoighty to be taken for sport, and Oi don't howd with fox-hunting neither."

"So I see." Mr. Charles Mott glanced glumly at the backs of the pictures.

"Ef you want to be riddy o' warmints, shoot 'em, says Oi, or nip their brushes in traps."

"Oh, oh!" came involuntarily from Will at this blasphemy. The Deacon transfixed him with his glittering eye, but went on without pausing: "And ef you want to be riddy o' rats, come to me. Don't set a-worshippin' your prize-terriers, like Ephraim jined to his idols."

"I did come to you to be rid o' the warmints, and now I want half-a-dozen spunky 'uns. Make your own price, but if you won't supply 'em I'll get 'em from Bill Nutbone."

"That's doubly sinful—to goo to the heathen." He turned to Will. "Ef you're so fond o' ferrets, young man, Oi could spare you this pair—cheaper than you'll get 'em from Nutbone." He let their pink eyes protrude from his pockets.

Will eagerly closed with the offer. If Frog Farm proved as dull as he was now beginning to fear—after this contrast of Anthony Flippance and Joshua Mawhood—ratting or rabbiting might be a providential diversion.

"But I can't carry them in my pockets," he said impressively. "Just made by Moses & Son, London. And I've got a long walk. Besides, I'd like them in cages."

"Oi'll send 'em by the carrier on Friday," promised the ratcatcher. "Frog Farm, you said. Good day to you, Brother Mott."

"Good day, Deacon. Sorry we can't do business. Queer old cuss," he said, winking at Will as the door closed. "Belongs to the Peculiars."

"I—I've heard of them." Will coloured a bit.

Tony, who had listened to the dialogue with enlightenment, here stalked out in half-genuine horror: "Holy Moses & Son! The publican and sinner prefers rats to Shakespeare!"

"Stow it, Tony!" called the landlord after him. "One preacher's enough." And, smiling, he changed the blanks into hunting pictures almost as deftly as his waiter would have done it.

He had scarcely effected the transformation, however, before the Deacon popped his head in again. Mr. Mott looked like a caught schoolboy, but though the beady eyes looked straight at the flamboyant hunters, Mr. Mawhood only said: "Oi forgot to lend a law-book."

"What sort of a law-book d'ye want?"

"Miss Gentry's got a counter-claim. Ef Oi won't pay for my wife's silk dress as Oi never ordered, she says my ferrets killed her chickens."

"That's not a counter-claim, Mr. Mawhood," advised Will.

"It's a lyin' claim, anyways. What killed her chickens was her own black devil, Squibs. Her and her angels!"

"You go down to the bar and see if the missus can find you a book—but wouldn't a lawyer be better?"

"The good Lord forbid! Oi'd sooner goo to a doctor. Well, thank you kindly, brother—one good turn desarves another. Foive, Oi think you said."

"Or six. First thing in the morning. Spunky 'uns, remember."

The Deacon sighed and disappeared again.

"Poor old chap!" Sure of his rats, Mr. Mott was now touched to sympathy. "His missus is a Tartar, no mistake. Still with them rounds of his, he dodges her a good deal." And he sighed like the Deacon and followed him—bear's-grease after aniseed—and Will, alone at last, followed too, though without a sigh, being still—as the waiter said—"one of the lucky ones."

In the corridor he turned the wrong way, finding bedroom doors instead of the staircase. He paused a moment to gaze at a stuffed specimen of the sacred animal that stood with brush rampant against a scenic background under a glass case, and a stuffed trout that swam movelessly through a mimic stream. Then he became aware to his surprise that Tony Flip, still in his dressing-gown and still hugging the balance of his posters, was pacing the corridor restlessly, like a caged lion, though it turned out to be really like a tame creature denied his cage.

"They won't let me in," he said miserably. And he indicated an open bedroom door opposite the fox, with a view of housemaids at work, angry at the hour. One was making his bed, thumping it viciously; another raised swirls of dust with a broom. Slops stood blatantly around.

"They won't even take free seats," he groaned.

VII

"What did I tell you?" said Will.

"Oh, it ain't because they think it wicked, the hussies. They turn up their noses at it, just because it's under their noses. If they had to go to Greenwich Fair to see it, they'd fight to get in. Candidly, cocky, have you ever seen a better bill?"

"It seems only too much," ventured Will.

"It don't say all at the same performance. In practice it all comes down to The Mistletoe Bough, the silliest of the lot, a bride who shuts herself in a chest for fun, you know, and moulders into a spirit. But think of Richardson's—what they cram into twenty-five minutes! You saw that at Greenwich, I suppose, Easter time."

"No, I only got to London in time for the Great Exhibition."

"You've been to that?" The Showman's eyes sparkled.

"What I came back for."

"That's a Show!!" And a note of immeasurable envy mixed with the rapture of the rival impresario. "But what a chance missed!"

"How so?"

"No drinks."

"I got lemonade."

"That's not a drink—that's a gas. Lord, I thought, looking at that bumper house, with a proper Christian bar, they could pay off the National Debt."

"You've seen it then?"

"Was there at the opening. Stood so near the Royal Party I patted the head of little Wales, and the Goldstick and Chamberlain walking backwards from the Presence nearly shoved me into the Chinese Ambassador just as he was salaaming on his stomach. Didn't little Albert Edward look sweet in his Highland costume?"

"I wasn't inside then," confessed Will, "and I only had eyes for the Queen and her cream-coloured horses. You've got a season ticket, I suppose."

"With the Prince Consort's compliments. The fact is, I supplied the elephant for the Queen's howdah."

"Did you?"

"Yes, didn't you see it in the Indian compartment? They wanted to show off the magnificent trappings she got from the Rajah, and they thought of getting a real live elephant, which would have been no end of trouble amid all those precious vases. But I happened to know of a stuffed elephant at a show down here in Essex, so I entered into correspondence with Buckingham Palace and loaned the beast for the season—buying him up first, of course—and sent him up in my caravan that had to be roused from its winter sleep and completely unpacked. Yes, trouble enough! But talk of the Koh-i-noor, that elephant'll be worth his weight in gold when he comes back—Queen Victoria's elephant as visited by the nobility and gentry of the world. I annex the Great Exhibition. See!"

"I wish I'd noticed him," said Will wistfully. "I only saw her statue in zinc, seven yards high. But there's so much to see—machinery and jewels and Mexican figures, it makes your head ache, and I couldn't even get a look at that Koh-i-noor, such a crush round it. But did you see the Preserved Pig?"

The Showman's eyes twinkled. "Mr. Woods, d'ye mean?"

"Mr. Woods?"

"The Chancellor of the Exchequer. Haven't you noticed how they've left off abusing the income tax now they've got the show to talk about? By Jove," he chuckled, "what a haul for the Exchequer if they bring the Crystal Palace under the window tax!"

"No, no! Best Berkshire breed. The real marvel of the Exhibition! None o' your stuffed creatures, but a natural pig cured whole. Weighs three and a half hundredweight; five foot and a half from tail to snout. 'Twas done by a provision merchant in Dublin—Smith—I took note of the name."

"That name will be immortal," said Mr. Flippance gravely.

"Yes, and there was a monster pigeon-pie!" said Will with the same unsuspicious enthusiasm.

The church clock, striking four at this point, made the Showman bound frantically to his doorway. "Not done yet, you snails and sluts! When am I to get these bills to the tent? Do you realize we open to-night? You'll ruin the show."

"I'll take them," volunteered Will. "My road lays by the field."

"A friend in need is a friend indeed." Tony thrust the heavy roll effusively into Will's hands. "Ask for my daughter—she'll help you to stick 'em up on the bill-boards."

"Your daughter?" murmured Will. He would have resented his sudden reduction to a bill-poster but for the romantic vision of the Bohemian petticoat.

"I can't pull the strings on both sides of the stage at once, can I? Not to mention the women's and boys' voices, and the piping Gaffers. Lord, she's got a head on her, has Polly. And pops in and out to play the piano too."

With pleasant flutterings of the springtide fancy, the young man lightly strode with his roll under his arm to the field where a long chocolate-coloured caravan—apparently the vehicle that had transported the elephant—stood horseless at an aperture in the mammoth mushroom described by Tony Flip. Labourers in shirt-sleeves were carrying in ropes and rough benches. Small boys and large dogs stood around, and there was a litter of straw, cardboard, shivered packing-cases, and dirty paper. Two trucks covered with tarpaulin, and a vast box with a high-pitched roof marked "Duke's Marionettes," completed the confusion. Will, peeping in, saw a stage already set, at the border of which a girl on her knees was tacking a row of tin footlight-holders. The rear was already roped off, and the benches seemed to rise like a gallery. Evidently the thing was done in style—crowned heads or no crowned heads. Not without a thrill he walked in, and across the grassy floor, but romance fled when the girl, raising her head, presented a face almost as massive as her father's, and ravaged by smallpox to boot. Polly had indeed "a head on her," he thought, though long pendent ear-rings preserved its femininity.

Politely concealing his chill, he murmured "Miss Flippance," and explained he had been instructed to deliver the bills to her.

She received them and him with an indifference that would have been galling had she been prettier, and was not gratifying even from a massive brain.

"Silly nonsense!" she grumbled, unrolling them. "To open before you've done your posting and circularizing. There won't be a soul!"

"Oh, surely—this weather!" he murmured.

Miss Flippance threw him an annihilating glance. "If dad once gets an idea into his head, you can't get it out with a forceps." Will stared at this vigorous young lady, who, with a poster unfurled in her hand, proceeded to yell directions and rebukes at the bench-arranging clodhoppers. It was an insult to his sex, he felt resentfully. No woman, however ugly, had the right to order men about, men who were not even married to her.

"Nincompoops! They'll never be ready for to-night," said Miss Flippance, acknowledging his existence again. "Would to heaven dad had gone up to London to see the Exhibition—and not hustled us like this."

"But he was there at the opening."

Miss Flippance stared at him. "Were you with him?"

"No such luck. I didn't even see the stuffed elephant."

"Has he stuffed you with that?" Miss Flippance emitted a mirthless laugh, and Will looked at once angry and sheepish. "Not that way, you hulking brutes! Turn 'em round. . . . And besides, it's ridiculous to give Hamlet. High art don't take south of Scarborough."

"Well, I saw Othello in London last week," he contradicted sharply—she should see he was no mere gull: "And the pit was packed."

"Yes—in April. But try it in the dog-days."

"Too warm, eh?" he sniggered. She turned away as from an idiot. That hurt him more than having swallowed her father's royal rodomontade. Did she then think the plot of Othello glacial? Or had she no sense of humour? Yes, that was it—the sex had been denied the sense of humour. True, it shrieked with laughter if you tickled it, but the tickling must be physical. Ah, she was at it again, bustling and bullying the superior sex. Well, he wasn't going to paste bills under her. Let that lazy liar of a Showman do his own dirty work.

"Good afternoon," he called out huffily, and walked out of the great tent in a far less romantic mood than when he had entered it. And then, as he came through the opening in the canvas, his eyes nearly started out of their sockets: Daniel Quarles's cart stood outside the tent, and there, perched on the driving-board, holding the reins, and calmly instructing the shirt-sleeved yokels to deliver the big drum to Miss Flippance, was the girl of the parcel-shed!

Before his eyes could return normally to their orbits or his breath to his windpipe, the incredible vision had vanished. Jinny had, in fact, had an overdose of commissions in the other purlieus of Chipstone, and having fetched the drum from its winter quarters as directed by Miss Polly Flippance that noon—it had, in fact, been pawned, and the piano was still irredeemable—she was hastening on her homeward circuit as fast as Methusalem could be induced to go.

"Who was that?" Will gasped.

The rustic who had received the drum looked at him with unconcealed contempt. A man who did not know that!

"That war Jinny!" he said.

It was as if he had given his drum a terrific bang. Jinny?—Jinny Quarles then! Who else? In the boom of that name reverberated a clamour of memories and of emotions, old and new. Images of a solemn-eyed mite, of a merry little maid, of a sedate Sunday scholar, and of the amazing creature of to-day, went all interflashing with one another. Yes, the little Jinny who had shared the wagon and his secret with him that fateful Sunday, and who if ever by a rare chance she had flitted across his thoughts, figured always as this same little girl in her grand pink Sunday pelisse, trimmed with pink velvet and fringes, was now grown up; bonneted, bewitching, incredible.

"But where—where was her grandfather?" he stammered. "Asleep inside?"

"Asleep?" The rustic grinned. "A long sleep, Oi should reckon. Whoy, we ain't seen the Gaffer for years."

"Don't stand there gossiping." It was the female martinet at her sternest.

"It's not his fault," said Will. "I was asking about old Daniel Quarles. Is he really dead?"

"Dead? Not to my knowledge. At least I have never noticed Jinny in black."

"Then where is he? Why isn't he looking after Jinny?"

"Eh? But he must be a hundred!"

"You don't mean to say he lets Jinny go out and do his job?"

"The most natural person I should think," said Miss Flippance. "Really I haven't time to discuss village carriers, if the show is to open to-night. . . . Do be careful of that drum. No, not inside, blockhead. Come back!"

As the tambour-laden slave did not seem to hear, his affrighted fellow-serfs yelled to him to bring the drum outside again, and when he was come, the despot's skirts rustled majestically back into the tent— they were long and hunched out quite fashionably, which accentuated the humiliation of the male element. But Will remained at the tent door, like Abraham after an angel's visit, thunderstruck and dumbfounded, but with consternation, not reverence. It was, he thought, the grossest carelessness that had ever occurred in the history of the globe. A respectable girl like that—why, what was the world coming to? Sent gadding about the country like a trollop, perched up horsily behind a carter's whip—this was what little Jinny had been allowed to grow up into! And that girl at "The Black Sheep"—she who had looked so innocent, whom he had mentally seen as a May Queen, crowned with garlands, dancing girlishly round a Maypole—this was what lay under her poetic semblance. And at the same time—pleasing and perturbing thought—both the unsexed Carrier and the maidenly May Queen were in reality little Jinny: no stand-offish stranger, needing deferential approach, but—in a way—his very own: the meek poppet whose cheek he had always pinched patronizingly, in whose eyes he had always seen himself as a grown-up god.

Miss Flippance, sweeping out again, and finding him still hanging about, immovable, had a new thought. "Pardon me—has my father engaged you?"

He coloured up in anger. "I brought his bills in passing—that's all."

"Oh, I thought you might be looking for a job. There's this drum, you know."

He could have knocked her down. But she was evidently quite in earnest, this outrageous, humourless female, only second in self-sufficiency to Jinny the Carrier. The world seemed suddenly emasculated.

"I'm no musician," he said surlily.

"But you look a strong young man and it's muscle we want, not music. You'd only have to stand here about half an hour a day. This afternoon, of course, you might join the Bellman round the town—I've ordered him for five."

"Miss Flippance," said Will, mastering himself and speaking with crushing dignity, "have you observed my clothes?"

"They don't matter," she assured him. "We provide the uniform."

"Do I look," he snorted, "like a drummer at a dime show?"

"If you've come as a walking gentleman," replied Miss Flippance simply, "you've come to the wrong shop. We're only wires."

"Oh, I know all about that." And he slashed savagely with his stick at the insulting tambour, which uttered a bass roar of agony.

"Splendid! But you might have smashed it!" cried Miss Flippance. "Where's the drumstick?"

"Am I the drumstick's keeper?" he answered, with an odd Biblical reminiscence.

"Nincompoops! Thickheads! Zanies! Where's the drumstick?"

But nobody had seen the drumstick. Jinny hadn't brought it, the slaves assured her. She assured them, still more emphatically, that they had dropped it off the drum in taking it out. And no inch of it being visible where the cart had stood, she drew the deduction that it was now speeding towards Long Bradmarsh.

She turned to Will. "Do run after her—the men are so busy—she can't be far, and she has to stop every now and again."

He glared at her. Then something inside him whispered that that was the obvious thing to do—impishly to pretend to obey her, and then to keep her waiting for the drumstick—eternally. Yes, he would be revenged on behalf of his sex.

"Yoicks! Tally-ho!" he cried with an advent of glee that he felt justifiably malicious. And, waving his own stick wildly, he bounded with mock frenzy towards the field gate by which the cart had gone off.

"You won't catch her like that," bawled Miss Flippance after him. "Across the fields! Head her off!" But he would not take orders from any woman, he told himself, so feigning deafness he ran doggedly into the Long Bradmarsh road, and turning a sharp elbow, felt his heart leap up to see the now familiar cart at a standstill before a wayside cottage. But even as he gazed it started afresh.

He tore on madly. The back of the tilt vanished round another bend. "Following a drumstick" passed grotesquely across his mind. What an odd home-coming! What a queer renewal of acquaintance with Jinny—after that solemn oath-taking in the wagon!

Presently he heard a wild scampering through the bushes on his right, and his canine friend of the inn was leaping and frisking and joyously barking beside him. They ran together—owing to the dog's leisurely tangents and curvatures he could just keep up with it. But with the sweat now pouring from his forehead, the inner imp began asking what he was running for, since he had already deceived and chastised Miss Flippance, left her eternally expectant. Why not now drop into the pleasant saunter home he had planned?

But the poor dog was panting in this heat—he answered the imp—it must have run miles since its meal in the parlour. Apoplexy threatened perhaps, hydrophobia even. Look at its lolling tongue! He snatched it up: it must be restored to its inconsiderate mistress, to whom, at the same time, a still more important rebuke could be administered, if indeed any vestiges of decency yet remained in the minx. But the little terrier struggled spasmodically in his arms—the ungrateful brute! He must save it from itself, then, just as he must save its mistress from herself. Clamping it to his breast with iron muscles, he toiled frenziedly forwards. Then the far, faint sound of a horn came like elfin mocking laughter on the sultry air, and with a sudden convulsion the animal wrested itself free, and Will was left hopelessly pursuing, not the cart, but the dog. He had indeed the pleasure of seeing the former slacken to receive the latter, but the vehicle was wafted away again so smoothly that to the poor perspiring pedestrian Methusalem appeared in his original Mazeppa rôle.

The chase ran along wide horizons—great ploughed lands or meadows with grazing cattle—the level broken only by ricks, roofs, and trees, mainly witch-elms, with a few poplars. Sometimes these elms clustered in groves, sometimes a few helped to make the hedge-line; as often they rose solitary in arrogant individualism. To the right was a delicious sense of the saltings and of mewing sea-birds; and mysteriously, as in the heart of the fields, red-brown barge sails or the tall, bare poles of vessels could be seen upstanding. And once where the road mounted, Will caught a glimpse of the Blackwater, and ships floating, and the dim, blue shore beyond.

But at the top of this hill he was too breathed to continue. He sat down, wiped his forehead, and surveyed the view; far from soothed, however, by its simple restfulness. If only his father had come to meet him, as his letter had requested, he thought savagely, all this wouldn't have happened!

IX

Anyhow there was no need to follow the glaring high road any longer. On the left he could see the clump of Steeples Wood, and he knew that once he had cut through that, he could find the swift field-path through Hoppits that would save miles of the high road and not bring him out on it till the Silverlane Pump. He strolled with a sense of relief towards the wood, but hardly had its green groves closed refreshingly upon him when, reminding himself he was a trespasser, he quickened his pace again, and hurried through the oak plantations and over the wonderful carpet of bluebells with but a slight eye to the sylvan beauty.

Even when he reached the field-path bounded by the ditch and the dog-rose hedge, he did not relax his speed, having bethought himself that the poor horse would surely be given drink at the trough of the Silverlane Pump, and that there would probably be a delay at "The Silverlane Arms," even if he should not have succeeded in heading the Carrier off altogether. And from that point she would surely need his protection, so lonely was the road till you sighted Long Bradmarsh with the drainage windmills and the bridge. And the no less necessary sermon could be combined with the protection.

He found the wheel of the village pump chained up. Evidently the water was running scarce. It looked not unlike a gibbet, this tall pump, and he could imagine a criminal dangling from the spout. There was little water in the trough, and the water-butt of the inn was almost equally dry; a wayside mudhole haunted by geese represented a pool. He remembered these arid villages in such strange juxtaposition with his own oozy birthplace—was it here or at Kelcott that he had made a boyish fortune, bringing water at a halfpenny a pint? His mother, he recalled with a faint smile, had been against the business because Jesus had said to the woman of Samaria "Give me to drink," though he had trumped her text with the injunction to the Israelites: "Ye shall also buy water of them for money." It all made him super-conscious of thirst, and he went into the inn, and ordering a pint of ale, inquired if the Carrier had passed by.

"Which way be you a-gooin'?" said the tapster. It irritated him to be questioned, and he replied tartly that he was going home. He gulped down his liquor and put his question to a group of children playing around the pump. They scratched their heads and gaped at him, and the youngest put shy, chubby hands to its smeary face. "The white horse and the girl!" he explained, and the shy child started screaming, and a woman burst from a cottage door and dragged it within, glaring suspiciously at the "furriner."

A labourer riding a plough-horse barebacked, and leading another, came from the Bradmarsh direction. "Has the Carrier passed you?" he asked.

"D'ye want a lift?" was the reply.

He lost his temper. "Haven't you got enough business o' your own?"

"Not much," said the labourer naïvely. "Ground be as 'ard as the road. Curous, baint it, arter all that soakin'."

He replied more civilly, glad his rudeness was misunderstood. "Yes, it's always either too little or too much."

"And ye can't sow unless 'tis none-or-both," added the philosophic ploughman, plodding on. "Gimme a followin' toime!"

The rustic meant a season in which rain and sunshine came in rapid alternation, but Will ruefully reflected that the "followin' toime," in the sense he was having it, was far from satisfactory.

But at that moment there was a cheerful bark, and that inconsistent dog was curveting around him, its tall thumping wildly against his trousers in an ecstasy of recognition. So he was too late, he thought with a strange heart-sinking; knowing its rearguard habit. He pushed it away with his foot. If the beast thought he was going to carry it again, it was jolly well mistaken. No more cart-chasing for him. His "following time" was over. And as the creature persisted in gambolling round his legs, he made a swish in the air with his stick to drive it on its way, and it uttered a fearsome yell; it being part of Nip's slyness to cry before he was hurt. But for once Nip was not a laggard, but an advance courier, and Fate brought Methusalem round the corner at the exact instant of his yell.

"How dare you strike my dog?" It was an inauspicious reunion. Jinny had checked Methusalem, and her grey eyes were blazing down from their dark lashes; her face framed in its bonnet glowed like a dark flower, and he was confusedly aware that that lonely hamlet's high-street was suddenly pullulating with people—the tapster and gapers at the inn door, the ploughman looking backwards, excited at last, the little children mysteriously out again with their mother, and other mothers and infants (in arms or at skirt) surging agitatedly from nowhere, whether at Nip's cry or Jinny's. Even the pump seemed to have spouted an old man, while an old lady arose, like an ancient Venus, from the pond. And every eye, he felt, was stabbing at the maltreator of Jinny's animal; the cackle seemed a sinister clamour as of vengeance mounting from that swarm of sympathizers.

"I didn't strike him," he answered sulkily. Clearly she had not recognized him—a position not without its advantages. Doubtless the raw youth of her childish memories was effectually buried beneath this manly form, set off by the elegant London suit, this well-barbered head, and the face that had exchanged freckles for the stamp of experience. "As a matter of fact," he added, "I fed the brute at the inn."

"Which brute?" retorted Jinny sharply. But at this moment Nip, who had been calmly lapping the dregs of the pool, intervened by leaping up to lick Will's hand.

"I beg your pardon," she murmured, coming to a standstill.

"Granted," he said, not to be outdone in graciousness, and beginning to enjoy the advantage her ignorance of his identity gave him. "But that's no proof I haven't beaten him. You remember the saying:

A woman, a dog, and a walnut-tree,

The more you beat them, the better they be."

"That's all nonsense," said Jinny, bridling up again.

He changed the subject quickly. "Have you got a drumstick?"

"Gracious! Do you want to try?"

He laughed. "It's for the drum at the show. Miss Flippance thinks you didn't deliver it."

"Why, it was tied on the drum. The fool of a man must have dropped it—if he hasn't poked it inside the drum. Did you look under the benches?"

"No. That's it! I remember now seeing the man take the drum inside by mistake. He must have dropped it on the way back."

"Don't you think it would have been more sensible to look before you leaped—especially such a long leap! And what a pace you must have come in this heat!"

He flushed faintly. "I'm a good walker. I know the cuts."

"Well, if you get back as quick as you came, there won't be much time lost." She clucked up Methusalem. "Good afternoon—hope you'll find your stick, and that you'll drum-in a good house."

What! She too thought him capable of being a drum-banger, a minion of marionettes. Had women then no eye—no perception of clothes—as well as no humour? The mob was melting away under their amiable parley, but he now rallied it afresh: "Stop!" he called desperately after Jinny. "Stop!"

But Nip's joyous bark at the resumption of the journey drowned all lesser remarks, and again the cart receded on the horizon—an horizon he knew houseless and arid, no region for a lonely, good-looking girl. Let poor pockmarked Polly Flippance brave the wild, if female carriers there must be: not his Jinny. No, he must reveal himself at the next stop, he must remonstrate, protest.

But the trouble was that the thing would not stop, and that there would be no stop now—he knew—for several miles. Perspiring, panting, hallooing and waving his stick and utterly oblivious of the scandalized street, he pursued at his swiftest, and Methusalem being no serious competitor in the long run, Jinny heard him at last, and looking back through the tilt over the dwindled packages, saw the pitiful, gesturing figure, and to his infinite relief the cart drew up.

"What have you lost now?" she called. "Your sandwich-boards?"

"I'm not going back to Miss Flippance," he panted, "I'm going Bradmarsh way."

"Then why ever didn't you say so?" she replied calmly. "Jump up!"

Jump up? She asked a strange young man to jump up? Then what else could she have done if he had said who he was—a fact of which he had indeed been just about to make royal proclamation.

"You take passengers?" he gasped. He remembered now that Joey had told him the cart would take him, but then he had had no idea that "her" was not the vehicle.

She was equally surprised: "Why else did you run after me?"

Run after her? He did not like the phrase. Girls ran after men—girls of a sort—to some extent girls of every sort: that was the doctrine in his set. And yet he had run after her—it called for explanation. "I wasn't running after you," he said slowly, "it was only that—that I couldn't believe my eyes to see you like that."

"Like what?" She was frankly puzzled.

"Driving about alone in this God-forsaken part. It's—" scandalous, he was about to say, but before the glimmering fire in her eyes he altered the word—"it's dangerous."

"Dangerous!" Her little laugh rippled out. "I thought you said you knew these parts."

"So I do—I'm an Essex man, even though I mayn't look it, having been half round the world."

"Have you now? Well, it's the big cities that are dangerous, Gran'fer says."

"Maybe he's right," he admitted, wincing a little before the candid grey eyes. "But don't you understand that a woman carrier is—" again he toned down his word—"outlandish."

Her amusement danced in her eyes. "Inlandish, I suppose you mean."

"Don't laugh," he said, forgetting that the unrevealed Will had no right to that tone. "You know it's an unwomanly occupation."

"Laughing?"

"You know what I mean. For one thing a woman can't know much about horses—and she oughtn't to have to do with 'em anyhow—it's not natural."

"May she have to do with donkeys?" Jinny inquired sweetly.

He frowned. "Chaff's no good."

"But I never give my horse any—do I, Methusalem dear?"

Such word-mockery was bewildering to his simpler brain. He opened his mouth, but nothing came, and his vexation only increased for finding no vent.

"May she have to do with pigs?" queried Jinny again.

"Pigs are at home," he conceded.

"Not always," she said demurely. "I meet lots on this very road."

"And you might meet worse than pigs on a lonely road like this—you might meet men—"

"Like I've met one now."

"Yes, but it happens to be me!" he said, again all but forgetting her ignorance of his identity. "Usually it would be dangerous."

"Well, but wouldn't it be just as dangerous for a male carrier?"

"Not at all. He can fight."

"And if he met a woman?" she said slyly.

"There's no danger in a woman."

"Then why are you running away from Miss Flippance?"

"Miss Flippance!" he cried in angry astonishment. "Who says I'm running away from Miss Flippance?"

"Well, you've run from her to me. And if you say you weren't running after me, you must have been running away from her."

"Don't you try to bamboozle me. I tell you I've been half round the world, and nowhere have I seen a woman carrier."

"If you'd ha' stayed at home you would have," said Jinny.

"So it seems. And in America there are those Bloomerites—come over here, too, I hear, nowadays, the hussies. Want to wear the breeches."

"Do they?" inquired Jinny with genuine interest. "I've often thought it would be more convenient for me jumping up and down, and there would be yards of stuff less. Some of those Chipstone ladies quite scavenge the streets with their long skirts, padded out by all those petticoats, don't you think?"

He grew almost as auburn as his hair: such secrets of the toilette, babbled by a young girl he still thought good at heart, outraged his sense of decorum.

"No, I don't think!" he answered angrily.

"Well, try," she suggested sweetly. "Put yourself into our place."

"It's you putting yourselves into our place that's the trouble," he retorted. "What will women be up to next, I wonder."

Here it was Jinny's turn to flare up. She had never—it has been already remarked—thought of herself as up to anything, rarely even thought of herself as a woman, least of all as a representative of her sex. But challenged now to her face for the first time, she felt she must hold the pass for all womanhood.

"We women will be up to whatever we please."

"Not if you want to please the men."

Jinny's young face flashed fire and roses. "And who wants to please the men?"

He laughed complacently. "I never met a woman who didn't."

The girl's fire died into cold contempt. "I don't think you know much about women."

"Me? Why, I've knocked about since you were in pinafores—and pelisses!"

"I shouldn't be surprised, Mr. Drummer," said Jinny with judicial frigidity, "if you knew less about women than I know about horses."

"I've seen half the world, I tell you."

She flicked up Methusalem. "But not the better half."

He winced again. "Fiddlesticks!" was all he could find to answer.

"Drumsticks!" rejoined Jinny gaily, and with a mocking flourish of her horn, she receded afresh.

Something stronger than his will now shot him forward crying: "I say, Jinny!" He meant by crying that old familiar name to disclose himself, and then to have it out with her, side by side on the driving-board.

She turned her head. "Do you want to jump on or don't you?" she called.

It was the last straw. Jinny—he had forgotten—-was not a name privileged for the friend of her pelisse and pinafore days: any male might use it, just as any wayside rough might abuse its owner. "I don't," he shouted savagely. "I'll never patronize a woman carrier."

"A dashing young lad from Buckingham!" She had started singing, whether to herself or at him, he could not tell, and he strode behind the cart almost as rapidly as Methusalem before it, to find out whether she was still answering back.

But apparently she had forgotten him—that was the most pungent repartee of all—and the gaiety of the chorus only added salt to the smart:

"Still he'd sing fol de rol iddle ol,
Still he'd sing fol de rol lay—"

The thin silver treble reminded him incongruously of her Sunday-school singing, and the revival of that long-faded picture of himself driving her home only emphasized the jarring present. He turned furiously down Plashy Walk, where the rollick of the chorus soon ceased to penetrate and the white fragrance of the wonderful hawthorn avenue made a soothing passage-way. His tongue felt acrid with anger, ale, and running, and Frog Farm, with the faces of his parents, now began to loom more emotionally before him, because of the tea as well as the tenderness awaiting him. For neither of these luxuries was likely to be absent, even if his letter—or his father—had gone astray. Let her protect herself, this minx of a carrier, Time's odd changeling for his sober little Jinny. Serve her right if some horrid instrument of fate should take down her pride!

By the time he had come through the mile of hawthorn, and defied the Plashy Hall dog with his stick, she had passed out of his thoughts, and his indignation against her had changed to indignation against the impudent attempt—obvious from the notice-boards—to deny him and the public this old-established right-of-way. Things would not have got even thus far had he remained in Little Bradmarsh, he was thinking, and he was already brooding over a plan of campaign as he was climbing over the stile back into the high road. And then his vaulting leg remained suspended an instant in air in sheer astonishment. Jinny was facing him from her perch of vantage, smiling sweetly from her witching bonnet, her cart athwart the road, in fact he could hardly step off the stile without treading on Methusalem's toes. Relaxing his motion, he sat down on the stile, staring at her.

X

"Why, Will!" exclaimed Jinny, and there was now a strange softness in her face and voice. "How stupid of me not to recognize you when I've got your box all the time!"

His mind, still perturbed about the right-of-way, and bent now upon home, could not adjust itself so suddenly to the new situation. Again his mouth opened without issue. Her smile faded.

"I'm Daniel Quarles's granddaughter," she said with a little quaver. "Little Jinny of Blackwater Hall."

"So you've remembered me at last!" His voice came out harsh, though inwardly he was melted by this new sweetness.

"Then did you know me all the time?"

"Of course—the moment I clapped eyes on you." He was not consciously romanticizing.

"That's what I've been thinking as I waited here for you. I'm so glad. Because that shows you were only teasing me, saying all those horrid things." Then a new thought struck her to self-mockery. "Of course—I'm getting silly—it wasn't so wonderful of you recognizing me, with the name of Daniel Quarles on the cart." And she laughed merrily. "Do you know why I didn't recognize you? It wasn't only Miss Flippance put me off, and that I couldn't connect you with drums and marionettes—it was you yourself that blocked the way."

"I don't understand."

"The old you, I mean—I was thinking about him all the time we were talking, and that funny new you wasn't like him one bit."

"Thinking of me!" He was touched. . . .
"Whatever made you think of me?"

"Didn't I just tell you I've got your box? And of course I knew you were coming back. We've been expecting you for days."

"Oh, then mother did get my letter!" His latent ill-humour flowed into the new channel.

"Of course."

"Then why didn't dad come to meet me?"

Her mouth twitched humorously at the corners with the suspicion the letter was still unread, but she replied: "I suppose because he's old and hasn't got a trap any more, and he knew that Tuesday was my day. Jump up, I'm ever so late!"

He shook his head. "I can't jump up."

"Why, what's the matter, Will?" Her voice was anxious and tender. "Have you hurt your ankle, running?"

"No, no!" he said petulantly. "Didn't you hear me say I'd never patronize a woman carrier?"

She smiled in relief. "Yes—I heard you say it. But that was the silly you."

His face hardened. "Silly or sensible, I stick to my word."

"Drumsticks!" she mocked again. "Jump up and tell me all about your affair with Miss Flippance."

"Don't be saucy, Jinny. It don't become you:"

For the life of him he could not accept her as grown up, much less as an equal, though she sat on high, dominating the situation, whip in hand and horn at girdle, spick and span and cool; while he, astride the stile, was a forlorn figure, with dusty shoes and hot, lowering look.

"It becomes me as much as silliness does you," said Jinny.

"I don't see the silliness."

"Why, you can't live a week at Frog Farm without patronizing me. Who else is there? There isn't hardly a trap to be had even miles around. Why there was a young man I drove out to Frog Farm last week, and a fine to-do he had getting home!"

It was not calculated to soothe him. "And what need had you to drive a young man?"

"It was for Maria—your mother's pig. She was ill; her whole litter might have been lost."

He frowned more darkly. Pigs, he had but just admitted, might reasonably come into the feminine ambit: still, if girls did get to know coarse facts, they might at least have the decency not to talk about them. "And did he call you Jinny?" he grunted.

"He didn't call me Maria."

"Well, traps or no traps," he said sullenly, "you'll get no orders from me. I've fended for myself in the Canadian backwoods, where there wasn't even a woman to sew on buttons, and I certainly don't need one now."

But she was still smiling. "Do you know the song of the dashing young lad from Buckingham?"

"I know you do. But what's that to do with it?"

She re-started the merry tune, but markedly altered the words:

"A dashing young lad from—Canada,
Once a great wager did lay
That he'd never use Jinny the Carrier,
But—he gave her an order straightway!"

"No, he won't."

"Don't interrupt. You've already given it.

But still he'd sing fol de rol iddle ol—"

"What order have I given you?"

"To carry your box, of course—

Still he'd sing fol de-rol lay—"

"But that was before I had the ghost of an idea—"

"Do join in the chorus:

Still he'd sing fol de rol iddle ol—"

"I'll have my trunk at once!" he cried furiously, and sprang off the stile.

"Fol de rol arilol lay!" she wound up with easy enjoyment.

"Give me my trunk," he commanded again.

"What—on this lonely road—in this weather!"

"That's my business!"

"No, it isn't—it's mine." She touched up Methusalem and turned his eager nose homewards.

Will ran round with the turning animal.

"Give me my trunk!" He was white with determination.

"And don't you call that an order?" She cracked her great whip.

He sprang to the tail-board, hanging on by one arm, and clutched at the trunk with the other, dragging it out. But he had forgotten to reckon with the faithful guardian. Nip, excited as at a rabbit, sprang from the basket in which he had been resting his four weary limbs and growled ominously, and as the burglarious arm did not draw back, the terrier—O almost human ingratitude!—sprang at it and made his beautiful white teeth meet in its fleshy middle.

"You little beast!" Alarmed more for his finery than his flesh, he snatched back the elegant London sleeve and dropped off the cart, which soon disappeared down a grim and lonely lane.

XI

He examined the wound in his coat, and finding to his relief that it could be neatly patched up, he stripped off the garment and surveyed his abraded skin, tooth-marked and red-flecked; Nip's signature in blood. Then the horrible thought of hydrophobia—he had witnessed a dreadful case in Montreal— popped again into his mind: after all, it was as hot as July, and no sane dog would have behaved so disgracefully! And then, pricked up by the sound of the horn, which came vaunting and taunting from the lane, he started running after the cart yet once more: he must find out if the dog would drink. But even the rumbling of the vehicle could no longer be heard, and he was slackening hopelessly when he became aware how involuted was this lane, and that by trespassing across a ploughed field he could gain several furlongs. Bounding over the ditch with his coat slung over his arm, and nearly tearing it afresh in breaking through the blackberry hedge, he ran as recklessly as a fox-hunter across the furrows, breaking out again like a footpad when he heard Methusalem's leisurely trot, and catching that unreluctant animal by the beribboned headstall. Jinny manifested no surprise.

"I thought you'd get over your silliness," she said, smiling. "Jump up then!"

"I'm not jumping up!" He was angrier and hotter than ever. "I've come to give your dog a drink."

"Eh? But we've passed 'The Silverlane Arms.'"

"This is no joking matter. He must have water."

"He doesn't need any. Surely I can look after my own dog—that's not a man's place, too, is it?"

"It's not a question of that—but if he doesn't drink, it may be fatal."

"Nonsense. A kind cottager offered him water only a mile back—he didn't want it. . . . What's the matter? You're looking so strange. . . . Have you had a sunstroke?" The alarm in her voice reflected the alarm in his face, and his alarm was in turn augmented by hers. He had a weird vision of that man in Montreal, thrown into convulsions by the sound of a splash and trying to bite his attendants, and a ghastly memory came to him of a Bradmarsh woman who had frizzled for her foaming child the liver of the dog that had bitten it. "Suppose your dog should be mad?" he asked, with white lips that already felt frothy.

"Nip? Nonsense."

"He bit me."

"Oh, I'm so sorry. Where? Let me see."

"I won't."

"But Nip never bites."

"All the more suspicious. Try him with some water, please."

"Where can I get water? Nip finds his own."

"You mean to say you don't carry water?"

"I'm not a water-carrier."

"How can you laugh? It's a question of life and death. Surely there must be a pond somewhere."

"You know there's nothing hereabouts. Why, you used to come to Kelcott to sell water at a halfpenny a pint. Don't you remember? You bought me a monkey-on-a-stick out of the profits."

"How you babble! Then I must go in suspense?"

"Drumsticks! Here, Nip!" The dog was in her lap in a twinkling. She pulled off her driving-glove and thrust her fingers into its mouth. "Bite, Nip, bite."

Will felt his first conscious flash of romance in all that fagging chase. It was like dying together.

But Nip's teeth refused to close on his mistress's fingers—instead he growled ominously at Will.

"Bite, you naughty dog!" And she pressed his reluctant teeth together.

"There!" She held down towards Will two fingers faintly ridged in red and white. But instead of feeling a reassuring sanity, an impulse he felt really mad streamed through his veins to seize the little fingers in his strong hands and to pull her down from the seat of the mighty, down towards the inner breast pocket that held his bank-notes. But his stick and his coat and Methusalem's bridle, all of which he was holding simultaneously, cluttered up his hands sufficiently to clog the impulse.

"That proves nothing," he said sulkily.

"And wasn't he lapping at the pool after you struck him?"

"Ah, that's true." His face lit up.

"Then you did strike him?"

"Don't tease. Yes, I'd forgotten, he lapped then, or rather I scarcely noticed it."

"I suppose you shut your eyes when going for him, just like a bull does."

"I didn't go for him, I tell you. I just swished my stick."

"Well, if you'd kept your eyes open, you'd have seen him drinking and saved your fright."

He was disappointed as well as irritated. "Then when you let him bite you, you knew there was no danger."

"There's never any danger on these roads—didn't I tell you so? Why, there was more danger in that monkey you gave me, for I sucked the paint off."

"I don't remember giving you any monkey."

"I didn't want a monkey, but you made me take it—like that oath in the wagon. Perhaps you've forgotten that too."

"I can remember giving you a kiss," he jerked defiantly.

"That I can't remember," said Jinny quietly.

"Suppose you've had so many since."

"Lots!" said Jinny. "Good-bye again, if you're so silly. Gee up, Methusalem!"

But he clung to the bridle and was dragged along, to Nip's shrilled agitation.

"Let go," said Jinny. "Don't be silly."

"Not till I have my trunk."

"That's sillier still."

"Give me my trunk."

"I think you have gone mad, Will."

"That's not your affair, Miss Quarles, I want my trunk."

"I was ordered to deliver it at Frog Farm."

"And I order you to deliver it to me."

"Let go." She cracked her whip in his direction.

"You little spitfire! If you touch me with that whip I'll have an action against you—as well as against your dog."

"Let go my horse then."

"I'm within my legal rights, as any male carrier would know. I demand my trunk."

"And I demand my horse. Let go!"

"I won't." He was running along with it now, keeping pace with the mystified Methusalem.

"Oh, Will!" she cried. "And you said that on a lonely road I might meet a man."

"Well—you have now!" he said viciously.

"Yes—the first in all my life to give me trouble."

That hurt worse than any whip. He loosed the festive bridle, staggering a little, and the cart rolled past him. Only what was that little object in the road?

Ah, in the altercation she had forgotten to put on her glove again after that dramatic offer of her fingers to the dog—it had tumbled down. 'Twould pay her out to lose it, he thought savagely. However, he thrust it into the inner waistcoat pocket where his paper fortune reposed so comfortingly. But as again he saw the tail-board with his now protruding box vanishing round a corner, a blind rage began to possess him. Surely he was not thus entirely to be thwarted and overridden. Surely, at least, he would not endure her actual delivery of his box at Frog Farm. No, he must head her off again, if only outside his own gate. Across his border a woman carrier must in no circumstances be countenanced. And once more the unfortunate Will Flynt ploughed through the hedges and meadows, not always remembering the prickly places; and finally chased by a bull on which he had to turn several times with his coat and his stick, just like a toreador; though, remembering what Jinny had just said about the bull shutting its eyes, he dodged it at the charging crises, and thus saved both coat and skin. But he was forced to scramble ignominiously over a fence into the high road, still a good mile from Bradmarsh Bridge, at the very moment the cart came clattering up.

But if Jinny had observed the Spanish bull-fight she gave no sign. What she said, as she reined in Methusalem, was much more surprising.

"I've been thinking you were within your legal right, Will. I'm sorry. A carrier must deliver goods as ordered. So if you're still silly—!"

If she had stopped before the final clause, he might have been touched by the unexpected surrender. As it was, he only said icily, "How much do I owe you?"

"Sixpence," she said as frigidly, "unless you'd like a reduction for my not taking it all the way."

"No, thank you." He passed the coin, grazing her warm fingers.

"By the way, you didn't happen to see my glove?" she said.

"Your glove?" he repeated. Why, indeed, should he fetch and carry for her? Let her be punished for her negligence. He moved towards his box.

"Oh, well—I suppose it'll be there on Friday," she said. "I'm the only person who ever goes that cut."

"Drumsticks aren't the only things that are dropped," he observed maliciously.

"No," she agreed simply. She did not even seem to remember how she had trounced "that fool of a man." No sense of humour in the sex, he reflected again.

"Do hold the brute!" he cried, for Nip was again showing his teeth in defence of the box.

"If you kept off a bull, you don't need protection against a terrier," she replied, and to his further amazement there was a note of admiration in her voice.

"The weaker the thing the harder it is to fight," he rejoined significantly. He had his back now to the cart, and he hoisted his trunk upon it.

"You're not going to carry it?" There was incredulity in her voice, for it was a box that looked nearly as long as himself.

"Who else?" He shifted the box to his right shoulder, which he had padded with his coat.

"I thought you'd go home and get a truck or something."

"And leave it on the road?"

"It's just as safe as my glove."

"There's no safety for either," he said oracularly, "if a man like me comes along." And he swaggered forwards with his huge load.

"Why, you're as strong as the bull!" said Jinny.

"I am." He was flattered.

"And as obstinate as a mule!"

He increased his pace.

"Good-bye, Will!"

He did not answer.

Methusalem caught him up. "Since you are going to Frog Farm," said the Carrier, "why not take your folks' groceries too? I don't usually get 'em till Friday, but when I got your order to go there to-day—!"

"Why should I do your jobs?"

"Just what I told you. You can't live a week at Frog Farm without me."

"Give me the parcel." His forehead was already beaded with perspiration, but his left hand heroically held out his stick: "Slide the string on this."

She shook her head. "Still he'd sing fol de rol lay," she trilled, and in a minute he was hopelessly left behind. The road had already begun the ascent towards Long Bradmarsh, but he heard her goading Methusalem to greater efforts, as though in fear lest he should repent under the burden of his obstinacy.

XII

As soon as she was safely out of sight, Will, breathing heavily, slackened his showy pace, and very soon lowered his load altogether and sat down upon it, while he wiped his streaming countenance. The physical relief was great. A lark was singing overhead and his eyes followed it restfully till he couldn't tell whether the throb was singing or the song throbbing. He must smoke his pipe by this wayside grass after all that scurrying and squabbling. Fumbling for his matches, he felt the bulge of the glove and softened still more. Anyhow he had been victorious over the vixen, and he was resting on his laurels, so to speak. Now that she realized he would never recognize her as a carrier, he could afford to give her one of the Canadian fal-lals he had bought at Moses & Son's for his mother, and which now reposed in the box arching beneath him. That would make her think he had not forgotten her even in Canada, and anyhow it would show her he bore no malice for the bite or even for her bark. Surveying the landscape, he recognized that by going on a little he would strike the turning to the bridge and "The King of Prussia," where he might possibly find a trap. The hussy need never know he had broken down. But as he sat there lazily smoking and evoking his boyhood and her part therein, the best part of an hour sped glamorously, and suddenly he saw red. Caleb Flynt, equally coatless, was hastening from the Bradmarsh direction as fast as his aged limbs could carry him.

"Hullo, dad!" he cried, startled. "Same old shirt!"

Caleb grinned. "Keeps her colour, don't she?"

"But why didn't you come to meet me?" said Will, recalling his grievance.

"Oi did—soon as Jinny come and told us she'd passed you carrying your chest and you might want a hand. Is that the hutch? Dash my buttons, you must ha' growed up like Samson! Fancy carryin' that all the way from Chipstone in the strong sun!"

Will did not deny the feat—the explanation would really have been too complicated. In his embarrassment, he overlooked that his father had not really answered his question. "And how's mother?" he said.

"Mother's in a great old state. 'Nation mad with Jinny."

"Why, what's Jinny done?"

"Sow neglectful. 'Bein' as you passed him by,' says mother to she, 'why dedn't you stop and pick up the chest?'"

He looked uncomfortable. "And what did Jinny say?"

"She said she dedn't reckonize the old you when she dreft by, and besides she was singing-like."

He winced at the reminder of the song, but was grateful to her for telling so truthful a lie: instinctively he felt that his folks having accepted a woman carrier with such brainless acquiescence would fail to enter into the fine shades of his feeling.

"Mother hadn't a right to make a noise with Jinny," he said.

"She only kitched of a fire for a moment. 'Twas more over you than over Jinny, Oi should reckon. Bust into tears, she did, and when Oi said maybe as Jinny was mistook she nearly bit my head off. 'Too lazy-boned to goo and give a hand to your own buoy-oy,' says she. 'Ain't he shifted for hisself nigh ten years?' says Oi. 'Can't you wait ten minutes more? Oi count he'll be here before the New Jerusalem,' says Oi. That dedn't pacify her much, bein' a female. Cowld-blooded—she called me. 'There's feythers,' says she, 'as 'ud be trimmed out with colours like Jinny's hoss—not leave it to a gal as is no relation to decorate even her dog in his honour.' 'That's for May Day,' says Oi. 'All wery fine,' says she. 'But May Day's over and gone six days'—she's a rare un for figgers is mother—'time enough,' says she, 'for God to create the world in.' 'Maybe you'd like flags flourishin' and flutterin',' says Oi, jocoshus like, 'but Oi ain't got no flags save my old muckinger.' And with that, bein' more shook than I let on, Oi blowed my nose into it, wery trumpet-like, and that seemed to quieten her, for her tantarums be over now, and the onny noise she's makin' is the fryin' o' them little old weal sausages for you."

"Good!" cried the Prodigal Son, his face transfigured. "She remembered my passion for veal sausages!"

"'And there's pickled walnuts too! Put them out likewise,' says Oi, 'for 'tis a poor heart that never rejoices.'"

"But that's your passion, not mine."

"That's what mother said. 'But baint Oi to get no compensation?' says Oi. And why dedn't you write to her all these years, Willie?"

His face darkened again. "I'm no great shakes with a quill. And there wasn't anything to say. I did write once to tell you I was safe across the Atlantic and was gone to make my fortune."

"We dedn't never get no letter."

"No—it came back months after. I forgot to put England on it, thinking maybe Essex was enough. But it seems there's a Mount Essex in the States, down Wyoming way, and the Yanks always think everything is for them. So I thought I'd best let things be, being on the go in those days."

Caleb fully sympathized with the plea. "And have ye made your fortune, Will?" he inquired meekly.

"That depends on your idea of a fortune," Will parried. But he had a complacent consciousness of those bank-notes behind the glove.

"My idea of a fortune be faith in God," said Caleb.

"Yes, yes, I know." The young man got off the box impatiently.

Caleb tugged at one of its handles.

"Lord, that's lugsome!" he said, letting the long heavy chest subside. "Ef you ain't come back rich, you've come back middlin' powerful. All the way from Chipstone!" He clucked his tongue admiringly.

Having once left the miracle undenied, and feeling the situation now altogether beyond explanation to the bucolic intellect, Will again silently acquiesced in the Herculean imputation and took the other handle. "But why didn't you bring a cart or a truck?" he asked as they began walking cumbrously towards the bridge.

"Ain't got nowt but a wheelbarrow," Caleb explained. "Times is changed—-Oi ain't looker no more, and there's two housen now. Old Peartree got to have a separate door, but 'twas a good bargain Oi put my cross to with the son o' the Cornish furriner what Oi warked for these thirty-nine year. Mother will have it she'd ha' made a cuter deal, she bein' a dapster in figgers and reckonin' out to a day when the New Jerusalem will be droppin' down, but Oi don't howd with women doin' men's business, bein' as your rib can't be your head."

"I quite agree," said Will, surprised to find such enlightened sentiments in his queer old parent. "But tell me about Ben and Isaac and the others."

"They don't write neither. We was lookin' to you to tell us about the others as went furrin. Ben should be a barber in America, and they say as Christopher's got a woife, colour o' coffee."

"Nonsense, dad!"

"Well, maybe 'twas Isaac."

"No Flynt would marry a nigger woman," said Will decisively.

"Oi'm right glad to hear it," said Caleb. "For Oi count the young 'uns 'ud come out streaky and spotty like pigeons or cattle, and though they likely turn white when they die, and their souls be white all the time, Oi could never be comfortable along o' finch-backed gran'childer."

With such discourse they beguiled the heavy way, trudging behind their tall shadows, till at the gate of the drive of Frog Farm they saw Martha peering eagerly along the avenue of witch-elms. In another instant Will, letting go his box-handle, was choked in her hug and wetted by her tears.

"I can smell those sausages right here, mother," he said, with a smile and a half sob. "How do ye howd?" And he emphasized the homely old idiom by patting her wrinkled cheek. She caught his hand in hers, and he was touched by the thin worn wedding-ring on the gnarled and freckled hand. His eyes roved round. "But surely this ain't the house I was born in. Why, that was a giant's castle."

Caleb looked a bit uneasy: "You're sure this be Will?" he asked Martha in one of his thundrous whispers.

"Why, I'd know him in a hundred."

"Well, there's onny nine or ten." And he laughed gleefully.

"Do be easy, Caleb. You're getting as unrestful as Bundock."

"I'm Will right enough," Will intervened. "Only everything seems to have got so small. Come along, dad." He took up his side of the box:

"Gracious goodness!" cried Martha, perceiving it at last. "My poor Will! Lugging that from Chipstone! Why didn't you call to Jinny to stop and take it?"

"How was I to know that that was Jinny's cart dashing by?" he said, moving forward quickly. "I suppose you didn't ask her to stay for the sausages?" he added lightly.

"I couldn't ask her, dearie," said Martha. "She was terrible late, she said, and I know how crotched her wicked old grandfather gets at feeding-time."

"How big she's grown!" he observed carelessly.

"Big!" They both repeated the word, but from a different surprise.

"You said you didn't see her," said Martha sharply.

"I saw a big young woman flying by in the cart—I didn't know then it was Jinny."

"But you just said everything's growed so little," chuckled Caleb.

"So it has—all except Jinny."

"And she isn't so very big," said Martha, "rather undersized, some folks would say."

"Well, I'm not so oversized myself," said Will.

"Will's seen her toplofty over Methusalem," explained Caleb. "Wait till he sees her on her pegs."

"But I did see her on her pegs," said Will, "at 'The Black Sheep'!"

"Then why did you goo and carry that little old box?" inquired Caleb.

"She wasn't in the cart then—how was I to guess she was the Carrier?" he answered crossly.

"But you could ha' ast for the Bradmarsh carrier."

"The coach was late," he snapped.

"But Jinny hadn't started yet," persisted Caleb. "Bein' as you seen her there."

"Legends, my boy, legends." Tony Flip's euphemism for lies rang in Will's brain. But legends, he was finding, are not easy to sustain. One lie breeds many, and he was sorry now he had allowed himself to be made a champion weight-lifter. "I thought being so late 'twas no use asking for the Carrier—'twas you I expected," he said, turning the war back into the enemy's country.

But they had now lumbered up with the box to the twin doors, and the task of dumping down the subject of discussion in a convenient place stayed the cross-examination.

The feast for the Prodigal Son had been laid in the parlour, and the scent of the fried sausages came appetizingly on the evening air, more poetic than any of Nature's competing odours.

"Why, there's my letter!" cried Will at the parlour door, beholding it on the mantelpiece. "You might have let me know you couldn't meet me."

He went in and took it down. "Not opened?" he cried crossly, the muggy atmosphere of the sealed chamber adding to his irritation. "And I told you exactly the day and hour I was coming!"

"We haven't had time to get it read yet, dearie," said Martha mildly. "I was going to take it to the dressmaker, but Saturdays I'm so busy and Sunday was Sunday, and yesterday I felt as if my ribs were grating together, and to-day was too hot."

"Well, I shan't write again in a hurry," he said peevishly, and was about to tear the letter in twain. But Martha snatched it from him with a cry and slipped it into her bosom.

"Sit down, Will," she pleaded. "Your sausages are spoiling."

But the Prodigal Son would not batten at once upon the fatted calf. He felt too dusty, he said, and then, imperiously pushing at the diamond-paned casement and realizing with disgust it would not open, vanished in search of soap.

"He can't be well," whimpered Martha.

"Don't worrit, dear heart," Caleb consoled her. "Oi count even Samson wanted a wash arter he'd lugged that little old gate up the hill from Gazy."

CHAPTER V

WILL AT HOME

Is not this the merry month of May,
When love-lads masken in fresh array?
How falls it, then, we no merrier be'n,
Like as others, girt in gaudy green?
SPENSER, "The Shepheards Calendar."

I

Time hung heavy on Will's hands the first few days of his return, as heavy as the meals heaped before him by the adoring Martha. There was as much for "bever" as for breakfast, yet quantity did not suffice him. He became almost as finnicking and fractious as Cousin Caroline, not content, for example, to strain the pond-water through muslin for the larger insects, but insisting on its being boiled: indeed hinting preposterously that the mortality among his unknown brothers and sisters might have been connected with potations on which Caleb and Martha had patently flourished. He held views on the house-refuse, ignoring Caleb's plea that "the best drain be a pig," and by making hinges the very first evening for the lower windows to open by, he had raised such a draught in the house that it was all they could do to keep their bedroom and their kitchen air-tight, and even Martha was glad when on the Wednesday afternoon he went off to get some fishing in the Brad, and the windows could all be closed up again.

But the few dace and bull-heads that rewarded his rod left too many intervals for reflection, and in the unsettlement of his thoughts, before settling down to a judicious expenditure of his ninety pounds, he felt he needed more deadening exertion. He tried poling against the stream to that ancient faery island—somebody's half-decked shooting punt was doing no good rusting on the bank in the off-season, he thought—but the process soon became automatic and his mind was still restless, while after the islands of the St. Lawrence this enchanted playground of his youth seemed tame and its prettiness trivial.

He fed his fancy on a salt-water expedition for the Thursday: recalled the great catches of flat-fish he and his brothers had made, the sport to be got out of the voracious if inedible "bull-rout," but it would be a very long walk, and what if when one arrived the tide should be too low? So he walked inland around Bradmarsh Common. But though it was, he told himself, the "old haunts" that he went out for to see, he omitted to revisit that venerable landmark, Gaffer Quarles. Conscience adjured him he ought to look up the old carrier, whether for respect or reproof—and he actually did hover around Blackwater Hall—but pride forbade his entering, lest he stumble upon the new Carrier. The Hall appeared even more dwindled to him than Frog Farm as he stood surlily surveying it; even the Common—after the Canadian prairie—seemed no longer to roll towards the blue infinities. He had a strong impulse to burst in on that careless old Daniel and give him a piece of his mind, even at the risk of meeting his gadabout granddaughter; but the bleating of the goats sounded forbidding, and as he was hesitating he found himself under the gaze of another gaffer, the crown of whose battered beaver tied on to its brim with coloured strings gave him a festal grotesquerie. Will remembered this ancient, though despite his gay headgear he now seemed inexpressibly grimy in his patched corduroys, his two ragged coats, and the dirty towel wound round his throat. It was the Quarles's nearest neighbour, "Uncle" Lilliwhyte, who lived in a cottage also on the Common; trading in cress, cherries, and mushrooms, driving home obstreperous cows and doing other odd jobs. This worthy was now exercising his equal right of gathering sticks on the Common, and the sordid association seemed to reduce Jinny to the same shrunken proportions as her cottage.

"Buy a nadder, sir?"

"Sir!" Yes, after all, his father had been a "looker," not a mere labourer, he himself had a waistcoat lined with bank-notes and cut by Moses & Son, why should he expect a sense of dignity from a girl of so lowly a status? Let her earn her livelihood as she wished—it was not his affair, except in so far as she should have none of his custom. A cock crew lustily, and it subtly heartened him up. Yes, he would go in now, give her back her glove, professing to have just picked it up, and wash his hands of her for ever.

"No, thank you, uncle," he said, with an irrelevant memory of the ancient's blind mother, "what should I do with an adder?"

"But that's a real loive nadder, just kitched, sir." He cautiously displayed its hissing head and darting tongue. "There's many a slowworm killed for a woiper, pore things. Onny fowrpence, sir!"

"Well, here's sixpence," said Will graciously. "No, no," he explained hastily, as the ancient began handing over the wriggling reptile. "Kill the beggar." And he hurried homewards. On second thoughts—inspired perhaps by some dim impression of a female figure flitting among the clothes-lines behind the Hall—he would not risk an encounter with Jinny, but make a special call upon poor, lonely old Daniel on the morrow. Jinny would then be out on her rounds. And if he took care to go at about the hour she was due at Frog Farm, he could avoid her at both places. Yes, that were tactics worthy of a man of the world.

Casual conversation with his elders reminded him, however, that Jinny was not expected that Friday. She had already left the parcel of groceries on the Tuesday. He was thus safe from her for eight days—he had only to remain at home. But the discovery that the whole of Friday was free from any possibility of her appearance at Frog Farm, and that Blackwater Hall was equally immune from her presence, seemed to remove the zest of his diplomacy. Neighbour Quarles remained unvisited, his solitude unmitigated, and Will wandered aimlessly on the high road between Bradmarsh and Chipstone.

The year was at its most beautiful moment. The hedges were white with hawthorn, and the fresh young leaves on the trees gave an exquisite sense of greenness without blurring the structural grace of the branches, while the unspoiled cadence of the cuckoo's cry came magically over the sunny meadows. But Will could only swish viciously with his stick at the hedges and litter the lanes with ruined blossom.

It was with no little surprise that, as he and his elders sat at high tea on this same evening, they heard the windings of Jinny's horn. The three sprang up: then Will sat down again.

"Ain't you comin' out to see Jinny?" asked Caleb.

"Let the boy drink his tea," said Martha.

"But you ain't never spoke to her yet," persisted Caleb. "And you used to give her eggs."

"Let the boy eat his eggs himself," said Martha sternly.

"Oi dedn't mean they eggs," laughed Caleb.

"Do go and see what Jinny can want," Martha commanded him. "I shouldn't be surprised if it is eggs—now that Mr. Flippance has opened his show he'll be wanting them regularly."

"Whatever for?" asked Will.

"He sucks 'em raw, like weasels, him and his darter," explained Caleb. "They should say it's good for the woice, and by all accounts showmen fares to have a mort o' pieces to speak."

"But why doesn't Jinny sell him her own eggs?" asked Will.

"How do you know she has them?" asked Martha quickly.

"Hasn't she?" he said lightly, reddening like the comb of the cock he had heard crowing.

"Not enough. That old sinner eats her out of house and home."

"Mr. Flippance?" murmured Will.

"No, no. Her grandfather. Why don't you go, Caleb?"

Will sat on stolidly, helping himself to more tea and pouring the milk into the slop-basin. Presently Caleb returned, announcing that Jinny had brought something for Will—she could only legally deliver it to Mr. Flynt, junior, she said.

Will turned redder than at the egg-talk. "But I never ordered anything," he said.

"You can't prewent folks sendin' you presents, same as they're foolish enough," Caleb reminded him.

A fantastic fear that the blue-eyed girl of the train was discharging some proof of devotion at him made him drum nervously with his teaspoon. "But who knows I'm back home?" he answered Caleb.

Through the open house-door came the gay strains of a fresh young voice:

"But still he'd sing fol de rol iddle ol!"

"Don't she sing pritty?" sighed Caleb.

"I'd sooner hear her singing about Zion," said Martha. "She's rather flighty, to my thinking."

"That's the first time Oi heard ye say a word agen Jinny," said Caleb, "leastways behind her back."

Will, tingling between the two tortures—the song without and the table-talk within—sprang up brusquely. "Drat the girl—my tea'll get cold. Sit down, dad, I'll see what she's brought."

II

Jinny sat stiffly on her seat, Nip clasped in her arms. The singing had ceased. Despite himself Will felt an odd pleasure in the sight of the trim figure so competently poised above Methusalem, and he was touched to note Nip's tail agitating itself amicably at the sight of him.

"Good evening," she said politely. "I am glad to see it has not developed."

"What hasn't developed?"

"Your hydrophobia. And I am keeping the dog tight, you notice."

He winced. "Oh, I'm not afraid of him."

"But I am—he's already bitten you once: get the cages, please, while I hold him."

"The cages?" He had a confused idea that Nip was to be caged, was dangerous after all.

"They're near the tail-board. Nothing to pay."

He went behind the cart, wondering, semi-incredulous; did indeed perceive a couple of cages in the dusk, and reaching for one, drew back his hand in a hurry from some darting, snapping, creamy, pink-eyed yellowness.

"Oh!" he cried involuntarily.

"What's the matter? Oh, I had forgotten they bite too."

"What is this practical joke?" he cried angrily.

"Eh?" said Jinny. "Didn't you order a pair of ferrets to be sent by the Carrier?"

His eyes grew wide. "I beg your pardon—I'd quite forgotten."

"I thought Deacon Mawhood wasn't a likely joker. Polecats, he said. Have you got the cages?" she asked, not looking back.

"I'm—I'm getting them," he stammered, and began cautiously haling them towards him.

"The Deacon asked me to say the hob and the jill must be kept apart."

"I know," he grunted, almost as shocked as over her mention of Maria's litter. The impudicity of her calling was again borne in on him.

"Anything else?" burst from him sardonically.

"No—except there's no need to cope them. I don't know what coping is."

"It's what you want," he said brutally. "Muzzling."

"Afraid of my bite, too?" asked Jinny, and turning towards the interior shelf that held the smaller parcels, she began to sing softly to herself:

"A dashing young lad from Buckingham."

He had been expecting "Canada" at the end, and felt somehow disappointed at its absence. "But when I gave the order," he rejoined notwithstanding, "I didn't know that the Bradmarsh Carrier was a girl."

"That didn't prevent you using her when you did know," she said quietly.

"When have I used her?" he cried hotly.

"Well, what about this?" She produced from the shelf in the cart a long parcel half enclosed by a string in broken, dirty paper, within which showed a layer of grimy straw.

"But what is it?"

"That's not my business." She tendered it downwards.

"I never ordered this."

"Hadn't you better open it?" she asked with a twinkle. He dumped down the cages violently, to the alarm of the ferrets, and tore it open, only to shudder back before the clammy-looking coils.

"An adder as well?" said Jinny. "You going to open a menagerie?"

"It's dead," he said.

"Did you want a live one?"

"I didn't want one at all—I never ordered it."

"Why, Uncle Lilliwhyte told me he sold it to you for fourpence and you gave him twopence extra to kill it."

"I beg your pardon—he misunderstood." It was his second apology. "But what a dirty way to deliver it."

"Did you expect me to nurse a viper in my bosom?"

Again this indelicate speech, hardly atoned for by its wit. "The old ragamuffin!" he muttered furiously. "How did the idiot know it was me?"

"Fellow-feeling, I suppose," said Jinny.

"Now you're saucy again. You must have told him it was me."

"Right for once. Honest uncle was upset at your forgetting to tell him where to send your purchase. I was milking my goats and saw you hanging about."

Again he flushed uneasily. "And how much do I owe you?" he asked hurriedly.

"Twopence for the viper, being only a short way. The Deacon says he prefers to pay the freightage on the ferrets, and to collect it from you himself."

He put down the straw-entangled snake on top of one of the cages, and pulled out a coin. "Have you got change for sixpence?"

"Not unless I loose Nip." She fumbled with one hand in her pocket.

He glowered. "Oh, next time will do," he said angrily.

"Oh, then, there is to be a next time!"

"Not so far as I am concerned."

"Sure you don't want any more wild animals?"

"No," he shouted.

"Don't be so fierce. The drumstick is found, you will be glad to hear."

He grunted.

"And the show is doing big business, Mr. Flippance tells me. He was so set up he gave me a pair of new gloves."

"That old braggart! What business had he to give you gloves?"

"Didn't I lose one through his drumstick?"

"But then 'tis me ought to pay for them," he protested.

"You? What nonsense! Why?"

"It was on my account you lost the glove—through trying to get a bite."

She smiled. "You talk as if I were an angler."

"I wish you were! Anything but a carrier."

"Don't say that. Would you like me to buy another pair of gloves—on your account?"

"If you would!" he said eagerly.

"Thank you!

But still he'd-sing fol de rol iddle ol.

"What size do you take?"

"Stow that fol-de-riddling—you know I don't mean gloves for me."

"Are you taking back the order?" she said, with feigned disappointment.

"I never gave you an order!" he said, goaded. "I'd cut my tongue out sooner."

"Keep your tongue between your teeth. You'll want it to give me an order with before you're a week older."

"Never! I'd as soon shoe a horse with a hairpin." He snatched up his cages decisively, one in each hand, and the adder rolled on to the ground, bursting its strawy cerements.

The girl's grey eyes flashed steel-like. "And can't I drive as well as Gran'fer? And don't I know the roads?" And she uplifted her horn from her girdle and blew a resounding blast of defiance. It set all the cocks crowing behind the house and brought Caleb bustling from within it.

"Did you summon me, Jinny?" he asked. "Gracious, Will, whatever you got there?" His eyes expanded to see the sinuous animals swirling fiercely against their wires; in coming nearer to peer at them, he stumbled over the snake and uttered a cry.

"It's all right," called Jinny. "It's dead."

"You killed it, Willie?" he asked.

"With a drumstick," said Jinny gravely.

"Fiddlesticks, father!" said Will angrily.

"Oi don't care what sort o' stick you killed that with," said Caleb, "so long as it's a dead corpse. But do ye come in now—mother's grousin' about the tea gittin' cold."

"I like cold tea. Go in, father. I'm just coming." He harked back to her blast of rebellion. "You may be able to drive, and you may know the roads. But can't you see how unnatural it is, you perched up there and blowing a horn like Dick Burrage of the County Flyer?"

"And do I blow it as fine as he?" she asked eagerly.

"Anybody can blow a horn," he answered curtly.

"Can they now?" She was piqued again. "I'd like to see anybody do it. Why, Gran'fer can't."

"Gran'fer hasn't got much breath left. I'm not talking of men in their eighties."

"He is in his nineties," she corrected.

"Exactly. I meant anybody with proper lungs."

"Can you blow it?"

"Why shouldn't I be able to blow it?"

"All right! Blow it!" said Jinny gravely. She unslung it with one arm and held it down. He gazed at it, taken aback, sandwiched between his cages.

"It's no good opening your mouth," she said. "I'm not going to stick it in. You'll have to put down those horrible beasts and do that yourself. Why don't they keep still? They make my head ache."

He moved to the back of the house to place the ferrets out of the way, kicking the poor adder before him—it was a needed relief to his feelings. Returning, thus purged, he took the proffered horn—it was not a professional coach-horn or post-horn, but just the little instrument of a master of foxhounds curling into a circle above—and with but scant misgiving put it to his mouth, and blew. But the silence remained unbroken. He puffed on and on with solemn pertinacity. Not a sound issued. His cheeks swelled to bursting-point, and grew redder and redder with shame and vexation. But silence still reigned.

"You mustn't put it inside your lips," corrected Jinny. "Think you're tum-tumming into a comb."

He readjusted it sullenly, but the music within was still coy.

"Slacken your lip," she advised. "Try to splutter br-r-r-rr into it."

But whatever he spluttered into it, nothing came out.

"I never realized it was quite so difficult, even the lipping," said Jinny simply. "Of course I didn't expect you to do the double or treble tonguing at once."

"What do you mean, tonguing?" he inquired morosely.

"Dividing the notes. Say 'Tucker, Tucker, Tucker' into it."

"But it's blowing, not saying," said Will obstinately.

But secretly he modified his methods, and at last a ghostly plangency or a staccato squeak began to reward his apoplectic agonizings, and the still prisoned Nip, who had been yawning in utter boredom, now accompanied the music with a critical and lugubrious howling.

Upon this spectacle and situation reissued the guileless Caleb, and had the Crystal City itself come down upon earth, his eyes could scarcely have orbed themselves more spaciously.

"He didn't summon you," observed the merciless Jinny.

"Go away, father! What are you staring at?" yapped the tortured young man.

"You do be a fine musicianer!" And Caleb grinned. "But do ye don't play now—mother's gittin' into her tantarums over your tea."

"The instrument must be out of order," said Will, handing it up crossly to Jinny. Remorselessly she drew from it a clarion call that made the welkin ring and the poultry-yard respond in kind.

"How the cocks crow!" she observed artlessly.

"Thinks because she blows a horn she's a devil of a fellow," Will remarked witheringly to his receding father. "Say, Jinny, why don't you wear the breeches?"

"Like those Bloomerites you told me of? I will," she responded sweetly, "if you think it more becoming."

"Me! You don't suppose I notice what you wear."

"Then how do you know I'm not wearing 'em now?"

"You have me there!" And he smiled despite himself. The smile lit up the face under the aureole of red hair—it seemed to Jinny a sudden glimpse, through a rift of Time, of the boy she had known. "All the same," he protested, "if I had a horn, I could learn it in an hour."

"Well, get one," said Jinny.

"Where can I get one?" he retorted fretfully.

"Dearie! Your tea—!" It was Martha herself now.

"Oh, I'd get you one," said Jinny carelessly, "but I'll wager you won't blow it properly in a week, much less an hour!"

"A week! What nonsense! In a moment."

"In a moment?"

"I was speaking to mother. What'll you wager?"

"A pair of gloves," said Jinny.

"Done!" said Will.

She clucked to Methusalem. "Good-bye," she called to the couple as the cart moved off. "I'll deliver your order next Friday, Will—without fail."

"Dearie, whatever are you running after her for?" cried Martha.

He came back sheepishly: "I thought the gate wasn't open."

From the Bradmarsh road the sound of the "fol-de-rol" refrain came sweetly on the quiet air.

"I wish she would sing of Zion," repeated Martha wistfully.

The pair of polecat ferrets—creamy white albinos, pink of eye and black of belly—hung in the cages on the back wall of the farmhouse, with a spare cage beside them as a retiring-place when a hutch was turned out. But only once—on the Saturday in the first ardour of possession—had Will taken them out a-hunting: on which occasion they had refused to rat or rabbit. Indeed their leaps and gambols persuaded Will that they pursued—as he remembered the Deacon once maintaining sympathetically about rats—their "private sports." Why indeed should sensible creatures, comfortably fed on chicken-head and blackbirds, and provided with straw to cocoon themselves against cold, go squeezing into holes or drains? Restored to captivity, these fainéant ferrets spent most of their day in squirming with desperate restlessness from one end of the cage to the other and perking their quivering noses and little black claws through the wires. And their master's own plight was much the same, for after the prairie, Frog Farm was only a hutch to him: his father, too, being so unexpectedly on the shelf, there was nothing that really needed him, nor was there any land for sale in the vicinity on which they might commence operations. Like his ferrets, if with a larger run, he swayed restlessly to and fro; from farm to river, from river to Common, from Common to Steeples Wood, from Steeples Wood to Frog Farm.

When he was not thus oscillating on the landscape, he was sweating in intellectual indecision in the parlour: trying to write a little note to Jinny to inform her that she was to come to Frog Farm no more, inasmuch as he intended to go into Chipstone himself once or twice a fortnight, and could easily bring home whatever was necessary. He had thought that when he had found a feather dropped by a green goose, cut his quill, concocted an ink out of soot and water, and discovered a piece of white paper wrapped round his bank-notes, that his difficulties were over. But the worst now remained, for he could not satisfy himself as to the phraseology of this note, being, as he had truly pleaded, no great shakes at letter-writing. Such glibness as he could muster in conversation was paralysed in fact by a pen. There was not even one of those word-books he had seen scholarly people use to ensure the spelling, and one must not unnecessarily afford material to a minx who—having obviously to do with bills and accounts—might conceivably be literate. He had a vague remembrance of her reading texts quite easily at the Sunday-school, young as she was. Even if she could spell no better than he, she might possess one of these spelling-protectors.

The only book at Frog Farm being his mother's Bible, he tried to secure accuracy by limiting himself to its words. But its vocabulary seemed strangely lacking. He had decided, for example, to begin with "Maddam." One could not call such a stranger as the new Jinny "Dear Miss," he thought, and "Miss" alone sounded thin and abrupt. No, "Maddam" was the mouth-filling resonance necessary: it struck a note of massive dignity. But did it really have two "d's"? And to his amazement and anguish neither "Maddam" nor "Madam" was to be discovered from Genesis to Revelation. Adam, the nearest analogue, who came in his reference volume with welcome promptitude, even precipitateness, had, he found, only one "d," but was he a sure guide to the orthography of the creature formed out of his spare rib? This and the many other curious and amazing passages that beguiled him on his route—presented thus to a fresh and world-experienced eye—ran away with so much time that Martha would be summoning him to the next of his many meals before he had even dipped his quill into the soot.

"Mr. William Flynt presents his complements" was another promising start—he had got a debt-demanding letter once at a boarding-house with this austerely courteous overture—but alas!—marvel on marvel—there did not appear to be a single "complement," whether in the Old Testament or the

New. Not a very courteous people, the Jews, he thought, under either dispensation. This happy-go-lucky hunt for words—an exciting steeplechase in which one skipped over spacious histories and major prophets with the chance of tumbling on the very word—began to be an absorbing substitute for ratting.

"The Epistles of James" suddenly caught his eye. Ah, here was a complete guide to letter-writing, he felt hopefully; what was good enough for James would do for William. But when written out, "William, the son of Caleb, of Frog Farm, to Jinny Quarles of Blackwater Hall, Little Bradmarsh, greeting" did not seem quite the correct opening. An Epistle of John was, even more misguiding. "The Elder to the Elect or Well-Beloved!" Clearly inappropriate to the point of absurdity!

Still, with modifications, Epistles must surely be valid models. So he started writing and re-writing, wrestling and hunting and polishing. But the word-chase had now to be supplemented by a paper-chase. How keep pace in paper with this orgy of penmanship? Every corner of the house was ransacked, with meagre results: he even meditated stealing back his own letter from his mother, knowing it had a blank fly-sheet, but it was always jealously guarded. It was not till he came on Farmer Gale's boy—schoolward bound   and paid him twopence for the remains of a penny copy-book that he could surrender himself freely to the labours of the file. An hour before this large laying-in of material, he had gone through a curious crisis. He had found in his purse, in a last desperate quest, a piece of paper which, unfolded, afforded a welcome white surface. He was composing quite a successful letter upon it when, on turning it over, he came upon the address of the forgotten blue-eyed charmer of the Chelmsford train. With frowning brow he tore it into small pieces. It was not merely that the letter was spoilt for sending: it was the juxtaposition with Jinny—back to back—that seemed suddenly profane.

IV

After several days' gestation, many words and turns of expression having to be rejected and replaced by phrases whose spelling could be ascertained from the Bible, the letter emerged as hereunder in a pale and aqueous ink:

"William Flynt to the Damsel of Blackwater Hall greeting. This epistle doth proclaim in the name of the generations of Frog Farm that Methuselah shall not come to pass here henceforward, inasmuch as behold here am I to purchase whatsoever is verily to be desired from Chipstone, be it candles or oil or spice or any manner of thing whatsoever, nor shall you carry forth aught hence, for lo! we will make no further covenant with you or aught that is yours. Peace be with you, as thank God it leaves me at present.

"Yours truly,
"WILLIAM FLYNT.

"P.S.—Let not your horn be exalted, nor speak with a stiff neck, for surely this is not the way to find grace in the eyes of the discerning."

But even this exalted effusion did not survive the first glow of satisfaction, for although it was treasured up as too good to destroy, and did not sound unlike the language that the Brothers and Sisters held in the meeting-house, he could not remember ever seeing a letter thus couched. It was succeeded by a homelier version, in which the word "Epistle" stood out as the only connecting-link. With a composition playing now for safety, and mainly monosyllabic, it would be a poor diplomacy not to work in one high-class word, of whose spelling he was sure.

"This Epistle is to say," the new version began abruptly, "that we don't need you to call on Frydays—"

Good heavens! Even Friday was not to be found in the Bible. Pursuing this astonishing line of investigation, he realized that Sunday itself was absent from its pages. The Bible without Sunday! O incredible discoveries of the illuminated!

He altered it, following Genesis, to the "sixth day," but then came a paralysing doubt whether it was not the fifth, for how could you rest on Sunday if that was not the seventh? He casually remarked to his mother that it was odd they did not rest on the seventh day, as commanded in Genesis. She explained to him that Sunday was the Lord's Day, but he seemed dissatisfied with the argument. Perhaps Moses & Son were not so wrong, he remarked, repenting of his resentment against them for being closed that Saturday.

He woke up the next morning with the solution of dodging the mention of the day and merely relieving Jinny of the duty of "markiting" for them. He felt sure that this word could be found, remembering a text about two sparrows being sold for a farthing. But to his chagrin it was not in the "markit" that they were sold. In steeplechasing for the word, he tumbled on a text in Hosea: "Blow ye the cornet in Gibeah, and the trumpet in Ramah," and that seemed like an omen. Yes, he would blow it in Bradmarsh, if not in Ramah. Let him wait till she came with the horn; then after whelming her with the wonder of his execution, he could, face to face and free of orthography, bid her trouble Frog Farm no more. And the postscript of his great letter, "Let not your horn be exalted, nor speak with a stiff neck," rang through his mind again, like a prophetic warning against overweening damsels.

"He's come back a new soul," Martha reported to Caleb, with shining eyes. "He's found God."

Caleb shook his head sceptically. "He's too boxed up for that—he don't open his heart enough."

"But he opens the Bible," urged Martha, "and he won't close it even for meals. I can never get it for myself nowadays."

"Dedn't you read me as the Devil can spout Scripture?" said Caleb shrewdly.

"For shame, Caleb. Anybody can see how changed the boy is—the only thing that makes me anxious is his Sabbatarian leanings. Suppose he should go and join the Seventh-Day Baptists."

"Dip hisself o' Saturdays?"

"No, no—'tis those that keep Sunday on Saturday. There's two in Long Bradmarsh, but I hope Will won't go straying into strange paths."

"You better enlighten him," said Caleb. "Them as is powerful enough to carry boxes from Chipstone ain't allus bright in the brain-pan. Oi count it 'ud be aukard if he fared to keep Sunday on Saturday, bein' as he'd want the Sunday dishes fust and we'd get 'em cold."

"There's higher considerations than the stomach," said Martha severely.

"The stomach ain't low and it ain't high," maintained Caleb. "The Lord put the stomach in the middle so as we shouldn't neither worship it nor forgit it."

"The only Sunday meal that matters," persisted Martha, "is the bread and the wine, and though there's no Lord's table nigh, such as I could find dozens of in London, nor nobody to worship with except you, yet if you go on scoffing, my duty to my Brethren and Sisters of the synagogue will be to withdraw from you."

"And where will you goo?" he asked in alarm.

"I won't go anywhere—'withdraw' only means that it is forbidden to break bread with you."

He was relieved. "Oi don't mind so long as you don't goo away."

"And what will you do in the day of Ezekiel thirty-eight, when Gog and Magog dash themselves to pieces against Israel? And when the eighth of Daniel comes to pass, and the Great Horn is broken and the Little Horn stamps upon the host of heaven?"

"Oi count it won't be just yet," he said uneasily.

"You count wrong. To my reckoning the two thousand three hundred days of Daniel are nigh up. In the great day of Isaiah four, when the Tabernacle rises again with the cloud and smoke and the flaming fire, the people of God shall rise too from their graves while the others sleep."

"Then you can wake me up, dear heart," he said, "bein' as you're sure to be up."

She shook her head. "You were always up first, sweetheart, but that day you'll sleep on and I'll have no power to rouse you—unless, says Isaiah, you 'look unto me and be saved.' 'Dust to dust'—that shows we're not immortal by nature."

"But ef it's comin' so soon, Oi shan't be in my grave at all," he urged anxiously, "and Oi can push into the Tabernacle."

"No more easy than for wasps to push into the hive. You've seen the bees push 'em back."

"But one or two does get in and Oi reckon Oi'll take hold o' your skirt, same as you been readin' me."

"I read you there'll be ten men to take hold of it," she said.

"Nine other men!" he cried angrily. "But they won't have no right to take hold o' my wife's skirt."

"That's what Zechariah says—'ten men of all languages.'"

Caleb's gloom relaxed. "He was thinkin' o' Che'msford and sech-like great places full o' furriners," he said decisively. "Here there's onny Master Peartree, and the shepherd ain't a Goloiath. Oi'll soon get riddy o' him, happen he don't hook hisself to you with his crook."

"But I'll pull in Will too," said Martha.

V

But Jinny did not appear on Friday with the musical instrument. Only the unexpected arrived—in the shape of Bundock. That royal messenger was visibly hipped as he delivered the letter to Will.

"A woman's writing!" he observed reproachfully. "That means dragging me here time and again!"

But Will had broken open the high-class adhesive envelope and was already absorbed in the letter.

"SIR,—Mr. Quarles thanks Mr. William Flynt for his esteemed order, but regrets to inform him that a coach-horn of suitable size for a man is not to be had in Chipstone. They have not even got a little hunting-horn like mine. I will, however, superscribe to Chelmsford and get you one without fail. Trusting for your further patronage,

"Yours truly,
"DANIEL QUARLES.

"N.B.—All orders carried out—or in—with punctuality and dispatch. Goods sent off without fail to any part of Europe, America, and Australia.

"P.S.—Please inform your hond. parents that as she brought q.f. of groceries that Tuesday I shall not call again till I deliver your instrument."

So Jinny had got in first in the pen-fight! And her letter bowled him over, not only by its bland assumption that she was already established as his carrier, but by the fluency and scholarship of its style, with its incomprehensible "superscribe" and "q.f." He felt baffled too and even snubbed by the signature, which gave her a businesslike remoteness, and even a legitimate status as a mere representative of the masculine, besides making him feel he had lost a chance by not sending off one of his many scrawls to the address of this same "Daniel Quarles." His answer would now require the profoundest excogitation, he felt, as he adjusted her missive between the bank-notes and the glove. There was, moreover, the material problem of vying with this real and fashionable correspondence paper. Ultimately he became conscious that Bundock was still standing at attention.

"Do you want anything?" he asked tartly.

"I'm waiting for the answer," said Bundock nobly, "or you won't catch a post till to-morrow night unless you trudge to Long Bradmarsh."

"Oh, there's no answer—none at all! Thank you all the same."

"Thank you!" said Bundock. "It's not often folks consider me nowadays—especially when there's a woman in the case. They just go on shuttlecocking letters till my feet are sore."

"But it isn't a woman!" said Will stiffly. "It's just a business letter from Gaffer Quarles." And he pulled it out, and the little glove fell out with it: which did not lessen his annoyance.

"Daniel Quarles never put his fist to a pen this ten year," asserted Bundock. "He was glad to be done with writing, says my father, for Daniel was never brought up to be a carrier, his parents never dreaming he'd inherit the business."

"Why not, isn't he the eldest?"

"The contrairy. Blackwater Hall and the bit of land is one of those queer properties that go to the youngest, if you die without a will."

"The youngest?"

"Ay, and that's what Daniel was. Borough English, 'tis called by scholars," said Bundock impressively. "However, he picked up a little from his brother Sidrach, who had already set up as a carrier on his own account round about Harwich, and a pretty business he did, old Sidrach, says my father, before he was discovered to be an owler and had to fly to America."

"Were they so persecuted?" murmured Will.

"And didn't they deserve it—smuggling our good English wool into France! Pack-horses they loaded with it, the rascals."

"Oh, I thought they were a sect!"

Bundock laughed. "That's with an aitch; though I dare say many a man owled all the week and howled on Sunday—he, he, he! Do you know—between you and I—who it is writes the hymns?"

"The village idiot!" answered Will smartly. "You told me so when I was a boy," he added, seeing the postman's disconcerted expression.

Bundock brightened up. "Ah, I thought 'twas too clever for you. But as for this letter o' yours, it's clearly a woman's handwriting, and if Jinny once begins writing to her customers, it's a bad look-out for me."

Bundock might well feel a grievance, for this was the first letter Jinny had ever written to a client, indeed to anybody with the exception of old Commander Dap, who, clinging to the friendship struck up at his wife's funeral, sent her birthday presents and the gossip of the Watch Vessel. To him she had written as her heart and her illiteracy prompted, but the elegant epistle received by Will Flynt was not achieved without considerable pains. She had the advantage, however, of not being limited to the Bible for her vocabulary, possessing as she did an almost modern guide in the shape of an olla podrida of a Spelling-Book, whose first edition dated no further back than 1755, the year of the Lisbon Earthquake. "The Universal Spelling-Book" had originally belonged to the "owler," and it was from the almost limitless resources of this quaint reservoir that, with a pardonable desire not to be outshone by her much-travelled neighbour, she culled both the "superscribe" defined as "to write over" and the q.f. (given in the "List of Abbreviations" as standing for the Latin of "a sufficient quantity"), except that she misread the long "s" for an "f." The immaculate spelling was, however, no mean feat, for the book's vocabulary was very incomplete and devoid of order, so that she had almost as much steeplechasing to do as her rival letter-writer. Moreover, she must fain study whole columns of traps for the unwary, where the terms of her own occupation appeared with disconcerting frequency. If there was not in the letter any necessity for distinguishing between "glutinous" and "gluttonous," "rheum" and "Rome," or any risk of confusing a "widow" with a "relic," still "seller," "fare," "due"—any of which she might have needed—all had their dangerous doubles, and she did not write "call" without carefully discriminating it from "Cawl, of a Wig or Bowels." "Punctuality and dispatch" was lifted bodily from Miss Gentry's billheads, and if she did not offer to send off goods to Asia and Africa, it was because only "Europe, America, and Australia" figured on Mr. Flippance's posters.

The recipient of this impressive communication was staggered by the strides in female education made since his boyhood. He betook himself at once—to his mother's joy—to the Bible, like a Cromwell before a great battle. Martha had stolen the book back to the kitchen and was pondering texts anxiously when he wandered in to hunt for it.

"Who sent you a letter?" she inquired uneasily.

"Old Quarles," he answered readily. "It's about an order he can't supply, and he asks me to tell you his granddaughter won't be coming to-day."

Martha's face lit up. "What a pity!" she cried. "She might have taken my bonnet to Miss Gentry to be re-trimmed." Martha had become reconciled to this minor vanity, now it was strategically unnecessary. "However, your young legs can do that, dearie, now they're back, can't they?"

"With pleasure, mother," he said, all unconscious of the lapsed plan. "Why waste money on carriers?"

She kissed him passionately, but seeing his anxiety to be at the Bible, she released him.

"I should look at Revelation, one, ten, Willie," she advised, "and you'll understand why the Sabbath—"

"Yes, yes," he interrupted soothingly.

"Also Colossians, two, sixteen and seventeen—the seventh day is but a shadow of things to come."

"I see," he said, escaping.

It took hours of hard theological study—indeed till Saturday morning—before the reply to Jinny shaped itself:

"SIR,—Mr. William Flynt thanks Mr. Daniel Quarles for his esteemed epistle, and regrets to learn that a coach-horn of suitable size for a gentleman is not to be had in Chipstone. I beseech you, however, not to superscribe to Chelmsford as Methuselah cannot fetch such a compass, and the righteous man regardeth his beast. Neither do I require a horn at her hand now or henceforwards.

"Yours truly,
"WILLIAM FLYNT.

"P.S.—Do you think that a maiden of your years aught to superscribe alone to Chelmsford, a city full of lewdness and abominations, where men use deceit with their tongues and the poison of asps is under their lips?"

"What are you writing, Will?" said his mother, coming in to sun herself in his holy studies.

"Nothing." He put his hand over the page of the copy-book, forgetting she could not read it.

"Are you writing to Jinny?" she inquired suspiciously.

"No, no—-it's Daniel," he corrected.

"Daniel!" she said in amaze. "About the Sabbath?"

"No, about the horn," he blurted out petulantly.

"The Horn!" She was wildly excited. "Is it the Little Horn or the Great Horn?"

He was amazed. "Well it began with the little horn—"

Martha was radiant. She poured forth her own theory of the Beast in Daniel, and emboldened by his silent agreement—when his daze changed into comprehension of her misunderstanding—she proceeded to elaborate her interpretation of the two thousand three hundred days of sacrifice. He, meantime, was finally deciding to turn "Daniel" into "Miss" except in the address.

VI

But Will's letter could not be posted—for many reasons. He possessed neither an envelope to vie with Jinny's, nor one that was closed with outside devices, nor any sealing-wax to make his letter its own envelope; he could only fold it into a cocked-hat and deliver it himself. Apart from these material reasons, he could not well let Bundock carry an answer, when he had denied there would be any, and he shrank from conducting his affairs under that official inquisition: moreover, haste was imperative if he was to save the girl from that difficult and dangerous journey, for "superscribe" conveyed to him a sense of precipitation, and he saw her cart almost stampeding to Chelmsford. At any moment she might set out in quest of the Great Horn. That was why he abandoned the idea of toiling to Chipstone to emulate her refined writing materials. He must hie to Blackwater Hall that very afternoon and play postman. He would not, of course, enter the house, but would find a way of slipping the letter in.

The surreptitious deed he meditated gave him almost a skulking air as he neared the Common, and he shrank from the observation of all he met, though with the exception of Uncle Lilliwhyte in a corduroy sleeved waistcoat, driving cows with a weed-hook, and an old crone who stopped and muttered with twisted head, he saw only frightened partridges whirring above or rabbits and field-mice scurrying at his feet. Near Blackwater Hall he encountered two of Jinny's milch-goats tethered, pasturing on the hedgerows, and their bleat had a cynical ring. The Common itself seemed almost to meet the sky, for clouds had gathered as suddenly as the crowd by the Silverlane Pump. He was feeling dispirited as he stole towards the house, but as he caught sight of the stables and barn at the rear, it seemed a happy idea to plant his note in some obtrusive coign. His heart beat like a raw burglar's as he stood surveying from afar the primitive sheds whose roofs were thatch, whose gates palings, whose sides faggots, and in one of which he could see Methusalem's head in a trough of oats. The stable-shed would be the surest place, he thought, or perhaps he could pin the note on to the harness he saw hanging in an adjoining shed from nails in the beams. Coming nearer to peer at Methusalem's manger, he was startled by the sight of a brown smock-frocked figure crouched on the littered, dungy floor and belatedly brushing Methusalem's fetlocks. Before he could escape he saw the wizened, snow-bearded, horn-spectacled face turned up at him, and heard himself recognized in a weakened but unmistakable voice.

"Why, bless my soul! Ef that bain't little Willie Flynt!"

Daniel Quarles rose and straightened himself to his full height, but nothing in Little Bradmarsh had seemed to Will so pitifully shrunken. "Little" Willie Flynt indeed towered over the patriarch who had once seemed Herculean to him. Yet if the robustiousness that the old carrier had preserved in his eighties had vanished at last, there was still fire in his eye and a fang or two in his mouth.

"Hope you are well, Mr. Quarles," said Will, recovering from the double shock of discovering and being discovered.

"No, you don't, my lad," piped the Gaffer. "Did, you'd a come sooner, seein' as Time is gettin' away from me."

"Did Jin—did your granddaughter tell you I was back?"

"She ain't scarcely told me nawthen else."

Will's cheeks burned.

"You ain't come back improved, says she."

Will's flush grew redder.

"But Oi don't agree with her—you've growed like a prize marrow. Come into the house and she shall make you a dish o' tay—Oi don't drink it myself, bein' as Oi promised John Wesley."

"No, thank you—I'd rather talk where we are."

"Well, Oi can't inwoite you in here—'tis too mucky." He gave Methusalem's tail a final flick with the brush. "And it's blowin' up for rine. We'll goo into the barn." And he led the way imperiously round by a great and ramifying apple-tree that hid a little black door secured by a padlock and infinite knots of string.

"One has to be witty," he commented, patiently undoing the complications, "with so many thieves about to steal my dole hay."

Will had not heard of these thieves, and thought Little Bradmarsh must be changed indeed, but he waited silently, wondering what to do with his note. And as he stood thus, there came from the cottage the sound of a girl's singing. Fortunately it was not satirical, so Will could hear it with pleasure:

"Of all the horses in the merry greenwood
The bob-tailed mare bears the bells away."

"Always jolly, my little mavis," said the patriarch, fumbling on, and, unable to resist the infection, his sepulchral bass voice took up the Carters' Chorus:

"There is Hey, there is Ree,
There is Hoo, there is Gee—"

"Oi wouldn't unlock the barn," he broke off to explain as the door swung open, "ef Oi hadn't such good company." He stood peering suspiciously into the tall raftered and beamed glooms; redolent of old hay and punctuated with a few cobwebbed and rusty instruments amid the endless litter. Will's eye was fascinated by an old wine-barrel flanked by a chaff-cutter and a turnip-cutter and covered with boards and weights. He divined it held corn and was thus closed against rats, and a whiff of aniseed came up in memory, and in a flash he saw the faces of Tony Flip and the Deacon—and himself flying after a carrier's cart.

"They've stole my flail," cried the Gaffer.

"Why, there it is, under that straw," said Will.

"Oh, ay. But there was more logs, Oi'll goo bail. Drat 'em, can't they chop for theirselves? It'll be that Uncle Lilliwhyte."

"Oh, but he's only too honest," said Will incautiously.

"There ain't nobody honest," barked the Gaffer.

"But he sent me an adder—" he began.

"Not he. 'Twas Jinny told him to send the adder. He'd ha' kept your sixpence and let you whistle for your sarpint. But next time you want an adder, you come to me."

"Do you sell 'em too?" he murmured, surprised.

"Oi be an adder!"

"What do you mean?"

His spectacles glowed strangely. "Read your Bible, young man—Dan is an adder in the path, what biteth the horse's heels, so that the rider should fall backwards—that's the blessing of Jacob—and let no man try to ride roughshod over the likes o' me."

Will shrank back before the passion of his words. Indeed in that gloomy old barn he began to feel a bit nervous.

"I've brought a note for Jinny," he said hastily. "Will you give it to her?"

The old man took the cocked-hat. "Mr. Daniel Quarles!" he read slowly. "But it's for me!"

Will's blush was now papaverous. "No—no!" he stammered. It was a conjuncture he had not foreseen.

The fire in the old eye leapt up at the contradiction, shot through the spectacles. "Plain as a pikestaff—Mr. Daniel Quarles! And then you has the imperence to say there ain't no thieves. But ye can't bamboozle me. Oi could read afore you could woipe your nose with a muckinger, ay, and my feyther afore me. Carriers ha' we been for over a hundred year, and my big brother Sidrach he had his own pack-horses loaded up with waluable stuff and writ me a piece ten year ago come haysel, sayin' as he hoped Oi should jarney to see him, and please God Oi will, he gittin' old."

"But where is he?" asked Will, glad that the Gaffer's monologue had drifted from its angry beginning.

"In Babylon!"

"Babylon?" gasped Will, whose recent theological excursions had made him almost at home in that purpureal city.

"That's my nickname for Che'msford, chuck-full o' lewdness and Church-folk. But Oi've been meanin' to goo and look Sidrach up and hear all about his travels, he bein' a rare one for adwentures, but somehow what with my carryin' work and one thing and the tother my days fly by—like the Book says—swifter than a weaver's shuttle. Happen lucky, though, Oi'll git over there to-year."

"I hope so," murmured Will vaguely.

"No you don't, drat you!" said the veteran with sudden viciousness. "'Tain't your care whether Oi ever clap eyes on my beloved brother agen. A 'nation cowld day it was he had to goo away—the Brad all ice and they should be tellin' of the Che'msford coach as come in without the driver, and he fallen down on the road, frozen stiff as a sparrow."

"What year was that?" asked Will, to keep the conversation on this more agreeable level.

"It was the year my brother Sidrach went away," said Daniel Quarles simply. "'Nation cowld. We heerd that in Lunnon the river was as froze as ourn, and flue-full o' sports—booths and turnabouts and pigs roasted whole, and great crowds to see a young bear baited. But feyther's cart went to and fro Chipstone just the same, and brought the news as how a woman was burned at Newgate for coinin'—it dedn't seem wery dreadful in that weather. Waterloo year that was another cowld winter—all the marsh ditches was solid ice, and all the eels was found dead and frozen. Couldn't eat 'em neither, not after the first day, they stank so. That numb was my fingers Oi could scarce howld the reins, and you'd ha' thought by my breath Oi was a wicked smoker. But 'twas wunnerful times, and we heaped up a deadly great pile o' fagots and bushes for the beacon, top o' yonder rise where ye see Beacon Hill Farm."

"Ah, the bonfire to celebrate the victory!" said Will, rejoiced to find irascibility cooled into reminiscence.

"Wictory! That was the name o' Nelson's ship as that silly old Dap should say he sarved in. Nay, this was but a bonfire to be lit when Bony landed. All along Blackwater we was ready for the inwasion, and when the beacon was fired, that was to be the signal. The soldiers was to goo to the coast and the ciwilians inland. But Bony never come, and 'twas a great waste. And Sidrach never come neither. 'Nation cowld the day he went away—Oi moind me gooin' through a foot o' snow across Chipstone poor-piece to the Church to see the Knight Templar what was dug up in the north aisle, pickled inside three coffins, but they'd put him back in the outer lead time Oi arrived. They should say it was a sort o' mushroom ketchup as kept him together for the Resurrection Day—a bit blackish, but wellnigh as sound and good-lookin' as you."

It was a compliment that made the young man shudder again.

"Ah, there is the rain!" he exclaimed, with relief at the hearty patter on the apple-tree.

But the old man would not be fobbed off so enjoyable a topic. "Three coffins—lead, ellum, and a shell—'twas a witty way agin them body-snatchers—you ain't safe agin thieves even in your tomb. And when you're above ground they tries to steal your wery letters." He pulled open the note.

"It's merely addressed to you as head of the business," Will explained.

"Ay, that Oi be, though the youngest. He that is last shall be fust, says the Book, ay, and the Law too, though 'twasn't fair to Sidrach to my thinkin', bein' agin nature. And next time a letter comes for me, do ye don't bring it and play your tricks, but let it come natural through Bundock's grandson. What's this? 'Mr. William Flynt thanks Miss Quarles for her esteemed epistle.' And who is Miss Quarles, and what's she been writin' to you?"

"About—about business," said Will.

"There ain't no Miss Quarles in the business," said the old man testily. "That be my business, and Oi lets Jinny amuse herself jauntin' to and fro, pore gal, she bein' that lonely on the Common and afeared o' dangerous charriters. Rare mistakes, she makes, bein' onny a gal, and costs me a pretty penny. But it 'ud cost me more ef Oi dedn't stop at home and guard the house from thieves. And now she wastes more o' my hard-earned dubs writin' to you as is a neighbour—drat the child, ain't that got a tongue? 'A suitable horn?' Dash my buttons! What do you be wantin' with a horn—you bain't a guard or a postman, be you?"

"No, but—!" he stammered. The explanation was not simple.

"'Oi beseech you, however, not to superscroibe to Che'msford' . . . 'the righteous man regardeth his beast.' Dang your imperence! Why shouldn't Oi goo to Che'msford? Oi ain't seen him these sixty year, and do ye don't come interferin' 'twixt brothers. Sidrach writ me a piece ten years agoo come haysel, arxin' me to superscroibe to Che'msford, and Oi'll not be put off by the likes o' you. You look here, my lad, ef you're come home to meddle or make, the sooner you goos furrin agen, the better."

"But it's not you—it's Miss Quarles I don't like journeying to Chelmsford. Look at the P.S."

It was imprudent counsel, for, as the Gaffer followed it, his face became a black cloud, the fire in his eye was lightning, the odd fangs in his mouth showed like tigers' tusks, and his beard seemed like a tempestuous besom sweeping all before it.

"'Lewdness and abominations.' You call my Jinny a Jezebel! Git out o' my house!"

"I'm only in your barn," Will reminded him, "and it's raining, and you just said yourself that Chelmsford is a Babylon chock-full of abominations. And you'd let a young girl superscribe there all alone!"

"Jinny shall superscroibe where she pleases!" roared the Gaffer. "For over a hundred year the Quarleses have superscroibed in foul weather or foine, with none to say 'em nay, and it ain't for a looker's son to come here dictatin'."

"I didn't dictate," said Will, with a fleeting schoolboy memory. "I wrote it with my own hand. Look here, Mr. Quarles," he went on, trying another tack, "you're a sensible old gent with great experience of the world, and it makes me frightened to see that grandchild of yours gadding about so far from home, and sometimes not getting back here till dark."

"That ain't timorsome—onny when she's alone here," he added cunningly.

"Maybe, but with such a pretty girl—!"

"Ay, she's like a little bird with her little fitten—and allus singin' like one too—all the day that goos about singin', 'Fol de rol—'"

"Yes, yes," said Will, wincing.

"And Oi'd best tear up your letter—she don't want to read about lewdness and abomination except in the Howly Book. And Oi count she has enough o' that on Sunday with you Peculiars."

"It is better she should read about it than scutter about seeing it. A cart ain't a suitable place for a girl."

"A cart's as suitable for Jinny as a horn for you," retorted the old man, bridling up again. "Oi suspicion you're plottin' to steal her away from me."

"What!" Will's cheeks burned with indignation.

"And Oi count you've got your eye on the cart too, like you bolted off to Harwich with your feyther's wagon. There won't be naught left for me but the poorhouse. But Oi'd die sooner." He was almost blubbering now with self-pity.

"Oi saved a mort o' money once," he said, "though it took a deadly time scrapin' the dubs together, what with the expense o' dinner at "The Black Sheep" and the hoss's feed—fower parcels or fowerty, Oi never stinted him o' his peck o' chaff, and three and a half pound o' oats and the same o' ground beans, and there's folks as grumble to pay accordin' to the soize and compass o' the parcel, though there's nights your hoss goos so lame and you're that pierced with wind and snow you got to knock up a farm and borry a hoss to git home with, and them days it was the barges took away custom. Old Bidlake used to goo along canals and cricks as ain't there no longer, thank the Lord, bein' as they sea-walls have made a many willages high and droy. But Oi had to pay all my savin's away to keep our name from disgrace, so as Emma should howd up her head in Kingdom Come. He hadn't the bed he died in, for all his traipsin' around in Tommy Devils; but time Oi went down to git Jinny, Oi made inquirations among the tradespeople and paid 'em to the last farden, aldoe soon as my back was turned, my own sister plots with her one-eyed little ship's monkey to pay for a stone, as ef Oi'd neglected my own darter, and all spiled with wicked words—did you ever see such words in a Christian churchyard?"

"No, of course not," soothingly murmured Will, to whom the long rigmarole conveyed nothing except: a sense of pathetic and loquacious senility.

"Ha!" said the Gaffer with satisfaction. "Oi says to Dap, says Oi, 'A Churchman like you may not see the blarsphemy, but think what John Wesley would ha' said to it.' 'Sir,' Oi says to the old gentleman, 'you jump into my cart,' says Oi, 'and not a sowl here shall harm a hair o' your wig'; and with that Oi wheeled round my whip, and bein' then an able-bodied young man ('twas the wery fust year arter feyther died), them as was throwin' stones and cryin' 'Knock his brines out' slunk away like blackbeadles, which was a pity, seein' as they missed the be-yutiful words he preached from my cart. From Chipstone to Che'msford Oi carried him—a dogged piece out o' my way, bein' as he wanted to preach there and his own hoss had gone lame—'twas the wile o' that great old murderer, Satan, says he, but the Almoighty sent you to confound his knavish tricks. That was a man of God, my lad, never out of heart, roighteous and bold as a lion, would preach even in front of a gin-shop where 'twas writ up: 'Drunk a penny, dead-drunk twopence, clean straw for nawthen.' Pounded glass mixed with mud the sons of Bellal threw in his face, but his eye-soight was not dimmed, nor his nat'ral force abated. Used to preach as much as foive times a day, gittin' up at fower o' the clock, and travellin' a bigger round than me, but wunnerful healthy, slept like a baby in my cart, and that saintly he said all his life he'd never done naught as 'ud bear lookin' at. He made me sing a hume with him and we was singin' it as we come into Babylon:

Oi the chief of sinners am,
But Jesus died for me."

As the sepulchral bass quavered out the tune, Jinny's fresh voice could be heard from the back door calling "Gran'fer! Gran'fer! Where are you?"

"She thinks Oi'm out in the rine," chuckled the old man, "but let her come and find me. His blessin' he gave me at partin', did John Wesley, and do ye don't never smoke nor drink that pison stuff, tay, says he. 'Oi'll promise ye tay and gin too,' says Oi, bein' as Oi liked beer best. 'But to give up baccy, that's main hard,' Oi says. 'There's harder,' says he, lightning-like. 'Promise me as ye won't be friends with a woman as is younger than your wife, for there's unholy sperrits about,' says he, 'as brings gales and earthquakes and temptitations, and the best o' men may git capsoized same as the Royal George, our best ship, t'other year.' Lord, that fair capsoized me, for how could this furrin ole gen'leman in his eighties know about Annie, as wasn't seventeen yet for all her wunnerful fine buzzom, and the missus older than me, in looks Oi mean, bein' as she was two years younger the fust time that worritin' census paper come along."

"When was that?"

"That would be the year Oi put new thatch on this wery barn for the new century."

"And what year did you meet John Wesley?"

"Ye'd best git Jinny to work that out. But it couldn't be many year afore the Jew Mendoza boxed Dick Humphreys for the Championship, for Oi wouldn't goo, ne yet bet on it, bein' as my sowl was saved, and when Oi lifted up my woice at the camp-meetin's and chapels in praise and repentance and shouted 'Glory! Glory!' dancin'-like, with the tears for my sins runnin' down my cheeks, that was more joy to me than Annie and the prize-ring and cock-foightin' rolled into one. And Oi ain't never backslided, praise the

Lord, bein' as Annie married a sedan-chair man and was hiked away to Cowchester, and Oi hope for your immortal sowl's sake, my lad, you bain't like what Oi was at your age."

"I hope so," said Will, not without uneasiness.

The patriarch shook his head. "There's the old Adam in you, plain to discern. Ye won't be safe till ye're married. But do ye don't marry an old gander of a widow like that potboy they should be tellin' of,"—he began to cackle—"that'll onny lead to wuss mischief. Wait till you happen on a clean little lass, rosy and untapped."

"A girl like your granddaughter, you mean?" Will heard himself saying.

The cackle ceased abruptly and the grin was replaced by a glare. "That ain't gooin' to be married! That's got to goo out with my cart, whenever Oi'm too busy workin'. Ef a rich man like Farmer Gale as drives her to chapel Sundays should be wantin' her all the week, Oi don't say Oi wouldn't goo with her to the big house, but that ain't likely, and she can't have nawthen to say to a rollin' stone as mebbe left a pack o' wives among they Mormons."

Will was nettled. "And who asked for your granddaughter?" he retorted. "Besides, you're quite right. I married dozens of wives in America—all widows too!"

The veteran chuckled afresh. "Dash my buttons! How you do mind me o' your feyther when he was your age—always had his little joke. Not that Oi count him growed up yet, he havin' never cut his wisdom teeth, but gooin' off as skittish as a colt arter peculiar doctrines and seducin' sperrits."

"Oh, there you are, Gran'fer!" And pat as to a cue a most "seducin' sperrit" flashed, like a shaft of sunshine, through the half-open door into the gloomy old barn. But she was aproned and bare-armed to the elbow, and rain-spotted, and a ringlet of hair was blown almost across her mouth, and the instant she perceived Will, she drew back in confusion, patting her hair tidy.

"Sorry, Gran'fer. I didn't know you had visitors."

But Will, to whom the sense she conveyed of brooms and dusters was sweetly reassuring of a still unsubmerged femininity, cried out as hastily:

"No, I was just going. You'll get drowned."

And he tried to pass her.

But the old man dramatically extended the uncocked hat.

"Howd hard, sonny."

Will, disconcerted, found his feet sticking to the floor.

"He's writ me a letter, imperent little Willie, and brought it hisself." Then a flash of amusement toned down the asperity. "Aldoe he had his tongue with him!" And the old man chuckled.

"Shall I read it?" murmured Jinny, putting forth her hand.

"Nay, nay!" He snatched the note back and tore it into careful pieces. "Ain't fit to be seen."

"No more am I," said Jinny with an uneasy laugh, and again she essayed to escape.

"Stop!" commanded the ancient, kindled afresh. "Willie's got to tell you what's in they scraps."

Will was silent.

"Don't stand gawmin'. Out with the abomination."

But no sound issued from the young man's lips. It was not merely that this new housemaidenly figure seemed safe enough even in Chelmsford, wrapped in its own sweet domesticity, and that adjurations designed for the minx bade fair to blunt themselves against this sober angelhood; but that the girl's radiance against the littered gloom within and the rainfall without, robbed him literally of breath.

"Speak out, Willie!" said the Gaffer, softened to contempt by his obvious confusion.

"Perhaps he hasn't brought his tongue," suggested Jinny, recovering herself.

"Then Oi'll lend him mine. You ain't to goo to Che'msford, he says."

"But I don't want to go to Chelmsford, Gran'fer. Why should I go to Chelmsford?"

"To get his horn, you baggage. And he don't be wantin' it."

"Oh, but he ordered it—it's too late now."

"Ay," said Daniel Quarles, "and goo you shall to git it ef the adder has to bite Methusalem's heels."

"But I don't have to go to Chelmsford for it!"

"You said you'd go to Chelmsford," burst out Will at last.

"Nothing of the sort."

"But I've got your letter!" He pulled it out, and again that awkward glove fell out. "Ah, there's your glove I've found on the road," he said, crimsoning furiously.

"Thank you!" She took both letter and glove placidly. "Now I shall have two pairs! But where do I say anything about going to Chelmsford?"

Thus invited, he came and looked down at the paper she held, and gripped an end of it himself, very conscious of her near fingers, and her bared arm, and her bending head. He was about to cry: "Why, there!" when a horrible doubt lest "superscribe" did not mean dashing away, or stampeding, or scurrying, or driving, or even going, checked the exclamation.

"I must ha' misread it," he said. "I beg your pardon."

"Spoken like a Christian!" said the Gaffer. "And Oi count John Wesley 'ud a said let bygones be bygones. Sow bring out the beer, Jinny."

"Thank you—I'm afraid I can't stay," said Will. He had a sullen sense of defeat, which the loss of the glove seemed to accentuate and symbolize. "My folks'll expect me home to tea."

"Your Mormon wives? Ay, Jinny, you may well blush," the Gaffer chuckled. "Willie's been and married a pack o' widows in America."

"And left them there!" said Will, permitting himself a faint smile.

"Left all those widows!" laughed Jinny. "How deadly dead you must be!"

But despite the merriment in which the episode had so unexpectedly ended, and despite the rain which had now grown torrential, he tore himself obstinately away, even refusing the "umberella" which the old man suggested and Jinny offered to fetch; though as he stepped under the plashing apple-boughs, he felt himself doubly foolish to refuse what would have been a literal handle for a return visit. And now that he had caught a glimpse of what he told himself was the real Jinny, not the Tuesday and Friday swashbuckler, but the Saturday-cleaning-up-for-Sunday house-angel, he did not despair of inducing her to shed these husks of bravado. But he had said "no," and "no" to his great annoyance it must be.

"When do you propose to superscribe?" he asked with crafty lightness, as he raised his hat.

"Oh, but I have superscribed," said Jinny. "But of course if it doesn't come soon, I shall write over to Chelmsford again."

VII

The first Sunday of Will's home-coming, nothing had been said about chapel. That, his elders thought, might be still a sore subject with the boy whose resentment at sacrificing his buttons on the altar had driven him "furrin." Still more delicate was the theological position into which the couple themselves had gradually drifted, and of which they now—before a spectator and critic—grew uneasily conscious. Martha's Ecclesia in Long Bradmarsh having collapsed almost as soon as she had been converted to it, she had no meeting-house to go to, and, almost simultaneously, Caleb, whose farm-wagons had recently been shifted to the new "looker's" headquarters, ceased to attend his Chipstone Chapel. This was partly to keep his wife company of a Sunday, partly because so many miles there and back was getting too much for his legs. In consequence the pair had arrived by compromise at a Sunday ritual of their own, a sort of Peculiar Christadelphianism, and Uncle Lilliwhyte, who never entered any of the many houses of God—it was popularly supposed he would not or could not remove his gay-stringed beaver—would often loiter outside Frog Farm in Church hours, listening to their loudly trolled and hybrid hymnology in a sort of pious eavesdropping. That was Uncle Lilliwhyte's individual contribution to the chaos of creeds that reigned in Bradmarsh.

But even this minimum of religion was denied the honest snake-seller when Will returned. The first Sunday, Caleb and Martha held their services furtively in their hermetically sealed bedroom, hardly daring to hum what they had so lustily intoned: by a common instinct they shrank from obtruding their departure from that straitness of doctrine in which Will had been reared. They were indeed secretly relieved that he made no reference to religion, nor seemed to expect them to go to the old chapel, nor even noted the Sundayness of the dishes that Martha served up with the same careful everyday air with which Caleb consumed them. They were equally relieved, however, that he did not go out rabbiting on the holy day with his new pet ferrets. "Oi've known some as dedn't consider that work," said Caleb, as they discussed this dread possibility. "But to my thinkin', if ye goo out with a spade, ye might as well be ploughin'."

That was what they said in bed on the first Saturday night. Very different was their conversation on the eve of the next Sunday. The problems all came now from Will's over-interest in religion. True, the Sabbatarian peril had not yet materialized: he had neither worn his best clothes on the Saturday nor demanded priority in the Sabbath dishes. But he had dropped more than one perturbing remark. Old Quarles, he supposed, was now too old to worship at his Wesleyan Chapel in Long Bradmarsh, to which Caleb had replied naïvely: "Ay, he sleeps at home Sunday mornings." Presumably, then, Jinny would not leave the old man alone on Sunday as well as on Tuesday and Friday: to which Caleb had answered cautiously—and without admitting that his observations were not up to date—that doubtless Jinny could only worship occasionally with the Peculiars and it depended on her getting a lift, Methusalem being a strict Sunday observer. Yes, he had heard Farmer Gale sometimes gave her a lift—who had told Willie? he wondered—but he supposed it was because the farmer, like her grandfather, was a Wesleyan. Later, Will had remarked casually to his mother that he didn't suppose Miss Quarles would be able to get to chapel on the morrow, as he had happened on her old grandfather, who seemed quite breaking up. Martha, murmuring sympathetically that Mr. Quarles must be getting old, was likewise compelled to gloss over her inacquaintance with Jinny's latest Sunday habits: she shocked and surprised herself by remarking that one's grandfather would hardly count against Farmer Gale, and hastened to add—especially as Will seemed shocked too—that such was Jinny's devotion to her grandfather that not for some years had she been able to stay longer than the Morning Service. Rejoiced though the old woman was at Will's mingled concern for the religion of the young and the weal of the old, she was a little uneasy at this personal turn of his theological thinking, and she quickly changed the conversation to the Great Horn and the Beast, a discussion which in her eagerness she hardly noticed was practically a monologue.

By nightfall that Saturday Caleb had gathered, with a sinking of the heart, that Will designed to accompany his elders on the morrow—and to Early Service! The boy had apparently failed to remark the breach in the old chapel routine the previous Sabbath: the Sunday had been hushed up only too successfully. It was as far as Caleb dared go, in the first plunge of confession, to say that, in the absence of a vehicle, Early Service at Chipstone was out of the question nowadays.

Such was the situation that faced the old couple in the sleepless watches of the second Saturday night, and dimmed even Martha's joy in the prodigal's return to religion.

"Best go with him, like when he was little," she decided. "We mustn't unsettle him so soon, now he's found God again."

"Ain't so sure he's found God," said Caleb shrewdly. "God ain't in a goose-quill, and writin' a piece about Daniel ain't the road to heaven, else where would me and most o' the Brethren be? To my thinkin' Will's onny lost the Devil."

"It's the same thing. What else does he want to go to chapel for, and Early Service at that?"

"To make trouble," said Caleb fretfully. "We was all so happy till he come—and you had Maria."

"Oh, Caleb, you don't deserve the Lord should give him back to you! And if you don't go to-morrow, I'll withdraw from you."

"That ain't right," said poor Caleb, puzzled by the unscrupulous threat. "But ef it's onny for Morning Sarvice he'll expect you to goo too."

"He knows about my rheumatics, dear heart," she said casuistically. "He knows I couldn't walk even to get my bonnet cleaned."

"But ef you were to tell him about the New Jerusalem—?"

"He'd best find that himself, now he's on the way. It's not far from Daniel."

VIII

Thus it was that Uncle Lilliwhyte was again defrauded of his ritual and that after a still more furtive and still earlier service in the sanctity of their airless bedroom, with hymns muted and prayers guiltily whispered, the couple appeared at an eight o'clock breakfast with an air of devotions unpaid, and Caleb, hurrying the meal, remarked that 'twas time to get ready for chapel or they would miss even the Morning Service.

At this, Will, who was in his fashionable London jacket—to the admiring awe of his elders—sprang up, and rushing to the back of the house near the water-barrel, brushed away hastily at a dull speck on his boot where a spurt from the boiling kettle had blotted out the shine he had so laboriously imparted. The male ferret, caged just above his stooping head, awoke at the agitation, and started rubbing itself under the neck as if in parody, but far more swiftly and persistently; then it jerked its nose and its thin whiskers through the wires.

"Not to-day," laughed Will, jabbing its nose with the blacking-brush. He felt very gentlemanly and happy, for the brief rain of the evening before had dried up, and the day was as fine as his clothes. As Caleb came out in quest of Will, the ferret was just snuggling back to slumber, and the old man, yawning with the loss of his Sunday morning sleep, looked enviously at the creature coiling itself so voluptuously in its straw.

"Lucky Jinny brought me sech a noice Sunday neckercher," he said, "or Oi'd ha' been ashamed to walk with ye. Ye look like our Member o' Parlyment." He himself looked, however, a respectable figure enough in his tall hat and finely stitched and patterned Sunday smock, his high-lows and gaiters, and it was not till they were getting over the stile that led to the short cut through the Green Lane that Will observed that his senior carried, like a tramp, a bundle in his handkerchief.

"What's that?" he inquired fretfully, becoming aware too that the Green Lane, even at its best, offered perils to his boot-polish.

"That's my hume-book and our dinner and tea. There's two packets for each on us, and we must be home for supper. Don't, your poor mother will be lonely."

Will had forgotten these meals: they had, in his boyhood, been carried decorously in the wagon. But the sunshine of the mid-May morning did not permit ill-humours, and they strode happily along the dappled by-ways, bounding over the shrunken sloughs, the son uplifted even beyond boot-polish by the intoxication of the Spring, and the father by the intoxication of the Spirit. For, the moment Caleb had crossed the stile, the old rapture of fellow-worship had returned, and the absence of Martha seemed to lift the shadow of her criticism; while doubts of his son's regeneration could hardly survive the sight of his springy step chapelwards.

Will was indeed living over again his childish memories of these Sunday journeys, and, somewhat to his surprise, something fresh and delicious seemed to emanate from them. It had after all been a pleasant change in the weekly round, this family jaunt with the big double-lidded provision basket, while the congregational picnicking in the chapel had not been without its jollity.

But Caleb did not leave him long to his memories. The old Peculiar was anxious to have a problem solved that had been weighing upon him these two years. In the New Jerusalem, whose descent to earth—ready-made and complete—was, according to Martha, imminent, to the impending confusion of disbelievers, there was to be "A street of pure gold, as it were transparent glass." Martha—as if to immunize him against his visit to the old Peculiar Meeting-house—had read out the text that very morning at their surreptitious service. And his ear had always heard "brass" instead of "glass." But how could gold be brass or either transparent? He did not like to shock her by questioning the letter of a text—his differences from her turned merely on the relative importance and significance of her texts as compared with those he had picked up from the Peculiars. Yet this puzzle was perhaps what really prevented him making the final plunge into Christadelphianism. It is true he might have demanded her solution of it—often through those long months of controversy as he looked at her saintly face so quiet on the pillow beside him, it was borne in upon him that in that bookish brain, under that frilled cotton nightcap, lay the explanation of the holy mystery. But possibly, with the subterranean obstinacy of the peasant, he shrank from an elucidation which might have left him irremediably at her mercy. A vindication of the text by Will, on the other hand, would give him time to turn round, take his new bearings. And a young man who was capable of composing a thesis upon the Little Horn and the Great Horn, could surely wrestle with this mystery.

"Oi hear you writ a piece about Daniel," he began tactfully, as they crossed the bridge.

Will frowned. He had forgotten Martha's misunderstanding. "Has he been round telling you?" he asked angrily.

"Me!" Caleb stared. "Oi bain't howly enough for wisions."

Will was puzzled in his turn. "You mean he can't walk so far!"

"Oi wouldn't say that: happen he can fly if he wants to."

"Fly!"

"Surely! A man so howly in his life—him what—"

Dead! So suddenly! Will stood still. This altered many things. The winged image of the Gaffer faded before the picture of a lonely Jinny. "When did he die?"

"You know that better than me," said Caleb meekly.

At this the thought that his "epistle" had over-excited the patriarch and stilled that aged heart, shot up, agitating the young man. That was why relief mingled with a vague disappointment when Caleb went on: "They lions couldn't kill him, but Oi reckon he had to die some time. But many of them what sleep in the dust of the earth shall awake, he tells us, and maybe"—he added with a flash—"they'll wake up in that golden city."

Will grunted a vague "Maybe."

"Touching that there city," said Caleb, "the gold of the street thereof will be transparent."

"I know," murmured Will, suppressing a yawn.

He knew! And the contradiction did not strike him! Instantly, as by another flash, the text solved itself in the old man's mind—gold in those millennial days, while it retained its sacred splendour would also lose its gross opaqueness, becoming rarefied, disembodied, spiritualized, so that gold was as brass since both were like glass, making thus a harmony of light with the jasper wall, clear as crystal, and the twelve giant pearls of the gates.

"It'll be a pritty sight!" he mused aloud.

"Yes, like the Crystal Palace," sneered Will.

"You seen that?" asked Caleb eagerly.

"A man couldn't be in London and escape seeing it," said Will. "Every cad drags you into his omnibus bound for Hyde Park. Such a crowd!"

"Yes, the chimney-sweep got his pocket picked, Bundock's buoy-oy was a-tellin'," said Caleb, "but the streets thereof, be they of gold?"

"The streets of London?" said Will, smiling.

"Noa, the streets of the Crystal City?"

"No, of course not, father."

"Then they can't be brass neither?"

"More like grass," Will laughed. "For there's real trees left standing inside."

Caleb joined in the boy's laugh. Though he had never really believed that the Crystal Palace represented the Millennial City, it was well to have the danger finally cleared away. And, abandoning the gold-brass puzzle, his mind flew back illogically but passionately to his Peculiar Brethren and the joy of the awaiting ritual.

"Ah, here's Plashy Hall!" said Will. "And the dog seems having his Sunday nap." He threw open the white gate marked "No thoroughfare!"

"But that's closed."

"Closed!" said Will in fiery accents. "I shan't even close it after us."

"I count they won't mind you in your Parlyment coat, but—"

"Go along, dad." And Will pushed the old man into Plashy Walk and strode forward like a village Hampden. Within a minute he missed Caleb, and looking back, saw him hurrying back from the gate.

"Must allus shut ga-aites!" he apologized with his rising accent.

"I'll burn it next time," said Will. "Why, this saves us a mile."

"But we'll miss the Early Sarvicers," complained Caleb. "You've forgot how they walk out to meet the Brethren, what come footin' it from afar, and have an extry sarvice at a half-way house back o' Long Bradmarsh."

"Surely the regular services will be enough."

"But 'tis noice to git an extry snack," said Caleb wistfully. "Many's the Sunday Oi've had foive sarvices." He sighed voluptuously.

"Well, better luck next time," said Will lightly.

The tone was not unkindly, but Caleb took it in full earnest, and his long secret grievance against Martha began to ooze into speech under the spell of his son's sympathy. Her warning against unsettling the boy was forgotten in this natural gravitation of male to male against female fantasy.

"Yes," he said, "I've allus been fast and faithful all along. 'Tis mother that's allus gooin' forrard. And woundily wilful—Oi never met nobody loike her, barrin' old Quarles. When we married we was both Sprinklers, but scarcely had we got six childer afore she says she must be baptoized. Wait till the summer, says Oi, for 'twas a black Feb'ary. But no—sow headlong is her natur' they had to break the ice. She give a deep soigh when the water took her—it a'most unhinged me. But she would have it she felt sow happy and contented. She drilled me hard to make me take the total immersion too—'nation obstinate is mother, but Oi've allus stood out stubborn for the Truth. Fast and faithful," he repeated, as if to reassure himself.

"Well, but you changed too!" Will reminded him less kindly. "You weren't born a Faith-Healer."

"That ain't my fault, bein' as the truth wasn't found out in my young days, though they warses o' Jeames was there all the time. But the fust day Oi met the Brethren Oi knowed they were the people for me. There was one on 'em among my own labourers. When Oi said as we didn't know 'zactly what God was, he said, says he: 'God's like you and me, bein' as He made man in His own image.' That was an eye-opener to me. But the others parsecuted him and called him Brother Jerusalem as a rewoilin' word. He had a fork to pitch a high load—cost foive shillin's, fancy what a good fork that must ha' been—and they went and broke it. Oi was grieved, but naught grieved him except to grieve the Lord. He dedn't drink neither, and you look so odd if you don't drink. But when they wanted to stand treat, he said he'd take bread and cheese. 'Goo to hell,' says they. 'There ain't no hell, even for you,' he answers soft; 'you'll be in the same darkness as now, that's all.' That was another eye-opener. Oi was taken with that hell—not bright and burnin', but all black and cowld—so Oi came out o' my darkness and jined the Brethren, and gave up beer, barrin' harvest-time, which rejoiced mother and was money saved for the childer. Be-yu-tiful things were brought to pass and be-yu-tiful things were said the day Oi went to my fust sarvice, and ef the Lord is with you to-day when you speak o' your experiences, Oi count be-yu-tiful things will be brought out agen."

Will shuddered. He stopped abruptly and was nigh turning back. He had forgotten that the Brethren would expect his soul-experiences and confessions—especially after this spacious and adventurous interval.

"What's-a-matter?" asked Caleb.

"Nothing, nothing," he said, remembering his own power of sullen silence. And to say something, he asked, as he walked on: "And what's wrong with mother now?"

"Wrong?" Caleb was shocked at this crude interpretation. "Oi don't be meanin' she ain't in her rights to hunt out new texts, she bein' a scholard. There was allus a bran-span-new one, Oi mind me, the Sundays I used to goo a-courtin' her. A wery long way she lived—they talk broad and careless where she comes from, not moist and proper like here—and Oi had to git up early and goo along the sea-wall—deadly dark and lonesome it was winter nights and mornin's, but her face was allus with me like the moon."

"Why, was she pretty then?" asked Will.

"Can't you see?" replied Caleb, with a faint surprise. "She ain't changed much, she havin' allus the peace of God in her heart."

Will was touched and astonished by this revelation of romance in the two elderly people foisted upon him as parents, whom he had all his life taken as eternally elderly. But still more surprising was the realization forced upon him that the religion which to him was a bore was to them a thrill.

"Shall I carry the parcel, father?" he asked gently.

"Nay, nay, that don't goo with Parlyment clothes. And it ain't as sizeable as the box you carried from Chipstone." He chuckled in freshly admiring glee.

Passing adown the long hawthorn avenue, they now issued from Plashy Walk, the rights of leg vindicated, and soon they began to see signs of other pilgrims faring towards Chipstone, that great gathering-place of faiths and creeds.

CHAPTER VI

SUNDAY AT CHIPSTONE

This zealot
Is of a mongrel, diverse kind;
Cleric before, and lay behind;
A lawless linsey-woolsey brother,
Half of one order, half another.
BUTLER, "Hudibras."

I

As old England has always been rich in "characters," in those grotesque or gnarled individualities that have escaped the common mould, the superabundance of sects, which, in conjunction with the paucity of sauces, amused Voltaire, has its natural explanation.

John Bull—himself a "character" among nationalities—could not long endure the Papal leading-strings, and ever since the days of Wycliffe a succession of free spirits has founded "heresies," not a few based on misunderstood mistranslations of Greek or Hebrew texts, torn from their literary and, above all, their historical context. But why during these five centuries Essex has been a breeding-place for Nonconformity, second to no other county, is a problem to tempt the philosopher. For its ministers have been silenced or ejected in numbers almost unparalleled; some indeed merely for tippling, dicing, carding, and womanizing, but the majority for the more serious offences of heresy or disrespect towards Parliament; while simple peasants—men, women, and girls—for their participation in seditious conventicles or practices, have been fined, jailed, transported to "His Majesty's plantations," and even nailed to stakes and burnt alive, clapping their hands the while with joy. Some of the most moving scenes of "Foxe's Book of Martyrs" and Bloomfield's "History of the Martyrs" are laid in Essex. Triumphant descendants of these opinionated saints were now converging on Chipstone from every quarter of the compass—it was but a toy-model of a town, yet it held in its petty periphery chapels, meeting-houses, or churches—ancient-towered or drably wooden or offering the image of a tinned congregation, tightly packed—for Baptists (Particular or General), Quakers, Wesleyans, Congregationalists, Peculiars, and Primitive Methodists, as well as your everyday Churchgoer; nothing indeed was wanting except an Ecclesia for the variation represented by Martha. And as most of these structures were in the High Street, or just off it, you beheld in that ancient thoroughfare of a Sunday a crowd of Christians, as like to the naked eye as a flock of sheep, sorting themselves into their denominational pigeon-holes, and disappearing as suddenly to right or left as the pedestrians in "The Vision of Mirza" vanished downwards through the trap-doors in the bridge.

Of all these types of Christian none seemed so indigenous to Essex as that aptly christened "Peculiar": it was as though peculiar to the marshes, an emanation of the soil. Though the first apostolic fervour was over in Chipstone, and the spirit was moving rather towards Woodham and Southend, the sect was still young and persecuted enough to be a devoted brotherhood, as Will soon realized from the greetings which his father exchanged with fellow-pilgrims, who grew more and more frequent as they drew nigh the outskirts of the theological town.

There was, among others, a cheerful-looking woman pushing a four-wheeled baby-cart, which held an infant back and front, and a food-parcel sandwiched between them. Caleb, addressing her as Sister, offered to wheel it, but she replied that the children would cry at a stranger. "Well, you'll soon be comin' to your destiny," said Caleb. But before Will and he had forged ahead of her, she had begun pouring out a premature confession. Two or three were gathered together, and the Spirit seemingly blew through her. That time last year she hadn't trusted the Lord: when they were wheeling the cart to chapel, she had wondered to her husband how she could fit in the coming baby. And the Lord had now made room by taking the prior baby, so that she was well chastised: moreover they had "parsecuted" her husband before a magistrate for not calling in a doctor for the child, but as it wasn't insured, they had only put him in prison for a little. All the same he was "broke up," having always been a "forthright" man. The Lord was indeed trying him by fire.

"Ay, 'twas the same, Willie, when your brother what's-a-name died," said Caleb as they drew ahead of the labouring baby-cart. "But the Brethren now exhort one another not to insure their childer, Satan being swift to cry child-murder."

"But isn't it child-murder if a doctor might have saved it?" asked Will coldly, for the woman's story had shocked him.

Caleb looked pained. "Ef the Lord wouldn't listen even to prayers, is it likely He'd regard doctors? Howsomever the Brethren stand fast and faithful—they goo to prison even at harvest-time when you're worth forever o' money. But the Lord's people are wunnerful good to one another, and the Elders look arter the families. Oh, what a joyous Harvest Thanksgivin' we had two years agoo, time the martyrs came out o' their cells. All in the open air it was, and Deacon Mawhood brought out be-yu-tiful lessons. No matter you lost your harvest money, he says, you won the palm and the crown, and 'tis the Second Harvest in the heavenly fields with angels to squinch your thirst from golden wessels that shall be yourn, says the Deacon."

Will received the rat-catcher's rhetoric with a snort, which put Caleb again on the defensive.

"Oi've never took no medicine for ten year," said Caleb. "And look at me!"

"Well, I've taken plenty," said Will. "And look at me!"

"Oi allow Oi ain't a Samson like you," admitted Caleb honestly, "nor couldn't carry a box that far. And when Oi say no medicine, Oi don't mean when Oi'm not ill. For same as Oi'm well, mother makes me take a little pill afore meals, bein' a wegeble as stops the gripes. There ain't naught about that in the Bible, seein' as the text starts onny when you git sick. And arter she lost your brother Jim—or maybe he was Zecharoiah—she did fetch a doctor for the tothers, argufyin' that when the child's too young to seek grace of itself, oil inside ain't no wuss than oil outside. And then they Christy Dolphins come along—"

"Who are they?" inquired Will.

But Caleb drew up with a sudden remembrance. "You'll find that out for yourself. They ain't far from Daniel."

"Live on the Common, do you mean?"

"Noa—there ain't none near us—there was two in Long Bradmarsh, but they've gone back to the Joanna prophet woman, so your poor mother ain't got—" he broke off again. "Oi don't say ef mother was took real bad, Oi shouldn't goo and git Doctor Gory, seein' as she threatens to goo for him same as Oi'm ill. It ain't the doctor, it's the faith, says mother, and so long as you don't believe in the doctor, there ain't no harm in lettin' him thump you about. So long as your heart turns to God, says mother, the doctor can listen to it all he likes."

"Then you do have the doctor!" Will was amused at these compromises exacted by his masterful mother, whose heretical evolution after the loss of offspring he could, however, well understand.

"Noa—noa, not for us—leastways not yet," Caleb protested. "That was onny for the childer. That made us feel free."

"Free?" Will queried.

"Not responsible like." He was somewhat embarrassed. "Faith-healin' ain't the main thing," he expounded anxiously, "it's faith-gittin'; it's lovin' God and seekin' His grace, just as you're doin' to-day."

Will was silent.

"Bless me!" cried Caleb suddenly. "Ef that don't look tempesty!"

Will's eyes went skywards and found indeed a livid patch of gloom, like a ghastly sag of sky, suddenly splotched in the warm blue. And as he looked, a zigzag flash stabbed through it.

"Quick," cried Caleb, indicating a fairly leafy oak, "git under that tree!"

"No, no," said Will, "it's dangerous." And a terrible peal of thunder accentuated his words.

"Oi'll hazard it," said Caleb, hastening towards the shelter. "The Lord is marciful—He can kill us when He pleases. He ain't got no need o' lightnin'. But that's gooin' to pour like billyho—and the rine falls alike on the just and the unjust—unless the roighteous man's got an umberrella."

Will smiled, though humour was as far as ever from Caleb's intentions. Unwilling to desert the old man, and perhaps weighing the improbability of an electric stroke against the certainty of spoiling his jacket, and the last surviving sheen of his boots, Will stood pluckily beside his parent, while, after another celestial salvo, great drops began to patter on the leaves and even to drip through them. "Lucky that thunder dedn't come in the middle o' last night," mused the old man gratefully as it roared on. "It's sech a bother dressin' yourself agen to set up till it stops. Hark at they Tommy Devils squealin'," he cried, indicating the startled swifts. But after a few minutes Caleb's patience gave out: the distant chiming of Chipstone Church bells, with which the way had been piously enlivened, was now chillingly inaudible; the thought that they would be late for chapel gnawed at his heart; and dryness seemed a poor equivalent for those missed moments of spiritual ecstasy. He was about to dash through the storm, when the rain ceased as suddenly as it came, the blackbirds began to whistle and forage merrily, and the sun, bursting out more brilliantly than ever, soon licked up the modicum of moisture that had percolated to their Sunday exterior. But Caleb's apprehensions were justified. He had overrated the pace of his aged legs, and despite the gain through Plashy Walk, he got no compensation for the missed

Half-Way Service, for when they arrived at the little meeting-house, the Morning Service proper had begun.

II

The chapel of the Peculiars was one of the minor religious edifices that did not aspire to the High Street. Behind an iron gate and a petty stone courtyard, it displayed a gabled front, with a roof of pantiles, and a row of dull windows of an ecclesiastical order on either side.

As Will passed through the door, all his tardily born sympathy vanished, and a wave of the old insufferable boredom smote him like a breath of the steerage on his Atlantic steamer. Almost ere his hat was off, his eye had taken in the whole once-familiar scene, the painfully crude walls, a little dingier with the passing of the years, the broad table-desk at the head of the hall, at which Deacon Mawhood and the Elders throned it in Sunday black, the rows of spruce wooden chairs sexually divided by a gangway, and exhibiting in its left section a desert of elderly females with a few oases of hobbledehoy girls. He thought of St. Paul's Cathedral, and calculated whimsically that if that cost twopence to see, how much ought one not to pay to escape seeing this!

But if his entry meant ennui to himself, it was a most dramatic event to the congregation. At first, indeed, this stranger in the fashionable jacket was not associated with Caleb, whose return to the fold was a separate thrill. It was believed for an instant that a veritable gentleman had succumbed to the Truth, and even when it was perceived that he was no other than Will Flynt, the news of whose home-coming had reached the majority, the sensation did not abate, for was not God still visibly with His peculiar flock, turning back the hearts of the wanderers, whether of the old generation or the young? A breath of new inspiration shook the hall, and the grey-haired Brother who had just begun reading the thirteenth chapter of Acts faltered in his mispronunciation of Cyrene. As he went on droning out the chapter—surely the longest in the Bible, chosen maliciously to depress him further, thought Will—its burden of the people of God, set for a light to the Gentiles, evoked a mounting exaltation, and those who had come with no thought of testifying, found themselves possessed of the Spirit. There was in particular a man with mutton-chop whiskers, on the bench in front of Will, whose body swayed with excitement, and who punctuated the reading with breathless jerks of nasal interpolation. "Be-yu-tiful!" "Yes!" "Amen!" "Thank Gord!" "Mercy!" and the like. And when at last the chapter ended on the verse "And the disciples were filled with joy and with the Holy Ghost," it lifted the man to his feet and he poured forth the story of his sinful past.

"Oi was Church of England—in the choir—and wore black and whoite gowns—and rang the bells—and was confirmed and all—but Gord had never pardoned my sins."

Will stifled a yawn and looked towards the door. But the rest of the audience hung upon the tale—the tale of a death-bed repentance of Churchmanship and the miraculous recovery to lead the better life of the Peculiar Brotherhood.

"Oi asked the Elder to howd up my hands, so that Oi might die praising Gord for the revelation."

Sobs came from the left benches, but they only fevered Will. He sat in a dull fury, dazed by words that passed over his brain without leaving a meaning.

"Oh, what a thronging boy and boy—a land where we shall never say 'Good noight'—engraved in eternal brass—the Lord shoines on your heart—sheep and goats—streets paved with pure gold as it were transparent glass!" It was not till he felt his arm clutched by Caleb in the old man's excitement at hearing this last phrase that Will connected such words with reality at all, and they faded back into mere religion till a sudden mention of "John in the oil of Patmos" shot up a quaint picture of a too profuse anointment.

Other speakers followed with the same transcendental vocabulary, and then hymns, in an interval between which, the black-garmented Deacon with a royal gesture, that seemed to sweep away the remotest effluvium of aniseed or moleskins, sent Will a hymn-book by a deferentially wriggling Brother. It seemed an ironic revenge for the book he had flung into the bushes, but it saved him from the oppressive proximity of his father's, which he had been sharing; for the old man, though he could not read the book, liked to hold it as he had always held it with Martha, and indeed could not have sung without feeling it at his fingers' ends. Will turned its pages with curiosity, thinking of Bundock's "village idiot," and noting that it was still published by a village barber. Then a gaunt, horn-spectacled man was seized of the Spirit.

"I've been looking for a han'kercher," he began, to Will's surprise. "I've been looking for a han'kercher," he repeated. "I've been looking for a han'kercher," he recapitulated with rising rhetoric, "to wipe my tears away." But the thrilling level, of this exordium was not maintained, and the stock phrases started again, merciless, unendurable, beating on Will's brain till they beat vainly against the depths of his reverie—or was it his doze? Ah, surely that was Jinny's horn at last! No, it was only his father blowing emotionally into his red cotton handkerchief—too huge to need looking for—a duplicate of that which held their meals. Besides, Jinny wouldn't be blowing her horn of a Sunday. But why didn't she come to chapel, the graceless minx? Was she careering around with that Farmer Gale, or was it her grandfather's illness?

If flighty young girls, with hearts sound at bottom, would come here and unfold the error of their independent ways, the practice of confession might be justified, and chapel-service become both useful and exciting. But these faded people, these ungainly men and fubsy females! Who on earth cared for their drab histories? Ah, there was Mother Gander, not so podgy as most—in the blue silk of auld lang syne—if only she would get up—or even Charley Mott—there would be some spark of interest. But no, the horn-spectacled bore held the floor pitilessly, and the phrases beat on.

"Be-yu-tiful, be-yu-tiful words—I thought I should die!—Poor me! What a comfort in them words!"

And the nasal voice, its fervour unallayed by its own outpouring, still punctuated the other speeches with jerky interpolations. "Praise the Lord!" or "Glory!" came with fiery iteration, and sometimes this saint with the mutton-chop whiskers said "Lord bless me!" or "Lord bless my soul!" and these frayed and almost meaningless ejaculations seemed full of a startling significance in his mouth and nose.

"Brother Bridges, they said to me, how's your soul? I couldn't give 'em a straightforward answer."

Will woke up again. It was not now the horn-spectacled speaker—he had apparently been wiped off the floor at last, and was not even visible—it was a man with a humorous twinkle and a red beard.

"But if they had asked me, how's your body—?"

There was a faint snigger from a thick-set girl, instantly repressed by her shocked mother; but after Will had extracted what relief he could from this incident, he tried vainly to extract from the anecdote the exciting edification it held for the others. "How can I go to Romford and tell people I haven't got salvation?" A dramatic crisis indeed for all save Will, who did not even stifle his yawn. The man's journey to Romford seemed infinitely unimportant compared with journeys going on every Tuesday and Friday, and despitefully checked on Sunday.

Once the door opened, but it was only for a shambling youth in his teens, and Will did not share the satisfaction of the congregation at this new, if belated, proof of their vitality.

"We're not afeared, no, not the humblest of us," pursued the red-bearded man, catching fresh inspiration from this continuous rise in their numbers. "And why? Because we don't go to work without a Partner."

Here at last was a definite image through the blur, and if Will in a vivid flash saw a working-partner for himself in a less sublime incarnation than the speaker had in mind, he was for once as a-quiver as his father, who now, albeit with the stock exclamation of "Be-yu-tiful!" proceeded to add real tears to the contents of his capacious handkerchief.

When Will became attentive again, it was a new voice testifying, and the matter seemed quite sensational.

"They used to be carried away and buried in a day. But when our Brother Bundock's boy got it, we had a special prayer-meeting, and even the marks were light!"

Oh! So it was only the postman's smallpox. He looked round in vain for Her Majesty's servant: indeed a general consciousness that the hero of the story was ungratefully absent, damped its appeal—only the man with the mutton-chop whiskers called out with unabated ardour, "Glory!" Will felt that the glory was to Bundock, thus valiantly sticking to his lack of convictions. More than even during the last week, life at Little Bradmarsh seemed impossible, as impossible as in his boyhood; better had he rushed with the mob of his mates to California; even now it was probably the best thing to do with his ninety pounds, unmanly though it were to flee and leave this girl carrier with her arrogance unbroken.

In her absence, if only one of the females would get up! That would be at least a change. But no! The sex was shy to-day, though the forenoon was, he remembered, the traditional time for its testifyings. Perhaps it was the presence of this stalwart young stranger that tongue-tied it.

But the males seemed to be telling their soul-stories at him, challenging his eye, appealing to his black jacket—or was that only a morbid impression of his? An outsider might have been touched by the thread of spiritual poetry in these outwardly commonplace lives, but Will, being of them, had the familiarity that breeds boredom, if not contempt. And contempt, too, was not wanting to this elegantly clad and much-travelled connoisseur of men and women and creeds, who had seen even French cathedrals in Canada, and knew that Roman Catholics were not the scarlet beasts his infancy had somehow imagined them. Once he caught Mr. Charles Mott's eye fixed upon him with a curious, wondering gaze, which seemed to change to a wink as eye met eye. Will's eye, however, remaining serious, a flush overspread the ex-potboy's face, and he looked away.

But Will's contempt passed into alarm when, at a sudden pause in the testifyings, all other eyes unquestionably converged on him. He turned as red as Charley Mott, and glued his eyes to his hymn-book, not daring to look up till another voice indicated that the Spirit had found a more willing tongue for its organ. But his relief was mixed with disgust, for it was the dry voice of the original grey-haired reader, and it seemed bent on a sermon which had not even the mitigated brightness of a confession. Then, autobiography seemed suddenly to break through it, for Will's wandering thoughts were fixed by an anecdote about riding to Rochester seven miles on a donkey on a winter's evening. "Lord bless me!" interpolated the nasal voice, so distracting Will that he never understood how the story led up to a doctor's remark: "I must have your leg off," a design the medical materialist appeared to have carried out.

Will tried to peer under the table to see the preacher's peg, but failing to perceive any signs of corkiness, concluded that the anecdote was not personal. He gathered that after this melancholy amputation by impotent Science, Faith had sufficed to keep the rest of the man together. Medicine had subsequently proclaimed he was in a galloping consumption, "but he ain't dead yet—he's still sound and whole," cried the preacher paradoxically, to the applausive "Glory!" of the tireless commentator.

Another illustrious example of regeneration—the preacher kept Will awake by recounting—had begun life as a parson. But none is beyond hope; even in the sacristy one is not safe from the Spirit, and unable to go any longer through the flummeries and mummeries of the Established Church, he had given up his living and fallen—at one time—so low that he was glad to become a potman in a public-house.

All eyes were here turned towards the unfortunate Charley Mott, and from his squirming figure to Mother Gander, sitting so stern and stiff; but the tension relaxed when the preacher—perhaps tactfully—went on to mention that it was at "The White Hart" in Colchester: where the landlord and landlady had both "parsecuted" him. They were now both dead. ("Glory!" from the nasal punctuator.) "I am sorry they are dead," said the preacher magnanimously. "But the Lord's arm is not short." And while they were well dead, Will learnt that their poor, persecuted potman had now a chapel of his own, where he preached "Full Salvation." Twenty or thirty were, it appeared, saved regularly and punctually every Sunday evening. "Glory!" trumpeted the nasal voice, and again Will, sullen and glowering, felt that the whole congregation was palpitating with expectation that he would leap to his feet and declare himself similarly saved, or at least not lost during his long absence. But he was not going to make a fool of himself, he told himself harshly. He would sooner face the ordeal of escape, of running the gauntlet of the Brothers and Sisters, and he looked round wildly towards the door, perceiving with satisfaction that the late youth had left it slightly ajar. Then, to his joy and the congregation's disappointment, another worshipper took the word, or was taken by it; Bidlake, the bargee, with his dog-eyes now shining and his shaggy face sublimated, who declared with touching fervour that he would praise God as long as breath was in him, and with the death-rattle in his throat he would cry: "You can do, Gord, what you like with me!" Ephraim recalled the coup by which he had converted his wife, whom family sorrows had made an infidel. "Ef you won't goo to heaven with me, says Oi, Oi'll goo to hell with you!" Now they both pulled and poled together and were happy—so happy, despite family losses and troubles. "Most men ain't fit to live nor ready to die. Just drifters. Throw 'em the life-line—the life-line afore they drift away!" And with a vivid gesture he threw an imaginary rope. By accident or design it was in Will's direction, and again the poor young man, with a stifling sense of being lassoed, became the cynosure of every eye. But, fortunately for him, Ephraim Bidlake did not pause here, and his rhapsody poured on; "Glorious truth"—"one generation to the tother"—"the prayer of roighteousness"—"come as you are"—"wain to trust in man"—a veritable cascade of phrases that, falling on Will's head, gradually lowered it in sleep. An impromptu speech is usually one the speaker cannot wind up, and the worthy bargee went on tangling himself up more and more, till it looked doubtful if he would ever have come to a stop, had not something happened which stole even his breath away.

Through the interstice of the door came suddenly sidling a little white dog. But this accession to the congregation produced no joy, merely a sense of profanity as it pattered up the central parting, leaving, moreover, wet prints of its paws. Springing without hesitation or apology upon the sleeper's best trousers, it curled itself up comfortably with a grunt. Assuredly Will was not fated to-day to escape the centre of the stage.

The young man recognized Nip instantly, and his yawn of awakening changed into a gasp, and his somnolent pulse into a precipitate beat. The animal's leap was indeed sudden enough to startle the strongest heart. Will turned his head instinctively towards the door—oblivious even of his damped trousers—but there was no sign of Nip's mistress. Still, whether she was in the vicinity or not, the dog was clearly out of place. Grasping his pretext of escape firmly by the collar and clasping his struggling opportunity to his breast, he stole from the meeting-house.

III

He expected to see Nip's owner outside. In his reading of the situation she had arrived so late that while she was hesitating whether to come in, the shameless dog had burst through the door, attracted doubtless by the aroma of all those dinner-packets, and this had made her still more ashamed to enter. But the quaint little street was bare of Jinny. So sunless did it appear without her, that he scarcely noticed that the sky was actually overcast again, and that the black cloud had regathered. He stood still, hesitating; in which relaxed mood of his the spasmodic struggles of the animal were successful, and Will became painfully aware that he was alone with his moist trousers and his London coat snowed over with little hairs, while Nip, after some preliminary gambollings and barkings at the recovery of the liberty he had himself abandoned, was vanishing into the High Street. So assured were Nip's movements that Will divined at once he had only to follow him to restore him to his mistress, and without waiting even to brush off the little white hairs, he darted towards the street corner, and was happily just in time to see the excellent creature trotting into the courtyard of "The Black Sheep."

His pleasure was not, however, free from surprise. What was Jinny doing at her business headquarters on the Lord's Day? Or had she come in her cart to chapel, and put it up there? He ran towards the picturesque stable-yard. There were a good many chaises, gigs, dog-carts and even carriages standing—the countryside drove to its churches—but there was no trace of either Jinny or Methusalem, while Nip was standing with hang-dog air by the doorstep, under a poster of "Duke's Marionettes." But as Will drew nearer, he turned tail, sauntered down the passage, surveyed the painted hand, and then with an air of decision bounded up the stairs. Ah, she would be in the parlour! And Nip's follower bounded upstairs too, keeping closely to heel. But no! Nip was not on dining bent, though the door was open. Rejecting all the appetizing scents that already emanated from the eating-room, Nip pit-patted along the dusky corridor and began whining and scrabbling outside a closed and numbered door. Very soon it receded before his pleadings; and as he scampered in, "You poor dog!" came out in the girlish voice that had so lacerated him with "Fol de rols!" But not the worst of that musical torment could vie with the jar to his heart-strings when, through the reclosing door, came another unforgettable voice with the jovial interrogatory: "Well, Nip, and what was the parson's text?"

He remembered now—with a cold sick horror—that this was the very bedroom from which indignant housemaids had excluded its tenant—yes, there was Reynard opposite with his glassy eye and his erected brush. Possibly Tony Flip was not even up. That was what came of minxes driving Methusalems! Instead of being at divine service, like all God-fearing humanity, she was coquetting—or worse—with a mountebank in an inn bedroom. Yet he felt he must not spy upon her—any moment, too, she might come out—and he hurried downstairs and stood on the step under the ironwork lamp, louring like the great black cloud, which he now perceived to be in heaven-sent harmony with his mood. And that drivelling patriarch had foamed at the mouth when he had hinted that woman's place was not a cart!

But Jinny did not keep him more than five endless minutes.

"Hullo, Will," she cried gaily, as she tripped from the passageway with Nip in her arms. "What are you doing here?"

How the broad frame of her bonnet set off the picture of her face! Small wonder a loose-living showman found it bewitching. Not so William Flynt—with his high ideals of womanhood! Even to be called "Will" was provoking rather than flattering: he felt it now less the perquisite of the old friend than the proof of an indiscriminating levity.

"I've come for the dinner," he said coldly. Nip gazed straight at him with his mild brown eye, but although Will did not suppose that the brute would open its mouth like Balaam's ass and give him away, he could not look it in the head. He turned his shoulder on dog and damsel and stared at the poster.

"I wish I could have dinner with you," replied Jinny frankly. "But I must be off to feed Gran'fer. Farmer Gale's trap should be here by now."

"He drives you home too?" He turned towards her, startled.

"Within half a mile—it is a treat for me to have another carrier."

"But he isn't a Peculiar," he observed severely.

"No, he's a Wesleyan like Gran'fer, who used to drive his father about. He puts up at 'The Chequers' hard by his chapel—his service ought to be over. I hope his horse hasn't taken fright again—we had just got to the High Street when the storm broke, and at the first flash the horse was off, galloped miles beyond the town before he could be got to a standstill."

"He might have killed you, the silly!" cried Will, meaning the farmer.

"Yes," said Jinny simply, meaning the animal. "By the time he was walked warily back, it was too late to go in. But I don't wonder Nip was worried about me. You see he likes to run behind the trap, poor fellow"—she wasted a kiss upon his unresponsive head—"and he always comes up in time to say good-bye at the chapel door, where he hangs about till I come out. But this time, of course, he must have been wandering about in search of me. He wasn't there when I passed just now. Mr. Flippance declares he must have gone to Chipstone Church, in the idea I'd suddenly joined it."

And the girlish laugh rang out, dissipating some of his humours as much by its joyousness as by the innocent mention of the Showman.

"But why shouldn't you join it, Miss Quarles?" he said. "It can't be duller than chapel."

"Now, now, Will." She shook a serious finger. "You ought to have gone to chapel yourself this morning. And don't call me Miss Quarles."

"But I prefer to call you Miss Quarles."

"But why not Jinny?" Her voice was plaintive.

"Because everybody else calls you that."

"Is that any reason why you should call me Miss Quarles?"

"If you can't see it—!" he began.

"I can't, and I hope you won't call me Miss Quarles."

"And why shouldn't I?"

"Because I won't answer to it."

"And why not?"

"Because, Will, it's not my name."

He gasped. "Not your name?"

She laughed merrily at his discomfiture. "It's a long story and Farmer Gale will be here. Hulloa," she went on, making his confusion worse confounded, "how did Nip's hairs get on you?"

He flushed, and flicked nervously at his coat. "There are other white dogs," he said evasively.

"Well, don't let him spoil your coat."

"And what about your bodice?"

"Oh, mine isn't new and Londony."

He was gratified at her perception: still more at her setting down Nip. That animal, however, was in the rampageous mood which always followed his restoration to freedom, and he began leaping up at his mistress's hand.

"Down, Nip, down! Oh, I do believe he's bitten through my new glove!" She pulled it off ruefully to examine the damage.

"Sensible dog!" Will growled. "He knows you oughtn't to be wearing Mr. Flippance's gloves."

Her own little white teeth flashed out in a mocking smile: "Lucky you are going to buy me another pair!"

"Me! Why, you wouldn't let me when I offered."

"Of course not. I'm thinking of the pair you'll be owing me."

"Owing you?"

"You don't suppose you'll win the wager, do you?"

"Oh, that!" He was disconcerted again. "Of course I'll win it," he said defiantly in a bombastic burst. "It won't take me a day's practice to blow down the walls of Jericho."

She laughed. "So you do remember your Bible. Well, I'll be satisfied if you blow Nip back from a rabbit."

"We shall see. Have you superscribed again?" he asked pompously, assured of his accuracy this time.

"Not yet—I expect the horn'll be at Chipstone by Tuesday—you shall have it the same evening."

"And the next day I'll be wanting gloves," he said loftily.

"We shall see—or rather hear. What size do you take, though?"

"Oh, I don't know—twice yours, I suppose."

"Oh, not twice!"

"Why, sure!" And he suddenly prisoned her little ungloved hand between his brawny palms. "I could easily crush it," he said, with a strange desire to do so, pressing it indeed almost to hurting-point. At that instant a far-palpitating blueness transfigured the courtyard, and from above-stairs came a terrific racket as if all the plates and dishes in the dining-room were hurling themselves at one another. Will felt the girl's fingers curl spasmodically round his and hold them tight: her face went white, and he seemed to hear her heart thumping.

"Don't be frightened!" he said, with his first manly satisfaction in her. Surely she was clinging to him for protection.

"That'll be a fireball down the chimney," she observed with disappointing coolness. "There was one came down last year in Long Bradmarsh and killed a poor little chimney-sweep who had got stuck in the flue. It'll set the chimney on fire, I expect."

"This rain will put it out," he said, still cheerfully conscious of her warm fingers, and feeling a joy in the deluge that had been so damp in his father's company. She drew back, however, into the passage to avoid the big plopping and ricochetting rain-drops and her hand got disentangled. "What fun if it's fallen down Mr. Flippance's chimney," she laughed. "Make him get up early."

Her laughter seemed to ring untrue, hysterical.

"Isn't he up yet?" he asked, trying to speak lightly.

"Oh, he never gets up on a Sunday—not properly, I mean. I saw him half up, but he's gone back to bed and is already snoring—I heard him."

"But how could you hear him?" he asked, with careful carelessness.

"Oh, I was in his daughter's room, whiling away the time of waiting—she's got ten times his sense—when, woke up by our voices, I suppose, in he trails through the communicating door in his fancy dressing-gown, yawning like a mouse-trap, and asks me to buy him a horse at the fair."

"A horse at the fair!" Scarcely had he enjoyed the relief of working out that he had taken the harmless adjoining bedroom for the Showman's, when this new blow struck him, like hooves on his chest.

"Of course I wouldn't listen to him," she said.

"Of course not!" His breast expanded again. "How can a woman understand buying horses?"

"Oh, I don't mean that." Jinny was distinctly colder. "I mean it's the Lord's Day. He'll have to repeat his order on Tuesday."

"But surely you wouldn't go to a horse fair?"

"Why not?"

"Because—it's—it's so horsey."

She laughed again. "And so fairish, too, isn't it?"

"What does he want a horse for?" he asked sullenly.

"I don't suppose it's for dinner—he isn't a Frenchy. But he's got a caravan, hasn't he?—and he has to begin his summer tour soon."

"And why can't he buy his own horses?"

"That infant? Why his last horse died of old age at four!"

"And what about that sensible daughter of his?"

"She hasn't got horse-sense," said Jinny, smiling.

"Well, I don't see how it comes into your business."

"A carrier has to buy whatever she's asked."

"Whatever she can carry. You can't carry a horse."

"No, but it can carry me. Besides, I've often carried a calf or a pig, and where am I to draw the line?"

"You'll be buying elephants next," he said, with a bitter remembrance of Mr. Flippance's story.

"I'm too old for gingerbread," she replied unexpectedly. "But I haven't forgotten the one you gave me once." He trembled under her radiant gratitude, with its evocation of the poetry of childhood. But a convulsive bound forward on the part of Nip broke up the argument. "Ah, here's Farmer Gale coming along," she said cheerfully.

Just like the fellow, he thought, to come just at that moment. And his resentment at the arrival of the dog-cart was not even mitigated by the watery spectacle presented by its red-faced driver, whose personable and still youthful figure rose from a streaming tarpaulin, to which a hat with an unremoved mourning-band contributed its drippings.

"You can't go in that rain," Will protested. "Let him go without you—I'll order a trap myself."

"But you said you were dining here—I can't wait."

He winced—his white lie had come home like a curse to roost.

"You can dine with me!"

"And what about Gran'fer?"

"Well, I can dine at home." But she scarcely heard him. She was already fastening a handkerchief over her Sunday bonnet—a fascinating process. "There's a good cover—I'll snuggle right in."

Shameless, he thought, riding about cheek by jowl and skirt by trouser with a young man not even of her own faith. That thin tiny boy sandwiched between was no real separation: why, the tarpaulin almost swallowed him under! They ought at least to sit back to back, and if there was any chivalry in the pudding-faced lout, he would transfer the tarpaulin to the back seat. How could Jinny forget that the magnate of Little Bradmarsh—cursèd Cornish interloper—was no fit company for the likes of her? He wondered that people did not warn her: but they were inured to her vagaries, he supposed. And even if the man meant honourably, in his reckless passion, how dare a widower with a great thumping boy approach a rosebud? Ah, now she was talking to this second-hand, warmed-up aspirant, who had already killed off one wife; inquiring sweetly about his animal's behaviour under the recent flash.

"Steady as a plough-horse!" came the cheery reply. "My eye, Jinny, you did handle him wonderful. I reckon you saved my life!"

"And what about my own?" With a laugh whose gaiety stabbed, she sprang upon the step. "Good-bye, Will. Hope you'll enjoy your dinner."

"Good-bye, Miss Quarles," he said coldly. "I mean, Miss—" But before he had realized he could not fill up the blank, the trap had started, and he could not even bound behind, like the joyous-barking Nip. Nothing tangible was left of the whole delectable and distressing episode except some white hairs on the fashionable fabric of Moses & Son.

"Hope you'll enjoy your dinner!" Her last words still rang in his ear. His dinner! Cold meat wrapped in a "muckinger," and consumed on chapel benches among drab Elders and elderly Sisters and better-lost Brothers and dismal rat-catching Deacons. No, sooner a crust and cheese at the bar. But why not roast beef and Yorkshire pudding in the parlour—why not make his lie true? Yes, lies were reprehensible: truth was always best, and his chaps began to water with ethical excitement. But alas, with a sudden misgiving he put his hand in his pocket. Not a farthing! In the agitation of his chapel-going, he had forgotten to transfer his purse to the Sunday suit—nay, even the ninety pounds were left in the discarded waistcoat, he remembered with an unreasonable chill. He was to be nailed to his lie, then. True, he might possibly get credit, but it was an awkward situation at best. No, better go back to his cold meat—besides, his poor old father would be wondering and waiting. It would be cruel to desert and distract him, and, the rain appearing somewhat thinner, he turned up his coat-collar and started out, almost colliding at the archway with the Mott couple, lovingly entwined under a spacious umbrella. They at least had no need to dine in chapel. Mr. Charles Mott looked at him again with the same curious wonder. "You're not going back?" he cried involuntarily.

"I can't desert my dad!" Will answered, somewhat shamefacedly.

"And he must eat, Charley darling," Mother Gander intervened. "You know how bad our Sunday dinners are."

"I haven't even got any money with me," he cried, with a last wild hope. But Mother Gander did not respond to his longing for truth. "Lend him the umbrella, dearest," she said ruthlessly. "We've another for the afternoon service."

Accepting it with mitigated gratitude—the umbrella he was trusted with was worth more than the dinner, he thought bemusedly—he moved more slowly to the chapel; wondering, too, how hotel-keeping could be reconciled with the Sabbatarian conscience.

He found the meeting-house now turned into an eating-house. The congregation had, however, visibly thinned: only those who had no hosts or homes in Chipstone remaining for this love-feast, with the exception of Deacon Mawhood, who, rather than go home to his wife, remained at the table as presiding dignitary, flanked by great glass jugs of water. The ravages in the ranks appeared to Will an eloquent testimony to the spread of the doctrine in Chipstone proper: in his young days the sect had been more suburban and rural, and the chapel at that hour had seethed with hungry pilgrims. Still, there was quite a happy hubbub, and the spectacle, with its real sense of brotherhood, struck from him more sympathy than anything in the service; and when a Sister told her cherub not to "goffle" so, he was mysteriously touched by the old word, and the memories it roused, to a sincerer respect for the creed which satisfied Jinny. What fun the boys had had in the wagon, driving home with her!

Caleb was chewing a hunk of bread and meat. The handkerchief-parcel—shrunk like the congregation—incarnadined the bench. "Oi had to begin," he explained apologetically, "seein' as Oi'd said grace, expectin' you back every second, and it seemed foolin' with the Lord to wait more than ten minutes. Pity that dog worried you. Be-yu-tiful things were brought out when you was gone. Where did you git to?"

He evaded the question. "I'm not hungry."

"Not arter that walk of ourn!" cried Caleb incredulously. "Oi count you've had your dinner somewhere else."

"Yes, off the dog!" he said a bit crossly.

Caleb smiled. "Oi'll not believe that," he said with an air of infinite cuteness.

"I'll have a drink," condescended Will.

"Do!" Caleb passed him a large tin mug of water. "And there's plenty more where that come from." Will knew it was Brother Quint—the "snob" or shoemaker who lived next door—who supplied these limitless streams.

"Ain't she beautifully polished?" Caleb went on naïvely, when his thirsty son set the mug down. "Holds noigh a quart—Oi never see sech mugs nowhere else! And Brother Quint'll fill it with biling for our tea. There, Will! There's your favourite sausages mother put in for you, special. None o' your dogs in that!" And he chuckled, brimming over with holy glee.

Cooled by the long draught, Will allowed himself to be seduced by the veal sausages, and, finding with surprise that the first slid down his throat in a twinkling, he was soon depleting the parcel into a mere "muckinger." And at this Caleb's innocent happiness was complete.

But the fate that stalks mortals at their culminating felicities now sped its arrow. In excavating a pickled walnut from the remains of the parcel, Caleb loosed a minute cardboard box, which sprang maliciously to the floor and then, to the agitation of the neighbours, rolled round and round towards the table under the very eyes of the rat-catcher.

The Deacon stooped down zealously to pick it up, and then held it on high. It was a pill-box! "Who brought this?" he cried in stern prophetic accents, across the table.

The happy hubbub ceased, the holy glee was frozen. In a tense silence all eyes were turned on the profane symbol. Will saw his wretched father's face go red and white, and his scraggy throat work painfully below the ragged white beard. Both the Flynts guessed at once that the careful Martha had slipped into the packet her husband's usual pill before meals!

It was a dreadful moment. For a space in which all nature seemed to hold its breath, Caleb sat rigid and dumb.

"Whose propity is this?" asked the Deacon still more sternly, and Will divined the mighty struggle going on in his father's quaint conscience; casuistic questions as to how far a pill-box conveyed unconsciously had been "brought" by him, or in what sense pills administered to him remorselessly from without could be said to be his "property."

Then suddenly Caleb's lips opened. "Oi count 'twas in my parcel," he said in tremulous accents.

The sublimity of the confession thrilled Will: he even felt a curious moisture at his eyes. But before the Deacon, sitting there like a judge about to pronounce sentence, could say a word, a blinding glare, followed almost instantaneously by an appalling crashing and smashing right overhead, showed that nature had indeed held its breath and had now spoken in flame and thunder. Will's first reflection when the daze had passed away, and the congregation found itself and its building providentially safe, was that it was indeed lucky his father had spoken first; otherwise his confession might have seemed extorted by terror. But Joshua Mawhood was not the Deacon to let such a situation pass without profit. "The Lord havin' spoke, brethren," said he, "there ain't no need for my opinion. The thing Oi hate most in this lower world is hypocrisy and dissemblin'. 'Roight up and down, Jo Perry,' as the sayin' goos. Ef we ain't been destroyed, as we sat here guzzlin' and guttlin', 'tain't no merit of the congregation, 'tis because the Lord bein' marciful don't destroy Sodom and Gomorrah so long as there's one roighteous man." He rose majestically and drew himself up to his full height, and held the pill-box even higher. "Brother Flynt, if you'll kindly step out, Oi'll hand you back your propity."

No fiercer punishment could have been devised for Caleb's gentle soul: the sinner, isolated, passing through his shrinking Brethren and Sisters, must come forward as to a confession table. No wonder the poor man held back.

"Oi don't need it now, Deacon," he said, with lips almost as white as his hair. "You can throw it away ef you like."

With malicious enjoyment the Deacon slowly and solemnly lifted the lid of the pill-box and dipped in his fingers, to hold up the impious contents to the public execration. Then his face changed.

"Why, it's salt!" he cried in angry disappointment. It was as if the devil were playing thimblerig with him.

"Oi was thinkin' the missus had ought to put some in," said Caleb, beaming again.

The woman of the baby-cart now found herself possessed of the Spirit. She sprang to her feet, a baby on either arm.

"We are the salt of the earth," she shrilled, "wherewith the others shall be salted."

"Hallelujah!" burst from the mutton-chop whiskers.

"Hallelujah!" responded the congregation, and a great anthem rolled out, outshouting the thunder.

V

To the disappointment of his father, who still hoped he would testify, Will would not stay for the Afternoon Service. But his worthy sire could bear a disappointment after the revulsion in his favour, he thought. He had to take back the umbrella to the Motts, he insisted, or, with this weather, the good Samaritans might be unable to return to their worshipping: in any case he had to see somebody at "The Black Sheep" on urgent business: business, he corrected hastily, of a spiritual nature, calculated to save certain souls from temptation.

"Well, Oi'm glad the Sperrit's workin'!" said Caleb, "and do ye git back to mother quick as you can, for it ain't fair as she should be left at home, time Oi'm enjoyin' myself. Not that 'tis my fault there ain't no chapel for Christy Dolphins—!" He checked himself and added hurriedly: "Do ye don't tell her about the pill-box: happen she'd think Oi was wexed."

"And do ye don't say you can't carry a box to Chipstone!" mocked Will gaily, glad to be released. "And of a Sunday too—you old Sabbath-breaker!"

Caleb did not smile: the episode had left too deep a scar. "Oi count the Deacon's in the roight," he said. "'Tis hypocrisy and dissemblin' to take pills at home and salt in public. Oi count Oi'll testify to the truth this arternoon."

"But you only take pills to keep off the indigestion, not to cure it," urged Will, giving him his own plea back. "Besides, salt is a sort of medicine too: without it you might get scurvy and goodness knows what."

Caleb shook his head. "Lot's wife wasn't turned into a medicine. Any man in his seven senses knows the difference 'twixt puttin' salt or medicine on his wounds."

Leaving his father to execute his sublime purpose, Will went off on his own mission under protection of the big Mott umbrella. In returning it, he learnt that even its great ribbed dome had not saved Mr. Mott from a wetting, in consequence of which and his delicate health he was now imbibing stiff glasses of grog in his bedroom, hovered over by the anxious Mother Gander. It was pathetically out of the question, Will gathered, for Brother Mott to attend chapel again that day. Will's "urgent business" lay, however, with Mr. Anthony Flippance: the soul to be saved being Jinny's, now menaced with still further soilure from the gross contacts of horse-copers, cadgers, kidders, butchers, drovers, shepherds, swineherds, touts, tramps, and all the tricksters and pickpockets of the cattle-market.

The mission did not loom unpleasant, for although he resented the fiction about the Crystal Palace and the stuffed elephant, the tall talk was harmless enough—he had heard taller in America—and he was not indisposed for ungodly society after the reek of the chapel. That the genial Showman would instantly see the matter from his point of view he did not doubt.

But Tony Flip was not in the dining-room even in dishabille, and the waiter was still so occupied with late or leisurely diners as apparently to be unable to conjure him up. "I've just taken him up his breakfast," he said, with an envious sigh. "No. 42. You'll find him."

But to intrude thus on the Showman's privacy seemed indelicate: he waylaid a chambermaid in the corridor and asked her to tell Mr. Flippance a gentleman would be glad to see him when he had finished his meal. She brought back a mysterious answer as from Miss Flippance that he never saw clean-shaven gents.

Will fired up as at an insult. Evidently the rogue was not going to be so malleable: that daughter of his, too, he remembered, had no proper respect for Jinny. "Tell 'em I'll wait here till my beard grows!" he commanded.

The chambermaid hung back, giggling. He felt in his pocket for a sixpence—again encountering only lining. "If you don't take my message, I'll kiss you," he menaced. It was a jest that never failed him, and it did not fail now, though the fleeing "tucker-in" giggled more than ever. He watched her enter the lion's den, but hardly had she done so, when the noble animal himself padded forth, grinning like a Cheshire cat, his fork protruded like a claw, and just-spluttered coffee dripping from his great jaws over the breast of his flamboyant hundred-stained hide.

"Where is he?" he roared genially to the dark corridor. "Come in! Come in!"

Will advanced defiantly.

"So it's you! I was wondering what wit heaven had dropped with the thunder! Yankee yumour—I ought to ha' guessed it." And he nearly spitted Will on his fork in his enthusiastic effort to shake hands. "'I'll wait till my beard grows'—ha, ha, ha! That goes in this very night—no, there's no show to-night, hang it! Don't go, Polly," he called, as he pulled Will into the room over a barrier of Bluchers and Wellingtons and even Hessian boots with silken tassels, "we must get that into Hamlet. When I say to Ophelia, 'Get thee to a nunnery; go, farewell'—I'll wind up 'Until thy beard grows.' That'll be your new cue, Polly."

"But that'll spoil the scene," Miss Flippance protested, poised in a morning wrapper in the open doorway between the two rooms. She was mysteriously mantled in aromatic clouds, like the spirit in The Mistletoe Bough, yet her father did not seem to be smoking.

"Not at all, Polly," he persisted, "it's just the right grotesque spirit."

"There'll be a laugh."

"The one thing Hamlet needs. Even the ghost don't carry it off."

"You'd better give me the line," persisted Miss Flippance. "It'll come better in the mad scene."

"Well, we'll talk about it—I think you've seen our American friend before."

"Before and behind," said Miss Flippance viciously, a scowl traversing her pockmarks. "And since he left me in the lurch, I wasn't sorry to think I'd seen the back of him."

"But as Miss Quar—as the Carrier hadn't got your drumstick, there was nothing to return for," apologized Will.

"Then why have you?" she snapped, and closed the door behind her with a similar snap.

VI

"Polly's in a pet," commented her parent. "She don't like being worried by actors in search of jobs, specially on Sundays. It's your hairless phiz, you know."

"But I'm not an actor."

"Of course not—she ought to have seen you haven't the face—only the razor: ha, ha, ha!"

Will was vaguely resentful. "But I dare say I could black my face."

"There's more to the drama than Othello, and more to Othello than burnt cork." And Mr. Flippance laughed again as he dropped into his wooden arm-chair and resumed his breakfast at a little table 'twixt the bed-canopy and the window. "Sit down, won't you? Excuse my back—I can hear all you say behind it. Ha, ha! That's another good gag, eh?"

Will, glancing round, saw that the chair not occupied by his host was hopelessly littered by his garments, mixed with papers: he therefore dropped on the high four-poster—it was now made—and cleared his throat for action.

"You'll have a drop of something," Mr. Flippance threw backwards, mistranslating the sounds.

"No, thank you!" He must not be bribed or drugged, Will felt: he had stern work before him. It was as well, however, to placate the adversary. "Glad to hear the show's a big draw," he said.

"And who told you that?"

"Er—the Bradmarsh Carrier!"

"Bless her—she carries all the lies I tell her."

"Aren't things rosy then?"

"I never lie on Sundays. Ha, ha, ha! Perhaps it's just as well Jinny won't do business with me to-day. No, old man, I ought to be middling mollancholy, as they say here. But I'm as happy as the day is long—and it's getting longer every day." He drained his coffee-cup voluptuously. "Never mind my business—what's yours?"

"Mine? I haven't come on business."

"Then you must have a brandy." He reached out and pulled the green bell-rope.

"No thank you. You see—" Will swung his legs hesitatingly. "Surely you don't think she ought to carry lies—?"

"Who?"

"The Bradmarsh Carrier."

"Jinny! She has to carry anything—at the proper tariff."

"But is it fair to her?"

"If you mean our doing bumper business, she don't know it's a lie, and her telling it helps to make it true. Why, you were itching to see the show yourself, as soon as you heard other fools were flocking." He turned a grinning face. "Come now, confess."

"I didn't come to see the show," Will contradicted, feeling vaguely baffled.

"Of course not, being Sunday. But what did you come for? Cut the cackle and come to the 'osses."

"I will," he said eagerly. "I hear you want to buy one."

Mr. Flippance swung round, chair and all. "Then you have come on business!"

"No, I haven't."

"Well, have you got a horse?"

"No, but I could get one."

"And you don't call that business!"

"I didn't mean to—!" Will was getting embarrassed. "It just slipped out. What I want to ask of you is—"

"Where the devil is that waiter?" broke in the Showman, reaching for the cord again.

"What I mean is," said Will, determined to get it out before the waiter popped up, "that there's a girl you're leading into brazen courses!"

"A girl! Me!" Mr. Flippance pulled himself angrily to his feet, and stood glaring at Will, with the snapped bell-cord in his hand like a green serpent. "You son of Ananias, if you've listened to any of those scandal-mongering swine you ought to be jolly well ashamed of yourself. There isn't a cleaner man—for a widower—in all the circuit. Why, I could pile up the dollars—as you call it—if I'd only darken my tent a bit, so that the lovers of the drama could go rubbing their noses and licking one another like the calves in the next field. But there isn't a brighter show this side of the Atlantic. Besides, my girls are all wood—there's not a flesh and blood female with me except Polly, and she's my own daughter, born on the right side of the blanket, too. Which is more than can be said for all of us. What may be your name, now?"

"What has my name to do with it?" He got off the bed.

"What has his name to do with it?" asked Mr. Flippance of the waiter, who now shot in with a well-divined bottle and appurtenances.

"Beg pardon, sir?"

"And so you may, you son of a slug. Here, take this rope and hang yourself with it! So you won't tell your name, you son of a flea," he went on, when the waiter had spirited off the breakfast-tray. "Well, here's my back—bite away." And with a high tragic gesture he turned to open the brandy-bottle.

"I'm not a backbiter," said Will angrily. "I'm a front-puncher, and my name is—"

"Never mind your name. I accepted you. You came like the spirit of the May Day—mixed with the Mayflower. I opened my heart to you. I gave you three names. I was Duke, I was Anthony Flippance, I was Tony Flip." He gurgled the brandy into his glass. "I demanded no references. I entrusted you with posters for my daughter."

"Which I delivered honestly."

"But anonymously."

"My name is—"

"Hush! Not for a million pounds would I hear it now. But the girl's name?" he turned round, glass in hand. "That at least I beg."

"I've mentioned it already. It's—it's the Carrier."

"Jinny!" Tony Flip burst into an explosive laugh of relief. "Fancy calling Jinny a girl!"

"And what else would you call her?"

"What you just called her—the Carrier."

"Then if she is a carrier, why should you degrade her into a horse-broker?"

"Oh, that's all you mean, is it?"

"Isn't that enough?"

"Don't be an idiot. Here, have a drink."

Will waved the glass away.

"Would you like to send your daughter bargaining among a lot of rough men?"

Tony grinned. "I don't think Polly 'ud mind the men. It's the horse she'd come a cropper over. Jinny's had a long experiance of horses, and she's smart enough to buy anything. If I wanted the moon, she'd get it for me—and cheap too!"

"And why can't you buy your own horses?"

"Why? Because I'm a child of nature—a simple player—who wears his heart on his sleeve for daws to peck at. My last mare crocked up in a week in the flower of her youth—seems to have been bought in a knacker's yard, shaved and singed and brushed and combed till she was as shiny as a Derby winner. They gingered her ears and jaws and cayenne-peppered her nostrils till she seemed clothed in thunder, like the war-horse in the Bible."

Will smiled despite himself. "And you expect a girl to see through all that! Look here, I'll buy your horse."

Mr. Flippance paused in the act of imbibing. "Oh, there we are," he said, looking shrewd. "Want to cut out Jinny's business!"

Will's cheeks became chromatically indistinguishable from his hair.

"Me! Do you think I want your dirty commission?"

"And do you think I want your stinking horse? Why the devil do you come interfering?"

Will was silent. Tony finished his glass like a victor.

"If it ain't the commission, what are you after?"

"That's my business," said Will sullenly.

"Just what I said!" crowed Tony. "But I'd rather pay Jinny a quid than you a bob. She's got her old grandfather to keep!"

"Yes, and he's as selfish and inconsiderate as you. But she shan't get you a horse, and there's an end of it."

"Oho!" Brandy had made him genial again. "Who's going to prevent it? Now don't say 'I will,' because that's in our dramas—attitude and all. Though judging by the way you've been going on, Mr. Anon, I'm not so sure you wouldn't make an actor! Perhaps Polly smelt right and you are one after all. But don't you come disturbing my peace of mind, you son of a star. Wild horses wouldn't drag me back to the legitimate."

"We're talking of caravan horses," said Will, at once mystified and mollified.

"You seem to know all about it. I guess you ran a show yourself in the States."

Will smiled darkly. "That's not your affair."

"But it might be. I'm not above a partner with capital. Duke's Marionettes are getting shabby. The ghost is nearly black; Ophelia wants a new coat of paint. Harlequin is out of joint and the Clown's cheeks are worn white. And we've got too few characters and too many plays. The public are on to it when they see Hamlet turning up again in The Beggar of Bethnal Green. Some new scenery too would smarten up the show. I shan't expect you to pull the strings—just put up the chinkers and we'll divvy up, you and me and Polly. Now don't say 'No' too quick. Drink it over." And, beaming beneficence, he again tendered Will the other glass.

This time Will took it, hearing himself clink it against Tony's through a daze, as he asked himself whether, after all, this notion—utterly fantastic and unexpected as it was—mightn't be as good a way as any other of investing his ninety pounds: he would certainly be in a position then to stop Jinny from buying the horse!

"Well, what do you say?" cried Tony.

"But you don't know my name?" murmured Will, with the stir of adventure and brandy in his veins.

"Pooh! What's in a name? A nose by any other name would swell as red." And, laughing, he clapped Will on the shoulder. "We'll spruce up the tent too, and slick up the caravan—a dingy old hearse ain't the best advertisement on a tour. And why shouldn't you take some of the parts? Pity to waste your twang. We'd get some American figures made—cowboys and slave-dealers and such—and spice our ghosts and goblins with Colonel Bowie knives and Yankee yumour. We might even turn the bridegroom in The Mistletoe Bough into a rich New-Yorker, and make the bride moulder away in an American trunk. There's a fortune in it. I don't mean in the trunk—ha, ha, ha!"

With a last instinct of sanity Will observed maliciously that it was Sunday. He merely meant to remind Tony that that was his day for truth. But the Showman's glass nearly fell from his fingers.

"You too!" he said. "And that Jinny—as lively a girl as ever stepped. And Mother Gander—as buxom a landlady as ever bussed a bagman. What's come over the East Anglian circuit? And I took you for a man of the world."

Unwilling to repudiate that status, Will remarked flabbily that precisely as a man of the world he didn't see any money in marionettes.

"No money!" Mr. Flippance swelled with indignation as he pointed out that Drury Lane and the mines of Golconda were not in it with marionettes, properly equipped and spring-cleaned; the public was simply panting for high-class puppets.

It goaded Will to emphasize his meaning. "Is this your Sunday talk or your week-day talk?" he interrupted dryly. "Didn't you just tell me that you're doing badly?"

Mr. Flippance admitted it almost without a wince. And had he not given the reason? To take money out you must put money in. "I tell you there's a fortune in it," he repeated.

"Sunk?" asked Will blandly. He added vengefully that he would consider a partnership when the stuffed elephant came home from the Crystal Palace. Tony, in crimson comprehension, rushed at the litter on the spare chair and dragged out a newspaper from under the neckties. "Read that!" he said sublimely, "the Essex County Chronicle!" And his semi-gilded forefinger indicated a heavily blued passage. "Our readers will be interested to know," read Will, "that it is a local showman who supplied the great stuffed elephant that holds Her Majesty's gorgeous howdah in Mr. Paxton's marvellous glass—"

He dropped the paper. "I beg your pardon!" he said, too disconcerted to realize that the "local" showman need not necessarily be Tony Flip. "But I really would rather not talk business to-day, and I don't know anything about yours—that wasn't my line in the States. I never even saw a puppet-show in my life, outside Punch and Judy. A real live drama now—" he concluded vaguely, meaning that he had at least seen real plays, and utterly unforeseeing the effect the remark would have upon his host.

For Tony Flip bounded like a large mechanical toy, plumped down again in his chair, turned its back and his own to his guest, and stuffing jewelled forefingers into both his ears cried out: "Get thee behind me, Satan! Avaunt! Avaunt!"

VII

"Me, Satan!" said Will, astonished. "Who ever heard of Satan refusing to do business on Sunday?"

If his last innocent remark had produced convulsive effects in a perpendicular direction, this set Tony Flip rolling from side to side in his chair. "Yankee yumour," he gasped between the spasms. "Lord!" he said at last. "You'll drive me to set up a minstrel show, only to get that in."

Will, though puzzled, could hardly help being flattered by these proofs of his facetious talents. It was strange, he thought, how different the conversation went when he was with Jinny. Then the laugh seemed always at his expense.

"I should think a minstrel show would be more fun," he observed.

Tony veered round with his arm-chair, ceased to laugh, and regarded Will with large, reproachful eyes. "And you cant about Sunday!" he said. "And then to come tempting me back to that Witches' Sabbath of a profession."

"Nigger minstrels?" Will murmured, more dazed than ever.

"As if nigger minstrels weren't half-way to your Othello. No, you son of Satan. To hell with your capital! Didn't you hear me say ditto to the rat-catcher? They are dens of the devil—theatres."

"Then why do you run one?"

"Me! I don't class my show as a theatre. Marionettes keep themselves to themselves."

"But you play Shakespeare."

Tony held up his fat glittering forefinger. "We pull Shakespeare's strings—Polly and me. But there's no actors the public can drag before the curtain."

Will admitted the difference, but not the moral distinction.

"You ever met any actors and actresses?" said Tony.

Will could not pretend to that privilege—if Mr. Flippance and his daughter refused to be counted—and there was a long silence, in which Tony seemed to the outer eye to keep sips of brandy-and-water lingering on his palate, though he was really—it transpired—chewing the cud of bitter memories. For suddenly he burst out: "I lived all my life with 'em. I've managed 'em for years—or, rather, failed to manage 'em. Born in a Green Room, rocked in a Witches' Cauldron, and baptized in grease-paint. My ma was a leading lady—she played heroines and my father wrote the melodramas. And they know a good melodrama at the 'Eagle.'"

"Yes—I've heard of the 'Eagle' in London," said Will.

"Ah, you know it by the song, perhaps:

Up and down the City Road,
In and out the 'Eagle.'
That's the way the money goes,
Pop goes the weasel!"

"I never heard a weasel go pop," Will laughed. "It was the mouse, if anything, though I did once see a stoat crack up before a cat."

Tony's mien relaxed in a faint smile.

The weasel was a tailor's iron, he explained, pawned by the reckless snip to raise money for treating the damsels who danced with him on that open-air platform to which the "Eagle's" audience streamed out betwixt the drama and the farce. He added simply: "That's where my Don Juan of a dad first clapped eyes on a girl, pretty, of course, but with no more acting in her than Mother Gander. Yet, would you believe it, he shoved her into the lead instead of ma, and wrote a piece all for her, and what was worse it was a big go. That was the last straw, and clasping me to her wounded bosom, she left him, poor ma."

"I should have thought she'd ha' left him sooner," murmured Will, vaguely uncomfortable under these frank domestic revelations.

"It isn't so easy to leave a man you're not married to!" said Tony.

Will gasped.

"Ah, that surprises you?" said the Showman complacently. With a cautious glance at his daughter's door of communication, he produced two cigars furtively from his washstand drawer—was he forbidden to smoke, Will wondered. "You'll find that good," he said, pressing one upon his guest.

"You see," he explained, as they puffed at these excellent weeds in a new intimacy, "if a woman leaves her husband it makes a scandal he don't like, whereas a man that's not tied is only too glad to be rid of her. Oh, I ain't defending ma, mind you—it only shows she was a born actress. I dare say she'd only sucked up to pa to get parts. But when he unstarred her, fine emotional actress as she was, she could never get her foot in again in London, to play leads I mean, for she was too proud to play anything else. 'I can play anything except second fiddle,' she used to say, and rather than cave in, she married a fifth-rate manager, called Jim Flippance, who had only a fit-up theatre (carries its own props, scenery, and proscenium, but not open-air, you know), and made him put up pieces with a kid in 'em to keep me out of mischief, but it wasn't long before I soared out of the parental nest, and by the time they both joined the majority, poor old birds, I'd been leading man or manager or both in half a dozen theatres, two of 'em London houses." Will receiving this information with a silent curl of his smoke, as though it were another elephantine claim, Mr. Flippance added vehemently: "Real London theatres, mind you, not those swindling gaffs for paying amateurs described by Boz—that's Charles Dickens, you know. You've read Dickens?"

Will shook his head. "Too heavy and high-class for me. They don't like him in the States either—I've heard he wrote a piece against them—"

"Ah, but you should hear him read his 'Christmas Carol!' There's a wasted actor for you! Lord, if I'd had the running of that chap!"

Will was more interested in the girl who cut out Mr. Flippance's ma. "I hope your father—your pa—" he substituted politely, "married his new flame," he said. Even through the glow of the brandy and the blur of the smoke he was dismayed by this dishevelled life.

"How could he? He had a wife in Cork. Yes, I forgot to say pa was Irish. I've always gone by my mother's married name, but you can have my father's name if you wish!"

"Not for a million pounds," said Will.

"You Yankee yumorist!" Tony blew a playful puff of smoke at him. "Well, you'll see it if you come across the old 'Eagle' playbills or those of Flippance's Fit-Up for that matter, for we did all pa's plays—ma had played them so long she knew all the parts. Pa sent her a lawyer's letter—for she didn't even trouble to change the titles or the author's name—but she defied him to wash his dirty linen in court, knowing how virtuous his 'Eagle' public was, and that it might ha' ruined him and his moral melodramas."

"They seem a funny lot—stage folk," Will commented.

"Bless you, there's no bearing of 'em."

Will, relieved, said he was glad Mr. Flippance didn't approve of such morals.

"Morals!" Tony glared at him. "Who's talking of morals? Men will be men and women women whether they're pro's or public. You didn't find America a Sunday-school, I reckon?"

Will, coughing over his liquor, supposed a man could have his fun anywhere.

"That's what I say!" said the Showman. "And on the other hand I've known actors as respectable as your rat-catcher. I'm one of 'em myself, as I told you just now. I'd seen too many dead flies in the honey—and my Polly's as pure as her poor dead mother. No, it ain't their morals that bother me, it's their ways. Holy Moses! To think of the time I had travelling round managing these sons of dragons and hell-cats! I envied ma and Flippance in the churchyard under their favourable stone notices. The jealousies! The cat-and-dog bickerings! The screams and hysterics! Who should play this or that, who should be largest on the programmes and posters, who should stand in the limelight, who should take the call—they never quarrelled who should take the bird: that's the hiss in our lingo. They were always hissing at one another, or at the poor manager, that's me! I've seen the leading man and the leading lady take their call hand in hand, and the moment the curtain was down resume spitting fire at each other. It wasn't that they had any vanity, they said, it was only that their position demanded they should take calls singly or be printed larger than each other. Cocks and catamarans! I tell you if I hadn't swopped with Duke for his marionettes, I should have had little rose-bushes growing out of me now, and that favourable stone notice over me. Oh, the peace of it—it's Sunday all the week!"

"I can see marionettes would be easier to manage," said Will, smiling.

"Ah, but to feel it as I do, you must have lived through it." Mr. Flippance rose in his emotion and paced animatedly. "You must have had a hornets' nest for your seat and a brood of vipers in your bosom, and shared diggings with the Furies. Oh, my radiant juvenile, your sun-coloured hair would have been snow if you had gone through what I have! If you'd had Ophelia in hysterics and Hamlet in liquor and even the ghost hardly able to walk, and the call-boy crying the curtain was up, and the audience stamping and whistling, and short-tempered people at the box-office demanding their money back, you'd be able to measure the feeling of thankfulness that comes over the cockles of my heart when I stand in my theatre and see my leading lady sitting so angelic on her wires unable to move hand or foot without me, or when I jerk my leading man out of the centre of the stage all in a heavenly calm; And to see the curtain come up and down with nobody scuffling behind it to bob and smirk—oh, the Jerusalem restfulness! There mayn't be as much rhino in marionettes as in flesh and blood—"

"You just said there was more," Will reminded him, unkindly.

"I meant compared with the capital put in," said Tony, without turning a hair. "You don't risk much when you don't have to pay your actors. But Duke wasn't mercenary, and it was the glory that appealed to him, poor man. He'd inherited the business, like me, but he'd always been ambitious after high art, he told me, and Flippance's Fit-Up was his boyhood's dream. We did the swop over mulled claret last Christmas Eve in this very inn. Peace and goodwill, thinks I, as we clinked tumblers on the deal. You've got the goodwill, but peace, no, that you'll never see again."

Will smiled. "I'll really have to come and see those blessèd puppets," he said, as the Showman replenished the glasses.

Tony replied that he should see the whole boiling of them either before or after the show, neatly packed in their big box. "And if there's any you'd like to kick, you're welcome," he said.

"What! Damage your property?"

"It would work off my bitter memories."

"But they're not the real live actors."

"No—there's the pity!" said Tony. "But they look so real—they're life-size, you know—that I sometimes yell at 'em and abuse 'em just for the satisfaction of their not answering back. And the leading lady looks as if she had a tongue to her—I promise you. A tongue—but thank the Lord it can only talk Shakespeare or noble sentiments—can't even nag the management for a new dress. As for the juvenile lead, I can't help tweaking his nose sometimes for the sake of auld lang syne. Polly can't understand my spoiling his beauty—I can't make her see I'm getting a bit of my own back—and when she catches me punching the low comedian's head with a boxing-glove she saucers her eyes, as though I was going dotty. But she never had to manage 'em. And I had to travel 'em too—don't forget that. Fancy carting around a menagerie, all in the same cage! But I have my revenge when I travel 'em now—into the box they go—leads below and the heavy man sitting on their heads, ha, ha, ha!—and utilities and supers on top of all! And it don't raise a whisper. Talk of the lion lying down with the lamb. Believe me, old cock, that there millennium will never come till we're all on wires." He drew vigorously at the cigar his eloquence had all but extinguished.

"There's a lot of the brutes," he mused between the puffs, "that don't know Tony Flip's escaped out of hell, and they write and call for engagements—same as Polly thought you did—and if it isn't Sunday I take 'em to see my company and rub their noses into 'em, so to speak. Look at 'em, I say, every man and woman knowing their place, and when to speak and when to hold their blooming tongue, every one knowing their parts too, which is more than you ever did, I'll be bound. No wigs, no make-ups, no dresses, no young bloods or decrepit dandies coming behind, no prompter, nobody missing their cue, or unpunctual or hysterical. No Bardell versus Pickwick. Nobody drunk, married, divorced, deceased, laid up, locked up, or run over, between the dress rehearsal and the first night. No understudies, eating their heads off: in the way when they're not wanted, and missing their cues when they are. No sore throats, no funerals to go to, no babies to get—if there's a baby wanted, I order it from the makers. And above all, my boy, say I to 'em, no treasury."

"What's that?" inquired Will.

"What's that? Well I'm blowed. That's pay-day. And kindly note, I say to 'em, that lead don't get more than utility, nor responsibles than walking gentlemen. It's Owenism, you sons of Mammon, I tell 'em, sheer Owenism. Everybody getting the same nothing, and nobody coming carneying for advance half-crowns. As for curtain-calls, the singing chambermaid's got the same chance as Lady Macbeth. And when it is a leading man that's come for a berth, I take him to the front of the booth where there's a retired village idiot I picked up, banging the drum. Look there, says I, he's not got much brains but he isn't wood, and that's the only flesh-and-blood job I've got left in this blooming shop. If you like to take it, why, in recognition of your position, I'll throw in an extra naphtha flare."

"And what do they say?" laughed Will.

"It can't be repeated on a Sunday! But you can picture 'em black in the face—all except the nose. That gets redder than ever! Hullo, Charley! Come in! Come in!"

Through the open door he had caught sight of the landlord in the corridor.

"Can't stop, Tony." Mr. Mott was, in fact, hurrying to take advantage of his spouse's return to chapel.

"Gander-pecked again, I suppose," laughed the Showman. "Ah, Charley, you'd be much happier if you had a wife on wires."

"There you go again!" And Mr. Mott, eager to join old pals at their fishing, sniggered past, leaving a reek of hair-oil.

"Poor chap!" sighed Tony. "But there's always hope for a man whose wife won't call in a doctor."

Will laughed, and cunningly took advantage of all this expansive geniality to escape from the room and the threatened transaction and to call from the doorstep as he took his farewell, "Then it's settled—I get the horse."

"If you bring it into the partnership," cried Tony after him, "not otherwise."

Will found himself waylaid by Polly as he passed her doorway. She beckoned him within with a mysterious, masterful forefinger, and he, seeing the moreen curtains of her four-poster discreetly drawn, entered, though not without Puritan misgivings. She drew another curtain over the closed door communicating with her father's room, and turned the key. "Don't waste my cigar," she said as he held it behind him. "I can see pa's given you one of mine." And taking up her glowing fag-end from the ash-tray, she resumed her suction of it, sipping in the intervals at a glass of milk. "I suppose you won't share my drink," she said simply.

"No, thank you," he said, hardly believing his eyes, though he now understood whence came the clouds in which he had found her mantled. Perhaps she was really a man in disguise, despite her long ear-rings. But then, would ever a male take milk with his cigar? What with tobacco and horsiness, what was the sex coming to? And yet there seemed something symbolic in this combination of stimulants, this masculinity mitigated by milk! "What do you want to say to me?" he asked, keeping the front door open with his hand.

"What's this about a partnership?" she said softly. "I couldn't help hearing."

"Don't ask me," said Will in tones hushed as cautiously. "Mr. Flippance did speak of it, but I've never thought of the theatre as a business, only as a spree."

"Did he want you to take a theatre?" she asked anxiously.

"Good heavens, no! He called it hell!"

Miss Flippance smiled sadly. "That's his way of consoling himself. He's dying to get a stock company again. But he mustn't have even a theatre for amateurs. I'd fight it tooth and nail."

"It's bad for him, I know."

"It's bad for me," said Miss Flippance. She puffed out a cloud. "You see, there'd be no place for me. I can wipe most actresses off the stage, but I'm not pretty—at least, not since my illness—and the public won't have me—except at the piano where I turn my back on them. Plain actresses must be heard and not seen."

"Oh!" Will was taken aback by such candour.

"Besides, one of the women would probably entangle him into marriage. I don't mind his having a wife on wires!" And a smile came travelling over the pits of her face.

"You don't mean to say he really wants to go back to hell?" said Will, dazed.

"Don't the moths after you've saved 'em from the lamp? And it was no easy task saving him. Christmas after Christmas I used to jest: 'Peace and goodwill indeed! You'll never have peace till you've got rid of your goodwill.'"

"But that's what he says himself," said Will naïvely. "So he can't be craving to go back—it's the marionettes he wanted me to stand in with."

"That's all my eye. He don't know how happy he really is nowadays, playing all the men's parts. That was always the trouble in a real theatre, especially when he was cock-of-the-walk—he never could make up his mind which part he wanted. First he'd try one, and then think another was better and throw it up in the middle and take away the other man's part. Nobody likes to give up a half-digested part, and it doesn't make things easier when, after all, you get it back again. Imagine the ructions he was always making, and I'm not going to have it all over again. He's got all the parts now, and so it's going to stay." With which ultimatum she held out her hand and gripped him with what he felt a manly clasp, and an honest. "Don't you be his partner," she counselled. "He's lost all his own money and it's not likely he'd multiply yours. He might have been a big London actor or manager, but the Bible sized him up before he was born. 'Unstable as water, thou shalt not excel.' If only at least one can keep him to water! No, you stick to your cash. There's no money in the show for more than him and me—my last jewellery will have to go for the horse—and if you've really got the dollars, he'd have a theatre, with you as juvenile lead, before you could say Jack Robinson, and then he'd steal your part and drive you to drink."

Will replied firmly, still holding her hand, that he was going to put his money into farming, and by the way, would she countermand that order to the Carrier for the horse?

"Oh, but we must have a horse," said Polly.

"Quite so, but why through Jinny?" He was prepared himself, he explained, to get them the best animal at the lowest price.

"And for what commission?" she queried.

"For love!" said Will.

Polly withdrew her hand. "No, thank you. We'd best let it go through Jinny—like everything else."

CHAPTER VII

COMEDY OF CORYDON AND AMARYLLIS

Among the rest a shepherd, though but young,
Yet harten'd to his pipe, with all the skill
His few years could, began to fit his quill,
Willie he hight. . . .

Fair was the day, but fairer was the maid
Who that day's morn into the green-woods stray'd.
Sweet was the air, but sweeter was her breathing,
Such rare perfumes the roses are bequeathing.
BROWNE, "Britannia's Pastorals."

I

It was the shepherd-cowman, and not Jinny, who delivered the horn to Will. She had "happened of him," Master Peartree explained tediously, in the remote field to which he had taken the sheep to feed off the winter barley. "Powerfully trumpeting" for him with it just when he was looking for fly, when indeed in the very act of discovering a maggoty rump, she had besought him to convey that "liddle ole horn," she being so late and Gran'fer likely to be "in a taking."

Now this "liddle ole horn"—when Will saw Master Peartree and his sheep-dog coming along in the evening light—he took to be the shepherd's crook or his great umbrella folded, so lengthy did it loom, and when he perceived that it was what he was expected to perform on, he was taken aback. It was not that he had not seen coach-horns in plenty, but he had seen them in their proper environment and at their proper altitude, their elemental straightforwardness making an exhilarating right-angle with the guard's mouth, a sort of streaming pennon. But a coach-horn in its bare quiddity, quite as tall as the shrunken old shepherd, and hardly a foot shorter than Will himself, dissociated from jovial visions of scarlet, rum-soused visages and spanking steeds, was as ungainly to behold and as awkward to handle as it was difficult to explain away. Evidently the jade had bought him the largest size on the market; he knew not whether to be flattered or vexed at her idea of the appropriately virile. But to send it by this alien hand—to make a village wonder and scandal of it! How, indeed, was he to explain to the bucolic mind his sudden passion for the instrument? Flutes and concertinas folks could understand, even tin whistles; but what could a man looking round for a farm want with a colossal coach-horn? He was glad at least he had met Master Peartree out of sight of his parents. There was a note attached to the case, and he opened it the more eagerly that it delayed the explanation which Master Peartree seemed to his morbid vision to be grimly awaiting.

"SIR,—Mr. Daniel Quarles has pleasure in forwarding per favour of bearer Mr. William Flynt's esteemed order. Bill enclosed. I hope you will find the stature agreeable to you—it was only by casualty I got such a protracted one, and as the compass protracts with the stature you could easily educe three octaves from it. Half-tones of course I shall not expect as without holes only a musical Arabian spirit like my granddaughter can evoke them, but when you can play the 'Buy a Broom' Polka with concinnity, I shall consider the gloves fairly conquered.

"I remain

"Yours obediently,
"DANIEL QUARLES.

"P.S.—The mouthpiece unscrews being mutable, so I can exchange it for another, if this does not suit Mr. William Flynt's lips."

How the deuce was he to play a polka he had never heard, especially "with concinnity" (whatever that might be), was the dominant thought in his perturbed brain. But as Master Peartree seemed still expectant—was it even of a tune?—Will stooped down to pat the dog, whose black-tipped tail was hoisted like a friendly signal. It was a ragged animal just between two coats—a canine counterpart of its shabby, straggly-haired master—but Will caressed it like a velvety lapdog while he inquired carelessly—his horn tucked like a telescope under his arm—how the Carrier had carried herself, what exactly she had said. But he only provoked—after the briefest glimpse of the girl—a rambling narrative about a sheep that had broken its arm in a "roosh," in the panicky restlessness of the thundery Sunday: it had fallen down a steep and another had rolled on top of it. And even with this "meldoo" the sheep were so pernickety you could do naught with 'em. Doubtless in this cloudy heat they felt the weight of their wool—he should be shearing some for the early market as soon as they could get the labour, which was not easy in these migrating days. Even young men who came back lazed about, he added pointedly, when they might be earning good money. Will hastened to inquire whether the shearers were as merry at their work as he remembered them. He could never forget the beautiful bass voice of Master Peartree, but he supposed time had now abated its resonancy, or was he mistaken? He was mistaken, he admiringly admitted, for the ancient was soon quavering out in a piping voice:

"There was a sheep went out to reap"

and Will, beating time with the great horn, was solemnly singing the chorus:

"Chrissimus Day, Chrissimus Day"

And now would the famous singer oblige with the "Buy a Broom Polka"? Alas, he did not know it, with or without "concinnity"! But young Ravens might know it, he who was as full of tunes as a dog of fleas, and with his perpetual flow of melody made bread and tea like harvest suppers, and shearing days as jolly as Chrissimus. But where was this musical box? Alas! he had "gone furrin," being somewhere beyond Southend. But master expected him back for the shearing; he was a rolling stone, was Ravens, but he usually rolled back this time o' year. No, not rolled with liquor, nor yet like the sheep that broke its arm. Had it been a fat sheep, he would have butchered it, but as it was only store he had set the arm himself. No, he had no need of a vet. for that, like the degenerate young shepherds nowadays; he wouldn't be beholden to cattle-doctors, not he, keeping for ever o' salts and gentians and bottles of lotion in his hut, although "suspicioning shab"—it might even be rot from the river-marsh—in one of the sheep which he had just been examining for fly, he had taken the opportunity to ask Jinny to send round Elijah Skindle. 'Tis a long talk that has no turning, and Will, when the narrative thus came, by a wide detour, back to Jinny, ceased fidgeting with the horn, and demanded what she had said to that. It transpired that she had refused to order Elijah, despite that Mrs. Flynt had recommended him as cheaper, alleging, drat her, that Jorrow was the better man. Will, curiously forgetting Mr. Flippance and his horse, concurred in the view that carriers cannot be choosers. He also started another current of indignation against carriers getting other folks to fetch and carry for them. Would the hard-working shepherd, who was too easily put upon, kindly not encourage the girl in future to shirk her job?

Touched by the sense of his own magnanimity and the sixpence slipped into his palm, the good shepherd promised to repress his obligingness in the interests of the higher ethics, and Will, bidding him farewell, slipped behind the row of stag-headed poplars opposite the gate of Frog Farm, and strove—before entering the house—to adjust his horn down his trousers and up his back. It was no easy process with such a "protracted" object: fortunately it was thin, save at the swelling end, but by keeping this bulge below, he could avoid humping his back. To walk with such a ramrod up it and adown one leg would, however, have taxed the talents of the most graceful damsel training for deportment. He hobbled painfully to the rear of the farmhouse, designing to hide the horn before entering, but lo! there was his mother filling the food-pot of his neglected ferrets.

"Oh, my poor Will!" she exclaimed. "I told your father you'd have rheumatics—sitting in chapel in your damp clothes." She tried to take him pitifully in her arms but he limped away, fearing she would imagine his backbone had come outside.

"It's only one leg a bit stiff," he said ungraciously. But she hooked her arm in his and drew her halt offspring towards the back door; a brief but parlous journey, for he felt the horn slipping towards his boot.

"Why, your ankle's swollen," said Martha tragically.

"It'll soon go down," he assured her.

A terrible struggle agitated the maternal heart. Even Will, preoccupied with his grotesque position, could see her face working.

"You're sure you wouldn't like to have the doctor?"

"Oh no, mother. What nonsense!"

Her clouds lifted a little. "But this may be Jinny's evening for coming—I could tell her to go for him to-morrow."

"To-morrow it'll be better—I feel certain, mother."

She beamed. "I'm so glad you've found faith, dearie. I knew when once you began studying the texts you couldn't miss it. King Asa, too, suffered from his feet. But he sought to the physicians and displeased the Lord. Have no confidence in man, dearie. There's days I get pains in my side as if my ribs grated together. But I'd be afraid to put myself out of the Lord's hands, after I've trusted to Him all these years."

Will winced. He seemed to himself vaguely blasphemous. As soon as he was alone in his bedroom, the swelling was transferred to the capacious box so miraculously carried from Chipstone. He dared not descend to supper: so speedy a miracle might have seemed too "Peculiar." But next morning (after a family breakfast which was for his elders a veritable feast of faith) he stole out with the horn and his fishing-rod and creel to the river, which in the watches of the night he had decided upon as the loneliest spot for practising, while the open ramshackle boat-house, where the rusty punt usually nested, was to afford a hiding-place for the instrument.

It was worth while going down that pastoral slope these days, even were one not bent on music, solitude, and the winning of gloves. In weather so prematurely sultry, the river was so sweet and still and green, with its shadowy reflections, its blobs of duckweed, the sedges and flags along its banks, and the willows—grey-white or silvery—along its borders: gliding so tranquilly in its reaches and lapping so lazily round its islands that only at bends did the water seem to flow at all. In the undulating meadows that sloped to it, silted with cow-droppings, Master Peartree's kine lay around chewing, and the sense of brooding heat gave to the landscape a dreamy magic, suffused with a sense of water.

It was to this idyllic retreat that our Tityrus or Corydon repaired to essay his metallic pipe. And, standing on the bank like a watchman, his horn to his lips, "Tucker, tucker," he breathed industriously into the unresponsive instrument. In vain did he lip and tongue the notes as instructed, nothing broke the sultry silence. Surely the mouthpiece could not suit Mr. William Flynt's lips. Suddenly, in his shamed impotence, he had a sense of a breathing presence. In his agitation the horn slipped from his nervous fingers and went souse into the water, while the startled beast—for the observer proved to be only one of Master Peartree's cows—lumbered bouncingly back along the pasture.

Fortunately the instrument had lodged in the shallow mud of the bank. Fishing it up—it was his sole catch that week—he found to his joy that it emitted a faint toot, and he rightly divined that a little water was just what it had needed. Encouraged by this intervention of Providence in his favour, his performance bore henceforwards some proportion to his pains.

It was embarrassing though to return from these painful puffings without a single bite. Every dinner-time he had to sneak in as best he could with empty basket after a morning of pertinacious tooting, successful enough to frighten off the deafest fish. Once, indeed, going home by a somewhat roundabout route that skirted Blackwater Hall, he chanced on a Chipstone fishmonger serving Long Bradmarsh, and was able to take home some fruits of his rod. But the only time our piscatorial swain ever tried for an honest bite was when he saw or heard somebody or something coming along. Then, drawing in his horn like a snail, he presented the picture of the complete angler. Usually it was only Bidlake's barge that disturbed his strenuous solitude, and the transient mockery of the twins was for the futile fisher, not for the unsuspected musician. Not even Master Peartree's cows ever munched their way again to the bank while the horn was at its fell exercises, for, like the horn which the fairy Logistilla presented to Astolpho in "Orlando Furioso," its blast seemed to put all creation to flight. His sole auditors were a pair of swans who refused to quit their normal haunt, though they hissed him fiercely. Possibly they were accustomed "to hear old Triton blow his wreathèd horn," and so had a standard of musical taste. Is not the swan's own song, too, celebrated, though it appears only to perform before it dies, as if to evade criticism?

But however soundly the swans might hiss, Will, after three days of red-faced rehearsal on the pleasant bank of the Brad, felt ready to challenge his female critic in all save the polka she had set for examination, and this he determined—after failing to hunt it out—was no fair part of the wager. A whole evening he had spent reknitting the thread of old acquaintanceship with carolling cottagers, gleaning much gratitude for his kindly attentions, but not the melody he was after, and being forced politely to abide while gaffers piped "Heave away, my Johnny," or gammers ruthlessly completed "Midsummer Fair" or "Dashing away with the Smoothing Iron." However, he could now turn out such complicated military flourishes that he excited his own military ardour, and felt like marching in his thousands, and doing such deeds of derring-do that the lips of all the damsels of Essex would vie to change places with that mouthpiece. It was high time then that this particular damsel should understand how vain was her hope that he could be baffled by a tube. Though he might not know that polka, he was sure that whatever "concinnity" might be, he could perform with it, and impatience began to steal over him at the delay in the test performance. For if Jinny had fobbed him off with the shepherd on Tuesday, she evaded service altogether on Friday. Even Nip might conceivably crop up with some small groceries tied on to him, and he could not try it on the dog. Also, unless he saw her soon, the cattle fair would be upon them, and she still unsaved. He must, with the relics of his copybook paper, compose a new note, formally citing her to stand and hear, and deliver the gloves.

But it was not easy to fix the place for deciding the wager. The riverside meadows she could not well get at in her cart, and for her to come specially on foot was hardly to be expected, in view of her household labours. To cut her off and perform to her on a high road was to run risks of being publicly ridiculous: even by-ways have ears. Suppose his nerve or his breath failed, suppose some impish accident muffled up the horn: there would he be with swollen cheeks, a mountain in labour, producing not even, a mouse-squeak; the mock of man and beast. But there was Steeples Wood—not too far back off the high road, but approached by a tangly brake that few ever penetrated: there—if he could persuade her to it—was the ideal place for the great horn solo. In a postscript he would express his willingness to take off her hands the purchase of the Showman's horse. To convey all this by correspondence involved almost as much effort as the practising, though his renewed call upon the Bible came to Caleb and Martha as the natural sequel of his faith-cure. It was no small feat of composition, this particular letter, in face of a people, which, however abundant its horses, appeared to have had neither "wagers" upon them, nor "gloves," riding or other.

II

That gloves were unknown to the ancient Hebrews, Will could hardly bring himself to believe, even by hours of searching, especially after coming upon a Fashion Catalogue for Ladies, which showed a surprising wardrobe. Bonnets they had, it would appear, and headbands and tablets and changeable suits of apparel, and mantles and wimples and crisping pins and fine linen and hoods and vails, and mufflers and girdles and stomachers: as for their jewel-cases, they seemed stuffed not only with rings and ear-rings and charms and bracelets and moony tires, but likewise with jewels that dangled at the nose or tinkled at the feet. How then should so elegant a world have dispensed with gloves? But so—after scouring the sacred Book from Genesis to Revelation—he must finally fain believe. Not a single patriarch, priest, satrap, shepherd, physician, apostle, publican, or sinner had ever sported gloves, and the Queen of Sheba fared no better in this respect than the Witch of Endor. Solomon in all his glory was not arrayed with even one of these. The Pharisees, it would appear, covered their foreheads with phylacteries—whatever these might be—but left their hands bare. And yet, Will thought wistfully, reading so early in the sacred Book how Rebekah "put the skins of the kids of the goats upon Jacob's hands," they might surely in all those centuries have gone on to the idea of gloves, especially for winter wear. But no, thousands of years after Rebekah, the knuckles of Dives were apparently as raw as those of Lazarus. Oh, why had he not betted something Biblical—a muffler now would have suited either sex: even handkerchiefs were available. Not that he could not risk spelling "gloves" to accord with "loves," which he found with no great difficulty in the holy text: he felt it romantic to throw himself thus trustfully upon "love," even should it prove misleading.

Yet the search was not altogether vain, for though he could find no gloves, the prophets, he found, were full of exhortations to Jinny, which he carefully dog-eared and committed to memory and kept up his sleeve for contingencies. "How canst thou contend with horses?" Jeremiah asked her. Ezekiel warned her against the cattle-dealer. "By reason of the abundance of his horses their dust shall cover thee." As for Isaiah, he remarked plumply: "Woe unto them that draw iniquity with cords of vanity, and sin as it were with a cart rope."

To himself, on the other hand, the prophets were kind; abounding in promises for the prosperity of his horn. And it was Amos who supplied his letter with its opening sentence, abrupt but dramatic:

"Can two walk together except they be agreed?"

But the letter written, there was the problem of sending it. The intervention of either Bundock or Daniel was intolerable. He must find an individual way. One verse that he came upon—it was in the Book of Esther—enchanted him with its images, telling how Mordecai wrote an order in the King's name "and sealed it with the King's ring and sent letters by post on horseback, riders on mules, camels, and young dromedaries." How he would have liked to seal his letter too with a royal ring, and send it "by post on horseback." He had a vision of the long procession of mules, camels, and dromedaries filing along the grass-grown lane to Blackwater Hall. How old Daniel would rub his eyes at the strange humped beasts—yes, and Jinny too. She would perhaps think that Mr. Flippance had acquired a new show and was paying her a processional visit. Possibly these animal images did lead him to the invention of his postal method, or possibly it was his prior apprehension of Jinny's utilizing Nip as a package-bearer. At any rate, after having wondered whether Martha's pigeons could be trained up in the way they should go, he hit on the device of tying his note to Nip's collar. The creature was friendly, and that Saturday afternoon it would be at home. He would only have to hover long enough around Blackwater Hall for his post-dog to fawn upon him. Of course there was no certainty the dangling missive would escape Daniel's spectacles, but Nip being providentially of the colour of paper, it was possible heaven had not blanched him in vain. Besides, this time the note was carefully addressed to Miss Jinny Quarles, with the "Quarles" scratched out by an afterthought when he remembered that it was not her name.

But, alas! Nip did not play up; that longed-for quadruped did not appear in the purlieus of the Hall. Will, tired of carrying about the note, thought again of sticking it up in the stable and ventured near, but his fear of encountering Daniel Quarles was too lively, and finally he essayed—with some obscure remembrance of Bowery melodrama—to fix it gleamingly in the fork of a tree by which Methusalem stood when harnessing and unharnessing. To his amaze a chaffinch flew out of the fork in violent protest, while her gaily coloured consort dashed up from another quarter, crying "U-whit" at him like an avine Flippance. Peeping into the hollow of the fork he saw a couple of rather belated youngsters, ugly, bald-headed, and featherless, apparently new-hatched and almost savouring of the egg: yet when he touched them with the note, opening great eyes and yawning with yellow beaks and kicking each other with skeleton legs. But before he could bethink himself of a new posting-place, lo! as sudden as the chaffinches but far more welcome, with a yelp of joy and a perpendicular tail wagging like a mad pendulum, Nip was upon him; and having succeeded with a desperate bound in licking the tip of his stooping chin, rolled himself on mother-earth with voluptuous grunts. Will profited by this supineness to attach the note by the thread he had passed through it.

The new postal system was a success. For when Will after high tea sneaked out to the Common and sounded his horn—with a happy combination of challenge, salute, and signal—Nip actually appeared with a reply.

It was, however, unsatisfactory. Miss Boldero—the very name, though he divined it denoted the same Jinny, came like a glacial blast—presented her compliments to Mr. William Flynt, but she had no time to be romantic in woods (she said) nor, even at their homes, could she ever pay more than volant visits to anybody, and that strictly in the way of Daniel Quarles's business. He could almost always find her at Blackwater Hall except Tuesdays and Fridays, but she trusted he would not be too turgid and thrasonical about his playing, even if his contumacious serenade should be puissant enough to extort the pair of gloves.

All these strange words came, of course, from "The Universal Spelling-Book." Will, though he would still have refused to toot before her grandfather, might have felt less crushed had he known that in that ancient authority, "romantic" was defined as "idle."

III

It is possible that persons of strict ethics—like Miss Gentry, say—would have lost sympathy with Jinny in these epistolary efforts of hers to stand on tiptoe, so to speak, and write beyond her education. But in thus titivating her style with gems of speech she knew not to be false, she was moved by the necessity of countering an overweening, overbearing, interfering young man, who was subtly assuming a sort of critical wardenship over her and her life: he needed a good vibration ("shaking or beating"), she must teach him by her gelidity ("coldness") to be less conversant ("familiar"), and that she was quite his parallel ("equal"). He must be made to feel that her company was not to be had for the rogation ("asking"), in short that she was no housekeeping ignoramus to be ridden over by world-travelled wisdom, however genuine. No, she was not going to incurvate ("bow or bend") to Mr. William Flynt.

This rigidity was the more necessary as, ever since in that thunderstorm his hand had tightened on hers—or was it the reverse?—the lightnings seemed to pass through her, the reverberations to shake her, whenever she thought of him, and even when she did not. What there was in him to rend her thus elementally she could not understand; doubtless it was the memory of the storm now for ever associated with him. He seemed—it was perhaps his life of adventure—to be in mystic unison with tempests and floods and that sea-creek of her childhood, now remembered exclusively as tossing and white-flecked. Even when she was turning over her Spelling-Book to find words to "vibrate" him with, it was the pages that vibrated: when she copied its gelid trisyllables, she felt her hand again in his, and her quill quivered as if the lightning were going through it.

And even Miss Gentry, though she would have derided Jinny's new vocabulary, might have admitted that there was a laudable side to her pursuit of learning: the Spelling-Book itself overflowed with commendation of such scholastic zeal. Jinny no longer knitted or sewed in her evening hour of leisure. It was occupied—even after the concoction of the grandiose letter—in a feverish study of the volume neglected since her first scholastic period. She must make herself a greater intellectual power, she felt: she must master all human knowledge. And that all human knowledge lay in the hundred and fifty pages of this little book, our simple village girl, who was not romantic in any sense of that word, who, except for Bible and hymn-book, had never read a book—not even a novel—and who approached life with senses fresh and virginal, sincerely and crudely believed.

Nor was the pose of "The Universal Spelling-Book" calculated to dissipate her delusion. This wonderful work, which was now destined to become Jinny's guide, philosopher, and friend, had nothing in common with those shallow productions of a later period, concerned mainly with correct combinations of letters. Dating from the age of folios and exhibiting, despite its diminutive size, the same solid solemnity, it did really take all knowledge for its province. (You learnt, for example, how to make the very ink you spelled with—and although you may rarely have possessed those best blue galls of Aleppo which formed the base of black, still you might hope to get the three pints of stale beer that were the substratum of red.) And not only all knowledge, but all morals formed the farrago of this book. Well might it ostentate among its "Patronizers" clergymen, private gentlemen, philomaths, writing masters, and heads of academies.

Originally published—as already related—in the year of the Lisbon Earthquake, and creating apparently as great a sensation (in England at least), it constituted an omnium gatherum so peculiar and extensive that there was no earthly (or heavenly) subject you could be certain of not meeting there, though there was one subject you could be certain of never escaping, for it cropped up in the quaintest connexions—and that was Virtue.

As the author—who hailed oddly from the Royal Exchange Assurance Office—justly claimed in his dedication to the Right Honourable Slingsby Bethell, Esq., Lord Mayor of the City of London, and One of its Representatives in Parliament (an encourager of everything tending to "the Practice of Piety" and "the Good of Mankind"), it was designed to do more than barely teach the young idea how to spell. "To inculcate into the Minds of Youth early Notices of Religion and Virtue, and to point out to them their several Duties in the various Stages of Life" was no less its aim. "And I should be very thankful," explained His Lordship's obliged, obedient, and most humble servant, "should I prove an instrument in the Hand of Providence in preventing but one of the rising Generation from falling a sacrifice to the pernicious Doctrines, secret Whispers, and perpetual Insinuations of Popish Emissaries."

It was a passage that had always swelled Jinny's bosom with emotion and the vow to ensure the gratification of this saintly aspiration by supplying in herself the minimum one member of the rising Generation to baffle these minions of the Scarlet Woman. It had been at first a little bemusing to reflect that for her Peculiar friends, the Established Church was little less pernicious: still, fended by the double buffer of her sect and Protestantism, she had thus far resisted the Emissaries she had never encountered (for certainly the Rev. Mr. Fallow, whatever the Chipstone curate might say of his Puseyite practices, had never tried to pervert her even to the Establishment).

With three generations brought up on this pious pabulum—the copy from which Sidrach the Owler had educated himself for smuggling was already beyond the fiftieth edition—-it seemed strange that the century should have had any declensions from virtue to note; that papistry should have progressed was incredible.

If in her dim, childish way, Jinny had ever felt a jarring note in this treasure-house of virtue and information, it was the assumption that both these existed primarily for little boys. True, among the fascinating woodcuts was one depicting little girls at school, but even there the mistress occupied the stiff chair, while the Dominie of the boys' school, majestic in a full-bottomed wig, sat throned on a chair with arms. "A good child will love God," she read with humid eyes, only to be pulled up short by "he will put his whole trust in Him." Everything seemed to be masculine, from God downwards: there was no place for women even in punishment: to be "well whipt at School and at Home, Day and Night"—a recommendation she found it difficult to reconcile with the definition of "Ferula," as "a foolish Instrument, used in some Schools"—was a Nemesis held out only to the boy who minded not his Church, his School, and his Book. Such a one would live and die a Slave, a Fool, and a Dunce. But as to the fate of bad little girls there was a mysterious silence. Even for their goodness there was no sure reward: for though presumably they were included in the well-behaved who would be clothed in Garments of Gold and have a Crown of Gold set on their Head, while Angels rejoiced to see them, these joys were never definitely attached to an exclusively feminine pronoun. A virtuous "woman" appeared once to her relief, but it was only to be a crown to her husband. Even in the foot-notes Jinny could not find a female. "If the young learner has learnt to read these lessons pretty perfectly," said one note, "let him go over them once more." As for the Useful Fables, it was the boy that stole Apples or went into the Water instead of going to School; and when it came to the longest story of all, "Life truly painted in the Natural History of Tommy and Harry"—the story that professed to show "Youth the ways of life in General," and did indeed show how wickedness wrecks you on the Coast of Barbary, where you are torn to pieces by wild beasts as per woodcut, while the pattern of Virtue and Goodness still lives happy—it appeared that even a realistic picture of life may be complete without girls.

IV

Behold, however, Jinny—despite her sex—embarked on a learned career, and burning the midnight oil in her fat little lamp instead of curling up in her chest of drawers. Puckering her brow she sat on a squat wooden arm-chair in that dun papered living-room, imbibing virtue and information, till the Dutch clock in the outer box-room startled her with its emphatic declaration of the hour, and the cracked mirror revealed her eyes heavy-lidded. Far out over the Common streamed the curtained light of that midnight oil, for the shutter could not be closed, owing to a pair of blackbirds that had set up house in the eaves. Jinny had found one of the young fallen on the grass: she had fed it with morsels of meat which it swallowed with great yellow gulps, following up the meal with a fluted grace. She had restored it to its nest—touched to mark the domestic virtue of its co-incubating parents. It had grown quite big now and flown hoppingly away with short sharp cries, but Jinny still cherished the nest and felt no need of the barring shutter. In the silence the creakings of the cottage often sounded like footsteps outside, but Jinny was not nervous, and a real footstep would rouse Nip, she knew. Sometimes, these warm May nights, she heard the cuckoo keeping hours as late as hers, sometimes the nightingales would sing passionately in the lane. There was one, she knew, that niched in a mutilated, ivy-swathed trunk bordering on the Common, and she would hear it answering the faint melancholy calls from afar with throbs and gushes of melody as well as with a series of quick, piercing notes. And sometimes when the air was clear she could hear the distant church clocks. But all these sounds, like Nip's and the Gaffer's snoring, were but a restful accompaniment to the acquisition of omniscience: even the nightingale, in her ignorance of literature, failed to romanticize her thoughts, painfully bent on mastering all there was to know.

Meanings, we have seen, played a great part in these studies: "Dollar—a Dutch coin"; "Engineer—an Artist"; "Gambadoes—a Sort of Boots"; "History—an Account of Things"; "Interview—Mutual Sight"; "Logarithms—Artificial Numbers"; "Mahomet—the Turkish Impostor"; "Replevin—a Writ so called"; "Stolidity—Foolishness"; "Tarantula—a Baneful Insect"; "Valentine—a Romish Festival"; "Upholsterer—an Undertaker"; "Zodiac—a Circle in the Heavens": such were the strange vocables she kept muttering and misunderstanding: believing indeed that "Paramour" was merely a grander word for "Lover" and connecting divorce with "Schismatic—one guilty of unlawful separation." It pained her to meet the "Sadducees—a People that Denies the Being of Angels," slurring, as did these unimaginable heretics, the status of her own mother. Surely it was for such that "Damnation—the punishment of Hell Torments" had been designed. Punctuation too she studied, growing learned in Apostrophes, Asterisks, Carets, Crotchets, and Obelisks; other hours were devoted to Grammar, Tenses, Degrees of Comparison (always between good and better Boys), Genitives, and even Scraps of Latin. Pronunciation, however, was her great stumbling-block. How was it possible to keep one's feet in the chaos, say, of four-syllabled words, each accented on a different syllable? Antiquary, Ambassador, Affidavit, Animadvert—it was heart-breaking and head-splitting. Her memory, so marvellous when vivified by realities, broke down before this procession of shadows.

With what relief she turned to the rich riot of "Moral and Satyric Poems"—though her sex was still distressingly ignored, and through every loophole the eternal male popped up.

He most improves who studies with Delight
And learns Sound Morals while he learns to write.

Still, where "Swearing, Gaming, and Pride" were rebuked in lashing lines, she was not sorry to find the petticoat conspicuous by its absence. It was a rare joy to come on Queen Anne in a "List of Abbreviations" under the unexpected guise of A.R.; in the list of kings, too, she appeared again, together with Mary and Elizabeth; not a large proportion, Jinny thought, rejoicing at the Victoria unforeseen by the learned author, whose "Chronological Account of Remarkable Things" stopped, like her friend Commander Dap's, at the Battle of Trafalgar.

This table was indeed one of her favourite pages—it gave her, she felt, a bird's-eye view of all history—and with her head for figures she never forgot that the Ten Commandments and the Ten Plagues were given in 1494 B.C., and that the sun stood still at Joshua's word in 1454, while Daniel was in the Den of Lions in 536. She was puzzled, though, at the destruction of Troy which intervened between Joshua's interference with the sun and Saul's anointment. Of the twenty-two great events that preceded the Christian era, this was the only one that the Bible forbore to mention. Subsequently to Christianity things seemed to her to have moved fast, for up till the year 1600 alone, fourteen "remarkable Things" occurred—two-thirds as many as had happened in the whole previous 4007 years since the world was created—while after 1600, extraordinary events sprouted like blackberries, no less than fifty crowding to their grand climacteric in Trafalgar.

In these fifty she was glad to see included the Confutation of Popery by Martin Luther—a personage with whom Miss Gentry had made her familiar—and she thrilled almost with local pride to find "Arts and Sciences first taught at Cambridge, 1119," for the Cambridge carriers sometimes penetrated eastwards as far as Chipstone itself. As a carrier, indeed, she was immensely excited by the "Eleven Days successive Snow" of 1674, the "Frost for thirteen Weeks" of 1684, "The Terrible high Wind of November 26, 1703," "the great and total Eclipse of the Sun, April 22, 1713," and the "severe Frost for nine Weeks" beginning on Christmas Eve, 1739. She could vividly sympathize with the unfortunate carriers of those days, and she did not wonder that these brumal phenomena should form so great a proportion of the few score happenings of Universal History, for frosts and winds must be terrible indeed to be recounted as on a level with the shooting of Admiral Byng, the American Declaration of Independence, the Birth of the Prince of Wales, and the "Attempted Assassination of George III at Drury Lane by Hadfield, a lunatic."

These studious vigils were invariably wound up with a prayer from this same limitless thesaurus: on her knees by the transmogrified chest of drawers, and with her hair hanging down her back, and the lamplight falling on the coarse grey-typed page of the Spelling-Book, Jinny repeated one or other of its masculine supplications, prose or verse, and only a cynic ("Cynic—a Sour, Crabbed Fellow") would have laughed at the solemnity with which she swallowed all those motley lucubrations, whether lay or clerical. An impromptu prayer for her grandfather was invariably slipped in, for this holy book of hers finished as terribly as the Old Testament, and what made it worse was that this awful culmination of the Spelling-Book was printed in black-letter. It was a gruesome recital of the miseries and follies of "the Seven Stages of Life"—none of which seemed worth living even with the correctest of spelling, while death seemed worth dying to escape the depravity and decrepitude of the final stadium. But although her grandfather, with all his peevish humours, could hardly be counted so steeped in sin as the old man of the text, while his infirmities were still rudimentary, yet the physical prognostication was terrifying— "for when we come to those years, that our Eyes grow dim, Ears deaf, Visage pale, Hands shaking, Knees trembling, and Feet faltering, then it is evident the Dissolution of our mortal Tabernacle is near at Hand."

Jinny could never read those dreadful words but she would creep anxiously to the foot of the dark, twisting staircase and listen for the reassuring sound of the Tabernacle snoring. And if she bore so patiently with his whims and crotchets, not none of the credit must be given to this sanctimonious Spelling-Book.

V

While Jinny was thus pursuing omniscience and equipping herself to meet the masterful young man, and while the young man in question was adding the mastery of the horn to his conquests, their roads failed to cross. Jinny went to chapel the Sunday following the thunderstorm, but Will was too alarmed by the communal expectation of public autobiography to venture there again, and his parents were only too glad to ignore his home-staying and to resume their private Christa-peculiar-delphian service, being sufficiently fortified by his preoccupation with the Bible. What had driven Will to the Book again was the outrageous appearance on Saturday night of Uncle Lilliwhyte as parcel-bearer. Recovering from his relief that the parcel did not contain snakes, but the conventional household stores, Will found himself angry on his mother's behalf. What right had Jinny to foist such a fusty ragamuffin upon them, the gay strings of whose rotting beaver only accentuated his griminess? Jinny must know that his mother ranked uncleanliness next to ungodliness. And Uncle Lilliwhyte would be a fixture too, unless violently shaken off—he was Jinny's neighbour; as natural a go-between as Will's own neighbour, Master Peartree. He had already bribed off the shepherd: must he be blackmailed by both?

And so, while Essex was at prayer, Will was concocting a furious Oriental epistle, demanding a clean envoy, if Jinny was too lazy to come herself. This was not so difficult to demand, though laziness seemed as unknown to the Hebrews as gloves. He had dallied, indeed, with his original idea of fetching the household parcels from Chipstone himself, but somehow he could not bring himself to so complete a severance of relations with Jinny, especially as after the appearance of Uncle Lilliwhyte in the new rôle of goods-deliverer, his mother had surprisingly suggested that to spare Methusalem's legs, the old nondescript might always in future bring the weekly parcel for a penny or two. Will had put this suggestion emphatically aside—it would mean exposing his mother to a contact she detested—but he wound up his letter to Jinny by threatening to become his own carrier unless the service was conducted with propriety. Nip duly returned that same Sunday afternoon with the answer that if he would send his esteemed order in writing, Mr. Daniel Quarles would have pleasure in executing his commission through a scrupulously scoured ambassador. Will started replying instantly that it was not his order: let her mark that he was not the householder, merely the "scribe." To write out the order, however, gave him unexpected pause. Who could have realized that "parrafin," "sope" and "shuggar" were alike unenjoyed by the heathen Jews? A pity that Frog Farm was itself so "flowing with milk and honey": with what confidence he could have drawn on the resources of Palestine! True, one might dodge—lamps and oil were abundant enough in Judæa, and purification and sweetness could be suggested with airy allusiveness. But in the end he only wrote grandly, "Household order the same as uzual."

Before this order had been executed, however, chance brought about a meeting. Not that Miss Gentry, near whose wayside cottage it occurred, would have called it chance. For that deft needlewoman, besides believing in her own stained-glass miracle, cherished, as we know, a naïve faith in "Culpeper's Complete Herbal"—a faith doubtless sustained by the attacks on the Pope or on infidel physicians that might lurk snakelike in its most innocent-seeming herb. Under the stimulus of this elementally indelicate work—never permitted to stray from her bedside, though imparted in filtered form to Jinny—she would tie woody nightshade round her neck for her dizziness, and buy watercress from Uncle Lilliwhyte to wash away pimples with the juice. And if these herbs were, as Culpeper testified, under the respective governance of Mercury and the Moon, how much more so human life! Miss Gentry had indeed remarked to Will that very afternoon (when he at last brought his mother's bonnet to be "bleached as good as new") that her own horoscope, cast in infancy by her aunt, had shown that the first time she went upon a voyage she would be drowned: a reading whose infallibility her happy survival demonstrated, since she had never been foolish enough to set foot upon a vessel. "But for the deciphering of this horoscope," she had pointed out, "I should surely now have been drowned, for I am naturally as fond of voyages as you."

It must be admitted that if Miss Gentry had thus pathetically perished, Will would not have taken his mother's bonnet to her, nor met Jinny that afternoon. But then would he have met Jinny but for the foolish sheep? Even the ovine fates, it would appear, are interblent with the human.

This sheep suddenly dawned upon Jinny's vision as Methusalem with his cunning nose was trying to open a gate that led over a private road, on either side of which its fellows grazed. Preoccupied with the task of clasping Nip so that he should not frighten the flock in his passage, she did not at first observe that in the gap between the hinge of the gate and the post, a sheep's head was jammed, and that Methusalem's success in lifting the latch bade fair to asphyxiate it. The silly creature, having escaped from the flock, had evidently tried to jump back again through this gap, at a point just large enough to admit its head, and with the failure of the leap, the head had descended into the narrowest portion and there remained in pillory. In the creature's terror at the approach of the cart and Nip's excited barking, its efforts to free itself became more convulsive than ever. Checking Methusalem in the middle of his pet trick, and fastening up Nip, Jinny jumped down and with soothing words seized the head of the frantic sheep, which was still thrusting itself backward and forward, though without the sense to jump upwards towards the broader space. But alas, its spasmodic struggles prevented her from getting a sufficient grip on it to lift the wedged and weighty head. She saw its ear was torn and bleeding, and to her imagination it was going black in the face. She looked round desperately. On the other side of the gate lay the flock, scattered apathetically over the pasture they had reaped and manured, chewing a tranquil cud, like self-righteous citizens before the writhings of one of their own black sheep: of a good Samaritan or shepherd there was no sign. She climbed over the gate and strove to lift the agonizing head from the other side, but she only increased the sufferer's frenzy as well as Nip's.

"Be quiet, Nip!" she shouted, almost hysteric herself. And as she raised her eyes to admonish the yapping terrier, she espied to her joy a puffing pipe and a stick advancing towards her cart; whether a young man or old she was not aware. He was simply man as saviour, and he was at the gate and working at the rear of the struggling head before she had quite realized it was Will, and a certain added pleasure at the sight of this man in particular had scarcely time to well up before it was swamped by the far greater pleasure of seeing the sheep deftly released. It staggered, however, as Will let it go, and lay sideways on the road, gasping, and Jinny observed with horror a raw ring round its throat where the wool was cut through as by a cord. But before she could get through the gate to its assistance, it had risen feebly, and as she came towards it, it trotted off timidly. Vastly relieved, she tried to coax or chevy the truant back to its companions. But it refused to go: on the contrary, it retreated, and in solitary self-sufficiency began to crop the wayside grass.

"Hasn't spoiled her appetite!" said Will, with a laugh.

"They don't seem to feel things as much as us," agreed Jinny.

"No, indeed." He knocked the ashes out of his pipe and pocketed it. "Fancy, if you'd got your head nipped like that!"

There seemed something aggressive in the suggestion. "I should have known to lift it up without waiting for a man," she said.

"All very well, but when one's head's caught, one is apt to lose it: one struggles blindly."

"We're not all like sheep to go astray," she said uneasily. "But thank you for your kind help." She jumped up and drove slowly through the gate. He closed it behind her and ran to open the gate at the opposite end of the private road.

"Thank you again," she said, passing through.

"But surely you'll come into the wood now you're so near," he cried through the arch of the vanishing tilt.

The cart unexpectedly slackened, Jinny's head was turned backwards. "If you won't be long," she said.

He shut the gate briskly and kept pace with her slow progress along the leafy lane towards the wood-path they both knew. Nip, untied, sprang to fawn at his feet, and then bounded into the hedge after something smelt, and barking raucously, wormed his way along like a weasel.

"Why didn't you come, Will?" said Jinny softly.

"Why didn't you?" he evaded. "Why did you send Uncle Lilliwhyte?"

"I didn't come because you didn't," she answered simply.

"I—I—your grandfather," he stammered. "I couldn't well play before him."

"You mean you couldn't play well," she flashed.

"That's all you know about it. I can blow better than Dick Burrage."

"Then why be nervous of poor old Gran'fer? He might have been umpire."

He was shocked again. "Good gracious, Jinny! Where did you get those betting words from?"

"That's my affair." She pursed her pretty lips. "But never mind—however you blow—you've deserved a pair of gloves to-day—in sheepskin."

He smiled. "I'm not above taking two pairs."

"If you win!"

"Of course I'll win."

"Don't brag. Save your breath for your blowing. We shall soon be there."

"Oh, but I'm not going to blow now," he pointed out.

"Not now? Then why have you lured me here?"

"But how could I guess I should meet you? How could I lure you? You could see I hadn't got my horn."

"I hadn't noticed," Jinny murmured.

"It's big enough," he said grimly.

"Then I certainly shan't go into the wood. I'm much too busy. Good-bye, Will." She flicked her whip, but ere Methusalem could quicken a leg, a terrible yelping came from the bushy hedgerow—it was the voice of Nip, but not of Nip the hunter, rather of a hunted, trapped Nip.

"Oh, poor Nip!" And in a moment Jinny had leapt down and was peering and pushing into the hedge. But she could penetrate scarcely at all: the wood behind was firmly guarded by a broad chaotic belt of thistle and nightshade, burr and bramble, furze and stinging-nettle, a veritable riot of prickliness; and this thorny tangle had closed upon Nip—trespassers prosecuted indeed!—though it was a relief to his mistress to find the trap was natural, not wickedly human. Stuck full of burrs, and looking like a spotted pard, her pet was shrieking for first aid. But even while she was hesitating to pierce farther, despite her gloved hands, Will brushed by her, thrilling her with the sense that this was his second feat of animal salvation; while the woodland savours and the rich prodigality and ruin of nature—for dead wood lay around as profusely as rank vegetation sprouted—seemed to stir in her the same sense of elemental forces as the thunderstorm. She scarcely noticed that Will had the aid of his stick in parting the jungle, and when he restored the whining animal to her arms, gratitude and hero-worship mingled in her emotion, though for a moment she was too occupied in picking Nip clean to say much, while Will, for his part, was engaged with equal industry in removing thorns from his sleeves and burrs from his trousers.

"Oh, you've hurt yourself!" she said at last, catching sight of blood and scratches on his hands and wrists.

"It's nothing." He tried to pluck out something from a finger.

"Shall I help you?" She pulled off her driving-gloves, took his finger and squeezed at the flesh, perceiving the microscopic protrusion of the thorn, but her own fingers were shaking and she could not extract it. He said it did not matter, it would work out; then he started sucking it. She somehow would have liked as with a child to kiss the place and make it well—the whole back of his left hand seemed reticulated in red—but instead she carried Nip back to his basket in the cart. He, too, was scored in red, though he did not seem to mind any more than the sheep. As she bent over her scratched pet, Will came up to the tail-board, still sucking at his finger.

"I shall need gloves now," he said, glancing with comic ruefulness at his scratches.

"You poor hero!" she said, with eyes softly flashing. "I will come into the wood and you shall win them."

His face lit up; then fell. "But how?" he asked.

"Isn't there my horn, silly?"

He laughed gleefully. "You're right to call me that." She leaped down, the horn dangling at her girdle, and fastened Methusalem to a tree. "Not that he's likely to move: still his head is homewards." Methusalem's head, however, was already grasswards: he was munching with gusto, while his great tail swished at the flies.

"But suppose somebody steals the parcels!" said Will with sudden compunction.

"This isn't Babylon—or America," said Jinny witheringly. "Besides, there's Nip."

Only a few yards farther was the opening they had been making for, but they now found it almost as overgrown as the entry chosen by Nip, and had it not been for the rare fern-leaf elders in the hedge, that marked their memory of the spot, they might have passed it by. "Might be in Canada," said Will. However, he pioneered with his stick, and, following him closely, she had a sense of safety and protection unknown since the days she was escorted from chapel. It was quite strange—yet not unsweet—to be thus guarded from the venomous vegetation thrusting at her from all sides, and she was not sure she was relieved when the menace and novelty were over, and they were in the wood. The struggle, moreover, had made the humanized part of the wood, on which they emerged, somewhat tame. The grove of young ash, beautiful as the slim silver-grey trunks were with their new green livery—too light to cast a shadow—suggested commerce to both of them, and the suggestion was emphasized by the charred remains of a bonfire of elm-loppings, and by a deserted charcoal-burner's hut in a clearing. But poetry had gathered on the mossy stumps of other trees, long since felled, and they came down a wonderful azure river of bluebells running as between wooded green banks. As they waded through the tall thin stalks, they chanced here on a patch of late-lingering primroses and there on green advance waves of foxgloves, with their long leaves. Primrose, bluebell, foxglove—what a beautiful succession, thought Jinny. How marvellous was earth in its changing loveliness, and Heaven in its unchanging bounty! On another slope, crowned by Spanish chestnuts, glittered a stream purling down to lose itself in scrub. Here rosemary was in bloom, humming with bees, and yonder was broom, its yellow blossoms showing against a lighter green than the earlier gorse, which flowered in great golden clumps.

"The gorse looks fine," said Jinny.

"And smells finer," said Will. "Let's sit down."

"Not here," said Jinny, coyly shrinking. "There's nettles."

"They're dead!" he said, grasping their yellow brittleness. But they walked on.

They came over baby bracken and crisp beechnuts to a sort of ring surrounded by blushing young oaks, and little silver birches with their flat green leaves, and tall aspen-trees, and one lonely mountain-ash with white flowers. Overhead, early as it was, the moon had long been hanging at three-quarters, white and magically diaphanous: a dream-planet. Unseen wood-pigeons purred, and a tomtit was singing.

"Here!" said Will, beginning to sit down.

"No, no!" She clutched his arm to keep him up. "An ant-heap!" This time her shyness had found sounder cover.

He gave a comical "Oh!" and stood watching the squirm of seething life, absolutely black at the central congestion, where ants walked indifferently under or over one another: they were like the moving grains in an hour-glass, Jinny thought. Will poked his stick into the great piazza.

"Don't," said Jinny.

"I'm not hurting them." The ants were, in fact, already using the rod as a causeway. "Why, they're like you, Jinny!"

"Like me?"

"All carriers and all busy."

She laughed, and followed their movements with a new sympathy, though she was rather disgusted by those that carried dead flies or dead ants.

"Those are not carriers—those are undertakers," she insisted.

They sat down at last on a mound of spongy moss, free from formic activity, and there was a silence. The little purling stream was too far off to break it, but they heard a chaffinch and the peep-bo-playing cuckoo, with that golden human note that floats through the warm, brooding May. And then the irrepressible and unbasketable Nip came rushing and tearing, not making straight for them, but appearing and disappearing like a giant fungus in the rich masses of blues or greens or yellows.

He made an opening for conversation, and presently when he came snuggling into Jinny's arms—poor scotched creature!—an opportunity for joint patting and petting: a process in which hands do not always succeed in partitioning out the pattable and pettable surface rigidly, but graze and brush each other, and even lie passively in abstracted contact.

"Why shouldn't I buy this wood?" said Will, after one of these sustained manual juxtapositions.

"Wouldn't that be lovely?" said Jinny.

"Yes—I must settle something soon. Those aspens, though, I'd cut 'em down. They're only a weed. And yonder ashlings weren't planted quite close enough—you've got to make 'em fight for air if you want 'em straight enough to sell."

Jinny was vaguely disappointed at the turn of this conversation; not following the romantic dream vaguely underlying it.

"But could you afford to buy such a big wood?" she murmured.

"Big wood? Why, in Canada you get forever of land for nothing!"

"Then why didn't you stay there?" she asked.

"This is better than America," and his hand touched Jinny's too consciously.

"Why, what was the matter with America?" she murmured, withdrawing the hand from Nip's flank with a little blush.

Everything was the matter with America, it appeared. He was, indeed, more anxious to explain how nothing was the matter with Essex, but under Jinny's physical bashfulness and intellectual curiosity he found himself headed off his native county and kept closely to Transatlantic territory. And under the spell of her eager attention he was soon discoursing fluently enough, sketching a discreetly selected picture of his adventures, beginning with the emigrant sailing packet in which he had gone out as a stowaway, but wherein he fared little worse than the emigrants proper, who in the first six of the thirty-seven days' voyage had had none of the stipulated provisions served out to them, despite their contract tickets, and no meat during the whole voyage. They had had to be satisfied with their daily water and the right of cooking, and complaints were met with oaths from the officers and doctors, and sometimes even with fists or rope-ends from the sailors. Once or twice the hose had been turned on them, but there were over nine hundred of them, he said, so she might imagine the Babel and confusion, though there were two great passenger decks on which the tallest man could stand, and on whose shelved sides they could all find sleeping-space, with never more than six to a berth. And then from the moment America had burst upon the vessel in the guise of touts, runners, and employers, all anxious to mislead or enslave, he had borne through the continent the banner of a steady disapprobation.

In the States, where his first clutches at Fortune had been made, peculiar perils awaited the British immigrant. If he gravitated, as was natural, to the cliques and boarding-houses of his countrymen, he was likely to be soon "used up" by the gambling and drinking sets that feigned to make him welcome. And if he escaped this pitfall by his resourcefulness, he would strike the native American prejudice against English immigrants, popularly supposed to consist of the paupers and wastrels whom the parish overseers of Old England, anxious to be quit of the burden of supporting them, bribed with free Atlantic passages and dumped on the struggling New World: a prejudice, Will admitted laughingly, which his own purse had done nothing to diminish.

At first he had got a job as car-driver and fed at the market-houses, but though the food was good and cheap, the company was rough of manner and language. And even when he was earning good money— at a boot-store with the sign of a gigantic boot made of real leather reaching to the first-floor windows—he had disliked the "go-along-steamboat" pressure of existence, and the Mechanics' Boarding House where gabbling Yankees gobbled at a pace both unhealthy in itself and unchivalrous to the unpunctual. The habit of loading the table with all the courses simultaneously took off the edge of his appetite if he was early, and left only universal ruins if he was late. He had no patience with clams that were not oysters, egg-plants that were not eggs, and corn that had to be munched cow-like. Accustomed to the clean linen of the paternal farm, he loathed the insect-ridden bedrooms one divided with a varying number of strangers. He liked to see pigs, but not perambulating and scavenging the streets; why, in New York they were more numerous than the dogs! Providence had designed tobacco, he opined, for smoking and not for chewing; and saliva for swallowing, not for spitting.

It was, in fact, a most unpleasant America that loomed up to Jinny's vision that day, especially in contrast with this lovely wood, overbrooded by the white moon now growing faintly golden: a sort of spittoon of a continent, mitigated by dollars and dancing. Even in Canada, for which Will had felt a more personal responsibility—accentuated by the British soldiers to be met at every turn—and in which he gladly picked out points of superiority to the States, a similar sense of massive untidiness had weighed upon him and jarred every home-born instinct.

He tried to convey to Jinny the desolation of zigzag rail-fences that took the place of these hedges now glorious with hawthorn and fool's-parsley and the starry stitchwort; the raw settlements, the half-built log huts hardly superior to yon derelict charcoal-burner's hut (their windows stuffed sometimes with old straw hats), the unachieved roads, full of mud or dust, the ubiquitous stumps that were once trees, the piles of logs that were not yet habitations, all that crude civilization arising shoddily out of the virgin forest on the sole principle of the cheapest practicable, with nothing whole-hearted but the lust for dollars. Caleb Flynt's slow English conservatism, Caleb's unworldly standards, spoke again through his son. But even Will was too inarticulate to put his feeling precisely into words—and when Jinny reminded him that in this very wood trees had been cut down and burned, and that he himself had spoken of cutting down the aspens, he could not quite make clear to her, who had never known any but long-humanized places, the peculiar indecency of a forest at the stage of semi-transformation into a mushroom settlement.

Beautiful enough the backwoods, he laboured to explain, where man's fight with the forest was only begun, where great beeches and maples, and wild flowers still possessed the black mould the settler was to lay bare for wheat; where his pioneer hut was circled by a green gloom, and the chink of his cow-bells or the laughter of his children alone vied with the ring of the axe and the thunderous fall of the giants. But later on—"it's like that plover's egg you opened once," he burst forth with a sudden inspiration. "No longer an egg, not yet a bird; only a smell!"

"But it was you who gave it me," laughed Jinny. There was a great content at her heart, sitting here and seeing her little world open out in forests and seas and emotions still stranger. And he—he for the first time enjoyed the society of woman as spiritual counterpart, had moments in which he forgot Jinny was pretty, in which her hand—now unconsciously nestling in his in her absorption in his narration—was felt as a friendly rather than as a physical glow. Unfortunately in this sense of a sympathetic Jinny lay the serpentine temptation which shattered their paradise. For, beguiled by her apparent subjugation, he went on to improve the occasion. "And it's just the same with women who are neither women nor men. A woman's place is the home."

The slipping of Jinny's hand out of his was the first sign that he had roused her to reality. Her cry, "How late it is!" was the next. And she looked at the sunset glowing in glamorous gold through the trees. There was a magic peace in the air, and a rare thrush sang as in a dream. It seemed a tragedy to move.

Will protested vehemently. "It's not late at all. You were unusually early this afternoon. No, don't go— you'll wake up poor Nip."

"Did your story send him to sleep? Rude dog! But I must go—a woman's place is the home!" She got up, smiling, with the snoring dog in her arms, but her mockery was friendly enough: the intimate atmosphere could not be dissipated at a jerk. He was constrained to follow her, if only to precede her through that jungly path: the prospect of driving home with her still shone rosy.

"By the way," he said lightly, "I've been talking with Mr. Flippance about getting that horse for him."

"What!" She stopped and turned on him, her eyes blazing.

"His last animal was faked," he explained mildly. "He was badly taken in, and you can't know all the tricks of the trade as well as a man."

"And isn't Mr. Flippance a man?"

"Yes, of course. But—but—"

"It all depends on which man, you see—and which woman."

"But I'm sure no woman knows properly about horses," he said. "How would you tell the age, for instance?"

"By the teeth, of course."

"Which teeth?"

Jinny flushed. She really did not know, and that made her only angrier: "If I wanted your help in my affairs, I should have asked you."

"Well, there's nothing to be mad about."

"There is everything to be mad about. How did you know he wanted me to get a horse? Only because I told you. And then you go to him and interfere with my business and insinuate I'm incapable."

"It's not so much you're incapable—" he began.

"It's because a woman's place isn't the cattle-market, I know. But why can't we buy cows as well as butter, and horses as well as horse-collars?"

"Because only men go—and it's rough."

"Well then, let women go and it won't be."

"And do you want women to be horsemen too, get up at four o'clock and go ploughing?"

"Why not?"

"They haven't the strength, for one thing. There's lots of things they can't do, and never will. Take thatching, for instance—you can't imagine a woman sprawling along a roof."

"Yes, I can."

"Of course you can," he sneered. "You can imagine her in breeches."

"If petticoats get in the way."

"There'll never be Bloomerites in England," he said grimly. "You mark my word. If a woman can't plough or dig without leggings, that's a proof she wasn't meant to plough or dig."

They had reached now the pleached and tangly path back to the road, but she darted ahead of him, battling with the branches herself in her revolt from dependence. He could not regain the lead unless he jostled rudely, and every now and then—not with wilful malice, but no less maddeningly—she held back for him the boughs she had parted. And all the while the sleeping Nip was protected too: clasped by one hand to her bosom.

Suddenly the circle of her little horn got caught in the bushes like the horn of Isaac's ram. "Why, Jinny," he cried, "we forgot all about the horn! Wait! Wait!"

She disentangled it calmly. "You shan't blow mine. You must blow your own now."

He fired up. "You want to get out of the gloves."

"Now you're going horn-mad," she jested icily, emerging on the high road. "Good-bye, Mr. Flynt."

It was the first time she had withheld the Will.

"Good-bye, Miss Boldero," he said as frigidly, removing his hat with an exaggerated gallantry. Each felt that the parting was final: never would they even speak to each other again.

But they had yet to reckon with Nip. For that intelligent creature, waking into the distressing atmosphere that had been generated while his vigilance was relaxed, would be no party to the breach. When he perceived that the cart was to go off without Will, he jumped down and tried to chevy him into it, and as the parties went off at a tangent, he ran desperately from one to the other, striving to shepherd them together, barking and pleading and panting like a toy engine. It was only a peremptory blast from a distant horn that at last persuaded the distracted animal where his first duty lay.

The dying day still flooded the earth with warmth and radiance: the little coffee-and-cream-coloured calves still frisked in the meadows that the buttercups turned into fields of the cloth of gold: the forget-me-nots were still gleaming in the cottage gardens, the lilac was still peeping over manorial walls, the laburnum still hanging down its yellow chandeliers, and the horse-chestnut upholding its white candelabras. But for these twain, obstinately and against the best canine advice going their separate ways, the colour had been sucked out of the landscape and the clemency from the air. Before Will, wandering deviously, had remembered his evening sausages, these also had grown cold; mist and clouds had turned the moon to a blood-red boat, and the bats were swooping and the wood-owls shrilling where larks had soared and sung.

CHAPTER VIII

CUPID AND CATTLE

Wit she hath without desire
To make known how much she hath;
And her anger flames no higher
Than may fitly sweeten wrath.
Full of pity as may be,
Though perhaps not so to me.
BROWNE, "Britannia's Pastorals."

I

It is to be feared that the sting of Mr. Will Flynt's offence lay precisely in Jinny's ignorance of horses, and that if her old companion had come to her aid more tactfully, she would have welcomed his co-operation in the great purchase. But her pride in her work would hardly allow her to admit even to herself that here was a commission perhaps beyond her capacities. Had she not enjoyed an almost lifelong experience of Methusalem? As a monogamist would resent being told he knew nothing of matrimony, so Jinny repudiated the notion that she knew nothing of equinity. Besides, the cattle-market was far from seeming so strange a world to her as Will had imagined. Had her cart not often conveyed thence or thither a netted calf, had she not marketed even his own mother's piglings? A fig for the masculine aura! If Mr. Flippance exaggerated after his fashion in declaring she would have undertaken to get him the moon—at any rate it was not the man in it that would have kept her back.

It was, therefore, with a bruised and burning but indomitable heart that Jinny went about her work these ever longer days. For women must work, though men may mope. Poor Will, who had nothing to do but to chew his bitter cud of memory, was the more pitiable, and his temper was not improved when early Friday evening the comparatively clean Master Gale, evidently caught on his way home from school, arrived with "the same as uzual." This apple-cheeked and white-collared understudy for Jinny was no less an eyesore than Uncle Lilliwhyte, and Will made Martha refuse the parcel on the ground that if they encouraged the lad, it would lead to truancy. Such was his solicitude for the schoolboy whose copy-book he had diverted from its scholastic function. But he was not less furious when Farmer Gale brought back the parcel the next morning on horseback and explained amiably that he had seen Jinny about it, and that henceforward this overburdened damsel would leave the Flynt parcel with his, and he would have pleasure in delivering it in the course of riding about his farms.

The rain and the cold snap, that had come so suddenly after the quarrel in the wood, was welcome to Jinny in her present mood. For her the summer was over. True, she espied its first wild rose, but it reminded her only of a round strawberry water-ice, such as her well-to-do clients spooned at the Chipstone confectioner's. Everything was gelid, except Nip's nose, and that but added to her depression. Was the darling feverish from the scratches of his spiny crawlings, or did he share his mistress's heavy humours? Her distraction might have led to a nasty accident had not the last of the trio kept his head, for in a lonely lane Methusalem, who in these days seemed to whinny his sympathy and nuzzle into her palm with enhanced tenderness, deftly avoided the prostrate antlered trunk of an oak-tree which had been split and splintered by lightning. Possibly it had lain there since that Sunday's storm, for her work had not brought her that way. The bark of the whole tree had been peeled off, save for a small patch where a few buds still suggested vitality, and Jinny had a grandiose sense that all nature sympathized with the strange desolation that had come over her joyous self.

Her mind turned to fate and constellations as she drew up at Miss Gentry's door and summoned with a blast that fantastic female, who was feeding the chickens with which she variegated life and tantalized Squibs. Miss Gentry did not need anything beyond her usual depilatory. It was a standing grief and astonishment to her that though white lilies (under the domain of the moon) will "trimly deck a blank place with hair," neither Culpeper nor the planets had provided against the contrary contingency: even fig-wort (owned by Venus) merely removing wens and freckles. Hence she was reduced to a mere chemist's prescription: a solution of barium sulphide swayed by no known planet. The stuff came in a pot.

Miss Gentry in ordering it did not shirk the word "depilatory." On the contrary she pronounced the five syllables with a pomposity which was the more impressive to Jinny because even "The Universal Spelling-Book" stopped short at four syllables. Not for worlds—whether to her client or the public at large—would Jinny have betrayed her knowledge that the hair-destroyer represented a never-ending battle with Miss Gentry's moustache. And for the sensitive dressmaker herself the polysyllable was a soothing cover. Ostrich-like she hid her head in its spacious sandiness.

There was, however, the little matter of Martha's bleached and new-trimmed bonnet, which Jinny might convey to Frog Farm, and the casual mention that it was Will who had brought it led to considerable conversation. Jinny's equipage was drawn up outside the little garden, where tulips (red, damask, and pink) stood like tall guards before a tropical palace; and Miss Gentry, despite the chill wind, leaned on her garden-gate, carefully nursing her black cat against Nip's possible swoops.

The excellent lady, whose erudition Jinny had always absorbed with the reverence due to a reader of The Englishwoman's Magazine, was always delighted to have the girl sitting at her feet—even though to the crude physical vision Jinny always appeared to be sitting above her head, and Miss Gentry to be looking up to her. Sometimes real information from the aforesaid magazine, which bore the sub-title of

"The Christian Mother's Miscellany," was thus transmitted to Jinny; but Miss Gentry's brain was obviously too cluttered up with archaic notions to be really beneficial to her young devotee. Thus, although Miss Gentry enlarged Jinny's mind, it was more a matter of range than of accuracy.

The conversation to-day, however, was on a more personal plane. Jinny was resolved to speak no further word to Mr. William Flynt: his interference was unforgivable. But when it transpired that he had brought the bonnet, she did not attempt to check Miss Gentry's flow of favourable comment, still less to contradict it. For a Peculiar he was quite the gentleman, Miss Gentry opined, especially after that coarse and flippant Bundock. Not tall enough for her taste, because she thought you ought always to look up to a man; still, handsome in a rough way, despite his ginger hair.

"Not ginger!" Jinny protested.

"It shades to ginger," the dressmaker replied severely, as an authority upon colours. "But it served to brighten up his face, which was none too cheerful. Born under Saturn, I should think, and the sign of the Scorpion."

"And what effect has that?" asked Jinny, alarmed.

"Well, for one thing it qualifies the unruly actions and passions of Venus."

"The goddess of Beauty," observed Jinny, airing her Spelling-Book.

"Of Love," corrected Miss Gentry.

Jinny's face shaded towards the colour under discussion, and she cried: "Down, Nip," to that recumbent animal's amusement. "He nearly jumped on the bonnet-box," she explained.

"He should eat herbs under the dominion of the Sun," said Miss Gentry.

"Nip?"

"No—Mr. Flynt. He needs vital spirits."

"Still, ginger is hardly the word," murmured Jinny.

"It looks ginger against his clothes," persisted Miss Gentry. "Of course a man can't understand dressing himself."

"Why, he's better dressed than anybody in Long Bradmarsh—except Mr. Fallow," said Jinny.

Miss Gentry was mollified by the compliment to her pastor. "All the same his coat wrinkles at the shoulders," she said. "You notice next time."

"I've got better things to do than to look at Mr. Flynt's coat-sleeves," said Jinny. "And I'll be going on."

"Well, if you do see him, give him my kind regards," said Miss Gentry, "and say that any time he's passing and would like a cup of tea, I'd be glad to discuss the tract I gave him."

"Oh, it's no use trying to convert him," said Jinny. "He's nothing at all."

"Then why did he go to your chapel the other Sunday?"

"Did he go?" said Jinny, amazed. "I dare say that's what has depressed him."

"He not only went, but with your peculiar ideas of the House of God, he had his dinner there!"

"Oh, no! Why he was dining at 'The Black Sheep.'"

"Nothing of the sort. A dressmaker has ears."

"But a carrier has eyes. And I saw him there."

"Then I'll never believe Isabella Mawhood again."

"I hope you haven't been making her more vanities," said Jinny, as she slowly turned Methusalem's nose the other way.

"Only a new bonnet, you funny little Peculiar. You see the case was coming on at the Chelmsford Sessions, and I should have got a verdict against Mr. Mawhood not only for his wife's silk dress, but for the chickens his ferrets killed—"

"You issued a replevin, I suppose," put in Jinny grandly.

"I could have had a tort or a subpœna or anything," assented Miss Gentry, with equal magnificence. "But the defendant thought best to compromise. He's got to clear this cottage of rats for nothing this winter—you know how they come gnawing my best stuffs—and in return my landlady has to pay for a new bonnet for his wife."

"But Mrs. Mawhood's silk dress—who pays for that?" asked Jinny mystified.

"Oh, Mrs. Mott pays for that."

"But why Mrs. Mott?"

"She didn't want to have a scandal in the community, and your so-called Deacon swore he hadn't got the money. They make Mrs. Mott pay for everything nowadays."

"It's too bad," said Jinny. "And Mrs. Mawhood comes out of it all with her dress paid for and a new bonnet."

"Well, she does become clothes more than her sister-Peculiars, I must say that—present company excepted! That old rat-catcher's lucky to have got such a young wife for his second, even though he was her third."

"She's not so young," said Jinny.

"She's no older than I am," persisted Miss Gentry. "And born, like me, under Venus."

Jinny suppressed a smile. Despite her respect for Miss Gentry she had never accepted her standing invitation to explore the Colchester romance. Unread in the literature of love though she was, the girl's natural instinct refused to see the middle-aged moustachio'd dressmaker as the heroine of a love-drama. Her affair with the angel seemed, indeed, to place her apart. "I think it's disgraceful to have had three husbands," she insisted.

"Not at all, when each is a Christian marriage, and the first two spouses have been duly taken by an overruling Providence. Of course the unhallowed romance one inspires is another thing. As I always say to Bundock—oh, we ought not to have mentioned names, ought we, Squibs dear? Please forget it." She stroked the cat in her arms. "But there, Jinny! You can't understand these things—you too were born under Saturn."

"How do you know that?" Jinny was vaguely resentful.

"You're so cold-blooded—perhaps it was even under the constellation of the Pisces—the Fishes, that is. You've never taken the faintest interest in Love. Do you know, I made a rhyme about you the other day."

"A rhyme!" Jinny was excited. "Do tell me!"

Miss Gentry shook her head. "You wouldn't like it."

"Oh, but I must hear it."

Miss Gentry continued obstinately to stroke Squibs. But finally, as if electrified by the fur, she broke out like an inspired pythoness, in a weird chanting voice:

"When the Brad in opposite ways shall course, Lo! Jinny's husband shall come on a horse, And Jinny shall then learn Passion's force."

Jinny was so overwhelmed with admiration at the poetry—quite on a par, she felt, with the pieces of "The Universal Spelling-Book," especially as the Rhyme or "jingle in the ear" was on the very pattern of the model verse there given:

Prostrate my contrite Heart I bend,
My God, my Father and my Friend,
Do not forsake me in the end

—that she could hardly take in the sense at the moment.

"How lovely!" she said.

"I'm glad you're satisfied. It means, of course"—Miss Gentry firmly explained the oracle—"that you'll never marry, being as incapable of Passion as the Brad of flowing backwards and forwards at the same time."

A strange protest as written in letters of fire crept through all Jinny's veins. Even her face flamed. She began "clucking" to Methusalem to start.

"And I've made one about Mrs. Mawhood too," pursued the pythoness, now irrepressible. "I don't wish her ill, but I'm afraid it'll prove true, poor thing." And without waiting to be discouraged, indeed, following the already moving cart, she chanted:

"She may look to South, she may look to North, But the finger of fate hath forbidden a fourth, And the rat-slayer, clinging to life and his gold, Shall dance on the grave where she lieth cold."

"Not dance!" laughed Jinny, relieved at this diversion.

"Well preach—it's just as bad, when a man's not ordained," said Miss Gentry, and this being the signal for a theological assault, Jinny drove off rapidly.

II

But she had no intention of bearing the bonnet to Frog Farm. Nor, despite the account that Farmer Gale had given of the new parcel arrangement, had she really agreed to establish him as sub-carrier-in-ordinary. He was too moneyed and important for that, and she found it hard enough to accept the favour of being driven to and from chapel in his dog-cart—a favour necessitated by her grandfather's and even her own ideas as to the indecorum of their business cart. Besides, she had almost resolved to seek his advice, perhaps his help, in the famous horse-purchase: anything rather than break down before Will! So she must not overdo it. No, Master Peartree, for all his novel churlishness, must convey the bonnet. He could scarcely be treated like Farmer Gale's boy, and if they did refuse it at his hands, still it would only abide next door.

The shepherd-cowman was not, however, to be found in his accustomed haunts, and she lost a good hour in hunting for him in the various mutually distant pastures to which he led his ever-edacious sheep. None of the men ploughing the great red fields for turnips had seen him pass. At last, by the aid of a taciturn lout, who was driving a tumbril laden with hurdles and backed with a tall crate, Master Peartree was located in the farm buildings at the other extremity of Farmer Gale's estate in a barn-like structure facing a long row of cart-sheds.

Skirting a sunless pond that was scurvy and ill-smelling, she drew up at the gate and blew a summons on her horn, but its only effect was to startle the chickens pecking in the litter, and the piglings fighting to snatch their mother's garbage from her tub or to nuzzle at her teats. There was nothing for it but to carry the bonnet-box to the barn, for the great farmyard was too mucky to drag her cart through. Picking her way among the strawy compost heaps, she divined why her horn had brought no answer: it had been deadened by a melody proceeding in a lusty tenor voice from the tall folding-doors, and this— somewhat to her surprise—was none other than the air of "Buy a Broom."

It forced her to polka to it the rest of the way, and although she must fain trip gingerly mid the manure-heaps and the melody had ended with applause before she reached the thatched structure, still it was with a brighter feeling that she found herself at the open doors. But the first glimpse within made her turn pale and draw back a little. The scene she had so unexpectedly stumbled upon was the stranger and grimmer for the silence that had now fallen, though the faces of the shearers astride the struggling sheep were still lively enough. Master Peartree had his boot over the head of a recalcitrant lamb, which but for her recent adventure she would have imagined choking.

But it was not the ungentle shepherd that made for her the centre of the picture, for among these men in dirty green corduroys and rolled-up check shirt-sleeves, whose legs gripped grunting, wheezing, struggling or feebly kicking sheep, was one in cleaner clothes, whose bare, brawny arms gave her a sharp sensation, almost as if he had nipped her with the shears he held in his palm. Was it boredom or the need for his labour that had enlisted Mr. William Flynt in this service? She did not know, but pale and dumb she retreated from the unconscious Will, whose sheep, wedged between his legs, hung limp with meek, helpless eye, the very image of a sacrificial victim, and was being sheared with the meticulous concentration of the outsider bent on showing he is not inferior to the professional. And indeed Will's was the sole sheep, she saw at once and with admiration, that though nearly bare of its wool showed without blood-fleck: a consummation to which its prudent lethargy had doubtless contributed. Young Ravens, on the other hand, who was now lying with both feet on his animal, had nicked it on ear, leg, and breast: apparently one could not serve two masters—song and scissors.

Perceiving Jinny with her bonnet-box, this young humorist now sang out the old street-cry: "Buy a band-box!"

The chaff stayed her retreat and stiffened her trembling form.

"Hullo!" she retorted, with less than her usual wit. "Back again like a bad penny."

Even as she spoke she saw Will and his sheep give a spasmodic start, and the first speck of blood appear on the flawless skin. But the shearer did not look up, although he automatically stretched out his hand for the ointment.

"Do ye don't struggle," observed Master Peartree amiably to his youthful ewe. "Oi'm not so strong."

As nobody said anything further, and Master Peartree, intent on his lamb, did not look up, Jinny too stood silent for a moment with her incongruous bonnet-box; recovering her sang-froid, and watching a catcher trying to drive in an unshorn lamb from the pen in which it had cowered and which it now ran round, bleating, terror-stricken and unseizable. She wondered if its heart were thumping more wildly than hers. Not that there was terror in her own breast—rather a strange exultation that her presence had had power to incarnadine the immaculate sheepskin. But her eyes roamed shyly from Will and his nipped victim, and studied with elaborate attention the divers coloured show-cards of the successful ram lambs that made their vaunt upon the beams or along the sloping walls, through which the thatching stuck pleasantly. Her mind went back to that sunny, bracing day in February, to the immense pastoral landscape of straw-roofed sheep-pens, ooze, mangold heaps, and haystacks, on which she had chanced when the lambs now so agitated were new-yeaned: some only an hour or two old, with long skeleton legs and bodies smeared as with yellow gold. How friskily they had soon learnt to leap on their mother's back! That day she, too, had been as untroubled, needing no outside melody to brisk up her pace.

Young Ravens, inspired by his new audience to a fresh burst of melody, started on "The Mistletoe Bough," the old ballad she had heard sung in the cottages at Christmas sing-songs, and which she now for the first time connected with the play on Mr. Flippance's posters.

"Hullo, Jinny," said Master Peartree at last, her presence slowly percolating. He finished his rebellious lamb and patted it forgivingly on the back, remarking genially: "Get up and let's have a squint at you." And as it trotted out happily, he threw its fleece—too small to wind up—on to a great heap in the corner and fell to work on a sheep.

"You've just done'em when it's turned cold," protested Jinny.

"Ay, 'tis a pity," said Master Peartree. "But first we couldn't get the labour, and then that rined and their wool was too damp, but Oi need 'em now for the early market."

"I know. I'm buying a horse there," said Jinny.

Another tinge of red appeared on the blameless skin of Will's victim.

"Methusalem ain't damaged hisself?" asked Master Peartree in concern.

"Oh, no, he's outside your gate, damaging your hedge."

"Then whatever do you need another for?"

"Oh, just to ride over somebody. But I wish I'd known you needed labour."

"Why, want a job?" grinned Jim Puddifoot, a giant in a brimless hat, who was sharpening his shears on a piece of steel. There was a snigger from his mates.

"What's the pay?" said Jinny, who had been thinking of Uncle Lilliwhyte, lately gravelled for lack of purchasers of his woodland pickings.

"There's half a suvrin a hundred," said Master Peartree as seriously, "and four quarts o' beer."

A great shout of laughter rose from the hired men: only Will went on shearing with apparent imperturbability, while a third carmine speck defaced the smooth surface of his martyred sheep.

"Where's the laugh?" inquired Master Peartree.

"Don't rob a poor man of his beer," carolled young Ravens. "She don't drink," he broke off to explain.

"Yes, I do, I drink like a fish. Water, that is, like that does."

This time even Master Peartree laughed, while Jim Puddifoot, raising his tin mug without a handle to his mouth, cried "Here's to you," and young Ravens lifting up his pleasant voice trolled forth:

"Robin he married a wife in the West,
Moppety, moppety, mono."

Little stabs and pricks were going through Will's breast, and still more through the skin of his sheep. As the chorus, from which Jinny's little trill was not excluded, took up:

"With a high jig jiggity, tops and petticoats,
Robin-a-Thrush cries mono,"

it seemed to Will as if Jinny was carrying on like a flash lady in a boon company. A high jig jiggity, indeed! Releasing his victim at last, he picked up its fleece sullenly and teased a tail out of it, wherewith, rolling up the rest, he proceeded to tie the bundle in a silence that the singing rendered still grimmer.

"What's that you've got there, Jinny?" asked Master Peartree, becoming suddenly aware of the bonnet-box.

"That's for you," she said.

"Me! Oi ain't got no womankind, thank the Lord."

Again Master Peartree had touched unintentionally the springs of laughter. Will pinned the frightened ewe-lamb, now caught and as dumb as himself, between his legs, and plucked a few preliminary bits from its breast with his fingers.

"But it's Mrs. Flynt's bonnet," explained Jinny, "and will you oblige me by taking it back to-night?"

The snick of young Flynt's shears sounded savage.

"That Oi won't," said Master Peartree, "seein' as here stands her boy Willie hisself."

"Oh, does he?" said Jinny. "I hadn't noticed."

"Ay, that he do. And even dedn't, he arxed me not to do your job agen, time Oi took in that liddle ole horn."

The new ovine martyr bounded. Quite a patch of its skin had been replaced by blood.

"Steady, Willie, steady!" cried Master Peartree. "Oi was afeared musicianers ain't no good for shearing."

"It's this silly, jumping beast," growled Will, breaking his obstinate silence.

Jinny was still tendering the bonnet-box to Master Peartree. "Well, give it to him then."

"Can't he take it straight?" asked the shepherd, clipping busily.

"That silly, jumping beast is too much for him as it is. He daren't let go. I'll leave the bonnet-box for him."

"Ain't no place here—'tis too mucky."

"'Buy a Broom,'" hummed Jinny, and young Ravens, smiling, seized a besom and swept vigorously at the stale and droppings. "Oh, I can't leave it here—the sheep might stave it in," she said.

"Leave it in the store acrost the yard—the key's in the padlock," said the shepherd. "Oi count Willie'll take it home, same as he ain't cut hisself to pieces."

Another roar from the others—this time Master Peartree beamed, and it might have gone ill with Will's lamb had the shears not slipped from his palm.

"Well, but when folks go woolgathering," remarked Jinny blandly, "they forget things. I'll put it in the store, but I won't be responsible."

"Tell her I won't forget it," roared Will, who was picking up his shears in the gymnastic attitude necessitated by the palpitating sheep between his legs.

"Oi reckon she can yer for herself," said the shepherd naïvely.

"Of course I can hear," said Jinny. "But tell him to tell his mother that the bill's inside."

"Oi reckon he can yer too," said the puzzled Peartree.

"He doesn't listen much to women," explained Jinny. "You ask him if his family wants anything else from Chipstone."

"Well, there he stands—you can arx him, can't you?"

"Well, don't I stand here, too?" said Jinny. "And why doesn't he answer?"

"He's too shy," sniggered Ravens, and burst out again:

"With a high jig jiggity, tops and petticoats."

"Shut up!" snarled Will.

"'Twas you asked me to sing," retorted Ravens.

"That's so, Willie," said the shepherd. "You should say you loved to yer 'Buy a Broom' and all them old songs. Why don't you answer, Willie?"

"Because there's nothing to say," Will roared. "We don't want nothing whatever from her." He was not often so ungrammatical, but anger knows no pedantry.

"Well, why couldn't he say so at once?" said Jinny, and whistling "A dashing young man from Buckingham,"—whistling was a new brazenness in Will's ears—she picked her way across the miry yard to the weather-boarded, tarred, and tile-roofed structure that stood on six mushroom-topped pillars, whose smoothness offered no purchase for rats. Ascending the steep steps, she deposited the bonnet-box betwixt the chicken-corn and the eggs. While padlocking the door again, she saw to her surprise that Methusalem was inside the gate, labouring towards her through the mud. The faithful animal, impatient for her, had evidently lifted the latch with its nose, aided perhaps by its teeth. The tears came into her eyes: some one at least did want her, and there was a long, affectionate contact between that clever, velvety nose and Jinny's palm. Then she returned to the shearing-barn and handed Master Peartree the key.

"Good day and thank you," she said. "I reckon I shall meet you at the cattle fair."

She did not wait to see if she had drawn blood from the sacrificial lamb; but, rounding her lips again, whistled her way jauntily back to her cart. As she drove along, the sun, struggling through a high cloud-rack, showed like a great worn silver coin, and the shorn sheep gleamed fairily white on the great green pastures. But there was an ache at her heart, which the delicious wafts from the early-mown hayfields only made emptier.

III

The shabby little cart with the legend of "Daniel Quarles," and the smart dog-cart of Farmer Gale, rolled side by side of a Monday morning in the restored June sunshine towards the Chipstone cattle-market. Jinny had timed this coincidence, and meant to extract the farmer's opinion of the horses for sale. She had already gleaned from her grandfather what particular teeth were chronological, but such confidence as she possessed in her own "horse-sense" had been rudely dissipated by a volume on the noble animal, which she had unearthed in Mother Gander's sanctum. The lists of diseases and defects from which it might suffer was paralysing, and even when it was a thing she had heard of—like grogginess—it grew more sinister by being called "navicular disease." Methusalem's maladies had been simple enough, and she had dared to drench or anoint him with divers remedies. But now that knowledge had dissipated the bliss of ignorance—now that warts had enlarged into "angleberries," rheumatism had darkened into "felon," and farcy, quittor, Ascaris megalocephala, and countless other evils were seen hovering around Methusalem, thick as summer gnats, she marvelled how he had staved them off. That poor Methusalem! An affectionate animal by nature was the horse,—the book told her—he wanted to please man, only sometimes he was in agony and the flesh could not obey. Good heavens, what if sometimes when she was in a hurry to get home, she had wronged Methusalem, even in her thoughts! Remorsefully, and with a new and morbid anxiety, she caressed his delicate, nose, amazed at her ancient, easy assurance of his immortality. It even shook her faith in the all-sufficiency of the Spelling-Book that it contained no intimation of the ills that horseflesh is heir to.

And the animal she had now to buy for Mr. Flippance might be affected with all or any of these ills, and even if one could detect such obvious defects as windgalls, spavin, thorough-pin, or broken wind, how avoid a crib-biter or a wind-sucker, how grapple with the bot-fly, two hundred of which could hook themselves horribly to a single equine stomach, or with the still more formidable Palisade Worm, which even its name of Strongylus armatus could scarcely worsen, a thousand of it having been counted by a patient authority on a surface of two inches, and its census taken at a million for a single horse!

Farmer Gale, however, failed to throw much light on these alarming questions, which he did not know, indeed, were being asked. His conversation kept gliding away to his grievances, for it consisted, like that of most farmers, of grumbles. Usually these started from the little string-tied sample bags of threshed grain he carried in his pocket to be blown and tasted by hard-bargaining customers. But to-day, though he was not bound for the corn-market, he was nevertheless not to be baulked of his grievances. They were not, this time, against Nature, but against Man; for, as the fields they passed showed, the corn was particularly forward. It was not Providence that had run down wheat to thirty shillings a quarter. Free Trade was in reality the ruin of free Britain. For the labour of Continental slaves, who went with the soil, and were sold with it like cattle, who subsisted on black bread, skim-milk, and onions, was brought into competition with that of the freeborn Briton, who must thus be dragged down to the same level.

The bluff, freeborn Briton was Farmer Gale's favourite rôle, and his ruddy face, grey bowler, and smart gaiters made him sympathetic enough superficially, while the potent landowner's consideration for Jinny's religious necessities had not failed to evoke a flattered gratitude in her humble breast when they drove together of a Sunday to their respective chapels. This amiable image of himself the breezy Briton was now destined to shatter. For after some critical comment on the ploughing of the fields they passed and the activities of the poachers—he would certainly have to get rid of that suspicious character, "Uncle Lilliwhyte," who occupied a cottage badly needed for a farm-hand—he pointed out the impossibility of building another cottage as Jinny had so crudely suggested. Prices were simply ruinous.

"I tell my labourers as man to man," he said emphatically, "that they can't have regular employment and their present wages. Take your choice, boys, says I. Look at other countries, do they get more than their six or seven shillings a week? No! Then that's what you'll have to come down to."

"But how can they live on it?" asked Jinny.

"How can farmers live?" he retorted. "We must go by the price of corn."

"But did you go by the price of corn after the Battle of Waterloo?" asked Jinny shrewdly. "For I remember Gran'fer once telling me you got—I mean your father got—a hundred shillings a quarter then, yet folks were so starved they went burning the ricks."

"I was only a baby then. I can't say what happened."

"But the same thing happened nearer our time," she reminded him, thinking of the Bidlake tragedy.

"Oh, that silly rioting and machine-smashing. That always came out of the poor not understanding politics. If things were bad after Waterloo, it was all Bony's work. And as for the unrest twenty years ago, we caught that from France, too, I remember dad telling me. They had risen against their king— such an unsettled people. But to-day it's our own British Government that's the enemy, and the money we farmers have lost this year is something dreadful."

"But you don't look as starved as some of our labourers' families. I've seen the Pennymole children crying for dry bread, and the father saying, 'I darsn't cut you no more—do, ye'll have none Saturday.' And Mr. Pennymole's always worked for you."

"You don't understand politics, Jinny."

"I understand poverty. The Pennymoles are better off, now they've got two boys grown up and earning sixpence a day. But I've seen Mrs. Pennymole making tea with charred bread, and her husband compelled to steal the cabbages left for the cows. . . . Oh, I oughtn't to have said that," she added in alarm.

"You certainly oughtn't! Compelled to break the Eighth Commandment—a pretty doctrine! And such liars, too. I saw quite a little girl munching a turnip she'd just filched from my field, and when I complained to her mother, the woman unblushingly said, "Tis me fats her up with swedes and turnips.'"

"They can't see their children hunger."

"They can put some of them in the poorhouse."

"Look at the mites there, white and half-starved. Sometimes I've got to deliver a parcel to Mr. Jims, the porter, and I hear the Master thrashing 'em with a stick."

"And it's what boys need—even my brat. Carrying parcels, indeed!" He stopped abruptly.

"Well, but they make the old folks of eighty and ninety scour the stone steps and do the washing!"

"They needn't go in—they can get relief from the parish."

"The parish! Eighteenpence a week for the family when the father's bedridden."

"There's the parish loaves!"

"Have you ever seen one? Half-baked, without real crust, all raw and soft, where it stuck to the next loaf."

"Beggars can't be choosers. Besides, there's plenty of work after harvest."

"Yes, even for babies of six," said Jinny bitterly. "And to keep boys from their beds after hard field-work. And at White Notley where they make the silk, there's little girls standing on stools to reach the weaving-desk."

"If you understood politics," Farmer Gale persisted, "you'd understand that prices make themselves, and that what we get with one hand we have to give away with the other. Have you ever heard of the Income Tax now?"

"No," admitted Jinny.

"Ha! You'd change your tune if you had to pay a shilling on every pound you earned. But that's merely the last straw that breaks the camel's back, for it isn't only as a farmer I'm put upon. But think of the Malt Tax! It's simply a scandal."

"Is it? I should have thought 'twas six shillings a week would be the scandal." Her eyes and cheeks blazed prettily, and she was beginning to shelve the idea of consulting her companion at the horse-market.

"I don't say you're altogether wrong," conceded Farmer Gale, admiring, despite himself, her fire and sparkle. "But it's the Government that's responsible. There was a great old meeting t'other day at Drury Lane Theatre in London. Two thousand people, if a man. The Duke of Richmond he up and said by Heaven we've got to have Protection, and we will have it. Oh, it was a grand speech. I went up for it express. And we've had a meeting of farmers down here, too, and we're going to wake up the country, we Essex chaps."

"Are you?" said Jinny, secretly amused at this "furriner's" complacent identification of himself with her county.

"You wait! We're going to come out with a Proclamation."

"But that's a Royal thing," said Jinny.

"Not always: besides we shall end with God save the Queen. Yes, that's it: 'Down with the Malt Tax and God save the Queen!' And the beginning: 'To our worthy labourers, greeting.' I'll draw that up soon as I get home."

"I should offer 'em ten shillings a week," said Jinny.

"You're joking!"

"I'm dead earnest. A family can't live under ten shillings a week. Then they wouldn't want to shoot your rabbits and steal your turnips and cabbages."

"Prices make themselves, I tell you. Folks can't have more than they're worth. Why, my dad paid as much as thirteen shillings a week to our old looker, Flynt, when he had his strength. Yes, though nobody ever suspected he got more than twelve."

"But besides his duties as bailiff he had to see after feeding the stock night and morning, including Sundays."

"That was why my father paid him the extra shilling. And you can't say I haven't treated him generously over the farmhouse."

"I wonder he could bring up such a large family so genteelly," mused Jinny at a tangent.

"The more the easier. A brat of four can scare the crows: the only pity is that his boys wouldn't stay on the land."

"What was there to stay for? I think there ought to be a law that nobody gets under ten shillings," persisted Jinny.

"What a blessing we haven't got women over us," said the farmer, smiling at a heresy too unreasonable for argument. "Men Governments are bad enough, but women would drive us to the workhouse."

"And what about the Queen?" asked Jinny.

"Well, what about the Queen?" he repeated vaguely.

"Isn't the Queen a woman?"

"The Queen a woman!" He was dazed. "But she doesn't really govern—not nowadays. It's Lord John!"

"Well then, what about Queen Elizabeth?"

"Ah, that was some time back," he said evasively.

"Yes, she put on the crown in 1558, November 17," quoted Jinny from that Spelling-Book.

"I didn't know you were so well up in history," he said admiringly. "I reckon you're ready at ciphering too?"

"How could I do my work without it?"

"Ah, that's true. And a good hand at a pen, I suppose?"

"I can scratch what I want."

"Ah!"

He fell silent.

"You don't play the piano?" he asked after a pause.

"No," said Jinny. "Only the horn." And she blew gaily upon it: whereupon to her surprise and satisfaction—for she had forgotten him, and it was necessary to tie him up against the sheep—Nip appeared, tearing from the rear. Farmer Gale watched musingly the operation of confining him to his basket by one of those pieces of hoop-borne rope that had excited the speculation of Mr. Elijah Skindle.

"I suppose you could play a polka on it," he remarked.

Jinny obliged with a few bars of the "Buy a Broom."

"If you had a piano," he observed with growing admiration, "I expect you'd soon learn to play it on that."

Jinny shook her head. "I shall never have the time. There's the goats, and the garden, and Gran'fer, and Methusalem—"

"Nearly all g's," laughed Farmer Gale, exhilarated by his own erudition.

"And isn't Methusalem a gee?" flashed Jinny, and exhilarated him further by her prodigious wit.

They were both smiling broadly as, just outside the market, they came upon Will leaning against a lime-tree, a pipe between his teeth and a darkness palpable on his forehead despite its "ginger" aureola.

Jinny's smile died and her heart thumped. Instantaneously she decided that as the farmer had seen them together at "The Black Sheep," to ignore Will absolutely would be to betray their quarrel to the world.

"Fine morning!" she cried as the vehicles passed. Will sullenly touched his hat.

He was amazed that the Cornish potentate should countenance her presence, so incongruous amid this orgie of untempered masculinity, this medley of unpetticoated humanity of every rank and class, of which drovers twirling branches or leaning on sticks formed the ground pattern: small farmers rubbing shoulders with smart-gaitered gentry in frilled shirts; blue-aproned butchers with scissors at breast jostling peasants in grimy smock-frocks and squash hats or ruddy, whiskered old squires and great grazier farmers in blue, gilt-buttoned coats, white flap buff waistcoats, and white pot or broad-brimmed hats; still more elegant town types in glossy, straight-brimmed cylinders and double-breasted, green frock-coats galling the kibes of bucolic, venerable-bearded ancients in fusty sleeved waistcoats and greasy high-hats, who blew their noses with black fingers. It was a fantasia of pipes and caps, of immaculate collars and dirty scarves, of broadcloth cutaways and filthy Cardigan jackets, of top-booted buckskins and corduroy trousers tied with string below the knee. As Jinny and Farmer Gale alighted, and mingled with this grotesque mob swirling around the pens in the sunshine, Will's heart was hot with resentment against the girl who, while rejecting the counsel and co-operation of her old friend in the great horse-deal, had brazenly accepted the guidance of a bumptious "furriner." How shamelessly she walked amid that babel of moos, baas, grunts, shouts, and bell-ringing, as if here was her natural place. Really, to see smoke puffing publicly out of her mouth, as it had puffed privately out of that Polly's, would hardly be surprising now. And the men were looking after her, there could be no doubt of that, appraising her as if she, too, was in the market. He could not but feel a faint relief that she was under substantial masculine escort, however abhorred.

The market-place, along which our quite unconscious Jinny was now making so indiscreet a tourney, was constructed outside the town proper, bordered on two sides by lime-trees and open to the sky save in the auction-room and bar, where walls and roofing gave a grateful shade, though the company in either did not contribute coolness. The cattle were shuffling about restlessly, jostling, mounting. The store calves and bullocks lay in pens; the fatted calves had already been sold: pathetic plumpnesses about to be butchered. Butchers, indeed, were already emerging from the auction-room leading struggling strap-muzzled calves by head-ropes, and holding on—for extra precaution—to their tails.

"Poor creatures!" said Jinny, with tears coming to her eyes.

"Yes, a poor lot!" assented Farmer Gale, and if Will could have felt the flash of scorn that went through Jinny's heart, he would have scowled less. There was a store calf, stamped in blue, so tiny that Jinny longed to mother it. Here again the farmer blundered: he doubted if anybody would buy it; at least it would be killed instanter to be mixed with pork for sausages.

He was a widower, Jinny remembered, and the line in the Spelling-Book defining that word floated suddenly before her illumined mind: "Widower—One who has buried his wife." There had always seemed to her something superfluously sinister in that definition—as if the husband had personally put his wife out of the way, or at least made sure she was disposed of. Was a man a widower whose wife had been burnt up, she had wondered whimsically. Or if Miss Gentry had been married and gone to sea and been duly drowned, would her husband have been free to remarry? But for Farmer Gale at least, how pat was the definition, she felt. He assuredly suggested the wilful widower: this man without entrails of mercy, whether for the poor or for beasts.

She moved away silently, trying to lose him, looking for the horses. She passed pens of sheep, and dogs (only a few of these, and tied), and cows with swollen, oozy udders. There was a sheep nibbling at a fallen lime branch outside its pen, and another shoving hard to displace him. Jinny picked it up and gave it to this covetous creature, who sniffed and then turned away. There seemed to be a sort of Spelling-

Book moral in it. Before the pigs (red-crossed and blue-marked) she found Master Peartree in rapt contemplation.

"The pegs be lookin' thrifty and prosperous," he observed, in response to her asking how he found himself. "They don't need no auctioneer's gammon."

"No pig does," punned Jinny.

"Ah, here we are!" said a less welcome voice—Jinny maliciously referred Farmer Gale's "we" to his juxtaposition with the pigs. The uneasy capping and ducking of the shepherd-cowman before his master, and his moving off towards his own animals, suggested that pigs were a private passion with Master Peartree. But he had brought up the memory of the shearing-shed, and with it the renewed thought of Will, and it was a tenderer thought than for the potentate at her side. Will might be stubborn and silly, but never, surely, would he deny that no family should have less than ten shillings a week: she felt relieved she had broken the ice between them, even though "Fine morning" was only a little hole in it.

As if echoing her thoughts, "Fine morning!" said the pig-auctioneer to Farmer Gale. It was a special mark of attention from this gentlemanly-looking man, elevated on a massive stool, who wore gaiters and a great gleaming signet-ring that showed as he turned the pages of a written catalogue. This was kept by elastic strings in a grand calf cover, though pigskin would have seemed more in keeping. Two acolytes, standing on the ground, scribbled in their lowliness. Buyers sat on the rim of the pens, with their feet dangling over the pigs, and the pig-drovers hovered near, in their long high aprons of coarse brown sacking.

Soon Farmer Gale became as fascinated as Master Peartree, for the pigs did indeed look "thrifty and prosperous," and as the penful was on the point of falling to a low bid, he nipped in and secured a bargain. While he was complacently cutting away bristles, signing his acquisition with his scissors, Jinny stole away, feeling he was safely penned.

IV

Will had long since disappeared from her ken, but when she came to the long roofed place, open at the side, where beribboned and straw-plaited hacks and draught-horses were tied to their staples, there he was, chained just as firmly by a sort of sentinel stubbornness. It was as if he was saying "Through my body first!" The thrill his proximity gave her was shot through with a renewed resentment against this obviously undiminished opposition of his. But she was resolved to meet him with banter rather than with anger.

"You buying horses?" she said genially.

"No, I am not buying horses!" he answered roughly. "But aren't you ashamed to be here—the only one of your sex?"

"Surely not!" said Jinny. "Where's your eyes?"

He looked round, wonderingly.

"Under your nose!" guided Jinny. "There, isn't that a mare? And I passed sows and ewes and heifers by the score."

"And that's what you class yourself with? And then you deny you are lowering yourself!"

"I always lower myself when I get off my cart."

"Well, you get up again! That's the best advice I can give you. Drive home!"

"And shirk my job!"

"I'll do your job."

"You! I thought you were not buying horses."

"You know what I mean. How much does old Flippance want to give?"

"Oh, he's not so old," she said evasively. She was scanning the horses with troubled eye, perturbed even more than by her own affairs by the thought of the innumerable diseases and defects and doctorings which might be lurking beneath their sheen of health and vigour. Her innocent faith undermined by literature and Mr. Flippance's experience, she had a cynical sense of horsey hypocrisy, of whited, blacked, or browned sepulchres, within which fearsome worms burrowed in their millions. She would have gladly consulted Will, had he not been so tactlessly intrusive. Even as it was, she murmured encouragingly: "There doesn't seem much choice to-day." Indeed, the animals were mostly huge shire horses with their heavily feathered fetlocks. Of hackneys there were only two or three.

"I should take that Suffolk Punch," advised Will, indicating a chestnut. "He'll have the strength to draw the caravan, and doesn't look so clumsy and hairy-legged as the others."

"I like the star on his forehead," said Jinny. "But I can't bear a cropped tail, it's cruel. Besides, Mr. Flippance hasn't got a caravan."

"Well, how does he carry all that truck I saw?"

"Oh, that goes in wagons with horses just hired from town to town. They don't even live in a caravan like Mr. Duke's got. No, but they have a trap that they drive over in, ahead, and then Mr. Flippance uses the trap to look for a pitch to hire, or to bring home naphtha for the lamps or timber for mending the theatre—something always goes wrong, he says."

"Then I'd have the Cleveland?"

"Which is the Cleveland?"

"That tall bay with black points and clean legs. I've hardly ever seen one at an Essex fair, but they're strong as plough-horses and handsome as hackneys."

"But don't you think that couple there are handsomer?"

"The black—of course! They're a pair of real carriage horses. Splendid action, I reckon. But Mr. Flippance won't want anything so showy as that."

"Just what a show does want," laughed Jinny. "You see he also rides about the town, blowing on the horn and scattering handbills."

"I didn't understand that. And can he blow a horn as well?"

"As well as who?"

"As me!" said Will boldly. "And when am I to have my gloves?" He sought her hand in the press and it was not withdrawn.

"When you go blowing it for Mr. Flippance in his next town," she laughed happily.

"Then I must choose the horse I blow behind," he said with an air of lightness. "What's the most old Flippance will go to?"

"Thirty pounds is his last word, I'm afraid."

"Much too little. But we'll see. Now I'll take you back to your cart."

"What for?" Her hand unclasped. "I've got to buy the horse, I must wait here."

"But they'll be taken in there." He pointed to the cattle auction-chamber. "And there's no need for you to bid personally."

"I shall enjoy bidding."

"Among all those men? You won't even get a look in."

The chamber was indeed besieged by a seething crowd, some standing on tiptoe, astrain to get their bids marked.

"I'll borrow one of those pig-dealers' stools," she said.

"Do be serious, Jinny."

"And do you suppose my work is a joke?"

"But you can't squeeze in that crowd? Suppose we find out the owner and get one of the black horses by private treaty?"

"And pay the market fee? Not me! Besides, he'll want a top price and there's more fun and chances in bidding. Oh look! that poor Cleveland's got himself all tangled up! Do help him!"

It was not easy to release the animal which, having encoiled its legs in the rope attached to its staple, was getting more and more frightened as its own efforts lassoed it the tighter. Jinny's heart beat fast lest Will should get kicked, and still faster at the nonchalance with which he accomplished his dangerous task.

"Thank you," she said sweetly, when the animal stood shaking, but quiet.

"It's not your horse."

"But I asked you to do it."

"Then you might do what I ask you?" he retorted.

She frowned. She did not like this tricky tit-for-tat. It was unchivalrous. It undid his deed of derring-do.

"You must not interfere with my business," she said severely, and swept to the nearest door.

"Jinny! Where are you going?" He had followed her.

"To the bar!" she said solemnly, perceiving the nature of the forbidden chamber. "Why can't I have a drink and a smoke? What will you take?"

He gasped, believing her serious. So female smoking even in public was no impossible foreboding. To this buffet, blockaded by laughing, swilling, tobacco-clouded masculinity, mitigated only—if not indeed aggravated—by a barmaid, Jinny was actually going to wriggle her way! And the buffet did not even sell milk!

"You shan't go," he said in a low hoarse tone, clutching at her arm. "By God, you shan't!"

But he succeeded only in grasping her dangling horn, and, in her dart forward, it was left in his hand. "I didn't ask you to 'take' that!" she laughed back as she crossed the threshold. "I meant, what's your drink?"

"Jinny!" he breathed, his voice frozen.

"Mine's ink!" she called out gaily, and the males, now aware of her presence, vied with one another to pass the bottle and pen on the counter to her, together with the little bowl of sand, all of which she bore to the quiet side of the room, where a protracted desk supplied facilities for notes and accounts. Reassured, but still resentful, Will stood at the door, awkwardly holding her horn with its bit of broken girdle, and watching her protectively as she scribbled on a piece of paper, and blotted it with the sand. Then coming back to him, she took away her horn—not without a reproachful glance at the snapped cord—and putting her folded paper into his hand instead, glided past him and was lost in the hurly-burly.

Disconsolate, yet excited, he opened the note, and read this wholly unexpected quatrain:

SWEARING

Of all the nauseous complicated crimes
That both infect and stigmatize the Times;

There's none that can with impious Oaths compare,
Where Vice and Folly have an equal Share.

This rebuke, drawn from the endless thesaurus of "The Universal Spelling-Book," and not original even in spelling, Will believed to be Jinny's own composition, and as inspired as it was, alas! deserved. Wonderful that Jinny could sit down in all that turmoil, in that smoky, gin-laden atmosphere, and pour out these pure bursts of song. Surely Martin Tupper, the mighty bard of the day, whose renown had reached even Will's illiterate ears, could not better them. And what was he, Will, beside her, he whose own claim to literature rested upon an imaginary exposition of Daniel! Smarting with self-reproach, he deposited the note where once her glove had rested—it should be a text of warning henceforward.

But if she was thus marvellous, still more necessary was it to withdraw her from these unfitting atmospheres, and he returned more tenaciously than ever to his equine watch, like a picket in a camp.

V

Meanwhile Jinny had blotted herself out in the crowd around the sheep-auctioneer, who towered in the midst of his dirty-white sea, yelling "All going at thirty-five shillings apiece!" or striding from pen to pen across the bars, while the buyers ruddled their lots with their mark, and the drovers cleared for him ever fresh passages among the swirling sheep, and acolytes kept parallel to him outside the fold with their ink-horns and notebooks.

But she had only fallen from the frying-pan into the oven, for suddenly she became conscious that Farmer Gale was again at her side.

"Got your horse yet?" he inquired, with his breeziest British smile.

"Sale not on yet," she answered coldly.

"Then come and see the bullocks sell."

Jinny, pleading she must go to the horse sale-room, moved away towards the congested chamber. He followed, smiling.

"Why, that is where they're selling the bullocks now," he said.

Her brain was seeking for a further pretext, when she caught sight of the sentinel Will frowning furiously in her direction. If she slipped in now, further argument from him would be nipped in the bud, and silently she followed the robustious widower through the hole he bored into the seething mass.

The entry of a female attracted no general attention, for it was impossible for the squeezed buyers to see more than the backs and sides of their immediate neighbours, even if all eyes had not been on the auctioneer and on the beasts which occupied the central ring, in the brief moments of their glory.

He stood at a raised desk, this master of the revels, in his shirt-sleeves, with a little stick for hammer: a clean-shaven man, with the back of his long head almost straight, and further lengthened and straightened by the continuation down it of the central parting of his neatly combed hair; the face bulging forward and into a massive mouth and chin. He was flanked by two young bookkeepers, one spotty-faced and spectacled in a Scotch cap and loud tweeds, and one bareheaded and demure; and around him on the rising benches of an amphitheatre rose a mass of masculinity surmounted by small boys. Drovers chevied in the "lots"—stuck with paper numbers—through large double wooden gates, and back—after their great moments in the ring—to their pens, through a smaller folding gate. The beasts did not always listen proudly to their praises: the more modest, instead of showing off their beauties, preferred to nose restfully about the straw of the floor, and had to be prodded into circular activity by the sticks of drovers who, as the bullocks went sullenly round, looked like a prose variety of picador in a toy arena. And throughout fell the auctioneer's patter, sometimes suave and slow, but for the most part staccato and breathless. "Who will say seventy shillings? Property of Mr. Purley of Foxearth Farm. And a crown. You all know Foxearth Farm. You all know the hurdle-maker. And his herds are even better than his hurdles! Who makes level money? Going, going—"

"No, don't you be going," said Farmer Gale smilingly. For the girl had begun to edge out. She felt herself uncomfortably pressed. Why, it almost seemed as if Farmer Gale's arm were round her waist. Good heavens, it was! And what was more, his body barred her movement outwards.

"Take away your arm," she whispered fiercely.

"I'm protecting you from the crowd," he whispered back. "They'll break your ribs in."

"Take it away!" she hissed. But he feigned not to hear, and his eye being now on the arena, not on her, she was too shy to struggle and make a sensation. The horn in her hand also impeded her efforts to extricate herself. Furious and flushing, she was forced to stand there, while the auctioneer's prosy patter beat down on her brain in a maddening ceaseless pour: "Selling to the highest bidder—no reserve. A big bullock. In your hands. Start the bidding, please. To be sold without reserve, I say. How much? Come on! Look at his fat! Thank you. Seven pound, fifteen—nine pound, ten—a great big bullock. I'm selling him without reserve. He is to be sold whatever he fetches. Ten pound, two and six. Going! No, not gone yet! Going—!"

"I must go!" repeated Jinny. "I must inspect the horses."

"You'll see them better in the ring here."

"Let me go! I'll never drive to chapel with you again!"

"Why not, Jinny?" He bent down with sudden passion, all the cautious Cornishman's long-wavering desires clenched by the discovery of her high educational endowments and concreted by actual contact with the desirable waist. "Why not go to chapel together and be done with it, once for all?"

"Done with what?" she murmured, reddening.

"Separating. Let me keep off the crowd always."

"Hush! They'll hear you."

"No, they won't. What do you say?"

"Be quiet! I want to hear the bidding."

"Shall we publish the banns?"

Jinny closed her lips obstinately.

"Won't you speak? You know I can buy out half Little Bradmarsh."

In her silence the voice of the auctioneer possessed the situation.

"The best heifer for the last—maiden heifer, beautiful quality. Fourteen pound. Marvellous creature, marvellously cheap. Won't anybody start me?" The drover prodded the prodigy up, and she trotted round dismally.

"Fifteen," cried a squeaky voice.

"Fifteen," echoed the auctioneer, cheering up. But his gloom soon returned. For the bidding refused to advance. "Being badly sold, this heifer," he wailed.

"By crum, he's right!" quoth the Cornishman, pricking up his ears. "Sixteen pound!" he cried aloud, and was already congratulating himself upon his bargain, when, like the voice of doom, came the squeaky "Seventeen!"

Farmer Gale was piqued. "Eighteen," he said surlily.

"Twenty!"

It was a staggering blow. But it only raised the farmer's blood. "Guineas!" he cried.

"Twenty-two pounds!" chirped the voice.

"Twenty-two pounds!" repeated the auctioneer insatiably.

Beads of perspiration and hesitation appeared on the farmer's brow. In his concentration on the problem his arm relaxed. Jinny stepped aside, and men unconsciously made way for her.

"Guineas!" cried the farmer.

"Twenty-two guineas!" repeated the auctioneer. "A beautiful maiden heifer—never had a calf. Going—"

But this time Jinny was really gone. She would not even risk waiting outside to hear the result, but in generous gratitude at her escape, she hoped he would at least secure the maiden heifer.

VI

The sight of Will still at his post suggested to her with a little qualm that he was not so wrong: these male environments were not without their drawbacks.

"Those horses seem to fascinate you," she said, with a little tremor in her voice. Whether Will or the violence just done to her was the cause of it, she did not quite know. But her mood was melting and her eye the brighter for a soft moisture.

But how was Will to follow her vagaries and adventures?

"That's my business," he answered gruffly.

"I thought it was mine," she laughed. She was quite prepared now to make it a joint affair.

"You know my opinion on that," he said icily.

"You haven't changed it yet?" she bantered.

"Why, what should happen in these few minutes to make me change it?"

"Things do happen in a few minutes," she said mysteriously. "Why, I might have come back and bought up the whole show." She waved her horn comprehensively over the horses.

"What rubbish you do talk!" he said impatiently.

"Do I?" She fired up. "There's others think differently."

"If they think differently, it's because they think lightly of you."

"Lightly, indeed!"

"Yes—they do. To drag you into an indecent sale-room!"

"Indecent?" She flushed, wondering if Will had seen that circumambient arm.

"It's all indecent—all that talk about heifers. I don't wonder you blush."

She laughed, relieved. "I'm blushing for you. You do talk such rubbish!"

"There you go with your cheek!"

"It's only what you just said to me."

"I said it because you do talk rubbish."

"And you talk rubbish in saying it."

"Well, go to those who talk sense, Miss Boldero!" And he pulled out his pipe and matches with a symbolic gesture.

"What an obstinate creature you are, Will!"

"Me obstinate! Why, ain't it your obstinacy that keeps you here, when I'm ready to do your job?"

"I told you I preferred to do my own jobs." And with that she went straight up to the black hackneys, and while Will puffed volcanically, she learnedly examined their teeth through tear-misted eyes that saw neither incisors nor age-marks. Then, after carefully prodding their ribs and punching and poking them about, as she had seen purchasers do with bullocks, she swept haughtily towards the auction arena, but afraid of encountering the farmer, she hovered uncertainly on the threshold, feeling like a bundle of straw between two donkeys.

Gradually she realized, and with enhanced resentment, that she was the donkey; that both these men had deceived her in representing the cattle-arena as the selling-place for the horses. By the crowd that began to accumulate round the horses, and to blot out the patient sentinel, as the hour for their sale approached, it became plain that they would be sold where they were tied, and presently the motley crowd, swollen by many of the cattle-auctioneer's audience, thrilled with the coming of this heavy-jowled worthy, who had not turned a hair of his neatly combed chevelure.

The biddings were not brisk. To Jinny's joy only the heavier animals, the plough-horses and the cart-horses, seemed in demand; the cobs and the ponies went for a song. The sable steeds she had selected as the only suitable ones came late—most of the animals had been released from their staples and led off by their new masters. To her dismay the hackneys were put up as a pair, and all her pride seemed falling into ruin. Fortunately, not provoking a bid, they were then put up separately, and Jinny set the ball rolling for the first with a brazen offer of ten pounds.

For a moment she thought gleefully that the horse was to be hers at that—for nobody there seemed in quest or in need of carriage horses—but under the auctioneer's scoff a few bargain-hunters soon raised it to twenty, and then to Jinny's alarm—for her margin was getting dangerously narrow—to twenty-four. At twenty-five the bargain-hunters fell off, and a new voice intervened—a husky voice that seemed to mean business, and whose every counter-bid filled her with dismay. At its twenty-eight pounds the auctioneer still upheld his stick with scorn and incredulity. She was almost at her bids' end. "Twenty-nine pounds," she cried crushingly. This time the voice seemed indeed silenced. She fully expected the stick to fall. But at the first "Going," though there had been no sound, the auctioneer cried cheerily, "Thirty pounds." Evidently somebody else had nodded or held up a finger. Inflamed by the fever of the struggle, she was impelled to risk even her own earnings, if Flippance would not go so far. "Thirty-one pounds," she cried ringingly. "Thirty-one pounds," echoed the auctioneer with a promising accent of finality. "Thirty-two pounds," he added instantly, and this silent competition was even more crushing than the huskiest bid. It put out her flame of recklessness, and her heart sank with the stick, as despite all the auctioneer's derisory deprecation, that wooden finger of fate fell finally at this truly absurd figure.

Then the name of the unseen silent buyer transpired. "Mr. William Flynt!" proclaimed a familiar voice. A blaze of positive hatred ran through all Jinny's being. The brute! The obstinate pig! To come interfering with her daily work, with her bread and butter! To ride his will roughshod over hers! And not only roughrider, but coward, sneak, traitor! Had he not wormed and wheedled out of her the limit of her commission and thus romped in, an easy winner! And he would take his purchase to Mr. Flippance, she supposed. Yes, he was already paying in full—she saw him now, near one of the clerks, drawing a pocket-book out of the region of his black heart; he was in a hurry, he would hasten with the animal to Tony Flip. But not so fast, O dashing young man from Canada! Flippance is a man of honour, he will repudiate the purchase. And the second hackney still remains. The biter is bit—the pit you have digged shall engulf you.

But what was Jinny's horror and indignation when this young man from Canada, now shamelessly revealed, instead of going off with his spoil to Mr. Flippance, remained and ran up the second horse with his serpent's tongue at still greater speed, as now cocksure of her limit. This time in her fury she ventured as far as thirty-five—it was useless. With a recklessness still more magnificent he cried "Forty," and with a chill at her heart in curious contrast with the glow of hate at it, she felt that all was over. Was it of any use bidding even for the few mediocre animals still possible? Would not this brutal monopolist buy up the whole bunch—even as she had, oddly enough, hinted a few minutes before about doing? Yes, there was nothing his masterful obstinacy would boggle at in its resolve to crush her will. He still stood by the horse-enclosure in unrelaxed vigilance. Before she could arrive at any decision, her mind was still further unhinged by the simultaneous appearance of Nip and the advent of pandemonium.

Whether it was Nip that had produced the pandemonium, or the pandemonium that had liberated Nip, Jinny never knew. The fact was, however, that Farmer Gale, waking to find himself outbidden for the heifer and disappointed of his maiden, had retreated fuming to his trap, and hearing Nip's revolutionary yaps for freedom in the adjacent cart, had loosed him out of some vague instinct of malice—kindness he called it to himself, so unacknowledged was his desire to thwart the will of the creature's mistress. A final kick administered to the retreating jump—also apparently as a kindly encouragement to the freed dog's progress—had not proved conducive to the equilibrium of an animal already deranged by a long-iterated grievance and an unexpected freedom, and his helter-skelter pelt through the market-place not unnaturally startled the nerves of not a few fellow-quadrupeds, already shaken by the strange journeyings and novel experiences of the day. But it was not until the sheep were reached, that Nip's passing became a public episode.

There had even before been numberless difficult scenes with the sold lots; the effort to muster them for their new journeyings had sufficiently taxed the lungs and tempers of men and sheep-dogs. When Nip appeared, the normally stolid Master Peartree was waving a giant red handkerchief and screaming wildly, while demented-seeming drovers, formed into a half-ring, danced and shrieked like savages at a religious service, and waved sticks with a ritual air, and the sheep-dog leapt round and round, chevying the flock in the desired direction. In this delicate crisis, Nip's rush of recognition at Master Peartree proved the last straw. One super-terrified wether threw the flock into a panic. The sheep rushed to and fro and everywhere (save where the sticks and shrieks pointed); and going thus everywhere, they went nowhere, jumping on and over one another's backs as in a game of leap-lamb. Some darted back into alien pens, and the sheep-dog, itself distracted, leapt from back to back of these, baying and menacing with feverish futility. It was like a stormy sea of sheep, in which man was tossed about as in a tempest. There were sheep standing on their hind legs as if dancing, there were men clinging on to these legs or to tails or to rumps, and pushing, pulling, and wrestling with them, but never ceasing to yell and chevy. Finally a rescue party appeared with a five-barred gate, which they moved this way and that, striving to cut off at least one of the ways of escape. But this only drove more sheep back into the wrong pens, where they seemed hopelessly mixed up with lots still unsold. Jinny had never imagined sheep such lively and individual lunatics. Now the intruders were being dragged out by the wool of the head or the rump, or half-carried, or wholly kicked; again the five-barred gate was brought into play, this time to keep them away from the pens, and then, wherever the eye turned, were these tempestuous billows of sheep. They bounded, reared, wrestled, danced, pranced, flew wildly at tangents: some escaped towards the town, and everywhere men screamed, scurried, bellowed, waved hands, or brandished sticks. Nip, his head equally lost, seemed to be doing every one of these things at once, whether ovine or human. And Jinny, in her anxiety to capture him, to remove him, unseen, from the Witches' Sabbath she feared he had called into being, forgot all about the other possible, if inferior, horses. By the time she had refastened Nip and returned to the sale, the stick had fallen for the last bid. She was just in time to see Will springing on one barebacked steed, and leading his beribboned brother by a cord. And despite all her anger and contempt, she could not avoid a thrill of admiration for the grace of his poise and the fearlessness of his carriage. And a dull aching pain began at her heart. She felt she wanted something; she had missed getting something—and obscurely she told herself it was the horses he was leading away. Yes, as a Carrier she was a failure.

VII

And then suddenly the jovial figure of the Showman panted into view. His face was unshorn, unwashed even, although abundantly irrigated with perspiration, and he wore a low-crowned vast-brimmed hat and an unseasonable fur-lined cloak reaching almost to his slippers and fastened at the neck by a brass buckle. Although Jinny always had a soft place in her maternal heart for Mr. Flippance, nobody could have been more unwelcome at this moment of her professional humiliation. But before she could confess her failure, Tony Flip gasped out: "A horse! A horse! My kingdom not to have it!"

"How do you mean?"

"Am I too late? Have you bought it yet?"

"Not yet!" said Jinny.

"Thank God!" He grasped effusively at her hand, but encountering the horn first, shook that instead, without apparently noticing the difference. "Just as I woke up, it popped into my nut that this was the morning of the cattle fair. Out of bed I flew like from that bed in the Crystal Palace that chucks you out by a spring, and though I mayn't have beat the half-mile record, I'm beat myself! Whew! Not a bad gag, that!" And mopping his brow, he grinned through a grimy handkerchief.

"I thought you looked odd," said Jinny, equally relieved.

"Yes, I know my collar's a rag. But better sweat than debt, eh?"

"It's not your collar—it's seeing you out of your dressing-gown at this hour!"

"You're a quiz, that's what you are," laughed Tony.

"Never mind! That cloak comes nigh it, and you've still got your carpet slippers."

"Have I? O Lord! I thought the road was feeling hard. Is that a bar I see before me?"

"It is," said Jinny severely. "But while you're still sober, perhaps you will tell me why you've changed your mind about the horse?"

"Because I've done with marionettes. I'm going back to the legitimate."

Jinny was puzzled. "To your wife, do you mean? I thought she was dead."

Tony roared with laughter. "You little country mouse! And yet you're right. The legitimate is the missus I should never have left—the drama with a big D. I don't mean the drama with swear words—ha, ha, ha! but the real live article. You see, Duke and me, we've agreed to swop back."

"What for?"

"What for? Why, that's just the trouble. For a consideration, says that son of a horse-leech. And I say that's blood-sucking. Good idea! Why shouldn't you be arbitrator?"

The word, which was unfortunately absent from the Spelling-Book, suggested nothing to her but being hanged, drawn, and quartered, like a rebel whom Gran'fer had once seen executed. But she was afraid of being again set down as a country mouse, so she replied cautiously: "I haven't the time!"

"Oh, I'll pay you your time. Yes, you'd be the ideal arbitrator," cried Mr. Flippance, catching fire at his own idea. "To begin with, you know nothing about it. So that's settled, and you shall drive me to Duke's caravan this very morning."

"Not if I have to wait for your drink."

"The way you drive a man not to drink is awful," he groaned. "Never mind. I've got cool again. Talking to you is as good as a drink. Guardian angel!" He squeezed her horn.

"You see," he narrated, as they drove townwards, "Duke turned up here with the Flippance Fit-Up on Saturday night, and struck an awful frost."

"So he told me," said Jinny. "I met him yesterday when I came out of chapel, and I told him what a roaring trade you were doing."

"My preserver! Then it's to you I owe it he's hankering for his own show back again! Not that he could expect to do any business in my own town, or indeed any other. He forgot that while I, unseen, can be Duke, the public won't look at him for a moment as Flippance. He takes the name of Flippance in vain— the public knows the difference between a barnstormer and their own Tony. To say nothing of that mincing little Duchess after my full-throated, full-bosomed Polly. Poor dear Polly—pining away pulling strings!"

"Why, she told me," said the astonished Jinny, "that she wouldn't go back on the stage for all the treasures of the Crystal Palace."

"Ah, that's her unselfishness—bless her!—her own crystal soul. She knows how the stage tries her pa's nerves. But haven't I stood by her side as we jogged the figures and seen her poor phiz working at the thought of being cut off from her public like in a diving-bell? She takes things hard, does Polly, not like the Duchess, who's got no more temperament than a tinned sardine. You've seen her, haven't you?"

"If you mean Mrs. Duke, she was with him yesterday. A pretty, blue-eyed woman, with golden hair."

"Oh, is it golden this season? But have you seen her act, I mean?"

"I've never seen a play at all!"

"Tut, tut, tut! Then you've never seen Me!"

"Oh—you seem to me a play all the time," she said candidly.

He was not displeased. "Then you do have an idea what a play is?"

"I've seen Punch and Judy—and the Christmas mummers."

He laughed. "Well, if Polly was working Punch and Judy from behind, there'd be more life and go in her than there is to the Duchess when she's on the stage playing Juliet. The public won't pay to see a china doll. But my Polly! I tell you that standing with the strings in her hand, with nobody's eye on her but mine and her Maker's, and in a space where there isn't room to swing a cat, I've seen that girl raging and shouting and tearing about with the passion of the scene till I've had to wake up too, and we've gone at it ding-dong, hammer and tongs. And with three figures each to work, and voices to keep changing, it's no mean feat, I can tell you. Duke and his Duchess now, when they worked the figures, used to just stand like stocks, saying the words, no expression or movement, except in the marionettes."

"But if the public sees only the marionettes—!" said Jinny.

Mr. Flippance shook his head. "There's no art in cold blood. Not that marionette art hasn't got its own special beauties, and I freely admit that in puppetry proper I'm not in it with Duke, who was born into the business, and who cut and fitted the figures himself. Lazy though you think me, how I've sweated to get those things right! What an ungrateful swine the public can be for one's pearls!"

"What kind of pearls?" asked Jinny.

"Why, when a character takes up a glass of wine, for instance, and drinks it."

"Well, I shouldn't applaud that," laughed Jinny.

"There you are!" he said with gloomy triumph. "The public can't see the cleverness of it. But if you remember the delicacy it takes to manipulate the figure from behind, to make it clutch the glass just right, instead of pawing the air, to make that glass come accurately to the mouth, you'll see the countless chances against perfection. Talk of the corkscrew equilibrist at Astley's! Why, Jinny, when that glass sets itself down again without accident, there ought to be applause to make the welkin ring. But not a hand, not a hand!"

"Well, but it can't seem very wonderful from the front," said Jinny.

"It would if people had brains to think. For every joint in the human body there's a joint in Duke's marionette, and for every joint in Duke's marionette there's a separate string to pull. Every art has its own ideal, and for a puppet to sit down safely is a greater success than for a Kean to play Shylock. Though, of course, all this must be Greek to you."

"But when I'm thinking of the fun of Punch and Judy," said Jinny shrewdly, "I can't think of the cleverness of the showman pulling the strings—otherwise I should forget the figures weren't alive, nor the story real—the two things contradict one another."

"By Jove! I think you've hit it," said Mr. Flippance, more gloomily than ever. "They take the standard of drama—not of mechanical miracles. And that's why they applaud most at the easiest effects, just shouting and blood and thunder, and that's why I'm sick, I mean, why Polly is sick of the whole business. Take our tight-rope dancer now. I don't say she's as graceful as a live dancer at Richardson's, or pirouettes like the Cairo Contortionist of my young days at Vauxhall. But she's far more wonderful. A live tight-rope dancer can, after all, only fall downwards if she makes a slip. But ours, instead of tumbling down, might fly up like a balloon, or even just miss the tight-rope and dance on nothing like you see a murderer at Newgate. But the public take the standard of the ballet or the queens of the tight-rope, and instead of giving us a hand for the cleverness in the making and dressing of the puppet, and another hand for the putting life into it, and a third hand for the dexterity of the manipulation, there's times when we get no more recognition than if 'twas a monkey-on-a-stick. I tried to educate 'em by letting 'em see the strings or the wires—I mustn't tell an outsider what they are exactly—I flooded my stage with light. Duke, now, used to keep his scene particularly dark with the fantoccini."

"What's fantokeeny?" asked Jinny, imitating his mispronunciation as best she could.

"They're the figures that are more mechanism than character—balancers, pole-carriers, stilt-walkers, spiral ascensionists, and this tight-rope dancer I'm telling you of. Duke's idea was to keep the mechanism dark."

"That seems to me best," said Jinny.

"I don't agree," said Mr. Flippance. "There's the scenic effects to consider. Darken your scene and you hide it."

"But if you light it, you show up the way it's done," Jinny urged.

"Unless you show 'em the way it's done, how can they appreciate the way you do it? But there, I'm done with it! Let Duke have his pony. Polly shall tread the boards once more."

"Does he want you to give him a pony then to change back?"

"That's it, the son of a Shylock."

"Then you will want a horse after all?"

"A pony—you little innocent—means twenty-five pounds. I suppose, though, that's about the value of a pony."

"It depends who's bidding against you," said Jinny ruefully.

"Well, anyhow, that's what the bloodsucker wants—the twenty-five pounds he gave me he wants back again."

"But if he gave it you, why isn't it fair to give it back?"

"Ah! You're beginning to arbitrate, are you? Well, then! It isn't fair because I get back the Flippance Fit-Up tarnished and depreciated by the performances of that howling amateur and his squeaking doll of a Duchess. Besides, I don't want the 'Fit-Up' particularly, only my trade-mark back, the world-famous word, Flippance, for I am going to stay the whole year here in Chipstone—you see what lots of people there are on market days—-Mother Gander's buying a bigger hall for you Peculiars—haven't you heard?—and me and Charley have worked it with her to sell me the old chapel. I'll easily get it mortgaged, licensed, knocked into shape, and enlarged—that piece of ground between the gate and the doors is wasted at present, and there's an American capitalist keen to come in—I met him just now riding a black horse and leading another—and what better omen could man desire? The Flippance Palace I shall call my theatre—suggests the Hyde Park success, d'ye see? And when that Crystal show is over—it won't run beyond October—I'll have the Queen's elephant standing in my lobby! Lord, it'll draw all Essex! Chipstone'll become the capital!"

These sudden pieces of information left Jinny gasping. The old chapel thus whisked away from under her feet, and turned into a gigantic Punch-and-Judy show sent her world reeling; while Will, transformed into a theatre proprietor, seemed rapt away to unimaginable heights—or depths. But she did not quite believe it all.

"And what does Miss Flippance say?" she murmured.

"Polly? She'll be off her nut with joy. Why, she's such a glutton for work, is that girl, that when we played The Mistletoe Bough she used to play Lady Agnes in Act I and her spirit in Act II (after she's killed by being shut up in the box, you know), and actually double the part with that of her maid, Maud, who has two quick changes from jacket and petticoat to tunic and trunks, and back again to bodice and skirt, not to mention slipping to and fro 'twixt spirit and flesh. She's pining away to a spirit herself, poor dear, for lack of her real work. Only we mustn't break it to her before the deed is done—or rather signed. The poor girl would insist on sacrificing herself. But after all I've saved thirty pounds—you realize I won't need a horse now—so even if I pay him twenty-five, I make a fiver. Not a bad morning's work, eh, my dear? We'll get a good stock company and give 'em everything from the Bard to burletta, and I've got some lovely ideas for taking plays out of Mr. Dickens's novels. Oh, we'll wake up the old place. Charley knows some local girls that would come in splendidly for ballets and choruses, and there's a wonderful scene-painter, too, down here—a chap I knew at the 'Eagle' in London—he's lost his job and come down to his folks to get cured—his hand shakes a bit still, but he's a marvel, I promise you, the days he's not sewn up."

Accepting this synonym for intoxication as referring to the medical operations upon the unfortunate artist, Jinny received the statement with an admiring commiseration.

"And haven't you got a friend, a wonderful expert in costumes?" Tony rattled on.

"Me?" she murmured, puzzled.

"A sort of bearded lady from a French convent, a cranky old Catholic who talks with angels, but is a dab all the same at dressmaking—!"

"You don't mean Miss Gentry?"

"That's the name. We'll appoint her wardrobe mistress." Never had Jinny known him so happy and gaseous—and, paradoxically enough, the more he poured out, the more inflated he got!

"Miss Gentry'll never enter a theatre," said Jinny assuredly.

"We shall see. Wardrobe Mistress to the Flippance Palace, Chipstone. Think how that will improve her billheads! And there's you, too! Why should you waste a first-class stage presence on carrying? You carry yourself too well for that, eh? Ha, ha, ha! A thinking part, perhaps, to begin with, but with your good speaking voice—"

Before Jinny had encountered the full shock of this new proposition, Mr. Flippance broke off and besought her frenziedly to drive down a side street. As she obeyed, she realized that they had just escaped Polly—though a Polly hardly recognizable in that houri in white, creamily jacketed, bonneted, gloved, and, above all, veiled, whom only her massive tread betrayed as charmless.

"You see," explained Polly's pa, "it doesn't do to argue with women you're fond of: you've just got to do what's best for 'em. Duke now, he's very weak with women: 'twixt you and I, he only got my Fit-Up because the Duchess, tired of working in the dark and of blushing unseen, wanted to show off what you call her blue eyes and golden hair. She tried pulling his strings—see?—and he, having no backbone, jigged about at her pleasure. But now, to my thinking, Duke's found out what a fool she's made of him and of herself, too. For, of course, she's mucked up his business. Polly mayn't be a Venus, but she's stunning in her make-ups—I assure you such a great artist is that woman, that seeing her standing in the wings at the first dress rehearsal, I've more than once fallen in love with her myself—till, of course, she opened her mouth. Yes, Polly can always have blue eyes and golden hair, but the Duchess will never have talent if she rehearses till doomsday."

"Then is Mr. Duke satisfied to go back to the illegitimate?" asked Jinny.

He laughed at the word. "To the marionettes? That's what Duke wants the twenty-five pounds for," he answered. "He's lost heavily, and he'll be able to show her a quid pro quo—or rather twenty-five of 'em—ha, ha, ha! All the same, we'd better not talk business if the Duchess happens to be at home. She may have her hand too tight on his strings."

"But what shall we do if she's in?"

"I shall only say I've looked in to congratulate her on her successes!"

"Oh!" Jinny was seriously shocked, and Mr. Flippance, realizing that her conscience was as "country" as her vocabulary, had the shrewdness to say he was only joking. "Besides," he added, "she's sure not to be at home in the morning."

"Why not?"

"Because she won't have her hair on."

"But how could she go out then without it?"

Tony made as if to pinch her cheek, as if nothing else could adequately express his acute sense of her simplicity, but she guarded deftly with the horn; rapping him, indeed, on the knuckles with it.

"Why, Jinny, you hurt me," he said ruefully.

"Well, remember I'm not a marionette."

"You're certainly not a woman of the world. The Duchess wouldn't let us in, I mean, but that's just what we want, provided we can get Duke to exit."

In another minute or two she drove him up to the back of "The Learned Pig," and alighting, they picked their way through the undulating and muddy enclosure, grass-grown, and strewn with logs, where the caravan was stationed. There was really a pig there (duly styed in his very dirty academy), besides pecking poultry and pathetic rabbit-hutches agleam with eager sniffing noses, and a flutter of washing, and two shabby traps, holding up their shafts like beggars' arms. But the caravan itself illumined the untidy space with its gay green paint, its high yellow wheels, its spick-and-span air, culminating in the lace curtain of its tiny arched window. Mr. Flippance dragged his slippers up the step-ladder, and Jinny, having by this time gathered what an arbitrator was, followed in his wake, prepared to undertake this or any other job.

But the Duchess did let them in—more, she opened the door herself, looking indeed too lovely for anything but a doll, and suggesting by her rising and falling eyelids, her smiling lips, and her mobile hands that she was equipped with all the most expensive devices.

Duke, habited in an old-fashioned blue coat with brass buttons, was discovered poring at a desk over a long, narrow account book: he was an elderly and melancholy young man, with bristly black-and-white hair and small pig-eyes set close together. The stamp of aspiration and defeat was set pathetically upon the sallow face he turned over his shoulder to his visitors.

Jinny was not edified by Mr. Flippance's pretence that she—Jinny—was the sole ground for the visit. She had, he said, been driving him home from the market, where he had gone to dispose of a horse, and he had taken the liberty of bringing her to see their "wonderful" caravan, finding, to his amazement, that she had never been inside. For once the stock Essex epithet was justified—it was indeed a "wonderful" caravan, and the interior so took up her attention that for some time she failed to follow the conversation, though she had a dim uneasy sense that it continued—as it began—with scant regard to the ethics of the Spelling-Book. The gay paint and the neat lace curtains had prepared her for an elegance, and even an airiness, that were not to be found within the caravan. But little else seemed lacking. For into this cramped wheeled chamber, looking scarce larger than her own cart, and certainly not so large as Commander Dap's cabin in the Watch Vessel, was packed not only a complete cottage with its parlour, living-room, bedroom, scullery, and kitchen, but the mantelpieces and chests of drawers were as crowded with china dogs and shepherdesses as Blackwater Hall itself, besides a wealth of pictures, objects of art, posters, and inhabited birdcages, to which Daniel Quarles's domain could lay no claim. Not that there was really more than one undivided space, or that you could tell where one room ended and the other began. Nevertheless, all the different sections were clearly visible, though a square yard here or there did double or treble service, forming part of this or that room according as you looked at it. Most clearly marked, of course, was the bedroom, consisting of a raised, neatly counterpaned bed, like an upper berth in a ship, and a chest of drawers topped with ornaments, though the kitchen with its grate and oven and flap-table ran it close, in every sense of the phrase. Amid these poky surroundings, the Duchess's blue eyes and golden hair shone so sunnily and veraciously—taken unawares as she seemed—that Jinny, ignorant she was expecting a visitor, felt that Mr. Flippance was as unjust of judgment as he was loose of statement.

But an interior so foreign to her experience affected her with all the pleasurable interest of drama, apart from the comedy of which she felt it to be the setting, as, awaking again to the conversation, she heard the two males still keeping it carefully away from the negotiation pending between them, and evidently hard exercised—despite gin from an improbable corner cupboard—to keep the ball of nothingness rolling. Painful silences fell, which a linnet and a goldfinch mule strove loyally to fill, but which remained so awkward that she herself was constrained to enter into the conspiracy, though only by way of genuine admiration. Admiration of the caravan—a ready-made thing that went with Duke—was by no means, however, the admiration the Duchess wanted, and as she failed to extract it from poor Mr. Flippance, fidgeting under Jinny's Puritan eye, she fell back on a tribute of her own to herself, recounting tediously the triumphs of her tour, and calling on her partner for corroboration, which he supplied in joyless monosyllables.

All Flippance's interjections with a view to stem the stream and divert the conversation to a pretext for Duke's exit with him were like straws tossed before a torrent. But presently there came relief—though the plot thickened, Jinny felt. There was a sound of footsteps on the ladder, and, "Ah, there's Polly!" the monologist broke off.

If Jinny was already steeped in a sense of the dramatic, if, stimulated by the novel setting, she had begun to feel that in such cross-currents and mutual deceptions must lie the substance of that unknown article of commerce these people lived by—a play—how strongly was this intuition confirmed and this sense enhanced when Mr. Flippance, whispering in apparent facetiousness, "I'm in my slippers—she'll rag me," kicked them off under a chair, slid back mahogany panels below the bed, disclosing a lower berth, and tumbled in, with his finger roguishly on his lips, closing the panels from within!

"The Mistletoe Bough!" he sibilated. So there it was! They were actually imitating a play before her very eyes. Duke and the Duchess, grinning, drew the panels tighter. The theatre was so in their blood, Jinny felt, that these things came as natural to them as carrying to her.

It was thus that Jinny saw her first farce—unless the high tragedy of Punch and Judy be degraded by that name.

VIII

Polly, it soon transpired, was come to the midday dinner with her friend, and the dinner itself was coming in presently from "The Learned Pig." The real purpose of the invitation was, it transpired equally, that Polly might explain to the Duchess the reading of a part alleged to be confused in the manuscript acquired with the Flippance Fit-Up: she was obviously fishing for tips. While these things were transpiring, poor Flippance in his fur was perspiring. Gradually Jinny saw a rift appearing in the bed-panels and widening to a cautious chasm of a few inches. It made her feel choky herself, especially as the caravan's little window was closed. She signed apprehensively to Mr. Duke, who, however, was already revolving feverishly how to clear the stage for himself and his fellow-negotiator. And presently he broke into the feminine dialogue with, "I'm sure, dearest, Polly wouldn't mind acting that bit for you.

But there ain't room for Polly's genius here—she'd be breaking up the happy home! Hadn't you better go into the inn-parlour, Bianca? There'll be nobody there yet."

The Duchess might have lacked talent, but she had not played in farces without learning how to behave in them: so without even needing a wink from her spouse, she made a kindly exit behind Polly, not, however, without turning back a grinning doll's head at Mr. Flippance's beaded countenance emerging gaspingly from his berth. But Jinny, who had already witnessed comedy and farce, was now more conscious of the tragedy of the situation than of its humours, as she saw the Duchess tripping down the ladder, with silken stockings revealed by the raised skirt. It seemed to Jinny that the poor lady was tripping thus blithely to her dark doom, behind the scenes of the puppet show; that her blue eyes and golden hair had flaunted their last upon the stage. And the irony of her grinning exit was accented by the manuscript in her hand: she was going off to study a part she would nevermore play. It all gave Jinny a sense of the Duchess being herself a puppet, with an ironic fate pulling the strings, and she was frightened by a thought hitherto beyond the reach of her soul; by a dim feeling that perhaps she too— and everybody else—was similarly mocked. Who was perpetually jerking her towards that young man, and then jerking her back? What force was always putting into her mouth words of fleer and flout, and pulling away the hand she yearned to lay in his?

"Whew!" exclaimed Mr. Anthony Flippance, as Jinny shut the door safely on the Duchess—for that lady never shut doors, partly because the process interfered with the sweep of one's exit, partly because what concerned a scene from which she was absent never entered her golden head.

"Whew!" repeated Mr. Flippance, scrambling out. "I know now what Lady Agnes felt like. 'Help, Lovel!— Father, help!—I faint—I die—Oh! Oh!' But I'm disappointed in Polly," he added, diving under a chair. "Fancy being all her life on the stage, and not espying these slippers!" He dug his feet into them.

"There's no time for joking," said Duke anxiously, as he tugged open the drawer of a desk in his "parlour." "I suppose Jinny is in the know?"

"Jinny's come as arbitrator!"

"What!" Duke wheeled round, his hair still more on end.

"Get on with your mystery-desk. It stands to reason a runaway financial imagination like yours needs a brake."

"Ain't you brake enough?" Mr. Duke's tone was bitter.

"And you want me to be broke!" retorted Tony. "I give you my beautiful marionettes, life-sized and life-painted, all carved by the best maker—"

"Oh, I know all about that!" interrupted Duke impatiently.

"Well, you're not going to deny your own skill, I hope?"

Duke glared impotently with his little pig-eyes.

"And with the costliest costumes," Tony went on blandly. "And all these puppets moreover with the latest mechanical contrivances, regardless of expense—"

"And don't I give you the finest goodwill in East Anglia," burst in Mr. Duke, "the Flippance Fit-Up with all its plays, prestige, and unique takings?"

"One thing at a time, old cock. Packed into a box that itself opens out and forms part of the stage, combining portability of props with—"

"Do dry up!" cried the maddened Duke. "If you're not quick, Bianca will be back."

"What's that to me? To cut it short, I give you the finest marionette show in the world, with scenery, sky-borders, and plays complete, and an old-established reputation, a show that has played before the crowned heads of Europe, America, and Australia, and, like the workhouse boy in Mr. Dickens's book, you ask for more. What say you, Jinny? Thinkest thou the Duke should have more?"

"We all want more," said Jinny. "Air! Mayn't I open the window?"

"Oh, excuse me." Mr. Duke, evidently trained by his big doll, rushed to do it. "But haven't I lost enough without losing my twenty-five pounds too?"

He turned back to his desk, and extricating from its remoter recesses another large narrow fat account book—the twin of that he had been poring over—held it up theatrically. "Here's my marionette accounts for sixteen years—look through 'em and see if you can find any single week—ay, even the week of King William's funeral—as low as the best of the weeks since I touched your wretched show."

"My wretched show!" Mr. Flippance lost his blandness. "Why, if that's the case, it's you that have depreciated it. You ought to pay me compensation."

But Duke had dramatically dumped the book down side by side with its twin. "Look on this picture and on that!" he said. "Duke's Marionettes, week ending March 10th, 1849, Colchester. Total, £23 18s. 10d. Flippance Fit-Up, Colchester Corn Exchange, week ending March 8th, 1851. Monday. Eleven shillings. There's an opening! Tuesday—"

"Oh, come to the damned total!" said Tony impatiently.

"There ain't any total," said Duke crushingly. "Tuesday, sixteen shillings and sixpence."

"Always rising, you see!" said Tony.

"Wednesday," Duke went on implacably, "nine shillings and fourpence—"

"Why, how do you get fourpence?" interrupted Tony severely. "You haven't been letting down the prices, I hope."

"That's noted at the side. See!" said the careful Duke. "A swindler passed off a groat as a tanner. Thursday, Eight and sixpence—imagine the Colchester Corn Exchange with eight and sixpence! Friday. Nine shillings—"

"Rising again, you see," chirruped Tony.

"Saturday. One pound thirteen and six."

"There you are! That pulls you up."

"Saturday evening," concluded Duke. "Two pounds eight."

"And then he grumbles!" Mr. Flippance raised his great ringed hands towards Jinny.

"Total, six pounds five and tenpence!"

"And isn't that enough to live on?" cried Tony. "Only two in family and a little bird or so! And if your box-office man had been smart enough to tell a groat from a tester, you'd have had six guineas!"

"He wasn't such a fool," said Duke dryly, "for on another night it's noted that a half-sovereign was passed off on him for sixpence."

"And then you outrage Providence by complaining of the takings," said Tony.

"Rent of Corn Exchange," continued Duke doggedly, "three guineas. Salaries (to company, including check-taker), four pounds eight. Lighting, a pound. Advertising (including bill-poster), three pounds ten—"

"But, my dear chap, what extravagance! No wonder—"

"Travelling expenses (company and scenery, excluding caravan), eighteen and ninepence. Drinks to Pressmen—one and sixpence—"

"Oh, not enough! No wonder—!"

"Net deficit, seven pounds sixteen and threepence, plus the salary of Bianca and me!"

"What! Why, you said salary of company, four pounds eight!"

"You don't suppose I included ourselves with the check-taker!"

"You didn't? Oh, my dear fellow," said Tony sympathetically, "no wonder you're down in the mouth. A wise manager always pays his salary before any other expense; then he's always sure of a stand-by!"

"It isn't the money that's the worst," Duke explained. "It's the dreadful loneliness."

"Why didn't you stuff the house with paper and put up 'Free List Absolutely Suspended'?"

"Easier said than done in a place where you don't know a soul. Why, Bianca had a Benefit Night, and how many do you think were in the stalls? Two women and a boy."

"I've known only the theatre cat—" began Tony cheerfully.

"And the boy went to sleep!"

"Wasn't it his bedtime? But I will say it's not entirely the fault of your acting. I've noticed ever since that Crystal Palace loomed on the horizon, it's unsettled the public within at least fifty miles from Hyde Park. I was talking to a showman who told me that in March and April this year business fell off everywhere— there was no interest in giants, dwarfs, fat men, pig-faced ladies, and even jugglers, animal magnetizers, lion-tamers, performing elephants, ventriloquists, prestidigitators, and professors of necromancy. Didn't you hear of the fate of poor Wishbone, the conjurer, at Chelmsford Fair? Not even a kid dropped into his booth, so he went out to perform outside, but before he could 'hey, presto!' the purse back to the owner, the peeler copped him. The magistrate wouldn't listen to his patter, and he can't tap himself out of quod either, poor chap. Besides, we all remember the awful weather in March, yes and up to the very opening of the Crystal Palace—rain, rain, rain."

"Well, take the March of 1849," said Duke, turning back his oblong pages, "and don't forget people'll sit in Assembly Rooms or a Corn Exchange when they won't risk a draughty tent. Now look at the weather that year—when I pulled my own strings. Tuesday, W.S.—that is, wet, snow. Wednesday, R.N. (rough night). Thursday, S.H.T. (storm, hail, and thunder). Saturday, W.T. (wind, tilt OFF!). Come now, you could hardly have a worse week, could you? Everything except B.F.1 or B.F.2 (black fog or big funeral). Yet see, my takings for that week were—"

Tony flipped away the book with his jewelled hand. "What you've got to compare with your Colchester week," he said, "is not your marionette week in March '49, but my Fit-Up week for that date."

"I don't see that."

"It stands to reason."

They debated the point warmly: finally Tony referred it to Jinny: that was what she was there for, he recalled.

"I certainly think," arbitrated the little Carrier, "that we ought to see what Mr. Flippance's live theatre could do in the same weather."

"Oh, very well," acquiesced Duke sulkily. "And what did you do that week?"

"Heavens, man, how on earth can I remember?"

"But haven't you got it written down?"

"What do you take me for?" asked Tony. "A tradesman? A bookkeeper? Unless Polly—"

"You told me the other Christmas that you averaged twenty-five," said Duke bitterly, "and I paid you one week's takings by way of douceur."

"Well, then you do know my weekly takings," said Tony loftily.

"I can't stay here for ever," put in Jinny. "I've got my work."

"I'm paying you, ain't I?" Tony rebuked her.

"But not giving me work." She assumed a judicial air. "Do you, Mr. Flippance, maintain that your theatre is a more valuable concern than Mr. Duke's marionettes?"

"Of course I do."

"Then," said the young Solomon in petticoats, "surely if you get it back, you ought to pay him the difference in value."

"Bravo! Bravo!" Mr. Duke's little pig-eyes gleamed. "A sensible girl!"

"Oh, Jinny!" groaned Mr. Flippance: "To desert your old pal!"

"And do you, Mr. Duke," went on Jinny imperturbably, "maintain that your marionettes are a better property than the Flippance Fit-Up?"

"Certainly not," said Mr. Duke, not to be caught.

"The marionettes are a worse property then?" she asked.

Duke banged his book. "Much worse."

"Then why do you want it back?"

Tony uttered a shriek of delight. "A Daniel come to judgment! Oh, Jinny, I could hug you!"

A sweep of her horn kept him at arm's length. "You say, Mr. Duke, that the Fit-Up property is the better, and yet you want to give it up?"

Mr. Duke leaned his elbows on the desk, and dropped his head in his hands. "You confuse me—I must have time to think."

"Hamlet!" observed Tony pleasantly. "But I don't think the ghost will walk." His hand moved towards the gin decanter, but again that baffling horn intervened.

"Look here!" said Duke, rummaging in his drawer. "I've got the transfer written out, ready for signature, two copies—the exact words of our last agreement, only turned the other way, of course. I'm a plain man—is it to be or not to be?"

"That is the question," said Tony sepulchrally. "But you see it isn't so plain as you. You've depreciated my theatre and it's not worth the extra pony. Why can't you make a reasonable compromise and just swap back?"

"What! And be a pony out of pocket?"

"You'll be an elephant out of pocket if you don't," Jinny reminded him. "Seven pounds sixteen and threepence a week mount up."

"Ah, that was a particularly bad week."

"Then there were good weeks?" flashed Tony.

"I tell you the best weren't as good as the marionettes' worst."

"Come, come, old cock, draw it mild!"

"If you don't believe me," said Duke, firing up, "look for yourself! And what's more, if you find I'm wrong, keep the pony and be hanged to you!"

"Easy! Easy! But I was never a man to refuse a sporting offer—tip us the tomes!"

Duke handed him the twin account books, but soon, tiring of the rows of figures, Mr. Flippance begged Jinny to pursue the investigation while he studied the document of transfer.

It was not without a thrill that, setting the volumes on a hanging flap that Duke had changed for her into a table, she went back over the pages of faded ink that told of toils and tribulations in the years before she had come into being: as a carrier she was peculiarly sensitive to these records of wrecked tents and ruined takings. Through the peace of the summer morning in that poky caravan, the winds from that pre-natal period seemed to be rushing, its snows falling, its hails and thunders crashing, and with these imagined tempests came up the thought of Will. What was he doing now, with his beautiful black horses? Was he looking for Mr. Flippance at "The Black Sheep"? But the thought of him was too agitating; she crushed it down and got absorbed in her task and the tales the figures told: the blanks carefully explained by Good Friday or royal mourning or the journey to some distant pitch; the varying cost of these pitches in publicans' meadows; the varying expense of cartage; the sudden jumps in the takings, due—as annotated—to high days and holidays, or to royal weddings, or to favourite pieces. She wondered why Mr. Duke ever played any others. "What is D.F.N.?" she asked suddenly.

"Dismissed. Fine night," said Mr. Duke in melancholy accents. It was the supreme tragedy. "Although a fine night," he explained, rubbing it in to himself, "not enough to be worth playing to."

"You didn't always do good business, you see," gurgled Tony from the gin-glass he had imperceptibly acquired.

"Accidents will happen," Duke retorted.

"And what is D.S.?" put in Jinny. "Dismissed. Snow?"

"D.S. is diddling show," explained Duke gloomily. "I struck one only last week at the very public-house I hired my pitch from."

"That wasn't playing fair," said Tony.

"No, indeed. They stuck a placard in the window, 'Great Water Otter. Free.' And when you'd had your drink they took you to the stables to see it in its tub. There were crowds every night. It was put in the paper."

Tony grinned. "'Lord, what fools these mortals be!'"

"But why?" asked Jinny. "I'd rather see a water-otter than a dancing doll."

"You're not even a country mouse," said Tony. "When the fools push and squeeze to get near the tub, they warn 'em, 'Don't go too near!' And all the while it's only a big iron kettle—a water-'otter. See!"

Jinny laughed.

"Yes, that's what they all do," said Duke dismally. "Laugh and help to gull the others. And between them the legitimate goes to the dogs."

"Or the otters." Jinny bent in lighter spirits over the twin volumes. "I'm afraid you've lost, Mr. Flippance," she announced at last. "I can't see any drama week of Mr. Duke's that goes as high as the worst of his marionette weeks."

"Right you are!" said Tony, cheerful under his liquid. "Sport is sport and the pony is yours. Here goes!" And picking up a pen from the desk, he signed one of the documents with a long thick line sweeping backward from his final "e." Duke signed the other copy more soberly, and Jinny witnessed both signatures with careful calligraphy. "It only remains, old cock," said Tony, "to deliver the twenty-five pounds."

"Hear, hear," agreed Duke.

"You don't suppose I carry it about with me?"

Duke's face fell. "But without money passing, it ain't legal."

"But I jumped out of bed in a hurry—Jinny'll bear me out. I mean," he added hurriedly, as a dramatic interest flickered across Duke's face, "look at my slippers!"

"Oh, I've seen your stinking old slippers!" Duke was getting unpleasant. "What I want to see is my money."

"Sorry, old boy—no use letting your dander rise—it's a case of H.G.I.—haven't got it, and M.O.I.U.— must owe it you! Still, I dare say we can rake up something on account, to make a legal consideration. Doubtless Jinny has got half a crown. Give me one, Jinny, till I get home."

Jinny, who had always hitherto dealt with Polly, and been scrupulously paid, had no hesitation in handing him the coin. She did not know it was the cost of her arbitration. Duke accepted it ungraciously as earnest money.

"And if I may advise you how to run your own show, now you've got it back," said Tony handsomely, "don't go so much by the fairs. There's not only the waste of time and travel in between one and t'other, it's lowering a fine art to the level of a merry-go-round or the talking lobst—"

"I can't wait for ever," interposed Jinny. "Are you coming?" She opened the door.

"Your time's paid," said Mr. Flippance severely. "However, Duke takes my meaning. Here's luck to him!" And with a last gulp at Duke's gin, he followed her to the door. "Send me my scenery and props and the same cart can take back yours and the box of figures."

"No, no," said Duke, "that'll need several journeys or carts. We divide the freightage."

"What! When I throw in twenty-five pounds! O Duke, Duke, if you ain't careful there'll be a show of the meanest man on earth." And shaking his fat jewelled forefinger waggishly at the caravan proprietor, he followed the Carrier. "Now for a last kick at the company," he observed to her, as the door closed upon the dismal Duke.

IX

But at that moment the ground resounded with gallant hoofs, and a handsome red-haired cavalier riding a barebacked black horse and leading another steed of Satan, and followed by a bounding little white dog, brought life and spirit into the scene. The rabbits poked their noses greedily through their wires, and the pig grunted in perturbation. Jinny, shrinking back behind Mr. Flippance, remained paralysed on the steps of the caravan, while Tony, unconscious that he was needed as a screen, hurried forward with a joyous greeting and a query which served the purpose as effectually, for Jinny was left unnoted on her pedestal.

"You looking for me?" asked Tony.

"I was," answered the horseman. "But now I'm looking for the stables. 'The Black Sheep's' full up, and I thought I'd put up my spare horse at 'The Learned Pig' till I could find you. However, here you are."

"But you crossed me, man, just outside the market!"

"Did I? Is Jinny here? I see her cart outside."

"Never mind Jinny—you're just in the nick of time. I want to talk business to you."

"And so do I to you. If I crossed you, 'twas because I was galloping to you with the horse you ordered through Jinny."

"And I was galloping to her to cancel it!"

"What!" cried Will. But the joyous rush and gambollings of Nip now directed his attention to Nip's statuesque mistress.

"I'm afraid you've let yourself in for those horses," she said, descending. She did not speak maliciously—the sting of her defeat was over, now that his victory had recoiled on the victor, and she was really a little sorry for him. But all other feelings were overwhelmed for the moment by this new sense of dash and grace, in which he and the beautiful pawing steeds were mixed up centaur-like, his figure looking so much taller on horseback that it almost corresponded to Miss Gentry's ideal. Unfortunately Will himself had no sense of the horses except as a costly and burdensome mistake: the iron issuing from Jinny's soul was entering into his.

"But surely you want one of 'em," he said, addressing Mr. Flippance. He had cherished a dim hope that the Showman might launch out into binary grandeur, but at the worst he was prepared to keep one horse—it would be useful for riding into Chipstone—pending its sale. But to have two horses on his hands, eating their heads off, after consuming practically the whole of his capital—this was too much. Nor could he believe that Jinny was not gloating over the Nemesis that had overtaken his attempt to crush her will.

"I don't see what I should do with a horse," said Tony, "seeing that I'm setting up the Flippance Palace Theatre as a local landmark. Of course I might have a play written round him," he mused, "or even round 'em both. They would certainly 'draw' all Chipstone, especially with a carriage behind 'em. Odd, isn't it? There'll be scores of carriages waiting outside my theatre, yet to see one on the stage gives everybody a thrill. Lord, how the public does love to see natural things in unnatural places! As my old pa used to say—my real pa, I mean—put an idiot on the stage and he gives pleasure, put him in the stalls and he writes dramatic criticism! Ha, ha, ha!"

"Then you do want 'em?" said Will eagerly.

"If you're ready to bring in the noble animals as part of the capital, I'll look around for a dramatist to work 'em in."

"You'd best look around for a capitalist," retorted Will in angry disappointment. "I've told you before, I'm going into farming."

"Then you'll want the horses yourself."

"They're no good for farming," Jinny corrected.

"Ain't they?" said Tony, surveying them with a fresh eye. "Then why did he buy them?"

Will got angrier. "That's my business. Do you want them or not?"

"I can always do with anything. A play's a pie you can shove anything into. You'd look bully yourself, as you Americans say, riding just as you are: just a cowboy costume, that's all you need. Will you do it?"

"Will I do what?"

"Play lead and supply your own horses."

"Don't be a fool—or try to make me one. I'm a plain farmer."

Tony grinned. "Jinny don't seem to think 'em suitable for plain farming. I reckon you'd better set up as undertaker. They'll go lovely with a hearse. All you need is a corpse."

"And I shan't be long finding one!" hissed Will.

Tony clapped his hands. "That's the style. Lord, man, what a wasted actor!"

Jinny could not suppress a smile. It brought Will's temper to breaking-point. "These horses at least won't be wasted," he said to her at a white heat. "For I'll take our friend's advice."

"Harness 'em to a hearse?" murmured Jinny.

"No, to a coach. I'll put an end, miss, to your mannish ways."

"Indeed!" Jinny bridled up, without, however, quite following the threat.

"You've done for yourself," he explained. "You've forced me into competition. You've got me the horses—there's no end of out-of-work coaches on the market to be got for an old song. I'll carry passengers and luggage faster and cheaper than you, and heavier stuff too, and I'll wipe you out."

Jinny grew white, but at the venom of his words, not their business significance. Her instinct retorted with a smile. "And I got you the horn, too, don't forget that."

"I don't—I was thinking of that. It's all your doing—and serve you jolly well right." He turned sneeringly to Mr. Flippance. "So I won't be a wasted musician either."

"Oho!" said Jinny. "And shall we see you on the box-seat all a-crowing and a-blowing?"

"I know you still think I can't blow—but you shall see."

"Seeing isn't believing," said Jinny.

"Had you there, old cock," said Tony.

"She knows what I mean, right enough. I'll start a coach-service 'twixt Little Bradmarsh and Chipstone, ay and farther too, passengers inside, luggage on the roof. I'll wake up this sleepy old spot." And his vigour seemed to communicate itself to his horses: they caracoled and stamped.

"Better let sleeping spots lie," said Jinny. "I thought you hated Yankee going-ahead."

"It'll save you going ahead, anyhow," said Will. "Why didn't you let things sleep?"

"Me! How could I help helping Gran'fer?"

"Women have always got an excuse. 'And the man gave unto me and I did eat.'"

"Lord! He's been reading the Bible!" laughed Tony.

Will flushed. All those hours in quest of orthography passed through his mind. And what had all his painstaking letters led to? Quarrels, recriminations, miseries. Well, let him have done with it all. Ignore her, crush her, that was the best way. Once he had driven her out of the business, that tongue of hers would wag more meekly. Then, perhaps—!

A rousing blast on Jinny's horn cut defiantly into his thoughts. It was at once a challenge and a mockery. Will turned his horses' heads sharply and trotted out, Nip at their heels. But at the edge of the enclosure Nip looked back wistfully to beg his mistress to join the party. She, however, lowering her horn, cried, "Come here, you naughty dog. Come here at once."

Nip stood in pathetic hesitation.

"It's that animal my play shall be written round," said Tony decisively. "How much do you want for him?"

"You know I wouldn't, part with him for love or money," said Jinny.

"Well, I haven't got any money," said Tony slowly. "But if you'd like the other thing—"

"Don't be silly!" Jinny moved towards her cart.

"I mean it—a wife like you would be the making of a man."

"Now you'll have to walk home!" said Jinny, springing into her seat. It was too ironic a climax to the morning.

"Not in my slippers!" gasped Tony.

"You should have put on your boots!" said Jinny sternly.

"But listen!" He clung to the cart as if he would stop it. "It's a heaven-sent opportunity."

"It must be sent back," said Jinny gravely.

"I mean for me," he explained desperately. "You know how Polly objects to my marrying again. But I've got to break the deal with Duke to her, so I could work in the two at once. It couldn't be worse."

"I shall never marry," said Jinny. "Gee up!"

"But whoa, whoa, you don't carry only your husbands," cried Tony. "Stop!"

He pursued Methusalem for some yards, but even Methusalem was too quick for him. And then, as he stood panting and perspiring and overcome by a dark upwelling of disbelief in life, he perceived the Duchess with her manuscript and his daughter returning from the histrionic consultation at "The Learned Pig."

"Thank the Lord, Polly's feeding out," he murmured, as he slunk into a doorway. Then his face brightened up. "After all," he thought, "I've only got to break to her about the theatre."

CHAPTER IX

TWO OF A TRADE

This comic story or this tragic jest
May make you laugh or cry, as you think best.
GAY, *Prologue to "The What D'ye Call It?"*

I

The darkest season in Jinny's life—outwardly a feast of light—was come to the crowning mockery of its August splendour. Day after day there was the lazy pomp of high summer; massive white clouds in a blue sky, a spacious voluptuousness, a languid glory. But Jinny felt less melancholy on the rare days when sea-mists rolled in from the marshes and spectral sheep were heard tinkling from dim meadows. The corn was now cut, and this too was a curious alleviation of the gnawing at her heart. When the far-spreading wheat-fields had rustled in the sun like the hair of the earth-mother, an auburn gold touched with amber and purple lights, infinitely subtle and suffusive, the beauty of it all had been almost intolerable. Now that remorseless reapers had turned the wheat into rows of stooks that were more suggestive of the hair of a village girl in curl-papers, Jinny found it easier to jog on her sorely diminished business along the sunbaked roads.

It was not merely that Will had turned from a swain into an enemy, and from a figure of romance into a business rival. It was not merely that his hated handsome visage kept coming up in her mind at the oddest moments, to the confusion of her work. It was the pressure of his competition.

Hitherto Jinny had believed in mankind. Despite "The Seven Stages of Life," by which her Spelling-Book combined instruction in old English print with detailed information on how the Devil blurs God's image in man; despite the testifyings of her fellow-Peculiars to their own wickedness, she had regarded her fellow-beings as in the main virtuous and kindly. What was she to think of human nature when she saw this dashing innovator literally "carrying" all before him?

In her pique and distress she failed to allow for the sensation created by the advent of the small second-hand coach with its pair of high-stepping black horses. Nothing so great and momentous had happened in Bradmarsh from time immemorial. Even in Jinny's own mind it loomed as large as any of the events in the Spelling-Book, from Noah's Flood to Trafalgar. Throughout all those somnolent Essex by-ways the passage of the novel equipage brought everybody to door or window. It was equal to the passing of the County Flyer on the main roads, a thunder of wheels and a jingle of harness and a music of the horn. True, two horses are not four, and a driver who blows his own trumpet has not the grandeur of a coachman with a scarlet-coated guard, not to mention the absence of relays to paw the ground and be switched without loss of a second to the fiery vehicle. Still, with scarcely a hill to negotiate before Chipstone, two horses and a man seemed velocity and magnificence to villages accustomed to a crawling two-wheeled tilt-cart and a girl.

And the Flynt Flyer—as it styled itself in vainglorious paint—had created a demand, as well as a sensation, even if the want had been unfelt before. Starting three services a week instead of two, it moreover dashed and zigzagged into corners and by-roads that Jinny had never pretended to serve, the denizens of which had been content to wait at cross-roads and landmarks, or to deal with her through intermediary neighbours or houses of call. And besides these attractions of convenience and novelty, there was the comfort for passengers of riding in the body of the coach with their feet in the straw, instead of dangling uneasily from the narrow side-ledges in Jinny's cart or sprawling in contorted adjustment to parcels and boxes. Persons who had always walked, now found it simpler to jump into the coach than to fag along in the heat. The carrying business saw itself transformed and extended.

In this elegant and epoch-making vehicle the non-human freight overflowing from the fore and hind boots was stacked on the roof, though the lucky first-comer had always space to sit beside Will and hear his stories of the great world. A shipmate from 'Frisco had boasted of driving in kid gloves a polished silk-lined cab and spanking fifteen-hundred-dollar steeds with silver-gleaming harness, and earning his three hundred dollars a month. The vision beglamoured Will's own status on the box, and reconciled him to lifting the luggage of his labouring inferiors. He aped it by driving in his best Moses & Son suit, as though more of a sporting charioteer than a menial, touting for custom. And parcels and clients flung themselves into his arms. What wonder if the high-piled load soon out-topped Jinny's, revealed in its nakedness on these sweltering days when she drove without her tilt! For gradually folk's eyes seemed opened, unsealed of a spell. Without a word spoken it was as if something unnatural and monstrous had been wafted away, and the simple order of nature—in the shape of a male carrier—had been restored. Without being quite conscious of how they had lugged their own boxes for the puny female, customers were aware of a new facility. They did not so much turn against Jinny as forget her in this gravitation to the natural centre.

At first Will had—with a touch of considerateness—fixed his days on Mondays, Wednesdays, and Saturdays, not to clash with Jinny's Tuesdays and Fridays. But as his supply created new demands, as he found he could widen his ambit as far even as Brandy Hole Creek or Blackripple, he took on new circuits, first for Tuesday and then for Friday and dropping his Wednesdays to give his hard-worked horses a solid rest in mid-week. It was not these new routes of his that galled Jinny, nor his impinging on her days—possibly she was not altogether displeased to meet the rival vehicle. No, the iron that entered her soul was the loss of her previous customers, who, despite Will's comparative magnanimity, had changed their day to suit the rival round. In the cases where she had imagined herself a friend rather than an employee, it was heart-breaking.

Hence this new and rankling doubt of her species, waxing daily as her business waned. Folk seemed to follow one another like sheep, and whenever now on a bit of miry road she came upon the serried footmarks of a flock, she shuddered with a sense of the ignoble pettiness of the pattern: no massive individual stamp like Methusalem's, not even a characteristic dent like Nip's, but an ignominious churning of mud by a multiplication of innumerable little identities. Pigs, too, supplied her with bitter comparisons when, with her cart void of passengers and almost empty of parcels, she passed at some cross-road the Flynt Flyer, stiflingly chock-full of both. For she had often noted in the feeding of swine that however abundant the food at its snout, master pig will always rush to the thickest jostling-point.

Such was the crowd, such was humanity, thought our little cynic; who was, however, no mere soured philosopher, but a harassed housekeeper, with a couple of aged dependents, whose rashers or oats were becoming seriously endangered. Methusalem had always lived from hoof to mouth, and as for her grandfather, had he not spent all his savings on her Angel-Mother's debts? There were still potatoes in the store, and half a flitch in the larder, and beer in the barrel, and vegetables in the ground, and milk in the goats' udders, but the reserves of provender, as of cash, were small, and Methusalem, whose appetite age could not abate, now began to loom as a deficit rather than an asset. Nip was the first to notice—and with pained astonishment—the parsimony of the new regime. Why keep a mistress if one is to be practically thrown back on one's own resources?

II

In these circumstances it scarcely seemed on a par with the ethics of the Spelling-Book, or of a piece with Jinny's character, that she should go to Miss Gentry and order a new Sunday dress of pink sprigged muslin of the latest design—a gown that but for its not hooking up at the back was absolutely ladylike. Still less that she should drive in it on Tuesdays and Fridays. Whether it was in emulation of her rival, on the theory that fashionableness was a factor of his success, whether it was to brighten up her spirits, or to exhibit a defiant prosperity, Jinny did not reveal, even to herself. But that it was worn at Will rather than on herself, may be deduced from the fact that the commission to the "French dressmaker" followed hard upon her first encounter with the Flynt Flyer at the cross-roads.

It was on this occasion—as at many subsequent meetings on Tuesdays or Fridays—that Nip was torn almost literally in two by his desire to be in both vehicles at once. That they should wish to pass each other without a halt or even a hail was amazing to the poor animal, and if his distraction usually ended in a leap on to the coach, where Will was never without a beguiling biscuit, he was always careful to rejoin the cart before the interval had become too spacious. Though a Nip-o'-both-sides, he was disloyal to neither: indeed, if ever creature did his best to bring two foolish mortals together, that creature was Nip. But they no longer even saluted each other. At first, indeed, the gentleman driver had doffed his hat gallantly, but Jinny's face had remained a stone, though that stone was a ruby. Will, therefore, when he had to meet or pass her, flew by at a rate which by its air of insolent superiority only increased her resentment. Later, he had begun to slow down when he espied her lumbering along his route, and to play the "Buy a Broom" polka on his horn with malicious accuracy.

By way of retort Jinny once tied a label to Nip's collar, marked "In charge of the guard." It was meant to taunt Will with lacking the dignity of a true driver, who never blew a horn. But the somewhat periphrastic sarcasm seemed to miss fire, for Will took the label literally, and when Nip had executed his usual leap on to the coach, he kept him prisoner for several days. The faithful animal, though fed as never before, was as unhappy, tied on the roof, as Jinny was, and when her cart at last passed, and her horn blew imperiously for him, he made such a supercanine effort that his cord snapped, and in an instant he was snuggling hysterically in the legitimate lap; regardless of that flowery summery fabric. His label, she found, now bore the words, "Pay Up The Gloves."

Alas, paying up—whether for wagers or fabrics—was out of Jinny's power. That very morning Miss Gentry had handed her the bill, delicately wrapped in a tract. Such a situation was quite new to her, though not unprovided against in the Spelling-Book:

Weigh ev'ry small Expence and nothing waste,
Farthings, if sav'd, amount to Pounds in Haste.

This had been a large expense, yet she had not weighed it. It was her debts and not her savings that had in such haste amounted to pounds. Woe to the pride that had seduced her:

What the weak head with strongest bias rules

Is pride, the never-failing Vice of Fools.

She did not need her book's reminder of her head's weakness—only too dismally she recognized that strange slipperiness of memory which made it more difficult to execute her commissions in proportion as their number dwindled. Was not the little notebook, to which she must now have recourse, the abiding symbol of this paradoxical humiliation?

She was not psychologist enough to understand that it was the very perfection of her memory which was now tripping her up. So many of her clients had for so long demanded the same things so seasonably that she was automatically compelled to carry out commissions that had now lapsed. She was like an actress who knows her part even backwards, but is broken up and confused when cuts are made; finding the too familiar words not to be ousted. Jinny would mechanically purchase items for clients who had forsaken her, and then—so scatterbrained was she become—leave them at other customers' houses! And on the other hand, she was capable of forgetting the orders of the few faithful. It was thus that under the combined strain of Miss Gentry's bill, the sultry August weather, the sight of the packed coach and its jaunty driver, the frantic return of Nip with his mocking message, Jinny, whom necessity had compelled to keep Farmer Gale as a customer, clean forgot his urgent need of a wedding-cake. It was not that she had forgotten to order it or even to fetch it from the leading confectioner's. The sudden union of Farmer Gale with the wealthy land-surveyor's widow, whose piano-playing had excited the far-off admiration of Elijah Skindle, was too sensational an event, especially to herself, to permit of complete oblivion. It was only that she forgot to deliver the cake at Beacon Chimneys. She was actually within sight of the stag-headed poplars that marked the horizon of home, when, turning her head as Nip suddenly leapt for a rabbit, she saw the great elegant carton in the cart. And the wedding was on the morrow. Conscience-stricken, and morbidly feeling as though the marriage would scarcely be legal without this colossal confection, she resolved, worn out as she was with the heat, to drive back to the house. But she had reckoned without Methusalem. To turn back within the very smell of his stable was unprecedented: it violated every equine code. Like Nip, he now became aware of the instability of things—of a new order. But, more obstinate, he refused to recognize it. Nothing short of the whip—which would have moved him, not out of pain but out of astonishment—could have sufficed to turn him, and how could a mistress who knew him in the right and herself in the wrong, resort to that, especially after such a sultry day? So after every effort to coax him or to lead him by the bridle had failed and almost twenty minutes had been wasted, she decided—in view of her grandfather's supper—to make a special journey the first thing in the morning.

As she gave Methusalem his glad head, she remembered that it was just before the turning to the hymeneal homestead that she had met that scandalously successful coach.

III

Before Jinny reached home that evening, a complainant had already called at Blackwater Hall to unload his grievance. Such visitors were, alas, no longer a novelty to Daniel Quarles, who had one day begun to find himself no merely nominal representative of the business, but a principal charged with derelictions. His virulent rebuttals of the reproaches did but increase the defections. The flouted customers made no allowances for the ferocities of senility, and, when told to go to hell, simply went to the Flynt Flyer—a much pleasanter alternative. Indeed, one suspects they welcomed the insult as justifying gravitation to the new star. The indelicacy, however, of divulging its existence to the nonagenarian was reserved for Mr. Elijah Skindle.

That rising practitioner's patronage was not the least of Jinny's humiliations. Even after his proposal of marriage, she had not been able to refuse to carry dogs to and from his establishment when so commanded by her clients, though she had drawn the line at orders originating from himself. Now, however, in justice to her grandfather, she could not but accept his commissions, even though she was aware they were largely artificial, mere canals for communication and courtship. Why, for example, could not Mr. Skindle, whose gig was often at gardens buzzing with beehives, not purchase his own honey? Why must she procure him an article linkable with "moons" and permitting fatuous references to "sweetness"? His protestations of lack of time were too brazen even for his own mouth: he stuttered and blushed like a schoolboy. It will be seen that Elijah's deeper self had not accepted his "lucky" escape from her. Hope springs eternal, especially when the desirable one's pride is bent, if not broken, by adversity. That proud stomach which had rejected his proffered luxuries with disdain now bade fair to be empty. While he, moreover, touched nothing he did not profit by, and through a lucky rise in animal sickness was fast overtaking the respectable Jorrow.

With an audacity almost Napoleonic he had conceived the idea of at once blazoning and curing his baldness, purchasing a hair-restorer through Jinny herself, so that she might be an accessory to the improvement at which he was—obviously for her sake—slaving. And there did actually begin to sprout on his cranium microscopic dots, like pepper sprinkled over an egg-shell. Elijah lost no opportunity now of lifting his cap at the sight of her, though he had not yet acquired the habit of removing it indoors.

"Whoa!" Elijah drew up his trap in the grassy lane before Blackwater Hall and jumped down. The afterglow of sunset was in the sky, but the Common was still torpid with the breezeless heat of the day. He was in his best flannel suit and smartest cap, though the same old pipe stuck in his blackened teeth. Removing it, he rapped at the door with it, knocking out the ashes with the same taps. As nothing happened, he tugged from his pocket a paper-wrapped pot and thudded at the door with that. He had been simulating rage, for he had come to denounce a mistake, though enchanted to have the opportunity of calling on Jinny. But now for fear she was not yet back—and vexed with himself for not choosing one of her domestic days—he began to get really ruffled. He lifted the latch unceremoniously, but the door seemed bolted. Re-pocketing the pot with an unsmothered oath, he moved towards the living-room wall and peeped through the wide-flung little casement. Pah! Only the Gaffer snoring in his favourite posture, head on the family Bible. The shabbiness of the ancient earth-coloured smock-frock, like the meanness of the furniture, added to Elijah's disgust.

"Fancy her slaving in this heat," he mused, "when she might be snoozing on my horsehair sofa!" He shouted angrily, "Wake up, you old codger."

The nonagenarian obeyed with a start. "What's amiss, my little mavis?" he yawned.

"I ain't a mavis," Elijah informed him irately, "I'm a veterinary surgeon."

Daniel Quarles sprang to his feet. "Marciful powers! Anything wrong with Methusalem?"

"No, no—" Elijah assured him through the little window, "I've come about Jinny."

The old man tottered and caught at his chair. "An accident to Jinny?"

"Stuff and nonsense! She'll be home any minute. Can I come in and wait for her?"

Daniel growled and grumbled. "Don't you see Oi'm busy readin' the Scriptures?"

"I won't interfere with that." He moved back to the door and rattled the latch masterfully. He suddenly saw the possibility of pushing his suit with the grandfather. "Why do you lock yourself in?" he demanded, as the bolts creaked back.

"Don't you see they've took the Dutch clock?" said the Gaffer pitifully. "She desarts me all day long, and Oi can't have my eyes everywheres."

Elijah glanced up at the clock in the ante-room, ticking as imperturbably as ever.

"Why, it's up there!" he said, puzzled.

"Do ye don't try to befool me. That's the same face, but they've took out the works and put in rubbidge. But it ain't works we're justified by," he added musingly.

Elijah, picking his way among the old cypress chests, followed him into the living-room, sat down unasked on the settle, and mechanically pulled out his pipe.

"Git out o' my house!" roared Daniel.

Elijah's pipe fell on the rush mat.

"Boldero hisself," explained the ancient, "never durst smoke in my nostrils. And who be you?"

Who was Boldero, Elijah thought a more sensible question. But he picked up his pipe with an apology. "All right, uncle, no harm done." He wiped his forehead. "Warm, ain't it?"

"Then why do ye want hell-smoke?"

"I shouldn't quite call this hell-smoke," Elijah deprecated.

"There's no smoke without hell-fire," Daniel explained. "Farmer Thoroughgood, he smoked just such a pipe as yourn."

"And he was thorough good, you see," said Elijah with an air of victorious repartee.

"Thorough bad," chuckled the Gaffer with a still greater air of wit. "Starved his missus to death. The neighbours as come, to see the corpse found her on a bed made out of a common sheep-hurdle, stood on bricks." He tapped the Bible with a dirty thumb. "Do ye don't yoke a hoss and ass together, says the Book. But that evil-doer used to plough a field with a cow and a donkey, and when it ploughed too hard, he'd harness an old sow in front of the donkey—there's currant-trees there now what pays better, not needin' no ploughin'."

"Quite like the old song," observed Elijah, still feeling superior and witty. "There was a cow went out to plough."

"Chrissimus Day, Chrissimus Day," hummed the old man. Set agoing, he quavered on:

"There was a pig went out to dig
On Chrissimus Day in the marning!

"Set ye down," he broke off genially, though Elijah was already ensconced, leg over knee. "Jinny'll be home in a jiffy."

"I wonder she's so long," Elijah began tentatively, "when she's got so little to do."

"Ay," assented the ancient, souring again. "'Tis me that's got the whole work o' the place. But gals likes to gad about in the summer, what becomes o' the old folks never troubles the young 'uns nowadays."

"They might just as well be married," ventured Elijah boldly.

"Ay, their husbands 'ud make 'em work," said the Gaffer, his eye gleaming maliciously. "But Oi don't howd with starvin' 'em, like Farmer Thoroughgood did his missus. When they come to see her corpse they found her on a bed made out of a common sheep-hurdle. Ay, and he used to plough his fields with a—"

Elijah, groaning inwardly, composed himself to hear the story again. Fortunately there was a fresh development at the finish. "One day 'twas a team o' bullocks and a blind hoss he started droivin'. Powerful warrum it war—wuss than to-day—and the flies sow worritin' that the bullocks set their tails up and bolted. The poor blind hoss couldn't see where to goo and fell down. The oxen couldn't drag him, and got tangled up in the traces." He roared with laughter at the picture, and Elijah grinned too.

"Those flies do worrit," he agreed, flicking at his forehead. "But about that Jinny of yours—" he added.

"She'll onny have them harmless fly-papers, you see," said Daniel, pointing to a coloured patch on the ceiling, blackened by a happy multitude. "Ef ye can't wait for her," he added amiably, "Oi'll give her your message. A wet you said?"

"A veterinary surgeon, Mr. Elijah Skindle," said Elijah grandly.

"Skindle!" The old man groped agitatedly in his memory. "That's a name Oi know."

"Known all over the Hundred," said Elijah complacently. "Ay, and they're hearing of my success at Colchester, too, where I come from."

"Cowchester!" The old man sprang up. "That's it—the man as married Annie! But that ain't you—he had more hair to him."

"Perhaps it was my father," said Elijah, flushing.

"Nay, nay. Annie couldn't have a son your soize," the Gaffer pondered.

"My mother's name is Annie," said Elijah.

A strange fire crept into the old patriarch's eyes. "A big-boned mawther of a girl, tall as the rod her father lit the lamps with, long raven hair and eyes as black as sloes, and a wunnerful fine buzzom," he said with slow voluptuousness. "Your mother ain't like that?"

"No," admitted Elijah.

Daniel Quarles heaved a sigh. "Oi thought not, or you'd be more of a beauty."

"Well, you're wrong," retorted Elijah. "For I've heard that my grandfather did use to light the lamps in Chipstone, and it's a great shame the way my brothers and sisters all dump her on me to keep."

The old man seized him suddenly by the coat-lapels. "She's back in Chipstone?"

"Been back over two years—ever since father died."

"He's dead?" Elijah felt the hands trembling against his breast.

"Of course—and I've got her to keep, though I'm the youngest," he grumbled.

"That's the same luck as Oi had," said the Gaffer, "with this bit of property, though Sidrach, he's the first-born." He dropped pensively back into his chair. "But Oi count Annie's better off where she is, bein' as Oi've got Jinny to keep and food gittin' dearer every day, she says, something cruel. And happen Sidrach'll come back too when he's old, not havin' landed property like me, ne yet no relations in Babylon. Never been sech a year since he went away—the Brad was all froze over."

Elijah imprudently recollected—to the old man's annoyance—that it had frozen equally in Queen Victoria's first winter, and he brought up "Murphy's coldest day," the proverbial lucky hit of an almanack-maker. Fortunately the Gaffer recalled an ancient jest of Bundock's: "Mother Gander's gin-bottle's froze over," and relaxed in genial hysterics. "Ay, she's conwerted now," he said, wiping his rheumy eyes. "But what an adulteress in them days! Ye couldn't get drunk at 'The Black Sheep' ef ye tried—beer without hops and wine without gripes."

Mechanically drawing out his pipe and popping it back in alarm, Elijah reverted to Jinny. Daniel now blamed Methusalem for her lateness. Horses, too, were lazy and ungrateful, same as granddaughters.

"Why don't you get rid of him?" said Elijah, with a sudden inspiration. That would cut her comb, he thought. Jinny docked of Methusalem would be ripe for the marriage-altar. "He's long past his work."

But Daniel Quarles shook his head. "Jinny wouldn't like me to part with that. Besides, who'd buy him?"

"I would," said Elijah, with a feeling of "All for love, or the world well lost."

"You? Od rabbet, what for?"

"I'd give you a fiver!" parried the knacker in his reckless passion. "Though most people let me have 'em for the trouble of killing 'em," he added incautiously.

The old man sprang up again. "Git out o' my house! And don't ye dare cross my doorstep agen!"

Elijah cowered back in his seat. "But I've come on business," he protested.

"Oi bain't a-gooin' to sell Methusalem."

"That's not what I came for," Elijah urged soothingly. "It's about Jinny."

"Oi bain't a-gooin' to sell Jinny neither."

Elijah winced. Was it divination or drivel, he wondered.

"You might as well sell her," he said boldly. "Look how she's mucking up your business, muddling everything." And rising and pulling out the pot again, he banged it down on the table.

"My Jinny muddle things! Git out o' my house!"

Before the Gaffer's blazing spectacles and furious fangs Elijah backed doorwards.

"Not before it's set right," he said, assured of his line of retreat.

"The Quarleses don't make muddles. For a hundred year—"

"Oh, Jinny's been all right the last hundred years," he interrupted impatiently. "It's the last few weeks I complain about! I hope it's not sunstroke."

"My Jinny!" The Gaffer's anger died. "She went away singin' as merry as could be, my little mavis," he said anxiously.

"Then what do you make of that?" Elijah indicated the pot.

The old man unwrapped it slowly, and readjusting his spectacles spelt out the label. "Oliver's Depil— Depil—" he stumbled on. "Is that pills?"

"No, it's for the hair."

"Well, that's what you want, ain't it?" he said naïvely.

Mr. Skindle coloured up. "But this is to take off the hair," he explained.

"Well, you can't do that," chuckled Daniel, "bein' more a 'Lisha than a 'Lijah."

"Oh yes, I can," said Elijah, his every dot bristling. "But if I hadn't been a noticing man, I should have undone all the good of months of my pots of hair-restorer."

"Whichever way it be, 'tis agen Nature," said the Gaffer. "The Lord giveth and the Lord taketh away. But pots be as like as peas. That's the shopman's fault, not Jinny's."

"Oh, indeed!" cried Elijah savagely. "And what about her bringing me hairpins?"

"Hairpins!" gasped the Gaffer. "Hairpins for a man without hair!"

"Even Samson in his prime didn't want hairpins!" Elijah pointed out angrily. "But that's what she brought me a packet of last week, instead of tobacco."

"Sarve ye right, ye unswept chimbley," the Gaffer growled, with a grin.

"That ain't serving me right," riposted Elijah. "That's serving me wrong," he added with redoubled wit. "And wouldn't take 'em back neither, the little minx, maintained I'd ordered 'em for my ma."

"Well, she'd want hairpins, wouldn't she, with all that beautiful raven hair," said the Gaffer, turning serious. "Happen you ordered 'em for her."

"I never order anything for her," said Elijah, waiving the description of her chevelure.

"More shame to you, then, young man. Ye don't desarve to have her. Same as ye're too stingy to pay for the hairpins, ye'd best give 'em to her with Daniel Quarles's love."

"I'm not stingy!" retorted Elijah hotly. "Would I be keeping my mother, with the poorhouse so handy, and me the youngest, too, if Elijah Skindle wasn't the most generous man in Chipstone? But I won't pay for Jinny's woolgathering. No wonder everybody's going to the coach!"

"The coach?" repeated Daniel Quarles. "What coach?"

"Hasn't Jinny told you?" cried Elijah, equally astonished. "The handsomest pair of black horses—"

"A funeral coach?" half-whispered the Gaffer, paling. The notion of slaughtering Methusalem had already brought the thought of death unpleasantly near.

"You and Jinny may well call it so, old sluggaby," said Elijah grimly.

The old man fell back into his chair. "Nobody never needed no funeral coaches here!" he quavered. "Our shoulders on the corpse-path was good enough for us. 'Twas onny that obstinacious little Dap, when poor Pegs laid by the wall, as wanted one."

"Who's talking of funeral coaches?" snapped Mr. Skindle. "Anyhow I've got to have that pot changed."

"Git out o' my house!" repeated the ancient for the fourth time, hurling the pot out of the window. Luckily it fell on grass.

Elijah's patience was at an end. Besides it had now occurred to him he might cut off Jinny on the route, away from this tiresome nonagenarian. The effort to woo her through him had been baffled by his inconsequence.

"Who's hankering after your wooden chairs? I've got horsehair at home," he retorted crushingly.

As he climbed into his trap he heard the bolts shot behind him. But just as he was clucking off his horse, the Gaffer's head popped frenziedly through the casement.

"Stop thief!" it cried. "Stop!"

"You be careful what you're saying, old cockalorum," said Elijah angrily, lashing his horse with vicarious wrath. "And pick up that pot. I shan't pay for it."

"You've stole my spectacles! Oi can't find 'em nowheres!"

"Why, you've got 'em on!" Elijah called back contemptuously.

So eagerly did his horse respond to the whip and the homeward impulse that Elijah had the satisfaction of passing the equally enthusiastic Methusalem before he could pull up. He was not even sure that this arrogantly gowned Jinny had acknowledged his salute. She would be at her door before he could turn—confound it! Why had he not waited another moment or started earlier and cut her off at a remoter point? To face that old dodderer again would be an anti-climax.

IV

So swiftly did Daniel Quarles nod again over his big Bible that by the time Jinny had got Methusalem stabled, she could not rouse him to undo the bolts, and all her merry whistling as she neared the latch was a wasted pretence. This protective habit of his indoors was a recent development, coinciding curiously with the advent of the coach she was concealing from him, and these closed doors—even his bedroom was now locked from within—annoyed and alarmed her. She had visions of him agonizing in his bed and herself reduced to breaking open the door. Perhaps even now he was ill, dying, dead! She dashed to the living-room window—stumbling over a pot outside it. Ah, thank God, that dear, peaceful grey head, that sonorous snore!

Pausing now to pick up the mysterious pot, she was distressed again. The passing of Elijah was explained! Miss Gentry's Depilatory she had brought to Mr. Skindle, Mr. Skindle's Hair Restorer to Miss Gentry. He had come to complain, but unable to get admission, he had flung the pot on the path. Oh, plaguy similarity of potted pomades—fatal double error—she had killed two clients with one stone. Her eyes filled with tears: even with a notebook she could not keep straight.

So guilty did she look as she scrambled noiselessly through the casement, that an observer would have thought her a burglar. Creeping past her grandfather, she opened the house-door,—the gigantic key that used to hang on the beam was now always in the lock—brought in the carton with the wedding-cake from the cart, and placed it on the chest of drawers for unfailing reminder in the morning. Then swiftly changing into her old frock and hanging up the new behind a corner-curtain, she donned her apron and stole into the kitchen. Finally, to lay the table, she must with loving hands uplift the venerable head.

The ancient had not slept off his perturbation, though he did not remember the cause of it, and seeing his supper still unlaid, he was righteously wroth. "A muddler, mucking up everything—that's what you be!" he said, repeating unconsciously Elijah's indictment. And Jinny, remembering the pot that now stood by the wedding-cake, went about wanly, unresentfully, with movements lacking their wonted deftness. Her grandfather had already forgotten the suggestion of sunstroke, much as it had shaken him: for her actual pallor he had no eye.

When she finally brought in the meal, she found him risen and standing tranced before the great wedding-cake, gazing dazedly at its elaborately frosted architecture.

"You didn't want to open it," she cried with irrepressible petulance as she hooked down the pasteboard lid.

He ignored the reproach. "Weddin's and funerals in one day," he brooded. "Pomps and wanities."

"Come to the table, Gran'fer," she said more gently.

"Pomps and wanities!" he repeated. "Who's this for?"

"It's for Farmer Gale's wedding—'twas too late to deliver it. Come along."

"In my day folks made their own weddin'-cakes. And dedn't want no funeral coaches neither. The church-path or the farm-wagon—"

"Come along!" She took his arm. "There's no funeral coaches here."

A whining and scratching at the door made a welcome diversion. Nip, back from the hunting-path, sneaked in, aware of sin, with ears flat, tail abased, and sidelong squint.

"Ain't seen that for days," said the Gaffer. "Where's that been?"

"I don't know," she lied, glad of Nip's guilty air, for to explain would reveal the coach. "On the razzle-dazzle, I suppose."

After supper, she remembered a box must be put in the ante-room that had been left with her to be called for. It was stupid not to have brought it in at once, ere the cart had been put in its shed—as stupid as her pot-swapping. In a sudden fear that if unremoved to-night she would carry it off to Farmer Gale's wedding just when the owner would be coming for it, she asked her grandfather to lend a hand with it. It was an unfortunate request, for as the still sinewy veteran was dragging his end over the sill, he said weirdly: "There ain't no man in Bradmarsh more lugsome'n that. Who wants your new-fangled coach?"

"What coach?" murmured Jinny, half puzzled, half apprehensive.

"The funeral coach." He stood still. "Where else 'ould a coffin goo?"

"Rubbish, Gran'fer. There's no funeral coach." Her little silvery voice rang out. "Heave away, my Johnny. Come along, Gran'fer, I've got to rub down Methusalem—you'll be too tired now."

"No funeral coach?" he repeated slowly, loosing the box.

"You've been dreaming, Gran'fer."

"But the two black horses—"

Her heart beat like a criminal's on the eve of detection. "Nightmares!" she laughed. "What did I say?"

"But he said—!"

"Who said?"

"Annie's buoy-oy."

"Annie's—?"

"'Lijah, he calls hisself."

"Elijah? And did he go up in a chariot of fire with the horses?" And more than ever incensed against Mr. Skindle, she hastily started her carrier's chanty:

"There is Hey, there is Ree."

Automatically his sepulchral bass exuded, and his arms reclasped the box:

"There is Hoo, there is Gee—"

Then together their antithetical voices rolled out joyously as the box moved forward:

"But the bob-tailed mare bears the bells away."

Inwardly she was thinking that a "funeral coach" was just what it was. Did its bells not ring the knell of all the peaceful past? Yes, it was the hearse of her past, of her youth. And somehow—somehow—she must readjust herself to the strange raw cruelty of the present.

V

She resettled him before his Bible. But when she returned from the stable, he had wandered again to the chest of drawers, and was now holding up the pot.

"And ye told me Oi was dreamin'!" he said angrily. "Why did ye lie to me?"

"What do you mean, Gran'fer?" she said, flushing.

"How did that pot come here?"

"I brought it, of course."

"No, you dedn't. Annie's good-for-nawthen son brought it."

"But I brought it in," she persisted. "It was lying on the path."

"Ah! Oi mind me now—he threw it at me."

"The wretch!" said Jinny, believing him. "Poor Gran'fer!" she cried with self-reproach, patting his hairy hand. "But it's bedtime. Come along!"

"Why did ye lie to me?" he repeated, unappeased.

"There's no funeral coach," she persisted. But even as she spoke, the faint tooting of a horn was heard from afar. Nip, idly gulping at flies, pricked up his ears; the ancient uttered a cry:

"The coach! The coach!"

Jinny's hand clutched his more tightly. They could now hear the distant rattling and jingling—the Flynt Flyer was incredibly coming their way, along that grass-grown road. What was it doing by that lonely Common, she wondered tremulously. What customers were there to steal here? Did the pirate hanker even after Uncle Lilliwhyte?

"You'll lose your beauty sleep, Gran'fer!" She drew him towards the corkscrew staircase. But he broke from her convulsively and hobbled out into the path, and stood with hand at ear towards the advancing clatter. To be seen staring at its meteoric passing would be too dreadful.

"Go in, Nip," she cried with unwonted harshness. "Are you coming, Gran'fer?" she said, following the dog, "or shall I bolt you out? Must bolt up against thieves, you know." And she began singing cheerily:

"There is Hey, there is Ree"

"Nay, 'tis the black hosses that bears the bells away, curse 'em. What should coaches be doing in these parts?"

"Same as me, I suppose," she said with desperate lightness. "It's only that young man who fancies himself a-driving and a-blowing."

"A young man come to steal my business!"

"Well, one can't lock that up! Come in, Gran'fer."

"Oi'll lock him up! What's the thief's name?"

"He's not a thief. It's the young man from Frog Farm."

"That whippersnapper! Come with a coach to drive over you and me—!"

"That's just what he'd try to do if we stand here! Come inside—the jackanips'll only think we're envying his bonkka turn-out."

The argument and the touch of idiom succeeded, though she could feel his form shaking with passion as she drew him in. "Why did ye keep it from me?" he asked pitifully.

"Because I knew you'd get in a state." As she shot the bolts, the better to shut Will out, she realized that her beating heart was somehow left outside, and that it was drawing her after it through doors howsoever barred and windows howsoever fastened, if only to watch the pageant of his passing.

"A funeral coach," the ancient was mumbling, "you and Jinny may well call it so, ole sluggaby."

"Yes, indeed, we may, Gran'fer," she said, smiling. "For it's his own funeral he's conducting. He'll soon come a cropper."

"Blast him!" growled the Gaffer.

"Hush!" Jinny was shocked. "It's all as fair as fair."

"For over a hundred year we've fetched and carried 'twixt Bradmarsh and Chipstone, and now this scallywag with his new-fangled black hosses—" A fit of coughing broke off the speech, and he suddenly looked so much like the last stage of man in the Spelling-Book that Jinny had to put him back into his chair.

"Didn't I say you'd get into a state? But you know there's more carrying than I—than we can manage. Haven't you sent lots of our customers away?"

"Curse 'em!" said the Gaffer comprehensively. "Warmin! And Oi told 'em sow to their head!"

"He's only got our leavings, you see." And she burst out in gay parody:

"There is black, both of black,
Let 'em run till they crack,
'Tis Methusalem bears the bells away."

But the bells were now jingling nearer and nearer—jingling in victorious arrogance. The old man started up again in his chair. "How dare Caleb Flynt's lad set hisself up agen me?"

"Don't, Gran'fer." She pressed him down. "Competition, folks call it. He's got to earn his living just like us."

"Nobody shan't come competitioning here." He broke from her again. "Daniel shall be an adder what biteth the hoss heels." He began unbolting the door.

"You'll never be able to bite his horse heels," she urged. "They fly by like the wind."

She had a sick fear the old man would hurl himself at the bridles, be dragged to death. But to her astonishment, ere he had lifted the latch, she heard the horses slowing down. The eight sounding hoofs, the clanging swingle-trees and harness, the great road-grinding equipage, were actually coming to a halt at her porch.

"Whoa, Snowdrop! Easy there, Cherry-blossom!" She knew the humour of these names of theirs, as she knew from a hundred channels of gossip everything about their owner, even to the identity of the blonde young female from Foxearth Farm who was so persistently a passenger.

So he had been forced to humiliate himself, to make the first approach—it was she who had, after all, been the conqueror, who had held out the longer! And in a swift flood of emotion she felt more than ever the injustice of her grandfather's standpoint. Will had not "come competitioning." It had all been unpremeditated. The horses had been left on his hands by that harum-scarum Showman. And anyhow, was he not serving the countryside better than she with her ramshackle little cart? But whatever the rights and the wrongs, a scene between the two men must be prevented.

"He's come to eat humble pie, Gran'fer," she whispered. "But we don't see people after office hours—and it's your bedtime."

"Oi'll show him who's who," said the Gaffer, disregarding her.

"But you can't do that like this!" she urged with the cunning of desperation. "Put on your Sunday smock."

"Ay, ay! Oi'll larn him to come crakin' and vauntin'." His face lit up with baleful satisfaction, as he thought of the rare stitching in the gathers and patterns of that frock of fine linen.

As Jinny, relieved, was sheep-dogging him up to his room, they heard the butt-end of a whip beating at the house-door.

"Daniel Quarles takes his time, young man," the Gaffer observed to the cobwebbed corkscrew staircase. And to Jinny, when she shut his door on him, he called back: "Do ye don't forgit to put out the beer. And two glasses."

VI

That imperious butt-end gave no time to change back to her own ostentatious costume. But she did not pause even to tear off her flecked apron. After all, in face of his surrender, she could forgo arrogance of appearance. Besides, he would scarcely have time to notice anything, so swiftly must she be rid of him—however she might savour his surrender—before her grandfather could re-descend upon him. True, the call for beer showed a relaxed tension, but who could predict the effect of quaffing it upon two hot-tempered males? Ignoring the injunction, she hurried to the house-door.

"Good evening, Miss Boldero."

She was a shade disconcerted by the formality. But a great waft of the old friendship seemed to emanate from his frank eyes and the red hair his hat-lifting uncovered. She felt herself drawn to that flame like a poor little moth: she wanted to fall upon his magnanimous morning-jacket, to sob away her sin of pride.

"Good evening, Mr. Flynt," she murmured.

He was astonished at the sight of her, and taken aback. Mentally he had shaken her off, had ridden over her by force of will, finding occupation and exhilaration in his new and prosperous adventure; finding consolation, too, in the creamy beauty of the girl who shuttled with such suspicious frequency in the Flynt Flyer. Blanche suggested not only cream but butter, so pliant and pattable did she seem, so ready to take the impress of Will's personality. That was very restful after the intense irritativeness of the rival carrier.

For irritativeness still remained to him Jinny's essence—even in their alienation. Her horn-blowing still jarred, her pink muslin dress was a new provocation. He was vexed at her jog-trot apathy when their vehicles passed, an apathy that took the sting out of his speed. He was piqued that she did not complain to any one of his competition, that she took no steps of reprisal, made no objection even to Nip's visits to him. But the central irritation in all these fleeting glimpses and encounters had been her prettiness.

Now, seeing her close for the first time since their quarrel at the cattle-market, and without her being whisked away, he had a shock. Why, she was not pretty at all: she was shabby and wan! Where was the sparkle that had haunted the depths of him? The real Jinny was, it suddenly became patent, a worn creature with shadows under her eyes and little lines on her forehead. How could he ever have imagined her attractive? Why, Blanche was like a sultana beside her.

But if the thrill he had expected to feel was replaced by this dull disappointment, another emotion did not fail to supervene. It was pity—pity not unmixed with compunction. Had it been so manly as he had thought, to come interfering with her business, violating the immemorial local tradition which assigned the carrying to a Quarles?

"Won't you come in?" she was forced to say, seeing him silent and petrified in the porch.

"Thank you—I've only brought this from Miss Gentry," he answered in awkward negation. He had come to jeer, but now he held the pot of Hair Restorer apologetically.

Jinny went from white to red. It was the supreme humiliation. Not only had he not come to make it up: he had come at the culminating moment of his triumph—sent as a carrier to her! And sent not merely with a parcel, but with the proof of her blundering!

"How kind of her!" she said, taking it, but neither her hand nor her voice was steady. "Did she send any message with it?"

"Not particularly." He had meant to rub in Miss Gentry's denunciations of female stupidity, to demand the other pot, but his heart failed.

"Well, thank her for her present," said poor Jinny, struggling hard for composure. "And tell her I'll be giving her something in return on my next round."

He suppressed a smile; shamed from it by the pathos of her courage.

"I guess she means it for your grandfather," he said chivalrously.

"Perhaps she does," Jinny murmured. She turned away to close the door on herself. The beautiful black horses pawed the ground impatiently. Will shuffled and squirmed less gracefully—there seemed nothing to do but to go. Had he not refused to step inside? But he had taken her at the end of his long round, he had deposited all his passengers and packages, and he felt loth to leave her thus. A resolution was forming within him—generating so rapidly in the warmth of compunction and renewed comradeship, that possibly the germs of it had already taken root in his subconsciousness when Nip's label brought him her sneer at his lack of a guard.

"It's very hot," he fenced, lingering. "Can I have a glass of water?"

She started, remembering the Gaffer's admonition.

"Oh, won't you have a glass of beer?"

"No, thanks, just Adam's ale."

Almost liquefied herself by feeling this son of Adam needed her,—even thus slightly—she moved swiftly to and fro, returning with the glass. But not so swiftly that she had not smuggled Oliver's Depilatory and the wedding-cake into the kitchen in case he should yet come in. He took the glass, managing to touch her cold trembling fingers.

"Much obliged," he said, after a deep draught, and this time it was her fingers that were drawn, though less consciously, to touch his round the returned glass. Then, swallowing something harder than water, "I've been thinking about it all, Jinny, and I'm sorry—" he blurted.

"Ha!" Her heart leapt up again.

"Sorry for you," he explained.

"For me?" Her face hardened.

"I—I—mean," he corrected, stammeringly, "sorry to hurt your business."

"You haven't hurt my business! There's room for both! It's a fair competition."

"It's very forgiving of you to say so. But I said I'd start a coach-service and I had to make my word good, hadn't I? A man can't say a thing and leave it empty air."

"No." In her new humility she was prepared to admire such solid manhood.

"But that's no reason why we should be bad friends, is it?"

She had thought that it was; now, that attitude of hers seemed childishly foolish. Self-abasement kept her dumb.

"No reason," he repeated, mistaking her silence for obstinacy, "why we shouldn't shake hands."

"Only this glass," she flashed more happily. But it shook in her hand.

"Ah!" He sighed with satisfaction. The way to his proposition lay open. He could broach it at once.

"Much better to pull together, eh?"

"Much," she echoed. How sweet to see the mists of folly and bitterness rolling away, to feel the weight lifting from her heart. Impulsively she held out her left hand, and as he clasped it, the warmth that came to him from its cold firmness somewhat shook his sense of Blanche's surpassing charm. Charm, in fact, seemed—to his bewilderment—to be independent of beauty. Or was it that what radiated from Jinny's little hand was a sense of capable comradeship, missing from that large limp palm which received but did not give? Well, but comradeship was what he wanted, what he was now going to propose. And if charm was thrown in, so much the better for the partnership.

"Aha, Son of Belial! So ye've come to bog and vaunt your horn here!"

It was her forgotten grandfather. Startled from her daydream, she dropped the glass and it shivered to fragments. In the dusk Daniel Quarles, wizened though he was, loomed prophetic over them in snowy beard and smock, his forehead gloomed with thunder and his ancient beaver.

VII

Will drew out his white handkerchief, and tying it on his whip waved it humorously.

The old man was disconcerted in his Biblical vein. "This be a rummy 'un, Jinny. Is he off his head?"

"No, Gran'fer—that's a flag of truce. A signal he's got something friendly to say."

The Gaffer turned on her. "Then why don't ye arx him inside like a Christian, 'stead o' breakin' my glasses?"

"Thank you, Mr. Quarles," said Will swiftly. He lowered the flag, and almost rushed across the threshold. Jinny retreated before him, and the trio passed silently through the ticking ante-chamber.

"Why don't ye loight the lamp?" the Gaffer grumbled. Jinny gratefully flew to hide her perturbation in the kitchen. True, she would only be throwing more light upon it. But the breathing-space was welcome.

"Hadn't you better have a look at my coach before it gets darker?" Will was reminded to say.

"Curse your coach!" He had reawakened the prophet.

"Easy, there!" said Will, untying his handkerchief. "It's to be a family coach now, you see."

"Family coach!" repeated Daniel, puzzled.

Jinny, fumbling at the lamp with butter-fingers, was glad it had not yet illumined her blushes. For, mingled with the rapturous tumult at her heart was a shrinking sense of impending publicity, of ethereal emotions too swiftly and masterfully translated into gross commitments. How had her mere passive acquiescence in a better relationship warranted Will's larger assumptions?

"Well, that's what it'll be if you accept my proposition, won't it?" she heard Will say.

"Set ye down, set ye down!" said Daniel. "What's your proposition? Jinny, why're you lazying with that lamp?"

"In a moment, Gran'fer."

She brought it in, its fat globe shedding a rosy glow over the dingy wall-paper, the squat chairs, and the china shepherdesses. But for herself she had no need of it. Everything seemed to her transfigured, steeped in a heavenly light.

"Where's that beer?" the ancient roared, its absence illumined.

She was glad to escape into the kitchen with her jug. Will moved towards the front door.

"You come and see the coach, Mr. Quarles," he persisted, "before it's too dark."

"Dang your coach!" But the imprecation was mild and the ancient shuffled to the door and surveyed the imposing equipage complete from box to boot, with its glossy sable steeds. Will, swelling with renewed pride, and mentally comparing it with the canvas-rotted, lumbering little carrier's cart and the aged animal on its last legs, awaited with complacency the rapturous exclamations of the old connoisseur.

But they did not come. "Ay, quite soizable, not such a bad coach, rayther top-heavy. Where's the leaders?"

"You don't want more than two horses on these roads. Ain't there plenty o' pair-horse coaches? Besides it don't set up for a coach exactly. I'm a carrier mainly!"

The old man winced at the word.

"You've called her the Flynt Flyer," he said, peering at the painted legend.

"And fly she does!" said Will, recovering his complacency. "There's life and spirit for you!" he added, as the horses pawed and tossed their heads.

"More like an adder biting their heels!" said Daniel balefully. "But Oi thought Oi heerd they was black!"

Will was outraged. "The Devil himself couldn't be blacker!"

Daniel shook his head. "Mud-colour Oi should call the offside hoss."

"Well, there's black mud, ain't there?"

"Nearside hoss seems wheezy," Daniel said sympathetically, as it snorted with impatience.

"Wheezy? Cherry-blossom? Why, he could run ten miles more without turning a hair."

"Why, he's sweatin' like one o'clock!"

"So am I." Will wiped his forehead furiously. "But that's only the weather."

"Hosses don't want to sweat when there's nowt to carry."

For a moment Will was knocked breathless. Recovering, he smiled complacently. "Why, it's all delivered. And it was a deliverance. A terrible load. Phew!"

"Nothing to ours! Lord, what a mort o' custom! Look at that whopping box we've just carried in." He pointed to the ante-room. "And all they other boxes!" he added with an inspiration, staring at the lumber of his deceased and scattered family.

"Oh, I know," Will conceded graciously, "that there are folks that stick to Jinny—I mean to you—for old sake's sake."

"Ay, and you're hankerin' arter our hundred years' connexion!"

"Eh?" said Will, dazed. He stole a reassuring glance at his magnificent turn-out.

"Oi could see what ye were droivin' at with your friendly proposition. Want us to take you into pardnership."

Will slapped his knee. "Well, I'm danged."

Daniel chuckled fatuously. "Ho, ho! Guessed it, did Oi? Ye can't keep much from Daniel Quarles." And in high good humour he laid his hand on the young man's shoulder and moved him back into the house.

They found Jinny, who had just deposited the beer-jug on the table, flitting up the stairs.

"Where ye gooin', Jinny?" the Gaffer called after her.

"You've got things to talk over," she called back.

"It ain't secrets," he crowed.

"Don't run away," Will added. "You're the person most concerned."

But his blushing rival had disappeared. It was all too unnerving, especially when the cracked mirror, aided by the fat lamp, showed her what a shabby unkempt figure was setting out the beer-glasses on the tiger-painted tray. As she could not change into her grand gown under the invader's eye, she was furtively carrying it up to her grandfather's bedroom.

VIII

"Set ye down," repeated the Gaffer. "Have a glass o' beer."

"No, thank you, I've had water."

"And the glass too," the old man chuckled. "That ain't much of a chate. Have a shiver o' cake."

Will did not like to refuse the slice till the Gaffer, after looking round with growing grumpiness, brought in the great wedding-cake from the kitchen, naked of its carton.

"Muddlin' things away," he was murmuring, as he posed it pompously on the table, whence its high-built glory of frosted sugar shed a festal air over the room.

"No, thank you!" cried Will hastily, divining a mistake—on the Gaffer's part, if not on Jinny's. He guessed Farmer Gale was concerned with it, for the whole countryside was agog with the meanness of a wedding that did not include a labourers' supper, nay, even a holiday for them. The old man glared, bread-knife in hand.

"It would give me stomach-ache," Will apologized.

The confession arrested the ancient. "Never had gullion in my life," he bragged, laying down the bread-knife. "But you young folks—!"

"It's like this," said Will, taking advantage of this better mood. "There's not enough business to keep both of us going. Suppose I buy you out."

"Buy me out!" The prophet of wrath resurged. His arm shot out for the bread-knife, pointing it door ward. "Git out o' my house. For a hundred year—"

Will got angry. "If I do get out, it will be a hundred years before I come back. However," he said, forcing a smile, "let's put it another way. Jinny shall come and help my business."

"Jinny'll never give up Methusalem."

"Well, Methusalem'll give up Jinny before very long—he can't last for ever. And she can keep him for Sundays—yes, that'll be a good idea. She can drive to chapel with him, not being a business animal." "And then she'd be clear of successors to Farmer Gale," a side-thought added.

"But Oi thought 'twas me you had a proposition for," said the Gaffer testily.

Will hastily readjusted his tactics. "Of course, of course. It's really lumping our businesses, instead of competing, don't you see?"

"Well, dedn't Oi say 'twas a pardnership you was arter?"

"Quite right. Only we'll give poor old Methusalem a retiring pension."

"He, he!" croaked the Gaffer. He added honestly, "But Oi don't droive much meself nowadays. 'Tis onny the connexion ye'd be getting and the adwice and counsel."

"Just what I want," said Will enthusiastically. "And I'm willing to share and share alike."

"Snacks?"

"Snacks!"

"It's not a bad notion," admitted the ancient.

"It's a ripping notion."

"Arter all, as you say, there's no reason we should come into colloosion." He dropped the knife back on the table, and looked out of the still open window.

"Ay, it's a grand coach!" he gurgled.

"The talk of the countryside—only needs a turnpike road to beat the train!" said Will, expanding afresh. "Snowdrop and Cherry-blossom I call these horses for fun—because they're so black, you see."

"Ay, black as the devil! And hark at 'em pawin'—there's fire and sperrit for you. That's as foine a coach as ever Oi took up from. It'll not look amiss with Quarles painted 'stead o' Flynt."

"I beg your pardon," said Will quickly. "Flynt must remain. The Flynt Flyer—you can't alter that."

"Why can't you?"

"You can't say the Quarles Flyer—the Quarles Creeper runs better off the tongue. The Flynt Flyer—that goes together."

"But it's you and me's got to goo together," retorted the obstinate old man. "Anyways it must be the Quarles and Flynt Flyer."

"That's too long. Besides the Flynt Flyer's become a trade-mark—known everywhere."

"And what about Daniel Quarles, Carrier? That's a better known trade-mark. We'll paint that."

Will shook his head. "I can't do that, but I'll paint Flynt and Quarles, Carriers, underneath the name of the coach. And that's the limit."

"Daniel Quarles was always a peaceable man. . . . Quarles and Flynt!" breathed the Gaffer beatifically.

"No, Flynt and Quarles," Will corrected. "Flynt must go first."

"Why must?"

"Don't F come before Q? Folks would think we didn't know our A B C."

"It would be more scholardy," Daniel admitted.

Will proffered a conclusive hand. "Then it's a bargain!" But Daniel let the hand hover.

"Oi don't droive much meself nowadays," he repeated with anxious honesty.

"We don't expect it of the head of the firm," said Will grandly; "there's substitutes and subordinates." But his hand drooped with a sense of bathos.

"Ay," said the old man, swelling, "subordinators and granddarters." He fished for the hand.

"Oughtn't we to let 'em know?" Will insinuated.

"Oi allus liked young Flynt, your father," answered the Gaffer, squeezing his fingers heartily. "And there warn't much amiss with your mother. A forthright family, aldoe Peculiar. Jinny droives a-Sundays to chapel with the buoy-oys!"

At which sudden failure—or rather resurgence—of memory, Will felt more urgently than ever the need of getting Jinny's consent rather than the nonagenarian's.

"You're mighty lucky," he said craftily, "to have a granddaughter so spry. I reckon we'd better have her down and tell her."

"Ay, that Oi be," replied the Gaffer. "'Tis heartenin' to hear her singin' up and down the house."

Indeed a little silvery trill was reaching them now. To Will it recalled more than one moment of mockery, but he felt nothing provocative in this song except its parade of happiness. It seemed to fling back his compassion, to be ominous of a refusal of his proposition. Perhaps, on second thoughts, it might be better to leave the old man to present her with a finished fact.

"Well, I must be getting home," he said. "Glad that's settled."

Daniel clutched the knife again. "And we'll cut the cake upon it."

"No, no." Mistake or no mistake, it seemed sacrilegious to slice into this quasi-ecclesiastical magnificence.

"But it's a bargain. Jinny shall cut it. Jinny!" he called up.

"Just coming, Gran'fer."

"That's too grand for a bargain," Will remonstrated. "Would almost do for a wedding," he added with sly malice.

"Well, ain't this for a pardnership?" the old man cackled. He moved to the door and stood looking out on the horses. "Steady, my beauties," he said proprietorially. He shuffled to them and rubbed a voluptuous hand along the satiny sheen of their skins. "Flynt and Quarles," he murmured.

Will had taken the opportunity to escape from the house. He now prepared to light his lamps. Bats were swooping and darting, weaving their weird patterns, but the air was still uncooled.

"Ye're not a-gooin' afore the cake's cut!" the Gaffer protested.

"I'd best not see Jinny—she might only fly at me."

"Rubbidge. When we've made it up!"

"But I'm late, and I shouldn't wonder if there's a thunderstorm."

"Won't take half a jiffy!" He dashed into the house and seized the knife. Will was only in time to arrest his uplifted arm, and Jinny, descending on the tableau, had a tragi-comic sense of rushing betwixt a murderer and her lover.

"What are you doing, Gran'fer?" she gasped.

He surrendered the bread-knife blinkingly to her, and Will released his arm, struck breathless by the change in Jinny. Not only were apron and shabby gown replaced by the Gentry masterpiece, not only was her hair combed and braided in a style he had never seen, but the face which reduced all these fripperies to insignificance seemed years younger and fresher. The little lines were gone from the forehead, the hard defiance from the eyes, and the wanness from the cheeks: the whole face was mantled with a soft light. How shrewd he had been to suggest this partnership, he thought with a pleasant glow, forgetting its origin in pity. For assuredly this softly radiant person made no call on that emotion. The old man was equally astonished. "Why, Jinny, ye're as smart as a carrot!" he cried naïvely. "Bless ye." He kissed her fondly. "Willie wants to goo into pardnership—Quarles and Flynt."

The young people looked at each other, both as carrots in hue.

"Well, Willie, where's your tongue? Tell her how we've settled it."

"He can tell me on Sunday," said Jinny, not utterly unresentful of their masculine methods.

"On Sunday?" the Gaffer gasped.

"After chapel," Jinny explained.

"Oi won't have no such talk a-Sundays. It's got to be now. Goo ahead, buoy-oy!"

"Oh, Gran'fer," Jinny pleaded. "Can't you go and light Will's lamps?"

"Ye want to upset it all behind my back," he said with a cunning air.

"No, I don't."

"Ye can't diddle Daniel Quarles. It's a fust-rate proposition, and don't ye dare say 'Noa.'"

"But, Gran'fer!" Jinny hung her head. "You might understand."

"Oi understand better nor you. Look at that coach now—a grand coach—Quarles and Flynt."

"Never mind the coach—light the lamps," Jinny cried paradoxically.

Daniel moved out reluctantly. "It's a hansum proposition, Jinny," he said. "Where's your tinder-box, Willie?"

"Here's matches," said Will. He looked uneasy. Her grandfather seemed to be irritating the girl—it boded ill for his proposition.

"Don't be afeared, Willie. She won't fly at ye now. Easy, my beauties. Steady, Snowdrop!"

IX

"You don't mind my clearing up," said Jinny, pouncing upon Farmer Gale's imperilled cake.

"Not if you don't fly at me," Will quoted with a nervous facetiousness.

Jinny smiled with equal nervousness: "Oh, I won't fly at you—nor jump at you, neither."

Will flinched. Had he not felt committed to her grandfather, he would have shrunk from the rebuff now menacing his proposition. Indeed, he was not quite clear as to how he could really amalgamate the two concerns. The notion of a girl guard, which had first flashed upon him as an inspiration, was now felt to be beset by obstacles. True, the operations of blowing such a long horn, taking so many fares, booking so many parcels, and locking and unlocking the boots, were a serious discount from the pleasures of driving, and a person familiar with the minutiæ of carrying, and a ready-reckoner incarnate, (and so agreeably incarnate) might well seem providential. But would the unfitness of so unconventional an occupation be glossed over by the existing acceptance of her in that line of business, and would his overlordship be a protection or an added scandal? Still, he was in for it now, unless she refused the post—which he hoped she would not! For after all, at the worst, with all these new circuits of his, he might still leave to her her little pottering round, counting it as a branch of the new Flynt and Quarles business. He would still have won the monopoly of the local carrying, and without the weight on his conscience of starving her out.

"I know you've got a deal of pride and all that," he began diffidently, "but you'll bear in mind your grandfather's tickled with the notion."

"It's hardly Gran'fer's business," Jinny murmured, blushing.

"Oh, I quite understand that. Of course it's your business really. Didn't I ask you not to run away? I didn't mean to reckon it settled unless you said 'Yes.'"

"I should hope not," said Jinny with a spirit that banished the blush. She carried the cake back to the top of the chest of drawers.

"Of course it's silly our going on separate, don't you think so?"

"I haven't thought." She took up the beer-jug to remove it.

"Well, I have—I've thought a good deal—that's why I figured that with you as my partner—No, not for me, thank you."

For Jinny was mechanically filling a glass. Flushing afresh, she poured the beer back. "But who's to look after Gran'fer?" she said, her eyes averted. "How can I leave him?"

"I've thought of that—naturally when you're so much with me, you can't be much with him. But, you see, there'll be plenty of dollars to share out—money, I mean—and we'd be able to get in a woman to take care of him."

To get in a woman! So he was prepared to let poor old Gran'fer live with them! O exquisite, incredible magnanimity! It solved all difficulties in a flash. "And what about Methusalem?" she asked, expectant of a similarly sublime solution.

"Poor old Methusalem!" he laughed. "Won't he like going to grass? Well, if he's so very keen, suppose he trots around once a week on his own little affairs—hair-restorers and the like."

Even the little dart failed to pierce. She was overwhelmed by this culminating magnanimity. This was indeed surrender. So she was not ignorant of horses, so her work had not been improper. She smiled responsively, but her voice shook. "You mean I can carry on?"

"Under the Flynt flag, of course."

"You wouldn't really mind?"

"All's grist that comes to the mill. Besides, it would leave me free to branch out to Totfield Major, and perhaps even Colchester. Tuesdays, say, if you like."

But she did not like. Her conception of a wife's dignity boggled at the notion of driving around as before. Unmaidenly it was not—he had handsomely admitted it—but unwifely it assuredly was. A wife's place, she felt instinctively, was the home. She shook her head. "I don't think I ought to drive Methusalem any more."

He gasped. "Well, you wouldn't expect to handle a pair of horses, would you?"

If he meant she could not, Jinny was not so sure. But why argue so irrelevant a point? "No, of course not," she murmured obediently. "I mean Methusalem will like going out to grass."

He breathed freely again. The path to his project was clear at last. "But as a sort of guard now—" he ventured, With an indulgent air.

Jinny beamed at so facetious a picture. She saw herself in red, with big buttons and shorn hair. "So I'm to blow your horn for you after all!"

"Sure—once you've paid up the gloves!"

She laughed merrily. Even Miss Gentry's bill was a dissipated nightmare now.

"But where shall I get the money?" she joked, for the pleasure of his reply.

"Oh, you'll take all the money," he instructed her seriously.

"I'll have to allow you some, though," she pointed out gaily.

"Half," he explained. "We divide the takings equally—that's my proposition. Snacks!"

"Oh, that's much too much," she protested as seriously.

The apparent admission pleased him, but increased his sense of magnanimity. "Share and share alike," he repeated magnificently.

"But you don't want to spend half the takings," Jinny persisted. "How could I manage on a half?"

"Why, you'll have much more than you ever had!"

Jinny was mystified. "But there'll be the house to keep up and—and—" She paused with shy flaming cheeks.

Will was getting a bit puzzled too. "And your grandfather? But I've already offered to pay for him and his minder too—out of the joint takings, I mean. Surely half and half is the most you can expect."

But it showed once more how little our Jinny had really been changed from early-Victorian womanhood by her exceptional experiences, that so unconventional a system of joint housekeeping made no appeal to her. "A quarter is the most you can expect," she retorted.

"What!" Will was even more revolted by her ingratitude than by her impudence. "When you only bring in your wretched little cart, and I sank all my capital in the coach!"

"Your capital?" Jinny repeated blankly.

"You know what I had to pay for the horses!"

It was an unfortunate memory to stir up, and it helped a flood of raw light to burst upon her.

"You're not really proposing I should be your guard?" she asked in a changed voice.

"Yes, I am," he reassured her.

"For money?" she breathed incredulously.

"Of course. You don't suppose I ask it for love! Business is—!"

Jinny turned on him like a tigress—anger was the only thing that could drown this dreadful sense of shame. "How dare you?" she cried. "How dare you ask me to work for you for money?"

Will winced before her passion. "You promised not to fly at me," he reminded her glumly.

"I didn't think you'd suggest that."

"And what's wrong in suggesting a partnership?"

"A partnership!" she sneered. "Do you suppose I'm going to pull you out of the mud?"

Will's blood was up in its turn. "You pull me?"

"What else? You find yourself stuck and you come to me to save your funeral coach."

"Funeral coach?"

"That's what Gran'fer calls it. And you will find yourself carrying corpses if you go on cooping up your passengers in this weather. Your silly concern hasn't got a tilt to take off, but at least you might put the luggage inside and the live-stock on top. Oh, don't be frightened, I won't charge for my advice. But you being young and raw—"

"Here! Stow that!" Will banged the floor with his whip. "Then you refuse my offer!"

"Offer? I call it a petition."

"Me petitioning—!" His breath failed.

"It wasn't me that came with a flag of truce."

He snorted. "You'll come one day with a cry for mercy."

"Me! You'll never see me at Frog Farm. I'd rather go to the poorhouse—to see you, I mean."

Will set his teeth. "Very well then—my conscience is clear. I did think I might have been hard on you. But now—!"

"Now," she echoed mockingly.

"I shall crush you."

She laughed tauntingly "Pride goes before a fall."

"I shall crush you without pity."

"You young rapscallion!" It was the Gaffer hobbling back. Having lit the coach-lamps, he had lingered in voluptuous contemplation of what they illumined. But the noise of high words had reached him, and now with the astonishing muscularity that still lingered in his shrunken frame, the ancient seized the whip and wrenched it from Will's grasp. Jinny flew between them, fearing he would strike as he stood there in prophetic fury, palpitating in his every limb. Her earlier intervention, though against a knife, had been comic: here was tragedy, she felt.

"You crush my Jinny! Why, Oi'll snap ye in two like this whip." And he hurled the pieces of the stock at Will's feet.

Nip leapt for the butt-end and brought it back in his mouth with high-wagging tall, demanding another throw. He broke the tension of foolish mortality.

"Don't excite yourself, Gran'fer," said Jinny, leading him to his chair. "I'll cut him out before he's a month older."

Will guffawed. "I offered her a fair chance, Mr. Quarles," he said, taking the butt from Nip's mouth. "You yourself said it was a handsome offer."

"We don't want your offers, ye pirate thief, nor your chances neither. Ye've only got our crumbles. Oi've sent a mort o' customers to hell, and you can goo with 'em."

"As you please." Will picked up the whip-end quietly. But the old volcano was still rumbling.

"You crush my Jinny—you with your flags and rags. Why, all Bradmarsh 'ould give ye rough music. Ye'd be tin-kettled."

"Very well! Only don't say I didn't give you a fair and friendly chance. Don't blame me if you come to want bread."

"Bread!" The old man sprang towards the chest of drawers and this time the cake was stabbed to the heart. "Have a shiver?" he cried magnificently, holding up a regal hunk on the knife-point.

Even Will was taken aback by this deed of derring-do. "Better save it up," he said sullenly.

"Save it?" repeated Daniel hysterically. Nip was already on his hind legs begging for it—with a superb gesture the prodigal grandfather threw it at the tireless mouth. "Never you darken my doorstep again!" he cried to Will.

Will cracked his bit of whip with a scornful laugh. "Before you see me in this house again, you'll have to carry me in!"

"Carry him in? D'ye hear that, Nip?" The ancient chuckled contemptuously. "That's a good 'un."

"Carry me in," repeated Will fiercely. And holding up his hand, "So help me God!" he cried.

"Spare your swearings, buoy-oy," said Daniel grimly, throwing the plaintive Nip another pile of sugary splendour. "Ye 'ont never cross this threshold agen save on your hands and knees." And sending his knife quivering into the floor, he brought down his hand on his Bible. "On your hands and knees," he repeated solemnly.

Will turned and strode out stiffly. He looked almost tall. A moment later they heard the clatter and jingle of the great equipage moving forwards and the jubilant winding of the long horn.

CHAPTER X

HORSE, GROOM, AND BRIDE

Then lay my tott'ring legs so low
That have run very far,
O'er hedges and o'er ditches,
O'er turnpike gate and bar,
Poor old horse! Poor old horse!
Somerset Song.

I

Normally the nonagenarian preserved scant memory of the happenings of the present, vivid though his youthful recollections were: But the great wedding-cake, served up at every meal for days, co-operated with the intensity of the scene to stamp his quarrel with Will upon his feebly registering brain. Especially did Nip's standing supplication for his quota revive and deepen the impression. "On your hands and knees!" he would cry savagely, as he threw the lucky dog a luscious morsel. And even when Nip was absent at meal-times—as his mistress contrived more than once, in her anxiety to pamper neither him nor her grandfather's resentment—the old man would growl grimly: "Carry him in!" Aching enough at heart from her own quarrel with Will, she had the wretched feeling that if by some impossibility she and her rival could ever again come together, the grotesque oaths of these two obstinate males would keep the family breach unhealed.

But sentiment cannot retain its acuteness under business worries and carking household cares. The rich cake eaten through so monotonously became to Jinny a sort of ironic symbol of the declining fortunes of Blackwater Hall. It contributed indeed no little to the decay of the old business, not merely by the great sum that had to be paid to the confectioner, but through the loss of the considerable customer whose hymeneal festivities its absence overgloomed. Marie Antoinette's advice to the starving to eat cake did not come into the Spelling-Book, otherwise Jinny might have reflected how near they were come to adopting it. Not that her grandfather had as yet occasion to suspect the bareness of the larder. Unlike Mother Hubbard he never went to the cupboard, the cupboard always comfortably coming to him. Moreover, some rabbits shot by the farmers as the falling crops uncovered them, and presented to the ancient by annual custom, served to postpone the evil day. Jinny was hardly conscious how much she stinted herself for his sake, so poor was her appetite become. It was only once—-when passing the big Harvest Dinner barn where Farmer Gale's men roared drunken choruses—that she felt a craving for food. This valuable freedom from hunger she attributed to the heat: in the winter, she told herself, she could always stoke for the week at the Tuesday and Friday meals so amiably provided at Mother Gander's. That worthy lady would also doubtless refill grandfather's beer-barrel at cost price. It was fortunate he did not smoke or snuff. Methodism had its points.

A more serious problem was presented by Methusalem—growing distended by overmuch grass—and even her goats coveted an occasional supplement to the hedgerows and the oak scrub if their milk was to run freely. But of hay or cabbages her store was small, and these finicking feeders, though they condescended to eat horse-chestnuts, would not even accept a gnawed apple. The poultry, too, must soon be eaten, if they could not be properly fed, and the thought of instructing her grandfather to twist a familiar neck made her blood run cold. With such a varied household to cater for, our little housekeeper began to envy Maria, who, according to Mrs. Flynt, raised her large and frequent families on everything and anything on earth, rhubarb-leaves being the one and only pabulum pigs turned up their snouts at. It was not the least painful part of this novel pinch of poverty that Jinny felt herself compelled to forgo those calls with little presents for the Pennymoles, the Bidlakes, and the poor and the bed-ridden in general, with which she had diversified her deliveries: she did not realize that her mere presence would have been a creature comfort.

But of these pangs and problems the world knew naught, hearing her little horn making its gay music and seeing her still jauntily perched on her driving-board in her elegant rose-pink frock and with the latest fancy whipcord edge to the straw of her bonnet. Her music, indeed, was far livelier than the wheezy notes of the Flynt Flyer's guard, though otherwise the red-coated clodhopper who had been stuck up on the coach a few days after its visit to Blackwater Hall, lent the last touch to its fascinations. But if passengers, other than Elijah Skindle and one or two equally unbusinesslike young men, were no longer content to crawl along in her cart, that historic vehicle showed scant sign of defeat. Already when the removal of the hoops in the hot weather had threatened to expose too clearly the nakedness of the land, parcels of stones on the model of the swain-chaser had begun to cumber it up, and when one Monday morning the Flynt Flyer came swaggering in new pea-green paint, the Quarles Crawler turned up on Tuesday mountainous with the old boxes and cypress clothes-chests routed out of the ante-room, and emptied of their litter.

It was at this point that the Gaffer had had to be put into the plot. He had long since begun to smell a rat—having a super-sense for his business, however his other senses might fail—and it would have been impossible to heave up the boxes without him, or to explain their removal without imparting some notion of the tragic truth. And the truth did not diminish his resentment against young Caleb's boy or his vigilance against further robbers. "Carry him in!" he would cackle and croak as he bore out the emptied "spruce-hutches" to the cart or carefully permutated their positions in it. Then with hoarse thunder: "On your hands and knees, ye pirate thief!"

But these ostentated boxes—while they saved the pride of the Quarleses—did but damage the remainder of their custom. The faithful few had been held back by solicitude for Jinny's livelihood: seeing her now so flourishing, the very tail-board lowered on its chains and groaning under protruding "portmantles," her last clients save Peculiars lapsed in silent relief, one after another. Daily, poor Jinny expected to see four horses on the rival vehicle and its circuit extended to Colchester. But that would have meant for Will a grandeur inconsistent with the petty commissions which he still deigned to execute: it would have allowed some of her old custom to return to her. And he was sullenly bent on driving her—literally—out of the business. But he enhanced the dignity of his profession by copying from an old inn of the pack-horse days its signboard of "The Carriers' Arms," depicting a rope, a wanty-hook, and five packing skewers. These, painted in black on the pea-green, seemed to proclaim his formal annexation and monopoly of the local carrying trade.

Jinny began to think seriously of buying up from the barns some straw from the reaped sheaves and competing with the cottagers in the all-pervasive plaiting industry. Splitting straws was no despicable occupation in the valley of the Brad, where it was done by enginery, and provided even children of six and old men of eighty with the opportunity of adding to the family income. Tambour-lace and other things also entered into her thoughts. The only thing that never entered into them was the idea of ceasing to ply. So long as the boxes and the cart held together, the Flynt Flyer should always see the rival vehicle imperturbably jogging. In every sense she would "carry on."

August was ending aridly. Methusalem's sensitive nose was protected from flies by green bracken. Calves snuggled in the hot meadows, meditatively chewing, an image of somnolence, their tails flicking whitely. Stooks or manure-heaps had reduced the fields to geometrical patterns. Tall hollyhocks leaned dustily like ruined towers. Bucolic conversation was of the absent rain. Rooks were more destructive than ever. Swedes were doing badly and every one had waited to sow turnips, rape, or mustard. They had no fodder even for winter stock. Master Peartree began to worry over his sheep as they munched the sapless grass. In the waterless little villages the ground was hard as iron, and Bundock strode over the swamps around Frog Farm as fearlessly as now frequently. "A regular doucher" was the general demand upon Providence, though it was couched—for church and chapel—in less vivid terms. These prayers enabled Bundock to work off one of his old aphorisms, saved for a rainless day. "It's no use praying for rain," he chuckled to the countryside, "till you see the storm-clouds." "But you don't scarce need to pray then," the countryside pointed out, to his disgust.

In Jinny's soul, too, there was drought, and she seemed to share Bundock's view that prayer was waste of breath. Not that her evening prayers were left unsaid, but in her apathy and weariness no private plea was added to the prescribed form, though the Spelling-Book commended the asking for extra mercies, provided also one begged for a perpetual continuance of the Protestant Succession. What deliverance could there be for her? God Himself, she felt obscurely, could not help her, any more than she had ever been able to help little mavises fallen from their nests and deserted by their mothers. Their thrilling-eyed vitality and exquisite flutterings had only made her miserable. But perhaps God was now as sorry for her.

One grown-up mavis, too, she remembered, a victim to the winter battle of life, the neck half severed from the half-plucked body, the liquid eye gazing appealingly at her, the legs stirring feebly in a welter of feathers. She had nerved herself to grant its dumb plea: she had stamped sharply on its skull and seen its eye fly out on the path like a bright bead. Could God do aught less drastic for her? Not that she ever dreamed of dying: she must live on, however mutilated, for it was impossible to conceive her grandfather getting along without her. Consider only his trousers! How loosely they were now flapping round his shrunken calves, almost like a sailor's. Soon the winter winds would be piping through them. Without her to take in a tuck, where would he be? And who would cut his hair and trim his beard?

It was her grandfather who was mainly responsible for the discontinuance of her chapel habit on Lord's Day. His increased fretfulness and fractiousness since he was become aware of the rival power, made it imprudent to leave him for long except unavoidably—not to mention the danger to herself of awkward meetings at chapel with that rival power—and there was the further difficulty of getting to Chipstone, now Farmer Gale's trap was out of the question. But she was not without a nearer place of worship—for to the scandal of the Peculiars, particularly Bundock, she now began to attend the parish church of Little Bradmarsh, whose emptiness with its parade of free seats after eleven o'clock was a standing pleasantry in the spheres of Dissent. The convenience of proximity was not, however, its main attraction for Jinny, and Miss Gentry would have rejoiced less had she understood that a change of heart or doctrine or the magnetism of the Reverend Mr. Fallow had as little to do with Jinny's apparent conversion; though the fact that Jinny had never forgotten her one childish glimpse of the prayer-absorbed pastor doubtless served to reassure the girl as to the not altogether ungodly character of his edifice.

She had entered to cart over to the Chipstone hospital some fruit laid before the altar at the Harvest Thanksgiving by the one prosperous worshipper. For Mr. Fallow was still an unwavering client of hers, almost the last outside her own communion, possibly because having neither family nor flock to distract him from his classics, he had scarcely observed the coach.

In the "Speculi Britanniæ Pars," in which he had once hunted out her genealogy—to his own satisfaction and nobody's hurt—Essex was compared to Palestine for its flow of "milke and hunny." And "hunny" was still her staple link with the tall fusty-coated, snuff-smeared figure, stooping over his hives or his Virgil, both sacredly fused for him in the Fourth Georgic. She marketed his surplus, exchanging it for firkins of butter and—O aberrations of the godliest—canisters of Lundy Foot. And it was after disposing of some of his smaller tithes—for the parish had remained outside the recent Commutation Act of 1836—that Jinny had been thus led to set foot in his church. There were in those days no floral decorations to mar the completeness with which the arches and pillars ministered to her troubled mood. The outside she had always found soothing, with its grey old stonework and its lichened tower rising amid haystacks and thatched cottages with dormer windows. But how much cooler the peace that fell upon her, when she passed through the old, spiky, oak door and under the long, wooden, vaulted roof into a dimness shot with rich stained glass. Mr. Fallow had been one of the earliest clergymen of the century to remove the whitewash from the old painted walls of his church, and though the royal arms—the lion and the unicorn—still lingered over the chancel, there was no other jar in the spiritual harmony except the stove, whose pipe went hideously up and along the ceiling. Ignoring that, however, in the effect of the whole and forgetting everything else, Jinny sank upon a pew-bench and abandoned herself to the unholy influences of architecture, so restful after her chapel with its benches and table-desk, ugliness unadorned. Not even a gradual consciousness of neglected duty could impair the divine tranquillity.

But the sober beauty of the place might not have sufficed to draw her again, but for a strange circumstance. One of the stained-glass figures, dully familiar to her from without as a leaden glaze, proved when seen from within in all the glory of art to be an angel of the very type under which her childish vision had imagined her hovering mother. And that it actually was mystically interfused with her mother, as her emotion had immediately intertwined it, was demonstrated by the fact that even when she at last went forward to gather up the plums and apples, the eyes followed her about in protection and benediction. Miss Gentry's legend of her moving angel lost its last shade of improbability, and it was with a new humility that Jinny repeated to her at the first opportunity her remorse for the permuted pot.

Nor did the angel's emanation of guardianship prove illusory, for outraged though Miss Gentry had been by the suggestion that her moustache needed a hair-restorer, she graciously intimated—after the second Sunday of Jinny's attendance—that the debt for the dress could be worked off in commission charges. It was a vast relief, for the Bundock-borne rumour of her apostasy had alienated the bulk of her co-religionists and exchanged the lingering remorse of earlier deserters for a sense of rectitude and foresight. Bundock's sympathy with the Brotherhood almost reinstated him in its good graces. "But it brings its own punishment," he pointed out consolingly. "Fancy putting a parson over herself to poke his snuffy nose into everything. That's a pretty dress, Jinny, he'll say, is it paid for? Or, that's a cranky old grandpa you've got—why don't ye put him in the poorhouse?"

It was as well poor Jinny did not overhear him, or she might have doubted whether her load of boxes was so uniformly imposing as she imagined. The Deacon, who did hear him, and who spent his life poking into holes and reprimanding sinners, was even more righteously indignant at the interference of parsons. "Inquisitive as warmin in a larder," he described them. "Fussing around the poor, but without a drop of rum in their milk of human koindness." Mr. Fallow—it would appear—had interfered on behalf of his parishioner in the threatened lawsuit with Miss Gentry: he had persuaded the guileless rat-catcher to promise to clear her cottage for nothing, and this although Mrs. Mott was paying her in full for his wife's silk dress, the responsibility for which he had righteously repudiated.

"Oi'll clear her cottage," he added darkly, and it seemed to Bundock that the parson had succeeded only in patching up the feud. But what was to be expected of the canting crew, the postman inquired. The new Chipstone curate had called on his father, and Bundock related with a chuckle how the bed-ridden old boy had patronizingly regretted that, being on his back, he could do nothing to help his visitor. "He sent him away with a bed-flea in his ear," gloated Bundock. Mr. Joshua Mawhood recalled a bigger flea in the same clerical ear. The hapless curate had offered him a ticket for a lecture on "Economy." "Come with me Bradmarsh way," the rat-catcher had retorted, "and Oi'll show you Mrs. Pennymole's cottage, and if you'll show me how she can bring up her nine childer on eleven shillings a week, Oi'll eat your shovel-hat." Bundock, unable to find a still larger flea, fell back on hypothesis. "If I'd been a Churchman and a chap in a white choker came to mine," he said, "I'd tell him to mind his own business, and I dare say he'd be insulted, though I'd be giving him splendid advice. You know where the door is, I'd say, for you didn't come in by the chimney. Now walk out, or else—!" And carried away by his own drama, Bundock administered a hearty kick to the apparently still-lingering phantom.

Needless to say, Mr. Fallow exercised none of this imagined prying into Jinny's affairs. Like his pew-opener, whose long caped coat with the official red border found now a fresh justification, he was only too glad of her uninvited attendance, and the considerable accretion she brought to his congregation. Her presence freshened up for himself his old sermons: for her sake he even put in new Latin quotations. But Jinny enjoyed more the three musicians in the gallery—'cellist, flautist, and bassoonist— whose black frock-coats and trousers made them as important in quality as they were in quantity, and when after they had played a few bars the congregation sang:

"Awake my soul, and with the sun
Thy daily stage of duty run,"

Jinny felt herself rapt far indeed from her daily stage of duty. Even the pew-opener shuffling about in his list slippers to poke up the stove or a small boy, or to snuff the guttering tallow candles on dark mornings, could not bring her to earth.

And another factor than the church and its mother-angel helped Jinny over this dreary time. This was her dog. For only now did Nip emerge into his full caninity, or at least only now did Jinny learn to appreciate him to the full. In howsoever leaden a mood she started her carrying work, Nip's ecstasy soon tinged it with gold. His blissful staccato barks, his tall inflated tail, his upleapings at her as she harnessed Methusalem, his gallopings and gambollings round that stolider fellow-quadruped, his crazy friskings and curvetings—who could resist such joy of life? Often it seemed to Jinny that he was returning thanks to his Maker for the sunshine or the good smells, rebuking unconsciously her heart-heaviness, bidding her cry no more over spilt milk, but just lap up what she could. "Cheer up, Jinny!" she heard him bark. "Men are brutes and women fools and gran'fers grumpy and customers cruel, but life is jolly and odours numerous and where there's a way there's a Will." And infected by these sentiments of his, she would crack her whip, and Methusalem would prick up his ears and pretend for her sake to go faster, and there would be a lull in the ache at her heart.

Nip, however, was less consoling when the rival carriers met on the road. Then his invincible persuasion that the two were one brought Jinny considerable discomfort. For Will persisted in his later tactics of slowing down, whether to take stock of her appearance or to rub in the odious comparison of their respective equipages, so that while these were in proximity, Nip was able to feel himself shepherding them, and he ran from one to the other, rounding them up. Even when Jinny manœuvred off down the first by-way, Nip, not to be baulked, would travel between one and the other, growing more and more desperate as they grew more and more distant, till at last, fearful of losing both, he exchanged his frenzied shuttling between them for a still more frenzied standstill midway between the mutually receding vehicles—you saw him almost literally torn in two. Finally, after plaintive ululations of protest, he would trot back, with hang-dog look and drooping tail, to the shabby cart, where his mistress throned, grim and pale, amid her manifold mock parcels.

III

But it was neither Mr. Fallows sermons nor Nip's that gave Jinny her first real sense of religion; not even the bass-viol and flute, though she heard them with ecstasy, nor the collects and litanies, though she perused them with interest. It came to her one pitch-black night when she had too confidently ventured out to bring first aid—a jug of real tea with some bread and butter—to poor rheumatic Uncle Lilliwhyte, whom earlier that day, while gathering mushrooms for supper, she had discovered in a deserted charcoal-burner's hut.

She had not known before that Farmer Gale had carried out his threat of evicting the nondescript from his cottage on the plea of needing it for a labourer, and although she had been compelled to suspend the ministrations which had set Mr. Fallow looking for the Lady Bountiful in her blood, she felt vaguely responsible for Uncle Lilliwhyte's declined fortunes, so parallel to her own. Would, in fact, the Cornishman have turned him out if Jinny had allowed that all-powerful arm to remain round her waist at the cattle-market; nay, could she not have cheered and nourished a subject countryside?

The unsavoury ancient was lying on some coarse sacking in a clearing still half charred. Literally "sackcloth and ashes," Jinny thought, as she groped her way along the glade by the twinkle of his candle through the chinks of his ramshackle hut. An old flintlock, some snares, nets and rods, and a cooking-pot seemed all its furniture. She was horrified to think—as she gazed at the gaps in the roof—that the prayer for rain might be granted. But to her surprise the old man was sharing the communal aspiration—"a good rine as'll make the seeds spear"—though not hopeful of the boon immediately. He did not want to be a "wet-'ead," he declared paradoxically, but the ground would be harder before the sun met the wind. Such solicitude on behalf of soil belonging so largely to the farmer who had evicted him seemed to Jinny touchingly Christian.

It was only when she had turned her back on his glimmering light and got into the thick of the woods that they became curiously unfamiliar. Great trees that she did not know existed came colliding against her, tangles of roots tripped her up on her favourite paths; she stumbled into unfriendly pricklinesses of every species. She seemed, indeed, ridiculously lost within a furlong of her own door: how this black labyrinth had got there she could not understand, but it looked as if she might be all night escaping from it. She was even uneasily expecting one of the snakes Uncle Lilliwhyte hunted to glide perversely under her feet, she bruising its head and it biting her heel as the curse in Genesis predicted. Of course, if she could spit into its mouth after chewing some Spanish bugloss, it would instantly die. So at least Miss

Gentry had assured her. But how find the rare bugloss in this blackness, or how spit accurately into the serpent's mouth?

Why had she not brought a lantern, she asked herself. Was it really because she was jug and package laden, or had it been only conceit? She asked the question still more self-reproachfully when, after smashing the empty jug in a stumble which left her knuckles bleeding, she heard the gurgle of a water-hen and realized that she was far off her track and nearly into the Brad. She could not swim, but even a swimmer in such a moonless, starless void would not see the shore. Cautiously feeling her way among the willows, she groped towards the pasture-land, paradoxically pleased when she fell over a sleeping cow. She lay there some minutes in the warm darkness, not anxious to move on, for the river wound perilously in and out, one could still hear it rippling deliciously in the reeds, and the odours of the night were as exquisite. And then through the measureless blackness a faint suggestion of grey began to make itself perceptible or rather divinable, so shadowy was it, a lesser shade of black rather than an adumbration of light; it was as if behind the blank firmament some star was striving to shine.

And suddenly, mystically, she felt that this hinted radiance was God, the Light behind life's darkness, and the words of the twenty-third Psalm came to her mind with all the force of a revelation. "The Lord is my shepherd, I shall not want. He maketh me lie down in green pastures. He leadeth me beside the still waters." How divinely apt was every word! So long as she had not wanted for aught, so long as she had not needed to be led, she had not really felt the meaning of the words: now that she was strayed and a-hungered, she knew overpoweringly that she had a shepherd. He was behind her watching, as surely as she watched over her grandfather. Now she understood what the Peculiars meant when they got up to testify. She must go back to them, bear witness this very next Sunday. Mr. Fallow's church had no place for such testimonies. Women could not speak even at Morning Service.

And as if to complete her conversion, there was a swift pattering, a joyous bark, and a cold nose in her fevered palm. She had only to attach her handkerchief to Nip's collar to be guided safely home. But it was Nip that was really her shepherd, she told herself, or at least her sheep-dog: it was Nip that was leading her beside the still waters. Dog was after all only God spelt backwards, she thought, with a sense of mystic discovery. And remembering all that Nip had done to bring her back to faith in life, she felt he was indeed a divine messenger. But then it was borne in upon her that if she testified her true thoughts, the Brethren would deem her irreverent. After all, it was Mr. Fallow who might understand better, he who spoke of his bees with love, and had once cited to her a passage from a Roman poet about bees being part of the divine mind. The Roman writer was not a Catholic, he had explained carefully, seeing her dubious face.

IV

In her gratitude to the dressmaker, Jinny had become more than ever her intellectual parasite, and a wealth of information from "The Christian Mother's Miscellany" and "Culpeper's Herbal"—to say nothing of the spinster's own sibylline rhymes—enriched the walk to and from church, which Miss Gentry graciously permitted her carrier and debtor to take in her society next Sunday morning. They parted indeed inside, Miss Gentry plumping herself unrebuked into the curtained three-benched pew of the dead and gone squire whom old Farmer Gale had dispossessed. Jinny was thus unable to exchange glances with her at the thrilling announcement read out by the cleric, who after the Second Lesson declared curtly—as if it were the most natural thing in the world—that Mr. Anthony Flippance, widower, of Frog Farm, and Miss Bianca Cleopatra Jones, spinster, of Foxearth Farm, both of this parish, proposed to enter into holy matrimony. At once a whirligig of images circled round Jinny and she saw dizzily the explanation of a disappearance that had puzzled her, for Tony had vanished from "The Black Sheep" without leaving a tip, the old waiter grumbled. What had led up to this adventure, she wondered, and how was Polly taking her intended stepmother?

"Isn't that the Showman you've spoken of?" Miss Gentry inquired, as the congregation of seven streamed out, swollen by musicians, sexton, clerk, and pew-opener. "The fomenter of ungodliness?"

"It certainly seems my old customer," replied Jinny, somewhat evasively. "But I didn't know he was living at Frog Farm."

"Didn't you tell me he was going to turn your chapel into a playhouse?"

"So he said once, but nothing seems to have come of it."

"More's the pity," Miss Gentry surprised Jinny by commenting. She added, "Even a playhouse would do less harm."

"I—I don't see that," Jinny stammered, protesting.

"It's as clear as daylight. The Devil stamps his sign plainly on a playhouse: he forges God's name on a chapel. And who is this Miss Jones?"

"I don't know. I never heard of any girl at Foxearth Farm called Cleopatrick—what a funny name!"

"Cleopatra," corrected Miss Gentry grandly, her bosom expanding till it strained her Sunday silk. "A great Queen of Egypt in the days of old. Born under Venus and died of the bite of an asp!"

"What's an asp?" said Jinny.

"It's what they call the serpent of old Nile!"

"Good gracious!" Jinny exclaimed. "Couldn't they have given Her Majesty agrimony wine?"

"Neither horse-mint nor wild parsnip could avail: there is no ointment against suicide," Miss Gentry explained. "She killed herself."

"A queen kill herself! What for?"

"What does one kill oneself for?" Miss Gentry demanded crushingly. "For love, of course. But I hope her namesake is more respectable. Cleopatra never published the banns. But how comes this Miss Jones to be at Foxearth Farm? I thought the people were called Purley—hurdle-makers, aren't they?"

"Yes—it must be a lodger. They do take lodgers. I must ask Barnaby—I meet him on the road sometimes." She stood still suddenly, going red and white by turns like the revolving lens of a lighthouse.

Miss Gentry stared, then smiled in sentimental sympathy "Is he a nice boy?" she cooed.

"Who? Ye-es, very nice," Jinny stammered. "But I've just remembered Miss Jones isn't his sister!"

"Who said she was? Oh, Jinny, Jinny!" Miss Gentry sometimes became roguish.

"She's only his stepsister," Jinny explained desperately. "Mrs. Purley's first husband was called Jones."

If the bride should really be the Purley creature—the fair charmer who rode so often in Will's coach as to be almost "keeping company" with him! What a lifting of a nightmare! What a sudden horizon of rose! But no, it was too good to be true!

"But I never heard she was called Cleopatra," she wound up sadly.

"People often have a second name hidden away like a tuck," said Miss Gentry.

"But her first name isn't the same either, it's Blanche."

"But Bianca is Blanche!" bayed Miss Gentry, like an excited bloodhound. "Only more grand and foreign-like."

Jinny's colours revolved again.

"Is it?" she breathed. But she remembered Mr. Flippance's address had been announced as Frog Farm. If he had thus ousted young Mr. Flynt, she urged, how could he be living so amicably under his rival's roof? Besides, how should Mr. Purley's second wife, a matron as famous for her cheeses as her spouse for his hurdles, have christened her girl so outlandishly? No, Joneses were as abundant as hips and haws, and this Miss Jones could only have come to their out-of-the-way parish—like Mr. Flippance—for reasons of statutory residence, though why the Showman should bury himself to be married, Miss Gentry declared to be an exciting enigma. Perhaps he liked a quiet wedding, Jinny suggested, having too many acquaintances in towns, and with that she dismissed the hope from her mind.

But it was not so easy to dismiss the topic from Miss Gentry's. That lady was rolling the hymeneal discussion under her tongue. She pointed out that Foxearth Farm was not in Little Bradmarsh and was prepared to discuss the romantic ramifications, if it should turn out on the wedding-day that the bride was disqualified. But Jinny cruelly took the sweet out of her mouth. Foxearth Farm was in the parish, she declared. "It's one of those funny bits, lost, stolen, or strayed into other parishes. I know because of the women from there who come upon our parish for blankets when they're laid aside—"

"Oh, Jinny!" deprecated Miss Gentry, to whom, maternity was as sordid and surreptitious as matrimony was righteously romantic.

But Jinny, innocently misunderstanding, persisted. "Why, I remember the fuss when the steam-roller tried to charge our parish for doing up a scrap of the road beyond Foxearth Farm."

They walked through the sunlit churchyard in constrained silence, Miss Gentry feeling as if the steam-roller had gone over roses. But stimulated by the iron pole and the four steps, by which ladies who rode pillion anciently mounted and dismounted, she began wondering who would be making the bride's dress. That gave Jinny a happy idea. How if she got Miss Gentry the work—that would be a slight return for all she owed her!

"Why shouldn't you make it?" she inquired excitedly. "I could speak to Mr. Flippance, now that I know where he is."

"Hush, child, don't profane the Sabbath! Men don't count in wedding matters," said Miss Gentry in complex correction. "Nor would I care about the patronage of stage people."

"But she mayn't be stage."

"Like runs to like," Miss Gentry sighed, and Jinny felt the Colchester romance hovering again. But it did not descend. Instead, Miss Gentry remarked that she ought to have known that it could not be a local beauty. No play-actor with any brains at all could be attracted by anything hereabouts, especially when they could not achieve the acquaintance of women of real attraction and intellect, these preferring the company of cats to that of strolling sinners. Nevertheless, far be it from her wilfully to rob Jinny of a commission.

"I wasn't thinking of my commission," Jinny protested with a little flush.

"I couldn't dream of it otherwise. Squibs and I need so little and have more work than we can manage."

"Squibs?" Jinny murmured.

"The place is overrun with rats," Miss Gentry explained. "What will it be when the cold drives them in from the ditches? However, fortunately that horrible old Mawhood stands compelled to clear the cottage before winter. That was the compromise our too kindly pastor let him off with."

"So you told me. Shall I order the Deacon at once?"

"The Deacon?" Miss Gentry sniffed. "Bishops they'll call themselves next."

"There is a bishop," Jinny reminded her. "Bishop Harrod."

"Wretched little rat-catchers!" Miss Gentry hissed. "Setting themselves up against the Church Established. I'm so glad you're done with them."

"But I'm not," Jinny confessed shyly. "I'm still Peculiar."

"You are, indeed!" Miss Gentry cried, startled. "Do you mean to tell me that after the glorious privilege of sitting under Mr. Fallow—!" Words failed her, and they also failed Jinny, to whom this unfamiliar metaphor conjured up a puzzling picture of the vicar perched on her Sunday bonnet. The girl was the first to recover her breath.

"Gran'fer told me my mother wanted me to be Peculiar," she explained. "I can't go against my Angel-Mother." Then she blushed prettily, never having mentioned the angel mother since childhood, and feeling somehow as if she had profaned a sacred secret.

"If your angel mother was alive," cried Miss Gentry with conviction, "it's to our church that she would come—to our grand old church with its storied windows!"

A divine thrill ran through all Jinny's frame. Her belief that her mother and the painted angel were mysteriously one was sealed. The oracle had spoken.

Miss Gentry, swelling at her silence—Jinny heard the silk crackling—felt herself indeed an oracle. Squibs had his pick of the plates at that Sunday dinner, enjoying a Sabbath rest from rats, and basking in his mistress's lap, a black curled-up breathing mass of felicity.

V

As Jinny jogged along next Tuesday morning, diverging from her usual beat to take in the hurdle-maker's home, that lay—like a geological "fault"—in the wrong parish, the plan that formed itself in her mind was to approach the question of the bride and the wedding-dress by way of Barnaby Purley, the youth who had so chivalrously come to her rescue by delivering at Uckford Manor the keg of oil overlooked by her on that memorable journey with Elijah Skindle. It was because Foxearth Farm possessed this hobbledehoy scion and a trap of its own that Jinny had never done its marketing, nor come face to face with the creature of whom with sidelong eye she caught tantalizing glimpses in the Flynt Flyer. "Not bad-lookin'" was the countryside's appraisal of her, which was rather ominous, indicating as it did considerable beauty, and conjoined as it was with a rumour of easy conquests, culminating in the coach-owner. But a good square look at her had not been attainable, even on Sunday, for though the family was Church of England—Mr. Giles Purley being even a churchwarden—it preferred to worship in the parish church to which it did not parochially belong. Jinny told herself she was hastening at this first opportunity purely in Miss Gentry's interest, for fear the bridal gown had been ordered elsewhere. But she could not quite disguise from herself her consuming anxiety to discover whether this everyday Miss Jones was really a Cleopatra, though she called her poignant emotion mere curiosity, and deemed herself as apathetic at heart as the bumble-bees now crawling miserably about her cart, which could be flicked into a feeble flight and drone, but which soon relapsed into their torpor.

In truth the suppressed hope of finding Blanche safely paired with the Showman was now quickening her pulses and restoring the wild rose to her cheeks. The September day, too, for all the long-continued drought, and despite the drowsy bumble-bees, was not devoid of animating influences, especially the delicious smell of burnings from the fields, where men tossed from their prongs brown masses of weed into red and smoking heaps, or carried like merry devils fiery forks from one pile to another. Monstrous fungi clove in pied picturesqueness to the elm-trunks, and a hawthorn grove with its scarlet berries was like a vast radiant smile. Overhead the sun, a shimmery thin-clouded sphere, showed like an eye in a great white peacock's wing. The hips and blackberries were interfused in the hedges, the ivy flowered on the squat church towers, the Virginia creepers were reddening the cottages, and the dahlias grew tall in the little front gardens. In the orchards the pear-trees and apple-trees were heavy with fruit. Around them the turnip-fields looked more like spreads of mustard, so thick were the slender yellow-flowering stems pushing between the crop proper. And everywhere was life; pecking poultry scattering before Methusalem's feet, and little frogs playing leapfrog; swarms of the Daddy-long-legs and gigantic spiders, great quarrelling families of rooks, quiet chewing cattle, pigs nosing for acorns or windfall apples, hares or great rats or weasels scuttling across the road, partridges straying fearlessly in the stubble, swallows darting unpromisingly high, and when Jinny passed over the little brick bridge, at which a black drainage-mill waved what seemed its four crossed white combs, a pair of superb swans hissed their proud protectiveness over a very drab cygnet.

Driving through an avenue of firs and hornbeam, and past a dirty pond with two flagged mounds in the middle, she reached the clearing where the hurdle-maker operated, with his farmhouse for base of his combined industrial, agricultural, and pastoral occupations.

Mr. Giles Purley, a rosy-wrinkled apple-faced ancient, stood in his shirt-sleeves, looking as pleasantly untidy as his farmyard, which was full of felled logs and split wood, and bean and corn stacks, and ramshackle sheds. He was planing off knots with a bill-hook, and as Jinny drove up to the gate of the old timbered red house, he greeted her with a cheery grumble at the drought which forced such winter work prematurely upon him. Jinny was abashed to find no pretext for her visit coming to her tongue, so she stammered out that she wanted to see Barnaby, and the droll look that twinkled across his father's face sent her colour up still higher. "Always wants a change, they youngsters," he chuckled benevolently, "whether 'tis of work or sweet-hearts."

At this point Jinny became aware of Barnaby himself, who, equally in his shirt-sleeves, was smiling sheepishly up at her from the ditch which he was discumbering with a hook. "Lilies of the walley they stick in their buttonholes," went on his father waggishly, "as if weeds was ever aught but weeds. There ain't one that showlders his sack o' corn or sticks to his dearie. Sheep's eyes they can make, but as for sheep-hurdles—!" The note was now earnest. It seemed an unpropitious moment to tackle Barnaby.

And to make it more impossible, Blanche herself suddenly bounded from the orchard, flourishing a great corroded pear.

"Nipped thirteen!" she cried gaily.

"Not bad-lookin'," forsooth! To Jinny she appeared in her bloom and colour like a rich peach dipped in cream: overripeness was the only flaw her beauty suggested to this girl in her teens. But the chill at Jinny's heart did not prevent her crying out with equal gaiety, "What an unlucky number—for the wasps!"

Barnaby laughed adoringly from his ditch, Mr. Giles Purley in simple joy of the slaughter. The pigs, he explained gleefully, had gnawed at the pear-bags and Blanche was "wunnerful masterous" at nipping the wasps as they crawled out of the forbidden fruit. Asps, Jinny found herself thinking, would have a bad time at such bold hands, though they made the Cleopatra likelier—she slued her eyes round to see the rings on them, but the engagement finger was hidden by the big pear, and Miss Jones, her gaiety checked, was eyeing her like the intruder she was.

"She can kill two at once," Barnaby called up.

"Like you with the lasses," flashed his father, to his confusion.

"It's nothing," said Blanche coldly. "They haven't time to curl their tails round."

"Who? The lasses?" asked Jinny, and to her relief the beautiful Blanche vouchsafed a smile.

"You won't be stung if you don't think you'll be," the girl explained more cordially. Then, unable to retain the proud secret longer, even from the Carrier, she burst forth, "I'm going on the stage with it."

"What!" Jinny gasped.

"Only as a beginning, of course. 'Bianca, The Bare-Handed Wasp-Killer,' it'll be on the bills."

"Rubbidge!" came explosively from Mr. Purley. "And where will Mr. Flippance get the wapses in the winter? A circus-slut indeed—I wonder what your mother can be thinkin' of! And what's Mr. Honeytongue going to bill you as, Barnaby? Not champion hurdle-maker, I'll go gaff!"

"Wait till you see me," said Barnaby with sullen mysteriousness. "You don't know a circus from a theaytre."

"You'll stick to your shackles and bolts," said his parent grimly, "and peel the bark off, too!"

At the mention of Mr. Flippance, Jinny's heart beat fast: she felt hovering on the verge of the revelation, and the Bianca and the stage-project rekindled her hope. But Mr. Purley's grievance had to be worked off first. "They're too lazy to peel the wood," he explained to Jinny. "But that's the main thing for hurdles—to strip 'em well against rain. Same as you was full-dressed in a pouring rain—the time it 'ud take you to dry! If you was naked now—"

"Oh, dad!" Barnaby remonstrated, to his parent's confusion, and enjoyed this tit-for-tat.

"When do you expect Mr. Flippance, Mr. Purley?" Jinny asked him hastily.

"Oh, he never comes in the mornings," Blanche replied, and this appropriation of the question seemed to Jinny to continue the promise of Bianca and the stage-project.

"Then can I speak to—to his intended?" she flashed brilliantly, with a clever smile.

"She's gone to her dressmaker," said Blanche simply.

It was a double blow, and Jinny winced before it. In that twinkling of her eye Blanche seemed years younger, diabolically handsome, a nipper of buds as well as of wasps. But a worse blow awaited her, for she had scarcely regained her composure when the distant sound of a wheezy horn and a sense of an impending avalanche brought Blanche into bounding activity again.

"Why, there's Will!" she exclaimed with a comic, happy start. "And me not dressed yet!" And without a word to the little Carrier, she ran gaily into the house.

Frantically clutching Nip who was about to spring to meet the coach, Jinny cried vague thanks to the hurdle-maker and hurried Methusalem down a by-way so narrow that she could hardly squeeze through the untrimmed "werges" neglected of Barnaby.

VI

When she heard the coach well on its way again on the Chipstone road, with Blanche divined within, she found herself possessed by an unexpected urging towards Mr. Flippance. She had no real round any longer—only the hours to fill and her grandfather to half deceive—and perhaps, despite Miss Gentry's own opinion, the bridegroom might yet be able to prevent her being cut out by the rival pair of scissors. The truth was, Jinny felt a physical need of the toning up the Showman somehow imparted to life. To drive around the rest of the day with practically no business but her own thoughts would be too dreadful. He must surely babble happily about his bride, and apart from the interest of her identity, some of his glow could not but radiate to her. And there was Caleb and Martha to see, too—how were they faring, these dear, simple creatures, too long unvisited? But then—thought that froze the heart!— had she not declared she would never set foot in Frog Farm again? No, she answered herself defiantly— and no memory of hereditary quibbling, nothing of her sense of humour, rose to trouble the reply—all she had said was that Will should never see her there. And Will was safely chained to the Chipstone road.

All the same she looked round apprehensively and with wildly beating heart before she allowed Methusalem to lift the latch of the familiar gate, and she had somehow expected so great a transformation in the farmhouse under its new and sinister activities, and was conscious of so vast a change in herself since she had last seen it, that its primitive black front almost startled her, so unchanged did it appear. True, the ferrets' cages were gone, but their absence only made it more its old self, and the moan of the doves was as reassuring as the singing of the kettle on her own hearth. Caleb's red shirt-sleeves looked for once in keeping with the scene, arising as they did out of yellow flame-tinged clouds from the rubbish-heap which he was burning, and the pleasant pungent smell of which filled her eyes with tears, half smoke, half emotion. Even in that glow the homely hair-circled face was capable of a new illumination.

"Gracious goodness, there's Jinny!" He ran to the house-door. "Mother! Mother!" he cried in jubilant agitation.

Martha emerged at a hobbling run, apron-girded. Despite the glow, her face darkened.

"You give a body a turn," she grumbled. "I almost thought 'twas the Golden City coming down."

"'Tis nigh as good," he retorted boldly, "bein' as Jinny was same as gone there. And bless me, ef she don't look ghosty!"

"Good morning, Jinny!" said Martha coldly. "We don't need a carrier now—with our coach to get everything."

Jinny's cheeks turned far from "ghosty." "I haven't come to you—only to Mr. Flippance."

"But he gets everything, too, through Willie."

"I know that—I merely want to speak to him."

"You can't now."

"The missus means he's abed," Caleb explained, rushing to Jinny's relief, and indeed the information brought a smile back to her twitching lips. "Minds me of a great old tortoise, diggin' hisself into his blankets. Do him good to be up with the sun, same as when Oi was a scarecrow, soon as the wheat was sown."

"You don't want to tell everybody you began as a scarecrow," said Martha frigidly.

"Ef we're rich now, dear heart, and can ride in our own coach, 'tis the Lord's hand, not ours. Oi watched over wheat and winter beans, and 'arly peas, and winter oats, and then spring barley, but all the time the Lord was watchin' over me."

"Not as a scarecrow," said Martha severely.

"Oi warn't a scarecrow ploughin'-time, bein' set on the middle hoss to flick the whip, and chance times when 'twas too frosty to plough Oi went to Dame Pippler's to school."

"I never heard that before," said Martha.

"Dedn't like to tell ye," he confessed, "being as 'twas too cowld to howd the slate-pencil, and the book-larnin' leaked out 'twixt the frosts. 'Twas a penny a week wasted."

Martha saw their visitor was amused at this revelation after fifty years of wedlock. "Jinny wants to be going on," she observed testily. "Look at all her boxes."

"Oi'm proper pleased to see 'em, for as Oi says to Willie, Oi hope as you ain't hart Jinny's business and grieved the Lord. Ye can't sleep, Oi says, ef ye've grieved the Lord."

"Then Mr. Flippance must be a saint," laughed Jinny. But she was touched to tears.

Caleb had, however, not finished his apologia for his lack of learning, and was to be diverted neither by Jinny's jests nor his wife's grimaces. "And in the summer," he explained carefully, "Oi got to goo out with my liddle old gun agin they bird-thieves, though peas and pebbles was all the shot my feyther—"

"Can't you try some at Mr. Flippance's window?" interrupted Jinny, fearful the fretful Martha would soon close her door upon her.

"Oi'd have to stand sideways for that!" He pointed to a hooked-back casement. "Fust he kivers hisself up, then he opens hisself out"—he chuckled contemptuously—"'tis 'in dock, out nettle,' as the sayin' goos."

Jinny lifted her little horn to her lips and blew a blast so literally rousing that hardly had its echoes died than from the black casement framework a red unshaven face, like the rayed rising sun on an inn signboard, dawned above clouds of flamboyant dressing-gown.

"Jinny! Hurrah!" cried the apparition in delighted surprise. "The very person I've been wanting for weeks!"

In the effulgence of that great rubicund sphere of a face Jinny's mists began to dissolve—after all, with all his faults he belonged to her rosy past, to the good old times ere black horses or red men had arisen to rend her. "Then why didn't you let me know?" she smiled.

"Just what I was thinking of doing. So glad you've saved me a letter. Never was so hard-worked in my life. Good morning, ma," he threw to Mrs. Flynt, whose set face now relaxed into a maternal mildness, "do I smell breakfast?"

"Ye could ha' smelt it afore seven, friend," said Caleb, growing dour as Martha grew soft. "And the missus a bit paltry to-day, too!"

"Am I late? I'm so sorry. Why, I thought it was Will's horn!"

"Mr. Flippance overslept himself, dearie," Martha said reproachfully.

"But you hate food spilin'," Caleb protested.

"Not so much as I hate spoilt food!" said Tony. "Not that a good housekeeper like Mrs. Flynt would really let food spoil—any more than you your wheat-patch."

"Ef ye had helped gittin' that bit o' corn in," retorted Caleb, "ye'd fare to have more to sleep on."

"There's more than one kind of work, Caleb," said Martha severely. "There's brain-work for them that have never been scarecrows."

"Yes, indeed, Mrs. Flynt!" said Tony earnestly. "I'm worked to a shadow."

"And there was no such hurry to get the corn in," Martha added.

"With all they prayers for rine gooin' on, ye can't be too careful," Caleb urged.

"But what work had you got, Mr. Flippance?" Jinny laughed.

"Getting married. Didn't you know?"

She was startled. "But you're not married already?"

"No such luck. When the lady says 'Yes,' you think all your troubles are over. But they're only beginning."

Caleb's face relaxed in a grin, whereupon Martha's hardened to a frown. "Marriage is no laughing matter," she said, with a glower at her husband.

"No, indeed, Mrs. Flynt!" endorsed Tony. "What with the forms and questions and ceremonies and witnesses and what not, and rings to buy and bouquets to order—it's worse than a dress rehearsal!"

"But you've had the rehearsal," Jinny reminded him.

"I was young and strong. Now you've got to help me."

"Me?" Jinny was enchanted at this smoothing of the path for Miss Gentry. "But I'm so busy," she protested professionally. "I can't wait till you're up."

"Jinny's too busy," Martha corroborated. And in her eagerness to be rid of the girl, she unconsciously clucked to Methusalem, and so exactly like Jinny that the noble animal actually started.

"Wait! Wait!" Mr. Flippance shouted down wildly. "Do wait! Such a lot to consult you about. Haven't even got a best man yet. Find me one and I'll call down blessings on your head!"

"I don't want you to call them down," she jested up. "That's the trouble."

"I'll be down before you can say 'Jack Robinson.'"

"I wasn't going to suggest him!" And she reined in her fiery steed.

Martha had hurried to her kitchen to bring in the belated breakfast, and the convulsion into which Jinny's last remark appeared to throw Caleb was left unchecked by wifely grimaces. The veteran alternated between gurgles and roars so continuously that Jinny, flattered as she was by the reception of her jest, began to feel uneasy.

"That fair flabbergasted him," he gasped, getting his breath at last. "How can Oi, says Oi, ef Oi'm a buoy-oy, Oi says." He wiped the tears from his whiskered cheeks and blew his nose into his great "muckinger."

"But he didn't ask you to be best man," she said, puzzled. "And you aren't a boy."

"'Twas master as called me a buoy-oy," he explained, his eyes still dancing, "so as to keep down my wages. Oi've got three hosses same as the min, Oi says, and can plough my stetch similar-same as them and cut and trave up my corn better'n Bill Ravens as felt the teeth of the sickle two days arter he started and couldn't work no more, though double-money time, as Oi can sartify bein' as 'twar me what tied my neckercher round his arm with the blood pourin' down like sweat, and lucky 'twarn't his wife, Oi says, but another woman gooin' behind him to be larnt how, she bein' in confinement. But master he wouldn't listen to nawthen. Oi'll give you easy ploughin' was all he promised, ye're onny a buoy-oy, he says, obstinacious like, and Oi stayed on a bit, not mislikin' the cans of tea the wives brought, all hot and sweet, and the big granary with pillars and fower on us thrashin' and rattlin' on the big oak floor, jolly as a harvest supper, and Bill Ravens—that be the feyther of the rollin' stone as shears chance times for Master Peartree—singin' like the saints in Jerusalem, all except for the words. But at last, bein' as feyther wanted the money and Oi needed time to look for a farmer not so nippy, gimme a week off, says Oi to old Skindflint. A week off! says master. What for? Gooin' to git married?"

At this point the convulsion recommenced, and Jinny, though she understood how the Flippance wedding had set his memories agog, had still to wait for enlightenment as to why they were agrin.

"Married, Oi says! How can Oi git married, ef Oi'm a buoy-oy?"

It was out at last, the great repartee of his life, and Jinny felt he was right to cherish its memory. She occupied the period of his renewed cachinnation in descending from her seat and giving Methusalem his impoverished nosebag. Her action reminded Caleb to offer to show her the enlarged stables, with the old roof raised to admit the coach. Then, colouring as if at an indelicacy, he hastily inquired how her grandfather was, remarking with commiseration that he must be getting a bit elderly.

Never had Jinny known him so loquacious—the absence of Martha was combining with her own advent to loosen his usually ruly member. And at last the pent-up flood of his grievances against the Showman burst forth. The return of Will, Jinny gathered, had been dislocating enough, even before his new-fangled coach had brought the stir of the great world and Bundock almost daily, but now the house and the hours were all "topsy-tivvy," worse than in Cousin Caroline's time. He would do Will the justice to say that it wasn't his fault—Will had been against putting up a "furriner" in their spare bedroom—but the "great old sluggaby" had come and ingratiated himself so with the rheumatic but romantic Martha, and offered such startling prices—a pound a week for board and lodging—"enough to feed the whole Pennymole family for a fortnight"—that she had forced her will upon both the male Flynts. "The trouble with Martha is," Caleb summed up, "she allus wants what she wants." Mr. Flippance, he explained, "got a piper for her from her Lunnon Sin Agog—funny name that for the Lord's House, even in Lunnon—and that piper fared to be all about the Christy Dolphins and their doin's—the Loightstand, Martha called it. And she read me a piece out of it how Mr. Somebody, husband o' Sister T'other, was baptized by Elder Somebody Else; and she wanted me to goo and do likewise."

"But you are nearly one of them, aren't you?" Jinny smiled.

He looked uneasy.

"Oi don't want to be baptized a Jew," he said plaintively. "Martha she argufies as Paul says we are the Jews, bein' Abraham's seed in our innards. So long as she calls us the Lord's people, Oi fair itches to be one, but that goos agin the stomach like to call yourself a Jew. Same as she was satisfied with the New Jerusalem part, Oi'd goo with her. For ef the Book says, 'No man hath gone up to heaven,' or 'Whither Oi goo, ye cannot come,' that proves as heaven's got to come to us, and happen Oi'll live to see it droppin' down with its street of pure gold same as transparent brass. But Oi won't be swallowed up whole like a billy-owl swallows a mouse."

"What's that you're saying, Caleb?" said Martha, now perceived back at her house-door.

"He was telling me about the Lightstand," said Jinny glibly.

Martha beamed again. "Ah, it won't be long before that light spreads, though now the world is all shrouded in darkness and superstition. But salvation is of the Jews."

"That ain't writ in the Book?" inquired Caleb anxiously.

"Salvation is of the Jews," repeated Martha implacably. "John iv. 22. There's nine of us now in Essex alone, the Lightstand says, not reckoning London. They don't know about another that's on the way Zionwards," she added mysteriously.

"Meaning me?" said Caleb nervously.

"Meaning a man with brains and book-learning," said Martha sternly, "and he's ready to see you now, Jinny."

"Well, nine ain't no great shakes," Caleb murmured.

"We are the salt of the earth," Martha reminded him. "A pinch of salt goes a long way."

"Ay, when it rolls in a pill-box," Caleb reflected ruefully. "And hows the old chapel, Jinny?" he said aloud. "Willy never goos now."

Jinny coloured up: one of her pretexts for apostasy seemed null and void.

"I'll see you when I come out, I suppose," she said evasively, as she followed Martha within.

VII

The parlour of Frog Farm had not the peculiar mustiness which greeted Jinny's nostrils when last she peeped into it that tragic morning of Maria's illness, but there was by way of compensation a reek of stale tobacco and the odours of the breakfast bacon and mushrooms, while in lieu of the sacrosanct tidiness there was a pervasion of papers, with a whole mass of scripts sliding steadily from the slippery sofa. The brown-lozenged text on the wall: "When He giveth quietness, who then can make trouble?" seemed to shriek for Caleb's answer: "Friend Flippance." Other documents bulged and bristled from both pockets of the dressing-gown as from greasy paniers.

"Bless you, Jinny," Tony gurgled from his breakfast-cup. He eyed her rapturously. "What a pretty pair you'll make at the wedding!"

"It's no use, Mr. Flippance," said Martha, beaming, "I've told you before I won't go into a church."

Mr. Flippance, who had been mentally coupling his bride and Jinny, replied with but the briefest muscular quiver, that the only thing that reconciled him to Martha's absence was that she was incapacitated by matrimony from the rôle of bridesmaid. This morning he would not trouble her to wait. "You can 'withdraw' from me," he said jocosely.

Martha was jarred by this profane use of the sacred vocabulary, and moreover felt it almost as improper to leave Jinny alone in her house, even with a budding bridegroom. "Jinny's got no secrets from me," she said tartly; and Mr. Flippance, divining his error, remarked blandly, "Nor have I." And as Martha started to dust the mantelpiece ornaments and to discover cigar-ash in her china shoes, he drew Jinny's attention to the "beautiful" silk sampler that hung over them. "And all worked with Mrs. Flynt's own hand! What a wonderful lion—and as for the unicorn, she's got it to the life!"

"Oh, it's only what I did when a girl," said Martha, blushing modestly. "Only I didn't like to hang it up then, because I'd left no room for the foreign trees like my sisters put in!"

"Well, but you've got in the alphabet, big and little, and all the figures! Wonderful!"

"That's where Willie learnt his A B C from," said Martha, radiant.

"Ah, that gay deceiver!" sighed Mr. Flippance. "He told me he was a Yankee, but now I find he's only a yumorist. Still he's a chap any woman can be proud of—what do you say, Jinny?"

Jinny, who had seated herself on the sofa, carefully steadied the slipping manuscripts as she replied with a forced lightness:

"I say, if you want a best man, you can't find a better."

"Ah, that's the trouble. He won't take part in a Church ceremony neither, he says he's got to consider the old folks—at the chapel," he added promptly. "But at any rate we shall have the best bridesmaid."

"You don't mean me?" said Jinny, colouring under his admiring gaze. "Because it's impossible. I haven't the time—or the money."

"Is it the dress you're thinking of? Surely the Theatre Royal, Chipstone, can run to that?" And pulling a protrusive scroll from a pocket of his dressing-gown, he unfurled it beatifically, exposing a poster with the coupled names of Anthony Flippance and Cleopatra Jones in giant letters.

"Anthony and Cleopatra!" he breathed in a ravishment. "The moment she told me her second name was Cleopatra I knew it was useless fighting against the fates."

"But have you bought our chapel then?" Jinny inquired.

"Bought your chapel?" Mr. Flippance was mystified. "Why on earth should I buy your chapel?"

"You—you might have turned it into a theatre!" she stammered apologetically.

He waved the suggestion away with a jewelled hand. "Only a new Temple of Thespis could live up to Anthony and Cleopatra. We are building!"

"Where?" Now it was Jinny that was mystified—she had seen no such enterprise afoot.

"Here!" He tapped the other pocket of his dressing-gown. "Plans!" He rolled up his poster reluctantly. "Cleopatra wanted to see it in print. Didn't I say what a work getting married was? But now that the bridesmaid's settled—!"

"But she's not!" said Jinny, more alarmed than when he was trying to cast her for the bride, perhaps because the danger of being sucked in was greater.

"Oh, Jinny!" He looked at her with large reproachful eyes and mechanically threw bacon to Nip, who had at last sniffed his way in, and who, fortunately for Martha's composure, caught it ere it reached her carpet. "You see she wants to have the thing all regular and respectable, and all her family are in Wales. She hasn't got a parent handy to give her away. And having led a wandering life, she hadn't even a parish to marry in. I never thought you'd desert an old pal."

"But I'm no pal of hers—I don't even know her."

"Oh, Jinny!" And just arresting a paper-slide, he extricated a photograph from the imperilled mass. "The new Scott Archer process," he declared proudly. "Knocks your daguerreotypes into the middle of last week. Good gag that, eh?"

But it was Jinny who seemed knocked into that period; and not only by this new triumph of the camera. For in this wonderful breathing image she recognized—in all save size, for this seemed a Cleopatra swelling to regal stature—the beauteous human doll she had last seen walking down the steps of a toy house, conning a part.

"But she's married!" she gasped.

"Not yet. Would to heaven it were all over!" said Mr. Flippance airily, but his great brow grew black for an instant ere he turned it sunnily on Martha. "Oh, ma, could I have more of these marvellous mushrooms?"

"I'll see, you greedy boy," she smiled, retreating.

"Well, who could help saying encore to such items?" He turned reproachfully on Jinny. "You nearly shocked the old lady."

"But didn't you—didn't you call her the Duchess?" Jinny stammered. "Oh, but perhaps it is Mrs. Duke's sister—she looks taller."

"That's because she's got no legs," he explained paradoxically. "But it's all right—The Loveliest Leading Lady in London." (Jinny heard the capital letters distinctly.)

He went on to explain that London didn't know this yet, and that some time must elapse before Cleopatra would be in a position to demonstrate it on the spot, owing to local jealousies. But Jinny came back remorselessly to her point.

"But surely she was married to Mr. Duke!"

"Hush! Appearances are deceptive. They were just close friends."

"You couldn't well be closer—in that doll's house," said Jinny scornfully. And her own words reminded her how he had denounced the Duchess as a "squeaking doll" whose "golden" hair was spurious.

"Now you shock me, Jinny," said Mr. Flippance severely. "Pure as the driven snow is my Cleo, stainless as the Lady Agnes, shut up in that great oak chest on her wedding morn, sweet as her namesake, Bianca, in The Taming of the Shrew."

"Why does she tame shrews?" asked Jinny, puzzled.

"That's a play by Shakespeare"—the name not occurring in the Spelling-Book, left Jinny unimpressed. "A shrew is a vixen."

This natural history left Jinny still less impressed. "That's nonsense," she said. "A shrew is tiny and lovely to look at, with darling rounded ears. I buried one the other day, and its eye was as bright as life."

"It's only a way of speaking," he explained, "as you call a woman a cat. Katharina's the polecat of the play that her husband has to tame with a whip, but Bianca is a dove, gentle and spotless."

"Doves are not so gentle," said Jinny. "They peck each other dreadfully. I like vixens better, at least they seem fonder of their family when you peep down their earths."

Mr. Flippance, who had never in his life seen either a shrew or a vixen or a polecat or observed the habits of doves, was taken aback. He had even a vague sense of blasphemy, some ancient religious images whirring confusedly in his brain. "Understand this, Jinny," he said sharply, abandoning the shifting sands of metaphor, "Cleo gave Mr. Duke her companionship and her artistic co-operation, but as for marrying him—bring me that Book!"

He indicated the precious volume which Mrs. Flynt had left in the parlour for his study of the text-evidence of the Christadelphian teaching. But Jinny took his Bible oath for granted. Sincerity and righteous indignation radiated from every round inch of his face, and Jinny, despite her farmyard experience, was too nebulous in her ideas of human matings not to be shaken. In truth he had been vastly relieved by the discovery that the couple had pretermitted the ceremony and that he was saved the tedium and expense of a divorce suit, though he wondered why Mr. Duke with his meticulous book-keeping and contracts should be so loose where women were concerned, while he, so averse from parchments and figures, had a proper respect for the marriage-tie. Human nature was devilishly deep, he thought: no wonder a man got drowned if he tried to fathom himself.

But Jinny, though she now believed she had misunderstood the ducal ménage, was not without an instinctive distrust. "She didn't want to live in the caravan," she protested.

"No," he agreed, misapprehending the local idiom. "It was that pig-headed wire-puller who wanted it. Duke's the villain of the piece, abusing my darling's innocence and exploiting her artistic aspirations. He got round the poor girl, knowing her aunt had left her all her money. Cleo, my dear Jinny, is the niece of the famous Cleopatra, the Cairo Contortionist, after whom she was christened, and whose death a year or so ago eclipsed the gaiety of Astley's and Mr. Batty's new Hippodrome."

"Was she so beautiful?" asked Jinny, somewhat awed.

"I was in love with her myself in my youth," Mr. Flippance replied simply. "But though you could gossip with her round the coke-brazier at the back of the ring, she always made you feel that no man was worthy to chalk the soles of her tight-rope shoes. And her niece, as you have doubtless perceived, has the same grand manner."

"Then why did she keep company with Mr. Duke?"

Jinny returned to the sore spot, Mr. Flippance felt, like a buzzing bluebottle.

"If you don't believe me," he cried, "show me the little Dukes and Duchesses. Where are they? Produce 'em."

He looked at her fiercely—as demanding a rain of coroneted cherubs from the air.

The bold stroke put the climax to Jinny's obfuscation. Marriage without children was practically unknown on her round, though the children often died. "Don't you see he wanted to compromise her?" pursued Tony triumphantly, after giving the cherubs a reasonable time to materialize. "He thought she'd never dare break away with her money, and that he could spend her last farthing on boosting himself into the legitimate. He's all right with the marionettes—a dapster as you say here," Mr. Flippance admitted magnanimously. "But as an actor he could no more expect to please my public than to keep Cleo hidden in a bushel. He might throw up the sponge and go back to his fantoccini—but what career was that for Cleo? She broke with him on the nail—the partnership, I mean. And I ask you, ma," he wound up, with an appreciative sniff as Martha re-entered, not only with mushrooms but freshly fried bacon, "what woman of spirit could do otherwise?"

Mrs. Flynt beamed assent, and her apparent acquaintance with the facts contributed to lull Jinny's uneasiness. Surely the pious Martha would not connive at scandalous proceedings. Relieved, she sat silent; wondering—while Mr. Flippance did jovial justice to the encore dish—what the Duchess would think if she knew that she, Jinny, could have anticipated her in the rôle of the second Mrs. Flippance. And what would Polly have thought of her as a stepmother, she wondered still more whimsically. Perhaps between them they could have made a man of him. She had never seen his daughter over her cigar and milk or her sense of Polly as a pillar of respectability might have been shattered.

"And how is Miss Flippance?" she said.

His face changed suddenly—rain-clouds overgloomed the sun. His fork fell from his fingers. "You don't know what daughters are," he blubbered. "She's left me!"

"Left you?"

"Ask ma," he half sobbed. It was infinitely pathetic.

"Don't let it get cold again," Martha coaxed.

"I can't eat." He lit a cheroot abstractedly, and the old woman and the young girl followed his silent puffings with a yearning sympathy, while Nip begged, unheeded.

"Mad on marionettes is Polly," he said at last. "The moment I got rid of 'em, she packed up my things and was off."

"Stole your things?" cried the startled Jinny.

"No—no. She knew I should be moving on for the banns—Cleo likes a quiet place—so she left me tidy. That was her sole conception of her duty to her legal pa. But she had always looked upon me as a thing to be tidied—not a soul to be loved and cherished." He wiped an eye with the sleeve of his dressing-gown and asked brokenly for his brandy. Martha hurried to his bedroom.

"But perhaps your daughter'll come back," Jinny suggested soothingly.

"God forbid!" he cried. "I mean they'd be at it hammer and tongs. Perhaps Providence does all things for the best."

"But where has she gone?" Jinny's sympathy was now passing to Polly, as she began to grasp the true complexity of her exodus.

"To her grandmother in Cork, I expect." He blew a placid puff. "Did I never tell you my pa's real wife—the one he didn't live with, I mean—was originally the widow of a well-to-do cheesemonger? Polly always looked up her nominal granny when we played Ireland. She likes respectable people."

"Is that why she won't come to the wedding?" Jinny inquired cruelly, for Polly's refusal to countenance it again stirred up her doubts.

Mr. Flippance was angered afresh. "I tell you, my Cleopatra can hold up her head with the whitest cheesemonger's widow in the land. But it's hard," he said, reverting to pathos and flicking his cigar-ash mournfully into the just-dusted shoe, "to be left without a daughter at such a crisis. Think how she would have stage-managed everything—even bought the ring." The tragedy of his situation mastered him. "Forgive my emotion—I was always one to wear my heart on my sleeve." He wiped his eyes on it again. "Nobody will ever pack like Polly. Ah, thank you, ma," he said, as Martha reappeared with the brandy bottle. "Have you half a crown?" he added, pouring himself out a careless quota. "You see," he explained, setting down his glass dolefully, and tendering Martha's half-crown to the astonished Jinny, "though old pals desert one at the altar, Tony Flip doesn't forget his obligations."

"But what's it for?" Jinny took the coin tentatively.

"You lent me it when that wicked Duke demanded money on the contract."

"Oh, thank you!" Jinny was touched—a half-crown seemed as large as her cart-wheel nowadays. Half remorsefully she suggested that a far better bridesmaid would be the girl at Foxearth Farm.

He shook his head. "I've been into that. But there are—objections. It doesn't do, you see, for the super to be taller than the leading lady. Now you being shorter—"

"But if Miss Jones were to wear very low heels—"

"But that would only make Miss Purley look still taller," he said, puzzled.

"I mean Miss Purley to wear the low heels—she is a Miss Jones, too."

"What?"

"Blanche Jones is her name—she's only old Purley's stepdaughter."

He started up. "Then Mrs. Purley was formerly Mrs. Jones?"

"Yes."

"Hurrah!" He seized the surprised Martha by the waist and began waltzing with her, while Nip barked with excitement.

"Quiet, Nip! What's the matter?" cried Jinny, smiling.

"A relation at last! Don't you see that Mrs. Jones can give the bride away?"

"But she's not really a relation."

"All these Joneses are one large family," he said airily.

"But you don't need a relation," Martha pointed out. "A friend will do."

"Really? I must study the stage-directions—I mean," he corrected himself hastily, "yours may be different from the Church of England."

"But I know all the same, for we weren't allowed to marry in our own chapels, leastways not till after Willie was born."

"Well, anyhow, I'm sure Cleopatra would prefer a relation. Mrs. Jones is a Churchwoman, I hope. It's necessary, ma, you know," he apologized.

"Yes—her husband's a churchwarden," said Jinny.

"A churchwarden! Hurrah! Better and better. Then he shall give Cleo away." He bumped the beaming, breathless Martha round again.

"But he isn't even called Jones," Jinny reminded him.

"A husband takes over his wife's Jonesiness. Bless you, Jinny!" He seized her hand and dragged her likewise into the circular movement. "Now we go round the mulberry-bush, the mulberry-bush, the mulberry-bush—"

Caleb, coming past the door at this instant, stood spellbound. Had Mr. Flippance been really converted, and was it the joy of the New Jerusalem? Or had Martha now "moved on," and was this the new dancing sect of which one heard rumours?

Martha's caperings ceased at sight of him. "It's the wedding," she said somewhat shamefacedly. "I'm just going to pickle your walnuts, dear heart," she added sweetly. "And Jinny must be getting to her work, too."

At which delicate hint, Jinny, faintly flushing, rose to take her leave, and Nip, who had been whining his impatience, was already gambolling hysterically without, before she remembered she had forgotten the very purpose of her visit.

"Oh, by the way, Mr. Flippance," she said, as she followed Nip, "I suppose the wedding-gown is ordered."

"Wedding-gown!" he repeated. "You don't think Cleo has any need of wedding-gowns! Why the Lady Agnes dress—Act One—is the very prop. for the occasion, and brand new, for she had just got Duke to put on The Mistletoe Bough. Otherwise I should have been asking you for the address of that wonderful French friend of yours—the bearded lady, you know. But if you won't be a bridesmaid, you've got to come to the show—yes, and the wedding breakfast too—I won't take any refusal. It'll be at Foxearth Farm, and I'm ordering oceans of sweet champagne. Well, thank you a million times for finding Cleo a father. Good-bye, dear. God bless you!" He had shuffled without and now kissed his hand to the moving cart.

"What about a new wedding-gown for you?" Jinny called back. "A dressing-gown, I mean."

"Yumorist!" came his chuckled answer.

VIII

Though not unconscious of a subterranean hostility in Martha, which she put down to the new business rivalry, and though still perturbed about the Duchess, Jinny felt distinctly better for this visit, not to mention the half-crown, that now rare coin. She was still more heartened two days later when Bundock brought a letter from Mr. Flippance stating that, strange to say, Cleopatra did not find the Lady Agnes dress suitable. It would make her feel she was only playing at marrying, she said, and she was too respectful of holy matrimony to desecrate it by any suggestion of unreality: indeed she was already being fitted by the leading Chipstone artist. The dress was, however, turning out so dubiously that she would be glad if Jinny's French friend would call upon her at Foxearth Farm with a view to preparing a "double." As for Jinny being bridesmaid, he must reluctantly ask her to abandon the idea, as Cleopatra considered her too short.

"That's the Flippance fist," said Bundock, lingering to watch her read the letter, "scrawls all over the shop. I don't mind your answering by post," he added maliciously, "now I've got to go there so much. I often kill—he, he, he!—two frogs with one stone now. So you're to be bridesmaid, Tony tells me."

"Nothing of the sort," said Jinny, "and mind your own business."

"It is my business," he said in an aggrieved tone. "Didn't he ask me to be best man? As if in this age of reason I could take part in superstitious rites!"

"I don't see any superstition about marrying," said Jinny.

"I'm not so sure—tying a man to a woman like a dog to a barrel. But anyhow, why drag in heaven?"

"Because marriages are made there, I suppose," said Jinny.

"Stuff and nonsense! And then the rice and the old shoes they throw!"

"I saw you throw one when your sister got married."

"Maybe. But I didn't believe in it."

"Then why did you throw it?"

He hesitated a moment. "They say if you don't believe in it, it's even luckier than if you do."

Jinny laughed heartily.

"I'm not joking!" Bundock declared angrily.

"If you were, I shouldn't be laughing," said Jinny.

"Oh well, go to church!" Bundock retorted in disgust. "And I hope the beadle will give you an extra prod next Sunday."

"What do you mean?"

"Don't pretend. Everybody knows that church is a double torture—first the parson sends you to sleep with his sermon, and then the verger wakes you up with his rod."

Jinny laughed again.

"Don't tell me!" said Bundock. "My own father was forced to go—all the labourers on the estate, poor chaps, dead-sleepy after the week's work, and that rod used to puggle 'em about. No wonder dad chucked both squire and parson."

"It doesn't happen in Mr. Fallow's church," Jinny assured him.

"Because nobody goes!" And Bundock hurried off with this great last word, and Jinny saw his bag heaving with the mirthful movement of his shoulders.

Somewhat to Jinny's surprise, Miss Gentry from being Cleopatra's alternative dressmaker developed into her adorer, it appearing that the lady displayed not only proportions most pleasing to the technical eye—"just made for clothes," Miss Gentry put it—but a positive appetite for tracts. She loathed Dissent, it transpired, and to be married by a minister would seem to her little better than living in sin. A very paragon of propriety and an elegant pillar of the faith, Miss Cleopatra Jones, spinster, worshipped regularly with the churchwarden and his family in the wrong parish church. Miss Gentry, ravished by this combination of respectability and romance, did not once compel the fair client to attend upon her, travelling to Foxearth Farm instead in Jinny's cart. It was impossible for Jinny's doubts of Cleopatra's immaculacy to survive Miss Gentry's encomiums. While Miss Gentry ascended to the bedroom of her beautiful and still golden-haired client, posed in an atmosphere of old oak bedsteads and panelled linen presses, Jinny would sit with the second Mrs. Purley in her dairy—a cheerful, speckless room which enjoyed a specially spacious window, dairies being immune from the window-tax—while that bulkier edition of Blanche made cheeses and conversation. Mrs. Purley made conversation irrespective of her auditor, for she needed no collaborator: indeed a second party coming athwart this Niagara of monologue would have been swept aside like a straw.

As a great musician can take a few simple notes, and out of this theme evoke endless intricacies, enlargements, repetitions, echoes, duplications, parallelisms, and permutations, and then transform the whole into another key and give it you all over again, so out of a simple happening, like her feeding of a sick chicken, or her discovery that a hen had laid her clutch in the hedge, Mrs. Purley, without for a moment interrupting the milling of curd or the draining of whey, could improvise a fugal discourse that went ramifying and returning upon itself ad infinitum. It reminded Jinny of Kelcott Wood, where every day from three to five, on these September afternoons, hundreds of starlings, perched like bits of black coal on the mountain-ashes, kept up a ceaseless chattering, shrilling, clucking, querying, cackling.

But she soon ceased to hear Mrs. Purley, was even lulled by the cascade. Very familiar grew every pan, dipper, vat, tub, press, cheese-cloth, or straw-mat, while the one readable article she knew by heart. It was the inscription on a china mug, in which Mrs. Purley sometimes put milk, and it recorded the virtues of a black-haired, black-whiskered head painted thereon. "The Incorruptible Patriot. . . . The Undaunted Supporter of the People's Rights. . . . The Father of the Fatherless. . . . The Pride and Glory of his Country" . . . such were a few of the attributes ascribed, with a profuseness resembling Mrs. Purley's conversation, to a certain Henry Brougham, Esq., who, as Jinny learnt from Miss Gentry, was really and truly "a love," having defended Queen Caroline when Miss Gentry was a schoolgirl. Queens were as liable to ill-luck as herself, Jinny began to suspect, recalling that Egyptian asp, and she became a little anxious for Victoria, who now came to figure in her dreams, as defended against French fire-eaters by this black-avised man, with the protruding nose, retreating forehead, and weak chin. Somehow—it was unintelligible when she woke up, but quite clear in her dream—the defended Victoria was also herself, for was not Henry Brougham "The Father of the Fatherless"?

Adjoining the dairy was a room, lit from it—to avoid taxation—by a pane in the door. Jinny sometimes had an uneasy sense that Blanche was inspecting her through that pane. Otherwise she hardly ever encountered the vespacide, who betrayed indeed no sense of rivalry, for the relations between Will and the little Carrier were unknown, and Blanche would, in any case, have considered so humble a personage negligible or at least nippable.

For if this handsome creature was—as she had struck Jinny-a shade overripe, it was not for lack of volunteer pluckers, and the mutability which Mr. Giles Purley had gently derided in his son had been even more marked in his stepdaughter. Fortunately Will was unaware of the episodes that had preceded his return to England. And not only did he regard himself as the first male that had ever squeezed that fair hand, but, untaught by its prowess as a wasp-killer, he believed her a passive victim to his own compelling charm. And the apparent perfection of Blanche's surrender was the more grateful to him after the granite he had kept striking in Jinny. But the mobility which had hitherto marked Miss Blanche's affections was now manifesting itself in a novel shape, for like Miss Gentry, she had come under the spell of Cleopatra, though a very different Cleopatra from the ardent Churchwoman who revealed herself to the dressmaker. The Cleopatra who magnetized the cheese-maker's daughter, and who, carelessly abetted by Mr. Flippance's sketchy promises, filled the ignorant girl with dramatic and palpitating ambitions, was a queen of the footlights, an inspirer of romantic passions, and in her unguarded moments—as when you sat on her bed at midnight with her hair down—a teller of strange Bohemian stories, a citer of perturbing Sapphic songs, the melodies of which she could even whistle. What wonder if Mrs. Hemans—Blanche's favourite poet hitherto—began to pall! She had been proud enough of her culture, leaving, as she felt it did, the parental perspectives far behind her; but now boundless horizons seemed opening up before her, and the London Journal which Cleopatra swallowed with her meals seemed to Blanche to contain nothing so alluring as Cleopatra's own career.

It was by quite accidentally overhearing a remark of Blanche's, and not by dint of Mr. Flippance's repeated invitation, that Jinny was finally strung up to attend the great wedding. The probability that Will and Blanche would be at the feast was a drawback that prevailed over the lure of a good square meal, and even over the glamour of that mysterious nectar—champagne. But when she heard Blanche instruct her mother that she would certainly not have to lay a place for "that common carrier," in a flame that might almost have consumed her letter-paper, Jinny wrote her acceptance to Mr. Flippance, and expended his half-crown, which she had laid by for a rainy day, on a wedding present which would do him good—a Bible, to wit.

In prevision of the great day she left off wearing her best gown, cleaned it, and by the aid of Miss Gentry and a bit of lace gave it a new turn. After the wedding it must, alas, be pawned! Jinny, though she had hitherto entered the pawnshop only to pledge or redeem things for her customers, had schooled herself to the inevitable. So had Mr. Flippance, whose idea of a best man had now sunk to Barnaby. But he was used to handling unpromising performers, he said, though he regretted the absence of a dress rehearsal, more especially for Mrs. Purley, who, having been induced to mother Cleopatra (nothing would induce Mr. Purley to father her), was unlikely, he feared, to confine herself to a simple "I do." That was not, he groaned drolly, her idea of a speaking part. He deplored, too, that there were not enough bells or bell-ringers in the Little Bradmarsh church to ring an elaborate joy-peal, as Cleopatra was so anxious to have every property and accessory of holy matrimony complete. It was for this reason, doubtless, that Miss Gentry, after reducing the rival dress to a rag, ultimately emerged as the bridesmaid.

IX

For the convenience of Foxearth Farm, as well as of Will, who, though a bit sulky about his mother's waiting on the Showman, was too entangled with Miss Purley to refuse to grace the festal board, the ceremony had been fixed for a Saturday at ten, and on that morning Jinny had meant to rise with the sun, so as to do the bulk of her day's chares in advance. What was her dismay, therefore, to open blinking eyes on her grandfather standing over her pseudo-bed in his best Sunday smock, whip in hand, and to hear through her wide-flung casement Methusalem neighing outside and the cart creaking!

"Am I late?" she gasped, sitting up. Then she became aware of a beautiful blue moonlight filling the room with glory, and of a lambent loveliness spreading right up to the stars sprinkled over her slit of sky.

"'Tis your wedding-day, dearie," said the ghostly figure of the Gaffer, and she now perceived there were wedding favours on his whip, evidently taken from Methusalem's May Day ribbons, which he must have hunted out of the "glory-hole" where odds and ends were kept.

Bitterly she regretted having excited his brain by informing him of her programme. He was evidently prepared to drive her to the ceremony.

"But it's too early," she temporized.

"Ye've got to be there for breakfus, you said, dearie," he reminded her.

"No, no," she explained. "The wedding breakfast with fashionable folk is only a sort of bever or elevener at earliest."

He chuckled. "Ye're gooin' to be rich and fashionable—won't it wex that jackanips! Oi suspicioned 'twas you he war arter the fust time he come gawmin' to the stable. Ye can't deceive Daniel Quarles. On your hands and knees, ye pirate thief!" He cracked his whip fiercely. "Up ye git, Jinny, ye've got to titivate yerself. Oi've put the water in your basin."

"But Gran'fer," she said, acutely distressed, "it's not my wedding."

"Not your wedding!"

"Of course not."

"Then whose wedding be it?" he demanded angrily. "'Tain't mine, seein' as Oi'm too poor to keep Annie though she's riddy of her rascal at last." He seized her wrists and shook her. "Why did you lie to me and make a fool o' me?"

So this was why Gran'fer had embraced her so effusively last night when she avowed her programme for the morrow; this was why he had given her blessings in lieu of the expected reproaches for her projected absence; this was why he had gone up to bed humming his long-silent song: "Oi'm seventeen come Sunday."

It was a mistake, she felt now, to have stayed at home for his sake on the Friday, changing the immemorial day of absence. He had been strange all day, without grasping what was the cause of his unrest, and Nip's parallel uneasiness had reacted upon him. It was not, however, till she had incautiously remarked that Methusalem too was off his feed, that he cried out in horror that she had forgotten to go on her rounds. Smilingly she assured him she had not forgotten: indeed the void in her whole being occasioned by the loss of Mother Gander's gratis meal had been a gnawing reminder since midday. But imagining—and not indeed untruly—that her work was gone, he had burst into imprecations on "the pirate thief."

As she sat up now on her mattress, helpless in her grief, her mind raced feverishly through the episode, recalling every word of the dialogue, unravelling his senile misapprehension; half wilful it seemed to her now, in his eagerness to clutch at happier times.

"It's nothing to do with the coach competition, Gran'fer. It's only because I've got to be out to-morrow for a wedding!"

"A wedding! She ain't marrying agen?"

"Who?"

"Annie."

"Annie? Which Annie?"

"There's onny one Annie. 'Lijah's mother."

"Old Mrs. Skindle! What an idea! It's a friend of mine, a gentleman you've never seen."

At this point she had had, she remembered, the fatal idea of showing him her furbished-up frock to soothe him, for he was trembling all over.

"Would you like to see what I'm going to wear?"

She understood now the new light that had shot into his eye as he touched the lace trimming.

"Similar-same to what your Great-Aunt Susannah wore the day she married that doddy little Dap! Ye ain't a-gooin' to make a fool o' yerself similar-same. Who's the man?" he had demanded fiercely.

"You don't know him, I told you—it's a Mr. Flippance!"

A beautiful peace had come over the convulsed face. "Flippance! Ain't that the gent what's come to live in Frog Farm? That's a fust-class toff, no mistake. Uncle Lilliwhyte should be tellin' me, when he come with the watercress on Tuesday, as Mr. Flippance pays a pound a week for hisself alone!"

That was the point at which her grandfather had kissed her with effusion, crying: "Ye'll be in clover, dearie!" while she, licking her chaps at the thought of the morrow's banquet, had playfully answered that there would certainly be "a mort to eat." The prospect set him clucking gleefully.

"Spite o' that rapscallion!" he had chuckled, enlarging thereupon to her on the way the Lord protects His righteous subjects, and enlivening his discourse with adjurations to "the pirate thief" to take to his hands and knees. Had followed reproaches for hiding the news from him, reproaches to Mr. Flippance for not calling on him, not even inviting him to the wedding: soothing explanations from her that Mr. Flippance knew he was too poorly to go that far; assurances she would be back as early as possible.

She ought to have understood his delusion or self-delusion, she thought, when he had clung to her in a sudden panic.

"Then ye will come back—ye ain't leavin' me to starve! Ye won't let that jackanips starve me out?"

And when she had reassured him, and caressed him, even promised to bring him something tasty from the wedding breakfast, he had gripped her harder than ever—she could still feel his bony fingers on her wrist—but of course they actually were on her wrists as she sat there now against her pillow—"ye'll live here with me—same as afore!"

"Why ever shouldn't I?" she had answered in her innocence. "We'll always live with you—Methusalem, Nip, all of us." What unlucky impulse of affection or reassurance had made her stoop down to kiss the dog in his basket—all her being burnt with shame at the remembrance of her grandfather's reply, though at the time it had touched her to tears.

"God bless ye, Jinny. Oi know this ain't a proper bedroom for you, but Oi'll sleep here if you like, and do you and he move up to mine."

She had put by the offer gently. "Nonsense, Gran'fer. You can't shift at your age—or Nip either."

"Oi bain't so old as Sidrach," he had retorted, not without resentment, "and Oi doubt he ain't left off bein' a rollin' stone. And Oi reckon Oi can fit into that chest of drawers better than when Oi was bonkka."

But the shrivelled form, with the hollow cheeks, flaming eyes, and snowy beard, was still shaking her angrily, and her sense of his pathos vanished in a sick fear, not so much for herself, though his fingers seemed formidably sinister, as for his aged brain under this disappointment. "Why did you say 'twas your wedding morn?"

The Dutch clock, providentially striking three, offered a fresh chance of temporizing.

"There, Gran'fer! Can't be my wedding morn yet, only three o'clock!"

He let go her hands. "Ain't ye ashamed to have fun with your Gran'fer?" he asked, vastly relieved. "But it's a middlin' long drive to Chipstone before breakfus."

"It's not at Chipstone—the wedding's at Little Bradmarsh."

"Oh!" he said blankly.

"So there's lots of time, Gran'fer, and you can go back to bed."

"Not me! Do, Oi mightn't wake in time agen."

"I'll wake you—but I'll be fit for nothing in the morning, if I don't go to sleep now."

"The day Oi was married," he chuckled, "Oi never offered to sleep the noight afore—ne yet the noight arter! He, he!"

"Go away, Gran'fer!" she begged frantically. "Let me go to sleep."

"Ay, ay, goo to sleep, my little mavis. Nobody shan't touch ye. What a pity we ate up that wedding-cake! But Oi had to cut a shiver to stop his boggin' and crakin', hadn't Oi, dearie?"

"Quite right. Better eat wedding-cake than humble-pie!" she jested desperately.

"Ef he comes sniffin' around arter you're married, Oi'll snap him in two like this whip!"

"Don't break my whip!" She clutched at the beribboned butt.

"That's my whip, Jinny! Let that go!"

"Well, go to bed then!" With a happy thought, she lit the tallow candle on her bedside chair and tendered it to him. It operated as mechanically upon his instinctive habits as she had hoped.

"Good night, dearie," he said, and very soon she heard him undressing as usual, and his snore came with welcome rapidity. Then she sprang out of bed, pulled on some clothes, and ran out to release the angry and mystified Methusalem from the shafts and to receive his nuzzled forgiveness in the stable. But when she got back to bed, sleep long refused to come; the sense of her tragic situation was overwhelming. Even the great peace of the moonlit night could not soak into her. It was impossible to go to the wedding now, she felt. When at last sleep came, she was again incomprehensibly Queen Victoria hemmed in by foes, and protected only by "The Father of the Fatherless" with his black whiskers. She awoke about dawn, unrefreshed and hungry, but a cold sponging from the basin her grandfather had prepared enabled her to cope with the labours of the day. She looked forward with apprehension to the scene with the old man when he should realize that the grand match was indeed off, but she could think of nothing better than going about in her dirtiest apron to keep his mind off the subject. The precaution proved unnecessary. He slept so late and so heavily—as if a weight was off his mind—that when he at last awoke he seemed to have slept the delusion off, as though it were something too recent to remain in his memory. As for the scene in the small hours, that had apparently left no impress at all upon his brain. In fact, so jocose and natural was he at breakfast, which she purposely made prodigal for him, that the optimism of the morning sun, which came streaming in, almost banished her own memory of it too: it seemed as much a nightmare as her desperate struggle against the foes of Victoria-Jinny. The lure of the wedding jaunt revived, and the thought of the domestic economy she would be achieving thereby, made her sparing of her own breakfast. She had a bad moment, however, when her grandfather suddenly caught sight of the horseless cart outside.

"Stop thief!" he cried, jumping up agitatedly.

Jinny was vexed with herself. To have left that reminder of the grotesque episode!

"It's that 'Lijah!" he shrieked. "He's stole Methusalem."

"Hush, Gran'fer!" she warned him. "Suppose anybody heard you!"

But he ran out towards the Common and she after him. His tottering limbs seemed galvanized.

"My horse is all right," she gasped, catching him up in a few rods. "I was too tired yesterday to put my cart away, that's all."

He turned and glared suspiciously at her. "That's my hoss—and my cart, too! Can't you read the name—'Daniel Quarles, Carrier.' But ye won't never let me put no padlock on my stable!"

"Your horse is there safe—come and see!"

He allowed himself to be led to the soothing spectacle.

"But Oi'll put a padlock at once, same as in my barn," he said firmly. "Don't, that rascal 'Lijah will grab him without tippin' a farden!"

X

The overlooked cart proved a blessing, not a calamity, for the operation of padlocking the stable-door before the horse was stolen so absorbed the Gaffer that Jinny found it possible, after all, to don her finery and slip off to the wedding unseen even of Nip, who was supervising the new measures for Methusalem's safety. Curiosity to see Miss Gentry's creation in action had combined with the pangs of appetite and her acceptance of the invitation to make temptation irresistible, and she calculated that she could be back by noon, and that, pottering over his vegetable patch or his Bible, the old man would scarcely notice her absence.

When she reached the church, she found the coach stationed outside, and though the liveried guard was lacking to-day, the black horses looked handsomer than ever with their red wedding-favours, while the pea-green polish of the vehicle reduced her to a worm-like humility at the thought of the impossibility of her cart taking part in to-day's display. Evidently Will had brought the bridegroom from Frog Farm. Out of the corner of her eye she espied Will himself, sunning himself on his box, and her heart thumped, though all she was conscious of was the insolent incongruity of his pipe with the occasion, the edifice, his new frock-coat, and the posy in its buttonhole. Fearing she was late, she hurried into the church. But nothing was going on, though the size of the congregation—far larger than usual—was an exciting surprise. There was no sign of any of the wedding-party, not even Mr. Flippance, and after imperceptibly saluting her Angel-Mother, she sank back into a rear pew, half pleased to have missed nothing, half uneasy lest there be a delay. Turning over a Prayer Book in search of the Wedding Service, she came for the first time, and not without surprise, on the Fifth of November Thanksgiving "for the happy deliverance of King James I and the Three Estates of England from the most traitorous and bloody-intended massacre by Gunpowder: And also for the happy Arrival of King William on this Day, for the Deliverance of our Church and Nation." King William's arrival struck her as providential but confusing—for though he had apparently detected the Popish barrels in the nick of time, how came there to be two kings at once? Suddenly she was aware, by some tingling telegraphy, that the bride and bridesmaid had arrived outside in a grand open carriage. Mr. Fallow in his surplice came in at the clerk's intimation and took up his position at the altar rails, the musicians struck up "The Voice that Breathed o'er Eden," and then there was a sudden faltering, and a whispering took place 'twixt parson and clerk, and Mr. Fallow was swallowed again by his vestry, while the clerk disappeared through the church door. It was realized that Mr. Flippance was not in the church, and it was understood that the bride's face was being saved in the vestry, where, however, as time passed, the agitated congregation divined hysterics.

Jinny—thinking of her neglected grandfather—was what he called "on canterhooks." Had Mr. Flippance not then come in the coach, had he been carelessly left in bed as usual? Catching her Angel-Mother's eye, she received a distinct injunction to go out in search of him, but she was too shy to move in the presence of all those people, though she had a vision of herself frantically harnessing Methusalem and carting the bridegroom to church in his dressing-gown—would carpet slippers be an impediment to matrimony, she wondered. Mr. Fallow came in again, looking so worried that she recalled an ecclesiastical experience he had related to her: how one of his parishioners, nowadays a notorious Hot Gospeller, had "found religion" on the very verge of setting out to be married, and had passed so much time on his knees, absorbed in the newly felt truth, that it was only through his friend the bell-ringer stopping the church clock that he was married by noon; if indeed—a doubt which ever after weighed on Mr. Fallow—he was legally married at all. What if at this solemn moment of his life Mr. Flippance should similarly find religion! She devoutly hoped the discovery would be at least delayed till he was safely married. Good heavens! perhaps the Bible she had given him was in fault! Perhaps she was responsible for his rapt remissness. Disregarding the congregation's eyes, she went boldly into the vestry.

Here, sure enough, she found the heroine of the day supported by a trio of ladies. The outstanding absence of Mr. Flippance left Jinny but a phantasmagoric sense of a bride, still composed indeed, but so ghastly that despite her glamour of veil-folds and orange-blossom she scarcely looked golden-haired; of a bridesmaid hardly recognizable as Miss Gentry, for the opposite reason that it was she with her swarthy splendour, opulent bosom, and glory of silk and flowers who seemed the Cleopatra; of a Blanche so appallingly queenly in her creamier fashion under the art of the rival dressmaker, that her own cleaned gown seemed but to emphasize her shabbiness and dowdiness. Acoustically the voice of Mrs. Purley expatiating on the situation was the dominant note, but through and beneath the cascade Jinny was aware of Miss Gentry explaining to the bride that the horses which had brought the bridegroom were not responsible for his disappearance. Not unpropitious, but of the finest augury were these sable animals, omens going by contraries. So they had brought Mr. Flippance!

They were tossing their bepranked heads, Jinny found, and champing their bits, as if sharing in the human unrest. Will was no longer smoking placidly on his box, but in agitated parley with Barnaby and his father. She heard the inn suggested, and saw the Purleys posting towards it. She herself ran round to the tower, fantastically figuring Mr. Flippance on his knees on the belfry floor amid the ropes and the cobwebs, but even the one bell-ringer seemed to have sallied in search of the bridegroom, or at least of the inn.

The churchyard was large and rambling and thickly populated—pathetic proof there had been life in the church once—and it was in a sequestered corner behind a tall monument that Jinny with a great upleap of the heart at last espied the object of her quest, though he seemed even more unreal than Miss Gentry in his narrow-brimmed top-hat, satin stock with horseshoe pin, and swallowtail coat, while his face was as white as his waistcoat.

"What are you doing?" came involuntarily to her lips.

"Reading the tombstones," he said wistfully. "So peaceful!"

"But they're waiting for you!"

"They're waiting for everybody. That's the joke of it all."

"I don't mean the gravestones."

"Look! There's a French inscription. And that name must be Flemish, see!"

"I haven't time!"

"Why, what have you got to do?"

"I mean, you haven't got time. It's your wedding!"

"Don't rub it in! What long grass! So we go to grass—all of us. Thanks for your Bible, by the way!"

So her apprehensions had been right. It was religion that was bemusing him.

"So glad you like it. Come along!" she said in rousing accents.

"All flesh is grass," he maundered on. "And rank grass at that!"

"It's only thick here because they can't mow this bit," she explained. "Too many tombs!" She plucked at his sleeve.

"So it's hay we run to!" he said, disregarding her "O Lord! Mr. Fallow's tithes, I suppose."

"Well, why waste good hay? He's waiting for you."

"Well, he's got plenty of time by all accounts."

"I mean, she's waiting," she cried, in distress.

"Is she there already? Look at that bird cracking its snail on the gravestone."

"It's an early bird—you'll be late."

"Don't worry. Tony Flip never missed his cue yet. Funny, isn't it, how it all comes right at night—especially with Polly there! Perhaps she'll come, if we give her a little time."

"But have you invited her? Does she know?"

"If she don't, it's not for want of telegrams to every possible address."

"But she may be in Cork, you said. You can't keep the bride waiting."

"She shouldn't have come so early—it's the first time I've known her punctual. The early bird catches the snail, eh?"

"But it's half-past ten! And there's a crowd too—I don't know where they all come from. Come along!"

"One can't consider the supers!"

"Well, consider me then. I've got to get back to Gran'fer!"

"The true artist always has stage-fright, Jinny. Give me a moment. I'll be on soon."

"All right." She was vastly relieved. "Have you got the ring?"

"Tony Flip never forgets a property. See!" And whisking it suddenly out of his waistcoat pocket, he seized her left hand and slipped it on her gloved wedding-finger. "That's where it ought to be, Jinny!"

She pulled it off, outraged, and flung it from her.

"On your wedding day, too!" she cried.

"Now it's lost," he said cheerfully, "and the bearded bridesmaid will have to go home with the unblushing bride."

"You ought to have given it to Barnaby," she said.

Anxious and remorseful, she went on her knees, groping feverishly in the long grass. "On your hands and knees" kept sounding irrelevantly in her brain. Mr. Flippance watched her like a neutral. "I'd forgotten that the woman runs away with the piece," he explained to her distracted ear. "I thought marriage was a show with two principals. But if there's got to be a leading lady, why not stick to Polly?"

"You should have thought of that before," she murmured.

"Correct as Polonius, Jinny. Even when I get the theatre, it'll only be hell over again. Why couldn't I stick to the marionettes? I charge thee fling away ambition, Jinny—by that sin fell the angels. But you've only flung away my ring."

"Here it is!" She pounced joyfully.

"Just my luck!" He took it ruefully.

"I thought you said she was so pure and wonderful!" she reminded him.

He winced. "That wouldn't prevent her bullying me," he replied somewhat lamely.

"What about the taming of the shrew?" she asked.

"By Jove! You're right, Jinny! Petruchio's the game! Whips and scorpions, what?" His face took on a little of its old colour. "It's getting up so early that has upset me. After all, Jinny, a lovely woman who loves you and puts all her money on you isn't to be picked up every day."

"Of course not. Anyhow it's too late to change now."

"Don't say that! As if I didn't want to change before there was anything to change—oh, you know what I mean."

"It's too late now!" she repeated firmly. She stood over him, a stern-faced little monitor of duty. "Come along!"

"Go ahead—the rose-wreathed victim will be at the altar."

They moved on a little. He paused as with sudden hopefulness. "You don't happen to know if there's a great oak chest with a spring lock in Foxearth Farm?"

"How should I know?" she murmured, apprehensive now for his reason.

He sighed. "Well, never mind—it'll all be all right at night. And what's it all for, anyhow? 'Wife of the above,'" he read out weirdly. "How they cling on!"

But Jinny had gone off into a reverie of her own. The tombstone formula he had recited struck a long-buried memory, and in a flash she saw again a quiet graveyard and a stone behind a tumbledown tower, and Commander Dap's black-gloved forefinger tracing out her mother's epitaph to a strange solemn little girl. All the wonder and glamour of childhood was in that flash, all the strangeness of life and time, and her eyes filled with tears. When the mist cleared away, Mr. Flippance was gone. She ran frantically around among the tombs like a sheep-dog till at length the sound of Mr. Fallow's ecclesiastical voice floated out to her, and hurrying back into the church, she felt foolish and tranquillized to find the service well forward.

XI

Jinny had misread Mr. Fallow's look: it was not fear of dragging on beyond the legal hour—noon was still too remote—but impatience at being kept away from his antiquarian lore by such trifles as matrimony, especially matrimony which was no longer, as in pre-Reformation days, preceded by the Holy Communion and symbolic of the union of Christ and His Church. Had there been a care-cloth to be thrown over the couples' heads, such as existed in Essex churches in 1550, even matrimony might have interested him. But as it was, his thoughts ran on old cheeses. He had been comparing his Latin edition of Camden's "Britannia" (1590) with the two-volume folio translation, a century later, by a worthy bishop, and was half scandalized, half excited, to find that the translator had introduced a wealth of new matter. Incidentally Mr. Fallow had learned the Hundred was celebrated for its huge cheeses—insitatæ magnitudinis—of ewes' milk, and that to make them the men milked the ewes like women elsewhere. And these huge cheeses were consumed not only in England, but exported—ad saturandos agrestes et opifices—"to satisfie the coarse stomachs of husbandmen and labourers," as the bishop put it. When had this manufacture of giant cheeses from ewes' milk died out in Essex? Mr. Fallow had already seized the opportunity of interrogating Mrs. Purley, whose reputation as a cheesemaker had reached him. But appalled by the voluminousness of her ignorance, he had taken sanctuary in his church and was still brooding over the problem as his lips framed the more trivial interrogatories of the ceremony.

For Jinny, however, it was a thrilling moment when Mr. Fallow lackadaisically called upon the couple "as ye will answer at the dreadful Day of Judgment" to avow if they knew any impediment to their lawful union. That in face of so formidable a threat neither came out with "Mr. Duke," though she still half expected him to pop up in person from the void, was for her sweet stupidity the final proof of the bride's immaculacy. And the whole service she thought beautiful and moving, having missed the gross beginning thereof. She was startled to hear the bridegroom addressed by Mr. Fallow as Anthony, and the bride with equal familiarity as Bianca Cleopatra. Otherwise the ceremonial seemed far too highflown for this terrestrial twain, though somehow not at all transcending the relationship in which her own soul could stand towards its spiritual comrade. But the replies of the three principals came all in unexpected wise. Mr. Flippance's "I will" was so ready and ringing, and his countenance so rosy, that Jinny wondered which was the actor—the Flippance of the churchyard or the Flippance of the church. The ex-Duchess, on the other hand, still pallid, faltered her affirmation almost in a whisper, at any rate it was not so loud as his comment: "I've told you always to speak sharp on your cue." Certainly no husband could ever have asserted himself at an earlier moment—was he perhaps already following Jinny's hint, or was it only the stage-manager responding mechanically to stimulus? As for Mrs. Purley, she showed even more stage-fright, her "I do" failing even as a gesture, and having to be prompted. "Too small a speaking part for her," commented Tony later, with a twinkle.

When everything was over and the register signed and Barnaby, breaking down under the weight of his financial duties, had wished the bride many happy returns—a felicitation only dispelled by his father saluting her as "Mrs. Flippance"—that now reassured lady, sweeping regally to her carriage, her train over one arm and her husband over the other—smiled at the admiring avenue of villagers and small boys as though they had thrown her the bouquet she held. When Mr. Flippance, gay and debonair, had handed Mrs. Flippance, looking golden-haired again, into their barouche, and been driven off with the hood up and his beautiful doll beside him, Jinny perceived Will handing the gorgeously gowned Blanche with parallel ceremoniousness into the coach, where the transmogrified Miss Gentry was already installed behind the bulwark of her great bouquet. And then Jinny became aware of Barnaby hovering shyly between her and the trap which held his parents, and indicating dumbly that the niche vacated by his sister was now for her. She had a sudden feeling that they did not want her in the coach beside those grand gowns hunched out with starched petticoats. As if she would have set foot in it! No, not for all the gowns in the world! But they were right, she thought bitterly—what had she to do with all this grandeur and happiness? The honeymoon was even to be in Boulogne, she had gathered. And she heard some force, welling up from the dark depths of herself, cry to Barnaby: "I can't come—I'm so sorry. But Gran'fer was upset in the night. Please excuse me to Mr. Flippance."

At this the bitterness passed from her soul to poor Barnaby's. Everybody was pairing off: the Flippances, his parents, Will and his sister: there was nobody left for him but Miss Gentry.

"But there'll be oysters as well as dumplings," he pleaded. "Will brought them from Colchester."

Jinny's famished interior—in making such a skimpy breakfast it had counted on the wedding meal—seconded his plea desperately. But the mention of Will was fatal. As a hermit's sick fantasy conjures up the temptation he knows he will resist, so Jinny saw yearningly, vividly, but hopelessly, the spread banquet, the dumplings soused in gravy, the brown bread and butter for the oysters, the juicy meats, the mysterious champagne-bottles, the sunny napery, the laughing festival faces, and, above all, the curly aureole of Will's hair.

"I'm sorry," she repeated veraciously.

In a panic the youth ran after the receding barouche. "Jinny won't come," he gasped.

"Don't stop, coachman," said Mrs. Flippance sharply.

"Tell her," called back Mr. Flippance, "she must—or I'll never ask her to my wedding again!"

Poor Barnaby tore back to the coach. "I say, Miss Gentry, you're a friend of Jinny's—do make her come."

"A friend of Jinny's!" It was an even unluckier remark than the reference to Will. A patron, an educator, an interpreter of herbs and planets, gracious and kindly, who might even—in private—admit the little Carrier to confidences and Pythian inspirations, yes. But a friend? How came Mr. Flippance to commit such a faux pas as to bring a carrier into equality with her and Blanche? Why had not the adorable Cleopatra been firmer with the man? "I can't order her to come," she reminded Barnaby majestically. "It's not like for a parcel."

As the horses tossed their wedding-favours and the coach jingled off with its fashionable burden, even the trap moving on under the stimulus of Mrs. Purley's rhetoric, the whole scene became a blur to Jinny, and standing there by the old pillion-steps, she felt herself dwindled into a little aching heart alone in a measureless misery. How tragic to be cut off from all this gay eating and drinking! There was almost a voluptuousness in the very poignancy of her self-mutilation. What a blessing we all do run to hay, she brooded, in a warm flood of self-pity.

But if Jinny thus saw the wedding-guests through a blur of self-torturing bitterness, their feast did not begin as merrily as she beheld it, despite that Mrs. Purley, as soon as she had exchanged her bonnet-cap with the net quilting for a home cap, served up unexpected glasses of gin. Anthony, no less than Barnaby, was upset by Jinny's absence, and Cleopatra resented this fuss over a super. But still more disgruntled by the gap at the table was, odd to say, Will. For his soul had not been so placid as his pipe. The glimpses he had caught of Jinny were perturbing. Overpowering as were the presences of the bride and Blanche, or rather, precisely because they were overpowering, they struck him as artificial by the side of this little wild rose with her woodland flavour, and the memory of their afternoon in the ash-grove came up glowing, touched as with the enchantment of its bluebells. Blanche, for her part, was peevish at Will's taciturnity. Miss Gentry, still rankling under Barnaby's suspicion that she was the Carrier's bosom friend, was particularly down upon that youth's naïve attempt to confine the conversation to Jinny, though it confirmed her suspicion of the state of things between those two. Mr.

Purley in his turn had been dismayed by Blanche's fineries: the young generation forgot that their fathers were only farmers compelled to take lodgers in bad seasons. Thus it was left to Mrs. Purley to sustain almost the whole burden of conversation. But her preoccupation with her little serving-maid and the kitchen, plus her uneasiness at eating in this grand room away from her hanging hams and onions, interposed intervals of silence even in her prattle, and the theme of her facetious variations—her fear in church that the bridegroom had bolted—did not add to the general cheeriness. The old wainscoted parlour, with its rough oak beams across the ceiling, had seldom heard oysters swallowed with gloomier gulps.

Fortunately the pop of the sweet champagne brought a note of excited gaiety into the funereal air, and glass-clinking and looking to one another and catching one another's eye were soon the order of the early-Victorian day. Mr. Flippance, acknowledging the toast of the bride and bridegroom, did not fail to thank Mr. and Mrs. Purley for the precious treasure they had solemnly entrusted to his unworthy hands, a being whose beauty equalled her brains, and whose virtue her genius. Mr. Purley deprecatingly murmured "Don't mention it," meaning of course his share in the production of this prodigy, but Mrs. Purley, fresh from her church rôle, began to feel that she had dandled Cleopatra in her arms. In replying for himself and his "good wife"—for the age assumed that Mrs. Purley could not speak—Mr. Purley could not wish the newly married couple anything better than to be as happy as they had been. "Literally 'a good wife,' eh?" interlarded Tony genially. "None better," asseverated Mr. Purley. "I'm close, but she's nippy." "You're thinking of Blanche," Barnaby called out gaily, through the laughter. "I don't say as your mother's nippy in words," Mr. Purley corrected, with a twinkle. He went on to wish as much happiness to all the unmarried people present, at which Miss Gentry giggled and markedly avoided Barnaby's eye; while Will, reconciled to fate several glasses ago, squeezed Blanche's hand under the table. Even when Mr. Purley, becoming a little broad, referred to the time when his "good wife" had first ventured into "The Hurdle-Maker's Arms," Miss Gentry joined in the hilarity. Her passion for the church-going Cleopatra had convinced her that the stage was not necessarily of the devil—The Mistletoe Bough, she had found, was only the same story that had been written as a poem ("Ginevra") by a Mr. Rogers, who, she had gathered, was a most respectable banker, and she was looking forward to her Mistress-ship of the Robes at the coming Theatre Royal, and even to witnessing her darling's debut as Lady Agnes from the front. Several hysterical embraces had already passed between her and the bride—somewhat to Blanche's jealousy—and all things swam before her in a rosy mist as she now pulled a cracker with Mr. Purley and read unblushingly:

"When glass meets glass and Friendship quaffs,
From lip to lip 'tis Love that laughs!"

a motto which caused the hurdle-maker to remark that it was lucky his "good wife" had left the room.

That loquacious lady had fallen strangely silent. The wine which had loosened all the other tongues seemed to have constricted hers. Perhaps it was merely the already mentioned preoccupation with her pies or other dishes still in the oven. Or perhaps it was the encounter for the first time in her life with a great rival tongue. It consorted with this latter hypothesis that she could be heard babbling now from her kitchen like a cricket on the hearth, and her elaboration of a temperature theme came distractingly across the larger horizons of Mr. Flippance's discourse, playing havoc with his account of Macready's Farewell at Drury Lane that March, and obscuring the moral of the vacant succession. Charles Kean? Pooh! Not a patch on his father. Had they seen him in Dion Boucicault's new play at the Princess's, Love in a Maze? No? Then before voting for Charles Kean he would advise them to go—or, rather, not to go. He had never denied the merits of the manager of Sadler's Wells especially as Sir Pertinax

Macsycophant, though he knew his young friend Willie preferred Mr. Phelps in Othello. "I say whom the mantle fits, let him wear it," summed up Mr. Flippance oracularly, and launched into an exposition of how he would run "The National Theatre." No Miss Mitford tragedies for him with Macreadys at thirty pounds a week, still less Charles Kean Hamlets at fifty pounds a night, but real plays of the day—he did not mean the sort of things they did at the Surrey, which were no truer to life than the repertory of the marionettes, but why not, say, the Chartist movement and the forbidden demonstration on Kennington Common? Or let Mr. Sheridan Knowles, instead of talking his Baptist theology at Exeter Hall, write a "No Popery" play, with Cardinal Wiseman as the villain. (Hear, hear! from Miss Gentry.) Of course there was the danger the censor would quash such plays as he had quashed even Miss Mitford's Charles the First, but then he, Mr. Flippance, knew old John Kemble, and would undertake to persuade him that times had changed.

Mrs. Flippance, who had displayed some restiveness under the long appraisal of male talent, displayed yet more when Mr. Flippance was now provoked to rapturous boyish memories of the censor's sister, Mrs. Siddons. But Blanche and Barnaby listened so spellbound that they ceased finally to hear their mother's inborne monologue at all.

It was at this literally dramatic moment that Bundock appeared at the banquet with the explanation that nobody would answer his knocking, and tendered the bridegroom a pink envelope which he had benevolently brought on from Frog Farm on his homeward journey. Miss Gentry, unused to these bomb-shells, uttered a shriek, which more than ever riveted the postman's eyes on her flamboyant efflorescence.

"Steady! Steady!" said Tony, opening the telegram with unfaltering fingers. "Take some more fizz. And give brother Bundock a glass."

He read the fateful message, and the anxious watchers saw strange thoughts and feelings passing in lines across his forehead, and in waves across the folds of his flabby clean-shaven jowl. Then his emotions all coalesced and crashed into laughter, noisy, but not devoid of grimness. "Listen to this!" he cried. "'Sincere condolences. Married Polly this morning. Duke.'"

Mrs. Flippance turned scarlet. "He's married Polly!" she shrieked. "The beast! The insulting beast!"

"Easy! Easy!" said the bridegroom to this second perturbed female. "It isn't him Polly's married—it's his marionettes. Chingford, the telegram is marked. I expect the caravan is honeymooning in Epping Forest. Give me Boulogne."

But nobody was listening to him any longer. The hysterics that had been only a rumour in church became a reality now. Miss Gentry had produced salts for her darling and was calling for burnt feathers, and Blanche and Barnaby, tumbling over each other kitchenwards, only set their mother's tongue clacking fortissimo. Even Mr. Purley was slapping the bride's hands as she shrieked on the sofa—he was deeply moved by her convulsions, never having seen a doll in distress. Bundock alone remained petrified, the empty champagne-glass in his hand, his eyes still glued on Miss Gentry, and the bubbles in his veins re-evoking that effervescence of the Spring in which even a rear-ward consciousness of green mud had not availed to blunt the charm of opulent beauty. Through the tohu-bohu Mr. Flippance calmly scribbled a counter-telegram: "Congratulations on your marriage. Condolences to Polly."

"Pity we ain't got some of that Scotch stuff to quiet her," said the agitated hurdle-maker.

"Whisky, do you mean?" said Tony.

"No, no! That new stuff they should be telling of—discovered by that Scotch doctor—puts you to sleep, like, and onsenses you."

"Oh, chloroform!" said Tony.

"Ay, that's the name. Masterous stuff for females to my thinking."

"So it is, I understand." Mr. Flippance smiled faintly. "But not for cases like this."

"The parsons won't let you use it!" Bundock burst forth. "They say it's against religion. I suppose they want the monopoly of sending you to sleep." He sniggered happily.

"I'll chloroform her," Mr. Flippance murmured. He could well understand Cleopatra's fury at being replaced by a woman so superficially unattractive as dear Polly, especially as she herself, catching at any stage career in her impecunious days, had not even been married by the fellow.

"Can you read my writing, Bundock?" he asked loudly, proceeding to read to him in stentorian tones as if from the telegram. "Polly, care of Duke's Marionettes, Chingford. Come home at once and all shall be forgotten and forgiven. Your heart-broken—"

But Mrs. Flippance was already on her feet and the telegram in fragments on the floor. "I won't have her here!" she cried. "You've got to choose between us!"

"My darling! Who could hesitate? Try a little gin." He hovered over her tenderly. "Take down a different reply, Bundock, please." He dictated the message he had really written.

"Condolences to Polly!" repeated Mrs. Flippance, smiling savagely. "I should think so. I doubt if he has even legally married her."

"Oh, trust Polly for that! She's got her head square on."

At this Mrs. Flippance showed signs of relapse.

"Poor Polly!" said Tony hastily. "Fancy her being tied to a man like that!"

"I don't know that she could have done much better," snorted Mrs. Flippance.

"But fancy Polly being wasted on a man who packs for himself! Another glass, Bundock?"

"Not while I'm on the Queen's business, thank you," said the postman.

"But you're not. Aren't your letters delivered?"

"What about your telegram?"

"True, true. O Bundock, what a sense of duty! You recall us to ours. We must drink to the Queen! The Queen, ladies and gentlemen—" he filled up Bundock's glass.

"I can't refuse to drink that," sniggered Bundock. "Wonderful what one day's round can bring forth!" he said, putting down his glass. "I began with a baby—I mean the midwife told me of one—went on to a corpse—and now here am I at a wedding! It's in a cottage by the holly-grove—the corpse, I mean—"

"We don't want the skeleton at the feast," interrupted Tony. Bundock hastened to turn the conversation to the grand new house Elijah Skindle was building—Rosemary Villa.

Blanche pouted her beautiful lips in disgust: "Don't talk of a knacker—that's worse than a corpse."

But Bundock was anxious to work off that Elijah called his house "Rosemary Villa" because rosemary was good for the hair, and having achieved this stroke, prudently departed before the laughter died. Blanche seemed especially taken with his gibe at that poor grotesque Mr. Skindle.

After his departure, flown with stuff for scandal and witticism, headier to him than the wine, the party grew jollier than ever. They played Pope Joan with mother-o'-pearl counters and then Blanche sang "Farewell to the Mountain," by ear, like—a bird, without preliminary fuss or instrumental accompaniment, and Mr. Flippance crying "Encore!" and "Bis!" spoke significantly of the possibility of including an annual opera season in English in his Drury Lane repertory. Why should Her Majesty's Theatre and the Italian tongue have a monopoly? Ravished, Blanche gave "The Lass that Loves a Sailor," her eyes languishing, and this led Mr. Purley on to dancing the old Essex hornpipe, whose name sounded like his own, with Barnaby banging a tray for the tambourine and Will's throat replacing the melodeon. To Miss Gentry, beaming in Christian goodwill upon the merry company, it appeared strangely multiplied at moments. But the more the merrier!

When the happy pair had departed for Boulogne via the Chipstone barouche, what wonder if Will, finding himself alone in the passage with Blanche, and not denied a kiss, felt his last hesitations deliciously dissolved. How restful to absorb this clinging femininity, this surrendered sweetness! With what almost open abandonment she had sung "The Lass that Loves a Sailor" at him, with what breaking trills and adoring glances! Marriage was in the air—two examples of it had been brought to his ken in one morning—and he now plumply proposed a third. A strange awakening awaited him.

Blanche grew suddenly rigid. Her imagination had already been inflamed by Cleopatra, clinging to whose aromatic skirts she saw herself soaring to a world of romance and mystery. She had swallowed credulously the exuberant play of Mr. Flippance's fantasy round her feats of wasp-killing, and was willing to do even that on the stage if it enabled her soles to touch the sacred boards. In her daydreams Will had already begun to recede. But now that Mr. Flippance had discovered a voice in her too, and operatic vistas opened out under his champagne and his no less gaseous compliments, she could not suddenly sink to the comparative lowliness of a box-seat. That song which Will had taken for the symbol of her submission was really the final instrument of his humiliation.

Rejected by the girl who has snuggled into one's heart, evoked one's protective emotions, exhibited herself all softness and sweetness! It was incredible! He did not know whether he was more angry or more ashamed, and he was tortured by this warm, creamy, scented loveliness which a moment before had seemed under his palms to mould as he would, and was now become baffling, polar, and remote.

"Blanche! Blanche!" he cried, trying to retain her hand, and tears actually rolled down his cheeks. But underneath all the storm he heard a still small voice crying: "Jinny! Jinny! Jinny!"

So he had been saved from this fatuous marriage, from this supple, conceited minx with her imitative scents and mock graces. The genuine simple rosebud of a Jinny was waiting, waiting for him all the time, the Jinny round whose heart his own heart-strings had been twined from mysterious infancy, who touched him like the song of "Home, Sweet Home," heard when miserable in Montreal, the darling lovable little Jinny as pretty as she was merry, no real exemplar of the unmaidenly, only a dutiful supporter of her grandfather and his business, at most a bit unbalanced by her mannish role; Jinny the girl with the brains to appreciate him, and whom he alone could appreciate as she deserved! How wonderful were the ways of Providence! How nearly he had been trapped and caged and robbed of her!

"I don't see what you mean by leading a fellow on!" he reproached Blanche hoarsely, with no feigned sense of grievance, as he gazed at the mocking mirage of her loveliness. But underneath the tears and the torment, his heart seemed to have come to haven.

"Jinny!" it sang happily. "Jinny! Jinny! Jinny!"

XII

On arriving home, Jinny's first thought after giving the Gaffer his dinner and swallowing a few mouthfuls to overcome her faintness—her mood of self-torture would not allow more—was to give Methusalem some oats extracted by stratagem from the old man's padlocked barn. She had scraped together a few handfuls and was bearing them towards his manger in a limp sack when she perceived that the stable-door was open and gave on a littered emptiness. Her heart stood still as before the supernatural. True, the new padlock was clawing laxly at its staple as if forced open, but then it had not been there at all till that very morning, and for Methusalem to leave his stable voluntarily was as unthinkable as for a sheep to abandon a clover-field. Yet there stretched the bare space, looking portentously vast. What had happened? She ran round the little estate, as though Methusalem would not have bulked on the vision from almost any point, and then she peered anxiously over the Common, as if he could be concealed among the gorse or the blackberry-bushes. The hard ground of the road, marked only by the dried-up ruts of her own wheels, gave no indication of his hoofs. It flashed upon her that padlocks were after all not so ridiculous, but examining more closely the one that drooped by the stable-door, she saw that its little key was still in it. Evidently the old man had forgotten to turn it. The cart was still in its shed, looking as dead to her now as a shell without its snail, though the image was perhaps a little too hard on Methusalem.

But to alarm her grandfather before she had made a thorough search would only confirm him in his delusions. Peeping through the casement of the living-room, she was relieved to see and hear him at the table, safely asleep on his after-dinner Bible. With his beard thus buried in the text, he might sleep for hours in the warmth and buzzing silence. Lucky, she thought, as she tip-toed past, that he had not made the discovery himself. He would probably have accused poor Mr. Skindle again, even set out after the innocent vet. with his whip. Then perhaps actions for assault and battery, for slander, for who knew what!

Horse-stealing was unheard of in these parts, and who save a dealer in antiquities would steal Methusalem? No; as in a fit of midsummer madness—under the depression of the drought and his depleted nosebags—he had bolted! After all, old horses were probably as uncertain as old grandfathers. Was there to be a new course of senility for her study, she wondered ruefully: had she now to school herself to the vagaries of horsey decay as she had schooled herself to human? But, of course, she surmised suddenly, it was the dragging the poor horse up in the middle of the night that had turned his aged brain, and the hammering-in of the staple had lent the last touch of alarm. He had been liable to panic even in his prime. Perhaps he had bolted before Gran'fer's very eyes, mane and tail madly erect. That might explain the uneasy look with which the old man had met her return—a sidelong glance almost like Nip's squint after an escapade—his taciturnity as of a culprit not daring to confess his carelessness, as well as his welcome blindness to the wedding fineries she had been too desperate to remove. But no, he would not have sat down under such a loss, or brisked up so swiftly under the smell of dinner, or pressed the food so solicitously upon her with the remark, "There's a plenty for both of us, dearie—-do ye don't be afeared." It would almost seem as if he had been noting her self-denial: at any rate such an assurance could not coexist with the loss of their means of livelihood.

It was a mystery. The only thing that was clear was that Methusalem must be recaptured before her grandfather was aware of his loss. Such a catastrophe, coming after the scene in the small hours, might have as morbid an effect upon him as that nocturnal episode had evidently had upon Methusalem himself.

Bonnetless, with streaming ringlets, in her lace-adorned dress, she wandered farther and farther in quest of her beloved companion. It was some time before she discovered that her other friend was at her heels. Surely Nip would guide her to Methusalem, as he had guided her through the darkness. But this abandonment to his whim only led her to the cottages with which he was on terms of cupboard affection, and dragged her into the very heart of the tragedy retailed by Bundock to the wedding-party, to the home of a dead labourer.

"His fitten were dead since the morning," the widow informed her with lachrymose gusto. "At the end he was loight-headed and talked about puttin' up the stack."

The neighbours were still more ghoulishly garrulous, and the odour of this death pervaded their cottages like the smell of the straw steeped in their pails, and as the housewives turned their plaiting-wheels they span rival tales of lurid deceases, while a woman who was walking with her little girl—both plaiting hard as they walked—removed the split straws from her mouth to proclaim that she had prophesied a death in the house—having seen the man's bees swarm on his clothes-prop. She hoped they would tell his bees of his decease. But desirable as it was to meet a white horse—that bringer of luck—nobody had set eyes on a wild-wandering Methusalem. Nor was he in the village pound.

She found herself drifting through the wood where she had once sat with Will, and through the glade where the tops of the aspens were a quiver of little white gleams. Had Methusalem perhaps come trampling here? That was all her thought, save for a shadowy rim of painful memory. Bare of Methusalem, the wood at this anxious moment was as blank of poetry as the lanky hornbeam "poles," or the bundles of "tops" lying around. One aspen was so weak and bent it recalled her grandfather, and the white-barked birches craned so over the other trees, she was reminded of a picture with giraffes in Mother Gander's sanctum. But of horses there was no sign. Picking up a wing covert of a jay, not because of the beautiful blue barring, but because it would make fishing flies for Uncle Lilliwhyte, she now ran to his hut with a flickering hope that he would have information, but it was empty of him, and she saw from the absence of his old flintlock that he was sufficiently recovered to be poaching. She emerged from the wood near Miss Gentry's cottage. But the landlady, who had the deserted Squibs in her arms, could only calculate that Methusalem had left his stable at the same moment as the dead labourer's soul had flown out of his body, and that there was doubtless a connexion. "Harses has wunnerful sense," said the good woman. Jinny agreed, but withheld her opinion of humans. She felt if only all the horses jogging along these sun-splashed arcades of elms could speak, the mystery would soon be cleared up. For Methusalem was of a nose-rubbing sociability. But it was only the drivers of all these lazy-rolling carts—fodder, straw, timber, dung, what not—that presumed to speak for their great hairy-legged beasts. To one wagoner lying so high on his golden-hued load that his eye seemed to sweep all Essex, she called up with peculiar hope: he confessed he had been drowsing in the heat. "So mungy," he pleaded. Indeed the afternoon was getting abnormally hot and stuffy, and Jinny had to defend her bare head from the sun with her handkerchief. Hedgers and ditchers had seen as little of a masterless, bare-flanked Methusalem as the thatcher with his more advantageous view-point. Leisurely driving in the stakes with his little club, this knee-padded, corduroyed elder opined that it would be "tempesty." And they could do with some rain.

That the rain was indeed wanted as badly as she wanted Methusalem was obvious enough from the solitude about the white, gibbet-shaped Silverlane pump and the black barrel on wheels round which aproned, lank-bosomed women should have been gossiping, jug or pail in hand. In the absence of this congregation Jinny had to perambulate the green-and-white houses of the great square and hurl individual inquiries across the wooden door-boards that safeguarded the infants. Only the village midwife had seen a horse like Methusalem as she returned from a case. She had been too sleepy, though, to notice properly. From this futile quest Jinny came out on the road again. But wheelwright and blacksmith, ploughman and gipsy, publican and tinker, all were drawn blank.

Beside trees tidily bounding farms, or meadows dotted with cows and foals, and every kind of horse except Methusalem, past grotesque quaint-chimneyed houses half brick, half weather-board, the road led Jinny on and on till it took her across the bridge. Here on the bank she recognized the plastered hair of Mr. Charles Mott, who was fishing gloomily. No, he had not seen a white horse—worse luck!—and would to God, he added savagely, that he had never seen a black sheep. Jinny hurried off, as from a monster of profanity, for Mr. Mott's disinclination for his wife's society, especially on chapel days, was, she knew, beginning to perturb the "Peculiars"; and with the sacramental language of the marriage service yet ringing in her ears, it seemed to our guileless Jinny ineffably wicked to be sunk in selfish sport instead of cherishing and comforting the woman to whom you had consecrated yourself.

She moved on pensively—the road after descending rose somewhat, so that Long Bradmarsh seemed to nestle behind her in a hollow, a medley of thatch and slate, steeple and chimney-stacks, hayricks and inn-signs, and fluttering sheets and petticoats. But the forward view seemed far more bounded than usual, deprived as it was of the driver's vantage-point: to the toiling pedestrian her familiar landscape was subtly changed, and this added to the sense of change and disaster.

She passed Foxearth Farm near enough to see again the barouche now awaiting the honeymooners, and to hear the voices of Will and Blanche mingling in a merry chorus. There was an aching at her heart, but everything now came dulled to her as through an opiate. Methusalem was the only real thing in life. She wanted to make her inquiry of the driver, but her legs bore her onwards to a glade where she could rest on one of Mr. Purley's felled trunks. Even there the chorus pursued her, spoiling the music of the little stream that babbled at her feet, and the beauty of willow-herb and tall yellow leopard's-bane and those white bell-blossoms of convolvulus twining and twisting high up among the trees still standing.

It was well past five before, footsore and spent, she stopped on her homeward road at the Pennymole cottage for information and a glass of water. This must be her last point, for standing as it did at the Four Wantz Way, it overlooked every direction in which Methusalem could possibly have gone, had he come thus far, while the size of the Pennymole family provided over a score of eyes. She found herself plunged into the eve-of-Sabbath ritual—all the seven younger children being scrubbed in turn by the mother in a single tub of water, and left to run about in a state of nature, or varying stages of leisurely redressing.

But neither the nude nor the semi-decent nor Mrs. Pennymole herself, with her bar of yellow soap, had seen even the tip of Methusalem's tail, and the extinction of this last hope left Jinny so visibly overcome that the busy mother insisted on her sitting down and waiting for tea. She urged that "father" would soon be home, as well as the two elder boys, all at work in different places, and "happen lucky" one of the three would have seen the missing animal. Jinny felt too weak to refuse the tea, and though the thought of her neglected grandfather was as gnawing as her hunger, she reasoned with herself that she would really get to him quicker if refreshed. The elder lads came in very soon, one after the other, each handing his day's sixpence to his mother and receiving a penny for himself. But neither brought even a crumb for Jinny. Mrs. Pennymole beguiled the time of waiting for the master and the meal by relating, in view of the labourer's death, how she had lost two children five years ago.

No fewer than four were down at once with the black thrush. Two boys lay on the sofa, one at each end, an infant in the bassinet under the table, and a girl in the bed. One of the sofa patients had swellings behind his ears the size of eggs, but they were lanced and he lived to earn his three shillings a week. The other, a fine lad of thirteen, died at three in the afternoon. The girl died at half-past eleven at night— beautiful she looked; like a wax statue. The undertaker was afraid to put them in their coffin; afraid to bring contagion to his own children. "Perhaps your husband would do it," he suggested to her. But her husband, poor man, couldn't. "How would you like to put your childer in coffins?" he asked the undertaker. The doctor wouldn't let her follow the funeral, she was so broken.

But it was Jinny who was broken now. These reminiscences were more painful for her than for the mother who—inexhaustible fountain of life—scoured her newer progeny to their accompaniment. Yes, existence seemed very black to Jinny, sitting there without food, or Will, or Methusalem, or anything but a grandfather; and the china owl with a real coloured handkerchief tied round its head, which was the outstanding ornament of the mantelpiece, seemed in its grotesque gloom an apt symbol of existence. She was very glad when cheery, brawny Mr. Pennymole burst in, labouring with a story in which whisker-shaking laughter bubbled through a humorous stupefaction.

He had begun to tell the story almost before he had perceived and greeted Jinny, and Methusalem's disappearance, on which he could throw no light, served to enhance it. To him, too, the day had brought an earth-shaking novelty—there must be something in the moon. For thirty years, he explained, as he took off his coat and boots (though not his cap), he had risen at half-past four. But waking that morning at one o'clock, he had got to sleep again, and the next thing he knew—after what seemed to him a little light slumber—was a child saying: "Mother, what's the time?" Half-past five, mother had replied—Mrs. Pennymole here corroborated the statement at some length; adding that it was Jemima who inquired, she being such a light sleeper, and always so anxious to be off to school: an interruption that her lord sustained impatiently, for this was the dramatic moment of the story. Half-past five! Up he had jumped, never made his fire nor his tea, never had his pipe, and instead of leaving home at twenty to six, still smoking it, he had rushed round to his brother-in-law's, where fortunately he was in time for the last cup o' tea, and then out with his horses as usual!

"And I made him tea and sent it round to the field," gurgled Mrs. Pennymole as she unhooked her bodice for the last baby. "He had two teas!"

Mr. Pennymole and Jinny joined in her laugh. "Sometimes I've woke at 'arf-past three," he explained carefully. "But then I felt all right." He recapitulated the wonder of his oversleeping himself, as he drew up to the table, where the bulk of his progeny was already installed, and it overbrooded his distribution of bread and jam in great slices.

"And I was up at four!" Mrs. Pennymole bragged waggishly.

"Yes, upstairs!" Mr. Pennymole retorted, sharp as his knife, and the table was in a roar, not to mention the four corners of the room, where those of the brood squatted who could not find places at the board. Everybody sat munching the ritual hunk, though for the black strong tea the adults alone had cups, two mugs circulating among the swarm of children, whose clamours for their fair turn had to be checked by paternal cries for silence. Mrs. Pennymole pressed both husband and guest to share her little piece of fat pork fried with bread, but they knew better what was due to a nursing mother. Jinny felt grateful enough for the bread and jam and the tea, cheap but at least not from burnt crusts, and sugared abundantly, despite that sugar—as Mrs. Pennymole complained—had gone up "something cruel." But though such a meal was luxury for her nowadays, she could hardly help wistful mouth-watering visions of the wedding-feast, from the known dumplings to the unknown champagne. It was for a strange company she had exchanged the wedding-party, she thought ruefully, as she refused a third slice of bread. She could not well accept it, when each child, solemnly asked in turn whether it would like a second, had replied with wonderful unanimity in the affirmative, and Mr. Pennymole, with his eye on the waning loaf, had remarked that children had wonderful healthy appetites, though that was better than doctors. She was glad, however, to be given a wedge of bread and cheese, though when her host jabbed his into his mouth at the point of his knife, it called up a distressing memory of a gobbet of wedding-cake thrown to a dog, and she became suddenly aware that Nip was no longer with her. She remembered seeing him last as she sat on the log, and she rightly divined that—wiser than she—he had gone to the wedding-meal!

Before she could get away from her Barmecide banquet, the brother-in-law and his wife came in, and then the whole story of the oversleeping had to be laughed and marvelled over afresh. The more often Mr. Pennymole told the story, the more his sense of its whimsicalness and wonder grew upon him, and the more his audience enjoyed it. "I made his tea," cackled Mrs. Pennymole. "I sent it round to the field. So he had two teas!" The cottage rocked with laughter. Only the owl and Jinny preserved their gravity. And even Jinny could not resist the infection when Mrs. Pennymole boasted to her visitors that she herself had been up at four, and Mr. Pennymole, with an air of invincible shrewdness, pointed out that it was "upstairs" she had been. So that though neither of the new-comers could throw light upon the Methusalem mystery, Jinny left the cottage refreshed by more than tea, and with the flavour of the corpse-talk washed away. The humour of it all even went with her on her long homeward tramp. In imagination she heard the oddness of the oversleeping and the duplication of the teas still savoured with grins and guffaws, while the little ones dribbled bedwards, while the elder boys were scrubbed in the scullery, and while the indefatigable Mrs. Pennymole was washing the hero of the history down to his waist. Her fancy followed the tale spreading over the parish, told and retold, borne by Bundock to ever wider circles, adding to the gaiety of the Hundred, abiding as a family tradition when that babe at Mrs. Pennymole's breast was a grandmother—the tale of how for thirty years Mr. Pennymole had got up at half-past four, and how at long last the record was broken!

Speeding along in this merrier mood, Jinny had almost reached home by a short cut through the woods, when she espied a gay-stringed, battered beaver and learned the tragic truth.

XIII

Uncle Lilliwhyte was carrying by its long legs the spoil of his rusty flintlock—Jinny was glad to see it was only a legitimate curlew with its dagger-like bill. He offered the bird for sale, but she was afraid it had fed too long on the marsh mud. She was glad to hear, though, he had called that very morning and sold her grandfather truffles—Uncle had a pig's nose for truffles, and her grandfather a passion for them.

"He hadn't got change for a foive-pun' note," Uncle Lilliwhyte reported. "And Oi hadn't, neither," he chuckled. "So ye owes me tuppence."

Jinny was amused at her grandfather's magnificent mendacity—his lordly way of carrying off his pennilessness.

"Never mind the twopence now," she said. "You haven't seen Methusalem, I suppose?"

She had supposed it so often that she took the answer for granted. This reply struck her like a cannon-ball.

"Not since 'Lijah Skindle took him away this marnin'!"

"Elijah Skindle took him!" she gasped, breathless yet relieved. "What for? Where?" Had her grandfather's fears been justified then?

"To his 'orspital, Oi reckon. Trottin' behind the trap he was, tied to it. A sick 'oss don't want to goo that pace though, thinks Oi. 'Twould be before bever," he added, when she demanded the exact hour.

"When I was at church! But Methusalem wasn't sick when I left home."

"Must ha' been took sick—or it stands to reason your Gran'fer wouldn't ha' let him goo!"

"But Gran'fer didn't know—!"

"Arxin' your pardon, Jinny—Mr. Quarles waved to 'em as they went off. And Oi'll be thankful to you for the tuppence, needin' my Sunday beer."

She groped in her purse. "But if Mr. Skindle took him back to Chipstone, how comes it nobody has seen him?"

"He went roundabouts by Bog Lane and Squash End, 'tis all droied-up nowadays. And took Bidlake's Ferry, Oi reckon, stead o' the bridge."

A sinister feeling, as yet formless, began to creep into Jinny's veins. Handing the nondescript his twopence and the jay feather, she ran out of the wood and then in the dusking owl-light by a field-path, and through a prickly hedge of dog-rose and blackberry that left her with scratched fingers, into her own little plot of ground. The stable door was now locked, though its aching emptiness was still visible through the weather-boarding as she passed by; the house-door was even more securely fastened, and all the windows were tightly closed. She rattled the casement of the living-room and heard her grandfather finally hobbling down the stairs.

He examined her cautiously through the little panes.

"Ye've left me in the dark," he complained, turning the window-clasp. "Oi'm famished. Where you been gaddin' in that frock?"

"Did you send Methusalem away?" she cried impatiently.

He put a scooped hand to his ear. "What be you a-sayin'?"

"Open the door!" she called angrily. "You mustn't shut me out."

"We've got to be careful, Jinny." He moved to the door. "There's a sight o' bad charriters about."

"Yes, indeed. What did Mr. Skindle want here?" she asked, as the bolts shot back.

"Skindle!" He pondered. "Young 'Lijah, d'ye mean? He brought me a pot."

"That was long ago—what did he want this morning?"

"This marnin'? Oh, ay"—the sidelong look returned with remembrance and was succeeded by one of defiance—"That's my business."

A terrible suspicion flashed upon Jinny.

"You haven't sold Methusalem?" she cried.

He winced. "That's my property. Daniel Quarles, Carrier. And by the good rights, Oi—"

"You have sold him!" she hissed in a fury strange to herself. And she found herself shaking the old man by the arms, shaking him as he had shaken her that very morning in the small hours. And he was cowering before her, the fierce old man, cowering there on his own doorstep.

"Oi couldn't see ye starve," he pleaded.

"Oh, it's not me you were thinking of!" she said harshly, not caring whether she was just or not. "You might have trusted yourself to me after all these years." Indignation at Elijah's supposed swindling mingled with her wrath—the idea of his getting Methusalem, an animal worth his weight in gold, for a miserable five-pound note! She gave the old man a final shake, imaginatively intended for Mr. Skindle. "Where's the money?" she cried, letting him go.

He recovered himself somewhat. "That's my money," he said sullenly.

"But where have you put it?"

Cunning and obstinacy mingled in his eye. "Oi've put it safe agin all they thieves!"

"I don't believe you've got any money!" she said, matching cunning by cunning. "You just let Mr. Skindle rob you."

"Noa, Oi dedn't. Oi got more than Methusalem was worth."

"Really? More than a sovereign?"

"A suvran!" He cackled with a crafty air. "More than double that!"

"More than two sovereigns?" said Jinny in tones of ingenuous admiration.

"More than double that!"

"More than four sovereigns?" Enthusiasm shone in her eyes through the dusk.

He hurried towards the stairs.

"You're not going to bed?" she called with mock anxiety. "You haven't had supper!"

"We'll have plenty o' supper now. He, he!" His gleeful cackle descended from the winding staircase. Before he returned, chuckling still, she had lit the lamp and put out some cold rabbit-pie and a jug of beer on the tiger-painted tray.

"A foiver!" he cried, waving it.

She snatched at the note and tore it in two and let the pieces flutter away.

"Help! Thieves! She's robbed me," screamed the Gaffer. He scrambled on his knees after the fragments.

"Hush! How dare you sell Methusalem?" He cowered again before her passion.

"That was eating us out of house and home!" he whimpered.

"Get up! There's your supper."

He rose like a scolded child, clutching the scraps of thin paper. She put on her bonnet.

"Where ye gooin'?"

"To Mr. Skindle, of course."

"Too late for that!"

"No, it isn't."

"But ye won't git Methusalem back."

"Oh, won't I, though!"

"But ye've tore up his foiver!"

"I don't care." But alarmed at heart over her insane deed, she took the pieces from his unresisting hand and put them in her purse. "Don't bolt me out or I'll break the window."

"But listen, dearie, Mr. Skindle won't be there—the place'll be shut up!"

"All the better. I'll break it in."

"But what's the good o' that? Poor old Methusalem's out o' his misery by now!"

Her heart stood still. "What do you mean?" She was white and shaking.

"'Lijah kills at seven," he said, "afore his supper."

"Oh, my God!" she gasped, the completeness of the tragedy impinging on her for the first time. "You sold him to be killed! No, no!" she cried, recovering. "He wouldn't give five pounds just for a carcase!"

"Then ef that ain't killed yet," said the Gaffer, "that won't be till to-morrow night."

A sensible remark for once, Jinny thought, subsiding almost happily into a chair. It had been silly even to contemplate setting out afresh after all the day's journeyings. In this weather the doomed horses would be shut up in Mr. Skindle's field,—she recalled their joyous gambollings—the first thing in the morning she would set out to the rescue. And yet what if her grandfather should be wrong, what if Mr. Skindle killed before breakfast! No, delay might be fatal, and she started up afresh and, unlocking the stable-door, brought in her lantern.

"Ye're not gooin' to Mr. Skindle at this time o' day?" protested the Gaffer from his soothing tray.

"I must." She lit the candle in the lantern.

"Well, give my love to his mother!" She thought it sarcasm and went off even more embittered against him.

She had not gone far before she met the returning reveller. Nip's ears were abased and his eyes edge-long, but in an instant, aware she was glad of his company, he welcomed her roysterously to it. But the blackness that now began to fall upon the pair was not wholly of the night. Great livid thunder-clouds were sagging over them, and of a sudden the whole landscape was lit up with blue blazings and shaken with terrific thunder. And then came the rain—the long-prayed-for rain, with its rich rejoicing gurgle. Providence, importuned on all sides, now asserted itself in a pour that was like solid sheets of water, and the parched soil seemed swilled in a few seconds. To plough along was not only difficult but foolhardy. Heaven had clearly thrown cold water on the project. She crept almost shame-facedly back to her still guzzling grandfather.

"Got a wettin'," he chuckled. "Sarve ye right to be sow obstropolus. And sarve you right too!" he added, launching a kick towards the shivering and dripping animal. Nip, though untouched, uttered a dreadful howl, and grovelled on his back.

"Do you want to kill them both?" cried Jinny. She was now sure that Methusalem was beyond reprieve—the point of Mr. Skindle's strategy in purchasing him, so as to leave her no sphere but matrimony, was penetrating to her mind, and, by the side of such "a dirty bit," Will's frank and blusterous methods began to appear magnanimity itself. To have found out, too, probably from Bundock, that she would be away at the wedding! The sly skunk!

XIV

For a full hour after Nip and her grandfather slept the sleep of the innocent in their beds, she sat up watching the storm, with no surprise at this unrest of the elements. No less a cataclysm was adequate to the passing of Methusalem. This sympathy of Nature indeed relieved her, some of her stoniness melted, and her face—as if in reciprocation—became as deluged as the face of the earth-mother. All the long years with Methusalem passed before her vision, ever since that first meeting of theirs outside the Watch Vessel: their common adventures in sunshine and snow, in mud and rain, her whip only an extra tail for him to whisk off his flies withal: ah, the long martyrdom from those flies, especially the nose-fly that spoilt the glory of July. She heard again that queer tick-tack of his hoofs, his whinnying, his coughing, saw the spasmodic shudder of his shoulder-joints, the peculiar gulp with which he took his drench. How often they had gone together to have a nail fixed, or his shoes roughed for the winter! What silly alarms he had felt, when she had had to soothe him like a mother, coax him to pass something, and on the other hand what a skill beyond hers in going unguided through the moonless, swift-fallen winter night! How happily he had nibbled at the beans in his corner-crib or the oats in his manger, what time he was brushed and combed—would that beloved mane get into rats'-tails no more? Was she never again to feel that soft nose against her cheek in a love passing the love of man? Could all this cheery laborious vitality have ended, be one with the dust she had so often brushed from his fetlocks? That joy which had set him frisking like an uncouth kitten when he was released from the shafts, was it not to be his now that he was freed for ever? Was he to be nothing but a carcase? Nay— horror upon horror—would he survive only as glove-or boot-buttons, as that wretch of a Skindle calculated? Would that triumphant tail wave only at human funerals, his own last rites unpaid? A remembrance of her glimpse at the charnel-house made her almost sick. Fed to the foxhounds perhaps! Could such things be in a God-governed world?

And her cart too would go—of the old life there would be nothing left any more. She could see the bill pasted up on the barn-doors: "Carrier's Cart on Springs, with Set of Harness, Cart Gear, Back Bands, Belly Bands—" But what nonsense! Who would advertise such a ramshackle ruin? "A Shabby, Cracked Canvas Tilt, Patched with Sacking"—fancy that on a poster! No, like its horse, it would be adjudged fit only to be broken up. Perhaps somebody wearing Methusalem on his shoes would sit on the bar of a stile made of its axle-tree.

She woke from her reverie and to the wetness of her face, streaming with bitter-sweet tears. The moon rode almost full, and in the pale blue spread of sky sparse stars shone, one or two twinkling. She opened the door and went out into the night. What delicious wafts of smells after the long mugginess of the day! The elms and poplars rose in mystic lines bordering the great bare spaces. Surely the death of

Methusalem had been but a nightmare—if she went to the stable, there would he be as usual, snug and safe in his straw. She sped thither, over the sodden grass, with absolute conviction. Alas, the same endless emptiness yawned, the manger looked strange and tragic in the moonlight. She thought of a divine infant once lying in one, wrapped in his swaddling-clothes, and then looking up skywards she saw a figure hovering. Yes, it was—it was the Angel-Mother, so beautiful in the azure light. At the sight all her anguish was dissolved in sweetness. "Mother! Mother!" she cried, stretching up her arms to the vision. "Comfort thee, my child!" came the dulcet tones. "Methusalem is not dead, but sleeping!"

At the glad news Jinny burst into tears, and, in the mist they made, her mother faded away. But she walked in soft happiness back to the house, and said her prayers of gratitude and went believingly to bed and slept as when she was a babe.

So long did she sleep that when she woke, the old man was standing over her again, just as the morning before, save that now he was in his everyday earth-coloured smock and wore a frown instead of a wedding-look, and the sunshine was streaming into the room.

"Where's my breakfus, Jinny?" he said grumpily.

"I'm so sorry," she said, yawning and rubbing her eyes. "I must have overslept myself." And then she remembered Mr. Pennymole's story, and a smile came over her face.

"There's nawthen to laugh at," he said savagely. "Ef ye goo out at bull's noon, ye're bound to forgit my breakfus. And that eatin' his head off too! Ye know there's no work for him. Ye dedn't want to bring him back."

"Back?" she almost screamed. "Is Methusalem back?"

"As ef ye dedn't know!" he said, disgusted.

Disregarding him and everything else, she sprang out of bed, rolling the blanket round her, and with bare feet she sped to the stable. But she had hardly got outside before the jet of hope had sunk back. It was but another of her grandfather's delusions.

But no! O incredible, miraculous, enchanting spectacle! There he was, the dear old beast, not dead but sleeping, exactly as the Angel-Mother had said, not a hair of his mane injured, not an inch of his tail less, and never did two Polynesian lovers rub noses half so passionately as this happy pair.

Jinny would have rubbed his nose still more adoringly had she known—as she knew later—the rôle it had played in his salvation. The threatening thunder-clouds had made Mr. Skindle put off his slaughtering till the morning, so that he himself might get home before the storm broke. The doomed horses he left shut in his field—who cared whether they got wet? But as soon as the coast was clear of Skindle and his latest-lingering myrmidons, Methusalem had simply lifted the latch of the gate with his nose and gone home. Mr. Skindle, oblivious of this accomplishment of his, though he had seen it practised on his never-forgotten journey with Jinny, had imagined him conclusively corralled. Mr. Charles Mott, returning with some boon companions from a distant hostelry where the draughts were more generous than he was allowed at "The Black Sheep," was among the few who saw the noble animal hurrying homewards, and he told Jinny the next Tuesday that she ought to enter Methusalem for the Colchester Stakes. His unusual rate of motion was also reported by Miss Gentry, who, lying awake with a headache after the excitement of the day, had heard him snort past her window just when the storm was ebbing. He must have sagely sheltered while it raged and have arrived at Blackwater Hall soon after Jinny had beheld her vision.

But as yet Jinny attributed the miracle to her Angel-Mother. And what a happy Sunday morning was that, with the church bells all clearly ringing "Come and thank God and her!" She did not fail to obey them, though not without a sharp turn in that padlock, and with the little key safe in her bosom. And having happily ascertained from Mother Gander that the five-pound note was valid in pieces, she dropped them into Mr. Skindle's letter-box together with remarks that drew heavily on her Spelling-Book's "Noun Adjectives of Four Syllables." Cadaverous (Belonging to a Carcase); Execrable (Hateful, Accursed); Sophistical (Captious, Deceitful); Sulphureous (Full of Brimstone); and Vindictive (Belonging to an Apology) were among her proudest specimens. They were not calculated to encourage Mr. Skindle's matrimonial hopes.

CHAPTER XI

WINTER'S TALE

Thou barrein ground, whome winters wrath hath wasted,
Art made a myrrhour to behold my plight.
SPENSER, "The Shepheards Calendar."

I

Pitter-patter was the dominant note of the rest of the year. The prayer for rain had been only too successful, and the blackbirds whistled their thanksgiving over their worms. But humanity grumbled with its wonted ingratitude. There were warm and windy days, and cold and sparkling days, but the roads never quite dried up. The short cuts to Frog Farm became impassable for Bundock; in the coursing season the long-grassed marshlands clove to the spectators' gaiters, and when the beagles were out, Jinny had the satisfaction of seeing Farmer Gale and breathless bumpkins floundering over sodden stubble-fields or ankle-deep in mud, what time baffled whippers-in piped plaintively, or jetted husky cries at their scattered pack. Glad as she was to eat of the leporine family, she detested sport for sport's sake, even the fox-hunting, though her poultry-run had just been raided and a dog-fox had snarled fearlessly at Nip from the ditch. Once, when the hare, crossing her cart with the dogs at his very heels, cleared the broad ditch with a magnificent leap, Jinny clapped her hands as though at a Flippance melodrama.

Sport for life's sake was another affair, and she looked back regretfully to the good old times described by her grandfather, when the farmer, having finished his day's work, would go out rabbit-shooting to preserve his crop, or when the fox could be shot, snared, or even hooked, as a dangerous animal. Now, when poor old Uncle Lilliwhyte had found Jinny's vulpine enemy dead in one of his gins, caught by a claw, that rising vet., Mr. Skindle, was called in to make a post-mortem examination, and it was only because he certified that the sacred animal had died of starvation, and not been poisoned, that the old woodman escaped the worst rigours of the unwritten law. As it was, his crime in setting the trap at all on land not his own, and his failing—through a new attack of rheumatism—to examine it before the fox died, almost resulted in his being officially driven from his derelict hut into the Chipstone poorhouse; a fate he only escaped by passionate asseverations that he had always been and till death would continue "upright," by which he meant "independent."

That was in one sense more than Jinny could call herself, for her store of barley or rye for her breadmaking was dangerously low, and she had come to depend a good deal on the food brought by this queer raven at prices more corresponding to his gratitude than to market value. She still peddled her goats' milk for a trifle among her neighbours, the abundant blackberries gave her fruit (though she could not afford the sugar for jam), she had gathered nuts as industriously as a squirrel, she ensured jelly for her grandfather by making it out of her own apples, while by exchanging the bad apples with a neighbour who kept pigs, she got Methusalem some "green fodder" in the shape of tares. But it was an unceasing strain to keep things going in the old style, and Uncle Lilliwhyte's spoils were more than welcome, for his activities varied from codling-fishing to eel-spearing, and from fowling on the saltings to collecting glass-wort for pickling. His rabbits and hares came with suspiciously injured legs, and Jinny seeing the bloody-blobbed eyes could only hope they had not been long in his wire loops. As she felt the long, warm, beautiful bodies, she had to tell herself how pernicious they were to the root-crops or the young apple-trees.

More legitimate spoils arrived when the old man was well enough to crawl to the nearest salt-marsh with his ancient fowling-piece, for, when the ebb bared the mud, countless sea-birds came to feed, and more than once a brace of mallards offered Jinny a vivid image of her inferiority to the rival carrier, so gorgeously shimmering was the male's head, so drab the female's. For while the driver of the Flynt Flyer had been blossoming out in the frock-coat he had first sported for the Flippance wedding, Jinny had been refraining even from her furbished-up gown, reserving it mentally for a last resource and feeling herself lucky that it was still unpawned. But one day when the vehicles met—for despite the heaviness of the going Jinny foolishly and extravagantly continued to plod her miry rounds—she caught Will looking down so compassionately at her spotting shoes that she straightway resolved to buy another pair at any sacrifice. Savage satisfaction at her defeat she could have borne, but this pity she would not brook. Better sell the goats, especially as Gran'fer would need a new flannel shirt for the winter. The animals were not very lucrative, and one out of the three would suffice to supply milk for herself and— by its bleat—her grandfather's sense of stability. But she had reckoned insufficiently with this last: he admitted he had no great stomach for her goats' cheese, and felt a middling need for flannel, but he clung to his nannies as though without them his world would fall to pieces. That her shoes were doing so, he did not remark.

In the end—though she shrank from the three golden balls on her own behalf—there was nothing for it but to pledge her wedding-frock under pretence it was a customer's. But in her dread lest the pawnbroker should recognize the dress, the sharpness which extracted the utmost from him for her distressed clients was replaced by a diffident acceptance of barely enough for the shoes.

This discussion about her live stock, however, gave her an idea. She carted part of her poultry to and fro in a crate, and their clucking and fluttering gave an air of liveliness to the business and made even Will Flynt believe it had woke up again, especially as he saw the smart new shoes on the little feet, supplemented presently by a new winter bonnet, which, despite his experience with his own mother's bonnet, he did not divine was merely an old one, whitened and remodelled by Miss Gentry.

Thus the equinoctial season found the little Carrier still upon her seat, defiant of competition and radiating prosperity from the crown of her bonnet to the sole of her shoe. Even the plainness of her skirt and shawl seemed only an adaptation to the weather. But she would have been better off by her log fire, making the local variety of Limerick lace with which she was on other days trying to eke out her infrequent sixpences. Though the rain abated towards the end of October, halcyon days and even hours alternated with hours and days of turbulent winds and hailstorms, and the sky would change in almost an instant from a keen blue, with every perspective standing out clear and sun-washed, to a lowering roof of clouds spitting hailstones, and a gentle wind would be succeeded by half a gale that stripped their flames from the poplars and sent the reddened beech-leaves whirling fantastically. In November these blasts grew more biting, Nip cowered in his basket within the cart, and the calves in the fields sheltered themselves behind the blown-down trunks of elms. Shivering, Jinny reminded herself that the real object of her rounds was the bi-weekly gorge at Mother Gander's.

They were indeed more generous than ever, these midday meals, so relieved was Jinny's hostess to find she had not really been baptized into Mr. Fallow's church. Mrs. Mott even had the Gaffer's beer-barrel replenished gratis. Not that she had any suspicion of the girl's straits. Though parcels were no longer left at the bar for Jinny, the poor woman was too taken up with her own troubles to draw the deduction from that. Beneath her imposing blue silk bodice beat a wounded heart, and in Jinny's society she found consolation for the lack of her husband's.

For a quarrel had begun between the Motts which was destined to shake all Chipstone with its reverberations. Mr. Charles Mott had profanely refused to be "Peculiar" any longer. The endeavour to draw him to the Wednesday services had proved the last straw. To him religion and Sunday were synonyms, and he had been willing to concede the day to boredom. He was a sportsman and was ready to play fair. But his wife was not playing fair, he considered, when she pretended that ratting, coursing, and dicing remained reprehensible even on weekdays. Expostulatory elders had vainly pointed out to him that it was only the Churchman who made so much of Sunday and so little of every other day, and Deacon Mawhood had been compelled to order several goes of rum at "The Black Sheep" to find opportunities of explaining to its landlord that his cravat-pin and plethora of rings were an offence. Let him note how his admirable wife had given up her gold chain. "Well, I don't want no chain," Charley had retorted, and his cronies still acclaimed the repartee. He had, in fact, broken his chain and would not even go to the Sunday chapel.

"You and me have both got our cross to bear," Deacon Mawhood sighed sympathetically to the distraught lady. "There's saints among us as won't even keep a cat or a bird because the thought of them may come 'twixt the soul and chapel. Oi sometimes suspicion it's a failing in roighteousness to keep a husband or a wife—partic'lar when they riots on your hard-earned savings."

The grievances which the poor hostess of "The Black Sheep"—now become a keeper of one—poured into Jinny's ear, fully confirmed all the Spelling-Book had told her of the wickedness of man—its preoccupation with the male gender had left woman unimpugned. But it was more under Mr. Mawhood's encouragement than Jinny's that this female pillar of the chapel now sent the Bellman round Chipstone with his bell and his cocked hat and his old French cry, to inform all and sundry that she would not be responsible for her husband's debts.

It was a procedure which scandalized Chipstone. Since the day when a neighbouring village had set up its "cage" for drunken men in the pound, with the other strayed beasts, no such blow had been dealt at the dignity of man. But Charley and his crew met it with derisory laughter. All Mrs. Mott's property was his—or rather theirs: he could sell the lease of "The Black Sheep" over her head, if she did not behave herself. Nay, he could sell her very self at the market cross, the bolder maintained, not without citing precedent. By many the Bellman was blamed for compromising the dignity of his sex: by none so contemptuously as by Bundock. For the Crier, not taking his own announcement seriously, had embellished it with facetious gags that set the street roaring. "I wouldn't say if they were funny," complained Bundock. "Anybody can play on the word 'Peculiar,' and certainly peculiar it is to put your husband in the stocks, so to speak. I don't deny Charley's legs sometimes need that support. But what can you expect if you marry your pot-boy? You must take pot-luck. He, he, he!"

To which the bulk of Chipstone Christendom added that however prodigal the ex-potman, he did not waste so much money as his wife lavished on that ridiculous sect of hers. A hundred pounds for the bishop at his jubilee birthday, it was said with bated breath—"a noice fortune!" Really, Charley was only too long-suffering not to take his property, including his wife, more strictly in hand, and when it was learnt that lawyers' letters were actually passing between the bedrooms of the parties there was general satisfaction. In short, public opinion was as outraged by Mrs. Mott's treatment of her husband as by her original acquisition of him. The only difference was that Mr. Mott was now a martyr.

The insult to the male sex was especially resented by the tradesmen to whom the martyr stood so profitably indebted, and under their incitement a new ban might have been put on "The Black Sheep" but for the reluctance of Will Flynt, who, though second to none in reprobation, refused to shift the headquarters of his coach to the rival establishment. That would only be hurting Charley's business, he pointed out, and indirectly themselves. The economic aspects of revenge had not occurred to these muddle-heads, and they were grateful to the coach-driver for the reminder. They did not know that his true motive for sticking to "The Black Sheep" was that Jinny was to be encountered in its courtyard on Tuesdays and Fridays. Nor was Jinny herself aware how profusely she was repaying Mrs. Mott for her meals.

As if this scandal among the "Peculiars" was not enough, Deacon Mawhood himself came into ill odour more literally. For in carrying out his agreement to clear the Gentry cottage of rats, he had committed the crime of which Uncle Lilliwhyte had been acquitted: he had operated by poison, to wit, and the stench of the dead vermin in their holes nearly crazed the excellent dressmaker, already sufficiently distracted by the silence of her bosom friend, Mrs. Flippance, swallowed up in Boulogne as in a grave. Miss Gentry, like Mother Gander, now wept on Jinny's shoulder, though it had to be done outside the garden gate, and even there the wafts caught one. If it had not been for the prediction that she would be drowned, did she ever set foot on a boat, she would have been in Boulogne weeks ago with her darling, but, like a ghost, she could not cross water. Indeed she would already have been a ghost but for her strong smelling-salts, her decoction of scabious against infection, and the fumigation of the cottage. Jinny did not shrink from bearding her spiritual superior in his bar and giving Mr. Joshua Mawhood a taste of her tongue. If that was his notion of religion, he ought to be cast out of his chapel, and she would let Mrs. Mott know of what a hoggish "illusion" he had been guilty—(Illusion, Sham or Cheat— "The Universal Spelling-Book").

But the Deacon, standing on the letter of his bond, was impermeable to reproach—nay, had a sense of righteousness, as having incidentally punished a distributor of tracts no less offensive than his dead rats. Not even the remonstrances of Mr. Fallow, who had arranged the compromise over Mrs. Mawhood's dress, could bring the Deacon to a sense of sin, still less of compensation. "Her rats were eating the pears like hollamy," he said, "and Oi've cleared cottage and orchard of 'em." Mr. Fallow was so interested to know what "hollamy" was, that he went away with a diminished sense of failure. But neither dictionaries nor octogenarians could throw any light on its etymology. The most plausible conjecture he could reach was that it must be "hogmanay," gifts made at the year's end.

But if the Peculiar Faith was thus involved in scandal, Churchmanship did not fail to provide its quota of gossip to the months that ended a fateful year. It was not only that Miss Blanche of Foxearth Farm had collected the scalp of yet another suitor (and one who, as Bundock's own eyes had witnessed at the Flippance wedding-feast, had been wantonly encouraged); it was that the minx, whose brother Barnaby went about in October saying Will Flynt was not good enough for her, became openly engaged in November to that obviously inferior specimen, Mr. Elijah Skindle. And old Giles Purley, tired of vagaries so incongruous in a churchwarden's family, was, said Bundock's father, imperiously hurrying on the match.

Although it was the postman who was the reference on the liberties permitted to Will at the wedding breakfast, it was his bedridden parent who became the leading authority on the new Blanche engagement. That was because Barnaby, disappointed of the wider life of the Tony Flip theatre, with no winter prospect but that of chopping down undergrowth and laying it out in long rows for hoops and hurdles, and receiving no consolation from Jinny when their vehicles passed, had discovered in the postman's youngest sister a being even more beauteous, and, when he had to take the trap into Chipstone, never failed in devoted attendance on the sick-bed. It was thus that all the world knew that the Flippances had not written once from Boulogne, not even to send on the promised cheque for the wedding-breakfast.

But even Bundock's father had not the true history of the engagement, constructing as he did from Barnaby's chatter a facile version of a "better match": how dear 'Lijah was coining money far quicker than Will with his petty fares and commissions, and fast ousting Jorrow, and with what elegant furniture he was fitting up the bridal bedchamber. Barnaby himself did not know that with the gradual vanishing of his sister's theatrical and operatic hopes, Blanche, immeasurably more embittered and disillusioned than himself, had sought in vain to win back Will, and had thrown herself first strategically and then despairingly into the arms of Elijah, who, summoned professionally to the Farm, had found unhoped-for consolation for his lost Jinny. Tongues would have wagged still more joyously had it been known that Will for his part was trying to win back Jinny, who in her turn was as adamantine to him as he to Blanche. The two Carriers met not seldom on the miry, yellow-carpeted roads awhirl with flying leaves, or in the rainy courtyard of "The Black Sheep," and for each the scene at once shifted to a sunny tangled fairyland where the wood-pigeon purred, and oak, elm, beech, and silver birch in ample leaf rose in a crescent, with crisp beech-nuts underfoot, and baby bracken. But not even Nip could effect any visible communication. Much more gracious was Jinny to Barnaby, as soon as she was relieved of his "passing" adoration.

The weather improved for a space in mid-November. There was a bite in the air and the sheep-bells tinkled keenly from the pastures. The morning hoar-frosts held till noon. A great red ball of sun and a pale yellow crescent moon would shine together in the heavens, early sunsets seen through bare branches seemed to fill them with a golden fruitage that changed slowly to lemon, and the haystacks rose magically through enchanted hazes. But the cold only made Jinny hungrier and the earth-beauty sadder. It was as if she had already forgotten the blessing of Methusalem's return, and as if carrying was not after all the heart's deepest dream—especially with nothing to carry.

It was a relief to be blocked occasionally by Master Peartree's sheep, billowing along like a yellow Nile, and to exchange conversation with the shepherd, now at the most leisured moment of his year.

Patiently she would hear how the sheep got ravenous in the high cold winds, why he was driving them out of yon danger-zone of rape and turnip, and how the only real anxiety between now and Christmas was that one might fall on its back, or the hunt frighten the ewes: for soon somehow he would be speaking of his next-wall neighbours in Frog Farm, and somehow the family would always narrow to Will. "A grumpy, runty lad," he described him once. "Sometimes he goos about full o' mum: other times you can yer him through the wall grizzlin' and growlin' like my ould dog, time my poor missus had her fust baiby. He'd ha' torn the child to pieces," he went on, diverging into an exposition of how sheep-dogs had to be trained to prepare for babies. But she cut it as short as she dared, inquiring, "But who'd he be jealous of?" "The baiby—Oi'm explainin' to you!" he said. "No, I mean, who's young Mr. Flynt jealous of?" she asked, wondering how Will could know that she had been shedding such gracious smiles on Barnaby. And when the shepherd replied "'Lijah Skindle, in course," she winced perceptibly. But though the sting of the reply rankled, she was not so sure as the rest of the world that it was true.

III

The abundance of black sloes, they said, foretold a hard winter, and as the winter approached, Jinny's outlook grew darker. Even to keep a roof over their heads was not easy with the thatch everywhere holed by starlings. Driblets came through the old man's bedroom ceiling and were caught in a pail. And as for the walls, Daniel Quarles cursed the builder who had put in such bad mortar that "big birds came and picked the grit out o' the lime." The rain drove even through the closed lattices. To keep the living-room dry, he had made Jinny purchase putty, of which he daubed no less than three pounds over the rotting woodwork of the window. A stumpy piece of log he also nailed to the bottom of the window to block up the crevices, though he could do nothing with the top of the kitchen door through the little vine that grew over it, and which in some years yielded several pounds of small white grapes.

And if it was high time that her Hall should be patched up, Jinny often thought with commiseration of poor Uncle Lilliwhyte in his leaky hut throughout all these rains. Even from a selfish point of view, his health was a consideration. If he broke up, a main source of supply would disappear, and any day he might be at least temporarily paralysed by his rheumatism, and need provender instead of supplying it. A frail reed indeed to rely on, and Jinny began to wonder if she had been wise in training Nip so carefully not to hunt rabbits. With food and shelter thus alike insecure, Jinny, remembering the formula of her sect, resolved to "ask in faith." Perhaps too conscious a resolution impaired the faith—at any rate Providence, even with an accessory at court in the shape of the Angel-Mother, proved stony, and the Angel-Mother herself appeared limited in her powers, however limitless her sympathy. She could not even make folks demand tambour lace. Jinny began to wonder if no terrestrial powers remained to be invoked in the old man's behalf. What had become of all the children, whose names were recorded in the fly-leaf of his hereditary Bible, and only some of whom had their deaths chronicled? Cautiously she probed and pried into corners she had never dared approach before, instinctively feeling them full of cobwebs and grime. And her instinct was justified—each child had been more "obstropolus" than the others. One of the daughters was always "a slammacks" and had married beneath her, another—a beauty even fairer than Jinny's mother—had, on the contrary, caught a London linen-draper on his holidays and looked down on her father, who would starve rather than eat a bit of her bread. One boy had "'listed," another been beguiled into the Navy by that "dirty little Dap," a third—a lanky youth nicknamed "Ladders"—had gone to London to see the coronation of King William, and had disappeared, while his devil-may-care younger brother had shot a rabbit at night and been transported to "Wan Demon's Land," a name that made Jinny shudder. This last was the only son of whose present locality he was even vaguely aware, though, oddly enough, the sailor son had once sent him word that, landing with a boat's crew upon an island called "Wan Couver," he had come upon "Ladders" in the service of the Hudson Bay Company, living in a stockaded fort called after the Queen, and surrounded by naked, painted Indians. But as none of these children were ever to dare cross their father's doorstep again, there did not seem much help to be looked for from any quarter of the globe that might contain them. And Jinny was sorry she had not left the cobwebbed corners in their original mystery, for as the stories multiplied, the old man began to loom as a sort of sinister raven that drives out its own offspring, though gradually she came to see behind all the stories the same tale of a cast-iron religion against which the young generation broke itself. Or was it only a cast-iron obstinacy, she asked herself, after working out that the first at least of these family jars must have occurred before her grandfather's oft-narrated encounter with John Wesley.

It was with a new astonishment that she learnt he had been careful to make his will, lest Blackwater Hall should fall into the hands of his youngest surviving rascal. "And who've you left it to?" she inquired innocently.

"Why, who has the nat'ral right to it? Sidrach, in course, as ought to has had it 'stead o' me, he bein' the eldest. He's been cut out o' the wote, too, what goos with the property and what's worth pounds and pounds."

He was so convinced of the righteousness of this will, and appeared so genuinely fond of his brother, that Jinny was afraid to suggest the strong probability of Sidrach predeceasing him. Indeed Sidrach began now to play a larger and larger part in his thoughts, his mind reverted to the early days of the "owler," and gradually the prosperity of those days shone again over the patriarch in "Babylon." Sidrach now loomed as a star of hope, and Daniel spoke constantly of paying his long-projected visit to him at Chelmsford, designing apparently to drive the cart himself, and to inform his brother of the magnanimous bequest that was coming to him—a legacy that would suggest to Sidrach corresponding magnanimity in the living present. Afraid the Gaffer would actually set forth on this dangerous and visionary quest, Jinny did her best to discredit the notion of Sidrach's opulence, and quoted "Rolling stones gather no moss," but the Gaffer argued tenaciously that if his eldest brother had not been comfortably off, he would have come to seek the shelter of their roof-tree, or at least applied for their assistance, as he must be getting old, or at least (he modified it) too old to work. Jinny offered to write to Sidrach to inquire, but her grandfather could not find the ten-year-old letter inviting the visit. No, he would go over and find Sidrach instead, and Jinny was reduced to pointing out from day to day how unfavourable the weather was for the excursion. As the days grew shorter and shorter, the project, finding no opposition to nourish it, seemed to subside. Jinny was almost conscience-stricken when one Sunday after church Mr. Fallow showed her a paragraph in the Chelmsford Chronicle, stating that "another link with the past" had been broken by the death "last Monday from a fall downstairs" in the Chelmsford poorhouse of a centenarian named Sidrach Quarles, who claimed to be a hundred and five, and who was certainly well over the hundred, his recollections, which were a source of entertainment to all visitors, going back to the days when England was still ruled by a "furriner," meaning thereby George II.

The shock Jinny received at this was more of life than of death. It made her realize she had never quite believed in Sidrach's existence, and this sense of his substantiality almost swamped the minor fact of his decease. She saw no reason why he should not remain substantial. Now that she had perhaps been guilty of baulking her grandfather's last chance of seeing his beloved brother, she did not feel equal to robbing him of his last hope of assistance. He might even agitate himself over making a fresh will, and it was far better to let Providence or the lawyer folk decide on his heir. No doubt when the dread necessity arose, the youngest son would be raked up from somewhere. But that dark moment still seemed far. The longer her grandfather lived, the more she had got used to the idea of his never dying. True, Sidrach had died, though his habit of living had been even more ingrained, but they did not take proper care of you in a workhouse, and besides he had died of an accident. She would keep Daniel from that fate, even as she would keep him from the poorhouse.

As she sat at his side by the fire that Sunday night, knitting him a muffler, her thoughts were playing so pitifully over poor old Sidrach in his bleak pauper's grave, that she was not at all surprised when her grandfather announced with sudden decision that he would go to see Sidrach the very next day. With a chill at her heart as though a dead hand had been placed on it, she told him gently that it was nonsense and that he must wait now till the spring.

But he shook his head obstinately. "Don't seem as ef Oi'll last out till the spring."

She laughed forcedly. "What an idea!"

"Not unless there's an election and Oi can buy grub with my wote-money," he explained. "And Oi ain't heerd as Parlyment is considerin' the likes of us."

"You've always had plenty to eat!" she protested, colouring up.

"That ain't enough in the larder when Oi looks, ne yet for Methusalem in the barn. Ye've got to have a store like the beer in my barrel. Where's my flitch? Where's my cheeses? Same as we're snowbound, like the year Sidrach went away, where would Oi get my Chris'mus dinner? 'Tis a middlin' long way to Babylon, but Oi'll start with the daylight and be back between the lights, and ef Oi'm longer, why the moon's arly. Oi'll be proper pleased to see dear Sidrach again—he larnt me my letters and Oi'll bring him back to live with us, now he's gittin' oldish. It ain't good for a man to live alone, says the Book, and that'll be good for us too, he bein' as full o' suvrans as a dog of fleas."

"Nip isn't full of fleas," she said with mock anger, hoping to make a diversion. "Why, you scrub him yourself!"

But he went on, unheeding. "Daniel Quarles has allus been upright, and he'd sooner die than goo to his darter or the poorhouse."

She thought miserably that the poorhouse was where he would have to go to find any traces of his beloved Sidrach, and she set herself by every device of logic or cajolery to discourage this revived dream of the journey. He might not even find Sidrach in such a big city, she now hinted, but he laughed at that. Everybody knew Sidrach, "a bonkka, hansum chap with a mosey face and a woice like the bull of Bashan and as strong too. Wery short work he'd ha' made of Master Will. Carry him in, indeed! Carried him out—and with one hand—that's what Sidrach would ha' done! Why, he's tall enough to light the street-lamps in Che'msford!"

These street-lamps, Jinny gathered, still figured in his mind as of oil, and she was able by dexterous draughts on his reminiscences to put off the evil day of his expedition. But whenever there was visible dearth at table, the thought of his rich brother, flared up again.

Could Blackwater Hall perhaps be sold, she thought desperately, and the money spent on his declining years. The thought was stimulated by a meeting of the Homage Court which came from railhead in the "Flynt Flyer," and before which Miss Gentry's landlady as a copyholder had to do "suit and service" in the Moot Hall to the Lords of the Manor.

But Jinny ascertained that Beacon Chimneys, a ramshackle place with much land, had been bought up recently by Farmer Gale for his new bride at fifty shillings an acre, farm and buildings thrown in; a rate at which Blackwater Hall would not even yield the forty shillings supposed to be its annual value as a voting concern—whereas the Gaffer's view, cautiously extracted, ran: "Ef you spread suvrans all over my land, each touchin' the tother, you pick up your pieces and Oi keep my land." Moreover, Mr. Fallow, to whom she had broached the idea, reminded her feelingly that old people could not be moved. He was keenly interested, however, to learn that the tenure was an example of Borough English and hunted up the local Roll of Customs (7th Edward IV) proclaiming that "Time out of the Mind of Man" the "ould auncient Custom of the Bourow" had been for the heritage to go to the "youngest Sonne of the first wife."

At heart Jinny was glad the idea of selling the Hall was impracticable: for what would have become of Methusalem and the business of "Daniel Quarles, Carrier"? To surrender before the "Flynt Flyer" would have been a bitter pill indeed.

IV

When all but the last swallows had departed, and Christmas began to loom in the offing, the Sidrach obsession resurged, and there being a spell of bright, clear weather, the only way she could devise to stave off the expedition was to pretend to undertake it herself. This was the more necessary as she was not certain the scheme did not cover a crafty design to drive Methusalem back to the knacker's for the five pounds. She would start very early and go, not to Chelmsford, but to "Brandy Hole Creek." Instead of waiting her Christmas letter to Commander Dap, she would visit him personally. He was, after all, a relative and would not like to see his brother-in-law starve—of course she would accept nothing for herself. Already she had intended to skirt the subject at Christmas, but to ask assistance openly was painful, while if one was too reticent one might be misunderstood. In conversation one could feel one's way.

So on a misty morning of late November, when the peewits were calling over the dark fields, she set out, the old man watching her off with a lantern.

"And do ye bring back Sidrach," he called after her, "sow we can all live happy."

For answer she blew her horn cheerily, feeling this was less a lie than speech. She would come back with help of some sort—that was certain. Whether she would confess that the help came from Commander Dap or would attribute it to Sidrach, or whether it would be wiser to come back with the discovery of Sidrach's death, trusting to its staleness to blunt the blow and to the news of Dap's assistance to overcome it, or whether it would be imprudent to mention Dap at all, not merely because it would be hard to explain how she had met the Commander of the Watch Vessel at Chelmsford, but because her grandfather in his inveterate venom against Dap was capable of refusing his favours—on all these distracting alternatives she hoped to make up her mind during the day. Here, too, she would perhaps have to feel her way. But she now miserably realized the wisdom of the Spelling-Book's "writing-piece": "Lying may be thought convenient and profitable because not so soon discovered; but pray remember, the Evil of it is perpetual: For it brings persons under everlasting Jealousy and Suspicion; for they are not to be believed when they speak the Truth, nor trusted, when perhaps they mean honestly." She meant honestly enough, God knew, but into what a tangle she was getting. She consoled herself with the thought that anyhow there would be no pretending that day in her business—to spare Methusalem on so long a journey the empty boxes had been left at home.

Single drops oozed upon her as she started, but as the mist lifted, though it revealed sodden, blackened pastures on both sides of her route, the underlying betterness of the weather manifested itself, and soon under an arching blue Methusalem was almost trotting over withering bracken and fallen leaves in a world of browns and yellows, while an abnormally friendly robin perching on the cart-shaft, and the scarlet-berried bryony festooning the hedgerows, contributed with the gleaming holly-berries to colour her darkling mood. There was a certain refreshment, too, in going off by this new route, where she for her part was as unknown. It was odd how the mere turning her back on the Chipstone Road transformed everything. Even the path—though this was not so pleasant for Methusalem—had at first an upward tendency, and her mere passing evoked stares and comments. This surprised her in turn till she remembered Will's disapprobation. She did not realize that the visible emptiness of the cart, with its implication that she was not plying, only driving it to some male headquarters, mitigated the sensation, and she congratulated herself there was no old client to observe the absence of cargo. In the first few miles she met no soul she knew except the taciturn lout who had once directed her to Master Peartree's shearing-shed, and who was now preparing a feeding-ground for the flock, pulling out mangolds with a picker and hurling them over the hurdled field from a broken-pronged fork. The sheep had to go to this higher ground for fear of floods, he informed her in a burst of communicativeness, and it wasn't half as eatable.

Passing a row of thatched, black-tarred cottages at a moment when the mothers were coming to the garden gates to speed their broods to school, she offered lifts till her space was packed with little ones. The old cart was now alive with youth and laughter, and the flocks of rooks from the elms were out-chattered. The road lay between great fields flanked by broad ditches, along which argosies of yellow leaves went sailing, and there were shooters with dogs, happy duck-ponds, old towers and steeples, black barns, gabled old houses with verge-boards over the windows, quaint inn-signs and mossy-tiled granges, and the ground kept humping itself and dropping more erratically than her home circuit, but never sufficiently to spoil the sublime flatness in which single figures stooping to turn over the soil showed like quadrupeds in a vast circle. She must needs go a bit out of her way to reach the school, which lay in a little town on the estuary, and it was a thrilling moment when from her seat she had her first far-off glimpse of the very waters that had beglamoured her childhood—outwardly it was only the gleam as of a white river with hazy land beyond, and on the hither side a few black huts looking almost like vessels; but over everything was wrapped a dreamy peace, which the clamour of the actual children could not penetrate, while in her nostrils—though it was surely too far off to be wafted to her—there arose the strange, salty, putrid odour of fenland, offensive and delectable. And as the road curved slowly towards the shore, all the charm and mystery of childhood seemed to be in those barges with the red-brown sails, those grassy knolls and unlovely mud-flats, in which rotting boats stuck half sunken.

Before she could deposit her charges in their classrooms some had dropped off and were looking for treasure in the flat, dyke-seamed fields. They had arrived too early for school, they explained. But she felt rewarded for carrying them to the waterside when she espied the long, low hull and great brown sail of Bidlake's barge. With a blast of her horn she summoned the trio of females, but only the twins mounted to the deck to wave hands at her as the broad wherry came tacking and gliding past, the shaggy Ephraim explaining in an indecorous shout that the missus was to be "laid aside" again, and this time he was looking around for a nice quiet lodging on shore for her and the girls. How handsome Sophy and Sally were growing, she thought, how charmingly they had smiled, just as if she had never left off bringing them presents. What a comfort they were so grown up now; they should soon be fending for themselves.

After the barge was wafted away, she remained on the shore a few minutes, fascinated by the lattice-work reflection of the clouds on the water, which through their scudding over it against the stream seemed to be going in opposite directions at once. She did not know why this phenomenon was agitating the recesses of her being; but suddenly there flashed up from the obscure turmoil the lines of Miss Gentry in her sibylline mood:

When the Brad in opposite ways shall course,
Lo! Jinny's husband shall come on a horse,
And Jinny shall then learn Passion's force.

Of course this was not the Brad, nor was it really going two ways at once, and in any case who wanted a husband or Passion? Clucking so suddenly to Methusalem that his movement scattered some poultry pecking around him amid golden straw, she turned up through the High Street. At a fishmonger's shop she got down and bought a pennyworth of bloaters for her grandfather's supper, the man sliding them off a rod where they hung like blackened corpses from a gibbet. She was half minded to inspect the shop of the "Practical Tailor" next door, to see if she could not pick up something cheap and serviceable for the old man's winter wear, but there was nothing in the little house-window, not even a roll of cloth, except illustrations of men's clothing so ultra-fashionable and dear that she was frightened to go in. "Pacha D'Orsay Chesterfields, Codringtons, Sylphides, Peltoes, Zephyr Wrappers, etc., etc., every description of Winter Coat"—here was assuredly what he needed. But one pound five? Who was there behind the sea-wall that could rise to such prices? Possibly it was here that Mr. Flippance had got his wedding equipment. She returned sadly to her cart, not even noticing that all these fashionable pictures were simply cut out of the catalogue of the great Moses & Son, London.

The road now led again through great grass-lands under shimmering clouds floating in a spacious blue, and with gentle slopes and hillocks, though little streams had replaced the broad ditches. There were rabbits taking the air that showed white scuts at the approach of Nip. Far to the right she left the saltings with their grazing cattle, but she could still see them from her driving-board, and the marshes stretched, humped and brown and infinitely interstreaked, a mud-maze with purple herbage and motley sea-birds.

Then suddenly there was a thunder and clatter behind her, and she pulled her horse mechanically to the left to avoid a coach, not realizing till it slowed down that this was the "Flynt Flyer's" day for the district. Her heart beat fast, almost painfully, and she went scarlet with the thought that Will would think she had come purposely on his track. Why, oh why, had she just chosen that day? There was no turning to be seen and desperately she steered Methusalem's nose towards a farm-gate, prepared to trespass, but it proved to be only a "lift" for wagons, opened by raising the rail from its slots, a feat which Methusalem's nose could not achieve. She leaped down and tried to pull it up herself, but her fingers were trembling, and in an instant Will was at her side, hat gracefully in hand, the rail lifted up, and the gate held aside for her passing. Blushing still more furiously under the gaze of the coach passengers, she led Methusalem through, and as she passed she said with a sweet smile: "Thank you."

This was all the audience heard or saw, but what was really said and substantially understood by both principals was:

WILL: "Oh, my dear Jinny, how pretty and kissable you look in that becoming new bonnet, and isn't it silly to be trying to compete with me along this road, when, though you get business from goodness knows who, you can't even keep your old customers on your own route? You haven't got the tiniest parcel, I see, nor any hope of one. Really you would do better to accept my offer of a partnership, or better still to get off the roads altogether, for the winter is going to be a hard one, and perhaps if we dropped our silly sullen silence and began to find out each other's good points again, who knows but what we might come to another sort of partnership? Anyhow I am delighted to open this lift for you, but what the devil you are going to do in a field just being ploughed is what I shall watch with amusement."

JINNY: "You perfectly unbearable Mr. Flynt! How mean of you to come spying into my empty cart! If you want to know, I am not out on business to-day at all, it's a little friendly call I am making on the farmer. I haven't, like you, to work all the week round to scrape together enough to feed my horses. Two days a week keeps me in luxury—ay, and Gran'fer too. And don't pretend to be so gay and happy—I know what a grumpy, runty chap you are at home, and how you're still hankering after that Blanche Jones who has thrown you away like an old shoe. Or if it's my refusal to be partners with you that's rankling, and you are even thinking after all of a closer partnership, then all I can say is, you must be the village idiot if you fancy I'll put up with Blanche's leavings. Don't imagine that silly old coach with the silly wanty-hook and skewers painted on it is very attractive to me. Why, if you were to come to me in a coach of gold like the Lord Mayor of London, with six milk-white steeds spruced up with flowers and ribbons like Methusalem on May Day, and say: 'I love you, Jinny, come and sit in silks and diamonds on my box-seat,' I should up with my horn and blow a blast of scorn, for I hate and despise you, and how dare you come ogling me before all the coach?"

And still retaining her sweet smile, Jinny gazed at the shirt-sleeved ploughmen, who though vaguely astonished at the invasion of their field, continued their stolid operations. Jinny arrested her cart to watch with equal stolidity the white whirls and long lines of fluttering gulls that followed the slow-moving ploughs, with such a twittering and circling and looking so beautiful over the reddish earth and under the blue sky. There was beauty, too, she felt, in the youth who from his white basket sprinkled seeds with a graceful motion, and when he smiled at her, she did not hesitate to remark in her sweetest tone on the rainy autumn, spinning out the hygrometric conversation till Will felt it almost a flirtation. Fuming and fumbling with the top rail, he took as much time as possible to readjust it in its slots. But in this game of patience he knew he must be beaten: however amusedly he might pretend to watch her pretences, his passengers would compel him to go on, and so, in no amused state of mind, at a moment when the gulls as by a magic clearance disappeared to a bird, he followed their example. When the whirlwind of his passing had died in the distance, Jinny came back again through the lift, with the feeling that Methusalem must think her a fool, and wondering if he were not right.

Soon after, she fell in with a carter who was going her way with sacks of flour for his master, and as they jogged along, conversing pleasantly, after the failure of his attempt to chaff and flirt, she was surprised to learn that he had till recently plied as a carrier on this very road, but had been ousted by the "Flynt Flyer." It had never occurred to her that there were other victims, but as he went on to denounce Will, she found herself defending the rights of competition and pointing out the service the coach rendered to the neighbourhood, and the carter fell back upon another grievance about which he was even more embittered. On one of his last journeys a man he had carried from the Creek had got off without paying, and he had foolishly let him go, thinking he was "a Brandy Hole chap" and would be returning by the same vehicle. But he had vanished from his ken. "Oi thought he was a Brandy Hole chap," he kept repeating plaintively.

She was glad to shed him at "The Jolly Bargee," a small inn with a sanded tap-room and no visible taps, where, amid a company she saw already gathered over frothing mugs, he would doubtless bewail the competition of the coach and the trickery of the fare he had taken for "a Brandy Hole chap."

Noon was tolling from the square church-tower when Jinny espied again her treasured picture of it, rising from a harmony of golden ricks and lichen-spotted tiles, just as on that happy, enchanted day when she had journeyed to the funeral of her mother's Aunt Susannah. How quickly one came—she thought with pleased astonishment—free of the detours and delays of custom, or the pretence thereof! There would be ample time to visit the grave of her father and mother before going on to the Watch Vessel, especially as it was thus on her way. But, remembering with a sad smile the dispute as to whether her grandfather could go to his sister's funeral in his cart, she took care to draw up her shabby vehicle in a nook beyond the lych-gate. Nip had vanished—like the "Brandy Hole chap"—she found; probably he was also at "The Jolly Bargee." Leaving Methusalem to his well-earned if not well-filled nose-bag, she returned to the gate.

The monkey-trees and weeping willows were unchanged, though in the path leading to the church-porch there was an avenue of young rose-bushes which she did not remember, and screened by them, to the right, a freshly dug grave which made her shudder. She hastened towards the crumbling tower—still more crumbled now—which her memory connected with the sacred spot. The blackberry-bushes still swathed it, though they were now stripped of their fruit, and in its shadow she found again, not without surprise, the familiar stone, the object of so much whimsical wrangling. Still Roger Boldero lay "safely neaped in Christ." She was almost certain that her grandfather had sent a couple of pounds to Commander Dap to have the stone changed, since the inscription, it appeared, could not well be emended otherwise. Yes, surely he had ordered that "neaped" should be turned into "asleep," for she remembered counting the letters and rejoicing to find them the same in number. But on the whole she was pleased the word had not been changed: her Angel-Mother had wanted it, she remembered, in memory of her happiness with Roger Boldero. As she stood there, musing on these two, feeling her mother's soft cheek against hers and recalling that smoke-reeking, hairier, burlier, yet somehow more shadowy figure, many pictures flashed and waned, and most vividly of all came the vision of her grandfather's strong shoulder supporting the coffin, and the kindly old Commander leading her off stealthily to this very spot, and she heard the death-bell tolling again with its long solemn pauses.

And then suddenly with a queer little thrill she awoke to the fact that the death-bell was tolling, that a company in black was bearing a coffin. She moved farther behind the tower, she was not in black, and felt almost an interloper. Presently there came from the rose-bushes the sonorous voice of a clergyman intoning the great words. She did not want to be delayed further, nor did she want to pass by the grief-stricken group, which consisted—she saw as she peeped from her hiding-place—of half a dozen men and women, all elderly and all weeping: with a small band of sailors in the background, whose left arms bore black silk handkerchiefs tied in a bow. She looked around for another way out of the churchyard, and finding a side gate escaped almost happily, jumped on her cart, and drove off towards the shore, thinking pleasantly of the genial little Dap and the dinner she would not be too late for; a meal which now, after this long drive, began to seem the paramount consideration.

The village rose russet from the trees, and she curved round exquisite corners of white cottages with Christmas roses in their gardens, and presently she came out by the grass-covered sea-wall. She hardly saw the sordidness of the shore—-the litter of pigs, poultry, boats, sheds, barrels—so great a seascape burst upon her, broken by a long narrow island, that added subtle shades and hazes to the far-spreading shimmer and fantasy, the water glinting and moving, dotted with red-sailed smacks and barges. Even the slimy posts that stuck up from it near the shore had a romantic air, being young tree-trunks that still stretched odd limbs.

But all this glory faded into nothingness when, catching sight of the Watch Vessel moored on the "hard" of gravel, at the place where she had first patted Methusalem, she saw that the flag was at half-mast. She scarcely needed to make the inquiry: the flag, the funeral, the nautical handkerchiefs, all rushed into a black unity. Dear old Commander Dap was dead.

V

A perverse imp kept telling her that the funeral meats would be unusually abundant. But she had no heart to board the Watch Vessel, to encounter these unknown fellow-mourners. She wanted to mourn in solitude. And her quest had failed. The last hope for her grandfather had been extinguished—Dap had followed Sidrach—and the best thing to do was to get home as quickly as poor Methusalem could manage it. He should rest, not here where she might meet the returning Daps and perhaps be recognized through Daniel Quarles's cart, but when they got to "The Jolly Bargee," where she must have a bit of bread and cheese brought out to her. Yet she could not tear herself away from this squalid, sublime waterside, and driving along the cart-route behind the sea-wall to a safe distance, she got out near a little wooden pier and walked on the rough earth of the sea-wall, which was luxuriant with pigweed and sea-beet, strewn with wisps of hay and straw from passing carts, and covered with dead little white-shelled crabs. There was something akin to her mood in the pleasant pain of the acrid mud-smell.

At "The Jolly Bargee" she was jarred by the slow easy laughter from the tap-room—the trickery of the "Brandy Hole chap" was still under facetious debate. Before her set face, the gorged Nip, rejoining her at the inn-door with conscious drooping tail, turned on his back and grovelled guiltily: but she ignored his abasement, and having gulped down her snack of bread and cheese—an unwelcome and unforeseen expense—drove on with the same brooding air. She was dazed by the wonder and pathos of the little Commander's death, the whole genial breathing mass become as insensitive as his glass eye: would he get that back at the Resurrection, she pondered, or would there be his original eye? Thence she passed to the thought of the dead Sidrach, the large handsome man of a hundred and five, strong as a bull of Bashan, whom she was supposed to be visiting, and she wondered dully what report of him she should bring back to her grandfather. Abandoning herself as usual to Methusalem's guidance in this deep brooding, she discovered after an hour or so that in his ignorance of these roads he had gone miles out of their way, down Smugglers' Lane, and when after half an hour of readjustment she had got on the right homeward road, her own subconscious gravitation to the waterside took her back to it. And while she gave Methusalem a rest here, the white moon and the early November sunset began to brood over the mud-flats, transfiguring them with strange scintillant gold, and Jinny felt a divine lesson in the transfiguration, and the solemn voice of the clergyman echoed in her ears: "I am the Resurrection and the Life." Doubtless the Commander was already in communion with the Angel-Mother.

The problem of Sidrach was still unsolved when the feeding-field she had seen preparing in the morning loomed again on her vision like a reminder of the urgency of that question. She envied Master Peartree's sheep munching so imperturbably in their hurdles while she had been going through all these emotions and perplexities. With their black noses and feet they looked, she thought, as though they had been drinking from a pool of ink, and her thoughts wandered again from her problem, and she let Methusalem drink from a pool of water. Though it was only four o'clock, the moon had turned a pale ochre and was shining full and high in the heavens, its continents clearly showing. There was no sound save the chewing of the sheep, the gulping of her horse, the wistful tinkling of a wether's bell, and from afar the fainter clanging of a cow-bell. Even Nip, feeling unforgiven, was subdued. Life was beautiful after all, she felt, as she watched the great splashes of sunset below the moon, the glimmering rose-tint on the horizon, the glint upon the pool, the tangle of magical gold in the branches. Somehow a way would be opened for her through this network of mendacity.

But by the time she got to her door, the Common was covered again with a grey mist, just oozing rain, and Blackwater Hall was a place of shrouded terrors. No light was showing through the shutters or through the chinks in door or window, and she had a sudden clammy intuition that her grandfather had solved her problem for her by the simple process of dying like Sidrach and the Commander. Silent and weird lay thatch and whitewash under the moon. She hammered at the house-door and then at the shutters, her heart getting colder and colder.

She tried the door again, then hearing Nip barking mysteriously from within, she went round to the kitchen-door. To her joy and amazement it was wide open, and a ray of moonlight resting on a little pool of beer on the brick floor showed that the tap of the beer-barrel which was kept there was dribbling. Even in that anxious moment her economical instinct prevailed, and as she was tightening the tap, there permeated through the living-room door a heavenly snore—no lesser adjective could convey the relief it brought. With a bound she was up the couple of stone steps and, unlatching the door, she sent a faint blue glimmer from the kitchen into the shuttered darkness, that was relieved only by the flicker of an expiring lamp and a last spark from a dying log. In that dim discord of lights she saw her grandfather's head on the thumb-holed tray, his hair and beard a dull grey spread, dividing a darker jug from two beery glasses. The absence of his Bible-pillow seemed symbolic of his degradation.

Who had been with him? she wondered. What boon companion had tempted him from his habitual moderation? She could not imagine. She shook him to awaken him, and lifted up his head. But it fell back in a stupor, and under the draught from the kitchen-door the lamp-flicker went out. She groped about, replenishing the lamp and trying to light it with a spill from the fire, but the greying log only charred the paper. She fumbled in vain among the china shepherdesses on the mantelpiece for her flint and the iron and steel gauntlet, and going out to get her lighting-up matches from her cart, she overturned the other arm-chair that stood in a novel situation at the table—probably the guest had drawn it up there. But the noise left the Gaffer's snore unweakened. Well, at any rate he had solved her problem—at least for the moment—she thought bitterly, as she groped her way back to the glimmering grate. But even the chemical matches would not light, whether by friction or when placed on the charred log: evidently the long damp had impaired them, and they even snapped under her fingers. How lucky it was one need not rely on such new-fangled gewgaws, she thought when—by a happy inspiration—she found the solid steel and stone with the tinder-box in the Gaffer's pockets; and soon the lamp was lit and the fire glowing ruddily under the bellows. Then she made herself some kettle-broth (hot water with bread soaked in it), which, sipped before the fire, was almost as cheering as the blazing logs, and resisting the temptation to cook one of the bloaters, she fed the still subdued Nip from the bread.

When he was cosily couched in his basket, and with a last summoning of her spent energies, she had rubbed down Methusalem, she tried to fold her third charge, but the old man still snored steadily, and when she sought again to raise his head from the tray, he swore inarticulately in his sleep, and she was too worn out to persist or even to remove the tray and glasses. She wanted to sleep herself, after all these emotions and the long day in the air, and her cracked mirror showed her a drawn face that yawned and closed weary eyes against itself. But it now occurred to her that she could not get to bed with Gran'fer in the room, she must sleep in an arm-chair or on the settle, or stretched on the floor with the cushion for pillow. But the floor through her early start was unswept, the settle was too narrow, and the chair soon got so hard that after a last attempt to rouse the sleeper, she put an old cloak over his shoulders, a stout log on the fire, turned out the lamp—setting her shadow leaping monstrously—and dragged herself up the dark, fusty staircase to his room, where she let herself fall dressed on his bed. She did not dare get between the sheets, for fear he might wake up in the night and come up to bed. Lying there, muttering the prayers she was too tired to kneel for, she had an underthought that Providence was giving her a hint: assuredly in the coming winter nights she must leave him in the room that was warmed all day by the fire, exchanging bedrooms, though not for the reason he had once suggested—a reason that made her last conscious thought a shame-faced memory. But her next thought was one of pleasant wonder—sunshine splashing the whitewashed sloping walls through the undrawn blind of a little lattice. What was this strange spacious room? How came she there in her clothes? Then memory resurged, and feeling she had slept dangerously long, she sprang up, unhooked the casement, and drew a deep breath of fresh air, as she gazed on this unfamiliar morning view of the Common and the hoar-frosted fields, dazzling her eye with floating colour-specks from the sun that cut redly through the foliage of a fir-tree. Particularly she relished the silver rim of the Brad now descried on the horizon. It made her feel sickish to descend from that space and freshness to the dark, airless, shuttered room with its musty, beery smell and its all-pervading snore. Swiftly she threw open the shutters and the casement, and let the light and air stream in.

The chill draught and the noise she made seemed to rouse the Gaffer at last, for as she was returning from the kitchen with some kindlings for the fire in her apron, he opened his eyes with a start and stared at her.

"Where's Sidrach?"

She was taken aback: she had not yet prepared her story. Indeed the waking in the big attic and the puzzle of his condition had driven her own problem out of her head.

"Sidrach?" she murmured. Should she out with his death and be done with it?

"Ay, he got riled 'cause Oi wouldn't let him smoke. Where's he got to?"

It was now her turn to stare at him. "Nonsense, Gran'fer," she said gently, "that's a dream you've been having."

"Mebbe." He blinked in the sunlight, mystified. Suddenly his face darkened. "Why do ye tell me lies agen? There's his tumbler!"

He pointed to one of the beery glasses she had left still standing. Commonplace as the glass looked with its lees, she was glad he had not pointed at it the evening before in the weird moonlight with her brain full of the poor dead Dap.

"Don't tell me!" she said in a voice she tried in vain to make stern. "It wasn't Sidrach that was drinking with you. Who was it?"

"It was Sidrach, Oi'm tellin' ye," he protested. "Oi put out his beer with his tumbler and his chair to be ready soon as ye brought him back, he bein' a rare one for his liquor. But the hours passed slow as a funeral crawl, it got owl-light and you not back, ne yet a rumble of your cart upon the road, so at last molloncholy-like Oi lights the lamp and makes a roaring fire and drinks by myself, and then Oi locks and bolts up and stoops down to put on another log, and when Oi looks up, there he sets in his chair in his best Sunday smock, all clean and white."

She thrilled again.

"But how could he get in, if you'd locked up?"

"That's what Oi says to him. 'Good Lord, Sidrach,' Oi says, 'how did you get here?' 'Come in the coach from Che'msford,' says he. 'The coach,' says Oi, wexed, 'ye didn't want to back up the jackanips what's come competitioning here, and Jinny gone to fetch ye, too. But how did ye get through the door?' Oi says. 'You draw me some beer, Danny,' says he. 'For Oi count ye've finished the jug.' So Oi goos to the kitchen with the jug, and there sure enough stands the door wide open—happen Oi hadn't shut it good tightly—and there passin' along the road by the Common Oi catches sight of the coach, lookin' all black in the dusk and glidin' away wery quiet, same as ashamed to be in our cart-racks. 'You pirate thief,' Oi says, shakin' my fist at the driver, 'ye'll never come into this house save on your hands and knees.' But when Oi goos back with my jug brimmin' over, Sidrach warn't there. 'Sidrach!' Oi calls, 'Sidrach!' No answer. Oi goos about beat out and crazy 'twixt here and the kitchen and then the clock strikes, and that remembers me to look in the tother room, and there Oi hears him chucklin' to hisself in one of they big empty boxes ye left at home this marnin'. 'Out ye come,' says Oi, laughin' too, for he was allus up to his pranks, was Sid. 'And Oi'm proper glad to see you, old chap,' Oi says. With that he comes out of his box, with a little o' the dust on his white smock, and he hugs and coases me—wery cowld his hands and face was from the long jarney—and Oi drinks his health and he drinks mine, and we clinks they glasses together and has rare sport gammickin' of the times when Oi was in my twenties and he taken me to see the cock-fightin' and that old Christmas Day his dog won the silver spoon in the bear-baitin' at 'The Black Sheep,' and Oi told him as Annie were free now but seein' as he was come to stay, Oi dedn't want nobody else and he needn't be afeared he'd be tarned out ef Oi died, bein' as Oi'd left the house to him by will and testament. 'Little Danny,' says he, 'you're a forthright brother, but no fear o' the poorhouse for neither on us, for Oi was born with that silver spoon in my mouth, and Oi've got a stockin' chock-full o' gold,' and he shows me it, hunders of spade guineas, each with the head of George III, fit to warm the cockles of your heart, and we clinked glasses agen and sang three-times-three, merry as grigs, and then the devil possesses him to pull out his pipe and baccar. 'No, ye don't,' says Oi, 'not for all the gold in Babylon,' and Oi runs to pocket the flint and steel on the mantelpiece, and to block out the fire, and he laughs and howds his pipe over the lamp and draws like a demon. Oi rushes to the lamp and tarns it out and then back to the fire, but aldoe that give a goodish light, Sidrach, he warn't there no more." He was almost blubbering.

"But how did he look?" said Jinny, whose kindlings had long since slid from her apron.

"A hansum bonkka man, Oi keep tellin' ye. Ain't ye seen him nowhere? Where's he got to? Just there he sat singin' with his great old woice:

'Two bony Frenchmen and one Portugee,
One jolly Englishman can lick all three.'"

The quavering melody ended with a big sneeze, and Jinny, fearing the brothers would indeed be reunited, rushed to close the window and light the fire. Though she felt confusedly that her grandfather, waiting for Sidrach, and drinking too freely in his melancholy, had probably dreamed it all, she was not sure that he had not really seen Sidrach's ghost. How else would the flint and steel have got into his pocket? In any case she was reminded that her secret was not safe. In concealing a death one forgot to reckon with the ghost, and Sidrach's might at any time divulge it suddenly to his brother, even if the present visitation was only a dream. Dap's ghost, too, was another possibility that must be taken into account. "I'll tell you where Sidrach's got to," she said desperately, as a yellow flame leapt up, "he's got to heaven."

"To heaven?" repeated the old man vaguely.

"To heaven!" she said inexorably. "He hasn't been in Chelmsford for weeks. He was very old, you see, a hundred and five."

The Gaffer began to tremble. "Ye don't really mean Sidrach's gone to heaven?"

She nodded her head sadly. "He fell down," she explained.

"Fell down to heaven?" he asked dazedly.

"His body fell downstairs—his soul went up to God."

"Then he come downstairs agen last night, dear Sidrach," he said solemnly; "he come to have a glass and a gammick with his little brother."

Jinny was not prepared to deny it, and though the idea jarred, it was after all difficult to see snoring senectitude with the poetry attaching to Angel-Mothers. She removed the dirty glasses silently.

"And where's his stockin' o' gold?" he inquired suddenly. "Why didn't ye bring back that?"

"There wasn't any," she said gently. "He died poorish."

"They've stole it," he cried. "They've robbed me. 'Twas me he meant it for."

"No, no—all he left was used up in the funeral."

"Ay, they ain't satisfied with carts nowadays," he commented bitterly. "Like that doddy little Dap. Did you goo to the churchyard to see the grave?"

"Yes," she replied unflinchingly, sustained by the verbal accuracy. "I've got you a bloater for breakfast," she added cheerfully.

"That's the cowld chill he caught as a cad, gatherin' eggs on the ma'shes," he said musingly. "Ague they calls it—never got over it. And tramped with his pack-horses in all weathers. And rollin' about here and there and everywheres. 'You'll never make old bones, Sid,' Oi says to him."

"A hundred and five is pretty old, Gran'fer," Jinny reminded him. "King David only says seventy, that's exactly one and a half lives your brother had."

"Give me the Book," he said brokenly.

With trembling hands she brought the great Family Bible he had inherited with the house. But his object seemed to be neither verification of the text nor prayerful reading, for he next asked for pen and ink, and then having ascertained the exact date of Sidrach's death, he adjusted his spectacles and chronicled it with a quavering quill opposite Sidrach's birth-date.

"He's gone to heaven," he said. "That's more than some folks'll do—even on their hands and knees. Do ye warm my beer for me this marnin', dearie, for Oi fare to be cowld and lonely in my innards, and Oi'd fain smoke a pipe myself, same as Oi hadn't promised the old man o' God."

VI

The year ended gloomily for Jinny. December was cold. In the mornings the fields looked almost snowy with hoar-frost, but the actual snow did not come till near Christmas. Her grandfather refused to be moved from his bedroom—one was safer from thieves up there, he now urged—so a fire upstairs every evening was added to her work. But the monotony of existence and of the struggle therefor was broken by two letters and an episode, albeit all interconnected.

Both letters were from Toby, the naval gunner, Dap's eldest son, and the one for her grandfather was enclosed in hers, as Toby was not sure the old gentleman was still alive, one of his sisters having heard that there was a piece in the paper about his death at the age of a hundred and five. He had only found her own address after the funeral, he wrote, a packet of letters from her having come to hand in the clearing up. For although his poor father with his last breath had asked that his telescope be given to little Jinny Boldero as a token of love and remembrance, he had died without telling them where to send it. It would now be forwarded in due course. For two months he had borne much pain with Christian resignation, she learnt with sorrow and respect. The other letter, addressed "Mr. Daniel Quarles," she had no option but to hand over, but did so with anxiety, for she had not yet broken the news of Dap's death, and whether he received it with regret or with unchristian satisfaction, it would assuredly agitate him. As she watched him open it, she saw a piece of paper flutter from it, and she caught it in its fall.

"That's mine!" he cried, snatching it from her fingers. "Pay the person naimed—" he read out dazedly. "What's that?"

"That must be a money order," she explained, though with no less surprise.

"A money order?" he repeated.

"You've seen post-office orders, surely," she said, not realizing that they had only become common a decade ago with the introduction of penny postage, and that nobody—not even his children—had ever sent him one before. "'Tis a way of sending money—you can send as much as two pounds for threepence. How much is yours for?"

Overlaid memories of his late eighties struggled to the surface. "Oh, ay," he said, not answering her. "That was a blow for the carriers—that and the penny post. Folks began to write to the shops; dedn't matter so much here, but the Che'msford carriers complained bitter as the tradesmen sent out their own carts with the goods."

"But how much is it for?" repeated Jinny impatiently.

He studied it afresh, holding it away from her like a dog with its paw on a bone. "Three pound!" he announced with rapturous defiance. "Ye took away my foiver. But this be for the person naimed on the enwelope, and that's Daniel Quarles."

"But what's it for?" she asked.

"It's for me," he said conclusively, and was going up to his room like a magpie with its treasure.

"Yes, but read the letter," she urged.

He consented to sit down and study it. "Good God!" he blubbered soon. "Poor Dap's dead."

"Dead?" echoed Jinny mendaciously.

"You read it for yourself, dearie. An awful pity, a man in the prime of life. 'Tis from his boy in the Navy as he ast to send me three pounds what he owed me. That was wunnerful honest of him, to remember, seein' as Oi don't, aldoe Oi count the Lord put it into his heart, knowin' Oi wanted money terrible bad. But Oi allus felt he was a good chap underneath: 'twarn't his fault he had a glass eye. That made him look at the nose, like, and git frownin' and quarrelsome. Three pound! That's a good nest-egg."

"Yes," said Jinny, glad the death was passing off so peacefully, "and he's sending me his telescope."

"He don't say that," he said, peering at the letter again.

She turned red. "I had a line too—didn't you notice yours had no stamp? I'll change your order for you at the post office," she went on hurriedly. Mentally she had worked out that two of the pounds represented the price of the new gravestone the Commander had never purchased, and the third his idea of interest for all these years. Doubtless he had been too tactful to send them back in his lifetime. Anyhow she agreed with her grandfather that it was really all the Lord's doing, for nothing could be timelier. Even her poultry was now being steadily sacrificed, and this great sum would get her beautifully over Christmas and New Year and start that with a handsome balance in hand. But she had counted without her grandfather.

"No, you don't!" The Gaffer's hand closed grimly on the precious paper. "That's a nest-egg, Oi'm tellin' ye."

"But what are you going to do with it?" she inquired in distress.

"That's for Annie."

"Mr. Skindle's mother! But he's rich as rich."

"He don't never buy her nawthen. He come here and told me sow out of his own mouth, the hunks. Oi had to pay for her packet o' hairpins."

"Well, anyhow she'll have her Christmas dinner, and that's more than you're sure of," she risked threatening.

"You've got the telescope, hain't ye?" he urged uneasily.

"I can't sell that. That's for remembrance."

"Ye can remember him without a telescope. And ef he had his faults, 'tain't for you to remember 'em, seein' as ye'd never a-bin here at all ef he'd done his duty by Emma and King Gearge. But Oi reckon he couldn't see everythink with that glass eye, and Oi ought to ha' carried silks and brandy myself 'stead o' parcels and culch. Did, Oi'd a-got a stockin' like Sidrach's and not had to deny myself bite and sup for your sake." And he hobbled stairwards, the post-office order clutched in his skeleton claw. "Do ye write to Dap's buoy-oy and thank him for payin' his dues, and say as Oi hope he won't put no fooleries on his father's stone, and he'd best copy what Oi had put on your father's and mother's."

Jinny duly wrote, if not in these terms. But when the telescope came, she felt anything but thankful. For, welcome as it was in itself, it came by the coach. She had been too distraught to foresee this, though she recognized that it was the natural way. And apart from the sting to her own pride, it agitated her grandfather profoundly. He had been nodding at the hearth, but the clamour of the coach aroused him, and ere she could get to the door he had sprung up with an oath.

"Don't let him over my doorstep!" he cried, pursuing her. "He's got to come in on his hands and knees." He jostled her aside and seized the bolt, but his hand trembled so, he could not shoot it.

"How can he crawl in, if you bolt the door?" she said tactfully.

He was staggered: the possibility of the opposition obstinacy relaxing had never even occurred to him. Recovering, he urged that the enemy would try to rush over the sill.

"No fear, Gran'fer. He'll never cross our threshold unless you carry him in!"

She spoke with unconscious admiration of Will's tenacity. Indeed the image of the young man crawling to her grandfather or even to herself would have been repellent, had it been really conceivable.

"Carry him in!" the Gaffer laughed explosively, and that burst of derision made him almost good-humoured. He let himself be pushed gently towards the inner room, while Jinny, with her pulse at gallop, opened the door.

The tension and friction of nerves proved sheer waste. The long narrow parcel was brought to the door by the hobbledehoy guard, and the driver remained, imperturbably important, on his box, looking almost as massive as an old stager in his new, caped greatcoat and coloured muffler, though the face under the broad-brimmed festively sprigged hat was very different from the mottled malt-soused visages of the coaching breed. It seemed but an idle glance that Jinny cast at it, or at the Christmas congestion of the coach, overflowing with passengers and literal Christmas boxes, and with hares pendent even from the driver's seat. Nevertheless, as ever when they met, long invisible messages passed between Jinny and Will, and not all her defiance could disguise her humiliation at this second triumph of the coach, coming as it did when the fortunes of the cart were at their blackest. For the Gaffer refused sullenly to part with his piece of paper—she did not even know where he had hidden it— and with Uncle Lilliwhyte too poorly to forage for her, she was almost tempted to apply for the Christmas doles that were by ancient bequest more abundant at Mr. Fallow's church than applicants for them. But her instinct of "uprightness" saved her: better that the last of her poultry should be sacrificed for the sacred repletions of the season. She did indeed dally with the notion of keeping Christmas not with, but from, her grandfather—possibly his failing memory might for once prove an advantage—but she had a feeling that apart from the profanity of ignoring it, the festival was too ingrained in the natural order to be overlooked, for did not Christmas mark the pause in the year, when with the crops in the ground and the little wheat-blades safely tucked under the snow, and the beer brewed and the pigs killed and salted, the whole world rests and draws happy frosted breath? No, the old man's instinct would surely trip her up, if she tried to run Christmas as an ordinary day.

She might, of course, as he had originally suggested, sell or at least pawn her telescope, but even if she could have brought herself to that, she could not have got it away from him, for he had annexed it from the first moment and sat peering out of it from the vantage-point of his bedroom lattice. He was at his spy-glass the moment he woke, enchanted when he could descry people or incidents far-off—it was as if his long seclusion from the outer world was over—and he would call out like a child and tell Jinny what he had seen. Sometimes it was Master Peartree and his dog, sometimes Bidlake ferrying on the Brad or a couple seeking warmth in a cold lane; now a woodman cutting holly branches with his billhook, anon Bundock bowed by his bag or Mott with his fishing-rod, and once he cried out he could see Annie coming out of Beacon Chimneys, though Jinny suspected that the tall figure with the "wunnerful fine buzzom" was really Farmer Gale's new wife. Particularly protected did her grandfather now feel against thieves, whose stealthy advent he would henceforward detect from afar. Delighted as she was in her turn with the new toy that kept him happy even on a reduced diet, she had to keep his fire going all day now, and to be up and down closing the window through which he would stick the telescope. Sometimes he directed his tube heaven-ward, though not for astronomical purposes. "Happen Oi'll see Sidrach coming down for a gossip," he said.

Just before Christmas he informed her he had decided that the right thing to do with the nest-egg was to purchase Sidrach a gravestone with it, and he instructed her to write a letter of inquiry to Babylon. But although this seemed to her a more logical use of it than he knew, she disregarded his instruction. The nest-egg was too precious. The time might come when he would ask for bread, and was she to give him a stone?

VII

Neglected on the coast in favour of New Year, Christmas was celebrated in the inland valley of the Brad with the conventional accessories, and every Christmas the mummers had been wont to attend on the Master of Blackwater Hall; as well as the waits. Jinny with no coin to offer to either, the last of her poultry doomed for the Christmas dinner, and Uncle Lilliwhyte also on her hands, had this year to beg both companies to refrain, alleging her grandfather was too ill. The weather was seasonable, the robin hopped as picturesquely on the snow as on the Christmas card Jinny had enclosed with her thanksgiving letter to Gunner Dap. The cottage, prankt with its holly and mistletoe, had a fairylike air—everything was perfect, even to the Christmas pudding. But only Nip and Methusalem were happy. To the Gaffer the breach of an immemorial tradition gave a troubling sense of void.

"Where's the waits? Where's Father Chris'mus? Where's St. Gearge?" he kept saying peevishly. Jinny put him off with vague replies or none. Once he alarmed her by asking suddenly: "Where's the Doctor?" She was reassured when he began spouting:

"Oi carry a bottle of alicampane."

He passed on to imagine himself as St. George, and seizing the poker for a sword declaimed vigorously, if imperfectly:

"Oi'll fight the Russian Bear, he shall not fly, Oi'll cut him down or else Oi'll die."

"Ain't we a-gooin' to see the mummers?" he inquired angrily as Christmas Day waned.

"Perhaps they are ill or it's too cold," she suggested feebly.

"But they're gooin' around to other folk!" he protested. "Oi seen 'em through my glass!"

"Well, then you have seen them," she said still more feebly. Inwardly she wondered if he had detected herself, on her way to church, carrying off some Christmas dinner to Uncle Lilliwhyte's hut. The telescope was a new terror added to life.

She had wanted to invite the prop of her larder to take his Christmas dinner with them, but her grandfather refused violently to sit down with such a "ragamuffin." His sense of caste was acute, and as Jinny's sense of smell was equally acute, she would not have persisted, even had renewed rheumatism not confined the ancient to his hut.

The day after Christmas that year was Friday, and after the comparative festivity of the holiday it required no small force of will to go round uselessly in the north wind, when one day a week would have more than sufficed for such odd commissions as still came her way. The snow had fallen thicker in the night, and robins, starlings, finches, blackbirds, little blue-tits (pick-cheeses she called them), and other breakfastless birds had all been tapping at her window for crumbs. But the remains of the feast made a good meal for her grandfather and he was in the best of humours, praising the acting of the mummers, which he did not now remember he had not seen this Christmas, and remarking upon the "wunnerful fine woice" of old Ravens' grandson among the waits. Apparently his memories of other years had fused together into an illusion concerning the day before. As Jinny set out, she found herself wishing he would forget his quarrel with Will. Not, of course, that she could forget hers!

There were grey snow-clouds in the sky, and as she ploughed past the sheepfolds, scarring the purity of the road with her cart-tracks, she beheld patriarchal sheep, standing almost silent with round, snow-white beards: only a green shoot peeped here and there from the speckless white expanse. Methusalem's muffled footsteps gave her a sense of dream, and, when the wind was not in her face, she watched her breath rising white in the air with some strange sense of exhaling her soul. But beneath this mystic daze went an undercurrent of wonder as to how she could meet the New Year.

Returned from her round—and she was glad, having shown herself and got her meal, to creep home under cover of the early darkness—she half expected to find the Gaffer as ill as she had feigned, but though he was still peering out into the night, there was no sign he was in the grip of the cold; on the contrary he seemed to have found fresh strength and brightness, whether from the nest-egg or this renewed ocular intercourse with his world. "Oi seen you all along the road," he chuckled. In this new mood she was easily able to persuade him to exchange a goat for Methusalem's provender. He would not part with his three pounds, but they gave him a sense of security, almost of gaiety. Indeed their existence made as wonderful a difference to herself as to him. Hidden away though the money order was, she felt the old man would be forced to produce it if ever hunger got too keen, and so the knowledge of it sustained her as the proximity of a boat sustains a swimmer. It was scarcely a paradox that without its assistance she could not have got through the first month of the New Year. For January brought the "hard winter" foretold by the sloes. Outwardly it was a bright world enough, with children skating on the ponds and ditches: indeed the frost brought out a veritable flamboyance of colour in the animal creation, and at one of her moments of despair when she had humbled herself in vain to offer lace to the new Mrs. Gale, Jinny was redeemed by the motley pomp of the cocks shining on the farmyard straw, and the glowing hues of the calves that bestrode it with them, all overbrooded by the ancient mellow thatch. Her heart sang again with the row of chaffinches perched on the white stone wall, and looking at the trees silhouetted so gracefully against the sky, she decided that winter bareness was almost more beautiful than summer opulence.

But she changed her mind when she watched—with a new sympathy born of fellow-anxiety—the struggle for food among the birds. Coots had flocked in from the coast to add to the competition of land-species, and frozen little forms or bloody half-feathered fragments, but especially dead starlings with lovely shades of green and purple, pathetically imponderable when picked up, all skin and feather—sometimes decapitated by sparrow-hawks—abounded on the hard white roads. As she began to feel the same grim menace brooding over her grandfather and herself, that social unrest which reached even Bradmarsh in faint vibrations began to take possession of her, and she arrived at a revolutionary notion which would have horrified Farmer Gale far more than her outrageous demand for a law that nobody should be paid less than ten shillings a week. She actually maintained that every man should be pensioned off by the parish on reaching the age of ninety! But the view found no sympathy in an age of individualism, to which the poorhouse was the supreme humiliation. Even Uncle Lilliwhyte, who was now on the mend again—though too weak to fend for anybody but himself—told her to her surprise that every man ought to put by for a rainy day. It was this slavish sluggishness of the poor that was the real stumbling-block to reform, she thought, though remembering Uncle Lilliwhyte's leaky habitation, she treasured up his reply as a humorous example of the gap between precept and practice.

Even more unsympathetic was Mrs. Mott's attitude. She scoffed at the idea that every man should be pensioned off at ninety. "Poisoned off at twenty," was her emendation.

"Well, you do your best," Jinny laughed.

Mrs. Mott's blue silk bodice crackled. "What do you mean?"

"Don't you sell them liquor?"

"It's good liquor," said Mrs. Mott, flushing.

"I was only joking. But joking apart, it doesn't do them much good." And Jinny thought of how even her grandfather had fuddled himself, with or without ghostly assistance.

"If I gave up my bar," said Mrs. Mott hotly, "who would pay the rent of our chapel?"

"Well, but the chapel got along before you joined," Jinny reminded her mildly.

"Heaping up debt!" shrilled Mrs. Mott, with flashing eyes.

"Then what's the good of poisoning off the men?" argued Jinny, smiling. "Where would your bar be without them?"

"Women could learn to drink," said Mrs. Mott fiercely, "and smoke too."

But the latter accomplishment seemed so comically impossible to Jinny—who had never seen Polly over her cigar and milk—that she burst out laughing at the image of it, and her laughter made Mrs. Mott fiercer, and that lady said for two pins she'd wear pink pantaloons like the Bloomerites. As Jinny did not offer the pins, but laughed even more merrily at the new picture presented to her imagination, relations with Mrs. Mott became strained, and when at their next meeting Jinny sensibly remarked that if the law really gave Mr. Mott his wife's possessions, it was useless going to it, all that lady's indomitable spirit turned against her whilom confidante. "You take his part like everybody else," she cried bitterly. "But don't think I haven't seen him ogling you!"

"Do you mean I've ogled him?" said Jinny, incensed.

"I don't say that, but you can't dislike his admiration—why else are you on his side?"

"I am not on his side—I detest him."

Mrs. Mott flew off at a tangent. "Then you ought to be grateful to me for protecting you against him."

Jinny was now as indignant as her hostess. "How have you protected me?"

"Haven't I kept you always out of his way?"

"Oh, is that why you've had me in the kitchen?"

"Of course."

Jinny felt at once chilled and inflamed. "It's not true," she cried recklessly. "When I first came to the kitchen, Mr. Mott was still in love with you, and I only went there because you didn't like to show yourself."

Such reminders are unforgivable, and Jinny would probably never again have enjoyed Mrs. Mott's hospitality, even had she not then and there shaken it off. It was only with an effort she could prevent herself declaring that Mrs. Mott would have to carry her into the kitchen before she entered it again. But when she got out in the cold air, she felt suddenly as foolish as Will and her grandfather had been. With starvation bearing down on Blackwater Hall like some grim iceberg, the loss of two full meals a week was a disaster. She was not even sure that the courtyard as well as the kitchen would not be closed to her, for Mrs. Mott seemed a woman without measure, whether in her religion, her affections, her politics, or her quarrels. Possibly, however, the poor lady overlooked her use of it, for the cart continued to draw up there with its air of immemorial and invincible custom. But if Jinny thus still kept up appearances, it was with a heart that grew daily heavier.

In looking back on this grim period, Jinny always regarded the crawling up of the wounded hedgehog as marking the zero-point in her fortunes. It was actually crawling over her doorstep like Will in her grandfather's imagination. What enemy had bitten off its neck-bristles she never knew—she could only hope it was not Nip—but catching sight of the dark, ugly gash, she hastened to get a clean rag as well as some crumbs and goat-milk. The poor creature allowed the wound to be dressed, and seemed to nose among the crumbs, but it neither ate nor drank. She packed it in straw in a little box and placed it in a warm corner of the kitchen, instructing Nip sternly that it was tabu.

"Caught a pig?" said the Gaffer with satisfaction, stumbling into the middle of this lesson in the higher ethics. "That's a wunnerful piece o' luck, a change from rabbits, too."

"You wouldn't eat it?" she cried in horror.

"Why, what else?" he asked in surprise.

"There's bread and there's jelly," she said, misunderstanding, "and perhaps Uncle Lilliwhyte will be round with something—he's about again."

"There ain't nawthen better than hedgehog," the Gaffer said decisively. "And 'tis years since Oi tasted one. Sidrach doted on 'em roasted, used to catch 'em in the ditch-brambles."

"But we've got to cure this, not kill it," she protested.

"Ye don't cure pigs that size," he laughed happily.

For once Jinny failed to appreciate a joke. "It threw itself on our protection," she insisted. "We can't take advantage of it like that. Besides, it's been bitten and might be unhealthy."

But he was contumacious, and it was only on her undertaking to get him a chicken for his dinner that he consented to forgo the dainty in hand.

To acquire this in the absence of coin involved the barter of the remaining goats in a large and complex transaction with Miss Gentry's landlady, and although this set Jinny and Methusalem up for weeks, yet since it meant the exhaustion of her last reserves, the wounded hedgehog became to happier memory a sort of symbol of desperation. True, there were still the telescope and the money order, but one could not easily lay one's hand on them—they bristled even more fiercely than the poor hedgehog.

All Jinny's care of that confiding beast proved wasted. In vain she renewed the dressing on its neck, in vain Nip and her grandfather were kept off. The third morning it was found on its back, more helpless than Uncle Lilliwhyte, with its hind paws close together but its front paws held up apart, as though crying for mercy. Its nose and paws came up dark brown on the lighter spines around, the eyes were closed and almost invisible, buried like the ears amid the bristles. The rag still adorned its neck.

Jinny gave her poor little patient a decent burial and a few tears. "'Tain't no use cryin' over spilt milk," the Gaffer taunted her. "Ye've gone and wasted good food, and Oi count the Lord'll think twice afore He sends ye a present agen."

The Gaffer was mistaken. Little Bradmarsh was about to flow, if not with milk and honey, with hares and rabbits and horses and sheep and haystacks and potatoes and mangolds and even chairs, step-ladders, fences, gates, watering-pots, casks, boxes, hurdles, hen-coops, and wheelbarrows. For after January had ended in a crescendo of rain, wind, sleet and the heaviest snowfall in his memory, came a diminuendo movement of sleet, thaw, and rain, though the wind raged unabated, and after that—the Deluge!

CHAPTER XII

WRITTEN IN WATER

For, in a night, the best part of my power . . .
Were in the washes, all unwarily,
Devourèd by the unexpected flood.
SHAKESPEARE, "King John."

I

The floods of '52 are still remembered in East Anglia. The worst and most widespread were in November, but "February Fill-Dyke" brought the more localized catastrophe in Little Bradmarsh. The village, lying as it did along the left bank of the Brad, was caught between two waters, the overflow of the streams to the north that ran down silt-laden towards this bank, and the backwash over the bank from the Brad itself, which, already swollen by rain, and by the waters pumped into it from the marsh-mills on its right bank, was prevented overflowing southwards by the dyke that further protected Long Bradmarsh.

It was Nip that brought Jinny the news, though she did not understand its purport till the service was over. For it was to church that he brought it. That ancient building, standing isolated on its green knoll flaked with gravestones, had begun to appeal to him as much as to Jinny, and despite her efforts to dodge or shake him off, he had become a regular churchgoer. Nobody seemed to mind his sitting in her pew or squatting by the stove: perhaps so exiguous a congregation could not be exigent, and in that aching void even a canine congregant was not unwelcome. But his mistress, despite the sense she shared with Mr. Fallow of divine glimmerings in the animal creation, had always an uneasy feeling of indecorum, especially when Nip snored through the sermon like a Christian, and she was congratulating herself that the "Fifthly and Finally" had been safely reached without him, when in he trotted—far wetter and muddier than on the day he had plumped on Will's knees in the chapel. The sight of him dripping steadily along the aisle towards the stove did not interrupt the hymn: the worshippers, though the morning had begun with a set-back to snow, were in no wise surprised by a return to rain. Only that Saturday night it had rained "cats and dogs": one dripping dog was therefore no alarming phenomenon. They did not realize that Nip had largely swum to church.

But when, at the church-door, they began to fumble with their umbrellas, they saw with wide eyes of astonishment and dismay that though a mere sleety drizzle misted the air, below the lych-gate a strange expanse of waters awaited their feet. Except for one broad finger of land pointing along the centre of a vast yellow lake, their world was suddenly turned to water, and Jinny had a weird wonder as to what the dead would think could they rise and see the transformation wrought in the earthy spot where they had laid themselves so securely to sleep.

But the first impression of plumbless depth was contradicted by the hedgerows standing up—despite their reflections—much as before, still with a light powder of the morning's snow, and when Jinny advancing to the gate, amid a chaos of ejaculatory comment that would have done credit to a full-sized congregation, probed the lake with the point of her umbrella, she exhibited barely three inches of moist tip. Reassured except for Sunday shoes, the bulk of the worshippers plashed forwards more or less boldly. But Miss Gentry refused to be comforted: she was already half hysterical and clutching at Jinny, for she recalled her anciently prophesied doom of drowning. What was the use of a lifelong refusal to set foot on the water? The water was come to her, as the Clown opined of Ophelia. Jinny could quiet her only by promising to see her safely to her door. With a jump the girl reached the four steps by which the ladies anciently mounted to their pillions, and running up, she surveyed the vista of waters, amid which the three pollarded lime-trees before Miss Gentry's cottage rose like a landmark. She could now make a mental map of the driest route. For from this observation-post, though she had a sodden sense of mist and rain and blowiness, the sense of an unbroken aqueous expanse disappeared. She could see water, water, but not everywhere, nor were even the watery parts submerged uniformly. It was like some infallible illustration of the ups and downs of Little Bradmarsh. Never before, not even under the varying strains of Methusalem, had she realized how undulating the village was for all its apparent flatness. She saw now how much a few feet counted, and how the majority of the cottages and the farmhouses—all the ancient ones indeed—had planted themselves along that dry finger: "the Ridge" they called it, she remembered, though the name had hitherto been a mere sound to her ear, for so gradual was its slope that she had never felt the ascent nor put on the brake in descending. But to see it culminating in the Common and her own dear Blackwater Hall was now a cheering spectacle. While a white-flecked, wind-whipped waste of yellow water was spreading where yesterday blackened pastures had stretched, here were brown fields quite untouched by the flood-water, with their furrows chalked out in snow. One field all winter white, with thin blades just peeping up, looked friendly rather than forlorn—such was the effect of contrast. Lower down the Ridge were stretches covered with a deposit of silt and leaf-mould, with plough-handles sticking up, and between these and the flooded regions was a half-and-half world that reminded Jinny of the salt-marshes: a maze of pools and pondlets and water-patterns in a greenish slime mottled with hillocks.

Taking off her precious shoes and stockings, Jinny descended from her observation-post and plunged the "little fitten" admired of her grandfather into the chilling muddy lake, which seemed to have risen since she gauged it. Miss Gentry, clenching her teeth, followed her example, but in the effort to grasp at once her skirt, shoes, and muff (with prayer-book couchant), and to prevent her umbrella from soaring off on adventures of its own, she made more twitter than progress, and when, at their first stile, Nip, plunging through the bars, dived into the field and swam boldly forward, Miss Gentry with a shriek perched herself on the stile and refused to come down. Jinny, baring her legs still higher, strove to laugh away her patron's fears, but her very precaution of tucking up had driven the dressmaker into a new frenzy.

"There's no risk so long as we dodge the ditches," Jinny pointed out, "and you can see those by the hedges. And look up there—there's your lime-trees signalling their feet are dry."

"Yes, but I can't get to them. Oh, Jinny, go and fetch me your cart. Do be a love."

"Sunday?"

"It's a question of life and death."

"Very well," Jinny pretended. "If I cut through that field with the cows I shan't be long," she said with cunning carelessness.

But she had not gone many yards ere, as she expected, she heard Miss Gentry plashing desperately behind her with cries of "Wait for me, Jinny! Wait!" Miss Gentry did not reflect that the cows would not be out in that weather; to face those fearsome inches under escort was a lesser evil than the possible dangers from panic-stricken cattle that now rose before her mind, and with one horn of the dilemma a bull's, her choice was precipitated.

At the Four Wantz Way new terrors arose for the poor lady. It was not from the swirl of waters that met there, for her road now stretched visibly upwards, but from the fact that the Pennymoles were occupied in moving their treasures to "the high room." The genial paterfamilias darting to his doorstep—with the kerchiefed owl he was rescuing in his hand—had his own flood of authoritative lore to pour out, but he could make no headway till Miss Gentry had blushingly apologized for her bare feet, and been assured that no respectable man would look at them. Then, though his hearers stood splashed and blown about, he held even Jinny spellbound with a description of Long Bradmarsh as he had known it in his boyhood before the embankment was put up, and when his parents had often had, even in summer, to open the back door of their cottage to let the water pour out. And what a work it had been, clearing up the muck afterwards! "That's a terrible thing, the power of water," he said solemnly. "People don't know what it means who ain't seen it. And it's rising every minute."

"What did I tell you, Jinny?" cried Miss Gentry. "Oh, Mr. Pennymole, will my house be safe?"

"It's one thing, mum, to be in the flood and another to be out of it," he responded oracularly.

"Come along!" said Jinny impatiently. "Your cottage has got two steps to begin with, and even if it gets up to your garden, you'll be safe inside."

"Beggin' your pardon, Jinny," corrected the oracle. "That fares to sap the foundations, and then crack! bang! you think it's a big gun, and down comes walls and ceilings. My gran'fer seen a whole row of cottages washed away. And then there's flotsam what bangs about and smashes you in."

Miss Gentry clutched wildly at Jinny, dropping shoes and muff into the swirl. "And Squibs does hate to get her feet wet," she babbled.

Alarmed at the effect of his pronouncement, the oracle hastened to tone it down and to pick up her things.

"No need to get into a pucker, mum. You're all right, same as you're in the high room. And Oi count ye've got a grate upstairs, which is more than we're blessed with this weather. That gre't ole stove can't git up."

"And you could sew in your bedroom," Jinny added soothingly. "You've never known it get higher than the ground floor, have you, Mr. Pennymole?"

"Not in my born days," answered the oracle.

"But there's always new things happening," wailed Miss Gentry.

"That's wunnerful true," Mr. Pennymole admitted, smiling. "Oi never thought Oi'd fare to oversleep myself. But the day there was that grand wedding at the church, Oi hadn't time to make my tea."

"And then he had two teas!" put in Mrs. Pennymole hilariously.

But before the story had proceeded far, they all became aware of people hastening from every quarter towards the unsubmerged regions, not for safety, but for salvage; carts and even wagons with teams began to come up, and the bustle and cackle recalled Mr. Pennymole to public duty.

Leaving his wife to finish telling the story, as well as transferring the furniture, he joined a party hurrying on to Farmer Gale's five-acre field, and as Jinny and Miss Gentry passed along, they saw potato clamps being dug up, cattle driven higher, corn and hay unstacked and transported, and even threshing in hasty operation. The Sunday clothes of those who hadn't stayed to "shiften," but emphasized the profanity of the scene.

"You see what Dissenters are!" said Miss Gentry in disgust.

"It's a matter of life and death," quoted Jinny maliciously. But Miss Gentry did not recognize her own words. Jinny went on to praise the true Christianity of these labourers, who though ground down to a miserable wage, were now dashing to Farmer Gale's assistance even in his absence—for he had apparently not yet returned from his place of worship at Chipstone. One cornstack saved, she calculated, would be worth more than he had paid Mr. Pennymole in the last five years.

"In this dreadful day of the Lord, it's souls that want saving, not stacks," said Miss Gentry.

Arrived at last on her own doorstep, she collapsed in Jinny's arms. What was the use of not going to Boulogne, she demanded, if she was to be drowned in her bed? At least she might have had the hope of seeing her dear Cleopatra again. And surely the darling must have written, must have sent her address. Bundock must have lost the letters, or, worse, suppressed them! He owed her a grudge because she had resisted his importunities. Yes, Jinny—dead to Passion—had no idea to what lengths people born under other planets would go—even though married! But, extricating herself, Jinny, with that cold blood of hers, left her patron to the consolations of Squibs; she must get home to her grandfather, she explained; he would be worrying over her fate.

II

She found him at his telescope, as outraged as Miss Gentry, and enjoying himself immensely over the spectacle that shattered his Sunday dullness. His big Bible had been lugged upstairs, and now lay on the bed, open at the Deluge; and the bucket that received his ceiling-drippings had been kicked over in his excitement. "That's the Lord's punishment on they Sabbath-breakers," he said gleefully. Nor could all Jinny's arguments—as she wiped up his private flood—bring home to him his inverted logic. "The Lord knowed 'twas in their hearts to break it," he persisted. "'And it repented the Lord that He had made man.'"

"Oh, it's not so bad as the flood of 2352," said Jinny, airing her Spelling-Book chronology.

"Wait till the Brad flows over the dyke," he chuckled. "That'll spill all over Long Bradmarsh, ay, and run down towards Chipstone."

"Oh, you don't think it will get over the dyke?" she said anxiously.

"Mebbe to Babylon itself," he said voluptuously.

"All the more reason they should try to save what they can," she urged. "Time and tide wait for no man, and why should any man wait for the tide? It's like with shepherds and stockmen that can't ever have their Sunday. Come down to dinner."

But the Gaffer's eye was glued to his tube. "That's as good as harvest!" he exclaimed in shocked exhilaration. "Dash my buttons ef they ain't thatchin' the stack they carted over from Pipit's meadow. And they're makin' new mangold and potato clamps."

"So long as they don't get largesse," Jinny maintained.

The Gaffer groaned. "Largesse or no largesse, Oi never seen sech a Sunday in all my born days. What a pity Sidrach didn't live to see it!"

When she at last got him to surrender the spy-glass, she could not refrain from taking a peep herself. She was astonished at the swift rise of the waters. Already the hedgerows were disappearing, while an avenue of elms rising mysteriously out of a lagoon was the sole indication of a road she had passed on her way to church. A swan and cygnets were now sailing upon it, with darker and less distinguishable objects tossing around. A bed of osiers seemed to be in its natural element as it rose from the waters that islanded a farm. The black, snow-powdered barn looked like the upturned hull of some squat galleon, and the haystacks thatched as with hoar-frost had the air of cliffs crumbling before the sea. One clump of bare trees rose out of the glassy void like the rigging of a sinking ship. Her world had suffered a water-change into something rich and strange in which only the rare protuberances enabled her to trace out the original earth-pattern. Even seagulls were floating, and frank-herons wheeling, and kingfishers diving. Her grandfather watched her like one who had provided the show. "That makes me feel a youngster agen," he cried. "'Tis like the good ole times when there warn't no drainage-mills ne yet Frog Farms."

"Frog Farm isn't swept away?" she cried with a sudden clamminess at her heart.

"Oi wouldn't give much for the farniture downstairs," he said, with sinister satisfaction. "That's the lowest house in the parish. And then ye deny 'tis the Lord's hand a-chastenin' the evil-doers. Oi reckon though they've packed their waluables in the coach, the pirate thieves, and scuttled off Beacon Hill way."

Without replying, she gazed through a tremulous telescope at the distant point where the Brad seemed to wind immediately behind the roof of Frog Farm but the convolutions and dip of the land, aided by an intervening copse, hid everything from her except the quaint chimney, though the smoke fluttering in the wind showed that if the Gaffer's hypothesis was correct, evacuation must have been recent. It was something, though, to see the farmhouse still uncollapsed, though her imagination surrounded it with water like the more visible farm. She was glad to remember that Master Peartree at least would have been in his hut on higher ground, keeping vigil over the lambing ewes.

"Somebody ought to go and see if they've really got away," she said anxiously.

"They'll be all right ef the Lord don't want to punish 'em," he said surlily. "And ef He do, 'tain't for nobody to baulk Him!"

After dinner he forwent his nap. The Lord had sent him not only a spectacle but a great new eye, and had even denuded the trees that might in summer have blocked his view, and he was not the man to "sin his mercies." Jinny had ceased to be anxious about his catching cold at the casement—evidently his life of driving had inured him—so, wrapping a blanket round his smock and the new-knitted muffler round his throat, she left him to enjoy himself while she cleared away the frugal meal.

Suddenly she heard a roar as of distant thunder, followed by a great shout from above.

"It's busted! It's busted!"

She rushed up in alarm, nearly upsetting his bucket herself.

"Behold!" he cried Biblically, handing her the glass. "That's busted a piece out of the bank."

She looked—and beheld indeed! In the embankment that guarded Long Bradmarsh gaped a breach of some fifty yards, while giant blocks of clay that must have weighed tons were swirling like children's marbles towards the Long Bradmarsh meadows whence panic-stricken labourers were now fleeing backwards.

"It's caught 'em, the Sabbath-breakers," said the Gaffer ecstatically. "That didn't wait to flow over the dyke."

"I've got to go and give help on the Ridge," she said resolutely. And not all his arguments or threats could stay her cart. "Christ said the Sabbath was made for man, not man for the Sabbath," she urged, and the text silenced him. But it was not so easy to dispose of the pietism of Methusalem, whose blank incredulity before her threatened disturbance of the holy day was only overcome by the convincing commonplaceness with which Nip barked around. The poor horse must have imagined that he had overslept himself and that it was Tuesday. Fortunately "the Ridge" lay downwards for him, and the crowds and the everyday bustle finally disillusioned him of his Sunday feeling, and he allowed his cart to be laden with the carrots, swedes, and mangolds that had lain in such snug rows packed betwixt hurdles and a sort of straw thatch kept down by long poles. At first Jinny kept looking round for the rival carrier, but either he would not demean his coach to such service, or he was water-bound.

Jinny asked several people whether they had seen the Flynts and whether Frog Farm would be safe, but if nobody could supply any information, nobody thought there would be any serious danger.

"They'll be all right," said Farmer Gale bitterly. "It's my land there that's drowned, and my stacks that are floating." He was on the scene now, directing operations, cursing his looker. For the first time the breezy Cornishman doubted his father's cuteness in buying up soil whose fatness was only due to its centuries of repose under water. "The land'll be out of heart for years," he lamented. Jinny could not help a secret satisfaction in seeing the hard-hearted farmer confronted by a force as remorseless as that which had swept Uncle Lilliwhyte out of his cottage. Nor could she escape a still subtler pleasure in thus heaping coals of fire on his head. But both these joys as well as her anxiety about Frog Farm were soon lost in the glow of service. It was such a delight to be no longer shamming work, while to give had become an almost forgotten pleasure.

When she returned to the field for a second load, the flood was already creeping over it, and the early darkness and a pale quarter-moon threw a new weirdness over these unknown waters. She found the lane outside still more flooded, and as Methusalem plashed homewards, she encountered Uncle Lilliwhyte rising from the waters like a disreputable river-god. He was dexterously spearing mangolds as they floated past, and stacking them, mixed with drowned hares, in a wheelbarrow, itself apparently flotsam. He had an air of legal operations, there was none of the furtive look that goes with bulges in smock-frocks, and Jinny, too, thought he was justly avenged on his evictor, though she refused to desecrate the Sabbath by buying any of his spoils. She could not help feeling rewarded when Nip appeared with a rabbit gratis. As he had not killed it, she refrained from rebuking him, and he came in subsequently for the bones. But his pride at having thus at last achieved his ideal almost turned his head, and all the more bitter was his humiliation when his next epoch-making capture—a dead rat—was rejected with reproach.

III

If Jinny had much to tell her grandfather over the rabbit stew, he in his turn had no lack of material for excited conversation. Both were exhilarated, rejuvenated by the metamorphosis of their landscape; it seemed, more pungently even than snow, to re-create the wonder of the world. It was a gay young grandfather that rattled off the farces and tragedies of the day's drama: a sodden haystack hurled into the Brad, a cart of mangolds overturned in a watery field, a bullock swimming for dear life and landing safely on a mound where stampeded horses cowered; dead ewes floating—and just in the lambing season too!—men in boats rescuing pigs and poultry from the grounds of water-logged cottages, and hauling clothes and bedding through the windows.

"There's hundreds o' Farmer Gale's acres drowned what was cropped with seed," he said with gloomy relish, "and regiments o' rats ha' saved theirselves atop of his stacks. When they've goffled their fill they wentures down for a drink, the warmints, and then up again. Same as 'twixt the devil and the deep sea for they onfortunit stacks."

That night a white mist rising from the waters blotted out everything, but the next morning, when Jinny went up to induce her grandfather to descend to breakfast, she found to her surprise and relief that though the Brad was still hurling itself through the breach, the bulk of Long Bradmarsh was still unflooded, still alive with salvage parties. The low arms of the marsh-mills were still working with frantic efficiency. What miracle had saved this village? Her grandfather explained that there must still be some righteous men there. But Jinny, looking through his glass for herself, discovered—after a preliminary peep at the Frog Farm chimney, whose smokelessness was a fresh relief—that the breach-water instead of flowing evenly over Long Bradmarsh had half found, half scooped out for itself, a sort of river-bed. Turning aside before a slight rise, it had veered round sharply eastward, and then curving back westward, when it met another obstacle three hundred yards later, it had finally poured itself over the dyke back into the Brad.

"That's a mercy," she said, expounding it.

"But now there's a chance of both they rivers flowin' over," he pointed out hopefully.

But as she gazed, she grew aware of a new phenomenon.

"Why, the Brad's going backwards!" she said.

He snatched the glass from her hand. "So it be!" he agreed. "But that's onny where the little river busts in agen the wrong way and pours along the top o' the real river."

Jinny was thrilling all down her spine. Again the sibylline prophecy of Miss Gentry rang in her ears:

When the Brad in opposite ways shall course,   Lo! Jinny's husband shall come on a horse,   And Jinny shall then learn Passion's force.

Overwhelmed by the uncanny divination of the dressmaker—a "wise woman" in good sooth it now appeared—she sank into a chair, her whole being aquiver with a premonition that she had reached the crucial point of her destiny. Who was it coming on a horse? Who but Will, that incarnation of equestrian grace? He was coming to rescue her, the dear silly, imagining her menaced by the flood. As if she had not got Methusalem! As if Blackwater Hall was not an Ararat! But his foolishness was part of the Fate— might he not even ride his horse through the doorway, lying along its back to avoid the lintel, and thus be practically "on his hands and knees"? In her grandfather's present happy mood, the old man might very well accept that solution. And Will himself would be "carried in," and might equally accept the compromise. Absorbed in her sophistic day-dream, she sat there till even the old man at his tube remembered breakfast. Nor did she again volunteer to help in the fields. All day she stayed at home over her Monday housework and wash-tub, awaiting the horseman, afraid to stir out.

And with equal patience her grandfather sat at his all-day show. Engineers and gesticulating figures appeared on the broken bank for his delectation, and a mile or so lower down labourers began to shovel gault (culch, he called it to Jinny), and lighters laden with it tried to sink themselves in the breach, but some were swirled away like bandboxes and others turned turtle—a comical sight that made him roar with laughter. At last exciting operations with ropes, stretched across the river, succeeded in keeping some in place. After that a big-sailed barge came to the rescue—he could even recognize the two punters with long poles who eked out the sail. Ravens' grandson, that ne'er-do-well, and Ephraim Bidlake, whose grandfather's barge used to "competition wuss than coaches," he told Jinny. They had brought a cargo of the blue-grey stuff—hundreds of sacks—and "dinged" it into the breach, wellnigh clogging it up. And then—oh side-splitting drollery!—the dyke had gone and "busted" in another weak place—near the bridge. And they were left "like dickies" with empty sacks, while the folk in the new-swamped fields went scurrying like rats.

So continuous were her grandfather's shouts of glee that Jinny ceased to attend to them, and would not come up to see even the new gap. She was the more amazed when at supper he talked of having seen

"'Lijah Skindle" fishing from the window of Frog Farm. "Oi called ye to come and see," he said reproachfully when she expressed incredulity. "He got his line danglin' from a broomstick!"

The sight of Miss Gentry astride a broomstick seemed far likelier to Jinny. In the first place, no window of the farmhouse was visible from theirs; in the second, how could Elijah Skindle be living there?

"What would Mr. Skindle be doing at Frog Farm?" she said.

"So long as he ain't taken Annie there!" he answered. "Oi shouldn't wonder ef the whole place comes tumblin' down like they fir-trees. For the more Oi set thinkin' on it, the more Oi see as it's to punish that competitioning pirate that the flood's been sent."

"Don't talk like that, Gran'fer. I expect you've been dozing."

"Oi tell you Oi seen him and his broomstick," he cried angrily. "And when he couldn't catch nawthen, he tied his han'kercher on it and signalled with it, too."

She did remember now that Elijah and Will had become thicker than their respective relations to Blanche seemed to warrant, and she had shrewdly divined that Will wanted to flaunt his indifference to his rejection, and Elijah to pose as the magnanimous conqueror. It was not impossible, therefore, that the horse-doctor, summoned to Snowdrop or Cherry-blossom on the Saturday afternoon, had been caught by the torrential rain and the gale and persuaded to stay the night in that spare bedroom once occupied by Mr. Flippance. But more probably it was only another of the old man's illusions. "Why, there wasn't even any smoke from the chimney," she reminded him.

"Mebbe there was too much water in it," he chuckled.

Jinny's blood ran cold, but not on account of the Flynts. She was still too obsessed with the vision of Will arriving on a horse to imagine him or his parents immured by the waters. No, the feeling that stole over her was that Elijah Skindle was not living at the farm, but that while the occupants had evacuated it, he had been drowned outside it—swept away with his trap—and that her grandfather had seen yet another ghost.

"If anybody was signalling," she pointed out, "the engineers and the wherrymen would have seen him."

"They can't see through a brick wall," he retorted crushingly. "Frog Farm ain't got no eyes on the Brad. Depend on't, 'tis the Lord's finger."

She was still incredulous. But the moment supper was over, she ran up to examine the farmhouse afresh. The wind had "sobbed down"; the sky was sprinkled with stars, seen through frequent rifts in the clouds; and the moon, though only a crescent, emerging through a cloud-rack, shed a silver radiance over the watery waste, and cast over it black rippling bands of shadow from the bare elms and poplars rising from it in such unearthly beauty. And there in the region of Frog Farm, perceptible even to the naked eye, a mysterious reddish-yellow light, like some new star, threw its far-reaching beams upon the softened flood. A closer examination revealed that some of the trees of the fir-copse had been sapped and now lay heaving gently—the old man, she remembered, had alluded to fallen firs—and that the ruddy rays came from a farm bedroom, no longer shut out by the foliage. The smoke, too, was rising again. It was clear that the house was not uninhabited, and that her grandfather might very well have seen Elijah Skindle, while the absence of smoke all day might be traceable to the inability of the occupants to get a light earlier from sodden matches.

"But if they are starving and signalling," she cried agitatedly, "we must tell people. We must send a boat."

"We can't get no boat," he said philosophically.

"But you've seen plenty of boats," she urged. "I saw two myself rowing over the five-acre field. And there's that fowling-punt on the bank."

"That! Oi seen that fleetin' bottom up! Ye can't goo out to-night. Ye'd be drownded. Why, look there! That's a dead cow from the Farm meadow!"

"Where? I can't see anything."

"There! Bobbin' near the copse." He pointed and snatched the glass from her. "Why, that's a hoss," he shouted exultantly, "a black hoss! That should be Snowdrop, ef it ain't Cherry-blossom!" He was on his feet now, quivering with excitement, his blanket falling from his shoulders.

"Why, how can you be sure in this light?" she said, trembling no less. "It may be a brown horse, or even a plough-horse."

"That's a black coach-hoss sure enough, black as his heart, the pirate thief. What did Oi tell ye? 'Wengeance is mine, saith the Lord. Oi will repay.'" He looked so solemn in the moonlight, with his white beard, and his white-sleeved arm pointing starward, that she almost felt his standpoint had a prophetic justification. But she shook off the spell.

"Sit down, Gran'fer," she pleaded, readjusting his blanket. "Mr. Flynt was in his right."

"Ef he was in his right, why has the Lord drownded his hoss?" he demanded fiercely. "Do ye set down, yerself." And he clutched her wrist with his bony hand.

"Let me go!" she cried. "There's Mr. Skindle to be saved too."

"There ain't no danger for them—'tis your boat what 'ud come into colloosion with trees and cattle and fences and—why, just look at that!"

He dropped her hand to scrutinize the strange object awash. "Hallelujah!" he cried hysterically. "That's the top o' the coach! Dedn't Oi say 'twas a funeral coach?"

She shivered, and a cloud, coming just then over the moon, seemed to eclipse her resolution to rouse the neighbours. The sudden pall of darkness made the old man clutch her again—his own evocation of the funeral coach had frightened him. "Oi won't be left alone by night," he quavered and wiped a watery eye. Jinny refused to take it as pathos. "You'll blind yourself with that telescope," she said sternly. But inwardly she felt he was not so wrong. In that dim fitful light there was more danger to the would-be rescuers than to the party so snugly gathered round some bedroom hearth in Frog Farm. That ruddy lamplight, still brighter by the extinction of the moon, beamed reassuringly over the waters.

Skindle's broomstick-rod might have represented merely an effort to break the monotony of imprisonment—it was no proof that they had been cut off from their larder. And with the waters now calmer, the house that had stood the gale was not likely to subside in the night. No, they were probably safer where they were than if "rescued." She must wait till the morning.

A loud thumping at the kitchen-door shattered her speculations. Jinny's heart beat almost as loudly. So the horseman had come at last, unheard in their excitement, choosing the back door as less of a surrender. Will had escaped then. He was not water-logged. She flew down the stairs three at a time. Poor Will! Poor Snowdrop—or was it Snowdrop that was saved and was now bearing his master to the heart that would give him compensation for all his shattered fortunes? Alas, no proud cavalier waited to bear her off clasped to his breast, no smoking steed—only a tatterdemalion before whose malodorous corduroys and battered beaver she recoiled in as much disgust as disappointment, though Uncle Lilliwhyte bore in his grimy claws a plump partridge, for which he demanded only twopence.

"But the season's over," she murmured.

"That's onny the tother day and 'twarnt me as killed it," he said. "The Lord don't seem to care about they game laws; He killed even on Sunday."

"Don't take the Lord's name in vain," Jinny rebuked him. "We can't understand His ways."

"They do seem wunnerful odd," admitted the nondescript. "Ever since Oi was a brat Oi've tried to puzzle 'em out, but it git over me. Same as a man now perished in this here flood, and went straight to hell. Wouldn't that be a cur'ous change for the chap—like the Lord larkin' with him!"

"Perhaps there'll be a flood that will put out hell one day," said Jinny evasively.

"Martha Flynt should be sayin' there ain't no hell to put out. That looks as if ye've got to goo to Heaven, do what ye will."

"Oh, I don't think she means that," said Jinny, smiling despite her heavy heart.

"That's what the humes sounded like as her and the looker used to sing of a Sunday afore Master Will come home and stopped 'em. Oi used to listen to 'em chance times—put me in mind of my young days like—but Oi don't howd with their doctrines."

"With whose then?" asked Jinny, interested.

"With nobody's. Dedn't Oi say, git over me? Ef the Lord was to offer me Heaven or Hell, which d'ye think Oi'd choose?"

"Is there a catch in it?" she asked cautiously.

"We've got to be catched in one or the tother," he said, misunderstanding. "But Oi mislikes 'em both. Will you be buyin' the bird?"

As Jinny produced two of her only three pennies, she began to realize for the first time the revolution in her fortunes implicit in the destruction of the coach. But her heart was aching too poignantly for any joy of victory. She could not savour, as her grandfather was savouring, the miraculous collapse of the competition. Victory or defeat—heaven or hell—she thought ruefully, she misliked them both. She was consumed with yearning, anxiety and compassion for the young rival who had failed to "come on a horse," who had perhaps no longer even a single horse to come on. Nor did the fate of Snowdrop or Cherry-blossom—that superb vitality turned into a floating carcase—leave her jubilant. In the morning, indeed, she was to awake to a sense of her triumph. But what endless hours of insomnia and nightmare had first to be lived through! Again Queen Victoria, who was also quite intelligibly Miss Jinny Boldero, was saved by "The Father of the Fatherless" from the gins and stratagems of the red-haired villain who cut away London Bridge just as Her Majesty was going over it in her gold coronation coach with its six black ponies and its canvas tilt. Struggling in the cold waters, she was held up by Henry Brougham, Esq., who helped her to scramble athwart the naked carcase of a black pony on which she floated to shore, when it stood upon its feet, and with Queen Jinny astride the saddle and Miss Gentry (in bridal attire) not at all surprisingly on the pillion, galloped towards Blackwater Hall across the dry Common where anglers sat with broomsticks. And while she was lying along the pony's mane to get through the door to the red-haired young man (now become the hero), just as she was beginning to feel Passion's force, that stupid Miss Gentry came crack with her neck against the lintel, and off rolled her head on the floor, its moustache dabbled in blood. Picking herself up, and her scattered bedclothes, and rubbing her bruised crown, Jinny congratulated herself on sleeping in a chest of drawers in such proximity to the floor.

But the bang, slight as it was, had cleared away the vapours of sleep and she awoke to a consciousness of victory brimming her veins with vital joy. Song, so long strange to her lips, unless simulated to lull Gran'fer, came back to them as she dressed, and when she prayed "Give us this day our daily bread," it was no longer an almost despairing cry to a deaf heaven.

Running upstairs to see if Frog Farm was safe, she was relieved to find it smoking imperturbably, though up to its bedrooms in water, and a glimpse of Caleb at the casement serenely lowering a bucket into the flood was still more reassuring. But she was thunderstruck when her grandfather gleefully pointed out that the bridge to Long Bradmarsh had broken down, almost as in her dream, and she half looked round for the coronation coach. Doubtless, she felt, surveying the broken bankside arch, which lay in uncouth masses impeding the current and sending it swirling through the still-standing central arch, the breach hard by in the dyke had helped to sap the bridge, and she was glad to see this breach being already repaired by her friends, Bidlake and Ravens, with a gang of labourers, for they were clearly heaven-sent minions for the expedition to Frog Farm.

But if she sang on as she cleared the breakfast things, her grandfather was in still higher feather. Not only had the morning brought to him as to Jinny a keener realization of the collapse of their mushroom rival, but he had discovered floating near the bridge a black horse which he persisted was the second horse, and though Jinny maintained it was the same horse, the old man had more faith in heaven. So occupied was he in gloating over this distant horse swirling against the ruined brickwork, with its stiffened leg pointing skywards, that he had not seen Methusalem harnessing under his nose, and it was not till Nip started his hysteric prelude to departure that Mr. Quarles was aroused to Jinny's proceedings.

"Ye can't goo out in the flood," he called down in alarm.

"It's Tuesday," she called up. The blood was dancing gaily in her veins. The frosty morning air was fresh and invigorating. She was young and unconquered. The long anxiety was over. Methusalem had survived the coach, even as he had survived the murderous wiles of Elijah! She put her horn to her lips and blew a challenge to the world.

"But there bain't no bridge," cried her grandfather.

"Daniel Quarles hasn't been downed by a coach," she said, "and he isn't going to be downed by a flood."

"No, by God, he ain't!" cried the old Carrier delightedly. "Oi'll goo round miles by the next bridge sooner than miss my day. And they false customers'll ha' to come to me on their hands and knees ere Oi takes 'em back. Goo to the coach, ye warmints, Oi'm done wi' ye! And Oi wish ye joy of your fine black hosses all a-jinglin' and a-tinklin'. He, he, he! Make muddles, do Oi? Oi never made no muddle like that, stablin' my hosses with the frogs. Do ye give a squint at that carcase, Jinny, as ye pass by and ye'll see it ain't the one but the tother."

"And do ye don't squint into that spy-glass no more," she called up in merry earnest. "Do, ye'll get a glass eye."

He laughed. "No fear. Have they writ ye yet about Sidrach's stone?"

Annoyed with herself at having called up that memory, she feigned deafness. "You'll find partridge for your dinner," she called out, and flicking playfully at Methusalem she burst forth joyously: "There is Hey—"

"There is Ree!" responded the sepulchral bass from above, and then as the old horse stepped out, both voices declared in duet that 'twas Methusalem bore the bells away. Jinny, waving her whip with a last backward glance at her grandfather, saw him wildly agitating his telescope, to which his coloured handkerchief was tied like a flag of victory.

IV

Methusalem waded stolidly towards the river, his cart nearly floating in places. On the drier artificial slope leading up to the bridge she drew rein, and, jumping down, walked cautiously over the two still standing arches to hail Ephraim Bidlake, now some hundred yards down the opposite bank. As she put her horn to her lips to summon him, she saw, quanted up-stream, another barge with a reinforcement of sacks, and as it must pass under the bridge she moved to the other side to send her message by it as it came along. But the posse of mud-grimed men with a last push of their submerged poles fell prostrate before her, as in some Oriental obeisance, and she heard the tops of the gault-sacks scraping against the brickwork of the arch as the boat passed under it, so high was the water. It reminded her again of her nightmare. But no heads came crack as they glided through, and running to the other side, she spoke the rising crew.

Turning, she became aware of Bundock standing, bag-bowed, on the dyke, amid a mass of sodden straw, gazing in horror at the ruins and the dead horse bashing against them, swathed in yellow weed. She advanced to the edge of the void and hailed him across some fifteen feet of eddying water.

"Ahoy, Bundock!"

"For God's sake, Jinny!" he cried, startled. "Go back! That'll give way."

"Not with my weight!" she laughed. "You going across?"

"How can I?"

"There's boats, barges, wherries, lighters, punts, and swimming," called Jinny, "and you've got to do your duty to the Queen."

"And haven't I done it?" he said pathetically, exhibiting his soused leggings. "But there's only three letters for Little Bradmarsh and all for the same man."

"I can guess who that is," she said. "And yet you won't kill three frogs with one stone."

Bundock burst into laughter. "So you've heard my joke," he said happily. "I do liven folks up, don't I, though few have the brains to appreciate aught beyond the Bellman's silly puns." Then his ruddy, pitted countenance resumed its melancholy mien. "But I can't joke about the flood, Jinny, you mustn't expect me to. There's poor Charley Mott!"

"Why, what's he got to do with water?" Jinny jested.

"Haven't you heard? He's drowned."

Jinny's laugh froze on her lips. Charley had obstinately gone to fish in the troubled waters of the Brad, the postman related, despite the weather. All the Sunday morning he had fished from the dyke, and was just walking off to dine with some pals at "The King of Prussia" when the bank burst, and he was caught by the torrent and smashed among the whirling blocks. It was exactly like the moral of the Spelling-Book, and Jinny saw before her as on a scroll of judgment the grey blurred type of Lesson XV: "Harry's Downfall." True, Harry had been torn by wild beasts as well as shipwrecked on the coast of Barbary, but in a country without the larger carnivora a complete analogy could not be expected.

"Poor Mr. Mott," she sighed. And then, remembering the case put by Uncle Lilliwhyte, had the luckless young man indeed gone straight from water to fire, she wondered. "It'll be a relief for Mrs. Mott anyhow," she said.

"A relief?" gasped Bundock. "Why, she's carrying on like mad. Says it's all her fault for trying to drive him to chapel. And that it was Deacon Mawhood that egged her on to drive him on the curb. And that he was worth a dozen Deacons, and she won't have any more to do with you Peculiars. Why, when I brought her the letters this morning, if she hadn't kept me such a time pouring out all Charley's virtues, I might have got across before this bridge broke down. Not that I could have delivered my letters anyhow."

"I think it broke in the night," said Jinny. Then she fell silent, disconcerted by these illogical manifestations of human nature, and she did not remember where she was till she found Nip tugging at her dress and cowering on the brink of the abyss, as if afraid she would be walking on. The wherry, she perceived too, was now coming up, and young Ravens' voice was floating melodiously across the waters:

"'Tis my delight of a shiny night

In the season of the year!"

"There's your ferry, Bundock!" she called.

"And what's the good of going across?" he asked. "By what I see I couldn't possibly get to Frog Farm."

"But I'm going there!"

"What!" He gazed towards her side of the river, the willows surging from which alone marked the former bank. Plover were flying with dismal cries over the unseen pastures.

He shook his head: "One inquest's enough for Chipstone."

"I'll take your letters," she said with a sudden thought that made her happier.

Bundock resisted the offer. His repugnance to seeing the Queen's mail sacrilegiously carried by a member of Her Majesty's sex was deep-seated, and it was only because he took seriously Jinny's threat to write to his sovereign that he finally handed the three letters by a compromise to Ephraim Bidlake. Needless to say that as soon as Bundock's pouched back was turned, that faithful henchman transferred them to Jinny.

When he took her little horse and cart on board his broad-built wherry, he imagined she only wanted to be ferried across, but she had soon spurred him to the great adventure across the "drowned" meadows. It was a question of life-saving, she said, and for the British Navy as embodied in Bidlake and Ravens, this was enough. Fortunately the females were now lodged on shore, awaiting Mrs. Bidlake's annual event. Moreover the wherry, relieved by the other barge, had a slack moment, and with Jinny to guide them from the vantage-point of her driving-board over hidden snags in the shape of submerged stiles, sheds, mounds or bushes, the two men punted boldly over the left bank. The mast had been lowered, for apart from the danger of boughs catching in the sail, the trees made a wind-screen to the pastures.

It was odd as the barge passed between two willows on the margin of the river, to see these trees reflected doubly, at once in stream and in flood. There was no difficulty in avoiding the larger flotsam, though one of Farmer Gale's haystacks was only staved off with Bidlake's pole, and it was not till they had quanted to the farmhouse itself that the steering became troublesome, for there were no windows at the back, at which they were arriving, there were farm-buildings and floating stacks waiting to embarrass them at the front, the so-called Frog Cottage presented a blank black wall at one side, while the windowed side-wall, from which Martha had once beheld Bundock marching through morasses, was encumbered, not only by the wreckage of the stable and the mangled body of the coach, but by Caleb's wild "orchard," in whose mystically rising oak-branches and pear-tree-tops poultry, to which fear had restored wings, were seen to be roosting. But by taking a wide course over the wheat-patch so as to avoid the stacks, the barge was able to double Frog Cottage safely, to glide triumphantly into dock, and lie alongside Frog Farm. The exciting manœuvre had been accomplished in grim silence—even Ravens forgetting to sing as they bumped over the chaotic remains of the old log-dyke and raised wagon-road— and it was not till it was over that Jinny found breath to blow her horn. And as she did so, she was startled to see behind the diamond panes of the closed casement of the central bedroom—now on a level with her driving-board and almost opposite it—a head that vaguely recalled Mr. Duke's.

But the next instant she recognized Maria, and the old black sow was pushed aside, the casement flung open and a red-haired head flung out. And if Jinny had stared incredulously at the sight of the pig, what word can convey the dilatation of Will's eyes as they now beheld the little Carrier perched on her accustomed seat, whip in hand, as though on the solid road! It was some seconds before he even perceived the barge sustaining her cart.

"What do you want?" broke harshly from his lips.

Such ungraciousness after the perils of her voyage jarred upon her. "Don't you want anything from Chipstone?" she asked, with a malice she had not intended.

"No," he barked.

"Well, here's your letters I've carried," she said demurely. "The postal service, like the coach service, has broken down." She hurled the letters through the window just as he was banging it to, but ere it could close it was thrown open again, and Elijah, Maria, Martha, and Caleb were tumbling over one another in their eagerness to greet her.

"Jinny!" came from all their mouths, even, it seemed, from Maria's, and she saw through dimming eyes that the bedroom was a chaos of furniture and fowls.

"Here, catch hold of that rope, one of ye," cried Ephraim Bidlake. "Tie it to a bedpost." He had already fastened the stem of the boat to an oak, but the current was swinging out the stern.

It was with a thrill that Jinny found herself gazing for the first time into Will's bedroom, though its normal character was disturbed by its emergency use as a sitting-room, poultry-run, pigsty, and salvage store. The wet crinkled motto: "When He giveth quietness, who then can make trouble?" was lying as if in ironic questioning atop a pile of parlour ornaments, and Martha's silk sampler lay stained and sodden on the very chair on which Mr. Flippance had sat admiring it. "Unstable as water," human destinies seemed to Jinny as she surveyed the jumble in the whitewashed attic. But there was too much bustle for reflection, nor could she even see clearly what Will himself was doing, for Maria and Elijah were jostling each other at the window in their efforts to get through, and the vet.'s cap fell on the deck in his agitation.

"Pigs first!" called Jinny, and as though obediently, Elijah clutching at the edge of her tilt scrambled on the foot-board of the cart and thence to the deck. "Nice behaviour, leaving us to starve," he grumbled in the same pachydermatous spirit, as he clapped his cap on his chilled cranium.

"How could you starve with all those fowls?" said Jinny.

"They weren't for weekday eating, the old woman said. Nothing since Sunday but dry bread!"

"As long as it was dry," Jinny laughed.

"It wasn't even that! Simply sopping."

"Well, all prisoners get bread and water," said Jinny in mock consolation. Ravens had hastened to pull out a greasy package. Elijah waved it aside with a sniffy air. "Thanks—I'll wait till we land now."

"Elijah not fed by Ravens," laughed Jinny. Outwardly she was in the gayest of moods, bandying words again in quite her old vein. But it was a feverish gaiety—underneath, every nerve was astrain for Will's reappearance with all it forboded of ecstasy and conflict. "Come along, Maria," she called, for the barge had drifted out a little on its window-rope, and the sow's eagerness was damped. Now encouraged, she allowed herself to be helped into the cart by Caleb above and Bidlake below. After the fowls had been chivied beside her, there was a delay.

"The missus be in our bedroom packin' some things for the night," apologized Caleb, returning to the window. "She can't sleep without her nightcap, it wouldn't be decent, and she likes me to change my red shirt for bed."

"But where will you sleep?" Jinny now asked, feeling suddenly responsible as for an eviction.

"Mr. Skindle's kindly offered to put us all up till we looks round," said Caleb.

"It's the big house I'm furnishing for my wedding regardless," Elijah explained. "And I'm going to give them their food, too, and it isn't the sort of food they've given me either. But when you're cooped up with folks in danger of your life, you get closer to them and don't grudge expense, especially when they're in low water."

"In low water?" echoed Jinny. "Oh, Mr. Skindle!"

"You know what I mean," Elijah replied. "Poor Will's lost his horses—such a come-down. Not that he ever had enough to appeal to a girl brought up to be a lady. In my new house now there's three spare bedrooms—I'll get my mother to make 'em all ready—that'll be one apiece for 'em if they care to spread themselves."

"But then how about Maria?" Jinny jested.

"Maria!" he grunted. "It's all her fault. I always said she was the fussiest pig I ever attended. A mere cramp, through not taking exercise all this rainy weather; fright cured her in a jiffy. But think of the valuable time she's cost me! I wouldn't have come but to oblige Will. No wonder they call the place Frog Farm."

"I don't hear any croaking but yours," flashed Jinny. "Why, if time is all you've lost, you're lucky. Where's your horse?"

"You didn't think I'd risk Jess on these roads in the weather we've been having? I only agreed to come in the coach Saturday night and go back Sunday morning with Farmer Gale and his wife when they drove in to chapel. Poor Blanche! She must have been in a terrible twitter when I didn't turn up at the Sunday dinner!"

"I wonder she didn't come out for you in a boat?" said Jinny slyly.

"She'd be thinking I'd been called to another patient. We medical gents can never call our time our own," he explained, but there was a tremor of uneasiness in his words. He pulled out his empty pipe and stuck it between his blackened teeth. Caleb here appeared with uncouth bundles, and Martha (embellished by sudden Sunday clothes) with a last frightened chicken, and as the barge had now quite tautened its window-rope and left a watery gap, Martha's descent was a fluttering episode.

"Not so easy as the New Jerusalem coming down," gasped Caleb, when she was safely installed inside the cart with Maria and the poultry and the dazed Nip.

Ephraim Bidlake, intimating he could not wait on this jaunt to lower any of the furniture, had gone off—in a little dinghy he carried—to rescue the fowls in the orchard branches, and their fearful cackling and the excitement of his perilous quest now drew all eyes, except Jinny's, which remained furtively bent on the window, from which the drifting of the barge had carried her away. It was with relief that she heard Martha suddenly exclaim:

"But where's the boy?"

"Oi count he's got such a mort o' new-fangled things," scoffed Caleb. "Tooth-brushes and underclothes and shavin'-strops—happen he'll want a whole portmantle. Oi offered to help him with his poor arm, but he's that fiery and sperrited—ye remember, Jinny, how he lugged his great ole box all the way Chipstone!"

"But what's the matter with his arm?" Jinny asked anxiously.

"Didn't you see his sling?" called Elijah proudly.

"Broken?" Jinny murmured, paling.

"Only a simple fracture." He puffed complacently at his pipe, forgetting it was empty.

"You've got to go back, Caleb, and help the poor lad," said Martha, with renewed agitation.

"Then you might as well get my hand-bag from my room," Elijah added. "I didn't think of it in the rush."

Ravens, labouring mightily with his pole to larboard, pushed the barge back to the window, and as Caleb obediently clambered in again, Martha, growing calmer, began telling Jinny how Will had swum out to the stable to save the horses, but had only got his arm kicked for his pains. And then, of course, he couldn't help her in carrying any of her furniture upstairs—it was a mercy he got back at all—and, it being Sunday, "Flynt" would help only to save life, though you'd have thought from Maria's squeals, as she was haled upstairs, that she was being slaughtered rather than saved. As for Mr. Skindle, he seemed stricter with the Sabbath than even the Peculiars, and would do nothing but try to light the fire.

"You were at home. I hadn't got but the clothes I stood in," Elijah explained. "What should I have done if I'd gone up to my neck in water?"

"Here's your bag," Caleb's voice broke in from the window, "but Will won't come, Martha!"

"Won't come?" shrilled Martha, and before Jinny could stop her, she was on the footboard and had disappeared through the casement.

"He's an ungrateful, ill-tempered fellow," Elijah commented, picking up his bag, and changing his collar as he talked. "I don't call him a gentleman. He can't forgive that his arm was set by a vet., and he sits about like a broody hen. Asked me not to mention it, which, of course, as a gentleman, I won't. What good do you suppose it would do me to have it known—I said to him—seeing I've already got the family connexion with Maria? But he got very cross," Elijah wound up innocently, "though I said I wouldn't even charge pig's price, but would swap the fee and Maria's too against his horses, provided I could recover the carcases."

"I've got to stay here," cried Martha, reappearing hysterically at the window. "He won't come."

"What nonsense!" cried Jinny, losing her temper. "We'll all go and pull him out."

"He's locked himself in my bedroom—the one with the side window—you can't get in from here." She wrung her hands; these days of durance and danger had evidently told upon her nerves.

"I'll smash the door in and his head too!" growled Ravens, his foot on the window-sill.

"No, no," Jinny commanded, swinging herself suddenly past him. "You take your wife down, Mr. Flynt. She's too excited. I'll rout him out."

Martha protested shrilly that where she had failed, a stranger could not succeed. No, she must stay with her boy, tend his poor arm! But the men overruled her and were returning her gently but firmly to the footboard of the cart when she cried desperately:

"Wait! Wait! I've forgotten something under my pillow." "I'll get it!" Jinny promised. "What is it?"

But Martha refused to say. It was very precious. It was in an envelope. It wasn't for Jinny to see. In vain Jinny declared she wouldn't open the envelope. Martha's hysteric protests mingled with the frenzied cackling of the fowls that Ephraim Bidlake was still chasing.

Leaving the males to pacify Martha and deposit her in the cart, Jinny stooped under the barge-rope and threaded the litter betwixt the bed and the right-hand door—the other door, she knew, gave on the bedroom bisected by Frog Cottage. Pausing but a moment to look down the now literal well of the staircase, in which dead mice floated, she rapped imperiously at the connubial chamber under the gable.

"Go away, mother!" came the fretful answer.

"I'm not your mother—if I were I'd slap you. A nice state you've got her into!"

"What do you want?" he said in a changed tone.

"Your mother's left something precious in an envelope under her pillow."

"I thought you said you'd never cross my doorstep."

"I didn't—I came by the window-sill." But even as her lips gave the obvious repartee, her mind beheld her grandfather scrambling into the room of the Angel-Mother, and it all seemed ineffably silly in view of the tragic realities of life. As if she would not have crossed even an enemy's threshold to bind up a broken arm!

"Well, suppose you return the same way," he retorted.

"That's what I mean to do," she said, angry again. "I've got my rounds."

"What! In the barge?"

"I don't want a boat. Long Bradmarsh has kept its head above water and Methusalem's going just as strong as before the flood." Then, afraid she had recalled his own dead horses, she added hurriedly: "How's your arm?"

"That's nothing, thank you. Good-bye."

"Not without the envelope."

Their words came muffled through the door-panels, and a barrier as obstructive seemed to divide their spirits, though they yearned dumbly towards each other.

"I'll put it under the door," he said surlily.

"I don't wonder you're ashamed to look me in the face."

Jinny was thinking of his behaviour to his mother. But it was an unfortunate remark. Will was ashamed, mortally ashamed of his defeat. He had come along from over the seas, he felt, swelling and strutting and jeering! Poor little Jinny! Poor, comical little village carrier! Oho, he'd soon crush her! Oho, he'd soon make an end of her! And now! His coach smashed up, his horses drowned, his capital gone, his savings—the bulk spent on his fine clothes—barely sufficient to carry him along while seeking some new employment, even his parents impoverished by the flood, their very roof perhaps about to collapse over his head! While she—! Here she was with her invincible old cart, walking the waters, posing as the saviour of the whole family, carrying on the postal service and the coach service, blowing her triumphant trumpet on her immemorial Tuesday round, her old clients doubly at her mercy! What humiliation could be more bitter?

And the worst of it all was that the ache of passion, nourished by her rejection of his new advances, had become intolerably poignant. Jinny! Jinny! He seemed to hear it all around him, Jinny! Jinny! from morning to night—and even all through the night, floating through his dreams like a strain of music. And Jinny herself was ever before him night and day, with her eyes laughing and her tongue stinging.

But now that she was there in the flesh, with only a door between them, he felt he could not open it. He must never look in her face again till he had rehabilitated his fortunes. No word of love had ever been spoken between them. But could he see her, stand near her now, and not speak it? And a fine story it would sound, even if his lips proved spiritless enough to attempt it. He had loved her from the first moment he had seen her in the courtyard of "The Black Sheep," nay, from childhood, and had tried to steal her business! Had loved her and might have driven her, with the grandfather she supported, to die in a ditch! And now that it was he who was in the ditch, could he come prating of love, add her enhanced scorn to his self-contempt? No, he had missed his opportunities! A nice hand to offer her—

even if there was any chance of her taking it—a hand swathed in a sling, symbol of his crippled fortunes! He must set out on his travels again—that was clear—work his passage—as soon as his bones had grown together—to those new Australian goldfields that everybody was talking of, and then, when his self-respect had grown together too, he would write to her and ask her to wait for him. And if she still said "No"—or had already said "Yes" to a better man—why what else had he deserved, monkeying around with a flirt who was not worthy even of Elijah!

As Jinny now heard him moving speechlessly to get the envelope, the voice of Ravens carolling the popular "Gipsy King," told her that Martha had been quieted down—unlike the fowls, which were still squawking under Bidlake's coaxings.

"I confess I am but a man,
My feelings, who pleases may know,
I am fond of my girl and my can,
And jolly companions a row!"

Suddenly she heard Will laughing.

"What's up?" she called, more brightly.

"Well of all the—!" And then an envelope was pushed under the door. "She hasn't opened it yet!"

Jinny stooped down. It was the letter from Will that Martha would not let her read in the Spring of '51!

"Well, she knew what was in it," said Jinny, her eyes misting. "And you oughtn't to laugh at such a proof of love. Nobody else would call that a precious treasure."

The word "love" sent vibrations through them both, despite the woodwork between.

"Well, there's money in the others anyhow," he said, and three opened envelopes came unexpectedly under the door—the letters she had just brought to him.

"What are these for?" she asked.

"You may as well have them—commissions for the coach."

"For me?" Jinny said, touched.

"Yes, I'd be obliged if you helped me out."

"Oh, Will!" Her voice was as broken as his pride seemed to be. But his mood was less of meekness than of self-scourging.

"Well, you said the coach service had broken down," he reminded her.

"I didn't mean to twit you—I'm sorry—"

"What for? You told me I'd get stuck and come to you to pull me out."

"But I'm so sorry, really. Poor Snowdrop! Poor Cherry-blossom!"

"Didn't you call it a funeral coach? Good-bye, you've got the treasure."

"You'd better come too."

"No, thank you."

"You needn't be beholden to the cart if that's what's sticking in your gizzard. You can get off at the dyke."

"Not me. You won't see me again—not for a long time."

"Rubbish! I can see you now through the keyhole."

"So long as I don't see you," he said gruffly.

"You'll see me before you're a day older."

"Bet my bottom dollar I won't."

"A dashing young lad from Canada," she carolled. "Once a great wager did lay— Why have you buried your face in your hands?" she broke off.

"I haven't—it's to shut you out!"

"Aha! So I do come in all the same."

Loud cries of "Jinny! Jinny!" now intimated, like the silence of the rescued poultry, that the barge was preparing to cast off.

"Just coming!" she called loudly. "Good-bye, you sullen, runty idiot. They can't wait any longer."

"Good-bye!" he growled.

Her look was mischievous as she ran off. But that he could not see: he could only hear the noisy banging of the opposite door. He had already forgotten his wager. But by hook or crook she meant to lure him out, if only for an instant. That was why she came as noisily back and thumped at his door again. "You can't be left without food," she said.

"That's my business. Let me be."

"Not till I know you won't starve. There's Ravens' dinner-packet you can have."

"Take it away," he roared.

Her eyes twinkled. He had played into her hands, empty as they were. "I won't take it away," she said. There was a sound as of angry dumping outside his door. Then the opposite door banged and silence fell.

After a moment Will, drawing a sigh, half of relief, half of despair, opened his door and the next moment—he never knew how it had happened exactly (still less did he realize that there was no dinner-packet there at all), but since he had only one arm it seemed to him afterwards it could not be he that had enfolded her, even if he had done so with his eyes when her merry mocking face shone so trickily upon the landing, while Jinny always felt that it was precisely the arm out of action that had come round her, just as it was his not coming on a horse that had made her feel Passion's force—but there they were (by some irresistible flood) in each other's arms, with Jinny's flower-soft cheek pressed with a wonderful warmth to his own, and her silvery little voice crooning: "Oh, my poor Will! Oh, my poor Will!" He knew immediately that there had been nothing like this in all his motley experience, nothing at once so pure, so sweet, so tender. This was the love that lifted, not degraded.

But Jinny, though she had no comparative lore of love and was all the more absorbed in the absolute wonder, uniqueness and completeness of it, knew more swiftly than her lover that this was no time for dallying. In what seemed to him a mere flash of lightning the whole episode was cruelly over, he was being helped into the barge, while Bidlake was in his bedroom untying the rope, and Jinny with motherly zeal and uncanny knowledge was scrambling together his things for the night. For her, too, the moment of breaking away had been hard, and as her face moved from his, it seemed like passing from a sunny clime to a polar world. But as she now busied herself with his little equipment, the glow was back again at her heart, and the transfigured world of that magic moment was hers again.

As the wherry began to move off at last, and Frog Cottage was doubled again, Martha, who had been laid snugly inside the cart surrounded by her live stock, with blankets from the bed thrown over her, threw them off, stretched her arms to her receding farm and burst into a new passion of tears.

"Dear heart! Dear heart!" cried Caleb, almost as agitated.

"Shall we ever see our things again?" she sobbed.

"That's nawthen to cry over, dear heart, even ef we don't. We've got to thank the Lord for givin' us the use of Frog Farm all they long years."

But Martha sobbed on, unconsoled.

"And Will's been taken from me too."

"No, no, Martha," Caleb reassured her. "There he is by the starn, smokin' his pipe. 'Tis middlin' clever to my thinkin' to fill it one-handed."

Still Martha refused to be comforted. So spasmodic were her gulpings that Nip set up a sympathetic howl and Maria a perturbed squeal. But none of these sounds—not even Ravens' singing—could drown the celestial music Will and Jinny heard in their hearts.

CHAPTER XIII

THE COURSE OF TRUE LOVE

As John the apostel sygh with syght,
I syghe that cyty of gret renoun,
Jherusalem so newe and ryally dyght,
As hit wacz lyght fro the heven adoun.
"Pearl" (Fourteenth century).

I

Jinny's passage through Long Bradmarsh with her overflowing freight of fares and live stock was like a triumphal progress. The loungers outside "The King of Prussia" actually raised a cheer. Fresh from the excitement of the Mott inquest, they knew the adventurous significance of her dripping cart-wheels and dry tilt, and were quick to see the symbolic significance of her carrying the disabled driver of "The Flynt Flyer," though its destruction was still unknown to them. At the instance of Elijah, she went round by Foxearth Farm, so as to put up Maria and the poultry there, as well as to reassure Blanche of his safety. Though the interview with the latter was naturally veiled from the occupants of the cart, it was obvious to them that it was Mrs. Purley who was doing the talking. Her voice, wafted to them through walls which dulled the actual words, was like an endless drone, each sentence fusing breathlessly into the next in a maddening meaninglessness. Elijah returned with a dejected mien: due not merely, it transpired, to the cascade that had broken over him, but to the fact that Blanche was just washing her head (that generation did not speak of its hair) and unable to see him. "As if you hadn't suffered enough from water," said Jinny sympathetically.

She had her first view that day of Mr. Skindle's bridal mansion. Its two stories rose in new red brick on the outskirts of Chipstone, in a forlorn field that was just being "developed," and its architecture, from bow-window to chimney-stack, was an imitation of the residence of Dr. Mint, the leading human doctor.

"There's Rosemary Villa!" said Elijah proudly, and Will smiled at the recollection of Bundock's jape and Blanche's merriment.

Ere Elijah, leaping down first, could mount his beautifully whitened steps, the door was opened excitedly and a gaunt grey-haired charwoman, with a smear on her cheek, dropped her grate-blacking brush and fell upon Elijah's neck in a spasm of emotion.

"Thank God! Thank God!" she sobbed.

"Here! Don't do that!" said Elijah, writhing in her grasp. He was blushingly disconcerted by this assertion of maternity before company: she had so long accepted the position of drudge that he had forgotten that his absence during the flood might reawaken the mother. "You're all black!" he explained, disentangling himself.

"That's mourning for you!" Jinny called merrily from her cart, and the jest relieved the situation. She looked curiously at the lank, aproned figure, fancying she caught a hint of grace in the movement of the limbs and a gleam of fire in the dark eyes. But this dim sense of the tragic passing of romance could not even faintly obscure her own happiness, on which the imminent separation from Will was the only cloud. Except for the thrilling contact achieved in helping him to alight, she had to part with him less cordially than with Caleb, who to her surprise and Martha's gave her a smacking kiss ere he stepped down. "Thank you, dearie—ye've saved our lives," he said. Jinny scoffed at that—the gratitude was due to Bidlake and Ravens. "Well, the missus'll have to kiss them," he sniggered. "You do your own kissing," said Martha sharply. "And keep your kissing for your own, too." All this talk of kissing but aggravated the pang of the frigid parting with the one person who mattered.

"Good-bye; see you soon," was all Will said.

"You bet your bottom dollar on that," she flashed, with a relieved smile, reading into his words a promise to come over the very next day.

"Oh, I'll pay you next time," he smiled back, and she had a delicious sense of his meaning to pay his lost wager in the currency with which Caleb had just acquitted his debt. She promised the old people she would come round on Friday and tell them how Frog Farm stood—if it did stand! But though her eyes exchanged with Will's secret promises for the morrow, an eternity of loneliness seemed to lie before her, as she drove back to the town, magnanimously blowing the "Buy a Broom Polka" to apprise her faithless clients.

II

So many commissions clamoured for her from folk with relations in the flooded area that she had no difficulty in redeeming her dress from the pawnshop that very day. But it was not on account of the many calls upon her that she arrived home in the dark. It was because she had forgotten to command her faithful ferry's attendance, and been forced to take the amazed Methusalem miles round by the farther bridge. Her grandfather would be anxious, she feared: then it occurred to her—not wholly with satisfaction—that he might have followed her day's movements by telescope. But she found him as happy as she had left him, and with the hearth blazing like a bonfire, reckless of logs. He had not observed her rescue of the Flynts, for, as she had warned him, his overtaxed right eye had become inflamed and throbbed with little darts of pain, and he had been compelled to fall back on the voluptuous venom of his reflections, supplemented by a text which he had hunted out with his other eye.

"It come into my mind all of an onplunge," he chuckled, putting a bony finger on a verse. "The horse and his rider hath He thrown into the sea," she saw with a shudder. "That won't be long afore he follows his hoss," said the Gaffer grimly as he polished his lens for the spectacle. "Oi will sing to the Lord," he read out, "for He hath triumphed gloriously."

"Don't be so wicked, Gran'fer," she cried.

"Wicked! That's roighteous—to sing to the Lord."

"You don't want people drowned!"

"Dedn't he want us to starve?"

"Looks more like his starving now. We can afford to forgive. You're reading the wrong end of the Bible, Gran'fer. We've got to turn the other cheek."

"Sow Oi would, ef anybody was bussin' me," he cackled.

Jinny flushed and turned both her cheeks away.

"Why, the day Oi met Annie at Che'msford Fair—" he began.

"I don't want to hear about Annie," she said severely. "She wasn't your wife."

"That's why I tarned from iniquity. But she ain't nobody's wife now."

"No, poor thing!" she said. "And it's a pity she's Mr. Skindle's mother, for he makes her do all the chares of his big new house."

"Well, but she's a woman, ain't she?" he asked with unexpected lack of sympathy. "She'd have to do her husband's chares."

"Not at her age!"

"At her age? Annie's a young woman."

"Compared with you, perhaps," she smiled.

"Git over me, her having a lad that size. Oi count she's worritin' over him, cooped up in Frog Farm."

"Not now. They're all safely out of it."

"What! That pirate thief's got safe!"

"Thank God!"

"That ain't God's doin'—that's some evil interferin' sperrit what comes out o' dead bodies, says John Wesley. Who took 'em off?" he demanded fiercely.

"They came off in Bidlake's barge," she said weakly. "And don't you be so unchristian. Isn't it enough he's—?"

"That ain't right, interferin' with the texts!" he interrupted doggedly. "Oi never could abide they Bidlakes. Ephraim's grandfather come competitioning on the canals, wuss than Willie Flynt."

"Well, Mr. Flynt can't competition any more, can he? I expect," she added with difficult lightness, "he'll be coming round now to make friends."

"Come round, will he? Just let him show his carroty head inside my doorway—he'll be outside like fleck, Oi promise ye."

"But if he wants to make it up—!"

"He's got to goo down on his hands and knees fust."

"Perhaps he will," she suggested. Indeed she had little doubt of it. That wonderful moment, with its climax of mouth to mouth, had reduced this long foreseen obstacle to a grotesque bogy. In the light of mutual and confessed love the perspective changed, and if she had once thought that she could not have borne to see him grovel even for her sake, that it would actually impair the love grovelled for, she had now been uplifted into a plane of existence in which for him not to humour her grandfather seemed as childish as the nonagenarian's own demand.

The old man now turned on her a red-rimmed probing eye. "He'd never come crawlin' to me ef he warn't arter summat. And he's been tryin' to git round you fust—don't tell me! What's his game?"

"Perhaps—he'd like—a partnership."

"Oi dessay he would!" he chuckled ironically. "He's got brass enough for anythin'. Why, the chap was arter you once. Ye dedn't know it, but there ain't much hid from Daniel Quarles. Oi suspicioned him the fust moment he come gawmin' to the stable. And what'll he bring to the pardnership? Cat's-meat and matchwood?"

His coarseness jarred every nerve, but she kept to his key of jocosity. "Didn't you say he had brass?"

"He, he, he!" he cackled. "But it's the wrong kind o' brass. Ef he wanted to be a pardner, why dedn't he come when he had his coach and hosses?"

"He did. Don't you remember?"

"Did he?" he said blankly. "Then why dedn't Oi take 'em?"

"That was all my fault, Gran'fer."

"No, it warn't, dearie. It was 'cause he said Oi'd made muddles. Oi remember now. He come and swabbled, and chucked a pot at me. And he's got to goo down on his hands and knees for it!"

Jinny saw it was hopeless to unravel these blended memories of Will and Elijah, as grotesquely interwoven as one of her own nightmares, on whose formation it seemed to throw light. She was glad, though, that the sharp edges of the actuality had now faded.

"Yes, yes—he shall," she promised soothingly.

"And then there was that weddin'-cake what Mr. Flippance sent us," burst up now from the labouring depths.

"Yes—wasn't that a lovely cake?" she agreed.

"Oi offered him a shiver—shows 'twarn't me as wanted to swabble. But he lifted his whip at me and Oi snapped it in two like my ole pipe when John Wesley stopped my smokin'. Oi don't want no pardnerships."

"Of course not, Gran'fer."

"Daniel Quarles it's been for a hundred year, and Daniel Quarles it's a-gooin' to remain."

"Of course. Daniel Quarles."

"And he's got to goo down on his hands and knees."

"And so have I," she laughed, "for we've let our bonfire die down. Poor Mr. Flynt—he's got a great admiration for you, spite that you've licked him."

"Oi guessed you and him been gammickin'. You can't hide much from Daniel Quarles. And ef that little Willie has got a proper respect for his elders and betters, that shows Oi larnt him a lesson."

"You did, Gran'fer. He's a changed man. There! Isn't that a nice blaze again? He's broken his right arm, too, poor fellow."

But here she had blundered. The old man's face lit up, not from the fire, but with a roaring flame of its own. "Thank the Lord," he shouted, "as hears the prayer of the humble. The high arm shall be broken, says the Book, and it's come true. The arm what dreft the hosses is broken like the coach!" He ended with a fresh cackle and rubbed his skinny hands before the blaze.

"You didn't pray for that?" said Jinny, white and rebuking. "That was unchristian."

"That's what King David prayed, Jinny, and he was a man after God's own heart. 'Break thou the arm of the wicked'—Oi'll show it you in the Psalm."

"I don't want to see it—King David wasn't a Christian yet. And we've got to forgive and forget, and not bear a grudge for ever, especially when a man's down. Think of John Wesley."

"Happen you're right, Jinny," he said, softening. "We've got to forgive the evil-doer, and ef the Lord's got him in hand Oi count we needn't trouble—he'll git all he desarves."

And with that Jinny felt fairly content.

III

But though the ground was thus prepared for his advent, Will did not come. "What are you prinkin' yourself for?" her grandfather asked in the morning. "It ain't your day." It was certainly not her day. It was more like a night—a long agony of expectation with every rustle of wind on the dead leaves sounding like his footstep. Towards dusk she even swept the water-logged landscape with the now neglected telescope. If she did not find him, she found—what was almost as soothing—a reason for his not coming. The broken bridge! How could he go all those miles round? Joyfully she called herself a fool, and awaited the letter he would send instead. The letter would fill up the Thursday and on the Friday she would go to him.

But even this milder expectation of a visit from Bundock went unfulfilled. At first she thought with some relief that Bundock was again shirking the circuit. But no! The glass revealed the slave of duty serving Beacon Chimneys. Throwing on her jacket, but bonnetless, she ran across the Common to meet her letter. But Bundock only gave her grumbles at the overstrain on his feet, and leaving him, to hide her dismay, she walked blindly up Beacon Hill till she was startled to come upon Master Peartree in the bosom of his new-born flock. It did not even occur to her that this was a proof he had escaped the flood, and that the occasion called for congratulation. But the sight of his lambs bounding and his ewes scooping out mangolds brought to mind his old account of a sheep that had broken its arm "in a roosh," and at once a second rush of joy at her silliness and a still more paradoxical pleasure in Will's broken arm flooded her soul. How could he write, the poor boy? It was not that she had really forgotten the state of his arm—indeed, she had thought of the sling as clogging the springiness of his walk, and making it still more impossible for him to come—only she must be going crazy again, she felt; just as in the days when she had taken home wedding-cakes and brought Elijah hairpins. Her eyes now filled with happy tears and, joyous as the yeanlings whose tails vibrated with such voluptuous velocity as they sucked, she gave chase to a little black lamb and kissed its sable nose.

That brought her thoughts back to the flood by way of Mother Gander's hostelry and its drowned landlord, and she inquired at last about Master Peartree's losses. They had been limited to one bullock, she was glad to hear, though no such glow of Christian feeling possessed her as she had recommended to her grandfather, when the shepherd-cowman proceeded to estimate that what with stacks, root-crops, and winter-wheat, Farmer Gale was the poorer by several thousand pounds. Other shepherds had been badly hit, but he himself—thanks to the Almighty—had got more twins and triplets than ever, and taking her round his plaza of straw he showed her the yellow-splashed, long-legged lambkins in the thatched pens, one set of which he would have to feed by bottle, for handsome mothers did not give the most milk, he moralized.

She ran homewards as full of the joy of life as the leaping lambs, though she was living only for the morrow. Through the frosty air she felt a first breath of spring, birds were singing, and even beginning to build, and the flood, she was sure, was falling. But when next day she reached Rosemary Villa, the gaunt drudge informed her that only the old Flynts were in! Her heart turned to lead. So he had not stayed in for her, though she, for her part, had raced to him by the shortest routes, irrespective of business, cutting through Chipstone proper by a single side-street. It was not till she had learnt that he was gone, like Elijah and all the world, to Mr. Mott's funeral, that her heart grew light again—she seemed to batten on tragedies these days. Of course Will could not avoid this mark of respect, he who had always put up his coach in the courtyard of "The Black Sheep," and perhaps she ought to have gone to the funeral too, and would probably have encountered it had she not skipped the High Street in her eagerness. She remembered now some lowered blinds in the street she had scuttled through, and a slow booming bell, whose disregarded notes now at last donged their message to her brain. But perhaps it was better so—her redeemed frock was too gay, her winter shawl and bonnet without a single touch of black. She ought to have borne the inevitable funeral in mind though, she told herself reproachfully. In her present guise she could hardly station even in the courtyard. It was fortunate "Mother Gander" no longer expected to see her within. How embarrassing it would have been for the widow to meet the confidante of her unmeasured denunciations! Probably the whole place would be closed for the day, though she supposed the Chelmsford coach with the passengers from London would have to come in as usual.

Apprised by the barking of Nip, the Flynt couple had descended, looking uneasy, for they had been speaking of her not long before. Their hostess-drudge had started the ball as she closed the door upon Will, outward bound for the funeral. "You'd think he'd found a fortune, not lost one," the melancholy creature had commented, warmed by that youthful sunshine. "I reckon he wasn't happy hartin' Jinny's business," Caleb had surmised. "And to be happy is as good as a fortune." Upon which Martha, who was equally in the passage "to see Will off," had surprised them by a sudden sob. "She's thinkin' of that poor drownded young man," Caleb had apologized, leading her gently upstairs. "Oi do hope Will'll keep a proper face for the funeral."

That appropriate face, however, had continued to be Martha's, and the explanation thereof when they were alone had surprised Caleb more than the sob.

"I knew she'd rob me of Will. I knew it from the first moment she wanted to read his letter to me."

"Rob you of him!"

"They're in love. Are you blind?"

"You don't say! Lord! Little Jinny! Why, she's a baiby!"

"A cunning woman. Came after him even when you'd have thought he was safe behind the flood! This letter will be all that's left to me! You mark my words!"

"Don't, dear heart. You're wettin' the letter—it'll spile. But dedn't Oi leave my mother to come to you, as the Book commands?"

"That's different. He's all I've got. I can't trust him to Jinny—she's too flighty—always singing."

"Sow's the birds, but look what noice nests they make! 'Tain't as if 'twas that Purley gal as Bundock warned us of, allus lookin' at herself like a goose in a pond. We ought to be thankful as Will's showed sow much sense. There's plenty o' good farmers along the road, but there's no weeds to Jinny even three fields back."

"I don't wonder you go kissing her! Pity you can't marry her yourself!"

"Oi'd have no chance agin Will's looks, dear heart. He takes arter his mother, ye see."

Dulcifying as this jocose finale had proved, it did not diminish the awkwardness of now meeting Jinny, but Martha, who had not even the consolation of finding an Ecclesia flourishing in Chipstone, was anxious to hear how far the flood had subsided from their beloved Frog Farm. They were both experiencing all the pangs of exile, aggravated by the discomforts of a house with monotonously boarded floors, forbiddingly fine furniture, and light and water coming unnaturally out of taps, and their grievances and yearnings for a return to reality now monopolized a conversation which Jinny strove in vain to divert to Will. She was reduced to looking at her cart for indications of the depths she had splashed through unobservantly, and could extract nothing about Will except that he insisted on paying for their board and lodging, and that this would surely take his last penny. "He'll have to look for a job now, he'll have no time or money to think of foolishness," Martha told her meaningly. But this broad hint conveyed nothing to her. In her affection for the old woman it never occurred to her that she would not make a welcome daughter-in-law, now the competition was over. And knowing as a scientific fact that your ears burned if people had been talking of you—whereas hers had been tingling with the frost—she went away, all unsuspicious, in quest of the coveted young man.

The funeral was over now, she saw from the many coaches returning singly or in procession through and from the High Street. Surely the grandest funeral ever known (she thought), doubtless out of consideration for so tragic a passing, though somewhat confusing to the moral of her Spelling-Book. Elijah, whom she met changing from a coach into his trap, confirmed her impression of grandeur, and looked forward—on grounds of special information—to the toning up of the churchyard with a monument as big as money could buy, surmounted by angels, "not weeping, mind you, but blowing trumpets like Will's." Elijah wore a beautiful new top-hat, flat-brimmed and funereally braided. "Very lucky I had just got it for my wedding," he confided to her.

"You won't forget to take off the braid?" she smiled. "And when is it to be?"

"We're having the banns read next Sunday. Blanche won't wait a day longer, though I'm so frightfully busy through the flood—it's a regular gold-stream."

"And how's Mr. Flynt's arm?" she asked.

"He won't let me see it now—I never knew such an obstinate pig. He's gone to Dr. Mint."

"What, just now?"

"No, no, he's gone home—to Rosemary Villa, I mean."

As soon as he was out of sight, Jinny turned Methusalem's head back to the Villa. She hung about uncomfortably for some minutes in the thought that Will might be coming along or would be looking out of a window. But after ten unpleasant minutes she descended from her seat and fumbled shyly with the new brass knocker, feeling far more brazen than it. She almost cowered before the upstanding figure of the septuagenarian Mrs. Skindle—it vaguely reminded her of Britannia with a broom—but stammering out that she had forgotten to ask if the Villa needed anything, she ascertained that Will had not returned. To pitch her cart at the door was impossible, to go to meet him might lead to missing him, so there was nothing for it but desperately to prolong the conversation till he should reach home. Her tactics proved fatal, for her cheerful reference to Elijah's coming marriage loosed upon her a deluge of hysterical tears, and she found herself the confidante of sorrows as tragic as Mrs. Mott's. Poor Mrs. Skindle, throwing herself upon this sympathetic outsider, so providential a vent for her surcharged emotions, vociferated that all her children had abandoned her, that she was to be put away in the poorhouse. In vain Jinny, standing in that bleak passage, her heart astrain for Will's coming, strove to assuage a grief which irritated rather than touched her. She could hardly bring her mind to bear upon this creature with the broom, so inopportune and irrelevant did the outburst seem, so sordid a shadow on her own romance. With surface words she assured the poor woman that all this was only in her imagination. But Mrs. Skindle, though admitting she had only divined it, kept iterating that a nod was as good as a wink, and that she wasn't even a blind horse. Her son had gone to see Blanche on the Wednesday and had come back with the announcement of his marriage next month, and Blanche had made it a condition that his old mother should be put away. "She'd pison me, if she wasn't afraid for her swan's neck. And so I've got to be put out o' sight. 'Tain't as if I can't earn my bread with this broom and duster, but she's too grand to have me charin' in Chipstone."

"Well, then, what prevents you going somewhere else?" Jinny asked impatiently.

"I can't go traipsin' about to new places and new faces at my age. And I don't want to go agin 'Lijah neither—he ought to ha' been married long since, and wasn't it me spurred him on to look that high? And won't he have the loveliest wife in Chipstone? What's your game, trying to drive me away? Why, if I leave Chipstone I'd never see my grandchicks."

"Well, but would you see them anyhow, even supposing they're hatched?"

"I reckon there's days I'd be allowed out and I could see 'em as they went by in their baby-cart."

"Well, at that rate you'd be happier in the poorhouse."

"Yes," with a burst of weeping, "I'd be happier there. Happen I'd better go there."

"But I don't believe your son will let you," Jinny reassured her, and tore herself away, miserably conscious of a sort of Nemesis for her strategic lingering. She dismissed the scene from her mind. But it added to the heaviness of her heart as she drove slowly about the streets with never a glimpse of the face she sought, and the ache of his absence began to be complicated by the fear that it was wilful, or at least not unavoidable. Surely it was not possible for three days to elapse without their meeting, had he been as keen as she. Even the funeral, she now felt grimly, was not an absolute necessity of life! He could have got out of it. No, there was something behind, more sinister than funerals. She went anxiously over her one brief episode of happiness. Had she done or said anything to offend him? Was it that, on reflection, he had resented the little trick she had played at the flooded farm in luring him outside his door? Yes, that must be it. And she had sillily rubbed it in with her last words: "You bet your bottom dollar on that!" But no, he could hardly be resenting the innocent device without which they would never have known the wonder of their first kiss. The wonder? But was it a wonder to him? Tumultuous thoughts of Blanche and more shadowy others tore at her bosom. He did not really care, did not really need her.

The sport of elemental passions, she drove vaguely around, hoping against hope to espy him. She was a creature of pure feeling—unsophisticated by fiction or drama—and darkling images of death came to her for the first time. And for the first time she let her work go undone. It was no mere apprehension of meeting "Mother Gander" that finally kept her from the courtyard of the inn, no mere sense that with the sweeping away of competition she could afford to neglect for once even the commissions she already held; it was the absolute distraction of her mind. She could have borne final separation more easily than this uncertainty.

As she jogged home, she realized miserably that Will had at last succeeded in stamping out her business, if only for a day.

IV

But on her way to church on the Sunday—thanksgiving was clearly due for her restored fortunes and the fast-falling flood—all her misery, which his Saturday silence had only intensified, melted away in a moment at the sound of his voice and the sight of his sling. To add to her rapture came the thought that, a turning later, she would have encountered Miss Gentry! But his exclamation: "Why, whatever became of you, Jinny? It's been hell!" radiated so much heaven that the closing of his lips upon hers was almost a retrogression, perturbed as it was by her shyness in the open air. And, of course, she ought to have gone to the inn-yard where he had been waiting, she saw the moment he began explaining; that was the natural station for her cart to have come to. "Do forgive me making you suffer so," she pleaded. "But I didn't like to go in, with Mrs. Mott in that state!"

But Mrs. Mott had not been "in that state" he corrected almost laughingly. On the contrary, with her usual unexpectedness and extremism, she had reopened the bar immediately and served there herself in her handsomest dress, with the gold chain heaving once more on the bereaved bosom. Will himself had been forced to clink glasses with her. "He wouldn't have liked to see us gloomy—like them Peculiars," she had said. "He was always one for jollity and life."

The anecdote enhanced the lovers' own joy of life, and though Jinny steered for church (if by a zigzag path to avoid other worshippers) they never got out of the fir-grove, where a tree sapped by the flood presented a comparatively dry seat amid the sodden gull-haunted ways. Perhaps it was the thrushes that encouraged them—despite the dankness—to "stick to it, stick to it." It was certainly more comfortable for kissing, Jinny shamelessly confessed, snuggling into the cloak he had bought to cover his sling. "When we stand up, you're too proud to stoop," she laughed blissfully. "You make me crane my neck up."

"That's only through the sling," he apologized.

"Never mind—you're not such a Goliath—nothing so tall as Elijah!"

His eyes blazed fiercely. "Why," she laughed, "you don't mind not being tall?"

"Of course not," he said mendaciously. "Only you haven't been measuring yourself against Elijah, I hope."

"Measuring myself—?" she began, puzzled. Then her silvery laugh rippled out. "Oh, you jealous goose! But his size'll be a bit awkward for Blanche, won't it?" Then a sudden memory flushed both their faces, and hastily drawing a copy of the Chelmsford Chronicle from his pocket, he directed her attention to the thrilling accounts of the great flood and the greater funeral, and her fitful attempts to peruse them constituted the only rational moments of the morning.

It was odd how the reflection of events in the mighty Essex organ seemed to redouble their importance, and how even Will swelled in Jinny's eyes when she saw him catalogued among "leading citizens" present at "the last obsequies of the popular proprietor of 'The Black Sheep.'" And if Will failed to loom as large as Charley—whose death, fortunate in its journalistic opportunity, instead of being swamped by the flood, came as its climax—nevertheless he appeared in print no fewer than three times. The second occasion was the destruction of "The Flynt Flyer," and this obituary was so long and complimentary that it almost made amends for his loss, even though he knew the details to be highly imaginative. In the third notice he owed his eminence to his father, who, Jinny learned with surprise, had been the beneficiary of a miracle. "Among the most singular of the effects produced by the Bradmarsh floods," ran the paragraph that drew Caleb from the long obscurity of his seventy winters and which was as prolix and breathless as a sentence of Mrs. Purley's, "may be cited the fact of a small cornstack some four yards long, recognized by a shepherd named Peartree as belonging to Mr. Caleb Flynt, of Frog Farm, father of Mr. William Flynt, the lamentable destruction of whose coach and horses under sensational circumstances is recorded in another column, having been lifted from its place by the waters that so suddenly burst upon this remote homestead; and, after floating about at their mercy, like a dismasted and rudderless ship, being deposited in safety in a higher field, wholly uninjured, save by the wet—in as firm and compact a condition as before the flood—and, apparently, without a single blade of straw in its body or its roof having been disturbed from its relative position, while other stacks in the same field, belonging to his former employer, Farmer Gale, were almost totally ruined."

"Oh, Will, I'm so glad," said Jinny. "I don't mean about Farmer Gale."

"I do. Mean hunks! Think what he paid dad all those years. But is it true about our stack, I wonder. Papers aren't always correct."

"Aren't they?" She nestled closer.

"Oh dear no. You should have been in America! Haven't you noticed it says Elijah rescued us? Such a mix-up with his housing us. That's why I didn't tell poor old dad till I could run up and see for myself."

She moved back. "Oh, is that what you came for?"

"Of course not, darling. But being here, I may as well have a look."

"Well, you'll be able to, while I'm at church. I suppose you wouldn't come," she added shyly.

"Church?" he laughed. "Why, it's nearly over!" He pointed to a pale, struggling sun that had well passed its zenith.

V

Mr. Fallow was, in fact, just at his Fifthly and Finally, with Nip for sole representative of Blackwater Hall. That faithful congregant, discovering that Jinny had dodged him as usual, had set out for church forthwith, and was utterly disconcerted to find her pew vacant. It was noted, however, that he remained awake during the sermon, pricking up his ears at the recurrent word "Methuselah," which no doubt sounded to him like his old companion's name. Mr. Fallow's timely sermon on Noah's Flood proved no less rousing to the human hearers, though it began unpromisingly with the text: "And all the days of Methuselah were nine hundred sixty and nine years; and he died." But Miss Gentry, already ruffled by Jinny's absence, wondered why so much honour should be done to Mr. Bundock "Why preach a sermon against a postman?" she asked Jinny afterwards.

The fact was, of course, that those "sceptical sophisms" which Mr. Fallow took the opportunity to traverse and confute came from "The Age of Reason," but as Miss Gentry had heard them only from Bundock, she did not know they were inspired by Tom Paine. At any rate it was satisfactory to have them demolished and the veracity of the Bible vindicated by the very arithmetical tests with which the atheists juggled. They had "set the story of Noah and his ark as on a level with the "Arabian Nights" and the ages of the Patriarchs as no less fabulous than the immortality of the giants of mythology." Well, but here was the text, Mr. Fallow thundered: "And all the days of Methuselah were nine hundred sixty and nine years: and he died." A statement splendidly bare—bare as Truth alone could afford to be. But let them follow it, these dear brethren and sisters, into all its ramifications, trace the scattered threads of chronology and exhibit their marvellous congruity. Noah's grandfather lived nine hundred sixty and nine years; and he died. But at the age of 187 he had begotten Lamech, and at the age of 182 Lamech had begotten Noah. Methuselah was then just 369 years old when the hero of the Flood was born. And the Flood came, we were told in a later chapter, in the six hundredth year of Noah's life; 600 added to 369 made 969. "And all the days of Methuselah were nine hundred sixty and nine years; and he died." Had the figures made 970, the Bible would have indeed ceased to be the infallible Word of God, and atheism could have crowed, unanswered. For Methuselah was not in the ark; and every living creature outside was destroyed from the earth!

Whether he himself perished in the Flood, or whether—as the preacher preferred to believe, the aged patriarch had been removed—like his father Enoch before him—from the evil to come, was a minor issue compared with the glorious certainty that 369 added to 600 made 969 and not 970. Had Lamech or Noah been begotten one year later, or the Flood recorded as one year earlier, what a catastrophe for mankind! How the sophists would have gloated over their perverse arithmetic! Happily such discrepancies were the mere dream of the impious. "And all the days of Methuselah were nine hundred sixty and nine years; and he died."

Nip refused to sit through the prayer for sceptics that followed. With the cessation of the word "Methuselah" his interest waned, and the dismal conviction overcame him that Jinny had gone back to the chapel. Tearing off at a great rate, he soon, however, scented the truants homing across the Common.

"Why, where have you been?" said his mistress, as if he were the sinner!

But his raptures at seeing united at last the twain he had done so much to bring together, served to suspend a debate that had brought the first cloud on the morning's happiness. Having to walk smartly to Blackwater Hall with no time for dalliance, they had come at last to a serious talk about their plans, and it transpired that Will's mind was playing about the new Australian goldfields. He seemed dangerously in the grip of the "yellow fever," which, spreading from a Mr. Hargreaves and Summer Hill Creek, had circled the world in less than nine months. He recited to Jinny the legends of the new diggings, the quartz that was three-fourths gold, the aureous streams, the nuggets the size of melons. When he spoke of purchasing shovels and blankets, it was not, alas, for their joint home, nor were the "cradles" of his conversation indelicately domestic. How could he talk of going away, she asked, with tears in her eyes, when they had only just got to know each other? Well, of course, he didn't mean to-morrow, with his arm like that! She needn't begin to cry yet, but obviously this hidebound old England was no place for a man without capital. Did she expect him to become a farmhand to Farmer Gale? Of course he could go on shearing sheep and doing odd jobs and sink into a Ravens, always singing, with nothing to sing about! But if they were to marry, he must find a decent livelihood. Hard, irrefutable truths! If only—she thought—they had both been less silly while he still had his coach and horses! Impossible to suggest to a man like Will that she might manage to earn enough for him as well as for her grandfather! Of course if he had lost his arm altogether—but that was too wicked a speculation to gloat over! Had Methusalem been younger and stronger, the cart might perhaps have taken on extra rounds, with Will in command. But even that would probably have jarred his pride. No, he was a ruined man, and adventure—as he truly urged—was his only chance. And yet she clung tighter to his one good arm, glad of the respite the other had given her, and hoping that the Angel-Mother would somehow intervene to keep him in the country—if not the county—she hovered over. Sufficient for the day was the good thereof; here was Will, and Nip, and the Sunday pie in the oven—the first good dinner since Christmas, the preparation of which for her lip-smacking elder had served to keep her sane during those days of torturing suspense. How glad she was the meal would be worthy of their visitor!

A faint uneasiness did indeed begin to creep under her happiness as they crossed the rutted road that divided the Common from her gate, but she was hardly conscious what it was, vaguely putting it down to Nip's dangerous attempts to caress them with his muddy paws.

"Here we are!" she cried gaily. "Lucky Gran'fer never asks about the sermon."

He drew her to him. Hurriedly ascertaining that there was no eye or telescope bearing upon her, she submitted to the long ardour of his kiss. Then she drew him in turn towards the gate.

"But I've kissed you good-bye," he said.

"Good-bye?" she repeated blankly. "Aren't you coming in?"

"How can I come in?"

Even then she hardly realized the situation. Foreseen as it had long been, it had so softened in her own mind—especially after her comparative success in soothing down her grandfather—that she did not realize it remained in Will's in all its original crudity. "You're not thinking of that nonsense!" she said, smiling. "We'll just lift up the latch and walk in! Won't Gran'fer be surprised?" But her smile was uneasy.

"You've forgotten, Jinny, he won't have me over his doorstep."

"Oh, is that the reason you didn't come all the week?" The greyness creeping beneath her happiness began to spread out like a clammy fog.

"Well, how could I have got to you? I couldn't stand about the Common in the wind and rain on the chance you might catch sight of me."

"I'd have stood about for you," she said simply.

"And didn't I stand about at 'The Black Sheep'?"

"Yes, that was my fault, sweetheart. But anyhow we won't stand about here." And she tugged at his arm. "Where else could you have dinner?"

"I can get some at 'The King of Prussia.' I'll be just in time if I go now."

"You desert me to get dinner!"

"You know that's nonsense, dearest, considering I could get both if I came in."

"Then why don't you come in?"

"You know I can't."

"Because of those few high words? How absurd!"

"We won't go into that now."

"Yes, we will. You don't want to eat humble pie. But it isn't humble pie," she laughed, with a desperate attempt at merriment, "it's steak and kidney pie! So there!"

"But, Jinny, he forbade me to cross his sill!"

"You old goose! He never thought we'd cross it arm in arm. Like this! Come along—won't he open his eyes and wipe his spectacles!"

He shook off her arm. "It's no laughing matter, Jinny. An oath is an oath."

"An oath!" she repeated dully. The violence of that grotesque collision had blurred her memory of its minutiæ.

"You can't have forgotten? He laid his hand on the Bible—he vowed to the Almighty I should never cross your threshold."

She essayed a last jaunty smile. "Unless on your hands and knees. Don't forget that part."

"Is it likely I could forget such an insult?"

"Well then, that's all right!" Her smile became braver. "We'll crawl in together, two little babies. Come along, petsy." And she stooped down comically.

"How can you be so childish, Jinny?"

"Isn't it all childish? Down you go, Willie!"

But he stiffened himself physically as well as morally. "Give in to such a humiliation?"

"You won't really be giving in," she said, with a happy thought. "With only one arm, you can only come in on your hand and knees. So you'll outwit him after all. Come along, poor little lopsided creature, Jinny'll help you—and Gran'fer will forget to count your limbs, my poor brave boy!"

"It's you that are forgetting," he said harshly. "It's impossible."

"What's impossible?"

"That I should crawl to your grandfather."

"I see! It's your pride you love, not me."

"No, it isn't."

"Yes, it is." She snatched her hand from his. "Nothing can bring you to your knees."

"It's not true. I'd go on my hands and knees to you, as if I was in chapel, and I'd crawl on 'em across your threshold and thank God for what laid on t'other side—but you see, Jinny, what breaks me up is that I made a vow too."

"You?"

"You don't seem to remember anything."

"I dare say I was a bit dazed at all the silliness. But if you swore too not to cross our threshold, why, I'll go and let you in by the lattice. And perhaps Gran'fer will be that tickled, he'll laugh and forget about his cranky old oath. Or perhaps he'll reckon you have scrambled in on your hands and knees. Oh dear, isn't it funny? See you in a moment, Will." She put her hand on the latch of the gate.

He shook his head. "Neither by door nor by window."

"Didn't I say I'd never cross your doorstep?" she urged. "And yet I came."

"You came through the window."

"Well, I'll come by the door. There! That's a fair offer. I'm not going to stick to silliness—when it's so silly!"

"All very well," he said coldly. "But you know you can't get through my door."

"Goodness gracious! Have I grown so fat?"

"Don't pretend. You know it's the flood. Besides, it wouldn't be any good my going through the window. What I said when I raised my hand to heaven was that your grandfather should never see me in his house—!"

"Just what I said—I remember now," she interrupted. "I said you'd never see me in Frog Farm. And yet you did—and lost your bet too." Her face was gay again. "So I gave in first, you see, sweetheart, and now you've got to play fair."

"You don't listen—you cut into my words. What I swore was that your grandfather should never see me in his house unless he carried me in!"

Her gaiety grew hysterical. "Ha, ha, ha!" she laughed. "Grandfather's given up carrying ages ago. I'm his deputy now. Oh dear!" She measured him with a rueful eye. "Well, I can but try!" And she put her arms round his hips.

"Don't make light of an oath, Jinny." He pushed her off with his left hand.

"'Twas you that made light of an oath—taking the Lord's name over trifles."

"I never took the Lord's name," he said sullenly. "I only lifted my hand."

"Well, you can't lift it now—and serve you right! You surely never expected Gran'fer to lug a sulky lout over his doorstep."

"Of course not. I never expected I'd want to cross it. Why, Jinny, though you were there in the room, I was that blind—!" And his hand sought hers again.

"Leave me alone!" she cried. "You and your miserable vows!"

"I'd cut my tongue out if I could unsay the words."

"You can unsay 'em more easily with your tongue in."

"A man can't go back on his sworn word. Women don't understand."

"So you said about horses. And nicely you managed yours! Oh, forgive me, I didn't mean to crow. That was your misfortune. But this is your fault. It's your pride you're in love with; not me. Good-bye; Gran'fer will be starving." She lifted the gate-latch angrily.

"But only good-bye for the moment," he pleaded. "I can't cross your threshold, but you can cross mine."

She answered more gently, but her tone was tired and helpless. "And what would be the good, unless you and Gran'fer make it up?"

"I'm not marrying your grandfather!"

Something patronizing in the sentence jarred afresh. "You'd better go back to Blanche—it'll be too late soon."

"I wouldn't touch Blanche with Bidlake's barge-pole!"

The magnificence of the repudiation had its effect—it swamped in both the recollection that it was Blanche who had done the refusing.

"You don't expect me to give up Gran'fer at his age?" she said more mildly.

"We'll get him a minder—when I come back from Australia!"

Australia put the climax to her weariness. "Oh, yes, I don't wonder it's so easy for you to go."

"It isn't easy for me to go, even as far as Chipstone," he protested passionately. "But it's your grandfather you love, not me."

"I love you both. Only think how old he is. It's like quarrelling with a child. And he is in his second childhood almost, though I wouldn't say it to anybody else. There are times when he seems quite his old self, wonderfully strong and sensible, but there are moments when he quite frightens me. He can't bear to be crossed, and he forgets almost everything that happens nowadays."

"Then perhaps he's forgotten our upset!"

"No, that's the unfortunate part. But we must just make a little joke of it. Down on your marrow-bones, Willie!" And she laid her hand on his shoulder with a last sprightly effort.

But even as his shoulder subsided, it swelled up again, like a pressed gutta-percha ball. "It's all grandfather with you, your husband doesn't count."

"Husband, indeed!" She withdrew her hand as if stung. "You're going quicker than your coach ever went."

"Oh, very well—I'm off to Australia!"

"As you please. I'll call for your box!"

"I'll have no truck with a cart of yours."

"There's no other way of getting things to Chipstone," she reminded him blandly.

"I'll shoulder it sooner," he burst forth.

"Ah, then you won't be going just yet!"

"Damn my arm! I'll not stay in this wretched country another fortnight! I'll never look on your face again."

She began humming: "A dashing young man from Canada—!"

His face grew black with anger, and he strode away even before she had passed through the gate.

VI

Righteous resentment saved Jinny from the collapse of the previous week. That dreadful gnawing of uncertainty was over. Whatever she had said, she was sure now that he did love her, even if she came second to his pride. That a way out of their difficulties would soon present itself to her nimble brain she did not doubt: her one fear was that he would find the way to Australia first, and it was a comfort to remember his helpless arm and his empty purse—"no money to think of foolishness," as his dear old mother had put it. Already on the Tuesday after the unheard sermon, she found a means of communicating with him without a lowering of her own proper pride. For the fourteenth of the month was nigh upon them, and the shops—even apart from the stationer's—-were ablaze with valentines, a few sentimental, but the overwhelming majority grotesque and flamboyant, the British version of Carnival. After long search she discovered a caricature that not only resembled Will in having carroty locks, but carried in its motto sufficient allusiveness to the quarrel with her grandfather to make it clear the overture came from her. Not that the overture looked conciliatory to the superficial eye. Quite the contrary. For apart from the ugliness of the visage, the legend ran:

To such a man I'd never pledge my troth,
I'd sooner die, I take my Bible oath.

Not a very refined couplet or procedure perhaps, but Jinny was never a drawing-room heroine, and the valentine was dear to the great heart of the Victorian people. Besides, do not the grandest dames relax at Carnival?

Jinny half expected a similar insult from Will by the same post, and though St. Valentine's Day passed without bringing her one, she still expected a retort in kind the day after. And when Bundock appeared with a voluminous letter, directed simply to "Jinny the Carrier, Little Bradmarsh, England," her disappointment at Mr. Flippance's flabby handwriting was acute, though otherwise she would have been excited, not only by his letter, but by the foreign stamp, the first she had ever received. "So he's still in Boulogne," Bundock observed casually, lingering to pick up the contents. "I hope he's sending you the money to pay Mrs. Purley."

"Why should he send it through me?" she said sharply.

"Well, since he's writing to you, it would save stamps, wouldn't it? I do think it was rough on Mrs. Purley, though, a wedding breakfast like that, though I expect he bought his own champagne—and clinking stuff it was, nigh as good as the sherry at poor Charley's funeral. However, she's marrying her own daughter now—Mrs. Purley, I mean—and lucky she is too to have escaped young Flynt, who is off to Australia without a penny—looks to me almost as if they're hurrying on the marriage so that Will may be best man before he goes, he and 'Lijah are that thick! He, he, he! Funny world, ain't it? You've heard my riddle perhaps—Why are marriages never a success? Because the bride never marries the best man! He, he! Well, she came near doing it this time—he, he, he! Though whether she's the best woman for either of 'em is a question."

"That's their own business," Jinny managed to put in.

"So 'tis, but with 'Lijah a member of the Chipstone Temperance Friendly Society, he'll hardly like a wife who washes her head in beer."

"What nonsense! How can you know that?"

"Fact. It's to make her hair wavy. There's nothing her brother Barnaby don't let out to my poor old dad. She was at it the day you all came to the Farm. It wasn't that she had her bodice off and her hair down after the douche,"—Bundock seemed to savour these details—"she didn't want him to smell it."

"Well, you seem to smell out everything," she said severely.

"I do have a nose like Nip's!" he chuckled. But although Mr. Flippance's letter was under it, he was forced to go off without even discovering that it did contain a financial document. Very amazed indeed was Jinny to see it drop out, this IOU, which was for herself and not Mrs. Purley, and represented half a crown! Retiring to her kitchen, she studied the large-scrawled pages.

"MY DEAR JINNY,—I have just read in Madame F.'s copy of her London Journal (which like Mrs. Micawber she will never desert, at least not till the present serial is finished) an extract from the Chelmsford Chronicle about the miraculous saving of a cornstack belonging to our mutual friend, Mr. Caleb Flynt.

"I gather that a flood must have devastated Little Bradmarsh, and I write at once to know if all my friends are safe, especially your charming little self. Strange to think that the parlour in which I breakfasted on bacon and mushrooms in your sweet society may have been washed away! But such is life—a shadow-pantomime!

"We are still at Boulogne, you see. For one thing—to speak frankly—it's a providential place to be at when funds are for the moment low, and it appears that Madame F.'s fortune—all that the villain Duke left of it—is in Spanish bonds. I need say no more. (I think I told you she was the niece of the famous Cairo Contortionist, and doubtless it was during the star's sensationally successful season at Madrid that she was thus misled.) The wily master of marionettes must have been aware of this when he got ["her off his hands" appeared quite legibly here, though scratched out with heavy strokes] back his show over her head.

"Our present plans are, before attempting London (which though almost barren of talent calls for overmuch of the ready), to launch an English season in Boulogne itself, where there is such a large English circle, that saves so much by being here immune from sheriff's officers that it can well afford the luxury of the theatre, not to mention the many French people here who must be anxious to learn English, especially after their visit to the Great Exhibition.

"Between you and I, I fear that Madame F.'s hopes will be dashed by the fact that the French have no eyes or ears except for a Jewess called Rachel, but as they have nothing near as good in the male line, we may yet—between us—show them something!

"If this fails—and I have seen too much of the public to be surprised at any ingratitude—there are always those wonderful new goldfields, where men of our race and speech are flocking, pickaxe on shoulder. Surely after their arduous toil for the filthy lucre, they must be longing of an evening for a glimpse of the higher life—I understand they have only drinking shanties.

"Imagine it, Jinny—a theatre for the rugged miners amid the primeval mountains with a practicable moon shining over the tropical scene. Pity I sold Duke that theatre-tent, but I suppose it couldn't be transported to Australia as easily as a convict. (Good gag, that, eh?) Admission, I suppose, by nugget. I don't see how you can give change—unless they take it in gold-dust—and anyhow, flush as they are, they will probably hand in considerable chunks at the box-office, reckless of petty calculation.

"So do not be surprised if one Easter morn you receive a golden egg laid by some Australian goose (I understand it is half a mole). Which reminds me to enclose herewith the half-crown I owe you. I dare say you have forgotten my borrowing it from you in the caravan of my blood-sucking son-in-law. But players have long memories.

"I suppose you see nothing of him or of Polly, for Chipstone is a poor pitch, but I am afraid from a Christmas card Polly sent me in reply to mine that the rascal is making her happy, so I can't hate him as much as he deserves.

"'I hope,' I scribbled across the picture of the snowy Mistletoe Bough I sent her, 'you are experiencing all that matrimony was designed for, when this institution was introduced into Eden.' Lovely, isn't it? And where do you suppose it came from? It was that delicious Martha's farewell wish to me on my wedding morning! I fancy she took it out of the number of the Lightstand that I bought her.

"Poor, dear Martha! Do give her my love and tell her there is a branch of the New Jerusalemites in Boulogne—no, best make it two, while you are about it, a French branch as well as an English branch, mutually emulous in 'Upbuilding!'

"And how is her dashing cavalier of a son who posed as an American? I expect he's married by now to the queen of the wasp-killers, judging by the warm way things were going at my own wedding-party. If so, pray hand him back his mother's Christadelphian wedding-wish with my kind regards.

"Oh, and don't forget to say amiable things (as they put it here) to Miss What's-a-name, the young and lovely bridesmaid! Tell her I haven't forgotten about her becoming wardrobe mistress, though if we go to Australia, I'm afraid it'll be too rough for her at her age, and even Madame F. may shrink from the snakes and the blacks and the convicts and the desperado diggers, in which case we shall have boys to do the female parts and revive the glories of the Shakespearean stage.

"Heavens, how I have let myself chatter on! My paper is nearly at an end—like youth and hope! Believe me, dear Jinny, in this world or the next (don't be alarmed, I only mean Australia),

"Your ever devoted,
"TONY FLIPPANCE.

"P.S.—I am so sorry but I find I can't find (excuse my Irish) any way of sending the half-crown by post, so I am compelled to send you an IOU, but if you send it to Polly (Duke's Marionettes, England, is sure to find her some day) I have no doubt she will honour it on my behalf. Safest address for me by the way is Poste Restante, Boulogne, as Madame F. likes trying different hotels.

"P.P.S.—There is a game here called 'Little Horses.' Most fascinating."

Many and mixed were Jinny's feelings as she ploughed through this bulky document, swollen by the opulent handwriting. Having no notion about investments, she vaguely imagined that Spanish robbers had impounded Cleopatra's money, and it added to her sense of the unsettled state of the Continent. As for the IOU, she was angrily amused to think that he had already paid her the half-crown on the very morning of the bacon and mushrooms so fondly recalled, and that she had bought him his wedding present—a Bible—with it. To pay little debts twice over while defrauding the big creditors (and she had reason to think Miss Gentry as well as the Purleys had been left unpaid) seemed to her only an aggravation of fecklessness. But perhaps the Flippances had not meant to be dishonest: it was those Spanish freebooters that were to blame, who had captured the gold destined for Little Bradmarsh. The humiliation of his reference to Blanche was hard to bear—it made her want to dismiss Will altogether—but oddly enough a still keener emotion was kindled by Mr. Flippance's obsession with Australia. Yes, Australia was in the air, it was a net into which everybody was being swept. Will was going from her—and to a place bristling with blacks and snakes and convicts and desperado diggers. Never had she received so perturbing a letter.

In the menacing silence of Will, she began to study this interloping and kidnapping Australia. For it was not only his silence that menaced: through the hundred threads of her carrying career—antennæ always groping for news of him—she learned that his resolve was fixed. Indeed, Frog Farm was almost the only place on her rounds where his departure was not talked of. At the fountain head she could collect no information, for Martha was the only person she now saw there and the old lady seemed anxious, after receiving her parcels, to rush back to the clearing up of the colossal mess of the receded flood: a work in which the scrupulously invisible Will was understood to be lending a hand almost as vigorous as his father's, albeit a single hand. But if the other was still in its sling, it was getting dangerously better, she gathered from Bundock's father.

That he would go without another word to her was highly probable. Was there not in Finchingfield a hot-tempered farmer who had kept silence for seven years after his wife's death? Miss Gentry, who in her Colchester days used to make his wife's gowns—the lady riding in behind him to be measured—said it was from remorse because he had once used an improper expression to her. And this same Essex obstinacy was liable to manifest itself in less noble forms, as her grandfather's feuds had proved abundantly. Will would shake off the soil of old England as surlily as he had shaken it off in his boyhood. As he had run away from his parents, so he would now run away from her, though far more unreasonably. But this time she would at least know where he was going, and her tortured soul reached out hungrily to picture his new world. The Spelling-Book was absolutely blank about Australia—how empty and worthless loomed that storehouse of information, with this gigantic lacuna!—but from a bound magazine volume of Miss Gentry's, borrowed for the first time, she drew confirmation of her worst fears. It was a place that needed many more stations and out-stations of the Society for Promoting Christian Knowledge, and there were mosquitoes that could only be kept off by lighted torches, and biting spiders as big as your palm; after frying at 105 in the shade, you might shiver the next moment in the icy blast of the "Southern Buster." And there were dust-winds to boot. If you went to the cemetery of Port Phillip, you would see that the majority of deaths were between the ages of thirty and forty. This premature mortality was due to the excessive drinking of cold water natural in so droughty a country. What a blessing that Will was not, like Mr. Skindle, a member of the Temperance Friendly Society! Nor was the labour market, congested as it was with ticket-of-leave men and bounty-emigrants from England, really superior to that of the old country, while house-rents were twice as high. As for the interior, another number of the magazine contained a story in which "an ill-favoured man with his arm in a sling" was pursued by a bull amid mimosa swamps in a setting of blacks with tomahawks and whites with pistols. "The Bull and the Bush," she murmured whimsically to herself, but at heart she was cold with apprehension.

Then by a strange coincidence she found reassurance. Calling on Mrs. Bidlake in her confinement, she found the mother well and the new child vigorous. But it was not from their condition merely that emanated the novel atmosphere of happiness that radiated over the household: perhaps, indeed, the well-being was only a consequence of the happiness. For the Bidlakes, too, were off to Australia, though not to the goldfields. The cloud over the family had lifted at last. Not that Hezekiah had been proved innocent, but that he was become opulent. Released on ticket-of-leave, the sturdy ploughman had got a position with a cottage and garden in that "splendid suny clim" as he now called it, and then, just as he was about to send for Sophy and Sally, he had won six hundred and forty acres on the outskirts of Port Phillip in a lottery run by the Bank of Australasia! If he could borrow the capital from the bank, as was not improbable, he would be able to cut up his prize into ten-acre allotments and build houses on it—by that you simply doubled or trebled your outlay in a few years. His sister should have a house anyhow, and in the meantime her husband could help him manage or farm the vast estate. As for the "dere gels" there would be no need for them to work now, though if they wanted pocket-money they would be snapped up for service, and get as much as sixteen pounds a year each. He had already sent fifty pounds towards the passage-money, and would raise more when he knew if they would all come out, and moreover he understood that there was a Family Colonization Society in London to which Ephraim might apply for an advance. What a change, this going out of theirs, from that dreadful departure in the prison coach for the hulks and Botany Bay! Jinny, sharing their tears of joy, was vastly relieved on her own account at the paradise the grotesquely spelt letter conjured up, and she rejoiced to reflect that all that ancient barbarous harshness of magistrates and judges had led under Providence to the enrichment of Britain's new soil with the sweat of her skilled agriculturists, and was even opening up new horizons for their innocent relatives. For assuredly this was a paradise on earth, if Hezekiah's letter was not a shameless lure for his brother-in-law.

Think of tea at eighteenpence a pound—even a shilling if bought by the chest!—think of sugar at twopence-halfpenny, and neck of mutton at a penny a pound, nay, a whole sheep for five shillings. Think of pork at twopence and the best cows' butter at sixpence; and after one has been reduced to turnips and dry bread, think of a land where ox-tails can be had for the skinning and sheeps' heads and plucks by the barrow for the fetching away. A land where, as he wound up rapturously, any man who worked could have his bellyful, and where everything was plentiful except women, so that his girls would be able to pick and choose among the "gumsuckers" and have "cornstalks" for husbands. They shouldn't marry among the "prisoners," please God, for he didn't reckon himself in that set, having done nothing to be ashamed of, though he did see now that threshing-machines were necessary when you had a lot of land.

"If they want women so badly, I might do worse than go myself," said Jinny laughingly.

"No, no, whatever would Little Bradmarsh do without you?" said Ephraim.

"They did without me well enough," she said bitterly. Indeed her first fine faith in human nature could not be mended as easily as the broken bridge, nor did the depreciatory allusions of her old customers to the deceased coach, and their compliments at her return, soften her cynicism. And as she spoke, she felt a sudden yearning to be done with them all: the infection of the new world began to steal into her veins too, but she knew her own exodus was impossible while her grandfather lived, and though she played with the idea and asked if she might copy Hezekiah's instructions for the passage, her real design was to gather information for Will's sake. It was very worrying though to copy the recommendations in the original spelling. "Of kors i don't now wot the shipps is like nowerdies, but the nu chums ses they dont give no solt, onni roc-solt (solt is peny a pound here, peper 2d. nounc) and you'll want thik warm close and moor beding." There was an elaborate list of provisions necessary to supplement the ship's dietary during the four weary months—it hardly needed copying, since it embraced a little of everything edible that would keep—but she was glad again that Will was not a temperance man when she found a bottle of brandy recommended as an indispensable medicine for the contingencies of the voyage.

Neglecting even the last instalment of her debt to Miss Gentry—had not the dressmaker given her the alternative of working it out?—Jinny began to acquire the longest-lived comestibles, storing them secretly in one of the ante-room chests. And it was by this concentration on Will's interests that she managed to live through his dreadful silence, nay, to enjoy long spells of day-dreaming in which these edibles were for their joint Australian larder. The goldfields her imagination dismissed as bristling with "desperado diggers." It was on the more idyllic images of her magazine article, written before the days of the discovery of gold, that her imagination fed. For though the writer denigrated the urban labour market, he admitted that there was plenty of room for rural labour, and then—with what seemed so uncanny a prying into her affairs that it flushed her cheek and made her heart beat faster—he postulated a young couple without capital setting up housekeeping together, and instructed them to take employment with a farmer while saving up enough to buy a small farm or herd of their own. The system, it appeared, was that the employer supplied rations as well as money-wages, and that while the husband worked on the land, the wife could do the farm cooking. (How lucky she had had so much experience, Jinny thought.) Nay, these rations, said the article (pursuing her affairs to what the blushing reader thought the point of indelicacy) would practically suffice for the children too, and when they grew up—-but her delicious daydream rarely went so far as this calculation of them as independent labour-assets.

The happy couple would also be permitted to keep a few cows, pigs, and fowls. Here the thought of Methusalem would intrude distressfully, and the difficulty of transporting him to the Antipodes. But when he had been left at Frog Farm in the loving hands of Caleb and Martha (become almost his parents-in-law), under promise of leisurely grazing for the rest of his life, with perhaps a rare jaunt to Chipstone market for their household needs, this ideal solution only reminded her of the phantasmal nature of the whole scheme, for Frog Farm could certainly not be saddled with her grandfather. But lest she should remember too cruelly its visionary character, the day-dream would at this point dart off swiftly on the journey through the Bush in quest of an idyllic spot free from blacks and provided with a generous employer.

Fortunate that this journey was to be so inexpensive, there being no inns (not even "The Bull and Bush"), but every settler being compelled by a wise decree of this wonderful State to give the bona fide traveller board and lodging for nothing. What a lovely journey that would be—if only one dodged the blacks and the diggers and the swamps with the alligators. She saw herself and Will bounding along like kangaroos (with Nip of course in attendance, she did not intend to take up with a dingo instead) through mimosa-bushes (like the scrub on the Common, only gaudier), and eating their dinner-packets under giant gum-trees, so enchantingly blue, whose tops, five hundred feet high, one might climb so as to survey the route for signs of native camps or friendly farmers. If there was no settler in sight by the time darkness fell, they would just perch themselves like birds in a nest of high branches out of all danger, and go to sleep under the starry heaven, which she saw vividly with the old constellations.

Closer to the real was her picture of the tenement with which the ideal farmer (when found) would provide his young couple. There would just be a few poles driven into the ground to support the roof of gum-bark, with its hole to let out the smoke. But of course one need not live much indoors in that climate—despite the occasional vagaries of the "Southerly Buster"—and it would be all the easier not to have to spend money on furniture. Why, put in Nip's basket, lay out Will's razor and slippers, set out her Spelling-Book and the Peculiar Hymn-Book the young rebel had thrown into the bushes, hang up his hat and her bonnet, and the place already begins to look like home. As for Will's box—presumably conveyed to the chosen spot by the local carrier in a bullock-cart—it is so large it will crowd out everything else and furnish the place of itself. Decked with a rug it will serve as sofa, covered with a cloth it becomes a table. Lucky she has not brought a box of her own, but has squeezed her things into his—in that wonderful, incredible fusion of two existences!

It was hard to wake from these day-dreams to the wretched reality, and yet Uncle Lilliwhyte profited from one of these awakenings, for her Australian hut had reminded her of his English specimen, and she hurried to see it and him. She found them both in a bad way. His wading overmuch in the flood in quest of salvage had brought back more than a touch of his rheumatism, while the winds and rain had left his shanty leakier than ever. They were both breaking up, the ancient and his shell, and she now did her best to patch both up. Already in her new affluence she had called in young Ravens to mend her grandfather's bedroom ceiling and redaub the gaps in the walls, and it was simple to turn this Jack-of-all-trades and fountain of melody on to the derelict hut in the woods. The poor old "Uncle" had hitherto built his fire as well as he could on the ground on the leeward side of his hut; Jinny now installed an old stove which she bought up cheap at the pawnbroker's and conveyed to the verge of the wood. But the hole in the roof that might serve for Australia would not do for England, and after Ravens had re-thickened the walls with fresh faggots and re-thatched the hut with shavings presented by Barnaby, Jinny was amused to find that what seemed an iron chimney turned out on closer inspection to consist of three old top-hats. Where the ancient had picked up these treasures—whether in the flood or in his normal scavenging—he refused to say. "Happen Oi've got a mort o' culch ye don't know of," he cackled, enjoying her admiration of his architecture. She wanted to have a floor to the hut, but this, like the exchange of his sacking for a pallet-bed, he opposed strenuously. "Gimme the smell o' the earth," he said. "Ye've shut out the stars and that's enough." He accepted, however, a bolster for a pillow.

By such interests and devices, aided by her regular rounds, Jinny staved off too clear a consciousness of the inevitable parting, which would not even have the grace of a parting. But the inexorable moment was like a black monster bearing down upon her—and yet it was not really advancing, it was rather something retreating: it could not even be visualized as a shock against which one could brace one's shoulders. There was the horror of the impalpable in this silent drift away from her.

But when at last the day of departure was named, and came vibrating to her across a dozen subtle threads, the negative torture turned to a positive that was still more racking. It was on the Friday—unlucky day!—that Will was to leave for London, and here was already Tuesday. Some of her threads conveyed even the rumour that, in order to save a little cash for his start at the Antipodes, he meant to work his passage. And here was she unable to pack his box or even to slip her provisions into it; doomed by all the laws of sex and proper spirit to watch—bound hand and foot as in a nightmare—the receding of the mate whose lips had sealed her his. By the Wednesday morning even her grandfather observed something was wrong.

"Ye ain't eatin' no breakfus."

"Yes, Gran'fer, lots!"

"Do ye don't tell me no fibs. Oi've noticed your appetite fallin' lower and lower like the flood, and now there's a'mos' nawthen o' neither. And ye used to be my little mavis!"

"You don't want me to eat snails or worms?"

"'Tis your singin', Oi mean."

"There is Hey!" she chanted obediently.

"Ye're the most aggravatin' gal—minds me o' your great-gran'mother. Ye need your mouth for eatin', not singin'."

After a sleepless night, unable to bear this inactivity, she ran round to the Bidlake lodgings to suggest that as young Mr. Flynt seemed to be sailing for Australia, it might be a neighbourly action to show him Hezekiah's hints to travellers. But she gathered from the happy mother that the absent Ephraim had already talked to Will about the heavier clothes and the bedding, and that Will had said how fortunate it was he had sold off his summer suits, so as in any case to get the latest make at Moses & Son's on his passage through London. Jinny suspected he had sold them off to raise funds for the voyage. Still the bravado of this pretence of a London outfit did not displease her. She learnt too that there had been a question of Will's convoying the ex-convict's daughters to their impatient parent, as the Ephraim Bidlakes would not be ready for ages, but it had been thought scarcely proper in view of their age and looks—a decision Jinny thought wise. Indeed, the idea that he was not to be thus companioned almost reconciled her, by contrast, to his departure.

When she got home she found to her surprise that her grandfather was entertaining Martha Flynt, who was far from the spruceness she usually achieved for outsiders of the other sex. She looked draggled and worn after her long and windy walk. What astonished Jinny most was that the old rheumatic woman should have trudged so far, and she opined that her business must be pressing and must be with herself. For it could hardly lie in the Christadelphian texts with which Martha seemed to be battering and bemusing the nonagenarian, whose great Bible lay open between them, and who was disconcerted to find her texts really there.

Martha had never set foot in Blackwater Hall before, so far as Jinny could remember, and very strange it was to see her sitting over her cup of tea which she must have made for herself at her host's invitation. With all his perturbation over the texts, he seemed only too brisked up by this amazing visit from a female, the first unwhiskered being, save Jinny, he had met for many moons. It was a fillip he did not need, Jinny considered: the old good food again, the sweet security, the satisfaction of revenge, had made his eyes less bleared, filled out his flacked cheeks and given him a new lease of strength and sanity—a sort of second wind—and this visit might only over-stimulate him. She did not like the undercurrent of excitement that showed itself in the twitching of his limbs and eyelids, especially when Martha declared he could not be really accepting the Book as all-inspired if he believed man's heaven lay in the skies. "Whither I go, ye cannot come," she repeated.

"We'll see about that," said Daniel Quarles fiercely, and clenched his fists as if he meant to storm the gates of cloudland. "And ain't ye forgittin' 'Lijah what went up to heaven with a chariot and bosses o' fire? That won't happen to 'Lijah Skindle, damn him—he'll have the chariot o' fire, but he won't git no higher. He, he, he!"

Martha was momentarily baffled by Elijah's ascension, but recovering her nerve, she dealt John iii. 13, "No man hath ascended up to heaven."

Partly to soothe the old man, partly to give Martha a chance of speaking out, Jinny here intervened with the suggestion that he himself should ascend up to his room and bring down the telescope to amuse his guest withal. Obviously relieved—for he felt himself in a tight textual corner—he hastened upstairs.

It was then that the old woman, bursting into tears, and clutching at Jinny's arm, sobbed out: "Oh, Jinny, you've got to come back with me—you've got to come back at once!"

Jinny turned cold and sick. What had happened to Will?

"But what for?" she gasped.

"To Willie!"

Her worst fears were confirmed. "Is he hurt?"

"I wish he was a little," Martha sobbed. "But even his arm's all right now." What Martha went on to say Jinny never remembered, for she was suddenly sobbing with Martha. But hers was the hysteria of relief, and when she at last understood that what Martha was asking was that she should come back and marry Will, so that he should stay near his mother, her heart hardened again. It was not that she made any attempt to deny her love—things seemed suddenly to have got beyond that—but Martha, she felt, knew not what she asked, seeming to have divined from her boy's demeanour a lover's quarrel, but without any inkling of the real tangle and deadlock. Even if she humiliated herself, as Martha half unwittingly suggested, it was all a blind-alley.

"My making it up won't keep him in England," she urged. "He's got no money. And no more have I."

She might have been more willing to make a last desperate dash of her head against the brick wall, had she understood how Martha had fought against her from the first and how pitiable was her surrender now, but no suspicion of that underground opposition had ever crossed her mind, nor did Martha now confess what indeed she no longer remembered clearly.

"But there's room for you in Frog Farm, dearie. We'd love to have you. We've always loved you."

"I can't," Jinny moaned. "It's all no use. And I've got Gran'fer!" Indeed, Martha's passionate plea had curiously clarified and steadied her mind, reconciling her to the inevitable. To go to Will was exactly what she had been yearning to do. But when the plea for such action came through Martha's mouth, she could see it from outside, as it were, realize its futility and cleanse her bosom of it. She felt strangely braced by her own refusal.

"But I've got some provisions for the voyage," she said, "that you might smuggle into his box—I know it's big enough. And I do hope, Mrs. Flynt, he's not going to work his passage."

"I only wish he was, for he mightn't find a ship. But you see Flynt would go and advance him the money and insist he must go steerage like a gentleman. He's got no heart, hasn't Flynt," she wept, "he only wants to settle down in peace after Will and the flood, and sit under his vine and fig-tree."

"Don't cry—here's Gran'fer coming down. I tell you what I will do, Mrs. Flynt, I will call for his box."

"Oh, bless you, Jinny!" Martha fell on her neck. "If you come, he won't go! That's as sure as sunrise."

"And then I can bring him his provisions," Jinny pointed out sceptically, as she disentangled herself from Martha's arms. Then both females were dumbed by the sight of the Gaffer returning in his best smock and with his beard combed! He tendered Martha the telescope with a debonair gesture. But Martha, her mission comparatively successful, departed so precipitately that the poor old man felt his toilette wasted, not to mention his telescope.

"She's a flighty young woman," was his verdict, "as full o' warses as our thatch o' warmin. Sets herself up agin John. Wesley as searched the Scriptures afore she was born." And laying down his telescope, he turned over the pages of his Bible, and perpending her textual irritants and questing for antidotes, fell quietly asleep.

He was delighted when she returned the next afternoon, and he played Genesis v. 24, with a snort of triumph, by way of greeting. Martha tremulously countered with Acts ii. 34, and denied that Enoch had gone up to heaven, but it was obvious her heart was not in the game, and Jinny was glad when Ravens' ladder was clapped against the casement and his padded knees appeared in an ascension of a purely terrestrial character, however celestial the melody that accompanied it. For the Gaffer had grown fond of this bird-of-all-work, now in the rôle of thatcher, and would hasten to hover about him, fussily directing the operations of his club, shears, or needle, correcting the words and airs of his songs, and even joining him in duets. Ravens' encouragement of the older bird had become almost as alarming to Jinny as his shameless delay in sending in his bill and his positive refusal to charge for Uncle Lilliwhyte's repairs, but this afternoon his advent was welcome, though the noise and jingle of the duets outside made her conversation with Martha difficult.

"He mustn't go—he mustn't go," Mrs. Flynt sobbed. "It's like the New Jerusalem coming down and going up again."

Jinny quite appreciated that. "I thought he wouldn't let me call for his box," she said quietly.

"No, the pig-headed mule! He's going to carry it himself."

"In what? It's not easy to get anything but me."

"He knows that. That's why he's carrying it. On his shoulders, I mean."

"With his arm just healed!"

"There won't be much inside—he's going to buy his things in London!"

"But the box itself—why, it's big enough to pack himself in!"

"I know, I know, dearie. But Caleb says he carried it himself all the way from Chipstone. And chock-full, too!"

Jinny suppressed a faint smile. "I remember," she said. "But perhaps he'll break down before he gets it to Chipstone," she added encouragingly.

"Oh, do you think so, dearie?" Then Martha's face fell. "But he only means to carry it to 'The King of Prussia.' There's a commercial traveller going from there in a trap to catch the same coach."

"Then let us hope he'll never get to 'The King of Prussia.'" Martha shook her head. "You see, Flynt's offered to bear a hand."

"Oh, well!" said Jinny. "Then it's all settled."

"But he won't have his father, either. Nearly bullied his head off. So Flynt's going to keep behind him all the way in case of a breakdown."

The picture of Caleb slinking furtively along the roads, behind his boy and the box, moved Jinny's risible muscles, and she burst into a laugh that was not far from tears.

"Don't, Jinny! I can't bear it. You can't love him, or you wouldn't sit there and laugh. I always knew you weren't the right girl for him!"

Jinny took this as the babbling of a mind distraught. "You'll get over it," she assured the old woman, patting the thin hand with the worn wedding-ring. "And he's bound to come back." The necessity of quieting Martha was fortifying: Jinny was like a queasy passenger saved from sea-sickness by having to look after a still worse sailor. She was the soul of the company at tea, staving off the duel of texts and sending Ravens into ecstasies over her quips and flashes. There was one bad moment, however, when Daniel Quarles candidly remarked to Mrs. Flynt: "Ravens should be tellin' me as your Willie's gooin' furrin. Ye'll be well riddy o' the rascal."

"Willie's an angel!" cried Martha hysterically.

"How could there be angels ef there ain't no heaven?" he queried, with a crafty cackle. "Noa, noa, Mrs. Flynt, it ain't no use kiverin' up as he's a bad egg. But one bad in a dozen or sow is fair allowance. Ye're luckier than me, what hadn't even one good 'un. Now ef Ravens here had been my buo-oy—!"

Jinny saw Martha a bit of the way home. She had now found a new compromise. "Tell Will that Ravens will come with my cart."

"And what will be the good of that?"

"It will save him the strain of carrying the box. And then as to-morrow's my day, I shall have to meet my cart at 'The King of Prussia.'"

"Oh, Jinny, then you will!"

"Yes—but don't tell him. Only say Ravens will call for the box at eight o'clock—that will give him time to walk if he jibs at the cart for himself."

It had all been arranged with the obliging bird-of-all-work, and Ravens had left Blackwater Hall that evening, carolling even more blithely than usual, when Jinny found—evidently pushed under the house-door—a mysterious cocked-hat addressed "Miss Boldero." With trembling fingers she opened it, her heart thumping. "To hell with Ravens! You can keep him!"

This utterly unexpected flash of an utterly unforeseen jealousy, and the thought that he had been drawn so spatially near again, was all that stood between her and despair that last dreadful night.

VIII

When the fateful Friday dawned, it found Jinny fast asleep, worn out after long listening to a wind that would soon be tossing a ship about. In those harsh hours she had felt it would be impossible to get up and go on her round in the morning. But no sooner were her eyes unsealed, than there sprang up in her mind the thought that, did she fail her customers to-day, gossip would at once connect her breakdown with Will's departure. So far, she had reason to believe, Martha's guess at their relations had not penetrated outside. But eyes were sharp and tongues sharper, and she must not be exposed to pity. Under this goad she sprang up instanter and did her hair carefully before the cracked mirror and dressed herself in her best and smartest. She would go around with gibe and laughter and fantasias on the horn, and whatever was consonant with celebrating the final retreat of the coach.

The morning was quiet after the blustrous night, but the year, like her fate, was at its dreariest moment—no colour in sky or garden, no hint of the Spring—and at breakfast a reaction overcame her. But this time her grandfather did not observe her depression: he was too full of the crime of 'Lijah, who—according to Martha—was putting his mother in the Chipstone poorhouse prior to installing his bride in Rosemary Villa. So garrulous was he this morning that Jinny—her mind morbidly possessed by a story of a miner who was found dead of starvation in the Bush with a bag of gold for his pillow—ceased to listen to his diatribes, retaining only an uneasy sense that he was twitching and jerking with the same excitement as when Martha had first come. "And Oi count ye'll be doin' the same with me one day," she heard him say at last, for he was shaking her arm. "But Oi'd have ye know it's my business, not yourn—Daniel Quarles, Carrier."

Jinny wearily assured him that there was no danger of her ever marrying, and she felt vexed with Martha for coming and starting such agitated trains of thought in his aged brain. Possibly the foolish mother might even have broached to him her desire to rob him of his granddaughter.

"Ye ought to be glad Oi've give ye food and shelter and them fine clothes ye've titivated yourself with," he went on, unsoothed, "bein' as there ain't enough in the business for myself. 'Tis a daily sacrifice, Jinny, and do ye don't forgit it."

The prompt arrival of Ravens made a break, but she had to cancel with thanks her request for his services with the cart, and then, when the old man was settled at his Bible, and her bonnet and shawl were on, she collapsed in the ante-room, sinking down on the chest in which she had hoarded Will's provisions, and feeling her resolution oozing away with every tick of the Dutch clock. Impossible to whip up a pseudo-gaiety, to make the tour of all these inquisitive faces! And through the lassitude of her whole being pierced every now and then her grandfather's voice, crying "Tush, you foolish woman!" She knew it was not meant for her, but for an imagined Martha whose texts he was confuting, but it sounded dismally apposite, and when once he declared "Wiser folks than you knowed it all afore you was born," she bowed her head as before the human destiny.

When the clock struck nine, he came stalking in. "Why, Jinny! Ain't to-day Friday?"

She raised a miserable face. "Yes, but I'm going to-morrow instead!"

"To-morrow be dangnationed!" he cried, upset. "Oi've, never missed my Friday yet."

"But I don't feel like going to-day."

"That'll never do, Jinny. Ye'll ruin my business with your whimwhams and mulligrubs. And it don't yarn enough as it is."

"There's no competition—it doesn't matter now."

"And is that your thanks to the Lord for drowndin' Pharaoh and his chariot and hosses?"

But she put her head back in her hands. "Do let me be!" she snapped.

"Don't ye feel well, Jinny?" he said, with a change of tone. "Have ye got shoots o' pain in your brain-box?"

"I'm all right, but I don't want to go to-day. I should only make muddles."

"We don't make muddles," he said fiercely.

"Let me be. I can't harness."

"Well, then Oi'll do it, dearie. You just set there—Oi'll put the door a bit ajar and once you're in the fresh air you'll be all right."

She heard him shuffle back into the living-room and thence into the kitchen as the shortest way to the stable, and then, almost immediately, she became aware of a little noise at the garden-gate. She was sitting opposite the clock, and through the slit at the doorway she beheld, to her amaze, a red-headed figure outside the gate, sitting on a box and mopping its brow as it gazed sentimentally at the cottage. Even in the wild leaping of her pulses, the grotesqueness of their both sitting gloomily on boxes—so near and yet so far—tickled her sense of humour. But as she sat on, smiling and fluttering, she saw him rise, cast a cautious look round, open the gate, and steal towards the living-room. In a bound she was within and waiting by the closed casement, and as his expected peep came, the lattice flew back in his face and her hysteric mockery rang out.

"I thought you'd never look on my face again!"

It was almost a greater surprise than when she had appeared with Methusalem walking the waters, for he had counted her just as surely set out on her Friday round as the sun itself, and his sentimental journey safe from misunderstanding (or was it understanding?).

"Oh, don't cackle!" he snarled. "I might have guessed you'd try to catch me."

She gulped down the sobs that were trying to strangle her speech. How glad she was that she had on her best frock! "I overslept myself!" she said gaily. "Gran'fer's harnessing. I see you've brought your box! You're just in time!"

"I haven't brought my box!" he snapped.

"Do ye don't tell me no fibs," she parodied.

"I mean, it's going from 'The King of Prussia.'"

"Really? Well I'll take it over the bridge for you."

"Thank you! I'm taking it there myself."

"This don't seem the shortest cut to Long Bradmarsh," she observed blandly.

He glowered. "Shows how easily I can carry it. I'm having a good-bye look at all the old places."

But below this surface conversation they were holding one of their old silent duologues. Jinny's heart was beating fast with happiness and triumph as her eyes told him he would never get away now, and he, hypnotized by that dancing light in them, dumbly acknowledged he was self-trapped. Yet how they were going to get out of their impasse, and how his pride was to be reconciled with their reconciliation, neither had the ghost of an idea. "I see," she replied, as if accepting his explanation of his visit. "But as to this old place, I'm afraid Ravens has rather changed the look of it with his new thatch."

He snorted at the name.

"But you'll find it unchanged inside," she added affably, "if you come in."

"Don't begin that again! You know I can't."

"Dear me! I had forgotten that old nonsense. Well, you can come nearer and peep in." Her face shone at the window.

His face worked wildly with the struggle not to approach hers. "I did have a peep. Good-bye, I've got the coach to catch."

"Well, the cart will be ready in a moment. Gran'fer is so slow harnessing. Hark! Nip's getting impatient."

He raised his hat. "Thank you, but I told you I was my own carrier."

"Good-bye, then. Pity you came so out of your way."

He turned, and his feet dragged themselves hopelessly gateward.

She waved her hand desperately through the casement.

"Good luck, Will! Hope you'll strike plenty of nuggets!"

"Thank you, Jinny!" He opened the gate.

"You'll let me know how you're getting on."

"If you like!" The gate clicked behind him. Her mother-wit leapt to stave off the moment beyond which all her frenzied questing for some solution would be waste.

"Oh dear me, Will! Where is my memory going? Put your box in the porch a moment, will you?"

"What for?"

"I've got a few little things for the voyage—I really forgot."

"Oh, Jinny!" He came back through the gate. "But I don't need to bring the box to the door. I'll take the things from you through the window."

"But I want to pack them in properly—I can't on the road."

"There's nobody passing."

"You never can tell. We don't want Bundock—"

"But I'll pack them in myself."

"I'd never trust a man—in fact I expect I'll have to repack all the rest. Look at Mr. Flippance."

But still he hung back. "There's lots of room."

"I know. Like a sensible man you're getting your outfit in London. Bring it along. Or shall I lend you a hand?"

"No! No!" He hurriedly shouldered the huge box and Jinny heard its contents shifting like a withered kernel in a nutshell. It was the same American trunk with the overarching lid, and as he swaggered up the garden with it, it seemed to her as if time had rolled back to last Spring. But what comedies and tragedies had intervened between the two box-carryings, all sprung from the same obstinacy! And yet, she felt, she did not love him the less for his manly assertiveness: how sweet would be the surrender when their sparring was over and her will could be legitimately embraced in his, held like herself in those masterful, muscular arms.

Her mind was really in her Australian hut as he dumped the box at her feet. No, it would hardly do for a table, she thought, with that lid-curvature. Then she braced herself for a tricky tussle.

"Well, where's the goods?" he said lightly.

"Don't be so unbelieving—they're in that spruce-hutch. Four months, you know, you've got to provide against."

"I know," he said glumly, unlocking his trunk and throwing up the lid violently. He would have liked to smash the springs. But the lid, lined with cheap striped cloth, stood up stiffly, refusing to give him a pretext for postponing his journey.

Jinny from her doorway gazed at the jumble in the great void.

"Shove it forward a bit," she said carelessly, moving backwards within.

"What for?"

"Your end of the box is not under cover."

"Why should it be?"

"It might rain and spoil your things—I'm sure I saw a drop." She tugged at the handle and the trunk slid along the porch and some inches over the sill. Unostentatiously he pulled it back a bit, but she jerked it in again. "Do leave it where I can see the things," she said with simulated fretfulness. "Good gracious!" She drew out the frock-coat he had sported for the Flippance wedding. "What's this grandeur for?"

"Oh, for funerals and things like that!"

"In the Bush? And fancy packing it next to the blanket. It's all over hairs. I'll brush it and sell it for you—Ravens will be wanting one for the wedding."

"What wedding?" he demanded fiercely.

"Mr. Skindle's, of course. Weren't you invited?"

He winced, and unrebuked she threw his wedding raiment over the provision-chest. "We'd best keep this on top," she said, drawing out the blanket, "else you won't get at it."

"I expect you'll be married by the time I'm back," he remarked with aloofness.

"Not I. I'll never marry now. I've seen too much of men's foolishness."

"Going to be an old maid?"

"If I live long enough!" Her vaunt of youth was dazzling.

"Well, I hope you won't!" he said fervently.

"Won't live? Oh, Will!"

"Won't fade into that. You know what I mean. The sweetest rose must fade."

"So will this muffler—fortunately. Haven't you taken your dad's 'muckinger' by mistake?"

"No, no—you leave that be."

"What a let of Sunday collars!"

"Weekdays too I like a clean collar."

"Ow, this onrighteous generation," she said in Caleb's voice, "all one to them, Sundays or no Sundays." She pulled up his cloak.

"You leave that cloak be!" he said, laughing despite himself.

"But now your sling's off, you don't need it."

"Yes, I do. Let it be, please."

But she unrolled it mischievously and a packet of letters fell out—her letters about the great horn.

"Well, didn't I say men were silly!" she cried. "Fancy taking that to Australia." And she made as if to hurl them towards the living-room fire.

"Give 'em to me!" He reached for them angrily, and that gave her an idea.

"But they're mine!" Standing at the end of the box, which made a barrier between them, she held them mockingly just beyond his reach. He came forward, then perceiving one foot was right across the forbidden sill, he jerked himself back violently. Then balancing himself well on his soles, with a sudden swoop he curved his body forward to the utmost. It only resulted in his nearly falling athwart the open box. He recovered his balance and the perpendicular with some difficulty and no dignity.

"Take care!" she cried in almost hysterical gaiety. "You nearly crossed that time."

"You give me my property!" he cried furiously.

"They're as much mine as yours."

"Not by law. You've no legal right to detain my property."

"And who's detaining it? You've only got to come and take it!"

His anger was enhanced by the sounds of Daniel Quarles returning with the cart, a carolling, lumbering, barking medley. It would be intolerable to be caught as though trying to cross the threshold.

"Give it me," he hissed. "I don't want to meet him." And as she tantalizingly tendered the packet nearer, he lunged towards her at a desperate angle, and overreaching himself as she deftly withdrew it, fell prone into the open box, his legs asprawl in the air.

"Curl 'em in, quick," she whispered, with an inspiration, tucking his legs in before he knew what was happening. But as the lid closed on him, he was not sorry to be spared the encounter.

"Get rid of him!" he implored through the keyhole.

"Business pouring in, Gran'fer!" she cried cheerily, as the Gaffer came up astare. "Bear a hand! No, no, not into the cart. It's to wait here. There is Hey," she began chanting.

"There is Ree," came his antiphone, as he grasped the other handle. "Lord, that's lugsome!" he panted, dropping it as soon as it was inside and letting himself fall upon it. "Whew!" he breathed heavily. Nip, too, all abristle leaped on the box and yapped hysterically, as though nosing for a rat. This was the last straw. Will, whose head the Gaffer was pressing through the far from inflexible lid, and who already felt asphyxiating, gave a vigorous heave.

"Why, it's aloive!" cried the Gaffer, jumping up nervously. Then as the lid flew up, Nip was hurled into space and Will's red poll popped up. "It's a Will-in-the-box," cried Jinny.

"Willie Flynt!" gasped the Gaffer.

"Yes, Gran'fer," she said in laughing triumph. "And you carried him in!"

"Ha, ha, ha!" A great roar of glee came from the jubilant junior, and in the act of scrambling up, his knees relaxed in helpless mirth and he let himself fall forward once more in the box, in a convulsion of merriment. "Daniel Quarles, Carrier! Ha, ha, ha!"

"And see, Gran'fer!" cried Jinny in still greater triumph. "He came in on his hands and knees!"

Daniel Quarles's bemused countenance changed magically.

"Ho, ho, ho!" he croaked. "On his hands and knees! Ho, ho, ho!"

Will's spasms froze as by enchantment.

"Come along, Will," said Jinny, hauling him out. "It's a fair draw and you've got to shake hands."

Will manfully put out his hand. "You nearly squashed me, Mr. Quarles," he said ruefully.

"Ye wanted settin' on," said the Gaffer, chuckling, and he took the fleshy young hand in his bony fingers. "Ye sot yourself to ruin us. But what says the Book?" he demanded amiably. "He that diggeth a pit shall tumble into—"

"A box," wound up Jinny merrily.

"Oi never knowed he was there, did, Oi'd a-tarned that key," said her grandfather, guffawing afresh.

"And everybody would have thought me in Australia, and then after long years a skeleton would have been found," said Will, with grim humour.

Jinny clapped her hands. "Just like Mr. Flippance's play, The Mistletoe Bough!"

She had closed the house-door. A timid tapping at it, which had gone unobserved, now grew audible.

"There's your dad!" said Jinny.

Will's eyes widened. "My dad?" he breathed incredulously.

"Git in the box!" whispered the Gaffer, almost bursting with glee. "Git in the box!" His sinewy arms seized the young man round the waist.

Will struggled indignantly. "I nearly choked!" he spluttered.

"Sh!" Jinny with her warning finger and dancing eyes stilled him. "Just for fun—only for a moment!"

Her instinct divined that to let the old man have his way would be the surest method of clinching the reconciliation. He could then never go back on her later, never resent the trick played upon him. It would become his trick, his farce, it would provide a fund of happy memories for the rest of his life. And as she cried "Come in!" and the latch lifted and Caleb's white-rimmed, cherubic countenance was poked meekly through a gap, while her grandfather, stroking his beard, composed his face to an exaggerated severity, Jinny felt that life was almost too delicious for laughter.

"Hullo, young chap!" was the Gaffer's genial greeting. "What brings you here?"

"Oi—Oi happened to be passin'," explained Caleb awkwardly, while his puzzled eyes roved from the girl to his senior, and then towards Nip, who was cowering in a corner, too nerve-shattered to leap on the lid again. "You ain't seen my Willie?" He moved forward questingly.

The older man tried to answer, then a guffaw burst from that toothless mouth, and turning his back he blew his nose thundrously into his handkerchief, while his lean sides shook like a jelly. "Why ever should we see your Willie?" cried Jinny, saving the situation. "Ain't he gone furrin?"

Caleb rubbed his eyes. "But Oi seen him at this door—he'll be late for the coach."

"At this door?" the Gaffer succeeded in saying, and then his handkerchief came into play again and he sneezed and coughed and blew like a grampus.

"Oi seen him just by the sill, swingin' forth and back like a parrot on a perch."

At that Jinny had some pains to keep a stiff lip, and even the box-lid quivered, but not with laughter, she surmised.

"I'm afraid you must have dreamed it," she replied.

"Lord!" quoth Caleb, and dropped dazedly on the box. To see the Gaffer's face when the lid shot up under his visitor was worth more than Mr. Flippance's finest show. The very soul of old English mirth was there. You would have thought that this crude device had never entered human brain before, was as fresh as the first laughter of Eden. And what heightened the humour of the situation was that Caleb was by no means overpleased to find Will had no intention of catching his coach. Nor did he begin to enter into the spirit of the thing till, admitting that Martha would "exult in gladness," it occurred to him what a surprise for her it would be to get her boy delivered back to her inside the box. Eagerly the two old men imagined the scene, catching fire from each other, improvising Martha's dialogue for her, from her amazement at seeing the box back, down to the colossal climax, till the mere idea had them both rolling about in helpless quiverings and explosions. Nor could Will, though he said he'd be danged if he'd stuff himself in again, and groused he'd got cramp in every limb, altogether escape the contagion, while to witness the roisterous merriment of the two hairy ancients gave Jinny such an exquisite joy of life as not even her lover's first kiss had given her. Such an assurance streamed from it of life being sound at the centre: a bubbling fount of sweetness and love and innocent laughter. It wiped out for ever the memory of that morbid doubt of the nature of things that had assailed her as she sat under the gaze of the stuffed owl in Mrs. Pennymole's cottage, the day of the rape of Methusalem. Tears welled through her smiles as Will at last bade his father lend a hand in transporting the box to the waiting cart. It must return to Frog Farm, even if he was not inside it.

"And I don't believe there ever were any provisions, Jinny," he grinned, with an afterthought.

"Oh yes, there are," said Jinny. "Look! And a bottle of brandy too!"

"You dear!" he began, but Jinny cut him short with warning signals. The sudden revelation of their relations might undo all the good of the spree, by reviving her grandfather's apprehensions of desertion. Indeed, when the hurly-burly was over, he could scarcely fail to ask himself what this sportive intimacy of the young couple portended, especially as he had even in the past suspected the answer. The truth must be broken to him cautiously, and with that reflection came the chilling remembrance that all this hubbub and laughter had solved nothing, that the situation, though superficially eased, was essentially the same as before, that the problem had only been postponed. Putting Will in a box was not keeping him in England. He would probably have to sail just the same, and the pain of parting be borne afresh, and even if he remained, she could not abandon her grandfather. But she shook off these thoughts. Enough for the moment that Will was hers again.

"Oi've never laughed so much since Oi seen that Andraa at Che'msford Fair the day Oi fust met Annie!" said her grandfather, wiping his eyes, as she set off on her delayed round, with Will at her side, and Caleb and the box in the cart, and Nip bounding like mad along the muddy road.

But it was impossible to keep Caleb in mind. Will was too impatient and too famished a lover for that, and it is not often that you sit at your sweetheart's side when you ought to be whirling towards the Antipodes. Caleb could not help seeing happy backs, circumplicated—in the more solitary roads—by arms, and the hope, first implanted by Martha, that he would be relieved of Will after all, and in so desirable a fashion, grew more and more assured, though the occasional rigidity of the bodies under observation unsettled him afresh.

"Aren't you late for the coach?" he heard Bundock's voice inquire at one of these prim intervals.

"No, too early!" laughed Will.

"But you're going the wrong way!"

"The first time I've gone right!" said Will, and with magnificent indiscretion he turned and kissed Jinny.

"Oh dear!" Jinny gasped, red as fire. "It'll be all over Chipstone by to-night."

"I wanted the banns proclaimed as soon as possible," he said, unabashed.

Then they became aware of a curious gulping sound behind them which drowned even Methusalem's tick-tacks. They turned their heads. Caleb—convinced at last—had buried his face in the famous "muckinger" mentioned between them only that morning.

"What's up, dad?" cried Will sympathetically. "Got a toothache?"

"It's the joy at you and Jinny," he sobbed apologetically. "And to think that some folk are near-sighted and can't see God, their friend."

"Meaning me, dad?" asked Will, not untouched.

"Meanin' mother, Willie. Lord, what a state Oi left her in—all blarin' and lamentation. 'Have faith,' Oi says to her. But Oi'm afeared she's got too much brains and book-larnin'!"

"Oh, I say, dad!" laughed Will. "Wouldn't Bundock like to hear that?"

"Bundock's of the same opinion," said Caleb, meaning the bed-ridden Bundock. "'Few texts and much faith,' he says to me once. And faith cometh by hearin', don't one of 'em tell us? Singafies the ear can't take hold of a clutter o' texts."

"Oh, but surely Mrs. Flynt has faith?" protested Jinny.

"She's too taken up with other folks' faith," Caleb maintained stoutly. "Wanted Mrs. Skindle to break bread with her and look for the New Jerusalem—she ain't found much of a Jerusalem, poor lone widder. And wanted to baptize that Flip gen'leman, but he never would come to the scratch. And tried her tricks and texts on your poor old Gran'fer, she let out. But when it comes to takin' a sorrow from the hand of God, her friend, she sets and yowls like a heathen what runs naked in the wilderness. Oi'm done with that Christy Dolphin stuff—it don't bring the peace of God, and Oi'll tell her sow to her head the next time she's at me to be a Jew!"

He mopped up the remains of his tears. "And same as Oi did jine the Sin agog," he added pensively, "how do Oi know she wouldn't goo on gooin' forrard?"

IX

If, in the very heart of the romp at Blackwater Hall, Jinny's insight could perceive that this reconciliation of her two males (or her two mules as she called them to herself) had left her marriage problem unsolved, still more did afterthought bring home the sad truth. There was no way of leaving the old man, no way of adding Will to the household. The latter alternative she never even suggested. It would bring her husband into public contempt to be thus absolutely swallowed up by the female carrier, and supported as in a poorhouse. So far off seemed the possibility of marriage that the Gaffer was considerately left in ignorance of the engagement—the only man in a radius of leagues from whom it was hidden, though Will was constantly about the cottage, having supplanted poor Ravens as a house repairer. But ever since the Gaffer had clapped him in the trunk—and the old man had forgotten he was not the first to do so—his affections had passed to the victim of his humour, and he often recalled it to Will with grins and guffaws as they sat over their beer. "Ye thought to git over Daniel Quarles," he would chuckle, poking him in the ribs, "but ye got to come in on your hands and knees! Ho, ho, ho!" He seemed to imagine Will called on purpose to be thus twitted with his defeat, though as a matter of fact the privation of his pipe was a great grievance to the young man, and supplied a new obstacle to his taking up his quarters there as son-in-law. But outwardly Will had fallen into Jinny's way of humouring the old tyrant, and this parade of affection rather shocked her, for she felt that Will was more interested in the veteran's death than in his life. Once when, recalling the delectable memory, the Gaffer remarked, "Lucky ye ain't as bonkka as Sidrach, Oi count they had to make him a extra-sized coffin," she caught an almost ghoulish gleam in her lover's eyes. He had indeed lugubriously drawn her attention to a paragraph in the paper saying that six thousand centenarians had been counted in Europe in the last half-century. Evidently the age of man was rising dangerously, he implied. The worst of it was that Jinny herself, though she would have fought passionately for the patriarch's life, found shadowy speculations as to the length of his span floating up to her mind and needing to be sternly stamped under. For she had told Will definitely that so long as her grandfather lived, she could neither marry nor leave England. Gloomily he cited Old Parr—he seemed to have become an authority on centenarians—who had clung to existence till 152. "At that rate I shall be over eighty," he calculated cheerlessly.

"Oh, it isn't very likely!" she consoled him.

"Well, it's lucky we aren't living before the Flood, that's all I can say," he grumbled. "Fancy waiting six hundred years or so!"

"I wish we were living before our flood," she said. "Then you'd have your livelihood."

"And what would have been the good of that without you? You'd have stuck to your grandfather just the same."

No, there was no way out. Australia resurged, black and menacing, and finally she even wrote herself to the London agents about his ship, consoled only by the entire supervision of his wardrobe and the famous trunk. And the only wedding that followed on their engagement was Elijah's. For—according to Bundock's father—till that had become certain, Blanche had refused to marry, despite the calling of her banns. "I didn't think that a man who once aspired to me could ever keep company with a common carrier," was her final version to Miss Gentry. "It shows how right you were to spurn him," said that sympathetic spinster, who had transferred her adoration of the Beautiful from the faithless Cleopatra to the clinging Blanche, and figured at the altar in her now habitual rôle of bridesmaid.

And it was on that very wedding-day—so closely does tragedy tread on the sock of comedy—that poor Uncle Lilliwhyte fell asleep in a glorious hope of resurrection. Jinny had not suspected the imminence of his last moments till the evening before, though she and Will had paid him several visits at his now weathertight hut. But she had become rather alarmed about him, and returning from her round one Tuesday, she set off alone, as soon as supper was over. Will had seen sufficient of her during the day, and it was understood he was to give his mother his company that evening, for Martha had fallen into a more distressful state than ever. "Will's got to go just the same," she kept moaning when Jinny came, "and Flynt vows he'll never be baptized into the Ecclesia, and turns round and tells me I lack faith. Me, who've learnt him all the religion he knows!"

There was a full moon as Jinny set out with a little basket for the invalid. Nip trotted behind her, and the trees and bushes cast black trunks and masses across her path, almost like solid stumbling-blocks. The bare elms and poplars rose in rigid beauty in the cold starry evening. Death was far from her thoughts till she reached the hut and saw the sunken cheeks in their tangle of hair illumined weirdly from the stove, which lay so close to the patriarch's hand he could replenish it from his bed of sacks.

"Just in time, Jinny!" he said joyfully. "Oi was afeared you wouldn't be." His excitement set him coughing and, frightened, she knelt and put her jug of tea to his lips.

"There! Don't talk nonsense!" she said, as a faint colour returned to his face.

He shook his head. "'Tis the tarn of the worms at last."

"Not for twenty years. Look at Gran'fer."

"Oi can't grudge 'em," he persisted. "Oi've took many a fish with 'em, and Oi've been about the woods from a buoy-oy, master of beast and bird and snake, and Oi know'd Oi'd be catched myself one day. And that's onny fair, ain't it?"

"Don't talk like that—it's horrible."

"Ye're too softy-hearted, Jinny, or ye wouldn't be here fussin' over the poor ole man in the trap. And ef ye'd been more of a sport, ye'd ha' understood it's all a grand ole game. Catch-me-ef-you-can, Oi calls it."

"It's dreadful, I think—the hawks and weasels eating the little birds."

"Then why do the little birds sing so? Tell me that! It's all fun, Oi tell ye, and they're havin' it theirselves with the flies and the worms. Take your Nip now. [Nip, hearing his name, wagged his tail.] Oi've seen that animal, what looks so peaceful squattin' there by the fire, stand a-roarin' like when you shuts the flap o' the stove time he tries to git at a rat-hole. Ten men couldn't howd him."

"He's never got a rat anyhow," said Jinny with satisfaction.

"More shame to his breed. Oi count he's frighted away my fox all the same. There's one what comes and looks in at me every evenin' just like Nip there, onny wild about the eyes like. Oi reckoned he'd be squattin' there to-night for a warm, too, friendly-like, but he'll find both on us cowld soon, the fire and me." And a racking spasm of coughing accented his prognostic.

"You mustn't talk like that. You mustn't talk at all. I'll send Dr. Mint to-morrow."

He raised himself convulsively on his sacking, throwing off the rags and tags that covered him, and revealing the grimy shirt and trousers that formed his bed-costume. His grey hair streamed wildly, almost reaching the bolster. "Ef ye send me a doctor," he threatened, "Oi'll die afore he gits here!"

"Do lie down." She pressed him towards his bolster.

"Oi won't take no doctors' stuff," he gurgled, as his head sank back.

"But why?" she said, covering him up with his fusty bedclothes. "You're not one of us, surely!"

"A Peculiar? Noa, thank the Lord. Oi told ye Oi don't believe nawthen of all they religions. Git over me, the whole thing."

"But if you won't have medicine, you must pray, like we do."

"Ye don't catch me doin' the one ne yet the tother. Oi count Oi can git along without 'em as much as the other critters in the wood. They don't have neither."

"Yes, they do—at least Nip and Methusalem have medicine when they're sick. I give it 'em myself."

"Oi reckon that's what makes 'em sick—relyin' on Skindles and sech. Oi never seen a stoat nor a squirrel take physic, and ye don't want nawthen livelier, and Oi never seen a animal goo down on his knees, unless 'twas a hoss what slipped. He, he, he!"

When the cough into which his gaggle passed was quieted, Jinny reminded him sternly that men were not animals, that he had an immortal soul, and she asked whether he would see Mr. Fallow or one of the various chapel ministers. That proved the most agitating question of all.

He sat up again, his face working in terror. "None o' that, Oi tell ye. Oi ain't afeared o' the old black 'un. He'll end all my pains, though Oi ain't tired o' life even with 'em—no, not by a hundred year. But do ye don't come scarin' me with your heavens and hells, for Oi don't want to believe in 'em."

"But I remember your saying once, we've got to have one or the other."

"And Oi told ye Oi mislikes 'em both."

"Not really? You wouldn't really dislike heaven."

He shuddered. "Lord save me from it! Oi've thought a mort lately about that Charley Mott—Oi used to see him drunk with his mates—and ef he's in heaven among they parsons and angels, Oi warrant he's the most miserable soul alive."

"Lie down! I oughtn't to have let you talk!" she said, so shocked that she charitably supposed his wits were going. This apprehension was enhanced when, just as her hand had pressed his relaxing form back to his bolster, she felt him grow rigid again with an impulse so violent that she was jerked backwards.

"Where's my wits?" he exclaimed in odd congruity with her thought. "Oi've nigh forgot the teapot!"

She hastened to offer again the half-sipped jug, which she had stood by the stove. He waved it away.

"Not that! Gimme the spade!"

"The spade?"

"Ay, it stands in the corner—Oi ain't used it since my old lurcher died. D'ye think he's in heaven— Rover—and all they rats we digged up together?"

"You're not going to dig up a rat?" she said in horror.

"No fear. But Oi won't have nobody else ferret it out." And from his bed he tried to shovel away the earth near the stove. But his strength failed. She took his spade. "I'll do it. What is it?"

"'Tis in the earth," he panted, "like Oi'll be. And Oi reckon Oi'd as soon be buried here as anywheres."

She turned faint. Did he mean her to dig his grave?

"This isn't consecrated ground," she said feebly.

"Oi count it's got as lovely a smell as the churchyard earth," he said. "But let 'em bury me where they will, so long as Oi don't wake up. Ye ain't diggin', Jinny."

Mystified and trembling, and wishing she had not come without Will, she stuck the spade in deeper and threw up the clods. Set her teeth as she might, she could not shake off the thought that she was digging his grave, and they began to chatter despite the warmth from the stove. The lurid glow streaming from it seemed sinister in the darkness of the windowless hut, and she paused to let in a streak of moonlight through a gap in the door. But the night outside in its vastness and under its blue glamour seemed even more frightening, and the cold blast that blew in made the ancient cough again. She reclosed the door, and with trembling spade resumed her strange task. Suddenly her blade struck a metallic object.

"That's it!" he cried gleefully. "And ye wanted to put boards over it!"

More mystified than ever, she drew up a heavy old teapot of Britannia metal—never had she handled such a weighty pot.

"Pour it out! Pour it out!" he chuckled.

She held the spout over her jug, which made him laugh till he nearly died. But by thumping his shoulders she got his breath back. She understood now what moved his mirth, for though nothing had issued from the spout, the lid had burst open and a rain of gold pieces had come spinning and rolling all over the hut. It seemed like the stories the old people told of the treasures of gnomes and pixies. There seemed hundreds of them, glittering and twirling.

"All for you, Jinny," he panted with his recovered breath. "All for you."

"Why, wherever did you get all this?" she replied, dropping on her knees to gather the shimmering spilth.

"That's all honest, Jinny, don't be scat. 'Tis the pennies Oi've put together, man and buo-oy this sixty year and more."

"But what for?" she gasped.

"For you. And fowrpence or fi'pence a day tots up."

"No, I mean why did you do it?" Her brain refused to take in the idea that all this fabulous wealth was hers. "Why didn't you live more comfortable—why didn't you get another cottage?"

"Oi ain't never been so happy as since Farmer tarned me out. To lay on the earth, that's what Oi wanted all my life—onny Oi dedn't know it."

"Then what was the good of the money?"

A crafty look came into the hollow eyes and overspread the wan features. "They'd have had me, they guardians, ef Oi dedn't have money. Oi wasn't a-gooin' to die in the poorhouse like my feyther, time they sold him up. Ef ye got the brads, they can't touch ye. Do, the Master 'ould git into trouble. They put mother and me sep'rit from feyther, and when Oi seen her cryin' Oi swore in my liddle heart Oi'd die sooner than stay there or tarn 'prentice. Oi dropped through a window the night o' feyther's funeral— for the Master had thrashed me—but Oi'd promised mother Oi'd come back for her, and 'twarn't many year afore she was livin' with me upright in the cottage. Happen you seen her, though she never seen you."

"Yes, I know," said Jinny softly. "She was blind."

"Cried her eyes out, to my thinkin'. But Oi says to her marnin' and night, 'Cheer up, mother,' Oi says, 'so long as we've got the dubs, they can't touch us, and ef they parish gents tries to lay hands on me, they'll git such a clumsy thump with the teapot they'll know better next time.' She never seen the teapot, mother dedn't, but she used to waggle her fingers about in it and laugh like billy-o."

Jinny felt nearer weeping as she culled these spoils of a lifetime. Many of the coins were curious; mintage of an earlier reign. She was peering in a cobwebbed corner when the barking of Nip as well as a familiar footstep in the clearing announced a welcome arrival. How glad she was Will had not been able to keep away! And then suddenly—at last—came the realization of her riches, of the solution of her financial problem!

"Quick! Quick!" whispered the old man hoarsely, and signed to her to hide the teapot. To soothe him she put it swiftly in her basket.

"You're sure there's nobody else ought to have it?" she asked anxiously.

"Oi ain't got no friend 'cept you and the fox. And ye don't catch him in the poorhouse. But Oi'll die happy, knowin' as Oi've saved you from it. Don't let 'em come in!" he gasped, as a tapping began.

"It's only young Mr. Flynt."

"Willie, d'ye mean?"

She blushed in the friendly obscurity. "He's come to see me home."

"He mustn't come in!"

"I'll tell him."

She set down the basket and went out into the blue night. It was no longer terrifying. Will with his ash stick seemed a match for all the powers of darkness. But she drew back from his kiss. Death was too near. In whispers she explained the situation, forgetting even to mention the gold. "I oughtn't to leave him—he oughtn't to die alone."

"Nonsense, sweetheart. You can't stay all night with a dirty old lunatic!"

"Don't talk so unchristianly, Will. You don't deserve—!" But she shut her lips. She could not go now into the happiness the "dirty old lunatic" was bringing them.

"Make him up a good fire and say you'll be back first thing in the morning. I'll come and take you. There!"

"Couldn't—couldn't you stay with him, Will?"

"Me? You said he wouldn't have me! And I haven't got enough baccy on me."

She went back tentatively. She found Uncle Lilliwhyte lying on his back on his sacks with closed eyes, and there was blood on the bolster. The earth had been shovelled in again and the soil flattened tidily with the back of the spade. The superfluous precaution—automatic effect of lifelong habit—had evidently cost him dear.

"He can come in now," he said feebly.

"But he doesn't want anything," she explained. "You lie still."

"Oi'd like him to come." She went softly to the door and called.

"Here I am, uncle!" cried Will cheerily.

"'Tain't you Oi want. But happen ef your mother 'ud come and talk things over—"

"My mother?" said Will, startled. Martha, he knew, would have the same repugnance as he to this feckless, grimy, impossible creature: an aversion which even the wasted features could not counteract.

"It don't seem to git over she," he explained, "but Oi never could hear proper, bein' at the keyhole in a manner o' speakin'. But ef she'd come and explain—!"

"Yes, she will," said Jinny. "She must, Will."

"I'll tell her," he murmured.

"He'll bring her in the morning," she promised emphatically. "You take a little more tea now and get to sleep." She covered him up carefully and stuck a great log in the stove.

"Do ye take that fowlin'-piece, young Flynt," he said, opening his eyes. "And be careful—it's loaded."

"Thanks, I'll take it in the morning."

"And there's the coppers and silver, Jinny. That's at the bottom o' the sack Oi'm on. And old tradesmen's tokens too."

"In the morning—you go to sleep now," she said tenderly. But she still lingered, reluctant to leave him, and was very relieved when Ravens (now become a woodman with an adze) looked in to see the old man, and, unembittered by the sight of the lovers, consented to pass the night in the hut he had mended.

X

Swinging home through the wood, through aisles flooded only with moonlight, the young lovers soon left the thought of death behind them. Indeed from the hut itself there had soon come following them the careless strains of the incurable caroller:

"'Tis my delight of a shiny night In the season of the year."

"What a hefty basket!" said Will at last. "Whatever have you been carrying the old codger?"

"It's what I'm carrying off," she laughed. "But give it me, if it's too much for your poor arm."

"It's not so heavy as my box," he smiled.

"But it saves carrying that," she said happily.

"How do you mean?"

"That's your farm in there—your English farm! Australia is off." She enjoyed his obvious fear that the scene in the hut had been too much for her brain. "Goose!" she cried. "Goose with the golden eggs. Just take a peep."

"There's only your jug and teapot." He was more mystified than ever.

But her happiness waned again when the riddle was read.

"You surely don't expect me to pocket your money," he said, as soon as his slower brain had taken in the situation.

"Oh, Will! Surely what is mine is yours!"

"Not at all. What is mine is yours."

"But that's what I said."

"Don't turn and twist—I know you're cleverer than me."

Her hand sought his. "Don't let us have a storm in a teapot!"

But he rumbled on. "With all my worldly goods I thee endow—it's the man says that."

"You've been reading the marriage service."

"And how would you know it, if you hadn't?"

That suspended the debate on a kiss. "You see I'd be almost as bad as poor Charley Mott," he pointed out.

"I see," she said humbly. Indeed she felt herself so much a part of him now that she wondered how she could have failed to look at it from his point of view. Her defeat of his coach—under Providence—had humiliated him enough. To have turned suddenly into an heiress was an aggravation of her success; now to make him appear a fortune-hunter would be the last straw.

"But couldn't I buy the farm and you rent it of me?" she ventured, with a memory of Hezekiah Bidlake.

"Everybody would think just the same—"

"Well, but somewhere else—where nobody knows us—?"

"You wouldn't come somewhere else—not till I'm eighty!"

"Don't be absurd! Anyhow you'll look beautiful with a white beard."

"Why not get him a minder with the money? Then we could go to Australia together."

"Leave him to a stranger! He'd die. But so long as the farm was in England, it wouldn't be so bad, even if I couldn't come just yet."

He did not answer, and as they walked on silently, her daydreams resurged, her nipped buds began bursting into wonderful flower. They parted at her door without further reference to money questions, but her face was brimming with happiness as the pot with guineas.

In that rosy mood—when her grandfather, nid-nodding over the hearth, roused at her return—she could not refrain from pouring out her teapot on the table, and changing his grumbles at her absence into squeaks of delight. She meant to pour out her story too, but he cut her short.

"That's mine!" he cried, exultant. "That's the gold Sidrach brought me!"

"No, no, Gran'fer. That comes from—!"

"But there's the wery spade guineas!" He dabbled his claws in the coins.

"Oh, is that what they are? But there's heads of Victoria, too."

"That's what he saved in Babylon. Dedn't Oi say as he died warrum?"

"But you must listen, Gran'fer. Uncle Lilliwhyte—" she recapitulated the story.

"They're mine anyways!" He scooped them up in his skinny palms and let them fall into the pot with a voluptuous clang. "Ye gits quite enough out o' my biznus."

This seemed so exactly the reverse of Will's attitude that she found herself smiling ruefully at the way she was caught again between her "two mules." But she could not thus lose her marriage-portion. "Uncle Lilliwhyte gave them to me for myself," she said firmly.

"And don't ye owe me back all the money Oi paid when your feyther died?"

Jinny was taken aback. "How much did you pay?"

"Hunderds and hunderds. Dedn't, he'd a-been a disgraced corpse, and your mother too."

Jinny was silent. The Angel-Mother seemed rustling overhead. The Gaffer closed shutters and bolted doors with rigorous precautions, and hugging the teapot to his bosom stumbled up to bed. Depressed by this unexpected seizure of her windfall, she found herself too utterly weary after her long day's work and excitement to open the shutters again, much as she disliked an airless room; she had scarcely energy to pull out her chest of drawers. For a few minutes she watched from her bed the blue flickering flame of the log, then knew no more till suddenly she saw above the dead fire a monstrous shadow curling over the chimney-piece and along the ceiling: in another instant she traced it to something still more horrible—her grandfather's legless trunk appearing over the hearthstone, with his nightlight in one hand and the teapot in the other. The rush-candle shook in its holed tin cylinder and set his grisly counterpart dancing. Jinny's blood ran cold. Evidently some one had murdered him for the gold and this was his ghost. Then she told herself it was one of her nightmares, and she looked around for Henry Brougham, Esq., to clear up the situation. But with a soft thud the trunk dropped as through a trap-door and there was nothing left but a great glimmering hole where the hearthstone should have been. Instantly she realized that it was only a secret hiding-place in which her magpie of a grandfather was bestowing the treasure—yes, there was the hearthstone slewed round as on a pivot. This must be that old smugglers' storehouse he and gossip had sometimes hinted at—with perhaps the long underground passages of ancient legend, reaching to Beacon Chimneys, nay, to the parsonage itself.

She closed her eyes carefully as his shadow heralded his re-ascent. He came up almost as noiselessly as that giant spectre, and between her lids she saw him scrutinize her. Reassured to see his shanks again, she emitted one of his snores, wondering whimsically if she did snore, or if any other girl had ever heard herself snore, and a smile almost broke the impassivity of her cheeks. Satisfied with the snore, he stooped down and she saw the hearthstone veer back to its place. "Well, I can always get it when I want it," she thought cheerfully, as his slow stockinged feet bore him and his more sinister shadow upstairs.

For some time she lay awake, pondering over the fate of her money, which seemed like Cleopatra's to be "in bonds," and wondering whether poor Uncle Lilliwhyte was still alive; then everything faded into a vision of Mr. Flippance jogging marionettes for rugged miners who poured out their teapots at the box-office, reducing it to such a swamp that its boxes floated in the tea.

At breakfast, finding her grandfather abnormally restless, she asked him a little maliciously if he had slept all right.

"Oi'll sleep better to-night," he said, and chuckled a little. He seemed indeed very happy at having his treasure so well warded, and though his exuberance was alarming, she felt that the excitement of happiness was a lesser danger than that long depression of penuriousness. If the defeat of the coach had seemed to give him a second lease of life, what might not his new wealth do for him? He might really become an Old Parr, and poor Will be kept waiting till the twentieth century!

It was thus with only a moderate uneasiness that she left him, stealing with her basket to the rendezvous at the hut. In the wood she met Ravens hurrying to find breakfast, and he sang out that Martha and Will had relieved him, and that Uncle Lilliwhyte was better. As she approached the clearing, she saw the old woman come out of the hut with a bottle in her hand and a face absolutely transfigured. The whining, peevish, latter-day Martha was gone: a radiance almost celestial illumined her features—it seemed to transcend even the bonnet and to rim it with a halo. This was a woman walking not on the dead dank leaves of a frost-grey wood, but through the streets of the New Jerusalem. Behind her came Will, with a little cynical smile playing about his mouth till he espied Jinny, when his face took on the same ecstatic glow as his mother's. Jinny could not but feel enkindled in her turn by all this spiritual effulgence, and it was three glorified countenances that met on this March morning.

"He's broken bread with me," breathed Martha, "and I've helped him put on the Saving Name." She displayed her bottle with drops of water beaded on the mouth. She had baptized—albeit only by an unavoidable reversion to sprinkling—her first convert. The dream of years had been fulfilled at last, and the apostolic triumph had lifted her beyond humanity, fired her with a vision in which, a conquistador of faith, she was to turn all Little Bradmarsh, nay, Chipstone itself, into one vast synagogue. This were indeed the New Jerusalem. "And it was Will that led my feet," she said, kissing him to his disconcertment. "And go where he may now, Jinny, he can't take that away from me. And I shall always have his letter to inspire me to win other souls." She touched the left side of her bodice, and poor Jinny, suddenly reminded that her grandfather had robbed her of her last chance of keeping Will in England, felt envious of Martha's exalted source of consolation.

"I've got to go now and cook Flynt's dinner," said Martha. "But he won't have much appetite for it if he's got any right feeling left, when he hears that another man, a stranger, has been before him in the path of righteousness. Maybe you'll write to the Lightstand, Willie, to say there's a new brother in Little Bradmarsh."

"I'll tell 'em the Ecclesia has doubled its membership," said Will, with a faint wink at Jinny, to which the girl did not respond. "Do you think, mother," he asked with mock seriousness, "the New Jerusalem will come down in Australia same as here?"

"Of course," said Martha.

Again Will winked at Jinny. But she frowned and shook her head. Her study of Australia had instructed her sufficiently that it was on the other side of the globe, and she knew that Will was having fun with the idea of the golden city coming down two opposite ways at once, but she felt it criminal to break Martha's mood, and indeed was not certain she herself understood how the Australians escaped falling off into space. Discouraged by her stern face, Will murmured he'd put his mother on the road and be back. She smiled and nodded at the promise, but her heart was heavy with a sense of inevitable partings as she went in to the lingering ancient.

The death-bed conversion was evidently a success, for she found him almost as radiant as Martha, though with a more unearthly light, while the gleaming as of dewdrops on his dishevelled hair, and the stains of damp over his bolster seemed to convict his spiritual preceptress of a dangerous recklessness. But he was probably beyond saving in any case, Jinny reflected, and what other medicine could have given him that happy exaltation? The logs roared in the stove, and all was joy and warmth that rimy morning.

"Oi've tarned a Christy Dolphin!" he announced jubilantly.

"Yes, I'm so glad. Drink this before it gets cold."

He waved it away. "Oi suspicioned all the time as that be the right religion. No hell at all, ye just goos to sleep, and when the New Jerusalem comes down for they righteous, ye don't git up."

"You'll wake up—you and your mother," she assured him, standing her jug by the stove.

"That's what Mrs. Flynt says. 'Ye ain't done no harm,' she says, 'and when the trumpet blows for the saints, your bones will git their flesh agen, same as now.'"

There was little enough on them to go through eternity in, she thought, gazing at his shrunken arms, which he had left outside the coverings in repudiating the tea. "Won't that be wonderful!" she said, the tears in her eyes.

"That'll be wunnerful wunnerful," he agreed. "That fares to be what Oi calls a real heaven—your own body, not a sort o' smoke-cloud ye wouldn't know was you ef you met it, your own flesh and blood, livin' on this lovely earth with the birds and the winds and the sun and the water, all a-singin' and a-shinin' for ever and ever. And no bad folks ne yet angels to worrit ye, no liddle boys to call arter ye—why it's just ginnick! Oi reckon Oi'll choose this same old spot."

"Yes, it's a lovely spot," said Jinny, but she wondered whether he had not made his own version of Martha's New Jerusalem, which she herself had always understood to be more jewelled than natural.

"Your mother will be able to see it too," she added gently, as she put the tea to his lips.

A beautiful smile traversed the sunken features. But suddenly a frenzy of terror swamped it. He sat up with a jerk that dashed her jug to the stove, shivering it into fragments. "But ef Oi waked, Oi'd need my money agen!" he shrilled.

What Jinny always remembered most vividly, when she recalled this tragic moment, was the red lettering on the sacks he lay on, exposed by his upright posture.

"Gay, Bird & Co., Colchester," her eyes read mechanically. When he fell back and hid that inscription, his face was at peace again. That acuteness of terror—the quintessence of the morbidity of a lifetime—had stopped his heart.

She was terribly shaken by this sudden and grotesque end. She felt his pulse, but without hope. She had never seen human death before, but she had a vague idea that you closed the eyes and put pennies on them. She had no pennies with her. She remembered there were some in the sack he lay on, pennies and shillings, but she did not dare disturb him to get at them. She was obscurely glad she had not to wrestle with the problem of whether she ought to get his teapot buried with him, for the contingency of his resurrection. Her grandfather would never surrender it, she felt, and if she descended into his mysterious underground and abstracted it, that might upset his wits altogether. Besides, Uncle Lilliwhyte's face was now taking on a strange beauty, as though his pecuniary anxieties were allayed.

But her nerves were giving way—she threw open the door and looked out eagerly, not for the lover, but for the man who seemed necessary in these rough moments. The dead must not be left alone, she knew that, or she would have set out to meet Will. Perhaps if she left him alone, his shy friend the fox would come trotting in, now he was so still. The parish authorities must doubtless be summoned to take charge of him. But ought he to have a pauper funeral—ought she not to steal back enough of his money to save him from that? But she remembered with relief that he had expressed indifference as to what became of his body—so long as it was restored to earth, its good old mother. As she moved a few paces without, in her peering for Will, she saw the blue smoke rising through the three top-hats, and in spite of the dead man's doctrines and apprehensions, she could not help fancying it was his spirit soaring towards the abode of the Angel-Mother.

When Will returned, she was relieved to find Ravens striding beside him. That sunny-souled factotum, who had meant to hie to the Skindle wedding, now found himself transformed instead into a corpse-watcher, while Will, taking Jinny a bit of his way, went off by the shortest cuts to Chipstone Poorhouse, as probably the centre of authority for parish funerals.

"There's the coroner, too," Ravens called after him.

"Will there be an inquest?" Jinny asked.

"Must be," said Will, and Jinny, alarmed for Martha's sake, ran back on pretence of her basket, and surreptitiously wiped the bolster. As they left the clearing, they heard Ravens singing in the hut.

XI

When their roads parted, Jinny insisted on returning to her grandfather, whose excitement now recurred to her mind. She was still a little uneasy about the pauper funeral, but Will had emphatically agreed with her that the teapot could not now be recaptured. Nor could it be drawn upon, he declared: the old grabber would assuredly have counted the contents. Jinny suspected that Will was pleased rather than sympathetic at her having ceased to be an heiress. The death of Uncle Lilliwhyte, so much the junior of Daniel Quarles, could not but set both their minds on the thought of a similar cutting of their Gordian knot, but the thought—dreaded or welcome—was not allowed to appear in their conversation, finding expression only in Will's aggrieved assumption of the Gaffer's immortality. "Even if I was to strike a nugget as big as a prize marrow, we'd be no forrarder," he had grumbled, and Jinny, with jangled nerves, had accused him of selfishness, when that poor old uncle was lying dead.

As she approached Blackwater Hall, a creepy conviction began to invade her that their knot was already cut: after that scene in the hut she was aquiver with presages of death and disaster. The absence of smoke—surely Gran'fer's hearth was not already cold—added to her alarm. She remembered again his effervescence at breakfast; why should his heart not stop too? And when she saw the broad garden-gate open, and the house door ajar, her own heart nearly stopped. Her intuition, she felt, had not deceived her. Yet he was nowhere in the house. Ante-room, living-room, kitchen, all were empty of him. The fire was out. In the bedroom lay his telescope, a discarded toy. She was about to sweep the horizon with it, when she had an inspiration. The smugglers' storehouse! He had gone down to count his gold, and the stone had rolled back—The Mistletoe Bough in another version. Tearing downstairs, she managed, after much fumbling with the poker, to make it revolve, and peered down into the dark clammy depths.

"Gran'fer! Gran'fer!" she cried. But only the dank silence welled up. He was undoubtedly dead, lying there stark among his guineas. She was scrambling down into the vault. But no! What nonsense! He must be pottering about with a spud, currycombing Methusalem, or doing some other odd job his renewed strength permitted. She hauled herself up—at any rate that would postpone the dread vision—and rushed round to the stable. That door too was open—Methusalem was gone! So was the cart. Nor was there any sign of Nip.

In her relief it was almost a pleasure to trace the wheels on the road. But soon she saw black again. It was his last drive—the last drive of Daniel Quarles, Carrier. That was the meaning of his excitement of the morning. He had gone out for the last time on his old rounds, and would meet Death on his driving-board, face to face, as he had met so many wintry storms and buffets. Staying only to roll back the stone, she raced out in his tracks.

But his course led unluckily to the Four Wantz Way and there she could no longer disentangle his cart-ruts. However, Mrs. Pennymole, reinstated in her scoured ground floor, had reassuring news enough, though it carried a new apprehension.

"I couldn't believe my eyes when I catched sight of him with the May Day favours all a-flyin' and a-flutterin' on whip and harness, and lookin' that strong with a great old smile over his dear old phiz, and Nip barkin' fit to bust. 'Where be you off to?' I cries as he dashes by, whippin' past like fleck—I never seen Methusalem go that pace, seemin' a'most as if he was glad to have his old master back agen, meanin' no disrespect to you, Jinny."

"No, of course not," said Jinny impatiently. "But what did he say?"

"I didn't rightly hear, I'm tellin' you, seein' how he tore towards the bridge. But 'twas summat about 'Lijah! I yeard that!"

"Good heavens!" cried Jinny, and thanking Mrs. Pennymole, she tore equally towards the bridge, wondering if she could get a vehicle at "The King of Prussia." It was clear the old wretch—there was really no other name for him—had gone to sell Methusalem again. Set up with all that gold, he meant to retire, and, inflamed by it, he could not resist the extra five pounds offered by the vet. And this time Mr. Skindle would not risk impounding her horse, he would slaughter instanter. Yes, her eerie premonitions had been justified, but they were warnings about Methusalem, not about her grandfather.

At the repaired bridge Farmer Gale's dog-cart came along with himself and his wife, but she was too shy to ask for a lift. Nor was there anything to be got immediately at "The King of Prussia." She toiled on through footpaths grey-silted from the flood till she reached the by-way that branched off to Foxearth Farm. Here she paused, wondering if it was worth while to go down it on the chance of finding Barnaby's trap available. And while she hesitated, there came bowling by from church the Skindle wedding-party in grand carriages. But though she cowered into the hedge, their insolent prosperity only soothed her somewhat by reminding her that Elijah had other work to-day than killing, and that, in any case, there was now no motive for it, unless perhaps revenge. To her surprise, in the rear of the procession, sharing Barnaby's bepranked trap, rode Will. His face beside Barnaby's seemed one large smile: even the unexpected sight of herself would hardly explain such broad cheerfulness in a man who, though profiting by a wedding, had come from arranging a pauper funeral, not to mention an inquest. But perhaps he was rejoicing at his escape from that overblown Blanche.

As if to corroborate this interpretation, he jumped down and caught her to him in the open daylight, while Barnaby's vehicle sympathetically disappeared after the others round the by-way.

"Oh, Jinny, Jinny!" he cried. "Such a lark!"

"But Gran'fer—!" she gasped, extricating herself.

He burst into a roar of laughter. "Have you heard it already?"

"Heard what? I'm looking for Gran'fer!"

"Haven't you met him on the road? He started back ahead of me!"

She drew a breath of relief. "With Methusalem?"

"And a fare," he grinned. "I had to go on to the coroner or else I too—"

But she no longer heard. "I must have missed him on the footpaths," she said happily.

"You'll find him at Mr. Fallow's," he said, and then laughter caught him again and rapt his breath.

"But do speak! Do speak! What's this mystery?"

"Your Gran'fer's eloped!"

"What?"

He wiped the tears from his eyes.

"Do speak!" She almost shook him. "Eloped with who?"

"'Lijah Skindle's mother."

"Annie?" she murmured involuntarily.

"Carried her off from the poorhouse! I was only in time for the tail-end of the fun."

"But how could he get at her?"

"Well, I tell you I only saw it at the point the Master came into it. But others saw more, and I've picked up spicy details from the paupers and the wretched porter—Jims, you know."

"Yes, I know Mr. Jims." A vision of the fat little man in his peaked cap and blue uniform rose before her. The dismal brick building in its iron enclosure was half a mile before you got to Chipstone—administered under the Gilbert Act by half a dozen parishes clubbed together.

"Well, your Gran'fer, rigged up to the nines with his best smock and beaver, and ribbons on his whip and a bunch of wallflowers and primroses sticking out of the spout of the teapot he carried, rings at the gate, and when Jims came to take in the parcel, as he thought, the old man pushes through and makes for the wards, Jims runs after him, and when he asks him what he wants, he answers, 'Annie! I've come for Annie!' 'Who's Annie?' asks Jims. 'We don't keep Annies—there's only old women, and it ain't visiting day.' 'Do ye don't tell me no fibs,' says your Gran'fer, and when Jims tries to stop him, he catches him in the stomach with his teapot and leaves him winded. Then off he scuttles to the stairs, and 'Where's Annie?' he cries to an old pauper woman sweeping them. This creature happened to know Mrs. Skindle was Annie, so she says, 'She's washing Mr. Robinson in his bedroom.' 'What?' shrieks your Gran'fer, swelling like a turkey-cock with jealousy. 'You just show me where that bedroom is!' The frightened old woman takes him up the stone stairs to the little yellow-ochred room where they had stowed the old dotard all by himself—I don't think he's as old as your Gran'fer, but he's quite a helpless driveller—and there, the old woman told me, your Gran'fer gives a great cry 'Annie!' and Mrs. Skindle drops the flannel, and there they were crying and laughing and kissing like two children, and he calling her 'My darling! My beautiful Annie!'"

"More than you've ever called me," said Jinny, herself inclined to laugh and cry and even to kiss.

The story was interrupted by an idyllic interlude. "But I expect Gran'fer's rather short-sighted without a telescope," she commented, disentangling herself blushingly.

"I was in the Master's room," resumed Will, "speaking to him about the funeral, and hearing a lot about the guardians and the parish authorities and such-like grand folk, when in rushes Jims and pants out his tale, and we all race around till we find the old couple coming down the staircase with arms round each other's waists, and your Gran'fer tells us fiercely he's taking her away, and opens the teapot to show he can support two wives if he wants to! 'Hold hard!' says the Master. 'I won't stop you, though I ought to have twenty-four hours notice, because I know the guardians haven't made such a good bargain with Mr. Skindle that they'll try to keep her, but you can't take away the parish clothes.' For of course the old woman was wearing that blue cotton dress—"

"It's got white stripes if you look close," put in Jinny.

"'Well, Oi can't take her away without clothes,' roared your Gran'fer. He said he counted it unrespectable enough that they should allow her to wash a strange old man, alone in a room, and that if they didn't mend their ways he'd have a piece put in the paper about it all. 'Well, let 'em give me back my own clothes,' says Mrs. Skindle. 'I've got to have twenty-four hours' notice about that,' says the Master. 'Ha, you've stole 'em!' says your Gran'fer. 'You be careful what you're sayin',' says the Master, bridling up. 'Who wants her rags and jags?' But in the end it was all settled friendlywise—your Gran'fer buying up some of the cast-off grandeur of the matron's (they drove a good bargain with your Gran'fer, the pair of screws, but he was free and flush with his teapot), and off the happy pair went at last, the bride as spruced up as the bridegroom, and I saw him hand her into the wedding-cart with her bouquet, while the old gentlemen in the corduroys and the old ladies in blue, and especially the little orphans, raised a cheer. Even Jims waved. I expect he'd had a drop out of the teapot."

"Daniel Quarles, Carrier-Off," laughed Jinny, half hysterically, for scandalized and startled though she was, a rosy light, whose source was yet unclear to her, seemed rising on her horizon.

"I went up to the cart under pretence of patting Nip," Will went on, "and asked the old boy where he was off to. 'Home, of course,' he answers friendly. 'You should be going to chapel first, you old rip,' I told him. 'We're going to be married in church,' answers Mrs. Skindle stiffly. 'I'm Church of England.' 'That's all right, Annie,' he says, patting her hand, 'we'll look in on Mr. Fallow about they banns,' and singing 'Oi'm Seventeen come Sunday,' drives off with her."

But Jinny refused to sympathize with the course of true love. "He's not really going to marry her?" she now cried. "But that's dreadful!"

"You scandalous creature! It would be more dreadful if he didn't!"

"But at his age!"

"Why, he's quite young yet," laughed Will. "One hundred and fifty-two is his little span, remember."

She let herself relax under his laughter. "Will they ring a peal of Grandsire Triples at his wedding?" she asked whimsically. Then with renewed anxiety: "Oh, but I do hope it hasn't all excited him too much," she cried. "I'd best get home as quick as possible."

"Home? You don't mean Blackwater Hall?"

"Where else?"

"You can't go there. As your Gran'fer remarked to the Master, that's no place for a respectable female."

She stared at him. "Besides," he said, "you don't want to interfere with the young couple."

"But I've not cooked the dinner!"

"Let the bride do that. She's as strong as a horse. It's the best thing that could have happened for both of 'em. After fending for all of us at Rosemary Villa, Blackwater Hall will be a holiday to her."

"But I must go and see about things. She won't know where anything is. And even if she cooks the dinner, she'll want my apron. She can't spoil her fineries."

"That's enough," he said sternly. "I don't often quote my father, but I'm bound to say some people are near-sighted and can't see God, their friend. You've done with Blackwater Hall."

"But where am I to go then?"

He laughed. "And what about Frog Farm?" He took her arm. "And we, too, must get tied up as soon as possible. No, Jinny, we can't do better than follow in your Gran'fer's footsteps. The way he held that grey-headed old woman's hand in the wedding-cart, while I—you're right, I haven't called you 'beautiful' enough." He paused to do so without words. "The old boy's taught me a lesson, dashing in like that, while I've been sitting growling and grizzling and wasting our best years."

"But you see, Will, it couldn't be before. And he was sacrificing himself to me, poor Gran'fer, if he wanted her so badly all the time. Just see how he waited till he could support her!"

"On your money! Under the roof you re-thatched for him!"

"It wasn't my money. And it was Ravens who did the roof."

"You paid for it!"

"No, I didn't," she protested.

"Why not?"

"He won't send me in the bill."

"Oh, won't he!" Will clenched his fist. "I'll jolly soon stop his singing if he don't hurry up with it! And why didn't you ask me to mend your thatch?"

"You couldn't come in."

"You don't come in to the roof."

"That might have been a way of coming in," she laughed, "it was so leaky. Anyhow you might have done Uncle Lilliwhyte's—it is his money that has saved us all."

"In a roundabout way," he admitted.

She snuggled to him. Happiness, which had hitherto seemed like the soaped pig at village sports, was seizable at last. "Won't it be wonderful when we're in the hut!" she said.

He opened his eyes. "You don't propose to live in Uncle Lilliwhyte's hut with the three top-hats!"

"Of course not," she said, blushing. "It's in Australia. There's just poles stuck in the ground."

"Why, when have you been in Australia?"

"Never you mind! You see, I've already saved up a little towards my passage and—"

But her words died on his lips. "I don't know that we need pull up our stakes," he said when he released her. "Farmer Gale's looking for a looker."

"You don't really mean that?" she said.

"He does, anyhow. I just met him in his dog-cart and he's mad about his flood-losses. 'You should have paid a good man,' I told the hunks to his head."

"Oh, but, Will," she said, shrinking, "you don't like Farmer Gale!"

"Well, he's safely married now, and after all, my father had the place first. . . . It belongs to the family. . . . Anyhow," he broke off masterfully, "I'd pay my wife's passage-money."

"Then I'll be able to buy Methusalem," she said in cheerful submission. "He's only five pounds—I suppose your father would take care of him."

"Rather! It would be a refuge from the New Jerusalem."

"But we'll take Nip with us, sweetheart—it won't be the goldfields, you know, just a farm. And we can take over the Bidlake girls too, if you like."

"Lord, what a crowd! But I don't see Nip on an emigrant ship."

"Haven't I heard of dog-watches?" she smiled.

"I guess you'd smuggle him in somehow," he laughed. "I've noticed you generally get your own way. And captains are but men."

"I thought they were sea-dogs," she laughed.

"You generally get the last word too," he grumbled with adoring admiration. "But I tell you, Jinny, though there may be more money, all these new countries are terribly raw."

"I know—'no longer an egg, not yet a bird, only a smell,'" she quoted with wistful humour, and these words of his in the English wood last May evoked again for both of them all the magic of their love at its dawning.

They walked on in silence towards Frog Farm. After all, with their united treasure of youth, energy, and love, their livelihood was no grave problem. Larks were carolling, the little wrens piping, and ringdoves calling, calling, for the Spring was near after all, and the daffodils had already come. It seemed indeed a vain snapping of the heart-strings to leave such a homeland.

"That'll be winter soon in Australia," mused Will tenaciously.

"Not if we were together," Jinny whispered, although the more she pondered during that wonderful walk the more the Antipodes receded to their geographical distance, the more shadowy grew the danger of falling off her planet. But, however they were to decide, she could see no reason—once her grandfather's wedding-bells had rung—why they should not all live—wherever they all lived—happy ever after.

Israel Zangwill – A Short Biography

Israel Zangwill was born in London on 21st January 1864, to a family of Jewish immigrants from the Russian Empire. His father, Moses, was from modern-day Latvia, and his mother, Ellen Hannah Marks Zangwill, from modern-day Poland.

Zangwill was initially educated in Plymouth and Bristol. At age 9 he was enrolled into the Jews' Free School in Spitalfields in east London. The school was for the children of Jewish immigrants and added to its teaching, of both secular and religious matters, with supplies of clothing, food, and health care.

Zangwill excelled here. He began to teach part-time at the school and eventually full time. Whilst teaching he also studied with the University of London and by 1884 had earned his BA with triple honours in philosophy, history, and the sciences.

He had already co-written a tale entitled 'The Premier and the Painter' when he resigned as a teacher owing to differences with the managers of the school. Zangwill now turned to journalism for his new career path, initiating Ariel, The London Puck, as well as working in various capacities for the London press.

His writing earned him the sobriquet "the Dickens of the Ghetto" primarily based on his much lauded novel 'Children of the Ghetto: A Study of a Peculiar People' in 1892 and its glimpse of the poverty-stricken life in London's Jewish quarter.

As a writer he was keen to reflect on his political and social outlooks. His simulation of Yiddish sentence structure in English aroused great interest. His mystery work, 'The Big Bow Mystery' (1892) was the first locked room mystery novel. Social satire flowed with 'The King of Schnorrers' (1894). A follow up to 'Children of the Ghetto' was 'Ghetto Tragedies' in 1894 and 'Dreamers of the Ghetto' in 1898 which included essays on famous Jews such as Baruch Spinoza, Heinrich Heine and Ferdinand Lassalle.

Zangwill was also involved with narrowly focused Jewish issues as an assimilationist, an early Zionist, and later a territorialist. In the early 1890s he had joined the Lovers of Zion movement in England. A few years later, in 1897, he took part in the "pilgrimage" of English Jews to Palestine. That same year he also joined Theodor Herzl (considered the father of modern political Zionism) in founding the World Zionist Organization and would take part in the first seven Zionist congresses. Zangwill was much admired as an orator and spoke movingly and eloquently on the issues he was passionate on.

In 1901 he had written that "Palestine is a country without a people; the Jews are a people without a country". On Herzl's visits to London, they worked closely together. In a debate at the Article Club in November 1901 however Zangwill was still mis-using the facts: "Palestine has but a small population of Arabs and fellahin and wandering, lawless, blackmailing Bedouin tribes." And made a direct plea to "restore the country without a people to the people without a country. For we have something to give as well as to get. We can sweep away the blackmailer—be he Pasha or Bedouin—we can make the wilderness blossom as the rose, and build up in the heart of the world a civilisation that may be a mediator and interpreter between the East and the West."

In 1902, Zangwill wrote that Palestine "remains at this moment an almost uninhabited, forsaken and ruined Turkish territory". But from this point on Zangwill began to see things differently which would, in 1905, result in his breakaway from Zionism.

Zangwill quit the established philosophy of Zionism when his plan for a homeland in Uganda was rejected and instead founded his own organisation; the Jewish Territorialist Organization. Its stated goal was to create a Jewish homeland in whatever territory in the world could be found for them. At that point in time suggestions were as varied as Canada, Australia, Mesopotamia, Argentina, Uganda and Cyrenaica.

Amongst the challenges in his life he found time to write poetry. He had translated a medieval Jewish poet in 1903 and his own volume 'Blind Children' in 1908 shows his promise in this new endeavour.

In 1908, Zangwill told a London court that he had been naive when he made his 1901 speech and had since recognised that the Arab population was twice that of the United States.

Zangwill was a supporter of both feminism and pacifism, but his greatest effect was as a writer who gained a wide audience with the idea of combining ethnicities into a single, American nation. The hero of 'The Melting Pot', proclaims: "America is God's Crucible, the great Melting-Pot where all the races of Europe are melting and reforming... Germans and Frenchmen, Irishmen and Englishmen, Jews and Russians – into the Crucible with you all! God is making the American."'

'The Melting Pot' made Zangwill's name as an admired playwright. The title itself was popularised as the phrase to use to describe American absorption of immigrants when it ran in the United States.

When the play opened in Washington D.C. on 5th October 1909, former President Theodore Roosevelt leaned over the edge of his box and shouted, "That's a great play, Mr. Zangwill, that's a great play." In a later letter in 1912 Roosevelt went further "That particular play I shall always count among the very strong and real influences upon my thought and my life."

'The Melting Pot' shone a spotlight on America's growth through the input of its new waves of immigrants. Zangwill was writing as "a Jew who no longer wanted to be a Jew. His real hope was for a world in which the entire lexicon of racial and religious difference is thrown away."

According to Ze'ev Jabotinsky, Zangwill told him in 1916 that, "If you wish to give a country to a people without a country, it is utter foolishness to allow it to be the country of two peoples. This can only cause trouble. The Jews will suffer and so will their neighbours. One of the two: a different place must be found either for the Jews or for their neighbours".

In 1917 he wrote "'Give the country without a people,' magnanimously pleaded Lord Shaftesbury, 'to the people without a country.' Alas, it was a misleading mistake. The country holds 600,000 Arabs."

With the end of World War I, and a more clearly defined idea of a Jewish settlement in Palestine, Zangwill once more returned to the Zionist effort and made efforts on behalf of the Balfour Declaration, proclaiming the right of a Jewish homeland in Palestine

In 1921 Zangwill wrote "If Lord Shaftesbury was literally inexact in describing Palestine as a country without a people, he was essentially correct, for there is no Arab people living in intimate fusion with the country, utilizing its resources and stamping it with a characteristic impress: there is at best an Arab encampment, the break-up of which would throw upon the Jews the actual manual labor of regeneration and prevent them from exploiting the fellahin, whose numbers and lower wages are moreover a considerable obstacle to the proposed immigration from Poland and other suffering centers".

Despite his advocacy on Jewish matters he would be disappointed to know that despite Israel now being established the quarrels of the Middle East continue to divide.

Israel Zangwill died on 1st August 1926 in Midhurst, West Sussex.

Israel Zangwill – A Concise Bibliography

The Bachelors' Club (1891)
The Old Maid's Club (1892)
Children of the Ghetto: A Study of a Peculiar People (1892)
Grandchildren of the Ghetto (1892)
The Big Bow Mystery (1892)
Merely Mary Ann (1893)
The King of Schnorrers (1894)
The Master (1895) (based on the life of George Wylie Hutchinson)
Without Prejudices (1896)
Dreamers of the Ghetto (1898)
Ghetto Tragedies, (1899)
"The Return to Palestine", New Liberal Review, (Dec. 1901)
Children of the Ghetto (1902)
"Providence, Palestine and the Rothschilds", The Speaker, vol. 4, no. 125 (22 February 1902)
Selected Religious Poems (1903) Translation of the Jewish Medieval Poet Solomon in Cabirol.
The Grey Wig: Stories and Novelettes (1903)
The Serio-Comic Governess (1904)
Merely Mary Ann (1904)
Ghetto Comedies, (1907)
Blind Children (1908) Poetry
The Melting Pot (1909)
Italian Fantasies (1910) Travel
Chosen Peoples, (1919)
The War For The World (1916)
The Principle of Nationalities (1917)
Chosen Peoples (1918)
Hands Off Russia: Speech by Mr. Israel Zangwill at the Albert Hall, February 8th, 1919. London: Workers' Socialist Federation, n.d. (1919)
The Voice of Jerusalem. (1921)

Filmography

Children of the Ghetto (1915, based on the play Children of the Ghetto)
The Melting Pot (1915, based on the play The Melting Pot)
Merely Mary Ann (1916, based on the play Merely Mary Ann)
The Moment Before (1916, based on the play The Moment of Death)
Mary Ann (1918, based on the play Merely Mary Ann)
Nurse Marjorie (1920, based on the play Nurse Marjorie)
Merely Mary Ann (1920, based on the play Merely Mary Ann)
The Bachelor's Club (1921, based on the novel We Moderns)
We Moderns (1925, based on the play We Moderns)
Too Much Money (1926, based on the play Too Much Money)
Perfect Crime (1928, based on the novel The Big Bow Mystery)
Merely Mary Ann (1931, based on the play Merely Mary Ann)
The Crime Doctor (1934, based on the novel The Big Bow Mystery)

The Verdict (1946, based on the novel The Big Bow Mystery)